CAJUN MAGIC MYSTERIES

BOOKS 1-3

ELLE JAMES

TWISTED PAGE INC

CAJUN MAGIC MYSTERIES

BOOKS 1-3

New York Times & USA Today
Bestselling Author

ELLE JAMES

Ebook ISBN: 978-1-62695-133-4

Print ISBN: 978-1-62695-134-1

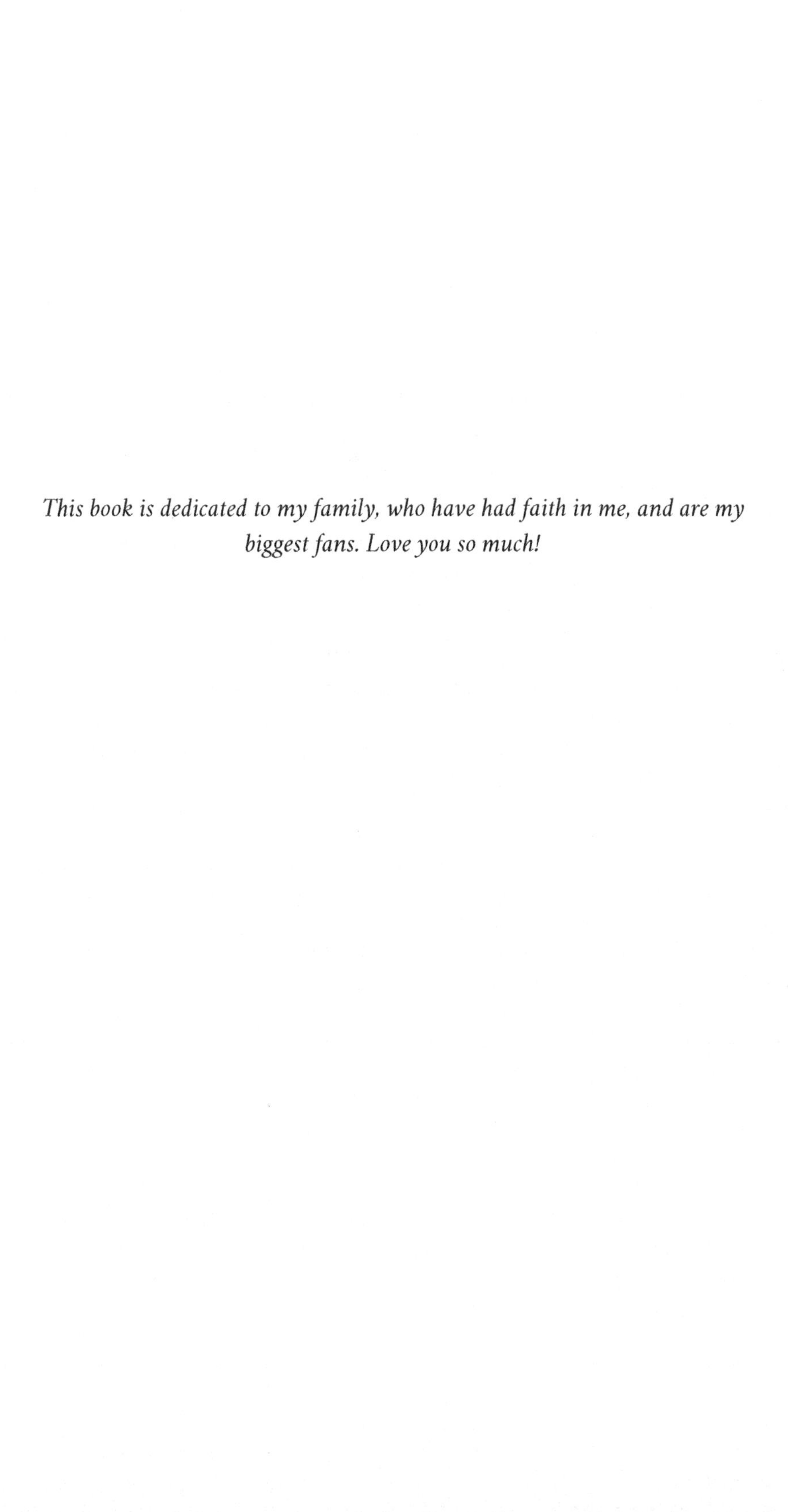

This book is dedicated to my family, who have had faith in me, and are my biggest fans. Love you so much!

AUTHOR'S NOTE

Enjoy the following books by Elle James:

Billionaire Online Dating Series
The Billionaire Husband Test (#1)
The Billionaire Cinderella Test (#2)

Texas Billionaire Club
Tarzan & Janine (#1)
Something To Talk About (#2)
Who's Your Daddy (#3)
Love & War (#4)

Visit www.ellejames.com for more titles and release dates
For hot cowboys, visit her alter ego

Myla Jackson at www.mylajackson.com

Don't piss off the Voodoo Queen ...

VOODOO ON THE BAYOU

A CAJUN MAGIC MYSTERY

VOODOO ON THE BAYOU

CAJUN MAGIC MYSTERIES BOOK #1

New York Times & USA Today
Bestselling Author

ELLE JAMES

CHAPTER 1

Bayou Miste, deep in the Atchafalaya Basin of southern Louisiana
June

Bound to a cypress tree, Craig Thibodeaux struggled to free his hands, the coarse rope rubbing his wrists raw with the effort. A fat bayou mosquito buzzed past his ear to feast on his unprotected skin. The bulging insect had plenty of blood in its belly—much more and the flying menace would be grounded.

What I wouldn't give for a can of bug repellent.

Craig shook his head violently in hopes of discouraging the little scavenger from landing.

The dark-skinned Cajuns who'd kidnapped him stood guard on either side of him, their legs planted wide and arms crossed over bare muscular chests. They looked like rejected cast members from a low-budget barbarian movie, and they didn't appear affected in the least by the blood-sucking mosquitoes.

"Hey, Mo, don't you think you guys are taking this a little too far?" Craig aimed a sharp blast of breath at a bug crawling along his shoulder. "I swear I won that card game fair and square."

The man on his right didn't turn his way or flick an eyelid.

Craig looked to his left. "Come on Larry, we've been friends since you and I got caught snitching apples from Old Lady Reneau's orchard. Let me go."

Larry didn't twitch a muscle, as if Craig hadn't uttered a word.

"If it will make you feel any better, I'll give you back your money," Craig offered, although he'd really won that game.

He'd known Maurice Saulnier and Lawrence Ezell since he was a snot-nosed kid spending his summer vacations with his Uncle Joe in the southern Louisiana town of Bayou Miste. He had considered them friends. Until now.

Granted, Craig had been back for less than a week after an eight-year sojourn into the legal jungles of the New Orleans court system. But his absence shouldn't be a reason for them to act the way they were. An odd sensation tickled his senses, as if foreshadowing something unpleasant waiting to happen. Sweat dripped off his brow, the heat and humidity of the swamp oppressive.

"Look guys, whatever you're planning, you won't get away with it." Craig strained against the bonds holding him tight to the rough bark of the cypress tree.

"Ah, *mon cher,* but we will." A low, musical voice reached out of the darkness preceding the appearance of a woman. She wore a flowing, bright red caftan with a sash tied around her ample girth and a matching kerchief covering her hair. Although large, she floated into the firelight, her bone necklace rattling in time to a steady drumbeat building in the shadows. Her skin was a light brown, almost mocha, weathered by the elements and age. Her dark brown eyes shone brightly, the flames of a nearby fire dancing in their depths.

Despite the weighty warmth of the swamp, a chill crept down Craig's spine. "Who's the lady in the muumuu?"

The silent wonder next to him deigned to speak in a reverent whisper, "Madame LeBieu."

Craig frowned and mentally scratched his head. Madame LeBieu...Madame LeBieu...oh, yes. The infamous Bayou Miste Voodoo priestess, a notorious mishmash of Cajun-Caribbean witchdoctor mumbo-jumbo and healer. No one really knew her background, but she was both feared and revered in the community. He studied her with more interest and a touch of unease. Was he to be a sacrifice in some wacky Voodoo ceremony?

"Are you in charge of these two thugs?" Craig feigned a cockiness he didn't feel.

"It be I who called upon dem." She dipped her head in a regal nod.

"Then call them off and untie me." Craig shot an angry look at the men on either side of him. "You've obviously got the wrong guy."

"Were you not de man what be goin' out with de sweet Lisa LeBieu earlier dis very evening?"

"Yes," Craig said, caution stretching his answer, as dread pooled in his stomach. He didn't go into the fact that Lisa wasn't so sweet. "Why?"

"I be Madame LeBieu and Lisa be *ma petite fille*. She say you dally with her heart and cast it aside." The woman's rich, melodious voice held a thread of steel.

Craig frowned in confusion. "You mean this isn't about the card game? This is about Lisa, your granddaughter?"

"No, dis be 'bout you mistreatment of *les femmes*."

"I don't get it. I didn't touch her. She came on to me, and I took her home."

"Abuse not always takes de physical form. You shunned her love and damage her chakras. For dis, you pay."

Craig cocked an eyebrow in disbelief. "You mean I was conked on the head and dragged from my bed all because I refused to sleep with your granddaughter?" He snorted. "This is a new one on me."

"Craig Thibodeaux, I know your kind." Madame LeBieu stuck a thick, brown finger in his face. "You be breakin' hearts all over, seein' all kinds of women, but got no love to show for it. You be showin' your loveless way for de last time." Madame LeBieu flicked her fingers, and the flames behind her leaped higher. Then, reaching inside the voluminous sleeves of the caftan, she whipped out an atomizer and sprayed a light floral scent all around him. The aroma mixed and mingled with the dark musty smells of the swamp's stagnant pools and decaying leaves.

"So you're going to douse me in perfume to unman me?" Craig's bark of laughter clashed with the rising beat of the drums. The humor of the situation was short-lived when the mosquitoes decided they liked him even more with the added scent. Craig shook all over to discourage the beggars from landing.

"Ezili Freda Daome, Goddess of love and all dat be beautiful, listen to our prayers, accept our offerings, and enter our arms, legs, and hearts." Madame LeBieu's head dropped back, and she spread her arms wide. The drumbeat increased in intensity, reverberating off the canopy of trees shrouded in low-hanging Spanish moss.

The pounding emphasized the throbbing ache in the back of Craig's head from where Madame LeBieu's henchmen had beaned him in his room at the bait shop prior to dragging him here. The combined smells of perfume and swamp, along with the jungle beat and chanting nutcase made his stomach churn. The darkness of the night surrounded him, pushing fear into his soul.

Craig had a sudden premonition that whatever was about to happen had the potential to change his life entirely. Half of him wished they would just get on with it, whatever "it" was. The other half quaked in apprehension.

The Voodoo priestess's arms and head dropped, the drums crashing to a halt. Silence descended. Not a single cricket, frog, or bird interrupted the eerie stillness.

Craig broke the trance, fighting his growing fear with false bravado. "And I'm supposed to believe all this mumbo jumbo?" He snorted. "Give me a break. Next thing, you'll be waving a fairy wand and saying bibbity-bobbity-boo."

Madame LeBieu leveled a cold, hard stare at him.

Another shiver snaked down his spine. With the sweat dripping off his brow and chills racing down his back, he thought he might be ill. Maybe even hallucinating.

A small girl appeared at Madame LeBieu's side, handing her an ornate cup. She waited silently for the woman to drink. Craig noticed that his two former friends bowed their heads as the Voodoo lady sipped from the cup then handed it back to the girl. Clutching the cup as if it were her dearest possession, the child bowed at the waist, backing into the shadows.

With a flourishing sweep of her wrist, Madame LeBieu pulled a pastel pink, blue, and white scarf from the sleeve of her caftan, and waved it in Craig's face.

"Mistress of Love, hear my plea.

Help dis shameless man to see."

"You know I have family in high places, don't you?" Craig said. Not that they were there to help him now.

Madame LeBieu continued as though he hadn't spoken.

"Though he be strong, his actions bold,

his heart be loveless, empty, cold.

By day a frog, by night a man,

'til de next full moon, dis cunja will span."

Craig stopped shaking his head, mosquitoes be damned. What was the old lady saying? "Hey, what's this about frogs?"

"A woman will answer Ezili's call,

one who'll love him, warts and all."

"Who, the frog or me?" He chuckled nervously at the woman's fanatical words, downplaying his rising uneasiness. His next sarcastic statement was cut off when Mo's heavily muscled forearm crashed into his stomach. "Oomph!"

"Silence!" Mo's command warned of further retribution should Craig dare to interrupt again.

Which worked out great, since he was too busy sucking wind to restore air to his lungs. All he could do was glare at his former friend. If only looks could kill, he'd have Mo six feet under in a New Orleans minute.

Madame LeBieu went on,

"He'll watch by day and woo by night,

to gain her love, he mus fight,

to break de cunja, be whole again,

transformed into a caring man."

"You didn't have to knock the wind out of my sails." Craig wheezed, and jerked his head in Madame LeBieu's direction. "She's the one making all the noise, talking nonsense about frogs and warts."

Mo's face could have been etched in stone.

The old witch held her finger in Craig's face, forcing him to look at it. Then she drew the finger to her nose and his gaze followed until he noticed her eyes. A strange glow, having nothing to do with fire, burned in their brown-black centers. Madame LeBieu's voice dropped to a low, threatening rumble.

"Should he deny dis gift from you,

a frog he'll remain in de blackest bayou."

With a flourishing spray of perfume and one last wave of the frothy scarf, Madame LeBieu backed away from Craig, disappearing into the darkness from whence she'd come.

Craig's stomach churned and a tingling sensation spread throughout his body. He attributed his discomfort to the nauseating smells and the ropes cutting off his circulation. "Hey, you're not going to leave me here trussed up like a pig on a spit, are you?" Craig called out to the departing priestess.

A faint response carried to him from deep in the shadows. "Dôn tempt me, boy."

As soon as Madame LeBieu was gone, the men who'd stood motionless at his side throughout the Voodoo ceremony moved. They untied his bonds, grabbed him beneath the arms and hauled him back to the small canoe-like pirogue they'd brought him in.

Forced to step into the craft, Craig fell to the hard wooden seat in the middle. When the other two men climbed in, the boat rocked violently, slinging him from side to side. One man sat in front, the other at the rear. Both lifted paddles and struck out across the bayou, away from the rickety pier.

"So what's it to be now?" Craig rubbed his midsection. "Are you two going to take me out into the middle of the swamp and feed me to the alligators?" He knew these swamps as well as anyone, and the threat was real, although he didn't think Mo and Larry would do it.

Would they?

"No harm will come to you dat hasn't already been levied by

Madame LeBieu," Mo said. Dropping his macho facade, he gave Craig a pitying look. "She done put de *gree gree* on you. Man, I feel sorry for you."

"Why? Because a crazy lady chanted a little mumbo jumbo and sprayed perfume in my face?" He could handle chanting crazy people. He'd represented a few of the harmless ones in the courtroom. "Don't worry about me. If I were you, I'd worry more about the monster law suit I could file against the two of you for false imprisonment."

"Going to jail would be easy compared to what you be in for." Larry's normally cheerful face wore a woeful expression.

The pale light of the half-moon shimmered between the boughs of overhanging trees. Craig could see they were headed back to his uncle's marina. Perhaps they weren't going to kill him after all. Madame LeBieu was probably just trying to scare him into leaving her granddaughter alone. No problem there. With relatives like that, he didn't need the hassle.

Besides, he'd been bored with Lisa within the first five minutes of their date. Most of the women who agreed to go out with him were only interested in what his money could buy them. Lisa had been no different.

The big Cajuns pulled up to the dock at the Thibodeaux Marina. As soon as Craig got out, they turned the boat back into the swamp, disappearing into the darkness like a fading dream.

Tired and achy, Craig trudged to his little room behind the shop, wondering if the night had been just that. A dream. He grimaced. Dream, hell. What had happened was the stuff nightmares were made of. The abrasions on his wrist confirmed it wasn't a dream, but it was over now. He would heed the warning and stay away from Madame LeBieu's granddaughter from now on.

He let himself in through the back door, flexing his sore muscles. The room was a mess from the earlier scuffle, short-lived though it was. Craig righted the nightstand and fished the alarm clock out from underneath the bed.

Without straightening the covers, he flopped onto the mattress in the tiny bedroom. It was a far cry from his suite back home, but he'd spent so many summers here as a boy, the cramped quarters didn't bother him. He was bone tired from a full day's work, a late night date gone sour, and his encounter with Madame LeBieu. What did it matter whether the sheets were of the finest linen or the cheapest cotton? A bed was a bed.

"Just another day at the office." He yawned. It would be dawn soon and his uncle expected him up bright and early to help prepare bait and fill gas tanks in the boats they rented to visiting fishermen.

Craig closed his eyes and drifted into a troubled sleep where drums beat, witches wove spells, and frogs littered the ground. A chant echoed throughout the dream, "By day a frog, by night a man, 'til the next full moon, this curse will span."

What a crock.

* * *

PROFESSOR AND RESEARCH scientist Elaine Smith moaned for the tenth time. How the staff must be laughing. Brainiac Elaine Smith, member of Mensa, valedictorian of her high school, undergraduate, *and* master's programs, with an IQ completely off the scale…and she hadn't had a clue. Until she'd opened the door to the stairwell in the science building to find her fiancé, Brian, with his hands up the shirt of a bosomy blond department secretary, while sucking out her tonsils.

The woman had seen her first, broken contact, and tapped Brian's shoulder. "Uh, this is a little awkward." She'd twittered her fingers at Elaine. "Hi, Dr. Smith."

"Elaine, I can explain," Brian had said, his hands springing free of the double-D breasts.

Without a word, Elaine had marched back to the lab. She'd only been away for a moment. If the drink machine on the second floor had worked, she wouldn't have opened that door. Thank God she'd made this discovery before she'd been even more idiotic and married the creep.

She crossed the shiny white floor to her desk and ran her hand over her favorite microscope, letting the coolness of the metal seep into her flushed skin. With careful precision, she poured a drop from the glass jar marked Bayou Miste onto a slide. With another clean slide, she smeared the sample across the glass, and slid it beneath the scope.

The routine process of studying microorganisms calmed her like no other tonic. Her heartbeat slowed and she lost herself in the beauty of microbiology. She didn't have to think about the world outside the science department. Many times in her life, she'd escaped behind lab doors to avoid the ugly side of society.

"Elaine the brain. Elaine the brain." Echoes of children's' taunts from long ago plagued her attempts at serenity.

Elaine snorted. *Wouldn't they laugh, now? Elaine-the-brain, too stupid to live.*

A tear dropped onto the lens of the microscope, blurring her view, and the lab door burst open. She scrubbed her hand across her eyes before she looked up. She'd be damned if she'd let the jerk see her cry.

"Elaine, let me explain." Brian strode in, a sufficiently contrite expression on his face.

He'd probably practiced the expression in the mirror to make it look so real. Elaine wasn't buying it. She forced her voice to be flat and disinterested. "Brian, I'm busy."

"We have to talk."

"No...we don't." She turned her back to him, her chest tight and her stomach clenching.

"Look, I'm sorry." Brian's voice didn't sound convincing. "It's just...well...ah, hell. I needed more."

Her mouth dropped open and she spun to face him. "More what? More women? More conquests? More sex in the hallways?"

He dug his hands in his pocket and scuffed his black leather shoe on the white tile. When he looked up, a corner of his mouth lifted and his gray eyes appeared sad. "I needed to know I was more important than a specimen, that I was wanted for more than just a convenient companion."

"So you made out with a secretary in the stairwell?"

"She at least pays attention to me." When she spun away, he grabbed her arm. "I should have broken our engagement first, but every time I tried, you'd bury yourself in this lab." He ran a hand through his hair and stepped closer. "It would never have worked between us. I couldn't compete with your first love."

"What are you talking about?"

"Your obsession with science." He inhaled deeply and looked at the corner ceiling, before his gaze came back to her. "Face it, Elaine, you love science more than you ever loved me."

"No, I don't." Her denial was swift, followed closely by the thought *'Do I?'*

He crossed his arms over his chest and stood with his feet spread slightly. "Then say it."

"Say what?"

"Say, I love you." He stood still waiting for her response.

She summoned righteous indignation, puffed out her chest and prepared to say the words he'd asked for. She opened her mouth, but the words stuck in her throat like a nasty-tasting wad of guilt. Instead of saying anything, she exhaled.

Had she ever really loved Brian? She studied his rounded face and curly blond hair. He had the geek-boy-next-door look, and he'd made her smile on occasion. She'd enjoyed the feeling of having someone to call her own, and to fill the lonely gap in her everyday existence. She hadn't had anyone in her life, no one to turn to since her parents had died four years ago. Having grown up too smart to fit in with kids her own age, she'd missed the much needed education only peers could provide and she didn't have any close friends. Had she wanted too much from Brian?

Had she really loved him? After all the years of living in relative isolation from any meaningful relationships, was she even capable of feeling love?

Her chest felt as empty as her roiling stomach. He was right. She couldn't say she loved him when she knew those words were a lie. And as much as she didn't like conflict, she disliked lying more.

How long had she been deluding herself into thinking they were the perfect couple?

"It's no use, Elaine. Our marriage would be a huge mistake. The only way you'd notice me is if I were a specimen under your microscope. It's not enough. I need more. I need someone who isn't afraid to get out and experience the world beyond this lab."

He turned and walked out, leaving a quiet room full of scientific equipment—and one very confused woman.

Afraid to get out? She glanced around the stark clean walls of the laboratory, the one place she could escape to when she wanted to feel safe.

Dear God, why can't I be like normal people? Brian was right. She felt more comfortable behind the lab door than in the world outside.

When she stared down at the litter of items on the table, blinking to clear the tears from her eyes, she spied the jar labeled Bayou Miste. The container had come to her in the mail, an anonymous sample of Louisiana swamp water. She stood, momentarily transfixed by the sight of the plain mason jar, a strange thrumming sound echoing in her subconscious, almost like drums beating. Probably some punk in the parking lot with his woofers too loud.

With an odd sense of fate, she leaned over the microscope, dried her tear from the lens with a tissue, and studied the slide. Her skin tingled and her heartbeat amplified. Here was her opportunity to get away from the lab.

She could help solve the pollution problems of an ecosystem, even if she couldn't solve the microcosm of her love life.

CHAPTER 2

LIGHT GLINTED OFF THE MIRROR ON THE EASTERN WALL OF THE TINY bedroom, nudging Craig out of a deep sleep. He cracked an eyelid and blinked at the persistent glare. Sunlight on the mirror? The sun never shone directly into this room in the morning, only in the late afternoon. Glancing at the clock on the nightstand, he jerked awake—groggy, but awake.

Six-thirty? As in six-thirty in the *evening*? He squinted at the clock. Yes, the little red light indicating PM glowed bright and the sun shined into his room on its way to the western horizon. *Damn*. His uncle knew he'd had a meeting with Jason Littington at one o'clock this afternoon. Why hadn't he gotten him up earlier?

Craig stretched and flexed his muscles, surprised how agile he felt after being tied to a tree. He felt woozy, not like from a concussion, but more like from a hangover from too much alcohol and not enough water to replenish his brain cells. But, all in all, no harm had been done in last night's fracas.

Fuzzyheaded, but definitely hungry, he rolled out of bed—and fell a long way down to the floor. Too late, he realized he should have put his feet down first. As he fell, his body tensed, and his muscles braced for impact.

He landed on all fours, the wind temporarily knocked out of him. When breathing returned to normal, he looked around.

Huh?

He hadn't been drunk when he went to sleep the previous night. But here he was, crouched on the floor looking up. The bed he'd just vacated and the wooden nightstand towered over him. He blinked to clear the haze. Something wasn't right. Perhaps it was because he was squatting.

Squatting? Why am I squatting?

He attempted to straighten, his muscles bunching in an unfamiliar way. When he tried to stand, he only leaped to another squatting position, and he was no taller than before. The nightstand and bed still loomed next to him.

Noises from the front of the store alerted him to his uncle's presence, and he crawled for the door, forcing his arms and legs to propel him. He'd never noticed how dusty and bumpy the wooden planks were. The going was slow and tedious, but eventually he made it to the doorway leading from the back room into the bait shop.

He opened his mouth to cry, "Uncle Joe!" but his voice croaked.

"I don't know where that boy gets off, leaving me here to answer to Littington," the old man muttered.

Craig forced air past his vocal chords, only to emit another croak. *I'm here, Uncle Joe,* he thought, willing his uncle to turn his way. *I was here all day. Why didn't you wake me up?*

Joe Thibodeaux had his back to him, rooting around behind the counter, shifting small boxes of weights and hooks, searching for something.

"Damn." Uncle Joe pulled back his hand. A hook protruded from his thumb, blood oozing around the gold metal. "This place needs a good cleaning. Couldn't find a snake if it stuck its head out and bit my ass."

He gingerly eased the hook from the digit and dabbed the blood against his T-shirt. Then he turned and circled the counter, practically stepping on Craig. "What the heck—" Uncle Joe used the tip of his sneaker to push Craig out of his way. "You don't belong in here. Go on. Get on out of here. I ain't got time to mess with you." His uncle strode for the door leading out to the dock.

A fly buzzed past Craig's head and he froze, his gaze tracking the insect's flight. An urge so powerful, a primal instinct older than time, erupted in his brain. He struggled to control it, fought to stop it, but he couldn't help himself. How could he deny what his body insisted on doing? He watched in horror as his tongue snaked out to snatch the fly from the air, and he swallowed it whole.

His eyes bulged. *Was that my tongue? I saw my tongue out in front of my face?*

Making the next logical connection, he gagged. *Bluck.* He'd swallowed a fly! He stuck his tongue out and pawed at it with his hand to remove the bug guts and germs. It was then he noticed his skin.

The room spun and he sat down on the floor. He blinked his eyes several times, then held out his arm again. It wasn't tanned and sprinkled with manly black hairs, as it had been the night before. His skin was smooth, shiny and—and—*green*!

Numb with shock, he crawled to the glass display cabinet with the expensive fishing reels. He bunched the muscles in his legs and jumped high enough to peer at his reflection in the glass. A mottled green water frog looked back at him.

Holy shit!

He jumped again. The frog came into view again.

This couldn't be happening. He was still asleep and this was just a continuation of the whole Voodoo thing—one long, crazy nightmare. People just didn't change into frogs overnight—no matter what that Voodoo witch would have him believe. He was asleep, right? He bunched his legs to take another look. Propelling himself off the ground, he realized he'd miscalculated a little and whacked his head into the glass.

Damn.

Not only did he see the frog again but, based on the pain in his head, he wasn't asleep either.

His legs trembled, and he leaned against the cabinet, feeling his miniscule frog heart pounding against his slick white chest. A chest like the one on the frog he'd dissected in high school. Not a chest a man could pound his fist against.

Holy shit. Now, what was he supposed to do? Somehow, he had to find that Voodoo witch and get her to undo what she'd done.

Shadows lengthened in the bait shop. The sun was setting and Uncle Joe hadn't turned on the inside lights.

Craig's skin tightened, stretching and pulling. He trembled with the force of every cell in his body splitting and changing in a miraculous metamorphosis. A roaring sound filled his ears and he watched as everything around him shrank.

* * *

Focus, Elaine. She had a mission to accomplish come hell or high water. By the looks of the long causeways she'd crossed getting to Bayou Miste, high water it was. Which was fine. If she concentrated on her mission, she wouldn't keep thinking of Brian's betrayal or of the millions of gallons of water surrounding her.

With a shiver coursing down her spine, she sent a fervent prayer to the heavens that she wouldn't have to set foot in it. Hopefully, everything she had to do, she could do from a boat or dry land.

Egad, *a boat*. Another shiver convulsed her body.

Elaine had inherited her mother's accursed fear of water. No specific incident could be blamed for her irrational panic in regard to getting in over her head, much to her chagrin. There was no logic in this crippling fear. Ever since she was a child, she'd been deathly afraid of entering water deeper than her bathtub, much preferring to shower.

Then why the hell hadn't she sent a graduate student to the bayou instead of driving here herself? She sighed. She'd face a thousand miles of swamp filled with water just to get away from the university and her disaster of a love life.

She had spent the entire trip from Tulane to Bayou Miste fuming and berating her blind stupidity. Why hadn't she seen through Brian's lies? Throughout their four-month courtship and ultimate engagement, he'd been kind, attentive, and accommodating of her need for space to do her work. What more could she want?

Passion? Gut-wrenching love? And most of all, fidelity? Was that really too much to ask? They'd been *engaged*, for heaven's sake.

She slammed her palm against her Toyota's steering wheel. If she hadn't seen it with her own eyes, she'd never have believed Brian was having an affair. Right under her nose.

No matter. Clearly, she was much better off without him.

When she pulled into the little town of Bayou Miste, Louisiana, on the edge of the Atchafalaya Basin, she had completed her self-coaching session. She was a worthy and intelligent scientist whose work was important to the protection of a fragile ecosystem. She would locate the source of pollution killing the creatures that lived in the swamps. Once her research was complete, she would document her findings and take whatever action necessary to close down the source and force them to clean up the mess they'd made.

But, as much as she tried to use logic and reason to mitigate it, Brian's rejection still stung. Was something wrong with her? Would she ever feel more passionate about a man than science?

The trip had taken longer than she had anticipated. She hoped the marina was still open. She wanted to move into her rental cottage and set up her lab as soon as possible.

Bayou Miste could barely be called a town. Main Street ended in the parking lot of Thibodeaux Marina, beyond which spread endless miles of swamp. Dilapidated houses lined both sides of the street for the equivalent of one city block. It was a good thing she'd made her arrangements before she came. Only one rental house existed in the entire town and it was all hers for the next three weeks.

An unsettling thought struck her and she glanced up, breathing a sigh of relief when she saw electrical lines. By the looks of the buildings, the town must have been built over seventy years ago, maybe a hundred. Peeling paint curled off the sides of a few houses. Weather and humidity had done their job to try to convert the structures into recycled compost.

The bait shop located at the center of the marina was in the same condition, except where someone had applied a fresh coat of white paint to a square patch about seven feet tall and seven feet wide. The bright white contrasted sharply with the graying boards. The can and paint brush stood against the wall, waiting for the painter to pick up where he'd left off.

The dock stretched off to the side and behind the bait shop. No one stirred in the lingering heat of the late evening. She understood why. She flipped her visor down and checked her appearance, attempting to smooth the frizzy mess her hair had become in the moist air. It was no use. Her hair knew no boundaries with one hundred percent humidity. She gave up.

Much as she hated to admit it, Brian had a point. She hadn't been out of the laboratory for a while. Mixing with people and being sociable was not easy for her in the best of circumstances. Invariably, she clammed up and stood there like a lump or, on occasion, she blurted out her opinions and alienated everyone within earshot. She preferred to read or walk alone. Sometimes she talked with other scientists, sharing information on past experiments or theories.

She felt like a fish out of water when she was outside the university environment. What did normal people talk about? What could she find in common with them? Hopefully, it wouldn't be an issue while she was in Bayou Miste. She would find her specimens, conduct her studies, and not be bothered by social obligations.

She pushed her glasses up her nose, gathered her purse and her courage, and climbed out of her practical, four-door sedan. After a few deep breaths of thick swamp air, she almost gagged. The rank smell of fish and stagnant water permeated the air. She squared her shoulders and marched up to the door of the bait shop, pointedly ignoring the water beyond.

Mr. Thibodeaux said she could find him here. Not only did he own the marina, dilapidated as it was, but he was also the landlord of the house she'd be living in during her stay. She hoped the house was in better shape.

She pulled at the rusty handle on the screen door, hoping the inside of the bait shop didn't smell as bad as the outside. When the door swung wide, she stepped into the dark interior and inhaled deeply. Again, she choked. A combination of earthy, fishy, musty odors assailed her nostrils.

Her eyes adjusted to the darkness left by the waning light of the setting sun. Soft thumping noises emanated from the far end of the store, but she couldn't see well enough in the dim interior to make out a person. Why hadn't anyone turned on the lights?

"Excuse me," she called softly.

More thumping and scuffling ensued. Elaine thought she heard a faint moan, but nobody appeared. Good lord. What had she interrupted?

She cleared her throat and tried again. "Excuse me?" Her voice echoed off the walls, and she cringed.

Still no response.

What was wrong with these people? She knew she'd spoken loud enough this time to wake half the town. Perhaps the person behind the counter wasn't a person. Maybe it was a dog or cat.

Whatever it was might be trapped or hurt and need her help. Her heart rate increasing, she strode across the room and had almost reached the other end of the building when a man rose from behind the counter, his back to her.

She stopped so fast she almost tipped over and her mouth dropped open.

Wow.

She'd never seen such a beautiful human male specimen in all her twenty-six years. His broad, bare shoulders were solid and tanned, each muscle neatly defined and precisely curved. His back tapered down to a trim waistline, disappearing below the top of the counter to what promised to be magnificent buttocks of firm proportions.

With his back still to her, he cleared his throat. "Am I...?" He held his hands up to the meager light from the windows and flexed his fingers. Then, holding his arms in front of him, he plucked a hair. "Ouch!" He laughed out loud and shouted, "Thank God."

Elaine stood in a silent stupor as the muscles in his shoulders flexed and extended with each movement. Her mouth went dry and not a single coherent thought surfaced.

He turned and treated her to the full force of his ice-blue gaze. Ebony hair hung long around his ears and curled down the nape of his neck in dark waves. A single lock fell across his forehead and he pushed it back into place with a broad hand.

Her fingers itched to pull the curl back down on his forehead. Her stomach did flip-flops at the expanse of hard-muscled chest only a few feet away.

Startled by her reaction to the half-naked man standing in front of her, she felt her eyes widen and she licked her lips. At least she *thought* he was half-naked. Was that a bare leg she could see through the glass case standing between them? Her ever-curious gaze slid downward.

The man glanced down, a faint red staining his cheeks. He folded his arms across his chest and quickly leaned forward against the counter. "Can I help you?"

It took her several seconds to locate her tongue before she could reply. "I need you," she stammered.

The man smiled and a wicked eyebrow rose up under the stray lock of hair that had fallen back over his forehead. He didn't comment, nor did he move, staying firmly in place, the counter covering him from the waist down. "You need me?"

Heat crept up her neck and into her face when she realized what she'd said, and what she'd tried to see. "I mean, I'm here about the bed."

His smile broadened.

She pressed her hands to her cheeks, her mortification complete. Where had her intellectual vocabulary and scientific mind gone? She felt like a giddy, hormonal teenager instead of a respected scientist with numerous research articles and a book under her belt. "Oh, good grief, let me start over."

"Perhaps you should." His words seeped into every pore of her skin like butter on a hot potato. He could have mocked her sudden inability to articulate. Instead, he graced her with an encouraging grin.

Her mouth opened, but her brain refused to engage. She had the overwhelming urge to run her tongue over his lips to taste his next sentence.

He cleared his throat. "Are you, or are you not, going to start over?"

She gulped, then stammered, "I-I'm Elaine Smith." Wiping the sweat from her palm, she stuck her hand out.

"Craig Thibodeaux." His rough hand enveloped hers. The simple gesture sent tingles through her digits, reminding every cell in her body she was female, single, and over twenty-one.

Myriad sensations raced from her fingertips to her lower extremities, moistening places that had no business being wet in the company of a strange man...a sexy-as-hell, strange man. Maybe shaking hands with him wasn't such a good idea after all.

When her senses returned, she jerked her hand back and rubbed it against her khaki slacks to still the spread of electrical impulses triggering an entirely chemical response throughout her body. Her reaction was pure physics and chemistry, nothing more, nothing less, she told herself. Besides, hadn't she just broken off an engagement? *Get a grip.*

"Mr. Thibodeaux, I spoke with you on the phone about renting a cottage for three weeks." She chose her words carefully, rather than uttering embarrassing nonsense as she had earlier.

"You must have spoken to my Uncle Joe. He owns the place."

"Oh, I see." She dragged her gaze from the vicinity of his chest and scanned the interior again. "Where can I find him?"

"I think he's out on the dock. Why don't you go see?" The man—Craig—didn't make a move from behind the counter. "I'd take you out there, but I have something I need to do first."

The thought of the dock paralyzed her. Docks were generally built around water. "I can wait," she said, quickly. "Go ahead and finish what you were doing."

Craig frowned and glanced away. "No, really, I don't want to hold you up. Just go on outside. He's sure to be within shouting distance. I'll be out in just a minute."

"Oh. Okay." She stared at the door he indicated with all the anticipation of one heading for a guillotine. "Are you sure you don't want me to wait?"

"Positive. Please, go on."

Geez. He sure was in a hurry to get rid of her.

Good. She didn't have time for men. Remember? Besides, she couldn't possibly have anything in common with an uneducated fish boy like Craig Thibodeaux. She was better off sticking with her scientific studies. She could have much more interesting conversations talking to herself. At least with her own company, she knew where she stood.

A little voice popped into her head, *yeah, hiding behind a microscope.*

She liked to think she was moving at a swift walk toward the door. If she was honest, it was more like a snail's pace. But she didn't stop, she kept right on going. Even though the dock was scary, the marina owner's nephew left her more unsettled than the murky swamp around her. She reminded herself that she'd come to study frogs, not the mating habits of the Cajun swamp dwellers. The less she saw of Craig Thibodeaux, gorgeous body and all, the better off she'd be.

CHAPTER 3

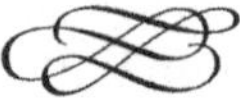

ONCE OUTSIDE THE BAIT SHOP, ELAINE STOOD WITH A HAND PRESSED TO her chest and breathed deep, calming lungsful of the sticky, warm air.

What had come over her? The sight of one bare-chested male shouldn't cause her to take leave of her senses. Even if he was one of the most beautiful specimens of hot, spicy Cajun males she'd ever seen. With those piercing blue eyes and more than his share of dark curly hair on his head...and on his chest...

She fanned the rising heat spreading up her neck into her face. Beads of perspiration blossomed on her forehead and upper lip.

No man had ever had this effect on her, not even Brian. And, frankly, it scared her.

Elaine Smith was a scientist, not a hormonally-charged teenager prone to mooning over attractive guys. Pushing loose tendrils of hair back from her damp forehead, she scanned the dock, looking for Mr. Joe Thibodeaux—hopefully a much older gentleman with less sex appeal than his nephew.

Darkness had cloaked the landscape and the water was even murkier and more menacing now than in the daylight. A boardwalk ran approximately fifty yards to either side of the bait shop with short piers jutting out at thirty-foot intervals to allow boats to pull alongside for refueling or overnight docking.

Lights dotted every other pier, providing a safe port for returning fisherman. At the end of the long boardwalk stood a grizzled old man in baggy tan shorts and a tattered T-shirt. He was deep in conversation with another equally aged man sitting in a fishing boat.

Anxious to get settled in the cottage, Elaine focused on her goal, not the water. Thank goodness she couldn't see through the boards to the swamp below.

You can do it, one step at a time. Don't look at the water to your right or left, just look to the next board in front of you. Thus schooling herself, she marched the length of the dock, slowing as she approached the men. She hung back far enough not to interrupt their conversation, but close enough for them to see her, and for her to overhear their words.

"I don't know what done it, Joe," said the man in the boat. "But, I tell you there musta been twenty or so fish floatin' belly-up."

"Now, Bernie, you sure you didn't see any sign of city folks in their flashy boats?" Joe scratched his scraggly whiskers. He lowered his hand to pat the faded picture of a leaping fish displayed across his shirt. "Sometimes they fish all day just for the sake of catching. Then they dump all those dead fish before they leave."

Bernie shook his head. "I thought about that, but not a one of 'em showed signs of having swallowed a hook. That's when I found this." He reached under the seat in front of him and pulled out a small alligator not much bigger than a baseball bat. Its body was already beginning to bloat and a milky film had formed over its eyes.

Elaine's heart sped up and she stepped forward. "May I see that?"

Two startled heads turned in her direction.

She inhaled the scent of decaying fish. Despite the rotting stench, she could barely contain her excitement. She held out her hand. "Hi, I'm Elaine Smith. Are you Mr. Joe Thibodeaux?"

"That's me." Joe took her hand. "You that doctor from Tulane who called about the house for rent?"

"I'm the one," she responded with a smile.

Joe frowned. "I thought you'd be older."

"Sorry to disappoint you. Is that going to make a difference?"

"No. Your money spends the same."

Bernie tossed the dead alligator onto the wooden dock and climbed out of the boat. "What's a pretty lady want with a dead 'gator?"

"I'm a scientist. I came to study the effects of pollution on the creatures that live in the swamp." She pushed her glasses up her nose and squatted next to the alligator on the wooden planks. "Where did you find it?"

"He found it in the swamp about five miles from here," Joe said.

Bernie frowned and stepped between Joe and Elaine, shooting a hard look over his shoulder at Joe. "I got a tongue. I can speak for myself." He faced her and pulled his fishing hat from his head, displaying oily, white "hat hair" and a gap-toothed smile. "Like Joe said, I found that 'gator and some dead fish in a lagoon about five miles from here. Durn shame, too. Used to be my favorite fishin' hole."

Blood pounded through her veins. She put her hand on Bernie's arm. "Would you take me there?"

His face flushed red and he twisted the hat in his gnarled hands. "Now, I'd like nuttin' more than to take you there, but my wife, Lola, would skin me alive if she found out I took a pretty young thing out to de swamp. She'd skin me alive and feed my flesh to them 'gators."

She turned to Joe. "Don't you rent out boats?"

Joe held his hands up. "Now, don't get some fool notion of going off on your own to find them dead fish. You'd get lost as soon as you left the dock. Besides, the swamp ain't no place for a lady."

"I'm no lady. I'm a scientist." She winced belatedly at her choice of words.

"Scientist or no, I don't rent my boats out to people I don't think can bring 'em back."

"Then perhaps you could take me?" She lifted the corners of her lips. "I'll need to hire someone for the next few weeks to take me out to gather frogs and fish for my studies."

"Folks around these parts do their frog-giggin' at night when the frogs are most active. If you're wantin' frogs, you'll have to go out at night to get 'em. I'm no night owl, but I know someone who is," Joe said, looking over her shoulder. "Here's your man. My nephew, Craig, can take you."

Fingers of sensation trickled down her spine. Without having to look, she knew he stood behind her.

"Craig can take who where?" His voice was as sultry as the humid air, oozing sex appeal with every syllable.

How did he do that? Did he have some way of emitting testosterone that, combined with her long-dormant hormones, caused spontaneous combustion in her lower abdomen?

She refrained from fanning her face, braced herself for impact, and executed a slow turn. The half-naked man from the marina stood in faded blue jeans, bare feet, and a cotton shirt, untucked and hanging open. This unkempt man had no right to look good enough to eat, one lick at a time, like a very tall ice cream cone on a hot day.

She was determined not to react as idiotically as she had previously. "No thank you. I'll eat another guide."

All three men gaped at her.

She clapped a hand to her mouth when she realized what she'd said. "I mean, I'll get another guide, or go alone."

Joe shook his head. "Dr. Smith, you don't seem to understand. Craig's your best bet as a night guide. And my rule is no guide...no boat."

"What are you more afraid of, the swamp or me?" Craig dared her with a half-smile and a hiked eyebrow.

She frowned. This was the second time a man had accused her of being afraid. She'd be damned if she'd take that lying down. Although, with him, lying down held a certain appeal.

Jumpin' genetics, what was she thinking? Heat surged up her neck and into her cheeks. Thank God he couldn't read minds. Straightening her shoulders, she stared straight into his eyes and replied, "Neither."

"So, when do you want to start?" Craig asked.

Boy, he moved fast. She felt a little out of breath. Although she struggled, she congratulated herself on keeping her inner turmoil from showing on her face. "I hope to have my lab set up by tomorrow night. Can you handle that, Mr. Thibodeaux?"

"Lady, I can handle anything you've got." He ran his gaze from the top of her curly brown hair, over her crisp white, oxford cloth shirt, down her neatly ironed khaki slacks, to the tips of her sensible Birkenstocks.

She gulped, forcing her chin to a defiant angle when she'd rather run like a scared rabbit in the face of a hungry wolf. "Good," she said, her voice squeaking. She cleared her throat and assumed her best professor voice. "I'll see you tomorrow at dusk. Please be on time and—" she eyed his open shirt, and raised an eyebrow in what she hoped was a disdainful look "—fully dressed."

"At your command, Dr. Smith," Craig said with a sweeping bow and several rolls of his wrist.

She turned to the elder Thibodeaux, who'd remained quiet throughout the exchange. "May we go to the house, now?"

"Yes, ma'am." He popped a smart salute, immediately softening it with an impertinent wink. Joe turned to his nephew. "You take care of Bernie's boat while I help Miss Smith with the rental house."

"Sure, but when you get back, we need to talk," Craig said, his expression serious.

She stared from the older man to the younger one. What was that all about? She didn't know, but she'd do well to keep a close eye on the younger Thibodeaux...and keep her hands and thoughts to herself.

* * *

An hour later, Craig had tied up Bernie's boat, topped off the gas tanks, and cleaned the seats and floors of all trash. Although it had been eight years since he'd visited his uncle, the activities were still second nature from all the summers he'd spent helping at the marina.

When Uncle Joe still hadn't returned, Craig paced the length of the dock. At every light pole, he stopped and held an arm up in the circle of light. He batted away moths and mosquitoes to get a glimpse of his skin to make sure he wasn't turning green. Occasionally, he ran a hand through his hair to reaffirm it was still there.

"What bug have you got up your butt, son? You're as twitchy as a trapped ringtail."

Craig spun to face his uncle, all the pent-up emotions of the past twenty-four hours gushing out in four words. "I'm in deep shit."

"Your daddy comin' down here?" Uncle Joe asked. "'Cause if he is, I'm leaving. I can't take two minutes of his high-and-mighty bullshit."

"No, it's worse." Craig said.

Uncle Joe scratched the gray stubble on his chin. "Can't think of anything worse than that stiff-necked brother of mine comin' for a visit. So, spit it out."

Craig pushed his hand through his hair again. "You're not going to believe this."

With a frown, Uncle Joe laid a hand on his shoulder, concern reflecting in his pale blue eyes. "Try me."

How did he tell his uncle that he was related to an amphibian? "Have you ever heard of Madame LeBieu?"

Uncle Joe nodded. "Seen her once or twice out in the swamps. She's been known to practice Voodoo on occasion. Had a buddy of mine who swore he'd never get hitched. Said he had too many women to love before he saddled himself with a ball and chain. But Madame LeBieu slipped him a love potion and he went and married dog-faced Darlene Dubois." Uncle Joe smiled. "Dangedest thang. Every one of their poor kids looks just like Darlene."

"Well, I had a personal invitation to visit with the priestess last night."

Uncle Joe's shaggy brows climbed up his forehead. "She asked for you in person?"

"No, she insisted on my coming. Mo and Larry delivered an invitation I couldn't refuse."

"Holy cypress knees." Uncle Joe clapped a hand to the top of his head, looking worried. "Did you do something to piss her off?"

Craig paced a few steps away. "Not that I can remember. I went out with her granddaughter, Lisa LeBieu, earlier that evening. When Lisa came on to me a little too strong, I took her home."

Uncle Joe scratched his whiskers. "That's gotta be a first."

"That's just it." Craig smacked his fist into his palm. "Lisa was mad I didn't take her up on what she was offering, so she got her Voodoo-practicing grandmother involved."

"Not good."

"No, it's not." An image of the old Voodoo witch materialized in his head along with the thrumming of the drums tapping a tattoo at his temples. He pinched the bridge of his nose to dispel the picture. "It's real bad. I think she put a spell on me. Last night when I went to bed I was a man. This afternoon when I woke up, I was a frog." His lips tipped in an ironic smirk. Jesus. He sounded crazy even to himself.

"Say again?"

Craig looked his uncle in the eye. "That old witch put a spell on me. When I woke up earlier, I was a frog."

"You don't say." Uncle Joe slapped his hand against his leg and hooted with laughter.

"Maybe you didn't hear me." Craig frowned as his uncle chuckled. "When I woke up this afternoon, I was a *frog*. As soon as the sun set, I turned back into a man."

"Got to admit that's the lamest excuse I ever heard for not showing up for your meeting with Littington this morning. Not sure I liked that guy, but I do like your story."

Frustration slammed through Craig. "I'm not kidding, Uncle Joe. I was as ugly a green water frog as you've ever seen in the swamp, and about this tall." He held his thumb and forefinger two inches apart. "Hell, you almost stepped on me a while ago when you poked your finger on that fishhook.

"That was you?" Uncle Joe scratched his head. "Didn't look much like you. Thought it was a stray from the swamps that got into the shop. Good thing I didn't step on you. How would I explain to your parents, I killed their only son when I stepped on him?"

"Uncle Joe." Craig's patience wore thin. "Perhaps you don't understand. This spell makes me a frog by day and a man by night. The old bat said something about having until the next full moon to figure out how to break it. That's less than two weeks." He snorted. "Otherwise, you're stuck with a frog for a nephew, forever. Hell, this sounds like some sick fairytale."

"Yeah, boy. You done messed with the wrong Voodoo queen. She don't give up until she gets what she wants," Uncle Joe said. "What'd she say she wanted?"

Apparently, living in the bayou made even the most down-to-earth men, like his uncle, believe in magic. Thank God. "I'm supposed to find someone who'll fall in love with me by the next full moon or I'm stuck being a frog."

Uncle Joe crossed his arms over his chest and tilted his head to the side. "Better get crackin'."

"What do you mean, get cracking?" Was his uncle insane? "You aren't suggesting I go along with this crazy swamp woman?"

"Don't see as you got much of a choice."

"I've got a choice, all right." Craig climbed into the skiff. "I'm going to find that witch and make her undo what she did to me."

"Won't do you no good." Uncle Joe lips twisted. "My cousin begged and begged, but when Madame LeBieu sets her mind to something, not even a hurricane as powerful as Katrina can budge her."

With his hand poised to yank the pull string on the motor, Craig paused. "What do you mean?"

"Only way you're gonna fix this mess is to follow her instructions."

Craig laughed without humor and rolled his eyes. "Like I'm going to find someone to love me in that short a time? Hell, I haven't found anyone in the past twenty-eight years. How will I find someone in less than two weeks?"

Uncle Joe tapped a finger to his temple. "You got a point, son. But you better try, unless you fancy flies and bugs for breakfast every morning."

Craig sat down on the hard metal seat of the little boat and buried his face in his hands. "Great, I'm screwed."

Uncle Joe scratched the whiskers on his chin. "What about the scientist lady? Can't you make her fall for you?"

Craig looked up and snorted. "She's not my type." Although, with eyes the color of Spanish moss and soft curls framing her face, Elaine had her own appeal, in a subtle way. She'd come across as vulnerable instead of the intimidating he suspected she'd been aiming for.

"And you've been more successful with the women you usually go out with?"

Craig's lips tightened.

Uncle Joe folded his arms across his chest. "Exactly. Maybe Madame LeBieu has a point."

Disgusted, Craig threw his hands in the air. "Oh, don't tell me you're on her side."

"No, but you gotta admit, your track record ain't so great."

"And since when have you started keeping score?"

"Since you first started noticing girls back when you were a smart-mouthed teenager comin' to visit me on your summer vacations. That's when. And don't tell me you're here strictly for work. I know you had a run-in with a woman back in New Orleans, and don't try to tell me different. Your daddy and I still talk, even though I don't know what he's saying half the time with all that lawyer jargon."

"I didn't come here to get away from a woman," Craig grumbled. "I have legitimate business with Jason Littington."

"Yeah, and I ain't partial to beer. Since when do you lawyers perform house calls? And when do you plan to head back to New Orleans?"

Resigned, Craig climbed out of the boat and walked a few steps toward the bait shop before he answered. "I'm not sure. Considering my present circumstances, I'm not certain I'll ever go back. You have got to help me out of this mess."

"You're ignoring my question."

"Look, if it bothers you for me to be here, I'll leave."

"Dug a finger in a festering wound, did I?" Uncle Joe dropped his arms to his side. "You know you're welcome to stay as long as you like. I can always use the help with the marina."

"Thanks, Uncle Joe," Craig said. "But that still doesn't fix my problem."

"Maybe an apology to Madame LeBieu and her granddaughter would be the place to start."

Craig ground his teeth. "The thought of apologizing to that old witch goes against the grain. I acted like a gentleman with her granddaughter and she considers that cause enough to sentence me to being a frog? I don't get it." His shoulders sagged and he sighed. "But if apologizing will get her to lift the spell, I'll do it. Anything to keep from changing back into a frog."

"That's more like it. Sometimes you got to get humble. And in the meantime, be nice to the lady scientist. She might be your salvation, the one to fall in love with you and break the spell."

Uncle Joe didn't seem to understand. Craig wasn't interested in love. As a high-dollar attorney-for-hire, he'd represented the gamut of divorce cases. He'd witnessed what he'd thought were reasonable adults do cruel and ugly things to each other in the name of revenge and greed.

Disillusioned, he had sworn to avoid the "D" word the only way he knew how...by thoroughly avoiding the "M" word. With his job and his lifestyle, he couldn't picture any one woman sharing his world for longer than half a year—max. And then what? Divorce, raked over the coals, dragged through the quagmire of he-said-she-said court.

No thanks, not for him.

Craig stomped back to the bait shop for bug repellent. He'd have to hurry if he planned to talk with Madame LeBieu before sunup.

Hell. And he'd thought his law practice was stressful. So much for coming to Bayou Miste to conduct a little business and snatch a bit of peace and quiet.

* * *

"My words stand." Madame LeBieu's melodious voice held a hint of steel. She stood with her arms crossed over her massive bosoms and her lips pressed into a stubborn line. The skirt of her Hawaiian-print muumuu billowed in the breeze blowing in off the gulf. "You must find a woman to love you before de next full moon, or your skinny little butt be a green hoppin' one forever."

"You can't be serious." Craig flung a hand in the air and paced the ground in front of the rickety porch. "How am I supposed to get a woman to love me when I'm a frog?"

"You got all night long to work yer magic, my friend."

He stopped in front of Madame LeBieu. "Most people sleep at night."

"Dat be *your* problem."

"And where am I supposed to find an eligible woman in the swamps?"

"Bayou Miste has plenty single women. What about de scientist lady I sent f—what come here on a mission? You be sure and help her find what she be lookin' for. Her heart is true and she cares, unlike you."

Craig stood at the foot of the warped wooden steps holding a lantern high to size up his adversary. He'd argued in some of the most hostile courtrooms and won cases against the best attorneys, but Madame LeBieu was in a league all her own. "I don't have time to date swamp women. I've got to complete the deal with Littington and get back to New Orleans. I can't go as a frog. Be reasonable."

"Looks to me as if your priorities have changed. If you don't do as I say, you won't have ta worry 'bout going to work no mo'."

"I could sue you." He cringed as he said the words.

Madame LeBieu snorted. "Go ahead. No judge will take you seriously if you can't even show up in court." She laughed and turned to reenter her ramshackle clapboard house. "Sue me, ha!" Her chuckles could be heard even as the screen door slammed behind her.

"I'm doomed," he moaned. He glanced at his watch. The sun would rise in less than an hour. He'd have to hurry to get back to the marina before the transformation.

The screen pushed open again and Madame LeBieu stood with one chubby finger raised. "One other ting. The magic don't work if she know about your problem."

On the ride back through the swamps, he thought through his options. Some options. He could do as Madame LeBieu said or stay a frog the rest of his life.

From where he sat, the vote was unanimous. He had to find a woman and make her fall in love with him in less than two weeks. Simple, right?

CHAPTER 4

WHOEVER SAID IT WAS QUIET IN THE COUNTRY OBVIOUSLY HADN'T SPENT time in the bayou. The raucous sounds of crickets, cicadas, and frogs were every bit as loud as the traffic outside Elaine's cozy house in the suburbs of New Orleans.

In a strange place with all new and sometimes frightening sounds and smells, Elaine spent a restless night tossing and turning. When she'd managed to sleep in short spurts, her dreams had run the gamut from scenes of Brian and the secretary to dark and sinister swamps filled with eerie croaking frogs. A steady thrumming laced each dream, as if drums beat to the rhythm of her heart.

When the pre-dawn grayness heralded the sunrise, she slipped out of bed and padded into the tiny kitchen to make a pot of coffee. Since she wasn't sleeping, she might as well get started.

She'd unpacked only the necessities the night before, one of which was the coffee maker. While the machine heated the water, she returned to the bedroom to change into khaki slacks and a ribbed T-shirt. She was tugging a brush through her tangled hair when she heard a knock at the front door.

With a quick glance in the mirror, she sighed. What was the use anyway, in this humidity? Her hair bushed around her in wild, wavy abandon. In a few swift motions, she swept the tresses back into a wide-toothed clip and raced for the door.

She turned the deadbolt and swung the door wide.

"Mornin', neighbor." A diminutive, older woman with hair the color of warm honey sailed into the room, a cloth-covered basket dangling from her arm.

Elaine stepped back, unsure how to react to someone barging into her home, temporary though it was.

"I smelled coffee a-brewin' and figured you were finally awake. Mind if I join you? I brought breakfast." The woman didn't seem to care that Elaine hadn't responded to her first words. She plunked the basket on the table and bustled through the kitchen as though she knew her way around.

The aroma of hot muffins wafted through the air, reminding Elaine she hadn't eaten. "Excuse me, should I know you?"

"Oh, bless my soul." The other woman held out to her hand. "I'm Mozelle Reneau. I live right next door to you. I just finished bakin' a batch of the best blueberry muffins you'll taste in the entire parish, if I say so myself, and I thought, Mozelle, it wouldn't be neighborly of you to keep them all to yourself, now would it?' So I marched myself right on over here to see if my new neighbor would be interested in sharin' a muffin and a chat with a stranger, although I hope we're not strangers for long."

How could any one person talk so long, and so fast, without taking a breath?

"And you are?" Ms. Reneau waited as if poised to pounce.

"Elaine," she gasped. She held out her hand and said more calmly, "Elaine Smith."

"And where might you be from, Ms. Smith?"

"New Orleans. And, please, call me Elaine."

"Why thank you. I'd be pleased to call you Elaine and I insist you call me Mozelle. The local boys and girls call me Miz Mozelle, if you're more comfortable with that. I don't mind, either way. There. Now that we're properly introduced, we can become quite chummy over a hot, fresh muffin and—" she sniffed, eyed the coffee pot and smiled

"—coffee."

Miz Mozelle moved around the tiny kitchen pulling down clean plates and coffee mugs from cabinets, more at home than Elaine. "We have an occasional visitor to these parts from New Orleans. Mostly, they come to fish. Once in a while, they like it so much here, they stay."

"Really?" Elaine asked politely when Mozelle paused to breathe.

"Certainly. Why our own Mr. Thibodeaux is a New Orleans transplant to these swamps. He and that nephew of his are quite the scoundrels. I like sugar in my coffee, no cream. Which do you prefer?"

Elaine sat at the small dinette table with a white-speckled Formica top. "The younger one."

"Pardon?"

Elaine's face burned and she mumbled, "Only sugar, please."

"Me, too. I like mine hot and black with a couple spoons full of the sweet stuff. As I was sayin', Joseph Thibodeaux is the black sheep, if ever there was one in the Thibodeaux family. And by the looks of it, that young nephew of his could be followin' in his footsteps."

"Why do you say that?" Elaine shifted in her seat, embarrassed by her bold encouragement of the gossip. But she could swear she saw a sparkle in the older woman's eyes when she said Joe's name and curiosity got the better of her.

"Craig used to come visit his uncle durin' the summer. He and his friends were always pullin' pranks and into things they ought not to be. Why, one time I had to shoo them away from my peach orchard. They must've thought I was a crazy woman swingin' my broom and whoopin' like there was no tomorrow. Good thing I did. As it was, they got a good bellyful of green peaches. Had them sicker'n dogs for a day or two."

A smile tilted the corner of Elaine's lips. She could visualize a younger version of Craig, racing through the peach orchards with a broom-wielding Mozelle close on his heels.

Miz Mozelle glanced over her shoulder toward the door. "Why, speak of the devil, there's Mr. Thibodeaux now."

Elaine's blood jolted through her veins and she reached a hand up to smooth her uncooperative hair before she turned.

"Ms. Smith, you up and about?"

At the sound of Joe Thibodeaux's husky voice calling to her from the porch, Elaine's heart skidded into a slower rate. She turned to answer, "I'm up, Mr. Thibodeaux, come on in."

He pulled the screen door open and stepped in. When he spied them sitting at the table, he scraped the floppy fishing hat from his head. He crushed the hat in his hand, raked his other hand through his wild, white hair and dipped his head politely in their direction. "Dr. Smith, Miz Reneau."

Mozelle popped out of her seat, smoothed her not-so-natural strawberry blond hair, and pulled a cup out of the cabinet. "I'm glad you took my advice and stocked this house with a matchin' set of dishes and silverware. Makes it mighty homelike for such a nice visitor as Miss Smith. Come join us for a cup of coffee."

Joe hovered by the front door, frowned, and stared down at his flip-flop-clad feet. "I just came to see if Dr. Smith wanted help unloadin' her car."

Elaine jumped up from her chair. "Oh yes, thank you. I could use a hand. Some of the items are heavy. Students at the university helped me load. I'm sure I could unload by myself, but your help would be greatly appreciated." Her lungs gasped for air. What had gotten in to her? She sounded as loose-jawed as the sweet Mozelle Reneau.

"Joseph, are you gonna stand there, or come in and have a cup of coffee with us?" Miz Mozelle stood with a cup in one hand and the coffee pot in the other, poised to pour.

He looked acutely uncomfortable. "No, thank you. I have to get back to the marina. Got a fishing tournament to launch. Can you wait for an hour, Dr. Smith? I'll be back to help then."

"Certainly." Elaine glanced around the room. "It'll give me time to figure out where I can put everything."

"Good enough." Joe nodded to her and Miz Mozelle, then backed out of the house. The door thumped loudly in its frame.

"*Mais, jamais d'la vie!* He took off outta here faster than a scalded cat. There's no gettin' into that man's head, now is there? If he were any kind of gentleman, he'd have sat down with us for a cup of coffee. Those

Thibodeauxs need lessons in manners. You'd think with their background and schoolin' they'd have learned some by now."

Elaine leaned against the front door frame.

The marina stood a few buildings away. Indeed, the Thibodeauxs could use a set of manners. What with the one rushing out the door as fast as he could, and the other running around half-naked in a place of business.

With the rambling prattle of Miz Mozelle in the background, Elaine allowed her memory to recreate the image of Craig standing behind the counter in the bait shop. As a scientist, she couldn't deny the kinematical perfection of the muscles rippling across his back when he'd flexed his arms high over his head. With her lips compressed, she mentally shook herself. But as a woman, she could certainly tighten the reins on her own chemical reaction to the man.

He was not her type, and she had no desire to plunge into another relationship doomed to go nowhere. Her love of science would stand in the way every time. No use going there.

"I'll be glad when he settles down with one woman. Me, and every mother of unwed girls in the parish. What that man needs is a woman who can knock his socks off. You know, rock his boat until he can't see straight."

Elaine's attention jerked back to Mozelle. "I'm sorry, who are you talking about?"

"Craig Thibodeaux, as if anyone wouldn't know. He's hell bent on sleepin' with every woman who catches his eye. Has every addlepated female around here vyin' for his attention."

A sudden disappointment settled over Elaine's sunny day, startling her. Why should it bother her to hear every woman around wanted to crawl into bed with Craig Thibodeaux? She didn't even know the man.

"Well, I'd best be moseying along." Mozelle set her cup in the sink. "I have a bridge game over at my house in one hour. Join us if you have a hankering to play a hand of cards."

"Thank you, Miz Mozelle." Elaine walked the older woman to the door. "And thank you for the muffins."

Fifteen minutes later, after a few accounts of how she'd trumped

Louella Landau in last week's bridge game, and reciting a list of the ingredients she'd used in the blueberry muffins, Mozelle finally made it out the door and on her way.

Elaine collapsed on the couch, winded by her encounter with the loquacious Mozelle Reneau. But, despite her new neighbor's constant chatter and enthusiasm, she was more relaxed now. The little cottage held a sense of home to her.

Not two minutes after Mozelle left, a tapping alerted Elaine to company at the door. She pulled herself off the old couch. Joe Thibodeaux hovered on the other side of the screen staring over his shoulder in the direction Miz Mozelle had disappeared.

"Hello, again."

"Thank God, she's gone." Joe swept his hat off his head and ran a hand through his thick, white hair. "That woman could talk the ear off a fish."

A hound dog the size of a horse nudged the door open.

Elaine smiled. "Does he belong to you?"

Joe turned and frowned. "Nope. He belongs to my nephew. Stay, Dawg."

"What's his name?"

"Dawg." Joe shot a stern look at the animal. "Stay out here and behave yourself." Joe muttered something else, but not quite loud enough for Elaine to hear. It sounded like "I'll handle this."

Now she was hearing things. "Just a minute and I'll get my keys."

Between her and Joe, they had the supplies unloaded and stacked in the living room in less than twenty minutes. The entire time, Dawg lay on the front porch, chin on his paws, his soulful brown eyes the only part of his body moving.

Elaine could understand why. After the first five minutes, the heat and humidity had her sweating profusely.

When Joe laid the last box on the floor, he straightened. "Need anything else?"

"I could use a little help setting up that folding table."

"Sure." While unfolding the legs of the table, Joe cleared his throat. "So, you got anyone back in New Orleans?"

Elaine blinked. "Excuse me?"

Joe's face flushed red. "You know, got a husband or fiancé back in New Orleans?"

Elaine studied Joe through her peripheral vision while shoving the brace into place on the table legs. "Why do you ask?"

Joe jerked the other leg out and smacked the brace before he answered. "Just curious. Not many young females come out this way by themselves. Seems kinda strange." Joe tugged at the collar of his T-shirt.

She couldn't tell what he was getting at, but relented and answered. "No, I don't have anyone special in my life back in New Orleans." Boy, that sounded pathetic. She felt awkward in a community where everyone was probably spoken for. And she, from a whole city full of people, couldn't even claim to have a serious relationship. Yeah, she truly sounded pathetic. Still. She had her career, science, and a cause to champion. What more could a woman want?

"My nephew, Craig..." Joe started.

She swiveled her gaze back to the older man and groaned inwardly. Why, when she thought she had her act together, did she continue to run into reminders of the half-naked Cajun with the coal-black hair and ice-blue eyes? Had it been so long since she's had hot, steamy sex that the first really good-looking man she saw had her ready to jump his bones?

She recalled sex with Brian. Those experiences had been nice, but hardly hot and steamy.

But here in the sultry swamp lands where beads of perspiration pooled between her breasts and rolled downward to the band of her trousers, all kinds of slippery images slid through her imagination. All of them included gliding her naked skin against Craig Thibodeaux's smooth, incredibly taut and bulging muscles.

"So, what do you think?"

She wasn't sure what Joe wanted. Was he asking her a question? "I'm sorry, what did you say?"

Joe's blush deepened to a ruddy russet. "Would you consider going out with my nephew?"

His words slammed into her gut and plummeted lower where they had no business plummeting. "Go out with your nephew? Craig?"

"Yeah." Joe looked up and smiled, his expression as pleading as Dawg's had been out on the porch. "He really is a nice guy, once you get to know him."

"Let me get this straight. You're asking me to go out with your nephew, Craig?"

Joe nodded, twisting his hat in his hand.

"Not that I'm interested, but why doesn't he ask me himself?"

"Oh, he doesn't know I'm asking for him. And, frankly, I don't think he'd be pleased to find out I had. But if he does ask you, will you give him the benefit of the doubt and say yes?"

Her breath quickened at the thought of being alone with Craig. "I'm going out on a boat with him tonight. Isn't that enough?"

"I know this may sound strange, but try to get to know him." Joe's gaze fixed on the hat scrunched in his fingers. "He's a little shy around the girls."

Elaine propped a hand on her hip. "That's not what Mozelle Reneau said."

Joe frowned. "Miz Mozelle likes to gossip. You shouldn't listen to her."

"She said you were the black sheep of your family. Is that true?"

Joe's lips tightened. "She's got no business telling that story to a stranger. What's happened in my family is my own business, not hers."

"By the looks of him, Craig could well be the black sheep of the family now. And you want me to go out with him?" Elaine gave the man a pointed look. "Why does he walk around half-clothed?"

Joe gulped and tugged at his collar. "It's mighty hot around here in the summertime."

"Since you're not going to tell me why you're the black sheep, I'm not guaranteeing I'll consider an offer of a date from your nephew."

Joe mumbled and turned toward the door. "That's what he gets for messing with a Voodoo queen."

Did he say *Voodoo queen*? Perhaps she'd heard wrong. "What was that you said?"

"Nothing." Joe waved a hand over his shoulder. "I gotta get back to the bait shop. I left a motor running or something."

"Thanks for helping me unload." When he didn't respond, she added, "I'll keep your request in mind."

The older man turned and smiled. "You won't be sorry."

She already was. If Craig wasn't the only guide she knew in the area, she'd keep as far away from him as possible. He unsettled her, and she didn't have any theory or hypothesis of why.

She stood at the door for several minutes watching Joe amble down the road toward the bait shop. When he was halfway there, Elaine realized he'd left Dawg.

She waved her hand at the animal and nudged him with her foot. "Go on, Dawg. Go home." The dog slowly stood, his tail thumping against the wooden planks of the front porch.

The animal's eyes were so soft and beseeching, she caved and opened the door to go back inside and unpack. "Fine. You stay on the porch. See if I care." She looked back at him, but he'd gone. She marveled at the comings and goings around Bayou Miste.

She had a lot of work to do before the evening and her rendezvous with the other Mr. Thibodeaux. At the thought of the Cajun hotty, the trail of perspiration between her breasts increased. *Damn my unruly hormones*. She marched to the window air conditioner and turned it down several notches to chill her skin.

Unfortunately, the temperature had nothing to do with the tingling sensations rippling through her body.

CHAPTER 5

"CRAIG! CRAIG!" THE LOUD SCREECH OF THE SCREEN DOOR HERALDED Uncle Joe's arrival at the marina.

Since he'd woken after sunup, all green and slimy, Craig had paced the floor. Well, as much as a frog could pace. He'd hopped a path back and forth across his bedroom throughout the day. Like an idiot, he'd closed the door prior to his transformation into a frog. Once he'd shifted, he was stuck in the bedroom until Uncle Joe came looking for him and let him out. His frustration level had topped out hours ago.

After his visit with Madame LeBieu, and before his metamorphosis, he'd sat down with Uncle Joe and covered all the bases if anyone came looking for him during the day.

His father was bound to demand to know his whereabouts and why he hadn't sealed the deal with Littington. His "working vacation" was supposed to be over in two days. With plenty of work piled on his desk awaiting his attention, the others at the family law firm would be less than sympathetic to his tardy return.

If anyone asked for him from Bayou Miste, Uncle Joe was to say he'd been summoned to a nearby town and he'd be back late. Craig would call Jason Littington the following evening to arrange for a night meeting.

If his father or brother called during the day, Uncle Joe was to tell them he was taking some time to catch up on his fishing and would return their call that evening.

Meanwhile, he was stuck as a frog during the day, which had its own set of challenges. He hadn't eaten since the night before and he was getting desperate enough to eat a twelve-pack of flies. But the back bedroom was fly-free and his froggy belly was starving. He'd tried to get his mind off his hunger by thinking of solutions to his problem, but he'd come up short of any foolproof answers. How did you argue with a spell —or a Voodoo queen for that matter?

To get a woman to fall in love with him would be a piece of cake. But he didn't want the lady in question to think he was committing to anything other than a convenient relationship to break an inconvenient spell. He may be a confirmed bachelor, but he wasn't out to hurt anyone.

He hadn't had a committed bone in his body since he'd dated Tracy, back in law school. From that incident onward, he'd made it a point to inform his lady friends he didn't want a long-term relationship. He'd told each one of them he'd drop her if she started making noises about happily-ever-after. Much to their disappointment, he'd done just that. Which was one of the major factors in his decision to take this pseudo-vacation.

Ah the lovely, Cassandra. One of the newest partners in his family's law firm. Beauty and a razor-sharp intelligence was a killer combination. What a shame she'd only been hunting a diamond engagement ring. And Craig thought she was going to be different, but she'd turned out like all the rest. He wondered if she'd ever really loved him. Not that he wanted her to...until now.

Hell, he should call her.

"Where are you, dagblast it?" Uncle Joe's voice called out on the other side of the wooden door.

Craig hopped away from it to avoid being pancaked.

"Craig?" The door swung open and his uncle towered above him. "There you are." Uncle Joe squatted down and peered at him. "That is you, isn't it?"

Craig nodded.

Uncle Joe grinned. "Takes a little gettin' used to, havin' a frog for a nephew. Almost thought I dreamt it all up." He clapped his hands together once.

The sound reverberated through Craig's head and he staggered backward.

"I've got good news. That scientist lady doesn't have any significant other hanging around New Orleans waiting for her to come back. You can ask her out. That is, as soon as you're up to it. Get it?" Uncle Joe laughed so hard he fell back off his heels and landed on his backside.

Craig wished he could claim credit for knocking his uncle over. How could the old man make fun of him when he was in such a dire predicament?

Now, what had his uncle said about the scientist lady? She was single? Craig cringed. As if he needed his uncle to set him up with women. He could do that all on his own.

Dr. Smith looked like someone with relatively little experience in the field of love. He grimaced. She'd definitely expect more than he was willing to give. Her moss-green eyes would look up at him and beg him to love her in return. *Damn.*

"I even softened her up for you."

Uh-oh. What did Uncle Joe mean by that?

"I asked her to consider going out with you, and told her you were all right and not to listen to anyone who says otherwise."

Craig croaked and fell over on his back. Just what he needed, a matchmaking uncle.

"Craig? Are you all right? Didn't get a hold of a rotten fly, now, did you?"

Craig flipped over onto his haunches and shook his head.

"Good. Gave me a damn heart attack." Joe straightened. "Could you use some fresh air? I'll let you out the side door. Here, let me carry you."

Craig hopped out of range of his uncle's hand and made his own hoppity way toward the door.

"Okay, okay. I get the hint. You always were a determined cuss. Have it your way." Joe opened the door and allowed him to hop down the steps and out onto the grass.

Inside, the phone rang. Joe glanced back at the bait shop. "Will you be all right out here by yourself? I'm going to answer that. Could be Littington."

Craig nodded.

Uncle Joe dashed back inside to answer on the fourth ring.

The overgrown grass needed cutting. Craig could barely see over the top of the jagged spears. He glanced down the road to where Uncle Joe's rental house stood on the other side of Old Lady Reneau's. No one stirred outside in the midday heat.

He wasn't so certain being outside was a good idea. The world was a cruel place for a small green frog. He peered back at the bait shop. He could see beneath the porch. He never realized how dark and sinister the underside of the porch appeared. What dangers lurked beneath? Was there a huge snake waiting to swallow him whole? Death by digestion. He shuddered.

"Woof!"

He jumped a full foot off the ground, his heart thumping against the thin wall of his chest. The grass cushioned his fall and he leaped to the side.

Behind him hovered a beagle, half the size of Dawg, but twenty times the size of a frog.

"Woof!"

The sound deafened his ears and he raced for the steps to the bait shop. He didn't stand a chance of making it up the steps, but he could duck beneath. Suddenly, the underside of the bait shop didn't look so menacing. Next to the slobbering black, white, and tan beagle, it was a haven—should he reach it before the dog decided to take a bite out of him.

Two inches from sanctuary, sharp teeth closed around him, locking him behind the canine bars of ivory. And the smell of dog food and dead animals permeated his senses.

Craig freaked and instinctively puffed out his body. His skin oozed a natural coating of bitter-smelling oil. The dog gagged and he fell from its mouth to the grass below.

He staggered to all four webbed feet and gazed up at the beagle. The dog's chomps foamed and he shook his head to rid his mouth of the nasty taste of scared frog.

Ha. Served him right. Eating defenseless frogs.

A deep-voiced bark sounded from the house down the street, and Craig looked up in time to see Dawg barreling down the road toward him and the beagle.

The beagle stared at the much larger animal, tucked his tail between his legs, and sped off in the opposite direction.

Way to go, Dawg. That's putting the fear of dog in him. When Dawg reached him, the hound ground to a halt so fast, his back end nearly flipped over the front of his body. He sniffed at Craig and whined.

Craig could swear the dog knew him. Dawg was apparently a lot smarter than he'd ever given him credit for.

Dawg nudged him with a cool, dry nose, knocking him over. Then a long, wet tongue snaked out to rasp against his chest. The ground trembled with rhythmic thumping. Craig's heart kicked into hyper-drive. Was it the Voodoo drums? He righted himself and noticed Dawg's tail whacking the ground.

Damned wishful thinking. That old witch wasn't going to let him off the hook that easy. She wanted him to grovel and suffer for a while. To hell with that. He'd think of something or someone to get him out of this.

Yeah, but who and what?

He glanced around. And spotted Mo and Larry ambling down the street, two very large characters in a small town. He'd always thought they'd make great bouncers in a New Orleans bar, but after their role in his abduction and ultimate cursing, he was convinced.

A slick black Camaro pulled to a stop beside them and the window slid down. Randall Pratt leaned out. "Who's the piece of ass renting Joe's cottage?"

Craig heard his question, even from as far away as he was and his blood boiled. Randall was a snake, a low down worm of a man and he had no respect for women.

"Dôn know," Mo said. "Why dôn you ask Joe?"

Randall snorted. "Clueless." The window slid up and he drove off spewing gravel.

"Man's got a problem." Larry's gaze followed the vehicle.

"Yup. Wonder how he can afford dat ride." Mo bent to pick up a rock.

"Didn't know Acme paid dat well."

"See him drivin' round in dat truck down by de plant."

Larry snorted. "Madame LeBieu need to put de *gree* on dat one."

Mo resumed walking as if Randall had never stopped to question them.

They halted when they saw him sitting there next to Dawg.

Larry leaned down and stage-whispered in a voice loud enough for Old Lady Reneau to hear, "Hey, Craig, is dat you?"

"Of course it ain't him. Dat frog dôn look nothin' like Craig."

"How you know what Craig looks like as a frog? Have you seen him yet?"

"Course not, fool. I tink he'd look like a lot smarter frog den dat. Dat one's hoppin' away like it dôn know me."

Craig croaked a laugh, heading for the bait shack.

Larry cupped a hand to his mouth and yelled. "Craig!"

Both men wore the maintenance uniforms of Littington Enterprises, crumpled and dirty from a hard day's work cleaning and performing maintenance on oil refinery equipment.

"Hey, Dawg." Larry pointed." You thank dat be Craig?"

Mo leaned down and inspected him again. "Nah, I told you, dis frog looks too dumb."

"Yeah, but you know how Dawg hangs wit' de man like he ain't got any better sense."

Mo scratched his head and frowned. "Dat you, Craig? If it is, hop twice."

Craig rolled his eyes, a technique infinitely easier as a frog. He hopped twice.

Larry grinned widely and rocked back on his heels. "What do you know? It is Craig."

"Yeah," Mo grumbled, "but he still don' look too smart."

Larry planted a hand on his hip. "Have you ever seen a smart frog, Mo?"

"Guess you got a point." Mo dropped to the step beside Craig. "Hey, man, Larry and I got dis ting figured out."

Craig nodded his head, hoping to encourage Mo to continue.

"We tink we got you some ways out of dis problem."

All right already, spit it out. Would they go and plead with the old bat to free his body to return to normal? Would they sacrifice themselves to allow him to be free?

Larry plopped onto the stoop and pulled a folded sheet of paper from his pocket, carefully straightening it. "We made a list of candidates."

Candidates? Oh no, not them too. Between Larry, Mo and Uncle Joe, they'd have him married off before the sun rose on a new day.

"Yeah, we figured you might need some help being as you're a little short on time." Larry snickered. "Short, get it?"

Mo elbowed him. "Get on with it."

"Anyway, we thought of every single woman in de parish who might fall for you. Top of de list is DeeDee DuBois." Craig's groan came out as a *ribbet*, and Larry lifted a hand. "Jes hear me out. She's twenty-four and available. Better still, she dôn have no prospects."

"Larry put her on da list. Me? I couldn't get past her slack jaw and pock marks, but she'd be willing and would fall in love within de first fifteen minutes of a date. Hell, she'd fall in love with a warthog, she's dat desperate."

Craig used his front foot to make a gagging motion.

"No?" Larry looked down the list. "Maddie Golinski."

"She be too young. Din' we scratch her off the list? She's only fifteen. Give it to me." Mo snatched the list and continued down.

"How about Lisa LeBieu?"

Craig swung his head side to side in a swift motion. *No way.* She was the one who got him into this pickle in the first place.

"Guess not." Mo ran his finger further down the list. "I'm sorry to say, but dis town dôn have many unattached girls. All de good ones done been spoke for. You gonna have to settle for one of de not so good ones."

Craig hung his head.

"Cheer up, buddy. At least you be seeing dem at night. If you find a dark enough place, you can pretend she's pretty." Larry smiled. "Dat's what I do."

"You be a sad, sad little man, Larry."

Larry frowned and stood. "Am not."

Mo rose, a full two inches taller than Larry. "Are too."

"Not."

"Too."

Larry's frown lifted. "Hey, how 'bout my sister, Josephine?"

Craig remembered a gangly pre-teen in pigtails. Josie, the little girl who used to kick him in the shins.

"You haven't seen Josie in eight years. She be all growed and not half bad to look at."

Mo crinkled his eyes into a narrow squint and touched a finger to his chin. Finally, he shrugged. "Hate to admit it, but Larry's right. She's jes returned from beauty school."

"Yeah, she's learned a trade and everytink. 'Bout to drive mama and de girls nuts doin' all deir hair and nails."

Craig couldn't get past the image of the twelve-year-old Josie. And his friend's sister. Since he didn't plan on a life-long commitment, he couldn't get involved with a friend's sister.

Mo tapped the paper in his hand. "Dat's all we could come up wit'. You could go to another parish, but dat'd take time. Time you don' have."

Overwhelmed by his lack of a viable solution, Craig hopped away from Larry and Mo, dejected.

"We feel for you, man." Larry called after him. "Can't begin to know what you're goin' tru. Never been a frog before."

"Yeah," Mo agreed.

Craig could tell him. It stank. Almost stepped on, chewed on by a dog, less than two inches high, no way to communicate... For a man with a law degree, his future didn't look so bright.

"Mo." Uncle Joe's voice carried through the screen door at the back of the bait shop.

Mo jerked his head toward the door. "Does your uncle know 'bout de Voodoo *gree?*"

Craig nodded.

With a grin, Mo yelled, "Yo, Uncle Joe, I be out here wit' your froggy boy." He pushed himself off the steps and turned toward the door.

Joe called, "Your grandmother just phoned. T-Rex is loose again, and your grandmother can't find Fifi. You better high-tail it home or she'll make handbags and luggage out of that 'gator."

"C'mon, Larry. Craig'll figure dis mess out. He's de one with all de diplomas. Need you to distract Rex while I sneak up from behind."

"Why am I always de distraction?" Larry groused. "Dat's jes a fancy way of sayin' I be de bait for dat darn fool 'gator."

"Yep, but he likes de way you taste better'n me. We better hurry afore he makes a snack out of Mamere's poodle."

Craig tried to laugh at the hulk of a human worrying about his grandmother's toy poodle, but all he could do was croak.

"Yeah, Craig, we know," Mo reached out a hand to haul Larry to his feet. "You dôn have to thank us for all our suggestions. Just get to work on followin' tru."

"I'll tell my sister you'll be callin'. Dat'll have de whole house in an uproar. Give dem somethin' to do besides gripe about Josie's beauty supplies all over de bathroom."

"C'mon, Larry," Mo said. "Good luck, Craig."

"Yeah, and watch out for snakes and 'gators. You ain't much of anythin' right now." Larry waved a hand, and the two hurried off in the direction of Mo's house where he lived with his gray-haired grandmother.

Craig gave a frog version of a sigh.

Thirty-three year-old Mo still lived with his mother's mother. The old woman was a hoot. She'd shared her moonshine and weed with them when they were hormonal teenagers full of themselves and bent on trouble. Craig knew Mo thought the world of his grandmother and woe be upon the person who upset her.

But Larry's departing words sank deep. He wasn't much of anything.

The simple phrase struck too close to home. How true it was. Not only in size, but also in accomplishment.

When was the last time he'd done something he could feel proud of? Mo took care of his grandmother. Larry, for all his complaints about his eight sisters, loved each and every one of them. He wouldn't have offered to fix Craig up with Josie if he didn't think highly of Craig.

Larry's was a gesture of trust and faith in Craig to do the right thing. Only problem, Craig wasn't looking for a commitment along with the love he had to find in some poor unsuspecting woman. He wanted her to fall for him, declare her love, break the spell, and he'd be on his way, a whole man—minus the heartbroken woman.

Jeez. It sounded heartless, even to him.

"Craig, I gotta service a few engines out on the dock. You're welcome to come with me." Uncle Joe paused on the steps. "Nah, you'd better stick close to home. No telling what could eat you by the water. Don't worry, it's not much longer 'til the sun sets."

Thank God. Although, somehow the anticipated transformation didn't hold as much appeal.

Not much of anything, huh?

He found a quiet spot beneath the step to wait and contemplate his choices. For the most part, he forced down the natural instincts to snatch the flies off boards, but a fat, juicy cricket managed to find its way past the shadows that hid him. The unsuspecting insect was toast with jam to his palate, and why not? People ate cockroaches in some countries.

As soon as he turned back into a man, he'd make some calls, set up a couple dates, test the feminine waters of Bayou Miste. Like Mo said, he didn't have much time and he couldn't afford to be picky.

Perhaps he really should ask Cassandra to come down from New Orleans. He could tell her it was some kind of emergency or other. She'd do it.

And with the pickings so slim in this part of the country, that choice looked more and more like the winner. But even if Cassandra said she loved him, would it be true? Craig didn't think Cassandra loved anyone but Cassandra. Could he afford to waste time on her?

Unfortunately, he couldn't afford not to.

If she didn't work out, he'd be stuck with the local lineup. He shouldn't care whether or not they had teeth or their butts were as broad as the bottom of a pirogue. But he'd prefer to find a woman who could pretty well stand on her own in the looks department. His conscience couldn't handle dumping the lovelorn if she had no hope of ever landing another fish in the sea.

If he remembered correctly, Josie wasn't bad looking as a teen. If Larry had no objections, he'd check out Josie.

With the decision made, Craig felt a little more in control. He'd start a campaign to woo Josie.

As the last wisps of sun sank over the horizon, washing the lush green swamps into gray, Craig hopped onto the steps. No sooner was he settled on the planks, the metamorphosis began. His skin pulled and stretched, the bones and muscles extending, flexing, and growing. His body unfolded, straightening, pushing upward. He closed his eyes against the pain shooting through his nerve endings. Just when he thought he would explode out of his epidermis, the pressure subsided.

He opened his eyes and his vision cleared. He towered above the steps he'd had difficulty climbing just moments earlier.

Steps?

Oh, crap.

Craig glanced down at his naked body parts and darted a quick glance toward the neighboring houses closest to the bait shop. Miz Mozelle stepped out onto her porch. As she turned toward the bait shop, he ducked in the side door.

"Whew. That was close." He'd have to plan his morphing location better next time. Apparently, there'd be a few more next times. But not many, if he could help it.

Time to find his lady love.

CHAPTER 6

ELAINE MADE HER WAY TO THE DOCK WITH A LARGE PLASTIC BUCKET banging against her knees, a satchel containing her journal slung over her shoulder, and a large, yellow flashlight clutched in one hand. She'd chosen to walk the short distance from the rental house to the pier thinking to stretch the kinks out of her legs. But if she were honest with herself, she'd admit she was procrastinating. The thought of spending a dark night in a boat on the water with a handsome man paralyzed her.

She didn't know which made her more uneasy—the man or the water. Either way, she'd plunged in way over her head. She had research to do and the source of the pollutants to discover. Wasn't that enough to worry about?

The thought of being surrounded by water made her stomach churn. Whatever happened, she couldn't lose her cool to a panic attack. This water was no different than what ran from her tap at home. Just a little more of it. But she would be safe in the boat, out of the wet stuff.

In the absence of street lights, the roadside blurred in the endless shadows of dusk. Elaine was glad she'd worn her shiny new mud boots. If anything lurked in the gloom, the calf-high rubber would protect her ankles. Unfortunately, the large boots didn't quite fit, and she clumped her way toward the marina feeling about as graceful as a lumbering elephant.

Arms aching, she hurried the last few steps to the bait shop, plunked her bucket on the porch and almost breathed a sigh of relief. Almost. Craig waited inside. Her heartbeat ratcheted up a notch. Perhaps if she repeated her mantra, she'd keep her wits about her and remain on track. "I am a scientist. I love science. I am a scientist. I love science."

She felt better already, even allowing a smile to curve her lips as she pulled open the screen door.

Just as the night before, the bait shop stood in near darkness, the lights not yet turned on. Her heart jumped into hyper-drive. The last time she'd come in here, she'd met Craig in the flesh, and not much else.

"I am a scientist. I love science."

The back door thumped and she heard soft shooshing of what sounded like bare feet on hardwood floors.

Bare feet. Um...

She eased along a shadowy aisle. By the meager light filtering through the few windows, she could make out a display of strings, hooks, and lead weights.

"I am a scientist. I love science."

A tall shadow emerged in the doorway behind the counter.

"Mr. Thibodeaux? Oh, there you are—"

The rising moon chose that moment to crest over the top of the trees and shine in a window, illuminating him in a bright moon glow. *All* of him.

She gasped, and her mind shut down all other information processing functions. A second after intellectual faculties ceased, every nerve ending in her body exploded in all directions. Her senses leapt into overload and her brain struggled to handle the volume of signals screaming along neural pathways.

Craig grabbed at the closest thing to him—a fish net.

All his perfectly placed body parts were on display. Broad shoulders narrowed to a tight abdomen and a thin line of black curly hair lead to his—

"Oh, my." Elaine froze, staring at the net and all it didn't cover.

He dropped the net and snatched a plastic bag of fake worms from the shelf beside him and covered his—

Good lord.

Elaine kept staring. Her mouth worked but the only words to emerge were, "I am a scientist. I love sex."

"What?" Craig asked, a harried smile tilting his lips.

"What what?" She resisted the urge to smack her forehead with her palm. Stupider and stupider. Who'd have thought she'd attained a double major in chemistry and biology, a master's and a doctorate and graduated at the top of every class?

Craig pushed the hair back from his forehead with his free hand and leaned against a counter, crossing his bare ankles. His pose reeked of confidence, as if waiting on a customer naked constituted perfectly appropriate behavior—at least in Bayou Miste society. "Can I help you?" he asked in a voice completely at odds with his current state of undress.

"Oh, yes." Elaine's response was a breathy whisper.

When he shifted the fake worms to cover more skin, she tore her gaze from his body and darted it up to his eyes. Heat rushed into her face. The hotter her face grew, the faster her breathing became. She had to get a grip or hyperventilate.

Oh, how much easier to sink to the floor in blessed oblivion! But she didn't faint, much to her chagrin. She closed her eyes, inhaling the potent smells of earthworms and fish. With her concentration shifted to the unattractive aromas, she managed to rein in her galloping hormones.

She opened her eyelids and pressed her lips together. "This is getting to be a habit, Mr. Thibodeaux. Do you provide such service to all your customers, or just me?"

"Are you embarrassed by nudity? I thought all scientists approached the human body in a clinical manner."

"Yes, of course." She didn't look at him. She stared at everything but him...shadows in the corners, light fixtures on the ceilings, packages of fake worms. *Oh, geez.*

She compelled her gaze to his face.

His lip turned upward on one side as if he was daring her to say anything more about his lack of clothing.

"Do you want me to wait outside? I don't mind in the least. In fact, I'll do just that." She backed down the aisle, but her bucket bumped against a shelf behind her, clipping the backs of her knees. Her legs buckled and she toppled to the floor in a heap of bucket, nets, and notebooks.

He leapt forward, tossing the worms aside and reaching out to grab her hand. "Are you all right?" He hauled her to her feet so fast she pitched forward and crashed against his chest.

Her fingers laced through his curly chest hairs and her breath caught in her throat. "I'm fine," she said, her voice a husky whisper. Then she noted something hard and stiff pressing into her belly. And it wasn't a package of fake worms.

What would it feel like to reach down and touch—

Elaine looked up into his face. Eyes as blue as a summer sky were hooded in shadow, but his lips curved in a knowing smile.

Embarrassment kept her close. If she backed away, he'd be on full display. But if she stayed where she was, no telling what her crazed senses would do. The scientific method escaped her when she most needed it. She should be reviewing alternatives and examining all angles before coming to the most logical solution to her rising problem.

And rising it was.

Perhaps a closer examination—

A loud click split the air, and the fluorescent lights above hummed to life.

"Craig? You in here?" Joe Thibodeaux's voice called out.

Elaine jumped back guiltily at the sound. What would Joe think if he saw her in a compromising embrace with his unclothed nephew?

Her face burned and she shoved away from Craig's chest, ducking behind a cardboard display of sunglasses. "I'll just wait outside," she whispered. And with one last look at the gorgeous hunk of naked male standing before her, she ran for her life.

Once outside the bait shop, she collapsed onto a weathered bench, pressing her hands to her fiery cheeks. She closed her eyes, but Craig's image burned in her memory. The muscled planes of his chest and shoulders, the narrow hips, tight abdomen and...and... *Oh. My. God.* All bathed in shimmering moonlight and nothing else.

How could she ever face the man again, when her body responded to him even when he wasn't standing beside her?

She really had to rein in her galloping pulse. She opened her eyes and looked around, realizing all her gear lay scattered across the floor inside the bait shop. Hopefully, Craig would bring it out. She couldn't go back in there. *No way, no how.*

Two very short minutes later, Craig banged through the screen door. Blessedly dressed in jeans, a denim shirt, and deck shoes, sure enough, he was carrying all her equipment.

She couldn't look at him without heat suffusing her cheeks. Thank goodness for the darkness of night and dim porch lights. She stood and held out her hands, looking at her stuff instead of his face.

"What is all this stuff?" he asked.

"I'll be collecting water samples, fish and frogs to study." She held out her hands. "I'll take those."

"No need."

"No, I insist. It's my gear, and I can carry it." She couldn't decide whether to smack her palm over her mouth or her forehead. Why couldn't she just shut up and let the man do his job?

"Suit yourself." He set the bucket, satchel, and bright yellow flashlight on the porch.

While he bent to accomplish the task, she couldn't help but notice how his hair glowed blue-black, reflecting the light above his head. She had to resist reaching out to touch the ebony waves.

He straightened and his gaze met hers. Briefly.

Her heart leapt to her throat and she dived down to gather her things. With her bucket looped over her arm, satchel over her shoulder, and everything else gripped loosely in her hands, she followed him down the steps to the dock.

An unavoidable challenge.

His narrow butt was just as tempting clothed as naked. His broad shoulders blocked her view of the water. Or was it she could only see him? In truth, if she looked up, she'd stare over the top of his head straight out into the swamp.

She swallowed, her thoughts an incoherent tangle of emotion and fear, with no logic to balance those unfamiliar, raw feelings.

He turned left and she got her first up close and personal view of the inky black water, not four feet away from her. She stood rooted to the wooden planks of the jetty, mesmerized by the swirling shadows created by the marina lights reflecting off the smooth surface. Her already speeding heart threatened to jump out of her chest.

Suddenly, Craig's retreating figure was a lifeline she desperately needed to grab onto.

Stomach in her throat, she ripped her gaze from the dark, liquid depths and locked in on the man she found completely distracting. Already, the growing distance between them seemed insurmountable. Much farther and she'd be paralyzed, incapable of following him.

Well then, get your pale white ass in gear and catch up.

She forced her feet to move, stumbling after him, keeping her eyes on her goal. Looking ahead instead of down, she charged forward. Then her clunky boot caught on something protruding from the jetty and she pitched forward.

With her arms too full to provide balance, she knew she was doomed. *Not again.* She tossed the bucket off her arm, chucked the flashlight, and threw her arms in front of her to brace for landing, praying she wouldn't fall into the water.

"*Oomph.*"

Her palms connected with rough boards moments before her chest and head, absorbing only a little of the shock. She hit hard. Winded, she groped to either side of her for the reassuringly solid planks of the dock. When she was sure she wasn't dangling over the edge, she lifted her head.

Her hair escaped its ponytail and swung into her face, blocking her view. When she pushed it aside and looked up, a pair of deck shoes stood inches from her nose. She let her hair fall back over her face, wishing it would hide her complete embarrassment.

Craig Thibodeaux squatted beside her and gently lifted the strands to peer underneath, concern written in his frown. "Are you okay?"

Elaine grimaced. "I think the only thing damaged is my pride."

His smile seeped into her bones, warming her to her toes and tempering some of her humiliation. "Don't worry. I've tripped on that same knothole at least a hundred times. Don't know why Uncle Joe hasn't done something about it." He straightened and extended his hand.

She reluctantly accepted the hand. Fear of rolling into the water outweighed her fear of her reaction to his touch.

With one strong tug, he brought her to her feet, and slipped his arms around her waist to steady her.

She breathed in the musky, intoxicating scent of male, her heart skittering into her belly. Everywhere she touched him electric shocks ran through her nervous system, racing through her body to pool with pulsing intensity between her thighs.

"Oh my," she whispered. Pushing the hair from her eyes, she dared to sneak a peek up at his face.

His arms were steel bands around her back, but his expression held a hint of laughter. "Are you going to make it from here to the boat, or do you want me to carry you?"

Startled at the tempting image his words evoked, she shoved against his chest and stepped a few inches away, willing her heart to calm its erratic beat. "I can manage, thank you very much." Laced with irritation, her voice sounded ungrateful even to her own ears. "I'm sorry. I shouldn't be so snippy. Thank you for helping me up. I'm not usually so clumsy."

"Is it just when you're on docks? Or when you're around men?"

Just with you. She bit her lip to keep from speaking the words aloud. Instead, she gathered her bucket and satchel, and scanned the dock for her flashlight.

The bright yellow torch had rolled to within an inch of falling off the edge. Her stomach sank to her knees at the thought of retrieving it. She couldn't ask Craig to get it, and she couldn't leave the darn light. With a thundering pulse and fingers tightly crossed, she inched toward the edge.

Before she came within two feet of it, Craig strode over and scooped it up. "Come on, we need to get going."

He pressed the flashlight into her hand and grabbed her elbow, hurrying her toward the boat. She felt as if she were caught in a river, headed toward the falls with no way to make it to shore. Her heart hammered in her chest and her hands grew slick.

She wasn't ready for this. *She couldn't do it.*

As they neared the end of the pier, she glanced around for the boat. Her expectations ran along the lines of an airboat or maybe a pontoon boat. Preferably an ocean cruiser, if only it would fit. What she found was a dinky metal skiff with an even dinkier engine mounted on the back.

Her world tilted and turned all hazy around the edges. "Breathe," she muttered to herself.

"Did you say something?"

"No, not at all." She'd hoped for light and airy, instead she sounded completely flaky—like a woman ready to fall off the deep end of sanity. Which, frankly, was exactly how she felt. She filled her lungs with air. *I can handle this.* She smiled and opened her eyes.

Larger-than-life Craig no longer loomed safely in front of her. He stood about a yard away, down in the tiny rocking boat, his hand outstretched.

She swayed.

Oh, God.

* * *

"TAKE MY HAND," Craig ordered firmly, instinctively sensing Elaine's fear. Although she hadn't said a word, he felt it in the way her hand shook when she placed it in his.

What the hell? Was she afraid of *him*? Twice now, she'd landed in his arms, and the experience had been...well...not unpleasant.

His groin tightened.

Okay, she'd sparked something carnal in him. Big shock.

He almost laughed out loud. Wouldn't she be appalled, if she knew?

He tamped down his lusty thoughts and tugged her gently to the edge of the pier. "Now all you have to do is step down. I'll do the rest."

Despite his uncle's opinion, playing tour guide to this lab-rat scientist wasn't going to solve his problem. Not if she was terrified even to touch him. But at this point he was stuck. Perhaps the solitude of the swamps would give him time to mull over his predicament. Come up with something better.

With her hand still in his, she stood staring down at the bayou. Her hair fell in gentle waves around her face, softening her features, making her appear vulnerable. The glasses perched on the edge of her nose couldn't begin to hide her expressive eyes.

When she had fallen inside the shop, as well as on the dock, every one of his protective instincts had shot to the forefront. And when he'd lifted her to her feet and into his arms, his body had reacted immediately, every cell instantly alert. Thank goodness she'd pushed him away. Otherwise he'd have surrendered to the overwhelming urge to run his fingers through her hair and kiss her surprised, pink lips.

Of course, kissing was the right idea, as far as Madame LeBieu was concerned, he reminded himself. If he wanted to break her spell, he'd have to woo someone into falling in love with him.

So, why not the clumsy, pretty scientist?

A dart of anger lanced through him. Damn it! He'd come to Bayou Miste to secure another client for the law firm, not to make some timid, unsuspecting woman fall in love with him.

She wanted nothing to do with him, and he sure as hell wanted nothing to do with love.

Damn that Voodoo witch.

Elaine stood frozen to the boards on the pier. The look of absolute terror in her eyes forced Craig out of his irate thoughts.

"What's wrong?" He searched the boat, the dock, and the bayou. Nothing appeared out of the ordinary.

"Do...do you have a life vest?" she whispered.

"Yes, of course." Craig dropped her hand and reached under a seat for the regulation orange vest. He pressed it into her fingers, and leaned forward to grab her bucket and stow it in the boat.

When he looked back, she stood exactly as she had when he'd handed her the vest, staring at the water, her eyes wide and worried.

"What's wrong?" he asked irritably. Then he noticed her trembling hands, clutching at the vest. She was petrified. But not by him, it seemed.

"I don't think I can do this." Her voice was barely above a whisper.

He jumped at the reprieve. "You don't have to. You could go home. I have other things to do."

His tone must have cut through her fear, because she stiffened her spine. Her lips drew into a tight line. "No. I have to do this."

"It's your choice. But if we're going, you have to get in the boat. Preferably sometime this century."

She stared down at the life vest and back at him.

"For Pete's sake." He climbed out of the boat. "Give me that." Grabbing the vest, he hooked it over her head. The subtle scent of flowers wafted in the air. He didn't know what he'd expected—formaldehyde or rubbing alcohol, maybe. But not the hauntingly familiar scent of wildflowers. He withdrew his hands and noted her skin was as smooth and delicate as silk.

When he realized he was holding his breath, he forced air into his lungs. At that point he should have backed away. But of their own volition, his hands moved forward to lift her hair clear of the vest. The strands cascaded through his fingers to lay wild and soft against the orange fabric. He wanted to gather it up again and bury his face in the shiny tresses.

"Does this strap do something?" she asked, her breath warm against his ear.

A river of awareness coursed through his veins and into his groin. He had to get control of himself before he did something both of them would regret. Elaine Smith wasn't his type. He preferred the tough as nails, what's-in-it-for-me kind of woman. A woman who could hold her own against his cynical views and single lifestyle. Elaine, however, was — He groped for the right word to best describe his impression of her. Soft? Vulnerable? Passionate?

The last word that sprang to mind struck him. Why would he think of her as passionate? Was it her full lips and wide eyes? Or was he only projecting his own carnal thoughts onto her?

He gathered his diminishing willpower and set her away from him. Then he looked down at the strap in her hands. "That hooks around your waist." As he reached for the strap, blood sang in his ears. Before he could take it from her, he stopped himself. His sense of honor warred with his lust. If he touched her again, lust might just win. He pointed at the strap and said, "It hooks around your waist and buckles there."

He did an about-face and practically leapt back into the boat, causing it to rock violently. He fought to stay on his feet, thankful for the distraction.

When he turned back toward Elaine, her face was white.

"Will it do that when I get in?" she asked.

"Do what?"

"That rocking thing." She swayed her hand back and forth, and her face paled even more.

Ah.

Around boats all his life, he hadn't considered she might be afraid of the pirogue. And all this time, he'd thought she must be afraid of *him*.

He smiled up at her. "No, I'll keep it steady. You just hold my hand and step in slowly."

Reaching up, he grasped her hand and tugged gently. At first she didn't budge. Then, one foot at a time, she inched toward the boat. When both her feet were at the edge of the dock, she looked down into his eyes.

As if he were her anchor, she kept her gaze fixed on his and stepped down into the little skiff.

The pirogue rocked gently and she threw her arms around his neck in a stranglehold.

He would have cursed, if he could have breathed. He braced his legs wide, absorbing the sway of the boat until it stopped. With one arm around her waist, he reached his other hand behind his neck to loosen her grip. "It's okay. You're not going to fall. I've got you." He kept his words soothing as he lowered her onto the hard metal seat.

Her arm around his neck only brought them closer when he bent over. His nose buried in her soft curls and he couldn't help but inhale. *Definitely flowers.* He liked that it reminded him of springtime and wild roses in bloom.

Once seated, she released her grip on him, grabbing her seat, her knuckles turning white. "I'm sorry." Her smile trembled and her green-eyed gaze darted around the pirogue.

"Why? Because you almost choked me to death?" He grinned wryly, his heart going out to her. "Don't worry. I'm used to having women throw themselves at me."

Her eyes narrowed. "I was not throwing myself at you." She sounded indignant, more like the self-assured scientist he'd met earlier.

He breathed a sigh of relief. He could remain objective around the confident scientist. Just don't let the frightened mouse reappear or he wouldn't be responsible for his actions.

He turned in his seat, reaching behind him to pull the cord on the outboard engine. After the second pull it sprang to life, chugging and coughing smoke until it settled into a steady rhythm.

With the tiller in hand, he turned to face Elaine. "Ready?"

Her hands clenched the cool metal on either side of her seat. She gulped, then nodded.

He smiled, feeling a grudging admiration for her. If she really was terrified, she was being pretty darn brave.

He eased the boat backward until it cleared the pier, then he swung the bow around and headed into the murky swamp. All the while, he watched the expressions fly across her face in the little bit of light shining from the boat lamps perched on long, narrow rods at the front and back of the vessel. Occasionally, a patch of moonlight filtered through the dense trees overhanging the waterway.

"I-I'm sorry about all the fuss...g-getting in the boat and all," she said. "It's just that I don't know how to swim, and I've a-always had an aversion to deep water." She peered worriedly over the side of the boat, shuddered, and then jerked her gaze back to his.

So it was the water she was afraid of. Not the boat. *And not him.*

For some reason, that cheered him.

He tugged at the collar of his shirt with a lopsided grin. "That would explain the stranglehold. I'll try real hard not to tip us over."

She stiffened. "Is it easy?"

"Is what easy?"

"To tip the boat. Is it easy to tip the boat over?"

"Not if you're careful. Just don't lean too far to either side."

"Don't worry, I won't," she said, her expression deadly serious. "Don't you have bigger boats?"

"*Mais, chère.*" A smile tugged at the side of his mouth. She probably wouldn't feel more comfortable unless the boat was a luxury cruise liner. He noted her fingers hadn't loosened their grip on the bench seat, and his smile softened. She really was scared spitless. "If you want to catch frogs, you have to do so in shallow water. The bigger boats are for deeper water. They'd get bogged down where we're going."

She fell silent, her gaze still locked on him.

He steered the pirogue through the twisting channels, carefully avoiding overhanging trees. The little bit of breeze their speed stirred kept the mosquitoes at bay. He made wide, sweeping turns so as not to tilt the boat and upset her.

At first, her rigid stare made him uncomfortable. He couldn't glance back or he'd risk running into a tree or small island, but he did glance at her from time to time. She wasn't bad to look at. Not at all like the flashy or business-suited women he spent his days with in the Big Easy. Her appeal was subtle. A quieter, deeper beauty you had to take a closer look to find.

Kind of like the bayou itself.

CHAPTER 7

"ARE WE GOING TO WHERE BERNIE FOUND THE DEAD FISH AND alligator?" Elaine leaned forward, eagerly.

"Yes, ma'am." Craig nodded. "Why exactly are you interested in dead fish and frogs?"

She chewed her bottom lip, thinking. Finally, she looked up. "Can I trust you?"

Craig hesitated, his brow furrowing. "Can you trust me?"

Elaine regarded him evenly, hoping she hadn't made a huge mistake in judgment.

"That's my question." *Could* she trust him? Besides being gorgeous in clothes and in the flesh, what else did she know about him?

"Yes, of course, you can trust me."

She swallowed hard. "I'm not good at this cloak and dagger stuff."

He nodded but didn't comment.

She explained, "I received a sample of swamp water from an anonymous source. It was labeled Bayou Miste."

"And?" he prompted.

"When I ran tests on the sample, I found high levels of uranium, thorium, and radium."

His blue eyes narrowed. "How much?"

"Enough to threaten the ecosystem in this area if it's not cleaned up immediately."

"Shit." He sat back and a muscle ticked in his jaw.

"Exactly. If the water samples and animal life I collect show the same toxin levels, the people and creatures in this area have a big problem."

At least his reaction appeared to be genuine concern. She had taken a gamble letting him in on what little information she had in her possession.

"That's why you're here." He stared somberly out at the dark, silent wilderness surrounding them. "This bayou is my uncle's livelihood. He's been here since before I was born."

"What about you? Have you lived here all your life?"

"No." He slowed the engine and nodded at her head. "Duck."

"Huh?"

"Duck." Craig reached across and pushed her head down. Something brushed against the back of her neck, snagged at her hair, then let go. It skimmed across her cheek with a mildly abrasive texture. Visions of snakes and spiders leapt into her mind. A scream bubbled up in her throat, but she clamped her tongue between her teeth and rode it out.

Craig let go of her head and sat back in his seat, leaning to one side. A low-hanging branch weighted by heavy Spanish moss whipped past.

Elaine sent a silent prayer of thanks to the teeth god for holding her tongue. He already thought she was a klutz and a wimpy nut case. No use adding fuel to the fire with an ear-splitting scream.

"You can sit up now, this area is fairly open."

She cautiously straightened, and stared at the man seated across from her. Studying him beat fixating on the inky, black waters, and curiosity about her guide helped distract her from her fears. "So, how long have you lived here?"

"Why do you want to know?"

On the spot, Elaine grasped for a reason. "Maybe I want to reassure myself you know where you're going."

"Don't you think it's a little late to be worried about that?"

"I suppose."

His gaze connected with hers and held for a few moments before he looked ahead of the boat again. "I've been around these swamps for the better part of twenty years. My uncle has had me guiding swamp tours and fishing trips since I was sixteen."

"Aren't you afraid of alligators or snakes?" A chill slipped down her spine.

"Nope, but I do have a healthy respect for them." He smiled and she felt warm all over, as if she could conquer any alligator or snake as long as he smiled at her like that.

"Why did you come to the bayou?" he asked. His attention focused on navigating, he didn't look at her.

"I told you, the water sample, toxins."

"I know all that." His gaze remained on the route ahead. "What I want to know is why you didn't send someone who isn't afraid of water to collect your samples?"

Perhaps because he wasn't looking at her, she felt more inclined to be open. "I guess I was tired of hiding behind my microscope. I wanted to challenge myself, and face my fears." And as much as she hated to admit it, she had her ex-fiancé to thank for opening her eyes to what she'd so recently refused to see.

Craig nodded with a half-smile. "Quite an adventurer. Didn't you do any fieldwork in grad school that required you to get near water to gather samples?

"Yes, but not anywhere near expanses of water as large as this. I stuck to small ponds around farm fields." She grinned sheepishly. "I guess I sound pretty wimpy."

"No. I'd say you're pretty brave for facing those fears. It can't be easy. That you're even in a boat surrounded by water is a testament to your sense of adventure and your courage."

Elaine rolled her eyes. "Now you're just pulling my leg."

He winked. He turned to the motor and flicked a switch. The engine shut off but the skiff continued to slide through the waters of the lagoon, illuminated by the boat lights. Silence descended for a brief moment before the cicadas picked up the beat of the night and roared to life around them. Although the water remained inky black, she could discern the shapes of cypress and willow trees towering above them,

Spanish moss draped from their branches, touching the water like feathery fingers stirring a brew.

Without the noise of the engine, the swamp version of silence deafened her. What did she have to say to the black sheep nephew of a backwoods bait shop owner? She was a scientist and he was...well...a fish boy. Besides being exceedingly handsome, and knowledgeable about the bayou, with blue eyes she could fall into, what did Craig Thibodeaux have that other men didn't? And, more important, what could she possibly have in common with him other than their shockingly intense sexual attraction?

She'd felt his gaze on her and the protruding zipper of his jeans when he'd held her close, both in the bait shop and on the dock. Granted, she'd tried not to think about it, but it was hard.

Oh, yeah. Hard and solid, and begging to be unleashed into her hands.

She sucked in a mortified breath, and stared down at her fingertips as if she'd find the subject of her thoughts pulsing and throbbing there. What was it about this man that inspired her to such lusty imaginings?

She'd never considered love anything more than a chemical reaction to the body's need to reproduce. But these feelings weren't something she could explain away as a mere chemical reaction.

She'd always assumed her hormones would tell her when it was time for children, and then she'd want to have sex. In the past, that passionate urge had never come, and even with her fiancé she hadn't really been all that interested in his lukewarm embraces.

Was her body faulty? Were her chemicals out of balance? Was that why she couldn't get excited to the point of orgasm with a man?

Daring to look up, she was captured by Craig's gaze. His eyes were as pale as the night was dark. She felt a tug in her lower abdomen and a strange throbbing between her legs. Was *this* the chemical reaction she'd been waiting for? If so, what an idiotic time to turn up!

The small boat slowed when they entered a lagoon half the size of a football field. She eased around in her seat and strained to see to the far side. Moonlight glinted off the silvery scales of floating carcasses.

"There they are." She ahead excitedly, her fear of the water temporarily forgotten.

The stench of rotting fish and vegetation filled her nostrils to the point she almost gagged. She pulled her collar up over her nose, as the boat drifted closer to the pool of death.

"So many dead fish," she whispered, her collar doing little to mask the unpleasant smell. She'd encountered her share of disgusting odors in the lab at the university, but this—

"How much of this stuff do you want?" Craig asked from over her shoulder.

"One of each species should be sufficient." She pointed at one floating fish. "Can we get close enough to collect that specimen?"

"Do you have bug repellent in your bag?"

"Excuse me?" she turned back toward him.

"Bug repellent."

Buzzing tickled her ear and sent a quiver down the back of her neck. She smacked at the buzz, hitting her neck. "I didn't think to bring any."

Craig grunted, reached under his seat, and pulled out a can with a green plastic lid. "Catch." With a flick of his wrist, he tossed the can to her.

She let go of the seat to catch it in both hands. The boat rocked. The motion rattle her so much, she dropped the can and clutched the seat again. The cylinder clanked against the metal floor and rolled to Craig's feet. *So much for being the grand adventurer.*

"Here let me." He snagged the can and flipped off the top. Positioning it in front of her legs, he sprayed a long steady fog around her knees and thighs.

The fumes gagging her, she pulled her shirt collar more firmly over her nose.

"Scoot over," he said.

She slid gingerly a little to her left on the bench.

He stood, twisted, and sat next to her, his hip touching hers.

Breathing became an issue, with or without the dead fish and bug spray. Her lungs worked in small, jerky gasps, insufficient to provide oxygen to her brain. Which would explain the disconnect with her powers of logic. All she wanted to do was to reach out and touch the muscular thigh pressed to hers.

"Lean forward," he said.

She complied, and Craig sprayed more of the smelly repellant across the back of her hair and down her back.

When she straightened, she looked up at him. Her gaze slid involuntarily from his eyes to his lips...only inches from her own. She cleared her throat. "Is that it?"

"Not quite." He reached out with both hands. With his fingers skimming the sides of cheeks, he leaned toward her.

Oh, God. He's going to kiss me.

Heart thumping in her chest, she hovered on the edge of a mighty abyss. She met him halfway, eyelids drooping, lips puckered, inexorably drawn to him.

His gaze coupled with hers and his cupped hand rose up the side of her face. Then he removed her glasses, pressing them into her hands. "Hold these."

* * *

WITHOUT HER GLASSES ON, Elaine's green eyes peered up at him, rounded and appealing in the light from the two boat lanterns. His gaze progressed from trusting eyes to full, sensuous lips. Even slathered in smelly bug spray, the pretty scientist tempted him. Too much. The urge to lean forward and press a kiss to those lush lips nearly overwhelmed him. His hand tightened on the can of repellent and a spray of the potent chemicals blasted out, serving as smelling salts to his senses.

Holy crap. He'd almost *kissed* her.

He sat up straight, sprayed a small amount in his palms and leaned forward again to wipe them against her cheeks.

The pungent smell took nothing away from those mystically green eyes or the silky smooth skin. And the breast rubbing against his sleeve ignited nerve endings best left dormant.

His fingers slipped beneath her hair to distribute repellent to the back of her neck.

Her eyes hovered half-closed, the rise and fall of her chest indicating the same difficulty breathing she'd had when he'd held her steady in his arms on the dock. The combination of silky hair against the backs of his hands, tender skin at his fingertips, and lips only a breath away, rocked his boat.

Moonlight chose that moment to filter through the trees to the little lagoon. Her face shone with an ethereal clearness, like an aberration... or an angel.

She blinked and, with jerky movements, leaned away from him until his hands dropped to his lap. She pushed her wild hair back off her forehead and slipped her glasses on. "How should we kiss the frogs?"

Craig frowned. From confusion over her words or from the sense of loss her movement created, he didn't analyze. "What did you say?"

Despite the dim lighting, he could see the rise of color in her cheeks. "I mean, how do we catch the frogs?"

Jolted back to reality, he shifted his weight to slide over to his seat. He dug a fish net from beneath the bench, handed it to her, and glanced at his watch. Eleven o'clock? With great effort, he stifled a groan. Six more hours to dawn, and he'd moved nowhere closer to resolving his problem.

With a glance across at Elaine holding the net, he realized he'd only added to his problems by agreeing to take the good scientist out for a late-night fishing trip.

No, she wasn't the right woman to break the spell. Unlike Lisa LeBieu, this one had a heart, one he'd surely break when he left this Voodoo-ridden swamp.

She glanced around from the safety of the middle of the boat. "Can we get a little closer?"

Craig did a double-take until he realized she wanted closer to the dead fish. He lifted a paddle from the floor and dipped it in the water, propelling the boat forward.

She twisted around in her seat, exposing the smooth, pale skin of her neck.

The vision twanged his growing awareness of her. He knew how soft the skin was, and thanked the stars it smelled of bug spray. He dipped the paddle again. The force of his stroke inadvertently turned them away from the fish and toward the shore. Moving to the other side of the skiff, he straightened the boat's direction with two compensating strokes. When they reached the fish, he dug the paddle in and slowed the boat to a stop.

"You have the net, scoop it up."

She leaned forward ever so slightly, her neck craning to see the fish, now bumping against the side of the boat. She scooted closer, the skiff dipping down on that side. Peering over, she leveled the net and scooped the fish out of the water, holding it high. A triumphant smile graced her lips. "I did it!"

Her exuberance brought a smile to Craig's face. "Very good. You caught a dead fish. Now, let's move on to the live frogs."

The excited smile turned downward and her nose wrinkled. She slid the fish into the bucket and closed the lid. "I've worked with a lot of stinky chemicals and samples, but this fish reeks."

"Happens when fish die."

Her lips twisted. "Where will we find the frogs?"

"Closer to the shore."

She turned to look ahead, her expression eager.

His perverse sense of humor made him want to frighten her just a little. "That's also where we'll find the snakes and other swamp creatures, so keep your eyes open."

His words had the desired effect. A shiver started at the top of her shoulders and wiggled down her spine. But she kept her back to him. Her spine stiffened and she focused her attention on the shore.

For someone afraid of the swamp, she had spunk. Even when he tried to scare her, she remained on course. She had purpose, a selfless purpose, unlike the people he worked with in New Orleans. There, they would chew her up and spit her out for fun.

His eyes narrowed and he studied her closer. *Or would they?* Somehow, he bet she'd hold her own if she believed in her cause.

"There! I saw one hop into the water." She turned, her face wreathed in an excited smile. "Did you see it, Craig? Can you get closer?"

Her use of his name caused his heart to skip a beat. Had the Voodoo queen done more to him than turn him into a frog by day? Why was he mooning after this cute but geeky stranger? She wasn't anything near his type. Maybe another trip to the witch was in order. Surely, his years as a skilled negotiator counted for something?

The skiff bumped against the shore, jolting him out of his musings.

She yelped and held tight to her seat. When the boat stilled, she looked around. "I don't see any frogs." After a moment she added, "What happened to the noise?"

As if someone had their hand on the master switch, the natural clatter of crickets and frogs had shut off. Silence surrounded them.

"Be still and quiet," he whispered. "They'll return."

The two sat quietly, barely moving except to breathe. At length, a cricket chirped, followed by another, and soon the entire swamp roared with activity.

She smiled up at him. A frog hopped into the lagoon next to the boat. Her focus shifting to the water, she held the net ready and leaned toward the edge.

With the smooth strokes of a natural-born swimmer, a frog the size of Craig's fist sailed on the surface. She reached over the side and slapped the net at the frog. When she pulled it from the water, it dripped empty. Her brows furrowed behind the rims of her glasses and her lips tilted in a pout. "Darn. He was a nice-looking one."

"Next time, set your net in the water just below the surface and lift up when the frog swims over the top."

"Like this?" She leaned over the side and lowered the net in the water.

"Yes. Now, hold still and wait for the next one."

Minutes passed. She held still throughout, determination written on her pursed lips.

Soon a frog swam within range.

Elaine's body tensed.

When the frog swam over the top of the net, she jerked the net up, frog and net dripping water all over the front of her white blouse. "*Woo hoo*! I got one!"

He gulped. The smile on her face combined with the water across her chest sucker-punched him in the groin. Lit by the lamplight, the lacy edges of her bra and the smoothly rounded globes beneath pressed against the transparent wet blouse.

Holding the net over the open bucket, she dumped the frog in with the dead fish, then slid the lid in place. The frog inside hopped, hitting the top with a bonk.

Craig flinched. He could sympathize with the frog. How frustrating to be so small and at the mercy of larger, carnivorous creatures! Not to mention stuck in a container with a stinky dead fish. His stomach clenched, then knotted even tighter at his next thought. "Are you going to dissect him?"

Her attention back on the water, she answered, "Of course. I have to study the effects of the pollutants on his skin, liver, heart, and other organs."

With a sick feeling, Craig looked away. Was his own fate to be someone's science experiment? If he didn't find someone to love him, that's what could happen. Either that, or he'd be snake or alligator bait. Which would be worse—having his brains scrambled or being slowly digested by a reptile?

Perhaps getting the scientist to fall in love with him wasn't such a bad idea.

As trusting and naïve as she seemed, it shouldn't take long. Would a few flowers and dinner in a nice restaurant work on a woman as smart as Elaine? And maybe after dinner they could make love into the wee hours of the morning...

The pert breasts shining through her blouse called to him. He could imagine his hands cupped over them, her dark, wavy hair splayed across his white pillowcase.

"What's wrong?" She glanced up at him and followed his stare to her blouse. "Oh, my goodness!" She crossed her arms over her chest. "Why didn't you say anything?"

Busted.

"I was enjoying the view."

Anger flashed from her green eyes. She turned away and plucked at the material to lift it off her skin. She blew down at the wet fabric, but it would take a lot more than that to dry. With a huffy breath, she kept her back to him. "I guess there's nothing to be done. If I want more specimens, I'll have to live with it." She threw a narrowed glance over her shoulder. "But you could have the decency not to look."

"Sorry." He grinned. "I'm just a man. Can't help it. You have a pair of right pretty breasts."

She swung her legs over the bench to the other side. But her clunky rubber boot heel caught the edge of the bucket, knocking it sideways. The lid flew off and frog and fish slid from inside.

"Get him!" She dove for the frog at the same time as Craig. But the amphibious hopper leapt beneath the bench she sat on. "Can you see him?" She lifted her feet and scooted back on the seat.

He could see one scared frog hunkered low. Just as he lunged for it, the frog hopped. Elaine toppled off the back of the seat, but he caught the escapee.

"I got him." He scooped the dead fish back into the bucket and tossed the frog in after it, closing the lid down tight.

When he looked around, Elaine lay on the bottom of the boat, her ankles dangling over the seat, shoulders shaking.

He reached out a hand. "Are you all right? Are you hurt?"

Her shoulders continued to shake, but she didn't answer.

Worried, he slipped onto her seat. "Did you break something?" His hands ran up her legs checking for broken bones. When he reached her hips and waist, she exploded in uncontrollable belly laughter.

"What a funny pair!" She clutched her sides and gasped. Tears streamed down her face. "My glasses—" more laughter "—can you find my glasses?"

"No. Oh wait, there they are." He plucked her glasses from her tangled hair and handed them to her.

"I'm sorry, I can't help it." She held the glasses in one hand and swiped at her eyes with the sleeve of her other arm. "I can't get up."

Craig glanced around. Her ankles were draped over the bench as she lay sprawled in the bottom of the boat. He slid her feet off the seat and wrapped his arms around her. "Just hold around my neck. I'll lift you up."

Her arms encircled his neck, her glasses still clutched in one hand. With their faces only inches apart, he could see the way the tears clumped in her long black lashes. Her pink cheeks glistened with moisture and her hair framed her face like fine black lace. And those lips...

The bug spray should have been enough of a deterrent to keep him away, but his gaze locked on her mouth and there was nothing he could do to stop his next action.

He leaned forward and pressed his lips to hers. The satiny texture drew him closer. His tongue pushed past her teeth and entered her open mouth to taste her sweetness.

He barely acknowledged the clunk behind him when her glasses dropped to the bottom of the skiff.

With her hands threaded into his hair, she pulled him closer. Her wet shirt soaked against his dry one, drawing attention again to her breasts. How he wanted to see them, touch them and taste them.

He cupped his hand over a firm rounded globe, reveling in the warmth generated through the wet fabric. Dare he toss aside her blouse and take those luscious—

Her fingers fumbled for his buttons, pushing aside the fabric to delve into his chest hairs.

Where had the prim and proper scientist gone? Who cared? As far as he was concerned, she'd just given him an invitation to reciprocate. *Hot damn, let the games begin.* With his lips still locked with hers, he reached a hand between them and unbuttoned the front of her blouse. Easing the shirt over her shoulders, he leaned back to take in the sight of perfect flesh encased in silky white lace.

She reached up and unsnapped the center clasp unleashing her breasts to his view. Dark, rosy brown aureoles puckered in the night air. He reached out to cup first one, then the other, tweaking the tips to hardened peaks.

Laying her back against the bottom of the boat, he leaned over her and took one luscious fruit into his mouth. The smell of flowers assailed his nostrils—a scent vaguely familiar to him. With his hands massaging her breasts, he moved up to press a kiss to her temple. "Not enough," he whispered into her hair.

"Want more," she moaned, nibbling at his neck.

He loosened the button at the top of her khaki slacks and slid the zipper downward. His knuckles grazed the smooth skin of her belly to the top of her curly mound.

His own pants felt like they'd explode he was so hard for her.

A buzzing sound pushed into his consciousness. He swatted at his ear, but the buzzing grew louder.

"What's that noise?" she asked, pushing his hand from her breast.

He skimmed his hand down her torso to duck into the waistline of her pants. "What noise?"

She pulled his hand from her pants and tipped him off her. "*That* noise."

Craig sat up and listened. The buzzing he'd assumed was a mosquito had grown into a loud, steady hum. "Sounds like a motorboat." He glanced down at her, regret sizzling in his gut—and lower. Beneath his pretty scientist's staid exterior burned a passion as hot as Madame LeBieu's Voodoo fire.

He reached out and pulled her to a sitting position. In one swift movement, he pulled the edges of her lacy bra together and snapped the clasp in place. His fingers lingered against her breasts. "We'd better go."

"What about the frogs?"

"We'll come back for more tomorrow night."

Her fingers paused in buttoning her blouse and she glanced up at him. "More?"

"Frogs, damn it."

He practically leapt to his seat, rocking the boat in his hurry to get away from those eyes. Those trusting, soul-stealing eyes. Eyes a man could easily lose himself in.

CHAPTER 8

STILL SITTING ON THE FLOOR OF THE BOAT, ELAINE FORCED THE embarrassment from her face. "What if the boat we heard is the one dumping the poison into the swamp?"

"All the more reason to get the hell out of here." Craig flipped the switch on the motor and pulled a rope. The engine rumbled, but didn't start. He squeezed a rubber bulb on a hose and then pulled again. The engine sprang to life, idling in the water.

She settled her glasses on her nose and carefully maneuvered to her seat. Instinctively, she leaned forward and touched a hand to Craig's knee. "We have to stop them."

He stared down at her hand, his gaze intense. "I read about some big shot company dumping pollutants into the swamps. People in the area said they'd hired thugs to take potshots at anyone who came near the dumpsite. No one was able to prove it in the courts, but the locals swore by it. Some criminals will go to all lengths to avoid being caught, even killing. I'm not willing to take the chance." He shifted in his seat.

His leg moved, and awareness shot all the way up her arm and down into her stomach. *Not a good idea, Dr. Smith.* She jerked her hand back to her lap, her fingers tingling. "We can't let them get away with poisoning the bayou."

He drew in a long, deep breath and made a show of panning the contents of the boat. "What do you suggest we stop them with? Have you got a gun in that satchel? Hell, you've got everything else."

"No." She ignored his sarcasm. "Everything but a gun. Can't we wait around and see who it is? Think about it. What better way to stop the polluting than to locate the source? We have to witness them in the act."

"Honey, if we can see them, there's a good possibility they'll see us. We don't have time to ditch the boat, and I'm not so sure you want to crawl around on the mud islands in the dark. They're full of snakes and alligators. Without a light..." He glanced over his shoulder as he backed the boat away from the shore.

A shiver wiggled its way down her spine. "Okay, next time I'll pack a gun."

His attention shot back to her. "You own one?"

She chewed her lower lip. "Not actually. Does Joe sell them in his bait shop?"

"Yeah, but they're not like fish nets." He flipped a switch on the engine, the motor revved and the boat shot forward. "There's a wait time associated with buying guns. Have you ever owned one?"

"No." She hadn't thought about wait time. What did she know about buying a gun?

"And you've never fired one either, right?"

"No." Okay, so maybe he had a point. But did he have to sound so superior? "How difficult can it be?"

"I can tell you right now, I'm not getting in the same boat with you if you're packing a pistol."

She tamped down her instant irritation. Not that she wanted a gun; she'd never even thought about owning one before. But his comment about not getting into the same boat cut to her pride. She'd worked with chauvinists who didn't think women belonged in scientific laboratories, as if they didn't have the brains God gave a gnat.

Just because she was afraid of water and clumsy in a boat, that didn't give Craig the right to treat her like a ditzy halfwit. Inexperienced, maybe, but not clueless.

She'd gotten used to the rocking motion and was more comfortable moving around in the skiff. Hell, they'd almost made love in the damned thing. Her tummy tingled and she ached between her thighs at the thought of how close they'd come. In a boat, for Pete's sake. In the water! He'd nibbled at her breasts and had his hand down her pants.

She cringed inwardly. Why did she suddenly have a propensity toward lusty thoughts about a man? She'd never fantasized about one before Craig. She needed to focus on her work. Men were nothing more than a distraction. Especially this man. And her own behavior—well she hadn't beat him off with a stick—or a net, for that matter. She mentally kicked herself for the next five minutes. How could she let her hormones take control? She'd practically thrown herself at Fish Boy.

At least, with her new awareness of dangers in the dark swamp, she quit worrying about the water and focused on what might be lurking *in* that water.

Still, alligators seemed to be the least of their troubles. If the boat they'd heard belonged to the ones responsible for polluting the swamp, what would they do if they found Craig and Elaine fishing for evidence?

Her skin chilled in the damp heat. Were they capable of inflicting harm on those who discovered their crime? Those being herself and Craig. She glanced across at her pulse-pounding boat guide.

Sobering. Absolutely sobering.

She didn't want him to get hurt because she was too foolish to recognize a dangerous situation.

The remainder of the trip back to the marina passed in silent contemplation of the dilemma she'd dragged Fish Boy into.

When the skiff slid up to the dock at Thibodeaux Marina, Craig jumped out while she held onto the rocking boat. As much as she wanted off the water, the climb out of the boat seemed such a risk.

While Craig was busy tying the lines, she scanned the wooden dock for steps or a gangway. As far as she was concerned, even a six-inch gap loomed dangerously close to a chasm.

Then he stood before her, his hand outstretched. "Take my hand." His low, commanding voice cut through her rising panic.

She stretched out her hand to his. All thoughts of water seeped out of her consciousness. She focused on the pale blue eyes in the dark, ruggedly handsome face.

Before she could say Atchafalaya, he lifted her out of the boat and pulled her straight into his arms. Pressed against his solid chest, she fought to breathe.

"I can't help myself," he whispered, and then he crushed her lips with his, forcing her teeth apart to allow his tongue entry. His hands slid up her sides to cup her breasts through her damp shirt.

Her knees melted and she clung to his shoulders, her arms finding their way around his neck. She felt sure the blouse was giving off steam from the amount of heat generated by his touch. She fully expected the fabric to burst into flames.

Had she really deluded herself into thinking she could ignore this man? *Yes*. Would she rue the day she got involved with him? *Yes*. Would she regret this kiss? *No*.

All too soon, he loosened his hold and backed away.

Rattled by her wanton response, she straightened her collar and cleared her throat. "Well, now. As good as that was, I'm thinking this might be a really bad idea."

Stupid. Stupid. Stupid. What must he think of her when she uttered such inanities? She held her breath waiting for him to crack a comment about not being interested anyway.

He smiled down at her in the lights dotting the pier. "Good, huh?" He lifted the back of his hand to her cheek and briefly touched her skin. "Next time, I'll go for better." Her eyes closed to his exquisite touch and opened again when the sensation disappeared.

He reached down into the boat and retrieved her bucket, flashlight, and satchel before he turned to face her. "Ready?"

More than he could begin to imagine. If he hadn't turned and walked away when he did, she would have embarrassed herself by panting or throwing her arms around his neck again.

This time, she didn't argue with him about who should carry the bucket, and he didn't ask. She followed him up the steps and out past the bait shop. Halfway across the road, Dawg joined them.

"Hey, boy." Without slowing, Craig reached down with his free hand and ruffled the dog's ears. "Been chasing any coons tonight?"

Dawg's tail wagged all along his body and he barked.

"I think you have a fan there," she said wryly.

"He's a good dog." He patted Dawg's head. "Aren't you, boy?"

As she walked beside Craig, the thick night air wrapped around her like a comforting blanket. "He came to visit me earlier today."

"Did he bother you? If so, just let my uncle know and he'll tie him up."

"No! No, not at all. He created a great roadblock on my front porch. Which, come to think of it, could prove advantageous. Once I begin analyzing the specimens, I'll want my privacy. With him spread out in front of the door, I'm sure visitors will think twice."

"Maybe anywhere else but Bayou Miste. Unfortunately, the whole town knows Dawg and his habits. He's been at it for the past ten years. They'd just push him aside and charge on through."

Elaine smiled at the obvious affection Craig had for the lazy dog. And considering the number of times Dawg bumped into Craig's legs and wagged his body, the feeling was mutual.

She'd never had a pet. Her life centered on her work. Outside the university she didn't have much going on. Unless you counted her one creative outlet, her herb garden. Sadly, she didn't have anyone with whom to share it. Nor had she wanted to.

Until now.

A gentle breeze caressed her skin and she leaned her head back and sniffed the fragrant aroma of blooming roses and honeysuckle. She glanced over at Craig. Walking with him in the early hours of the morning seemed so right.

As they neared the porch of her rental house, she glanced at the luminous dial on her watch and yawned. "I didn't realize how late—early—it was getting. Thanks for taking me out in the boat."

He set the bucket on the porch, then handed her the satchel and flashlight. When their fingers touched, Elaine snatched her hand away. Entirely too aware of him already, she wasn't sure she wanted to finish what they had started earlier. The man overwhelmed her with his sheer masculinity.

"Will I see you tomorrow?" she asked.

Craig lifted a tendril of her hair, and tucked it behind her ear. "I'm not sure. Check with my uncle tomorrow at dusk. If I'm not available, my uncle will take you out."

Though disappointment burned in her chest, she forced a smile. "That would be just fine." She wanted Craig to take her out again, not his uncle. Question was, did she want Craig to take her with the expectation of collecting more specimens…or of stealing another moonlit kiss?

"Elaine?" He touched a finger beneath her chin. "It would be a big mistake to get involved with me."

"I know." And she did, but she couldn't help the way she felt around the man.

"No, really." He brushed a finger along the side of her cheek.

Elaine leaned into his palm, lured by its warmth and the crazy sensations it sent skittering through her insides.

"I'm a confirmed bachelor with no intention of settling down anytime soon."

So he wasn't the settling down kind of guy. With a mission to accomplish, she didn't have time to play around with the local bad boy. Besides they were completely wrong for each other. She straightened her body and expression, hopefully presenting a poker face, when her heart felt decidedly bruised. "Did I ask you to marry me?" His lips twisted as if he didn't know whether to frown or smile. "No." She stuck out her hand. "Well then, thank you for your assistance."

He engulfed her hand in his larger one. Instead of shaking it, he tugged, bringing her up against him. With his free hand, he cupped the back of her head and brushed his lips over hers.

Logic completely shattered into so many ions blasting through her veins. She stood on her toes to get even closer. Her hands slid up his chest to circle around the back of his neck and delve into his thick, black hair.

How could kissing him be so wrong when it felt so right?

She pulled him closer, determinedly fighting off doubt—and

common sense. After all, when you had a chance to eat lobster, you didn't settle for a peanut butter and jelly sandwich. She kissed her very tasty lobster, enjoying the sensations, wishing the satisfaction would last...but knowing it wouldn't. *Couldn't.*

He was a Fish Boy—she was a scientist. He lived in Bayou Miste—she lived in New Orleans. He loved women, had them falling all over him. She...well...

She pulled back. *What am I doing?*

"Kissing me," he said, a smile curving his lips.

Heat rushed into her face, burning her cheeks. "Oh! Did I say that out loud?"

"Yes." Craig's hands retained their hold, warming the small of her back as his jeans zipper pushed against her tummy.

Thank goodness the cottage door was still closed behind her, a solid wood barrier between them and the ancient iron bed she'd slept in alone last night.

What would it be like to invite a complete stranger into her bed?

Or... Did he still qualify as a complete stranger? They'd shared a boat ride, a steamy kiss, and she'd seen him naked.

Twice.

All she had to do was unlock the door and invite him in. Let nature take its course. So what if he wasn't into commitment. He might be worth a one-night stand. No, he'd *positively* be worth a one-night stand.

Come to think of it, he'd probably run screaming as soon as he sampled her inexperience. She and Brian had kissed and made love, of course, but those times had given her anything but these explosive, sizzling sensations she was feeling now. Staring into Craig's eyes, she couldn't imagine his lovemaking as anything less than exciting, mind-blowing, turn-the-furnace-to-full-blast, rock-your-boat ecstasy.

The cool night air closed in around her, suffocating her ability to breathe. *Or think.* She pushed against Craig's chest and backed away until her ankles bumped into the porch steps. "Well, I have work to do."

"Don't you want to go to bed first?" His eyes twinkled in the light from her porch.

He was teasing her, and she didn't know how to respond. Her body warred with her mind, and her mind won out. "I have to take care of the fish and frog before I can call it a night." She backed up onto one porch step. "Thanks, again."

"My pleasure."

His warm words seeped into her pores, igniting the blood in her veins. All this sexual tension was turning her insides into a confused, raging inferno. Good grief, if she stood there much longer, she'd be begging him to take her to bed. *To hell with the fish or the frog, let's rock the bedsprings.*

She pressed a hand to her abdomen. *Omigod. What am I thinking?* She fumbled in her satchel for the keys, jammed them in the lock, and raced through the door. "Bye," she said without looking back into those mesmerizing blue eyes.

Oh, lord.

Perhaps having Craig's uncle take her out was a much better idea, after all.

* * *

THE DOOR SHUT behind the intriguing Dr. Smith, yet Craig found it difficult to leave. What was it about the scientist lady that riveted him to the spot?

Must be getting punchy thinking about all that Voodoo witch's talk of love. He had to remind himself Elaine was probably a woman who fell hard for a guy. It wouldn't be fair to use her to get him out of this mess.

Her pretty green eyes staring up at him from behind those disguising glasses left him feeling a little unsteady. No other woman had ever had that effect on him. *Damn.* Should he go after her to break the spell? Or set his sights on a local girl as he'd planned?

The lights switched on one by one inside the house. He could see Elaine's shape silhouetted against the window shades as she moved around.

It would be wrong to woo her. Not that he'd committed to that route. There were plenty other fish in the swamp. He could check them out as well. But he was running out of time...and he actually *liked* her. God, which made it worse. How could he even consider making her fall in love with him and then dumping her?

He glanced at his watch and his heart jumped in his chest. One o'clock. Four hours to sunup.

Craig strode to the end of the road and turned into his uncle's yard. Much like every other structure in the small community, the little clapboard house had seen better days. A fresh coat of paint held the harsh effects of mold and humidity at bay. Two whitewashed rocking chairs sat on the porch in the moonlight, as a welcome to visitors.

He knocked on the door. No answer.

He knocked louder. Still no answer.

Where the heck could Uncle Joe be? He never stayed out late except on Saturday night.

For that matter, what day was it? Craig prided himself in controlling his schedule. Not knowing what day it was added another stick to his frustration bonfire. He rubbed his chin. What did he do yesterday? He'd taken Lisa out on Thursday, which would make that Voodoo-day. Friday, he'd spent the day as a frog, and that would make today Saturday, or early Sunday morning.

How many days had already passed since the Voodoo queen cursed him? Too many, out of the two weeks he had to undo the damage. Geez, time was running out.

Catching flies for the rest of his life was not an option.

Speaking of options, now would be a good time to contact Cassandra. He swung by his car for his cell phone. On the fourth ring, her answering machine picked up.

"Hi, this is Cassandra. I'll be out of the country for a couple days. Leave a message and I'll return your call when I get back."

Damn. He didn't have a couple days to waste. Still, if it came down to the wire and she was his only option...

"Hi, Cassandra. I know we didn't part on good terms, and I'm sorry about that. Maybe I can make it up to you. I'm in Bayou Miste. Call me as soon as you can." He hung up, his gut churning. He didn't love Cassandra, but what else could he do?

Now for Uncle Joe. He had to be at his favorite honky-tonk on the outskirts of Bayou Miste. Craig debated driving his BMW, but the two-mile walk would do him good. Enjoying the feel of human leg muscles propelling him forward in an upright position, he walked faster and faster until he broke out in a run. Damn, it felt good to jog again. He hadn't exercised much since he arrived at Bayou Miste.

He missed his usual early morning run through the streets of New Orleans. The brightly painted houses and a cup of his favorite coffee always helped to jumpstart his day.

He raised his arms and jabbed at the air. He couldn't do this as a frog. The best he could hope for was a decent leap without splatting into a wall. He had to get a handle on frog movements. Not that he planned to be one for long.

Craig heard the music before he'd come within two hundred yards of the Raccoon Saloon. The parking lot was jammed with nice cars, old pickups, and a few rusty bangers. Yeah, the locals liked their beer and music. The die-hards turned out like clockwork on Saturday night.

He stepped into the smoke-filled bar and practically gagged. The smoke bothered him more than usual tonight. He scanned the room looking for Joe's scraggly white hair. With the small bar so packed and hazy, he couldn't see him right away.

A meaty palm smacked him on the back.

He staggered under the force.

"Hey, Craig." Mo stood with a beer can in one hand and a cigarette in the other. "Good to see you, man. *Mais,* I mean, it's good to see you as a man, anyway." He tipped the can, draining the contents in two gulping swallows, then crushed the aluminum in his fist.

"Hi, Mo." Craig continued his perusal of the room's occupants. "Seen Uncle Joe?"

"Yup." Mo jerked his head to the left corner. "Back dere with Bernie and Oscar."

"Thanks." Craig squinted through the tobacco fog until he located the table. The three older men sat at the back of the room as far away from the speakers as they could get.

"You know, Craig," Mo said. "Larry's right. You should go after his sister. She's had a crush on you since practically forever."

Craig's heart raced at the thought. Not out of anticipation, but panic. She was nice, but he liked choosing his own dates. The thought of Mo and Larry finding women for him curled his intestines. "I'm still thinking about it."

Besides, there was that bro-code friend's-sister thing...

"Don't wait too long. Afore ya know it, that full moon will be a-risin'."

"Craig, honey." A thin hand slipped under Craig's elbow and a buxom breast pressed to his arm.

Hell.

"Hello, Lisa."

Lisa LeBieu, with her long straight black hair and olive skin, would turn any man's head, but Craig had been scorched once already. He didn't feel comfortable standing in the same room with her, much less with her lounging all over his arm.

She walked two fingers up his chest and tapped his chin. "I hear Mamere LeBieu put a hex on you."

Craig extricated his arm from her clutches. "Back off, Lisa."

She tried to hook his arm again.

With another backward step, he came flush up against a wall, his head bumping a sconce, causing the light to shimmer.

"What's the matter, Craig?" She stalked him until her full breasts pressed against his chest. "Afraid of poor little me?"

"Yup." Her approach reminded him of a black widow spider. Black hair, red lips, all the soft feminine curves luring a man into her trap, then *zap*! Just like the bug zapper on his uncle's back porch. "Do you mind? I'm here to see my uncle."

"I don't mind at all," she purred, running her fingers across his shoulders. Her hand stopped and she plucked something off his shirt. "What's this?"

Craig stared down at her hand. In the light from over his head, a long wavy hair glimmered. *Elaine's hair*. His mind conjured the image of her against the bottom of the boat, her hair spreading wildly around her. Although he willed it not to, his groin tightened.

Lisa's eyebrows snapped to a V. "Who is she?"

"I don't know what you're talking about." Inside, he cringed. God forbid Lisa LeBieu should get her claws into Elaine. The shy scientist wouldn't even know what hit her until Lisa had her stunned and cocooned. Protective instincts surged within him—something he hadn't felt toward a woman since his mother. *Damn*. This was not good. He didn't want to feel that way, and she sure as hell didn't need his protection.

Lisa's eyes narrowed even more, and he could swear she read his every thought. The room closed in on him. He had to get away from her, find Uncle Joe, and get the hell out of there.

With a smile forced to his lips, he played Lisa. "Sweetheart, I really need to see my uncle. Would you excuse me, please?" He laid his hands on her shoulders and gently pushed her away.

Then he ducked and ran.

Right into his uncle.

"Craig, there you are. Been wonderin' when you'd get off the swamp with that scientist lady."

Craig stifled a groan. As vindictive as Lisa was, all she needed was the identity of the hair's owner and she'd be wreaking havoc all over the parish. He turned to gauge her response.

She focused down at the hair between her fingers, a corner of her lip curling upward, and not in a pretty, sassy way.

"Leave her alone," Craig warned.

Lisa's eyes rolled up to gaze into his. "A little too punchy, aren't we, frog man? What were you two doin' out on the swamp at night? Catchin' a little swamp nooky?"

A slow burn rose around Craig's collar and up the back of his neck. What had he been thinking when he'd asked Lisa out in the first place? Sure, she was cute and had a great body, but she was trouble with a capital "T". As his uncle had told him so eloquently when he was a young teen, "Think with your brain, not with your balls, and you'll stay right with the girls."

With Lisa and those cute curves, he hadn't been thinking with his brain, which was apparent.

"Did you come lookin' for me?" Uncle Joe stepped in between Lisa and Craig.

"Yeah. We've got to talk."

"What's eatin' you, son? Besides that mangy beagle?" Joe snickered. When he saw the look on Craig's face, he coughed and straightened. "No, really. Whatcha need?"

"Can we get out of here?"

"What, and miss the two-bit beer from two to four a.m.?"

Craig frowned.

"Okay, okay. The one day a month they offer beer at a tenth of the cost and you have to go and be a frog about it." Uncle Joe burst out laughing at his own joke, slapping his knee and doubling over with the force of his guffaws.

At the moment, Craig saw no humor in his uncle's words. "I'll meet you back at the bait shop when you're finished cracking jokes."

"Did you walk?"

"Yeah."

Uncle Joe swayed and lurched toward the door. "I'll drive you home."

"No, I'll drive *you* home." Craig snatched the keys and stalked toward the door.

"Spoilsport. Won't even let a man have a little fun. Can't enjoy a good buzz without someone ruinin' it for me."

"My heart bleeds for you." Craig's retort dripped with sarcasm.

"No heart. None whatsoever. Drag me off in the middle of night to talk to me and won't let me drive. It's not as if the Raccoon Saloon has two-bit beer every night."

"Only every Saturday night."

"The highlight of my week." His uncle belched.

"Come on, Uncle Joe."

Before they'd gone a mile, Uncle Joe lay fast asleep against the passenger seat door, snoring loud enough to rival the cicadas.

Craig parked the truck in his uncle's driveway. When he got out and opened the passenger seat door, the inebriated old man almost fell out.

With an arm hooked under an elbow, Craig helped his uncle into the house and to the kitchen table.

Uncle Joe slumped onto the speckled Formica tabletop and continued where he left off in the truck, snoring loud enough to shake the eaves.

"Uncle Joe?" He shook him anxiously. He needed Uncle Joe to wake up long enough to listen. "Uncle Joe."

Joe lifted his head.

"Listen to me," Craig shouted loud enough to rattle the windows.

"Whadda you want?" Joe said, his voice slurred, his eyes barely open.

"You have to watch out for the scientist lady. I think she might be in danger."

He blinked. "From what?"

"Well, Lisa, for one. I don't like the way she looked at me in the bar. She's trouble." Lisa's evil smirk worried him. "Elaine's also investigating toxins in the swamp. There may be someone dumping stuff in there. If they find out she's snooping around, they might come after her."

"Whadda you want me to do?"

"Just keep an eye on her. Don't let her go out on that swamp alone."

"Okay." Joe's head slumped back to the table, hitting it with a thump.

Craig clenched his teeth and counted ten. Then he hefted his Uncle out of the chair and dragged him into the bedroom, dumping him on the bed and slipping off his shoes. He was out like a light. *Damn.* The bait shop wouldn't open early this Sunday.

"Never mind. I'll keep an eye on her myself."

But how he'd keep her safe as a two-inch tall frog, God only knew.

CHAPTER 9

Elaine slept like the dead until the sun crept into her window and warmed her face. With her eyes still closed, she savored the feel of clean sheets, country air, and a late-night kiss from a tantalizing Cajun. The mattress in the rental house was soft and comfortable. A bed made for lying in later than usual, preferably with the one you love.

Her eyes popped open. What was she thinking? As if love and Craig were at all compatible. They'd mix like oil and water.

Completely awake, she sat up and swung her legs out of the bed. No time for fantasies, she had work to do. The fact that her mind had superimposed Craig's naked body in the sheets beside her had nothing to do with her rapid ascent from the bed.

Needing caffeine to help her maintain focus, she trudged barefoot into the kitchen wearing a short nightie and not much else. Two scoops of coffee in the filter, water in the top, and she was on her way to a luscious cup of go-juice.

Scratch. Scratch. Scratch.

Through the glass of the kitchen door, she could see the screen door wobble.

Scratch. Scratch. Scratch.

She crossed to the door and peered out. Dawg stared up at her, droopy brown eyes imploring her to let him in. She cracked the door and peeked through the screen. "What do you want?"

"*Woof!*" The dog tapped the screen door again with his toenails.

"You want to come inside?" She opened the door wide enough for the dog to slip past. When she would have let the screen slam shut, the dog twisted around and stuck his nose in it.

"So what's it to be, in or out?"

The dog stood still, his nose holding the door ajar. Then a mottled green bullfrog hopped over the threshold and into the kitchen.

She darted her gaze from the dog to the frog and back again. "Is this bullfrog a friend of yours?"

As if in answer to her question, Dawg wagged his tail all the way up to his nose and swiped his tongue over the frog, knocking the amphibian over on his side.

"Yeah, and with friends like you, who needs enemies? I get it." She knelt close to the frog and scooped him up in her hand, bringing him to eye level. "Can't say I've ever known a dog to have his own pet bullfrog, but I'm told anything can happen in the bayou." She studied the creature. "Do you have a name?"

"*Woof!*" Dawg, nudged her hand, licked her cheek, and wagged his tail so hard his body whipped from side to side.

"His name is Woof?"

Dawg nudged her hand again.

"Oh, you don't like me holding your friend, do you?" Elaine carefully placed the frog on the floor and patted Dawg.

The big dog lapped at her cheek and sat, pounding the floor with his tail.

"You're easy to please." She shoved the dog out of her face and laughed, feeling light and carefree. Is that what a couple days away from the university could do for you? What Brian was talking about? Had she gotten too carried away in her work and forgotten how to smell the stump water?

She rose and glanced down at the pair. A dog and a bullfrog. "You two can stay, as long as you don't leave me any yucky presents."

"*Woof!*" Dawg gave his standard reply, licked her knee, and flopped on the nearest rug, as if all that wagging and woofing had worn him out. But the frog still stood where she'd set him on the floor. He seemed to stare up at her legs.

She swore she saw a hint of intelligence in his little black eyes. She frowned. *Wow*. Bayou Miste was really getting to her. "If you're staying, you have to have a name other than Woof." She tapped a bare toe and tilted her chin. "Freddy?" She waited. What was she expecting? A reaction?

The frog's head swayed side to side.

Holy crap. Was that a "no"? She studied the frog, never having known a frog to answer questions. Had she hit on some type of intra-species communication? *Nah*. She was so losing it. "How about Bully?"

Again, the frog swayed side to side.

She crossed her arms over her chest. This type of frog must have a natural swaying motion. "This is really strange. I'm talking to a frog." She wagged a finger at the creature. "See what you're doing to me? I'm calling you Todd, like it or not."

The bullfrog didn't sway this time, instead its front legs jerked in a shrugging motion.

"Good. Now, I need to get a shower and get to work. Make yourself at home."

She headed for the bathroom, but something made her turn to check the frog. Sure enough, he'd taken a hop after her.

She gave him a withering look. "And no peeking."

* * *

GRINNING, Craig tilted backward to take in all of a giant Elaine sashaying from the room. Ah, well. It had been worth a shot. Her short, filmy pink nightgown did nothing to hide long, silky legs—legs smoother than whipped cream and probably as tasty. The cheeks of her pretty backside peeked from beneath the hem of her babydoll, encased in black silk panties—a naughty contrast to the innocence of her top.

She disappeared through the bedroom door and soon the rush of water could be heard from the bathroom.

When Elaine had squatted next to him, all he could think of was licking her knees. Damned if Dawg didn't get that pleasure.

Dawg had stood by him at sunrise when he'd transformed back into the frog. He'd decided it was a good idea to have the dog close as protection against snakes and other creatures. But Dawg had proven even more useful when he'd helped him gain access to the scientist's house.

Note to self: Tonight, give Dawg a nice, juicy steak.

Craig hopped around the room, hoping to get an idea of what Elaine was like by the things she'd brought with her. But all personal items were either high on a couch or table. He couldn't see a thing.

He glanced toward the open bedroom door. Should he? Craig hopped by and shot a quick look inside. The light from the bathroom door shone like a beacon guiding a ship in the fog.

A quick tour of her bedroom while she was showering wouldn't hurt. He wouldn't peek. Honest. He hopped into the room and began his search for some insight into this woman who talked to dogs and frogs. When he hopped around the side of the bed, he landed square in the middle of her pink nightgown.

He froze, wrapped in the tantalizing scent of a flower garden. *The same aroma the Voodoo queen had sprayed in his face.* What kind of coincidence was that? The silky nightgown felt good to his sensitive frog skin. For a few brief moments, he languished in the folds, imagining Elaine still inside the babydoll.

Water splashed enticingly in the bathroom. More than anything, he wanted to sneak a peek. But what kind of man would he be if he did that? He'd promised not to.

Sort of.

He stared down at his green skin. As a frog, what harm would come of his seeing the scientist in the shower? She'd never know "Todd" wasn't a real frog unless he told her after he turned back into a man, and he had no intention of doing that.

But his conscience warred with his desire and won.

The water shut off and he heard the plastic against metal sound of the shower curtain rings sliding across the curtain rod. He could imagine her reaching for her towel, stepping from the tub onto the mat and wrapping the terry cloth around her body. Even as a frog, his body tightened.

Quick, so as not to arouse her suspicions, he hopped off her nightgown and made for the door.

"Hey, little guy," her soft voice called out behind him.

He stopped, frozen to the spot. Caught sniffing around a woman's bedroom.

"Did you get lost, or something?" She stepped up beside him and crouched down.

He ventured a sideways glance and saw soft, creamy white feet with pink toenail polish. Her skin smelled of fragrant soap and radiated heat from her shower. His cool amphibian body leaned closer to her warmth. Then he looked up.

Tight calves crooked at the knee, turning into smooth, naked thighs. A fluffy white towel wrapped precariously around her hips and breasts did little to dispel his rising awareness. He opened his mouth to growl in frustration.

"*Gribbit*." Now that was about as satisfying as getting a splinter in one's webbed foot. He squatted next to a woman whose body could start a riot and all he could do was croak.

"It's okay, I'm not going to dissect you. You're welcome to stay here and visit with me. I'm just going to get dressed."

She stood, her hands rising to the edge of her towel, opening...

Conscience overruled and Craig spun away, but not before he saw the rounded swell of her breast. Unable to take any more, he beat a hasty retreat through the bedroom door. How much more exciting this scene would have been, if he were in his man-form.

Then again, she wouldn't have let him past her bedroom door.

Guilt weighed heavily on his mind. He felt like a damn peeping Tom. Elaine deserved better. At least she was fighting for a worthy, unselfish cause—the environment. He was just fighting to save his own skin, and not of the green variety.

Was spying on her fair? No. So why the hell was he lurking in her home?

Just admit it.

He still needed to find someone to fall in love with him to break the spell, and Elaine Smith was a prime candidate. *Damn the situation. And damn that Voodoo priestess.*

Dawg rose from the rug and trotted over to him.

"*Woof!*"

I know, I know. I got myself into this situation. If I had taken the women I dated more seriously, I wouldn't be where I am today.

"*Woof!*"

Dawg trotted past him to the door.

Knock, knock, knock.

"*Woof!*"

"Now who could that be?" Elaine walked out of the bedroom, tugging a pale blue, snug-fitting shirt down over a lacy white bra, smoothing it over the top of her khaki shorts. Her hair was combed straight back from her forehead, and hung in loose, wet ringlets past her shoulders to the middle of her back. She slipped her owl glasses onto her nose and reached for the doorknob.

"Well, now, what have we got here? Good morning, beautiful." The oily, cocky words oozed out of the one person in the parish Craig had always wanted to smash in the nose—Randall Pratt.

Her back stiffened and she peered at him through her glasses like a stern schoolmarm. "Excuse me, should I know you?"

Randall pushed past her into the small living room. "Absolutely, you should know me. I'm the most eligible bachelor in the parish, Randall Pratt. And you are?"

Elaine gave him an even look, and crossed her arms over her chest. "Not impressed."

Chalk one up for the scientist. Craig liked her more and more every minute. She wasn't quite as naïve as he'd originally thought. And she could spot a snake when he walked through her door.

"*Tsk, tsk.*" Randall walked around the room, fingering books on the coffee table. "We don't want to start out on the wrong foot, now do we? I came to see if I could help you with anything. Unloading your car, moving furniture in the bedroom. You name it, I'm your man."

"Unless you like scrambling frog brains and dissecting stinky dead fish, I don't think so."

Randall looked up, his nose wrinkled. "That's an exciting occupation for a woman. What are you some kind of frogtologist? Or are you dreaming up new recipes for a cookbook?"

"The cookbook, definitely, the cookbook." Her voice dripped with sarcasm.

Throw the bastard out, Elaine. Craig wished he could do it for her. If he were in human form, he would.

The snake drifted over to her worktable and leaned over her microscope. "What's this, a microscope?"

"No, it's a frying pan." Elaine marched over to stand in between Randall and her equipment. "Yes, it's a microscope. If you're through with your inspection, I have work to do."

Yeah, buster, beat it. Craig hopped over to stand next to Elaine.

Randall leaned closer and touched a finger to her collarbone. "Why don't you and me go by Maggie's Café for a bite to eat?"

Elaine slapped his hand away. "I'm not hungry."

"Oh, come on, you have to eat sometime." He tucked a lock of hair behind her ear. "How about for dinner tonight?"

Craig's blood boiled. If the man didn't get his filthy paws of the scientist, he'd...

He'd...what? Croak?

"No thanks," Elaine replied, ducking around Randall to march over to the door. "Besides, I already have a date."

Craig did a double-take. She had a date?

Randall frowned. "With who?"

Yeah, with who? Craig couldn't think of a single man of Elaine's level of intellect in the entire parish, barring his truly. He didn't like that she'd agreed to go out with someone else. The thought curdled his insides. He didn't like the idea at all.

"Who I go out with is none of your business." She opened the door and motioned for him to leave.

Randall swaggered toward her, stopping short of the door. "I make everything that goes on in this parish my business."

Yeah, Randall had a knack for getting into everyone's business, all right. A couple years younger than Craig, he had been a real pest growing up. He'd found pleasure in tagging along behind Larry, Mo, and Craig, and anytime he had the chance, he got them in trouble. Like the time he'd sunk the fishing boat at the marina. Since Craig and Larry had been the last ones to use it, they'd gotten the blame. Later, they'd caught him with the plug in his pocket.

"Mr. Pratt," Elaine began.

"Call me Randall."

"Mr. *Pratt,*" Elaine repeated with more emphasis. "Please leave."

Craig and Dawg hopped and trotted to stand beside her. The dog growled low in his chest. Craig found himself wishing the old Voodoo queen had changed him into a dog, instead of a defenseless frog. He could have sunk his canine cutlery into the jerk to speed him along his way.

"I don't take no for an answer. I'll be back." Randall leaned forward and kissed Elaine's surprised lips.

She reached up and popped him. The smack of palm to cheek rang loud against the walls.

"*Woof!*" Dawg stalked forward.

Randall pressed a hand to his cheek and backed toward the door. The shocked look on his face was almost comical. "You shouldn't have done that."

Elaine stood taller, her lips pressed into a straight line. "No. *You* shouldn't have kissed me."

"I'm not through with you, lady." Randall's voice promised retribution.

But Elaine held firm. "Leave. Now."

Before Randall's heels cleared the door, Elaine slammed it shut.

She glared at the door as if it had committed the offense instead of the man who'd gone through it. "The *nerve.*"

She swung around, almost stepping on Craig, and paced across the room. With an angry yank, she pulled the glasses from her face and waved them in the air. "I can't stand a pushy creep who thinks he owns the place." She scrubbed her fingers over her lips. "And he *kissed* me. Yuck!"

Craig hopped out of the way on her next pass. Twin flags of pink flew high on her cheekbones and fire blazed from her moss green eyes, sparking like a forest in flames. Tendrils of dry hair drifted up from the wetter strands and danced around her face.

Damn, she was hot when she was mad.

He'd risk making her angry just to see her reaction—exciting and enticing as hell. Where had she been hiding all that passion? If she could get this riled over a stolen kiss, imagine her passion in bed. Craig's little froggy heart couldn't take much more of this. When the hell was dusk?

Just as quickly as she'd started pacing, she flopped onto the couch and leaned her elbows on her knees. The fire died from her eyes and she stared at the books on the table.

Dawg left Craig's side and trotted over to her. He nosed the hands clasped in front of her. Her fingers parted and the dog stuck his nose between them.

Craig hopped toward her, wondering what had happened for her to stop ranting so suddenly. Like Dawg, he sensed her sadness even before a tear slid down her cheek to fall on the dog's nose.

"What's wrong with me? Am I really that rigid?" She leaned forward and wrapped her arms around the dog's neck. "Can't I be kissed without treating it as an assault?"

No, you were right. The guy deserved your slap. Craig wished he could take her in his arms and hug away her hurt expression.

"*Woof!*" Dawg pulled out of her clinch.

"See, even you don't think I'm loveable. Hell, maybe you're right. Who could love someone with frizzy hair, who looks like a frump and hides from life behind her microscope? Brian sure didn't."

Who was Brian? Craig had a mind to pummel the jerk's face for making Elaine cry.

"How can you date someone for four months and never really see them?" She flipped onto her side on the couch, and tucked a throw pillow in her arms. "It's no use. I'm afraid of water, I'm afraid of relationships. All I have is science. Which makes for a cold bedfellow."

"Woof!"

"You said it. It's a rough life." She rolled back up into a sitting position and punched the cushion into the corner. "But I'm here for a reason and I might as well get started. I can work on my love life later."

She pushed off the couch and strode to the refrigerator. She pulled a large lump of silver wrapped in plastic from the freezer and took it over to the table.

"At least frozen, it doesn't smell quite as bad, huh Dawg?"

Dawg sniffed at the fish in her hands and nuzzled the plastic.

"Sorry, fella. You don't get to eat the evidence yet. Let me take some samples from it first. Although, the thought of eating this should turn your stomach. Oh," she glanced guiltily toward Craig. "And you might want to let your frog friend outside before I start dissecting his cousin.

Craig's empty frog belly clenched as he imagined a sharp scalpel slicing through the tender green skin. She was right. He wasn't up to seeing a fellow frog sliced open for science. She found it necessary, but he found it way too frightening.

He'd leave her to the specimen samples and find something else to do.

Like decide once and for all how to get out of this mess.

As time slipped away, he didn't feel any closer to resolving his difficulty. If he didn't move fast, the full moon would seal his fate, and he might end up under Elaine's microscope, after all, just another cell to analyze or heart muscle to slice a cross-section from.

Could he make Elaine love him and get him out of this mess? Her mention of Brian-whoever indicated the relationship was over. That made her available. And a prime candidate.

The image of the lone tear trickling down her cheek seared a path from his mind straight to his heart. Only a bastard would make her fall in love with him when he had no intention of ever returning her love. He couldn't do it.

And why the hell did he have this overpowering urge to pummel Brian's face for making her cry?

Jesus. He needed to find someone less vulnerable. Someone who wouldn't look at him with genuine tears in her eyes when he told her it was over.

Was there such a woman?

Lisa. But Lisa couldn't love anyone but herself. And she knew about the spell.

No, he had to find someone to love him, and it had to be real. He didn't relish eating flies the rest of his life.

CHAPTER 10

"UNCLE JOE!" CRAIG STRODE INTO THE BAIT SHOP FROM THE BACK ROOM just after dusk. He'd made good his escape from Elaine's cottage when Dawg whined to get out. Once again, transformation caught him on the back step of the shop. This time, Miz Mozelle hadn't been anywhere in sight. Thank God. "Uncle Joe!"

"You don't have to yell, for Pete's sake. I ain't deaf, you know." Uncle Joe squinted one eye and touched his hand to his head with a groan. "Did you get the number of the truck that hit me?"

"Ha ha." Craig smirked at his uncle's scruffy clothes and bed hair. "Try Mad Dog twenty-twenty."

"Oh, yeah." Uncle Joe turned toward the commercial refrigerator and yanked out a bottle of water. "Dang. I need a couple dozen pain killers."

"Prevention is much more effective than the cure. You should avoid the Raccoon Saloon on Saturday nights."

Uncle Joe lifted three fingers, Boy Scout style. "I'm swearing off, I promise."

Craig grinned. "I've heard that before."

"Right now, just the thought of booze turns my stomach."

"Good, keep it that way." Craig walked to the window, his gaze gravitating to his uncle's rental house. He wondered when Elaine would arrive at the bait shop. "Heard anything from Littington?"

"Yup. Got a meetin' set up for tonight at eight at the Lake View Restaurant in Morgan City."

"Good." Although he would be glad to finish his business with Littington, Craig would rather be with Elaine out on the swamp.

Uncle Joe ran a hand through his hair, making the long white tufts stand on end. "Bad news is, I also got a call from your father."

Craig shot a sharp glance at his uncle, familiar tension settling in his neck and shoulders. His father was already pushing to acquire this deal. His life was all about the business—no time to enjoy family and friends. Craig inhaled and held his breath. "Is he coming down here?"

Uncle Joe looked up, his bloodshot eyes feigning horror. "God forbid, no."

Whew. All he needed was his father's interference at this point to make the situation a complete nightmare. As if a Voodoo hex, pollution, and funny feelings about a scientist weren't enough. "I thought you said it was bad news."

Joe scratched his chest. "Just hearing from your father gives me the hives. He can be such a pushy son-of-a-bitch, acting like he's got a corncob shoved up his—"

"Yeah, well..." Craig interrupted his uncle's colorful language. With his back against the wall and one foot crossed over the other, Craig struck a casual pose, his gaze never leaving his uncle's face. "I take it, he's still trying to get you to clean up and come back to work for the firm."

"Never a call goes by without him pluggin' for me to come back."

"Why don't you?"

Uncle Joe lifted his palms upward. "And give up all this?"

Craig looked around at the shop's interior. "What? A beat up old bait shop and marina?"

"You may see it as nothing but a rundown bait shop. But I look at it as my salvation." He winced and dug around under the counter until he came up with a bottle of ibuprofen. "Ahhh."

"Why did you give up the law?" Craig asked.

"Had my reasons." Uncle Joe uncapped the bottle and shook four tablets into his hand.

"Name one."

"I don't want you getting' no ideas about quittin' the firm. Your father would skin me alive. It's bad enough one of the family dropped out. Can't have another Thibodeaux desert the ship."

"Come on, Uncle Joe. You can tell me anything. I'm not walking out on the firm. I'm aiming for partner within the next two years."

Uncle Joe tossed the pills into his mouth and swallowed a swig of bottled water before he replied. "Let's just say, I had a change of heart."

Craig's curiosity wouldn't let his uncle alone. "It was a woman, wasn't it?"

"Now don't go puttin' words in my mouth." Joe walked a few steps away. "I never said it was a woman."

"It was a woman." Craig smacked the wall next to his hip. "Exactly the reason why I haven't shackled myself with one to this day. They're trouble."

"You'll sing a different tune when you find the right one, boy." His uncle said. "And, if you're anywhere near as smart as you profess, you'll fight for her, no matter what."

Craig stared back into intense blue eyes, so similar to his own. "Is that the problem? You didn't fight for her?" he asked softly.

The older man turned his back to him. "Go away, boy, I got work to do."

"Okay, Uncle, but we're not through talking."

"If you know what's good for you, you'll let this sleepin' dog lie." Uncle Joe grabbed a broom and, with short, sharp strokes, swept his way toward the front of the store.

"One other favor, Uncle Joe."

"Ain't you had more than your share for the day?" Joe muttered.

"I need you to stall Dr. Smith until I get back from my meeting with Littington."

"No need. I could take her out myself, if I have to."

"I thought you didn't do night tours?"

Uncle Joe's face reddened. "I just told her that 'cause I had a card game with the boys that night. I'll take her."

"No." A jolt of unexpected panic seized Craig. He'd told Elaine Uncle Joe could take her out, but the thought of her and the older man out on the water without his protection chilled him to the bone. No telling what would happen if whoever was dumping the toxins found them snooping around. "I want to take her out myself. Frankly, I'm concerned about the entire situation."

"Afraid she'll take more than her limit of frogs?"

He snorted. "I believe there are enough frogs in that swamp to supply a whole slew of universities."

Uncle Joe scratched his chin. "Although, more and more of 'em seem to be going belly up lately. Bernie came by again yesterday with news of more dead fish around that same lagoon."

"It's not so much the frog supply I'm worried about. I'm more worried about who else is out there on the swamps at night."

"You're getting punchy, boy." Joe crossed his arms over the tip of his broom. "People fish at all hours on the swamps. No crime in that. Done it myself for the past thirty years."

"Maybe so." Craig rolled his shoulders to ease the tension. "Times are changing, and not everyone out there has fish on his mind."

Uncle Joe regarded Craig. "There something you're not telling me?"

"Let's just say I'm looking into it. Leave the scientist to me." He turned back toward his uncle. "Stall her, tell her I'll be late, but don't take her out there without me."

A smile curled at the edges of the older man's lips. "Sounds like you got a hankerin' for the gal."

Craig stopped in mid-stride, turned, and looked out the window, again. "Call it whatever you like, just don't let her go out," he responded in low, clipped words.

"Okay, okay, you don't have to bite my head off."

Craig glanced at his watch. "Damn. I better get moving if I plan to meet with Littington."

"Yeah, that's another thing."

"What?" Craig asked without turning away from the window.

"Your father asked about the Littington deal."

Craig shot a glance at Uncle Joe. "What did you tell him?"

The old man grinned. "You're workin' it."

"Good." With a nod, Craig looked out the window one last time, then headed for the door. "All I need is for him to race down here and find out what a mess I'm in."

"Spare me. I'd make a deal with the devil himself to keep your father from comin' down."

"Be careful what you wish for. That Voodoo queen just might be the devil incarnate. Don't give her any more ideas."

* * *

JUST AS ELAINE gathered her gear for another night on the swamp, the phone rang. Having only left the number with the dean's secretary, she wondered what was wrong at the university. Her heart skipped a beat. Why else would the university call? "Hello?"

"Elaine?" A familiar male voice crackled over the line.

"Brian?" Elaine's apprehension diminished, replaced quickly by annoyance. "Are you on a cell phone? I can barely hear you."

"Yeah, it's me," he answered cheerfully, as if their last words had been nothing out of the ordinary.

"How did you get this number?" she asked curtly.

"The dean's secretary gave it to me. I told her it was a family emergency."

"So you lied to Annette." Why should that surprise her?

"I consider you family. Pretty romantic, huh? I had to talk to you. I don't like the way we ended our last conversation. I'm sorry, I miss you, and want you to come back."

Elaine held the phone away from her ear and rolled her eyes. When she brought it back, she spoke in slow, deliberate syllables. "Brian, we not only ended the conversation that day, we ended our relationship."

"I wanted you to know I was wrong about Cynthia and she means nothing to me and—"

"She dumped you."

"Actually, she didn't tell me she was married."

Elaine emitted an unladylike snort. "So you called second stringer Elaine to fill in while you find another secretary to bounce?" Wow, she had been naïve.

"No, that's not it at all." He sighed. "I guess I was pretty harsh and I understand if you're still mad, but I did call to apologize."

"No need to apologize." Elaine almost felt sorry for the man. He really did sound sincere. Although, she questioned what she'd ever seen in him in the first place. "I think you did me a favor."

"Really? How?"

"You opened my eyes to my appalling lack of a life outside my work."

"I did that? Glad I could help," he said, sounding hopeful. "So, when are you coming home?"

"Not until I've completed my research." The thought of going home didn't hold nearly as much appeal as it had the first day. Could one tall, drool-worthy Cajun have anything to do with her current feelings?

"How much longer will your research take?" Brian persisted.

"At least a couple more weeks." Fourteen more nights with Craig in the dark, just the two of them. Too bad it had to be in a boat.

"Two weeks?" Brian's voice rose slightly. "That long? What if I come down next weekend? We could spend some quality time together. You know, sit on the porch, and sip mint juleps or whatever the locals do on their day off."

"Brian, we're through." That idea didn't bother her nearly as much as it had two days ago, either.

"Come on, Elaine. I made a mistake. Since the argument, I've had time to think." He actually whined. "I really miss you. How about it if I come down there next weekend?"

"Look, I'm busy with my research. I'll be working through the weekends." With the distance between them, it was easy to put him off. But when she went home, would she take up where they'd left off? Did she really want Brian back in her life?

Sure they'd had some nice evenings watching his favorite shows in her living room. They had quiet, comfortable sex on occasion. Brian had been everything she thought she'd wanted in a relationship. He had been comfortable—and generally predictable.

But with understanding gleaned from meeting a man who totally knocked her socks off, she realized she'd only been attracted to Brian because he'd paid attention to her. She deserved better. She knew that now.

One fiery kiss from a black-haired Cajun in the Louisiana bayous changed her entire perspective. She'd tasted the excitement. He made her blood burn through her veins, igniting her senses. She had never, ever felt that way with Brian.

"You're still angry." Brian broke into her erotic musings.

A couple days ago, she'd been mad and very disappointed. Now, she actually felt relief.

"Think about it." Brian went on. "I don't mind making the trip. It could be fun."

"Look, Brian..." How did she tell him it was over and they had no future?

A pair of light blue eyes swam into her thoughts. She wasn't sure of her feelings for Craig. But, with fourteen more days of research left, she might have more of a clue by then. Not that it mattered. He wasn't interested in her. But just the fact that she could entertain these thoughts told her she had no business being with Brian.

"I'll take that as a yes," Brian said. "I'll talk to you later in the week. Take care and watch out for snakes."

"Wait. No. Brian—"

But the line was dead.

Great. Now she had to convince him she really didn't want him there. Annoyed, she called him right back, but it went straight to voicemail. *Damn.* She set the phone in its cradle and tapped her fingernails against the counter. She'd call him tomorrow and tell him not to come. Her relationship with Brian was truly finished, and she suffered no disappointment over that. Only a minor bit of regret for not having seen the truth earlier.

How liberating! She deserved more than comfortable, and she meant to get it.

She thought of Craig, and her surge of energizing euphoria slipped a notch. Was a ladies' man any better for her than comfortable? With his striking looks, he could have any woman in the parish. Why would he be interested in a frizzy-haired scientist for anything more than a fling? For that matter, why would she willingly entertain a relationship knowing it wasn't going anywhere?

Okay, one revelation at a time, one hurdle to cross at a time. She had work to do, a swamp to save. She gathered her buckets, nets, satchel, and flashlight.

Night cloaked the land as she clunked along the road to the marina. Would Craig be waiting impatiently? Or had he gotten his uncle to fill in for him, after all?

The back door to the marina opened and a tall, dark figure emerged in a tailored suit. He marched to a shiny black sports car, climbed in, and spun out of the parking lot. Something about the way he moved seemed familiar. But who did she know in Bayou Miste who'd wear a suit or drive an expensive sports car?

Her heart kicked into overdrive when her hand touched the door handle to the bait shop. Would Craig be waiting in the shop? Would he be naked again? She found herself silently wishing a "yes" to both questions. The man was way too attractive for her own good.

Her mouth watering, she entered the building. Lights lit the aisles and shelves. No deep shadows to hide naked men. Darn.

"Mr. Thibodeaux?" She didn't see anyone moving about. The place looked empty.

"Yo. Back here," Joe Thibodeaux's voice called out, and he emerged from behind the back counter. "Can't find a damn thing in this place."

"Hello, Mr. Thibodeaux. Are you taking me out in the boat this evening?"

"No. Craig'll be takin' you when he gets back." Joe ducked below the counter again.

"Oh, he's not here?" A lump settled in her stomach.

"No, just left."

"Was that him in the sports car?" Somehow, she hadn't pictured Craig owning a sports car on his income. Let alone a suit...

"Yeah." Joe answered from behind the counter. He surfaced with a box. "He had an appointment to keep before he could take you out on the swamp. He'll be a couple hours."

Disappointment warred with relief. Hours? "Couldn't you take me out, Mr. Thibodeaux?"

"Nope." Joe set a box full of assorted fishing paraphernalia on the counter. "Don't do much fishin' in the dark. Gave it up on account of my night vision pretty much stinks. Don't worry, he said to tell you he'd be back." He rifled through the box without looking up. "Can't find my favorite filet knife."

She reached into the box and pulled out a long thin knife. "Is this it?"

Joe made a face. "If it had been a snake, it woulda bit me." He looked up. "You're welcome to hang out in the bait shop until he gets back. Although, I'm not much entertainment."

"Thanks, but I have work I could be doing back at the cottage. Mind if I leave my things here for now?"

"Not at all. Set them behind the counter." Joe pointed with his knife.

She piled her bucket, nets, and satchel on the floor and turned to leave.

"Craig treatin' you right out there on that swamp?" Joe casually shaved a fingernail with the filet knife.

Warmth spread up her neck and into her cheeks as she relived the feel of Craig's hands on her breasts and the touch of his lips to hers. "Oh, yes. We're finding specimens."

"Good, good." Joe peeled off another fingernail, then looked up. "Did the boy get around to askin' you out?"

Her cheeks burned. "No. Of course not. I'm not here to date, I'm here to conduct research."

"Yeah." Joe hefted the knife. "A woman as smart as you has gotta be pretty dedicated to her work. Not much time for fun and dating."

Ouch. His description hit the nail square on the head. Actually, it made her sound just as Brian had described-—without a life. "I like to have fun." Damn, she sounded defensive. She didn't want to give Joe the impression she was a pathetic recluse.

"Craig's been known to be serious about his work, too, something you can appreciate. But he's got a sense of fun buried in there. He, Mo, and Larry used to pull some pretty wild stunts around here during the summers." Joe hands stilled and glanced up. "Not that he does that anymore."

"No?" A smile curved her lips. She could picture a younger Craig racing through Miz Mozelle's peach orchard raising hell. Even then, he had to have been a complete heartbreaker with those dark good looks and ice-blue eyes. "Does your nephew always wait on customers in the...um..." She coughed, suddenly embarrassed.

"In what?"

She studied the corners of the shop as her face heated. "Nude. Does he always serve the customers in the nude?"

"Huh?" Bushy brows disappeared into the white thatch of hair hanging over Joe's brow.

She waved a hand. "Never mind."

The old man's face split in a grin. "Don't know if he serves customers in the nude, but Craig does have a way with the women."

Her smile faded. "I bet he does." Women. Plural. As in, more than one. Just like Brian.

"Now, don't get me wrong," Joe stared into her eyes. "The women always liked him right back."

"So he's dated a lot of women, then?" she couldn't help asking.

"Yeah, but the boy needs to settle down." Joe ducked his head and whittled at another nail.

That surprised her. "He does? Why?"

"He needs someone to love him." Despite Joe's attention to his hands, the conviction came through loud and clear in the tone of his voice.

What was the old man up to? Why was he trying to get her to go out with his nephew? "And are you saying I'm the one who should?"

"Yeah. He needs a serious, settled woman to ground him in reality."

She coughed to hide her immediate denial. *Settled woman?* That made her sound old and not at all alluring. With her ego beaten to a pulp, her self-opinion began to smell worse than the dead fish in her freezer. "If your nephew is such a ladies' man, why would he want to "settle" with a woman like me?"

"Because the other girls don't matter to him. They never did."

"Then why should I?" She couldn't believe she was discussing Craig's love life with his uncle.

"Because, despite what he might think, he needs someone like you."

"Settled," she said, her voice flat. Not intelligent, or pretty, or interesting, or sweet. But *settled*.

"Yeah, settled." Joe's words slowed. "Not in an ugly way. What I mean is, not flighty."

"Sounds more like he needs a mother, not another date," she muttered, and turned toward the door. "You can count me out of that equation."

"Dr. Smith." Uncle Joe laid a hand on her arm. "I'm afraid you got me all wrong."

She stared into Joe's face assessingly. "Your nephew sounds like a womanizer incapable of committing to a relationship. Any sane woman would run screaming from such a man."

The older man's hand dropped to his side. "Maybe so, but he's changing his ways." In a low murmur he added, "He has to."

"And you want *me* to help him change his ways?" *Unbelievable.*

"Yeah." An implied "please" emanated from Joe's anxious face.

"I don't have time to tame a wildman, Mr. Thibodeaux." Although, the idea had its appeal. Her heart jolted before she could rein it in again. "I'm here to study the swamp, not your nephew."

"But he really is a nice young man."

"And a ladies' man who can't take women seriously."

Uncle Joe grimaced. "Did I say that?"

"Pretty much."

His lips curved downward. "That's not exactly how I meant it to come across."

"Nevertheless, I'm not interested in your nephew, his women, or his needs. I'm only interested in the swamp." She turned toward the door. "Now if you'll excuse me, I'll go back to the cottage until Craig shows up to take me out."

"I screwed up, didn't I?" The corners of his mouth dipped.

Elaine couldn't be mad at the well-meaning man. He reminded her of a sad basset hound. She smiled despite herself. "Depends on what you were aiming to accomplish."

"I want you to go out with my nephew."

"Okay, I will."

Joe glanced up hopefully. "Really?"

She continued, "I'll go out with him in the boat. But I won't go out on a date. Frankly, he's not my type." Who was she kidding? That was exactly the reason why she gravitated toward him. That bad boy aura intrigued her.

"Now, don't let my words turn you off. He's got a good heart."

"I'm sure he does." But he liked women. Lots of them. How could she compete with others who had to be more comfortable with flirting and small talk? Did she even want to? "Mr. Thibodeaux, I'm really not interested in your nephew."

Liar.

"Maybe you aren't right now, but if he asks, will you at least think about it? That's all I'm going to say. I'll keep my big mouth shut from now on."

Elaine stared at Mr. Thibodeaux. She could see how much he meant his request. What the heck. Craig would never ask her out, so why not make the old man happy?

"Tell you what," she said with a smile. "I'll think about it."

CHAPTER 11

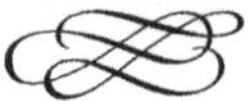

"I want a firm I can trust to represent my interests both here in Cypress Springs and in New Orleans." Jason Littington tossed his napkin on his plate and sat back.

"That's why I'm here, Mr. Littington." Craig twirled the stem of his wine glass. "I've read about Littington Enterprises. You've built quite an empire on oil refineries in southern Louisiana."

"Yes, and it hasn't been easy. Maintaining a delicate balance between the EPA, tree-huggers and local unions gets tricky. Do you realize the Cypress Springs factory employs over four-hundred locals? That's four-hundred possibilities for lawsuits from Bayou Miste to Morgan City."

"I'd like to think Littington is one of the largest and most responsible employers in the surrounding parishes." Craig's expression challenged the other man to dispute his words. He didn't. "Why did you choose our firm?"

"Your father and I go back to Tulane. We were roommates. I still consider him a friend."

Craig nodded. "He would have come himself, but he's tied up in several high-profile suits in New Orleans." He tapped his fingers on the wine glass. "Are you having any legal difficulties at this time, Mr. Littington?"

"Oh, the usual. An occasional disgruntled employee, balancing emissions standards and costs and legal waste disposal. Face it, people want jobs, they need gas to run their cars, but no one wants the refineries in their back yard. With all the state and federal regulations, it's hard for a corporation to make a profit."

With a slight nod, Craig tried to appear sympathetic. Littington didn't look like he suffered from financial constraints. His Armani suit and Rolex watch showed no signs of wear.

Craig stole a glance at his own watch. He'd already been with Littington for an hour and a half. Normally, he spent that and more if the client's financial worth warranted the effort. But tonight, he could only think of Elaine and going out on the swamp.

Time crawled. Littington gave him the same background information he'd heard a hundred times before from other wealthy clients. Started with nothing, built a huge empire with the help of a few political aces played along the way. Yada, yada, yada. With a stifled yawn, fifteen minutes later Craig glanced at his watch again. "Mr. Littington—"

"Call me Jason."

"Jason." Craig smiled. "I can have the paperwork drawn up by Wednesday. Do you mind if we meet at the same time and place? I'm unavailable during the day."

"Not at all. Evenings work better for me, as well." Littington pushed away from the table and stood. "Tell your father I said hello."

Craig rose and shook hands with his father's friend. The man's smooth white hair, tailored suit, and manicured nails reminded him too much of his father. Almost a carbon copy. Hell. Would Craig look like that in twenty years? Would the bottom line be all that mattered to him? He brushed aside his wanderings. "I'll see you on Wednesday, Mr. Littington."

The drive back to Bayou Miste raced by in a blur. The smooth-running engine and sound insulation left Craig twenty uninterrupted minutes to think. And what did he think about?

Elaine.

Barring the frog curse crisis, they'd come to Bayou Miste for completely different reasons, the irony of which was not lost on Craig.

He'd come to secure a deal with a wealthy client bent on lining his pockets and finding loopholes in EPA regulations. Possibly helping to leave that client's refineries clear to dump more pollutants into the environment.

Elaine had come to Bayou Miste to research pollutants and save the environment from would-be "killers". And she thought he was nothing more than the uneducated nephew of the marina owner. What would she think of him if she knew the truth?

His foot lifted from the accelerator and the car slowed. A hard, sickish lump formed in his gut. Did her opinion matter? He'd only known her two days, for Pete's sake.

He jammed the gas pedal to the floor again, and the BMW shot forward, taking the curvy roads much faster than what was legal or safe. He didn't care. Some situations called for rule breakage.

If he dissected—he shivered at the unfortunate word choice—his thoughts over the entire evening, he'd discover they centered around one dark-haired scientist with her heart in her work.

He should be worrying about how to solve his amphibian love dilemma.

Note to self: Concentrate on your priorities.

With a mental kick in the butt, he forced his mind back on track, straightened his shoulders, and focused. Cassandra was out of the country for who knew how long. He could look up DeeDee DuBois, Maddie Golinski, and Lisa LeBieu. Craig sighed. Holy crap, he was in deep shit. DeeDee and Maddie gave him the hives, they were so...so...well, not his type. Lisa chilled him to the bone with her Voodoo grandmother. He'd already thought of Josie, yet somehow thoughts of Elaine kept pushing Josie to the back of his mind. Representing high-dollar divorce and corporate law cases seemed a snap compared to finding someone to love him. Limited to the night made the difficulties even more pronounced. He was a man for the few hours a night when most people slept. How could he woo someone so quickly in the narrow timeslot allowed?

For one, he could get that someone into bed as soon as possible. If his love candidate could be lured under the sheets, he could keep her awake into the wee hours, getting her to know and love him. Or he could hunt for an insomniac, hang out in bars, or engage in all-night dinners. These last options seemed too risky and may take more time—a commodity he didn't have much of. Craig parked the BMW at Uncle Joe's house and trotted back to the marina where he slipped out of his suit and into jeans, a long-sleeved denim shirt, and deck shoes. He entered the bait shop.

"That you, boy?" Uncle Joe called out.

He and Bernie sat at a rickety card table with a chessboard between them.

"Elaine come by?" Craig asked.

"Sure did, about two hours ago." Joe's fingers lingered over a black knight as he studied the board. He moved the piece forward and to the left, removing a white pawn from the game. "She left her things behind the counter. Wanted you to come get her when you got back."

"Thanks." He located the familiar bucket, satchel, and net, swept them up in his hands, and headed for the front door.

"What's this about you serving customers in the nude?" Uncle Joe called out. "Can't afford a sexual harassment suit against the marina."

Craig's face warmed but he kept going. "Don't worry about it, we'll talk later."

When he cleared the door, he trotted down to the dock and tossed the items in the boat. Adrenalin shot through him as he walked up the steps to the road and aimed for Elaine's cottage. Memories of their last kiss, and of Elaine in a towel, replayed in his mind.

In human form, the correct body parts responded, causing him significant discomfort. If he didn't get a grip before he got to her door, further movement would prove difficult. He'd be tempted to throw her to the floor and—

Don't go there, buddy. Remember Josie? Your plan? Is Elaine anywhere in your plan?

No.

Regret formed a tight knot in his chest and he questioned his decision to exclude Elaine from the list. Of all the candidates, she interested him the most—which scared him down to his toes. Perhaps he had a masochistic tendency to deny himself pleasure.

Lights from the cottage windows shone into the night, illuminating his steps. He searched through the panes until he spotted Elaine's silhouette in the living room, bent over something.

As he knocked on the door, blood pounded in his veins. To get his physical reactions in check, he rotated his shoulders, and stamped his feet. His upper lip broke out in a sweat, as it had on his very first date at the tender age of sixteen.

At the ripe old age of twenty-six, he shouldn't be feeling so overwhelmed with lust. Elaine was just a woman. True, a woman with a to-die-for body disguised in khaki. She was the only female he knew who'd go out on a boat in light-colored, ironed slacks.

The door opened and Elaine stood there in her neatly-pressed white oxford shirt and khaki slacks. Although she was covered from head to foot in starched clothing, Craig could still envision her in the bath towel, her hair slicked back in neat, wet waves down her back, a rosy hue to her fresh-washed cheeks.

"Ready?" he asked, staring into moss-green eyes made even bigger by her tortoise-shell owl glasses.

"Yes," she said, her voice a breathy whisper.

"Me too," he said, and turned away before she could see how ready he really was.

* * *

ELAINE SAT BACK in the boat, smearing bug repellent on her neck, hands and ankles.

Craig hadn't spoken more than two words since he'd helped her into the boat. He kept a distance between them, and made their brief contacts short and impersonal.

Now he sat in brooding silence, guiding the skiff through the black waters, his attention fully focused on the channel ahead.

What had happened to the easygoing man from last night?

She couldn't stand the silent gap widening between them. "I identified the frog we caught yesterday as a *rana sphenocephala*."

A frown dipped between Craig's brows.

The frown made her all the more determined to get him to talk. "It's more commonly known as a Southern Leopard Frog."

He looked at her, briefly. "How can you tell them apart?"

Not exactly a warm response, but open-ended. Encouraged by his question, she decided to give him an answer. For most people she'd keep it short, but she wanted to see his reaction to detail. "We can identify the different species by location, coloring, shape, and sounds. The leopard frog, found in Southern Louisiana, is an orange-brown color and makes a low-pitched guttural sound, similar to a chuckle."

A smile tilted the corner of Craig's lips. "Laughing frogs. Did you stay up all night waiting for the leopard frog to chuckle?"

Elaine returned his smile, warmed by his response. "No. But did you know Dawg has a pet bullfrog?"

Craig's body stiffened and he shot her a glance. "Oh?"

Confused by his tense reaction, she leaned forward. "Does that bother you?"

"No, not at all. Dawg makes friends with everyone. It really doesn't surprise me that he's made friends with a frog." Craig negotiated a turn before he spoke again. "Are you going to dissect him?"

"Dawg?"

"No, the frog."

"No, I don't think Dawg would appreciate my cutting on his pet frog." She chuckled. "Funniest thing I've ever seen, though. A canine protecting a bullfrog."

"Like you said, strange things happen in the bayou."

"Did I say that?" She knew she'd said those very words to Dawg earlier that morning, but not to Craig.

"Must have heard it somewhere else." He nodded ahead of them. "Duck."

This time out, she didn't hesitate. She pushed aside the drooping Spanish moss as they'd entered the same lagoon where they'd found the dead fish.

When he cut the engine, the boat skimmed silently through the water.

She strained her ears to listen. "Hear that?"

"What?" He lifted the oar from the bottom of the boat and dug into the water to slow the craft.

"Exactly. Nothing. I don't hear another motor. Hopefully, we'll have plenty of time to collect as many specimens as we want."

"Get your net ready, we're about to bump into a small island."

As the boat slid into the bushes and vines crowding the shore, she braced herself. A rounded bump in the water loomed ahead of her. Her heart skittered to a stop. "What's that?"

Craig shone a flashlight beam at the dark brownish-black knob about the size of the dog's head. "You're a scientist, don't you know a cypress knee when you see one? They grow out of the roots of the cypress trees here in the swamps."

Embarrassment rose in her cheeks as she realized how stupid she must appear. But her chagrin was short lived as frogs hopped into the water, diving deep to escape the massive beast of a boat disturbing their evening song.

With her heart pounding in her chest, she readied her net and leaned over the side of the boat. Her face stared back at her in the reflection of light from the boat lanterns. The inky black depths mesmerized her until her head spun and her vision blurred. The familiar panic and fear of water rose up into her chest, threatening to overwhelm her calm.

Craig leaned across and touched a hand to her knee. "Do you want me to do it?"

With conscious effort, she ripped her gaze from the reflection and stared down at the hand warming her skin through the khaki fabric. When she didn't respond, she felt his hand squeeze gently.

"Elaine?"

She glanced up into eyes so blue she fell right in, drowning in their depths. He'd called her by her first name. How resonant and beautiful his voice made it sound.

"Do you want me to help?" He smiled into her eyes and warmth spread from his hand up her thigh to throb gently in her center.

Molten blood coursed through her veins, scorching her insides and making her body tingle with awareness—awareness she'd sworn to ignore. "No."

"No?"

She straightened away from him. "I can do this." All she needed was to focus on the task. She stared at the water, again, and completely forgot why. All her consciousness centered on the dark-haired Cajun mere inches away. Like a celestial body drawn to the sun, her body gravitated toward him.

The boat tilted as he shifted to straddle the bench seat. A leg appeared on either side of her and she leaned back against his chest, his heat enveloping her.

"I want to help," he whispered into her hair, his breath stirring the tendrils around her ears. "Don't deny me the opportunity to be macho."

She stilled, her body a racing engine, heating to dangerously explosive levels. She'd never felt this alive and aware of her own sensuality.

"Look." Craig reached around her and pointed to a frog swimming in the water close to the skiff. He wrapped his fingers around her hand with the net and leaned into her until the mesh rested in the water. Together, they waited until the frog moved closer.

Unable to breathe for fear of moaning, she basked in the solid muscles pressed against her back. A brawny arm wrapped around her middle and his hand cupped hers, guiding the net through the water.

Even through the pungent odor of swamp and bug repellent, she could smell his aftershave and minty-fresh breath. Closing her eyes, she imagined him pressing a kiss to her temple. With the image so real, she could almost feel his lips brush her skin in a butterfly-light kiss.

Her eyes popped open as she felt the caress again.

He kissed her temple.

What should she do? A girl could get lost out here. Lost to her purpose, lost to herself. And with a man like Craig—a man content to be a fish boy all his life, cutting a notch in his bedpost for every woman he bedded and left heartbroken.

She jerked away. His warmth burned her like the moth in the candle flame. If she hovered too close, she knew her wings would catch fire. Fear born of self-preservation urged her to struggle.

"Whoa, steady now," he said, as if gentling a spooked horse. He spread his arms and legs wide to still the rocking boat.

Without his arms to hold her back, Elaine lunged for the other seat. But the rocking motion threw her off balance. Teetering near the edge of the boat, she flung out her hand toward Craig. The boat tipped and she toppled over the side.

The legendary slow-motion switch kicked into gear. She absorbed the details of the overhanging trees, marveling at the long strands of moss stretching three, sometimes four feet in length. Craig stood, his mouth forming around her name. His fingers reached for hers, tips touching tips, with no purchase found.

His beautiful blue eyes were the last image she committed to memory before water embraced her, sucking her down through the duckweed and muck, to the silt and aquatic vegetation on the bottom. Vile liquid filled her nostrils and throat as she opened her mouth to scream.

Terrified of water, she'd never learned to swim. So she sank like a rock. Her lungs starved for air felt ready to burst, and her head grew light.

Water churned beside her. Strong arms grasped beneath her shoulders, hauling her up. Up to the surface, to air and light. When her face broke through, she struggled to crawl higher up the torso holding her. Panic filled her and she flailed, afraid she'd sink beneath the surface again.

A grunt was followed by strong arms clamping hers to her sides. "Stop kicking, woman."

She coughed and spluttered, "Can't swim!"

"You don't have to," he said, his voice calm and steady. "Stand up."

Elaine kicked and flailed to keep her head from submerging again.

"Damn it woman, stand up." He struggled to keep her from drowning him too. Finally managing to turn her in his arms to face him, holding her tight against his chest. Where she floated, he stood solid and still. "Try it. Put your feet on the bottom. It's only about chest deep."

"Can't swim," she whispered, tears trickling down her cheeks along with the swamp water.

"You don't have to, Elaine." He leaned forward and claimed her lips with his.

Shocked into stillness, she clung to him. She wrapped her arms around his neck, pressed her breasts against his hard-muscled chest. With her lips locked to his, her feet found the bottom. Relief quickly transformed into desire and she returned his kiss fervently, her tongue meeting his, thrust for thrust.

When they came up for air, she fell gratefully under the spell of his eyes. "You saved me."

He smiled. "No, the water wasn't very deep. You could have saved yourself." He reached up to brush the moisture from her cheek with his fingers. "However, if we don't get out of here soon, we'll be alligator bait."

Fear charged through her veins again and she practically crept up Craig's body, wrapping her legs around his waist. "Ohmigod, where are they?"

"They could be anywhere. And as much as I enjoy you crawling all over me, I don't relish the idea being dinner to a reptile."

"Oh, yes, of course. I'm sorry, I'm acting like a blubbering baby. It's just—"

"It's okay. Just loosen up on the neck so I can get you back in the skiff."

Mortified and still shaking from her near-death experience, she shut up and let him lift her back into the boat. She clung to the seat as the vessel dipped down into the water when he pulled himself aboard.

When they both settled on the metal benches, she let out a shaky sigh. *Thank god.*

"Look over there." Craig pointed to the water about ten feet from the boat. Light reflected red off two golf ball-sized bumps on the surface. She peered closer and saw the water swirl in long waves behind the bumps. "What is it?"

"Alligator."

"Wow." Her stomach flip-flopped. "That was close."

"Yeah. And that's a big one."

"Could it have—" she gulped "—killed a grown man?"

Craig nodded, his expression grim. "One that size could. He must be fourteen feet long."

Despite the warm night, a chill coursed down her spine and set into her bones. Her teeth chattered so loud, the sound echoed between her ears.

Craig looked over at her. "We need to get you back to the house."

"But we didn't catch anything." What about her research? She hadn't caught a single frog or fish. The evening was a complete loss.

Well. Except for one fiery kiss.

"It doesn't matter. You need to get out of those wet clothes and into something dry or you'll get sick."

"I'm okay," she insisted. Another shiver rocked her entire body, belying her words. Why was she arguing? All she could think about was that alligator. Maybe a hot shower would warm her bones and erase the smell of swamp water from her hair and skin.

"Yeah, you're okay. If that water is polluted, it's not doing you or me any good." He turned to pull the rope on the motor. He tugged with such force, the engine leapt to life the first time.

She hunkered low as he turned the skiff and headed out the way they came. The wind from the boat's movement cut through her wet clothes, making her even colder.

He glanced over at her and caught her shivering again. He slowed the boat to a stop, reaching his arms out to her. "Come here." His words were a command, but spoken with tenderness.

She placed her hands in his and allowed him to pull her across to sit on the bench beside him. He wrapped his arm around her and, with the other hand, increased the speed on the boat, navigating toward Bayou Miste.

Was his embrace a prelude to something more? Or just a friendly attempt to comfort her? Although she felt warm and secure, and was no longer drowning in the swamp, she was suddenly struck with an unsettling, but certain knowledge.

She was in way over her head.

CHAPTER 12

WHEN THE SKIFF BUMPED AGAINST THE DOCK, CRAIG JUMPED OUT AND tied it in place. Reaching down, he pulled Elaine up to stand beside him. He rubbed her arms and turned her face to the light from the single lamp, whose dingy yellow glow was besieged by every bug in the parish.

Her body quivered beneath his fingers and her lips were a sad shade of purplish-blue. She looked like a pathetic drowned rat with big owl eyes. Nothing to stir a man's desires. Yet, he wanted more than anything to taste those full lips and hold her in his arms, warming their bodies.

A mighty tremor racked her and she stared up at him apologetically. "I'm sorry. I just can't stop shaking." A tear trickled from the corner of her eye. The single drop traced a path down her cheek and became his undoing.

Without a word, he scooped her into his arms and marched across the pier and up to the road.

She squealed and hooked an arm around his neck. "You don't have to carry me. I can walk."

"Hush," he said, breathing hard after the climb.

"Craig, put me down," she said in her matter-of-fact voice.

"Just shut up and let a man be macho, okay?" He tempered his words with a brief smile. Then he concentrated on breathing all the way to her cottage. When he reached her porch, he set her on her feet. Seeing her embarrassment, he lightened the mood by doubling over, making a show of gasping for air.

Her mouth quirked upward and she fisted her hands on her hips. "You sure know how to make a girl feel all feminine and petite."

He straightened and winked, no worse for the wear after his uphill trek. "Light as a feather, I assure you."

After a failed attempt to shove a cold hand into her wet pocket, she muttered, "I can't make my fingers work to get the key out."

"Here, let me." He moved up behind her and pushed her cold hand aside, sliding his into the soggy opening.

She leaned back against him, her shivers creating small tremors against his chest and groin. Even with two layers of wet clothes pressing against his body, he felt warmth spread from where her back touched his chest downward.

When his large hand snagged on its way in, he wiggled it free and pushed deeper.

She gasped, and her body stiffened.

At last, his fingers touched metal. With his hand cupped over the keys, he could feel her thigh through the thin lining. His grip tightened, and he pulled her snug against him, reveling in her feminine form and the feel of her backside rubbing his front.

A soft moan escaped her lips, her muscles relaxed, and her head dropped back against his shoulder.

Fire raced through his veins, and he felt the moisture in his clothes start to steam. *Sweet mercy*. He jerked the key free and shoved it into the lock.

With his arm around her, he guided her inside and closed the door behind them. When he stared down at the trembling waif of a scientist, all he could think of was making mad, passionate love to her.

Why?

"You need to get out of those wet things and take a hot shower." He said the words, but he made no move to leave her to go it alone.

She reached up to unfasten a button, her fingers shaking and stiff. After several attempts, her arms dropped to her sides and she looked up with half a smile. "Maybe I'll just shower with my clothes on. Thanks for save—getting me out of the water and carrying me up to the house. You didn't have to."

"Don't mention it." He should have left, but he found himself reaching out to flip the top button of her blouse. "Here, let me help."

Her hands came up to stop him. When he hesitated, she tentatively caressed his forearms. It was all the encouragement he needed.

He loosened the next button, and the next, until he reached the waistband of her dripping khaki slacks. He slipped his fingers beneath the big button and pushed it through, then slid the zipper down.

A gentle tug freed her shirt from inside the trousers. With his hands poised over the edges of her blouse, and he finally looked up.

Behind the rims of her glasses, her eyes darkened to a forest green. Her lips, having regained their natural rosy tint, parted, and her tongue snaked out to wet them.

"Need more help?" he asked, his voice gruff with the effort to control his more primitive instincts. He wanted nothing more than to rip the shirt from her back, toss her over his shoulder, and carry her off to bed. Was he possessed? Had the Voodoo witch cast a love spell on the scientist? Or him...?

"Please," she whispered.

That's all it took.

* * *

CAUGHT IN A HAZE OF FIRE, Elaine stared up into Craig's eyes as he shoved the blouse over her shoulders. His desire-filled gaze raked over her and she trembled, wondering if he liked what he saw.

Slowly, she reached up behind her and unclasped her bra.

He smoothed the straps over her shoulders and down her arms until her breasts were bare and free of constraint. The bra dropped to the floor.

The hunger in Craig's eyes sparked a similar need inside her. When he lifted a hand to cup her breasts, she leaned into him.

He frowned when his warm fingers touched her skin. "You're still cold."

"I'm getting warmer by the second," she said, her voice low and husky.

"You still need that shower." His hands dropped to her waist and he pushed her slacks over her hips and slid them down her legs, trailing his knuckles across her thighs, calves and ankles. "Come to think of it, so do I."

She shivered at the thought of them naked together under the hot, streaming spray, soaping each other's bodies until—

"See? You're still shaking."

She didn't bother to tell him she wasn't shaking from cold. She stepped out of her slacks and stood in front of him dressed only in her lacy white bikini panties, feeling incredibly feminine and, for the first time in her life, truly desirable. She pulled her glasses off and set them on the table. Everything was soft and fuzzy around the edges.

Now, what? Her skin warmed from within, the fire inside her building to a raging inferno. Would he follow through? She hoped he'd continue his he-man tactics and sling her over his shoulder, carrying her off to bed, where they'd shake the cottage's very foundation. Whatever move he decided to make, he'd better make it quick, before she chickened out.

He raked a hand through his hair and backed up a step.

No. *Hell*, no.

He couldn't be getting cold feet now! Her body was ablaze, and he was the one who'd lit the match.

"Don't stop now," she whispered and closed the distance between them. Had she ever been so bold?

"I don't think we should," he said.

"Then don't think."

Her words shocked even herself. Since when had Elaine Smith ever not thought? *Since Craig Thibodeaux appeared naked in front of her*, that's when.

He looked into her eyes. "You know it can only lead to hurt."

She slipped a button loose on his shirt, spread the damp fabric apart, and kissed his chest. "I'll take my chances."

"I told you, I'm not one to commit." He leaned forward and pressed his lips to her forehead.

He lingered until the imprint seared a permanent place in her memory. A slow burn knotted her stomach. She'd always known he was a player, but frankly, at this moment she didn't care. *She wanted him.*

"I'm not asking for any promises." With a flick of her finger, she worked another button free.

His hands stopped hers and he held them until she looked up into his eyes. "I don't want to make you cry."

She stared up into his light blue gaze and wondered at her ability to push all else aside for a brief moment of pleasure. But push she did. "I'm a big girl. I can handle this. Now, will you shut up and lose the clothes?" She wound her fingers into his hair and pulled him down to her lips. Before she kissed him, she whispered against his mouth. "I want you, Fish Boy."

With a groan, he crushed her to him, slanting his mouth across hers. Her lips opened wide enough for his tongue to slip through. He traced a line of kisses across her jaw to her earlobe, sucking at the tender skin.

She moaned. *So good.* Her hands flew down his chest, urgently popping buttons free and tugging his shirt from his trousers. He shrugged out of the garment and stood bare-chested in front of her.

For the second time that night, he scooped her up in his arms.

Ahhhh...wishes do come true.

He carried her to the bathroom and set her on her feet. With a few quick movements, he had the water steaming and the rest of his clothes lying in a heap at his feet. He stood proud and naked in front of her, and this time, she took a moment to study every gorgeous feature of his magnificent body. From his wavy black hair to broad muscled shoulders, down the hard planes of his tight stomach, to the stiff evidence of his desire.

Omigod. She gulped. His desire for *her*. A heady sense of power surged through her veins and a smile curved her lips. She hooked her thumbs into the elastic of her panties and slid them down her legs. Then with a wink at him, she ducked behind the shower curtain.

He followed her in.

They both reached for the soap at the same time. Her hands wrapped around the pink bar of Caress, and his hands wrapped around hers. Together they worked up a lather, gazing heatedly into one another's eyes.

She set the bar back on the edge of the tub and started at his shoulders, working her way down his chest to his stomach, avoiding his engorged member for the moment. She wanted to make him as hot as he made her.

While she lathered his front, he wrapped his arms around her back and lathered her shoulders and down her sides to her buttocks. He cupped her cheeks and pressed her pelvis against his hardness.

Electric shocks jerked through her veins, all culminating at the juncture of her thighs. She wanted nothing more than for him to ram himself into her and satisfy her needs. But he poured shampoo into his hands and turned her around to lather her hair.

Umm. Nothing felt better than someone rubbing your scalp, except—

Don't go there, honey, Elaine warned herself.

He smoothed the suds from her hair and lathered his hands with soap again. He pulled her shoulder blades against his chest and lathered her belly, sliding upward to cup her breasts. He pinched and tweaked until her nipples stood at attention and she thought she'd fall apart from want. Then his soapy hands slid downward to tangle in the damp hair between her thighs. His fingers slipped between her folds and touched her nubbin of desire.

She forgot to breathe. Her hands covered his as he flicked and fingered her to a fevered pitch. "Omigod. I'm on fire."

The water heater picked that moment to run out of hot water. The temperature changed from steamy to lukewarm in a matter of seconds.

"Better hurry and wash the soap off," he whispered against her ear.

Welcoming the cooling effect, she rinsed quickly, the pelting cold water barely tamping the rising heat within.

Craig reached around her and twisted the faucet knob. With infinite care, he turned her around, cupped her face in his hands, and lowered his mouth to hers. She tasted the water on his lips, and slid her tongue across his teeth to delve in and dance with his. Her hands roamed over his back in a frenzy, angling downward to cup his buttocks and jam him against her.

"I want you," she whispered into his mouth. "I want you inside me."

He lifted her legs and backed her up against the wall of the shower. The cool, hard ceramic tiles shocked her skin, a sharp contrast to the heat generated between their bodies. He wrapped her legs around his waist, while she locked her arms around his neck. And he lowered her onto him, penetrating slowly, until she took all of him.

"Oh, crap." Abruptly, he jerked her off him, and winced.

"What?" Fear of a looming rejection swirled around her when her feet touched the bottom of the tub.

"Protection. I almost forgot."

She leaned her forehead against his and moaned. "I'm a scientist. I should have thought of that. I can't believe I didn't."

His hands smoothed up her sides, to cup her breasts. Bending low, he took one into his mouth. "I can’t get enough of you." He pulled hard, sucking the tip between his teeth.

Elaine clutched his head, holding him close. The cool tiles against her back did nothing to chill the molten energy roiling inside. "You’re a guy, don’t you carry one in your wallet, or pocket, or something?"

"Let me check." He slapped the shower curtain aside and dove for his jeans. In the back pocket, he found his wallet, held it up and leafed through the wet papers and leather. "Oh, thank God." He held up a foil pouch and pressed a kiss to it.

She stepped from the tub and wrapped a towel around herself, suddenly a little shy. In the throes of passion, being naked with Craig felt natural. With the interruption, the passion had cooled slightly. How did you rekindle? She ached to finish what they’d started, a need throbbing low in her belly.

Girlfriend, don’t lose it now. Good Lord, how many opportunities did she get to rumble with a sex god? With the edges of the towel clutched in her hands, she turned toward the bedroom door.

He followed.

When she reached the bed, she swung around and drew in a deep breath. Never in her life had she wanted to be with a man as much as she wanted to be with Craig. She dropped the towel. Oh, how liberating to stand nude and not feel self-conscious!

The look on his face scorched her naked skin. Moving with the grace of a predator stalking his prey, he growled low in his chest and swept in on her, tossing her to the mattress. Climbing on the bed, he straddled her hips.

She squealed and giggled, feeling strange about laughing while making love. Brian had taken sex so seriously. "You're an animal."

"You bring it out in me." He lapped at her neck and nibbled his way to her breasts.

His hands and lips worked their magic down to her stomach. With his knee, he nudged her legs apart and lay down between them.

Heart thumping, she leaned up on her elbows and watched him as he scooped his hands under her buttocks and buried his face in her femininity. When his tongue touched that certain spot, she fell flat on the bed and arched her back. Her world burst apart in a cataclysmic explosion.

His tongue flicked again and she moaned. "Omigod, you're killing me."

He lifted his head. "Does that hurt?"

"Don't stop!" she cried out. Reaching down to clutch his hair, she pressed him back to the task he'd begun. "Ah, please, don't stop."

He tongued and licked, sending her over the edge again. One long finger slid inside her, swirling the moistened opening.

Her body spasmed, jerking and exploding with sensation, lifting her higher and higher. "Now," she gasped. "I want you inside me, now."

She heard a rustle and a tear, then he pressed the tip of his swollen member to her opening. He hiked her knees up and planted a hand on either side of her. Swooping low, he stole a kiss and slid into her, slowly, steadily, until he filled her.

He pulled halfway out and paused.

Impatient beyond reason, she wrapped her legs around his waist and brought him home.

In, out, he pumped against her. She matched him thrust for thrust, rising off the bed to take him all the way into her. She'd never felt so complete, so full, and so right.

Now that she knew what making love should really feel like, she couldn't go back to the lackluster, black and white past. Craig was vibrant, Technicolor, here and now.

His body stiffened, he threw back his head, and he rammed into her one last time. Balancing on his hands, he held steady for a long, exquisite moment and then collapsed on top of her.

For several seconds she couldn't breathe, and didn't care. She could die like this and have no regrets.

But eventually, he rolled to his side, taking her with him, neither of them willing to sever their intimate connection.

She sighed and snuggled against his chest, allowing the curly hairs to tickle her nose. She inhaled his scent, a mixture of her soap and his musk, a heady combination. "Mmm. I could stay like this forever."

* * *

CRAIG HELD Elaine in the crook of his arm and sighed.

Forever.

Suddenly, his body sprang to alert. An adrenalin rush poked his heart into overdrive and he breathed like a marathon athlete at the finish line. Self-preservation mode threatened to kick in.

He studied Elaine in the light from the bathroom door. Her face glowed a creamy pink, warmed by the heat generated from their skin-to-skin contact. Incredibly long lashes brushed her cheeks.

He lifted a hand to the smooth line of her jaw. Her skin, soft and smooth, did funny things to his stomach. His breathing slowed to match the steady puffs of air stirring the hairs on his chest.

Funny. He couldn't picture her standing up against him in a divorce court. Closing his eyes, he tried to envision her in a tailored suit, briefcase in one hand and divorce lawyer at her side. The only image he conjured was her in a lab coat, her glasses perched on the end of her nose, a smile curving her lips as she looked up at him from her microscope.

With little more effort, he envisioned them at sixty, lying in bed. His hair would be gray or gone. Hers would be a frizzy mass of salt and pepper. Her green eyes would look up at him, crinkled at the corners from years of smiles and laughter.

Instead of repulsing him, the image warmed him. He pulled her closer. On the edge of consciousness, three-quarters of the way to dreamland, in the far distance he heard the steady beat of a drum.

CHAPTER 13

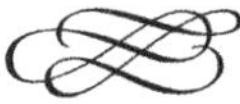

ELAINE STRETCHED, ROLLED ONTO HER BACK, AND SLUNG AN ARM ACROSS the pillow next to her.

The *empty* pillow.

Her eyes blinked open and she sat up. "Craig?"

Where'd he go?

A quick scan of the room and through the door to the small living area revealed nothing. No dark-haired, blue-eyed, hunk-a-hunk-a-burnin'-love roaming around naked in her little cottage.

The Cajun sex god had flown the coop.

With a half-mortified, half-disappointed groan, she flopped flat on her back, the sheets against her bare skin a sensual reminder of the mattress acrobatics she and Craig had performed into the wee hours. She punched the pillow. How could she be so foolish to think he'd stay? He probably hopped in and out of so many beds he didn't know where he was half the time.

The scent of him drifted up from the pillow. Without thinking, she hugged it to her breasts and inhaled deeply. A soft sigh escaped her lips, and the twisty-gurgling feeling in the pit of her stomach settled into a hungry rumble.

Why should she be annoyed with his disappearance? Hadn't he said more than once he wasn't into commitment? She'd gone to bed with him with her eyes wide open.

So, why did it hurt so much that he'd disappeared?

You're a big girl, Elaine, get over it.

With a glance at the clock on the bedside table, she realized it was well past noon, which explained his absence. He probably had to go to work today. Out of courtesy, he'd let her sleep.

Cheered by the deduction, she shoved aside the blankets and trotted to the bathroom. The small white-tiled room looked like a tornado had hit it. Jeans and shirts littered the floor along with several empty foil packets.

Craig left without his clothes?

Elaine scooped up the items, still heavy with moisture and smelling strongly of swamp water. No wonder he didn't want to put them back on. He probably slipped out in the dark so as not to embarrass her or himself in the light of day. Not that he seemed all that self-conscious about being nude.

She flicked open the shower curtain. The soap bar lay in the bottom of the tub, a fragrant reminder of the two of them beneath the warm spray, sliding together, slicked with suds.

With a nervous jerk, she closed the curtain and leaned in to turn the faucets on without looking. A cold shower ought to dispel any lingering fantasies.

While the water pattered against the plastic shower curtain, she peered into the mirror at the reflection of a stranger. With her hair mussed, eyes sparkling, and cheeks flushed pink, she looked more alive than she'd ever seen herself before. The sight of beard burn across her breasts only increased her awareness. An image of Craig sucking one rosy tip at a time into his mouth sizzled in her mind. Her nipples hardened into peaks and fire seared into her belly.

She opened the medicine cabinet and grabbed for toothpaste. With clean teeth and fresh breath, she could conquer the world. In less than ten minutes, she accomplished her morning ablutions and a brief shower.

Dressed in a light floral dress and ready for anything, she gathered the damp clothing and stuffed it into the washing machine hidden behind louvered doors in the kitchen.

Now what?

She scanned the miniature lab scattered across the folding tables erected in the living room. You'd think after two trips into the swamp she'd have a larger selection of specimens to work with. One dead baby alligator, a fish, and a frog. Not much. But a start, nonetheless.

She pulled out her notebooks and went to work.

Two minutes later, a scratching sound at her front door alerted her to a visitor.

Setting aside a slide, she walked across the living room and opened the door to Dawg.

"Good morning." She leaned down and ruffled the dog's ears. "It's a beautiful morning. Huh, boy?" With a glance around she noted his frog wasn't with him. "Where's your friend?"

"Woof!"

The mottled green bullfrog of the day before hopped into view from around the door.

"There you are. I thought maybe you'd decided to ditch the dog."

Dawg's tail thumped the floor, and he slurped the frog with a long, juicy tongue.

She laughed out loud when the frog fell over, completely slimed in dog saliva.

"Woof!"

"You are a special case, aren't you? If you two don't mind, I have work to do."

* * *

CONSIDERING the world outside the cottage doors loomed as a dangerous jungle to a bullfrog, Craig contented himself watching Elaine.

Completely absorbed in dissecting her specimens, she studied samples of tissue beneath her microscope and scribbled notes in a journal all afternoon. She'd barely noticed when Dawg flopped down on the floor against her feet. But when he laid his head against her legs and looked up at her with an open-mouthed yawn, she finally glanced down.

"Am I boring you?" She reached down and patted the dog's head. Her stomach rumbled and she glanced at the clock over the mantle.

"Lordy, already four o'clock and I haven't even had breakfast." She glanced back at Dawg. "I don't suppose you're hungry too, are you? How about a peanut butter and jelly sandwich?"

Mmm... A peanut butter and jelly sandwich sounded like heaven to Craig.

Dawg rolled his eyes heavenward, and his tailed thumped in agreement.

Elaine walked the few steps across the room to the little kitchen area. The dog lurched to his feet and followed. Craig hopped over to stand close by.

"I'm sorry, but I'm fresh out of flies for Todd."

Good. Craig would rather starve than eat another fly. He'd have to fill up on human food at night.

Armed with a sandwich and a glass of ice water, Elaine sat at the Formica table. "I'm not liking what I'm seeing, Dawg."

Dawg nudged her leg and pounded the floor with his tail.

She tore a piece of crust off the side of her sandwich and absently handed it over to the dog. "The toxin levels are dangerously high in all the samples. Frankly, I'm surprised the leopard frog was alive when we found him. His liver was only half the size it should have been. Remind me to ask Craig about factories in the area, will you?"

The dog's mouth dropped open in what resembled a grin and his tail swished across the floor knocking into Craig.

He steadied himself and looked back up at Elaine.

She had a sad, faraway look on her face. Her fingers plucked at the crust of her sandwich, but she didn't eat. "Do you think he will avoid me, now?"

Taken off guard by her change in subject, he felt as if he were eaves-dropping.

"I mean, after all, I'm no prize catch when it comes to looks." She slipped her glasses off her nose and self-consciously tucked a loose curl behind her ear.

He recalled nibbling on that delectable ear. But what did she mean, not a prize catch? Seemed the good professor didn't even know the amazing bounty she had hiding beneath her lab coat. His gaze followed her hand down the side of her long, creamy white neck.

"I wonder why he's so afraid of commitment." She slipped the glasses back on. "Not that I'm interested in a lasting relationship with the man. Even if he is great in bed. I mean—" she stared down at Dawg and Craig "—he flat out told me he wasn't into commitment. And what good is a relationship based only on sex?"

Craig opened his mouth to argue, but snapped it shut before he croaked and embarrassed himself. What they had wasn't just about the sex. They also fit together perfectly, him inside her, her snuggled up against him in bed. Hell, the woman had enough passion—in bed and out—to light the skies on fire. He'd never been with someone so instinctively natural and...and...sensual. And she didn't even know it.

"Okay, okay, so we have one night of incredibly hot sex."

Yeah, you know it. His chest swelled with the certain knowledge he'd given her as much pleasure as she'd given him. When he looked down, he realized not only had his chest swelled, but his neck had swelled too. He opened his mouth and belched out a loud croak.

"You know, Todd, I think you're right." She leaned back in her chair.

Huh? All he'd done was croak. How "right" could he be?

"Me being with Craig makes about as much sense as a dog keeping a pet frog. Last night was probably a mistake." She paced across the room, tapping a fingernail to her bottom lip. Finally she came to a halt. "Look at me. I don't have time to worry about my love life. If I'm going to make a difference in the swamp, I'd better get cracking." She knelt beside him and the dog. While she ruffled Dawg's neck, she gazed down at Craig and chucked a finger beneath his green chin. "Can't have all your cousins getting sick out there and dying because some sick bastard is dumping poison into the water."

She plowed back into her work with a vengeance, barely looking up until the sun disappeared behind the treetops.

Throughout the afternoon, Craig had watched for a chance to escape the tiny cottage, but she'd gotten so wrapped up, she'd even forgotten to put out Dawg. And the lazy canine stretched out on the braided rug in front of the couch, completely content to spend the afternoon sleeping.

As the sun crept out of the sky, Craig grew increasingly nervous. If he didn't get out of the house quickly, he'd transform right in front of her. He couldn't afford to do that. If there was even a slim chance that she was "the one," she couldn't know about his condition.

A heavy weight settled on Craig's chest, and he fought to shake it.

He glanced at Elaine, recalling her earlier lament. What idiot would think she was rigid or boring in bed? The woman was completely uninhibited. Knowing what he knew about her zeal for lovemaking only made him hot.

She stood in front of her microscope, her pretty dress brushing her calves, her delicate ankles peeking from beneath the hem. She displayed passion not only in bed, but also in her work. She truly cared about finding the source of the pollutants and determining the damage such an infraction could have on the ecosystem of the swamp.

He stared at her, her hair pulled back into a ponytail, her attention focused on the slide under the microscope. And a huge realization hit him square in the gut.

She had what he lacked.

Passion.

Passion to fight for a cause she believed in. Passion enough to challenge her crippling fears to discover the truth. Passion to root for the underdog—or under*frog,* in this case.

And what did he have? A place in his family's law firm defending clients with more money than brains, vindictive people who didn't care about anything or anyone but themselves.

People like himself.

The clock on the fireplace mantle rang seven times, piercing his depressing musings. *Oh, hell.* His body tensed, and he darted a glance to the clock and then to the window.

The sun had disappeared behind the trees, sliding its way through the forest to the hidden horizon.

Damn. Only a few minutes stood between him and Elaine discovering the truth about him. He had to get out of the cottage, and quick.

He bounced up and down on Dawg's floppy ear.

The dog twitched but didn't budge.

With a mighty leap, Craig hopped straight up in the air and came down on Dawg's forehead. *Time to wake up, boy*.

Dawg opened an eye, spotted Craig, and thumped his tail against the floor.

Craig butted his head against the stubborn canine trying to nudge him to his feet. *Come on boy, get up*.

Finally, the dog lumbered to his feet, stretched, and yawned his mouth so wide he whined.

"Hey, Dawg." Elaine scribbled something in the journal, then looked up. "Nice to see you're still with the living. You slept so long I thought maybe you were dead."

With another hop, Craig bumped into Dawg, hoping to steer him in the direction of the door.

But Dawg had other ideas. He trotted over to Elaine, sat down, and gazed up at her with soulful brown eyes.

She reached down to pat the dog's head. "Did you work up an appetite sleeping for so long?"

"*Woof!*"

"I'll take that as a yes. Come on, I've got some leftover lunchmeat." She led the way into the kitchen.

The dog followed her without a backward glance at Craig.

Traitor.

What was he going to do? His heart pattered hard against his chest. The damp clothes were in the washer, in the kitchen with Elaine.

Suddenly, his ears started to ring and his skin tingled. *Uh-oh*. He shook so hard he swayed, the tremors moving from to tip of his nose to his webbed feet. *Damn, the change was happening*. With three giant jumps, he landed just inside the bedroom door before the transformation gripped him.

His bones and skin stretched, the chemicals in his body burning like billions of miniature electrical shocks. Slowly, his flesh unfolded, reshaping until he stood tall and straight.

The room tilted. He braced his feet and turned to peer across the room at the mirror on the wall. He was back. *Thank God.*

Knocking sounded at the front door, jerking him out his muzzy-headed state. Who the hell was visiting Elaine after dark? He ran for the bathroom and snatched a towel to wrap around his waist.

"Do you think it might be Craig coming back for his clothes?" She hurried past the open bedroom door, Dawg close at her heels.

Did her voice sound eager or nervous? He wondered if she regretted their romp in the sack.

He hid behind the bedroom door and waited nervously to see who it was, watching for a chance to use this distraction to make good his escape.

Elaine opened the front door. Mo filled the entry, his broad shoulders seeming to stretch from one side of the doorframe to the other. He wore his factory maintenance clothes, but his shirt hung loose from the waistband. With a shy smile, he stuck out his hand. "Hi, I be Maurice Saulnier. You don't know me, but I be a friend of Craig Thibodeaux. Do you know where dat boy be?"

What the heck was Mo doing here? Craig needed to escape, but curiosity got the better of him and he leaned closer, straining to hear and see.

With her back to him, Elaine answered, "Actually, I don't. But I expect we'll go out on the swamp again tonight. Do you want me to give him a message?"

"*Oui,* tell him to come see his old friend Mo."

"Is it an emergency?" Her voice was polite and inquisitive.

"I guess in some ways dat what it be."

"Anything I can help with?" She leaned toward Mo.

"Just tell him, I arrange him a date with DeeDee Dubois for tonight. She'll be waiting at Catfish Haven at eight."

Elaine's back stiffened. "Oh."

Craig cringed. *Thanks, Mo. You have the insight of a moose.*

"I have de night shift at de factory, otherwise I'd tell him myself."

"I understand." Her voice sounded strained.

If Craig had entertained ideas of showing up naked in her room and picking up where they'd left off the night before, he squashed those ideas now. Some serious damage control had to be done in the wake of hurricane Mo.

The big Cajun clod backed away from the doorway. Elaine followed him out on the porch with Dawg close at her heels.

While she and Mo stood outside the front door, Craig found his shoes in a corner and slipped them on. He sneaked around the bedroom door and dashed for the back kitchen entry. No time to grab his clothes, the towel would have to do.

With all the speed of a hurdle jumper in Olympic competition, he flew through the backyards of the neighboring houses, hell-bent on getting to the bait shop.

As he passed the house next door, he spied Mozelle Reneau with her broom, poised in the light over her back porch. She gaped at him, her mouth dropping open.

Heat burned up his neck to his cheeks. Hell, what did you say to an old woman when you streaked by her in nothing but a towel? "Hi, Miz Mozelle!"

"Craig, what do you think you're doing, running around in nothing more than your birthday suit?"

"Can't talk now," he yelled, leaping over her azaleas into the next backyard.

He didn't slow down or look back, but he heard Mozelle's exclamation, "Good Lord. What's the world a-comin' to?"

When he finally stood in the safety of the little room off the back of the bait shop, he hauled in deep breaths. The situation had reached the point of ridiculous.

He had to find someone to love him, and soon, or he'd go stark-raving mad. Perhaps a date with DeeDee Dubois would be the trick. Surely, she would be desperate enough to fall in love with him on sight. He hated what it would do to Elaine after they'd shared such an incredible night together, but she'd be better off without him.

Climbing into a clean pair of jeans, he paused. A vision of Elaine asleep that morning, her hair spread against the pillow, her mouth full and tender from a night's kissing, plagued his mind.

Get over it. She's not your type.

Elaine Smith was out of the equation now. Craig had no desire to drag her any further into the quagmire of his life. She deserved to find true love.

No matter how much the thought of seeing her with another man tore at his heart.

CHAPTER 14

SO. CRAIG HAD A DATE WITH DEEDEE DUBOIS.

Elaine shouldn't have been so surprised. He'd told her he wasn't the commitment type. And she'd said she didn't care.

Which she didn't.

Then why did she feel so rotten?

She sat at the Formica table, her hands curled around a cup of tea. Normally, she'd be heading over to the bait shop at this time, ready to go out on the swamp with Craig.

Given the circumstances, why bother? He had a date with DeeDee. That would take a couple hours at the least. If they didn't decide to have dessert at her place...

A knot of pain tightened in Elaine's belly. She pushed aside the tea and dropped her forehead to the table. Hopeless. That's what she was. Her track record with men stunk. She'd dated Brian because he was within her comfort level. With Craig, nothing about comfort entered her mind. He made her burn all over.

"Why am I such a fool?" She banged her forehead on the smooth, speckled tabletop.

A knock at the screen door made her turn her head sideways against the table.

The screen opened and Craig stepped through, a perplexed look on his face. "Are you okay?"

She jerked up her head, her cheeks flaming. "Of course, I'm okay. Why shouldn't I be?" *Just because you have a date with DeeDee shouldn't make me want to crawl under a rock.*

"I got worried when you didn't show up at the shop. Aren't we going out on the swamp tonight?"

The clock on the mantle chose that moment to bong eight times.

"Didn't your friend Maurice find you?" she asked.

"No. Why?"

"He dropped by here earlier with a message for you. He said you had a date with DeeDee DuBois at the Catfish Haven. Shouldn't you be there by now?"

His lips curved upward and his oh-so-blue eyes twinkled. "I had the same message from DeeDee. But after last night, how could I go out with someone else? I called and told her I had a prior engagement."

Sudden joy surged through Elaine's body. She quickly squelched it. Craig was a ladies man and she was only one of his ladies, she reminded herself. Just because he'd cancelled his date with DeeDee didn't mean anything.

Did it?

His gaze roamed over her shoulders and down to her legs. "If we're going, you better change. The mosquitoes would have a heyday on your body in that outfit."

Warmed by his perusal, she averted her eyes. "I'll only be a minute." She leaped from her chair and dashed to the bedroom. After closing the door behind her, she collapsed against the wooden panel, her heart pounding in her chest.

He's here. He's here!

Three feet in front of her stood the white iron bed they'd shared the night before, the sheets still tangled from their lovemaking. She hadn't been able to face making it after he disappeared that morning.

Now, the sheets called to her and her breasts tingled against the fabric of her sundress. Wickedly sensual possibilities raced through her mind, and her breathing quickened. What would he do if she opened the door and invited him in for an encore?

But he hadn't come to make love. He'd come to take her back out on the swamp. He hadn't so much as hinted at a repeat of their passion-filled night, let alone attempted it. She pressed a hand to her stomach.

Could what they'd shared have been only one-sided? She'd thought their passion magical. Didn't he? Had he been bored with her, like Brian? As the ultimate failure hit her hard, tears welled. Good God, she was unexciting in bed. More than anything she wanted to run and hide. Just as she'd done to get away from Brian.

A single tear leaked out of the corner of her eye and trailed down her cheek. When the lone droplet reached the edge of her chin and dripped on her hand, her foggy brain kicked in gear.

What the hell am I doing? Was her spine made of swamp goo?

No.

She scrubbed away the tear and straightened, reminding herself why she'd come to this podunk town in the first place. Not to run away, but to help solve the mystery of what was killing the swamp at Bayou Miste.

Not, repeat, *not* to sleep with Fish Boy.

Her only logical course of action was to ignore the man completely. Or at the very least, her attraction to him.

With a decisive sweep of her arm, she stripped the sundress over her head and tossed it across the room. In a few efficient movements she slipped into jeans, a long-sleeved white blouse, socks, and her oversized rubber boots. Thus fully covered, she felt more equipped to face the incredibly hunky Cajun waiting to take her out for a boat ride.

After a deep breath, she flung open the door, ready to march into battle.

Craig stood in the middle of the living room in his tight jeans, long-sleeved chambray shirt, and a smile hot enough to initiate a core meltdown in her nuclear reactor.

Listing to port with the wind sucked out of her sails, she almost ducked back into the bedroom. How could she avoid responding to him? No woman in her right mind could ignore such a perfect male specimen.

"Are you ready?"

Elaine forced a flippant tone into her voice. "As far as I'm concerned, the sooner we get to the bed, the better."

A chuckle from Fish Boy made her rewind what she'd just said. *Damn.* She slammed her eyes shut briefly, then opened them. "Boat. I meant boat."

His nod and slightly curled lip didn't ease her embarrassment. Not only did he find her boring in bed, he thought she was funny even to suggest they jump back in the sack.

Mortified, but determined, she grabbed her bucket, nets, and satchel, and stomped to the door. When he didn't follow, she turned back with one eyebrow quirked up. "Well, are we going or not?"

His lips widened into a full-fledged laughing grin. "We go, *chère*."

She charged ahead, staying two feet in front of him. As she passed Miz Mozelle's house, the old woman stuck her head out the door and shouted, "Watch out for that pervert, Elaine. He's up to no good. I can tell you that. I'm gonna have a good long talk with that uncle of yours, Craig Thibodeaux." She waived her fist at him and ducked back inside.

Elaine slowed and looked at him, then back at the empty porch. "What's that all about?"

He spread his hands wide. "I have no idea. None whatsoever."

A sideways glance at his less than guilt-free face confirmed he was lying. Typical.

Still angry—mostly at herself—she clung to her ire, stalking ahead of Craig all the way to the dock. Once her feet hit the boardwalk, she stopped and stepped aside to let him lead the way. Anger could be carried too far. No need in setting herself up for another fall into the water.

When they sat safely in the skiff, she realized she wasn't as petrified of the boat or the water as on the first day. Bolstered, instead of facing toward him, she turned her back and faced forward. As they slid through the murky swamp, the gentle breeze stirred by their progress caressed her face.

She closed her eyes and imagined his fingers curling around her jaw line and down her throat.

"Duck."

She opened her eyes in time to see a willow branch laden with Spanish moss. Dodging to the left, she just avoided being slapped in the face. When they cleared the overhang and entered the polluted lagoon, she saw a light gleaming from the bow of a much larger, modern airboat. On its broad deck, two men wrestled a barrel to the edge and shoved it overboard.

She leaned back and placed her hand on Craig's leg. "Look! There's someone out there," she whispered.

As the barrel sank into the water, so did the realization of what she'd just witnessed. "Omigod." She clapped a hand to her cheek. "It's them! The ones polluting the swamp."

Just then, one of the men looked up and spotted their skiff. He turned to his partner and pointed in their direction.

Craig swung the skiff in a tight circle.

"Where are you going? We have to stop them!"

"No, we have to get the hell out of here before they shoot us and dump us in with that last barrel."

She glanced back at the airboat. One man jumped into the driver's seat and revved the engine. The other slid in next to him. The boat swung around and aimed right at their tiny skiff.

"Hurry, Craig!" Elaine shouted. "Oh crap, oh crap. They're coming straight for us!"

"Keep your head low. They might have guns."

"Would they shoot as us?"

In answer, a popping sound penetrated the steady drone of the motor.

"Get down!" Craig yelled.

Elaine bent double, her heart in her throat. "What are we going to do?"

"Do you think you can flip the switch on the front light?"

"I can try." She dropped to her hands and knees on the floor of the skiff and inched forward, swaying with every sweeping turn. Cool water soaked through her jeans, chilling her until her teeth clattered together. When she made it to the front of the boat, she ran trembling fingers up the metal pole until she encountered the switch. *Click*. The light went out.

Craig flipped the switch on the back light, plunging them into darkness.

"We don't stand a chance of outrunning them," he shouted over the whine of their overburdened motor and the quickly approaching airboat. "We have to find a place to hide."

Meager moonlight trickled through the dense canopy. She strained to make out what was ahead, wondering how he could see enough to steer.

A branch loomed in front of her and she leaned sideways. "Duck!" she shouted.

She hoped the low branch would be more of a hindrance to the larger vessel. She glanced back to see if their pursuers would slow.

The airboat, lights blazing, blasted through the leaves.

Craig steered into a smaller waterway. She kept a close eye on what lay ahead to keep from getting knocked from the craft, while glancing back to gauge the distance between them and the gun-toting villains on the faster boat.

As the channels narrowed, the airboat slowed. Several gunshots cracked the air. Something whizzed by Elaine's ear and hit the water a few feet away.

"Get on the bottom of the boat. Now!" Craig called.

With her heart pounding in her throat, she dove for the hold, bumping her knee on the bucket. "But what about—"

Another shot rang out.

Craig's arm jerked off the tiller and the skiff wallowed to a stop.

Why was he slowing? A glance behind them sent her heart skittering down into her stomach. "They're getting closer."

He grunted and shifted to the other side of the bench seat. With his other hand, he grasped the handle, gunned the motor, and whipped the skiff around a bend in the maze of islands. The thick trunks of dozens of cypress trees blocked them from the airboat's view, but Craig didn't let up speed until they could no longer hear or see the light from the other craft.

Uncomfortable against the metal ribs and rivets, she lifted her head and peered behind them. No airboat, no villains shooting bullets their way. She swiveled to look ahead.

The skiff angled slowly toward what looked like a willow tree. Before she could open her mouth to cry out, the bow parted the slender leaves and they entered a natural grotto. The leaves fell back in place behind them blocking out the meager light from the moon.

Craig cut the engine and the skiff drifted to a stop.

She sat up in the bottom of the boat, feeling around like a blind man for the bench seat. "Do you think we're safe?" she whispered.

No answer.

With her eyes opened wide to let in any light whatsoever, she spotted his outline hunched at the rear of the boat. "Craig?"

He shifted and muttered. "Damn."

"What's wrong?"

"Nothing." A grunt gave lie to his words.

"Bullshit." She hauled herself up to the bench next to him and felt her way up to his shoulders.

Her right hand connected with something warm and sticky.

He flinched.

A heavy weight settled in her chest and she scrambled to find the light and snapped it on.

"You're wounded!" Her heart threatened to choke off her air supply.

My God. Those bastards may have killed him!

* * *

CRAIG GRITTED his teeth to keep from groaning. His shoulder burned like the devil. "It's nothing. The bullet grazed me. I'll be fine."

The back light swayed. The reflection off the water bounced off the canopy of leaves transforming the grotto into a greenish-yellow cocoon.

Elaine's face had blanched and her eyes were round as saucers. "Omigosh."

"Really, it looks worse than it is. The bullet just grazed the skin." He flexed his arm, wincing again at the pain. "No damage to the muscles or bones."

She seemed to gather herself. "Let me get a better look." With shaking hands, she unbuttoned the chambray shirt and gently pushed it over his damaged shoulder. "You're right. It's just a flesh wound. However we need to stop the bleeding. Did you bring any towels?"

"Use the knife in the tackle box to rip off a piece of my shirt."

She dove for the box next to his feet and surfaced with the knife. Instead of slicing into his shirt, she ripped her shirttails from the waistband of her jeans and unbuttoned the front. Thinking she'd cut a piece off the bottom, Craig was surprised when she slipped the whole shirt over her shoulders and held it in her lap. Dressed only in a lacy white bra and jeans, she sliced through the fabric of her blouse.

Craig gulped and tried not to stare at her full, rounded breasts. Breasts he'd nibbled on with such delight the night before. "Careful with that thing. I use it for filleting fish. It's sharp."

"Hush and let me take care of you." Grabbing the sides of the sliced blouse, she ripped it in two. With a few quick movements, she slit and cut it again into a smaller piece. Then she folded the corners of the square and pressed it against his wound.

He winced, drawing an apologetic smile from her. "Can you hold this and apply pressure while I make a strap to hold the bandage in place?"

With his tongue too dry to articulate, he reached up with his good hand. She guided his fingers into place, and then bent to the task of cutting the rest of her shirt.

Armed with a long strip of cotton material, she wrapped the makeshift bandage over his shoulder and under his arm.

When she circled around the back of his shoulder, her breasts pressed firmly to his chest and her hair brushed against his cheek. He inhaled her fragrant floral scent. Blood pumped through his veins to the rhythm of Voodoo drums.

He must not be that badly injured if he couldn't keep his mind—and hands—off her.

Once she'd knotted the strip over the wound, she started to

straighten. He caught her bare back with his good hand and pulled her tight against his chest. "*Mon Dieu,* you drive me wild, woman."

She made a half-hearted attempt at pushing against him. "Craig, you're in no shape to do anything."

"Then I'll bleed to death a happy man." He closed his mouth over hers, his tongue pushing past her teeth to deepen the kiss.

The silky lace of her bra tugged at the hairs on his chest. He found the back clasp and worked the hooks free. With slow deliberate movements, he slid his fingers under the strap and slid it from one shoulder, then the next, so her breasts were freed.

With a groan, he tried to bend to take a rosy tip into his mouth, but pain shot through his shoulder. "Ow!"

She backed away in alarm. "We can't do this. You'll—"

"The hell we can't." He grabbed her wrist and pulled her over to sit in his lap, bringing her breasts to within lip range. "Mmm." He kissed a peaked aureole. "Better."

Her fingers laced through his hair and pressed him closer. "I didn't think you found me attractive," she said between several breathy gasps.

He stopped short of sucking her breast full into his mouth and lifted his head. "Come again?"

Cheeks aflame, she muttered "Nothing," and tugged his head downward.

"Not find you attractive?" He leaned away and glanced down at her body. Her thigh was pressed hard against his crotch, the warmth of her fueling deeper fires within him. "Are you out of your mind? What's not to love?"

Whoa.

Had he really spoken the "L" word? Did she notice? He stole a glance at her face.

Her brows had furrowed. Not a good sign.

How could he gracefully take it back?

Did he really want to?

"Then, why did you leave before morning?"

Oh hell. She'd blamed herself for his ducking out. He desperately wanted to tell her he'd been with her all day, but he couldn't. She'd think he was a lunatic. He thought quickly. "What would Miz Mozelle say if she saw me sneaking out of your house early in the morning with no clothes on?"

"I don't care what Miz Mozelle says. I do, however, care what you think." She looked away, biting her lip. "I think."

His heart warmed. "Well, I care what Miz Mozelle thinks. She can be —" he searched for the right word "—well...determined when she thinks you're doing wrong."

Elaine smiled and traced a finger across his lower lip. "And you've had occasion where she thought you were in the wrong?"

"Once or twice." With a swift move, he snagged her finger with his teeth and sucked it into his mouth.

"Can't be all bad. You survived. Therefore, I'll take my chances." she plucked her finger from his lips and leaned down to press a kiss to his temple. Then she guided his mouth back to her breast.

With a hum of relief and pleasure, he pulled her nipple between his teeth and flicked his tongue over the puckered tip. She tasted so damn good.

Thank goodness she hadn't probed further into his "L" word slip. Unsure how he really felt, he didn't want to discuss it.

He moved to the other breast to devote as much attention as he had to the first. He'd just kissed it when Elaine twitched.

Then she jerked her head and twitched again. "Um, Craig?"

"Yeah, *chère*," he answered, his focus on the luscious mound in front of him.

"I think the mosquitoes found me."

* * *

LATER THAT NIGHT—*MUCH* later—Craig slipped into his jeans and bent to kiss Elaine. He paused when the dim glow of the half-moon shone through the cottage window onto her slumbering face. The bluish light caressed her pale cheeks and an errant curl lay across her jaw and lips.

He smoothed the strand behind her ear. She turned her face into his hand and moaned softly. A fraction of the sound she'd emitted a few short hours before. She stretched her arm across the bed, the sheet shifting to reveal a full, creamy breast.

His groin tightened and he reached for the zip on his jeans. He wanted to rejoin her in the bed for a few more minutes of bliss in her arms and between her silky thighs.

The clock in the living room chimed the hour. Six o'clock. If he didn't hurry, the sun would rise and he'd be nothing more than a frog to this woman. Sweeping low, he pressed his lips to hers in a gentle kiss and, at the last moment, tasted the tip of her breast. With a final glance, he slipped out the back door and stole silently through the pre-dawn shadows.

The room at the back of the bait shop felt even smaller and more confined than he remembered, the single bed a far cry from the comfort of Elaine's. Strange. He'd never been concerned over his sleeping arrangements before.

Pink and orange fingers of light shot through the dense undergrowth of trees as the sun crested the horizon.

His vision blurred and he dropped to the floor. His transformation had begun.

Another day, and he was no closer to breaking the spell.

CHAPTER 15

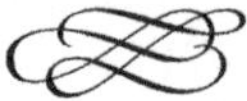

THE LINGERING SCENT OF CRAIG'S AFTERSHAVE ASSAILED ELAINE'S SENSES, lifting her from her dreams. Mmm. She smiled and sat up, letting the sheet fall to her waist. The cool morning air soothed her skin, tender from hours of lovemaking.

Craig Thibodeaux was fast becoming a very addictive stimulant. Although she somehow knew he'd be gone, she couldn't help scanning the room, just in case. Disappointment tainted the sunshine streaming into her window, but she hugged the night's passions close, recalling in vivid detail—

A knock sounded at the front door, jarring her from the memory. Who the heck would be at her door at— Good grief! A glance at the clock revealed she'd slept past noon. Not in the mood for guests, she flopped back down and buried her face deep in the pillow, pushing the sides up to cover her ears.

The knocking grew louder.

So much for basking in the morning afterglow.

With an impatient jerk, she tossed the sheets aside and swung her legs to the floor.

Persistent pounding reverberated through the house and her head. She had no choice but to slip into slacks and a T-shirt. By the fifth round of pounding, she catapulted from mild annoyance to outright anger. She grasped the door handle and yanked it open. "Where's the fire—" The last word trailed off when her gaze collided with a Cajun siren standing with a hand on her hip.

The female was every woman's nightmare. Creamy mocha-colored skin radiated youth and vitality. Midnight black hair fell in loose waves down to the middle of her back. A petite body sported perfectly proportioned breasts, a tiny waist, and a smoothly rounded bottom.

The young woman wore a black leather mini-skirt with silver chains looped low on the front and a black tube top barely covering her perky, braless boobs.

"Hi, I'm Lisa. Got any coffee?" She pushed past Elaine and entered the cottage.

What was it with these people barging into her personal space? "Excuse me? Do I know you?" Elaine didn't bother disguising her irritation.

"No, we haven't met." Lisa's gaze panned the room and then returned to her. "I just wanted to come over and meet the competition."

Elaine's thoughts tumbled like a loose shoe in a clothes dryer. "Competition for what?" She could picture a contestant runway at a Bayou beauty queen contest. She had better odds of winning an alligator toss or swamp vine swinging contest against this woman.

Lisa turned in the middle of the living room and regarded her. "Competition for Craig Thibodeaux, of course."

Elaine's heart plummeted into her empty stomach. She knew Craig was not a one-woman man. But to have one of his other conquests barge boldly into her house, especially after last night, smacked her in the gut.

Lisa and her perfect everything served as a grim reminder of the impermanence of Elaine's hold on Craig. How could she compete with Miss Cajun Swamp Princess, whose face and body could launch a thousand ships? Elaine glanced down at her own wrinkled clothes, disguising any feminine curves beneath. Her body would only sink those ships.

Coffee. She needed coffee. She stumbled for the kitchen.

The sex kitten moved around the room lightly touching books and equipment. "Are you from N'Awlins, too?"

"Yes." Elaine concentrated on scooping coffee grounds into the filter.

"That's where I'm going as soon as I can shake this place," Lisa said, her tone more of a spoiled teenager than an adult.

"What about Craig? Aren't you going to hang around and see who he chooses?" Must be lack of caffeine. Had she really asked another woman, a complete stranger, that question?

"Craig Thibodeaux?" Lisa's dark brows crinkled. "No use waiting around for him, *chère*. He doesn't believe in commitment."

The Cajun beauty's matter-of-fact statement reinforced Elaine's observations of the day before. But hearing someone else voicing the truth aloud made her stomach clench.

"I've known Craig for years," Lisa continued. "He likes playing the field. If you know what's good for you, you won't let yourself fall in love with the bastard."

"He's not a bastard." Despite Craig's disappearing act, Elaine didn't believe he deserved Lisa's name-calling. "And I have no intention of falling for him. But even if I did, it's none of your business."

The black-haired woman lifted a shoulder. "Did he tell you we went out?"

Elaine's heart bottomed out in her shoes. The man knew how to pick them.

"No? *Tsk, tsk*. He's such a naughty boy." The way Lisa said "naughty boy" made him sound like a sex offender.

Still. In Elaine's case, he'd been anything but offensive. "Look, I don't know why you came over here, nor do I care. But I certainly don't want to hear any details about your relationship with Craig Thibodeaux. I'm not now, nor have I ever been, in love with him."

Lisa's mouth curled upward on the corners, but the semblance of a smile didn't quite reach her eyes. "Oh, I'm not warning you or anything. I'm just saying it'll be a waste of time. The man is a confirmed bachelor. Women are nothing more than playthings to him."

She knew everything Lisa said was true, but on some deeper, more hopeful level, she'd ignored reason up until now, preferring to live in denial. And, although every logic cell in Elaine's body screamed for her to hold her tongue, emotion won out. "Did you ever think that maybe he simply hasn't found the right woman yet?"

Lisa's eyes narrowed. Her gaze ran the length of Elaine's body from the top of her frizzy brown hair to the tips of her unpolished toes. One of the Cajun woman's plucked eyebrows winged upward. "And you think you got what it takes to capture that man's attention. *Chère,* if I couldn't keep him, what makes you think you can?" She jutted her breasts out just a little more as if to emphasize her point.

Then she tossed her glorious black mane over her shoulder and sauntered to the door. With her hand on the knob, she paused and glanced back. "Oh, I wouldn't mention this conversation to Craig. He doesn't like to talk about his old girlfriends with the girlfriend *du jour*."

Lisa's parting words left Elaine with a depressing image of thirty-two flavors of girls at an ice cream shop.

She stared at the door for several minutes after Lisa left. The magic of what she'd experienced with Craig the previous two nights now seemed...tawdry.

Lisa's words echoed in her mind. If the dark-haired Cajun beauty couldn't hold Craig's attention, no way in hell could she. Yet, as much as she tried to tell herself it didn't matter, she knew it really did. With Craig, she'd felt beautiful and accepted, not an awkward geek to be laughed about later.

"You're not going to take any bunk from that bayou bimbo are you?" Mozelle Reneau stood framed in the screen door. "Mind if I come in?"

Elaine waved her hand. "Please, do."

"That girl's trouble." Miz Mozelle turned to glare at Lisa climbing into a turquoise '67 Mustang convertible. "I said the same to Craig less than a week ago. But would he listen? No siree. Went ahead and took her out, he did. What's this world a-comin' to? Young people disrespectin' their elders. *Hrmph*."

Sadly, Miz Mozelle's words served only to confirm Lisa's claim. Craig had gone out with the Cajun vixen less than a week ago. Had he taken her to bed, too?

The older woman stepped into the cottage. She peered closely at her before shaking her head. "You feelin' okay?" Miz Mozelle placed the back of her hand against one of Elaine's cheeks. "No fever, but you don't look so good. What did Lisa say to you?"

She looked away, unwilling to share her disappointment with her kindly neighbor. "Nothing."

"Nothing, ha." Miz Mozelle walked closer and lifted her hands. "She said hurtful things, didn't she?"

A traitorous tear sneaked out the corner of Elaine's eye and trailed down her cheek. "I'm a geek. I'll never attract a man."

Mozelle looked scandalized. "No you're not! You're a very lovely and intelligent woman. Come here." She pulled her into a hug.

It had been four years since Elaine's parents passed away...four lonely years without someone to hug her and tell her everything would be all right. With Miz Mozelle's arms wrapped around her, she let the floodgates open and cried her heart out. She cried for all the years of trying to fit in. She sobbed for the death of her parents when she'd only been twenty and in the middle of her undergraduate degree. She even shed a tear for Brian's betrayal. But most of all she cried because she knew she didn't stand a snowball's chance in the bayou with Craig.

Miz Mozelle patted her back and whispered, "It'll be all right, *chère*. It'll be all right."

When the storm passed, Elaine lifted her head and sniffed. "I'm pathetic. I shouldn't feel so sorry for myself."

"You got every right." Mozelle grasped her by the shoulders. "But there's no use wallowin'. Whatcha gonna do about it?"

"What can I do?" Elaine scrubbed a hand over her damp face.

"Fight for what you want." The older woman let her go and planted her fists on her hips. "Iffn' you want Craig Thibodeaux bad enough, ain't he worth fightin' for?"

"Craig?" Elaine blushed furiously. "Who said anything about Craig?"

"Girl, it's written all over your face. You're crazy about the boy."

Elaine groaned in mortification. "Is it that obvious?"

"As plain as the nose on my face." Mozelle looked down the length of her nose, then refocused on her. "Why do you think Lisa felt so threatened?"

"Lisa...threatened?" Elaine laughed. "No, no, you've got that backwards."

Mozelle hrumphed. "Why would she come over here and feed you full of a bunch of hooey-balooey, if she didn't feel threatened by you?"

"I don't know. But she's so much more beautiful than I am. How could Craig possibly be interested in me? She's so stunning, voluptuous and perfect. I'm—" she took in her baggy T-shirt and frowned, "—just me, a scientist. I don't even know how to act like a girl."

"You don't?" Mozelle snorted and glanced toward the bedroom. "I'm not blind. I saw Craig sneakin' out of this house in the early morning hours on more than one occasion. If I'm not mistaken, he's more than a little interested in you."

"But not enough to hold his attention. I don't have gorgeous hair like Lisa, and I don't even know how to flirt." Her shoulders slumped and she turned away.

"We can do something about the hair and I can help you with some tips on flirting."

"I don't know how." Elaine's chin lifted. "Once a geek, always a geek."

Miz Mozelle rolled her eyes. "*Hrmph*. That's no way to act." She touched a finger to Elaine's chin, lifting her face. "How did you get through all those degrees?"

"What's my education got to do with this?" she asked.

"You didn't succeed at all that schoolin' by quittin' when the going got tough, did you?"

"Of course not."

"You persevered and tried harder, didn't you?"

"Yes, but—"

Mozelle planted her hands on her hips. "No buts. You just have to set your mind on what you want and go after it. Iffn' that's Craig, you have to load your guns with the right ammunition."

"Huh?" Elaine blinked. "I don't understand."

Mozelle rolled her eyes. "Get your pocketbook and keys. You're drivin'."

"Where are we going?" Elaine grabbed her purse and car keys.

"You'll see."

Like a lamb to the slaughter, Elaine allowed her neighbor to lead her out of the cottage and to her car. Once they were inside, she turned to ask, "Where to?"

"There's a shop in Morgan City with just what we need."

Not at all reassured by Miz Mozelle's mysterious words, she pulled out of the driveway and set the car in motion. She had plenty to do with her experiments, but she knew if she stayed at the cottage, she wouldn't be able to concentrate anyway. Definitely, a first. She had always prided herself on her ability to focus on work, no matter what.

The dense foliage of southern Louisiana flashed by in a blur of green. Miz Mozelle kept up a steady stream of chatter the entire way. About what, Elaine couldn't begin to remember.

When they reached the edge of Morgan City, Mozelle pointed to a sign strangely fitting for the Atchafalaya basin. The background was a mixture of tiger stripes and jungle foliage with the words, *Shear Safari Beauty Salon* looped across in vines.

Elaine's stomach knotted. Whenever she'd taken time to have her hair professionally styled, she'd felt even more inept. She'd walk away without a clue of how to recreate what the beautician had mastered. Within hours, her hair reverted back to the same unruly mop. "You have your hair done on safari?"

"No, but it's about time I started. One of my dearest friends works here and she's been after me for years to try something different."

"And you're going to do it on my account?" Elaine glanced at her with misgiving. "I don't know if I want to carry that kind of responsibility."

"Fooey. I'm responsible for my own actions, and I choose to change. What about you?"

The gauntlet had been tossed. Would she pick it up and rise to the challenge? Or would she wimp out and run back to the security of her microscope, as usual?

Craig's blue eyes and the hard contours of his body seared through her memory. "It's not just about hair. What could a man like him see in me?" They were from different worlds. How could he respect what she did, who she was, if even her former fiancé didn't?

"*Chère*, if you can't see your own value, how do you expect him to see it?" She smiled. "It's not about the outside. But the outside can give you confidence, can reflect what's on your inside."

She'd never thought about her appearance like that before. It made sense, but...

"Still, I don't know if I'm ready for a radical change."

"Suit yourself. But me, I have a hair dye with my number on it. See you inside." Miz Mozelle jumped out of the car and strode into the shop.

Which left Elaine sitting staring after her, feeling like the dingy cut loose from the ship.

What the heck. She was here, so she might as well get a trim. She got out of the car before she could change her mind, and shoved her keys into the bottom of her purse.

She hesitated, halting below the jungle-printed sign. Did she really want to have her hair done by someone with jungles on her mind? What would they do? Blow it up with an elephant gun?

She raised a hand to her ponytail. What's the worst that could happen? Her hair couldn't look any less attractive than it did already. *Could it?*

She let out a noise of frustration. She was entirely too consumed by her appearance. Her mind should be on the true task at hand.

What was she doing, anyway, reacting like this to the threat of a beautiful woman who'd once had Craig's attention? As if a new hairstyle could improve her chances with the man. Was she out of her mind? Out of her league, yes, but did she have to lose her marbles as well?

She spun back to unlock her car door.

"Oh, don't leave. We get so few visitors in this town, I'd do your hair for free just for the practice." The sweet Southern drawl called out from the glass doorway of the salon.

Elaine turned in embarrassment toward a young woman with big, bleached blond hair. "I changed my mind."

"Well, change it again, *chère*." The woman's voice was pleading and welcoming, all wrapped up in a friendly smile.

Elaine hesitated. "I really don't think..."

"That's just it. You're not supposed to think when you go to the hair salon. You're supposed to relax and leave the thinking to the pros."

Accustomed to using her brain all day long, she still couldn't string two coherent thoughts together to make a sensible protest. Fine. Why not let someone else do the thinking for once?

On second thought, the blonde's bleached tresses and thick makeup didn't instill confidence. What had she been thinking to poof her hair out so big? Having battled natural curl all her life, Elaine couldn't imagine anyone actually wanting such big hair. The woman's short leopard print skirt and black tube top hardly seemed appropriate for daytime attire.

No, this was a really bad idea.

The beautician stepped out and hooked her arm through Elaine's, giving her no choice but to follow. "Come on, I promise not to do anything drastic. A cut and maybe some highlights. That's all."

The pungent scent of perm solution and hairspray assailed her senses the moment she set foot in the salon.

"Mirna Mae, look what I got," The blonde yelled across the room.

A thin, older woman of indeterminate age stood behind a black vinyl chair, brushing the tangles out of Miz Mozelle's brassy, strawberry blond hair. Mirna Mae raised her arms in a touchdown motion. "*Woo hoo!* Way to go, Josie. Got yerself a live one."

"What's yer name, *chère*?" Josie propelled her toward a chair.

"Elaine."

"Aren't you the scientist been goin' fishin' with Craig Thibodeaux?"

She nodded, not at all excited about discussing Craig with yet another woman, especially after Lisa's visit. She just wanted her hair done. No questions asked.

Josie sighed. "Girl, what I wouldn't give to be in yer shoes."

"If I were twenty years younger, I'd take a crack at him myself." Mirna Mae, clad in a skintight leopard print jumpsuit, and her wrinkles camouflaged in five coats of base makeup, called out. She was ushering Miz Mozelle to a sink in the back.

Like a fish thrown in a tank full of alligators, Elaine was pulled into the salon and plunked into a swivel chair. On third thought, maybe her hair was fine the way it was. She leaned forward to get up, but a hand pressed her firmly back against the black vinyl.

Trapped, her heart kicked up its pace into pre-panic-mode, similar to the way she felt around water. Or *had* felt, anyway. She hadn't been nearly as bothered by her phobia last night. But here in a salon filled with other women, she knew she was in way over her head. Beauty shops were for girly girls, the ones that spent hours at the mirror fussing with makeup or hair. Such machinations were a complete mystery to her.

Josie turned her to face the mirror and pulled the ponytail out of her hair. With deft fingers, she fluffed the long strands out and around Elaine's shoulders. "You've got a lot of lovely natural curl."

Elaine gaped at Josie's reflection in the mirror. "Kinky, curly, unruly mop would better describe it. My hair is hopeless. I should just shave it off."

The bottled-blonde's eyes widened. "Are you kidding? I have a dozen clients who'd give their left breast for hair like yours. Right, Mirna Mae?"

"Both breasts." Mirna Mae shut off the water and slung a towel over Miz Mozelle's hair. "Wouldn't you give both breasts to have Elaine's hair, Mozie?"

Mozelle sat up in the shampoo chair and nodded across at Elaine. "In a New Orleans minute."

Elaine heaved a sighed. She knew they were just being nice. "Is there any hope of taming the beast?"

Josie smiled. "What? Your hair or Craig Thibodeaux?"

Warmth spread up Elaine's cheeks into her hairline. "My hair, of course. I have no interest in Mr. Thibodeaux."

"In that case, yes. The hair is doable." Josie fit a plastic cape around Elaine's neck and velcroed it snugly against her skin. "The man is an entirely different matter."

"You got that right," Mirna Mae agreed.

"Come on." Josie grabbed Elaine's elbow and urged her out of the chair. "It's off to the shampoo bowl for you."

Mirna Mae switched on a blow dryer aiming it at Mozelle's hair. The noise drowned out any chance of small talk. *Thank goodness.*

With the spray of water sprinkling her forehead and the cool porcelain sink against the back of her neck, Elaine relaxed. Josie didn't bring up the subject of Craig during the entire shampooing process. Maybe she wouldn't discuss him for the rest of the makeover.

Fat chance.

The blond beautician draped a towel over her hair and patted it dry. "I usta have the biggest crush on Craig Thibodeaux when I was thirteen." She smiled dreamily and her tone held a hint of nostalgia. "With that coal-black hair and ice-blue eyes, he was a god a girl could easily sacrifice her virginity to."

"Did you?" *Crap.* Elaine could have slit her own throat as soon as the words popped out of her mouth. What had she been thinking to utter such a personal question? Perhaps the flash of jealousy scorching her veins had a little to do with her outburst.

"Oh, heavens no." Josie led Elaine back to the swivel chair and pulled the towel from her hair. "He was my big brother's best friend. Larry threatened to tell Mom if I so much as flirted with him." She sighed. "But that didn't stop me from dreamin'."

Yeah, Elaine'd had a few of those dreams herself. Some of which weren't only dreams. *Think ice. Think ice.* She concentrated on quelling the warmth rising in her belly and face. Revealing her current relationship with Craig to this woman was no way to win friends in this part of the state, as evidenced by Lisa's nasty visit.

Josie checked the labels on several cans on the counter and lifted one marked "conditioner". With a flick of her wrist, she sprayed a liberal dose into Elaine's hair. "You know what's crazy?"

She shook her head rather than answer. She could think of any number of crazy things that had occurred lately.

"After all those years of tellin' me to back off Craig, the last couple days Larry's been pushin' me to go out with him. Makes me wonder what he's up to."

Elaine felt her fingernails flex against the arms of the chair. She knew she had no hold on Craig. But this was the second woman in the past two hours to talk about going after Craig. Craig, the man she'd slept with for the past two nights.

"I don't know what's got into that boy." Josie set the can on the table, ran her fingers through Elaine's hair, and picked up a pair of scissors. "Maybe he figures I'm all grown up now and Craig's a mighty fine catch, after all. What do you thank, Mirna Mae? Should I go for him?" Josie never looked up, just kept on cutting.

Elaine held her breath. Whether or not the beautician went after Craig shouldn't bother her in the least. Hadn't she told Craig his lack of commitment wasn't a problem for her?

But suddenly it felt like a problem. A *big* problem.

Josie sighed and stepped in front of Elaine to cut the top of her hair. "A guy like that could break a girl's heart in a wink of one of his baby blues."

Tell me about it. Elaine feared she was half way there already.

"You should go for him," Mirna Mae said, spraying a layer of hair-spray across Mozelle's growing web of tangles and curls.

Miz Mozelle shoved an elbow into Mirna Mae's side. "Iffn' she don't care for the boy anymore, don't go puttin' ideas into her head."

"Do that again, and I'll shave you bald." Mirna Mae rubbed her side and glared at Miz Mozelle.

"Even if I wanted to go after him, Craig's way out of my league." The blond beautician set down the scissors and pulled a brush through Elaine's hair.

Fish Boy was out of Josie's league? Elaine couldn't stop herself. "How so?"

Josie plunked a fist on her hip, studying Elaine critically in the mirror. "I'm a small-town girl. What could he possibly see in me when he has high-powered city women fallin' all over themselves to catch his eye?"

Elaine looked around the shop and out through the window. What high-powered women? "Around here?"

Miz Mozelle answered before Josie. "Sure." She seemed eager to change the subject. "Josie, you're young and date a lot. What do girls do nowadays to snag a man's attention?"

"Why, Miz Mozelle?" A sly smile slid across Josie's face. "You thankin' of going on the prowl?"

"Maybe I am, maybe I'm not, but that's not here nor there." She motioned her head toward them and said, "Elaine's got a hankerin' for one of the local boys and hasn't had much practice in man-catchin'. Seein' as you've had plenty—practice, that is—you'd be the best coach to teach her."

"Oh really? Which boy?" Josie's hand paused en route to the wire brush caddy.

Elaine wished she could sink through the floor. How embarrassing to have your social limitations aired in front of complete strangers. And she couldn't tell Josie she had the hots for Craig, not after all the blonde had said of her dreams about the man. "I'd...rather not say."

With a comb, Josie smoothed her wet hair, swiftly parted the waves into sections, and then twisted the long strands, pinning them out of the way. She combed the bottom layer of hair as straight as the curly tresses would allow, and lifted a strand, pulling it tight. She picked up the scissors again and waved them in the air. "Since you won't fess up on who, I won't be able to give you specific pointers. But dere are a few techniques sure to attract any red-blooded, heterosexual male." With a crisp, clean stroke, Josie snipped off three inches of hair.

When the curls fell to the floor, Elaine barely noticed. She listened with interest to what the younger woman had to say.

"You got all the right equipment." Josie snipped her way across the bottom layer. Then she unclipped a section, letting it fall over the shorter strands. "You just need to package it properly and display it to your best advantage. I learned that in beauty school. Somethin' to do with marketing."

Great. That advice was really useful. Elaine still didn't have a clue. "How?"

Josie removed another clip and cut her way through more curls. "We're doin' it right now. A new 'do' will go a long way toward instillin' confidence and sex appeal."

"Surely, looking good isn't enough to sustain a relationship."

"No, but you can hardly get one started if he doesn't even see you.

And if you don't have some kind of sex appeal, you're not going to hold his attention for long. Maybe only long enough for a quickie in the sack."

Damn. The people in this place sure had a way of zapping to the core.

Josie's words struck entirely too close to home. Was Elaine merely a two-night stand with the local Cajun sex god? Her heart dropped like a lead weight into her stomach. She glanced down at the shapeless smock she wore, picturing the khaki slacks and plain white shirt under it. "I don't think I have what it takes."

"*Dites moi la verité!*" Mozelle shouted from beneath Mirna Mae's attack with the back-comb. "Listen to what Josie's got to say. She knows what she's talkin' about."

Miz Mozelle's adamancy was infectious. And she was right. Elaine could sit there and list all her faults or she could come up with a way to compensate. What did she have to lose?

She glanced up apologetically and smiled. "You're the expert, what should I do?"

"You need a little makeup, a figure-huggin' outfit, and a great hairdo, of course. Then you need a few pointers on how to act to get and keep a man's attention. Let's start with – Knowing your Man. Here's where you gotta do a little homework."

"Homework?"

"Yeah, you need to know a little about your man. What's his favorite sport and food? What does he do for a living? Occupation tells a lot about a man, his dreams and aspirations."

Elaine nodded, soaking it all in. So far, everything Josie said was common sense.

"Take Craig, for instance. I know a lot about him already on account he usta hang out at the house during the summers. If I wanted to go after him, which I'm still thankin' about, I already know the basics. He's a lawyer, his favorite food is shrimp gumbo, he likes football, and the N'Awlins Saints are his favorite team."

One word jumped out of Josie's chatter, clunking against everything Elaine thought she knew about Craig. "He's a *what?*"

"A lawyer." Josie frowned at Elaine in the mirror. "Didn't you know that?"

"I thought he worked for his uncle at the marina." Her head spun with this new bit of information.

"That's just him helpin' out. He usta spend his summer vacations with his Uncle Joe. Larry says he came to Bayou Miste to meet with Mr. Jason Littington on business."

Craig wasn't a fish boy? Elaine's brain grappled with the revelation. "So, you're saying he's only in town on business?"

"Yeah."

"Where does he normally live?"

"N'Awlins."

Elaine's heart turned flip-flops in her chest. *Craig lived in the same city as she did*. Their relationship didn't have to end when they left Bayou Miste. The flip-flops stilled. But Craig considered her only a passing distraction.

"I'm surprised you didn't know all this. You two have been out on the swamp for the past few nights. What did y'all talk about?"

"Nothing much." What talking they'd done hadn't included a word about Craig's professional life. He'd led her to believe he was nothing more than a helper at his uncle's marina. *The louse.* Like the little silver ball in a pinball machine, Elaine's mind bounced between the joys of knowing Craig lived in New Orleans to the hurtful knowledge he'd lied to her all along. *Ping. Ping. Ping.* She massaged the bridge of her nose to still her ricocheting thoughts.

"Anyway. Back to lessons on love—Packaging One-oh-one." Josie dropped another section of hair and continued cutting. "You just need a look that will knock a man on his butt. *Chère,* the khaki slacks have gotta go."

Elaine's hand dropped to her lap. "They do?"

"Definitely. You could wear a brown paper bag with more appeal that those. What you need is something that's form-fitting and shows every curve to its advantage. I've got just the dress for you."

"Dress? But I work in a lab. Dresses aren't practical in a lab."

"Maybe not in a lab, but definitely at the Raccoon Saloon."

"Huh?" Now she was really confused. Josie's energy and thought processes left her head spinning. "You lost me."

"Tonight's ladies' night at the Raccoon Saloon. You're coming with me." Josie waved a comb at Mozelle. "You too, if you have enough gumption to crawl out of the Bayou."

Mozelle pursed her lips consideringly. "I'll go if you go," she challenged. "Been needin' to get out for a long time." She puffed out a breath. "Haven't set foot in that place since 1991. I'm way past due for a night of foot-stompin' fun."

"What exactly is a Raccoon Saloon?" Elaine asked.

"*Chère*, it's only the most happenin' place in the basin on a Tuesday night. It's just outside of Bayou Miste, so it's close to home. All the guys come out on ladies night cause that's when the women put on their finest and strut their stuff."

"Strut?" Knots formed in Elaine's stomach. "I don't know how to strut."

"Girl, by the time I'm through, you'll have every man in the parish panting after you."

Elaine nearly choked. "I don't want every man's attention."

"Honeychile, every single, able-bodied man will be there. Your man, whoever that might be, most likely will be there too. Which brings me to the next love lesson—making your man jealous."

"This is getting way too complicated."

"No, this is the easy part. All you gotta do is pay attention to someone else while your guy is watching."

"Isn't that duplicitous?" she asked, appalled.

"I don't know what duplicitous means, but it gets a guy's blood boilin' if he's interested." Josie snipped one last time and stepped back to look at her handiwork. "Oh, my."

With the beautician standing between her and the mirror, Elaine couldn't tell what she meant. Her heart pounded in her ears as she expected the worst. "Is that a good 'oh, my' or a bad 'oh, my'?"

"Sometimes I simply amaze myself. Take a look, *chère*." Josie stepped out of the way.

In the mirror, a stranger stared back at Elaine. Gone was the bush of hair spread in a V from the tip of her head to below her shoulders. In its place were soft, layered curls brushing the tips of her shoulders and providing a frame around her face. She lifted a hand and actually ran her fingers through the tresses without getting hung up in snarls. "Wow."

"*C'est magnifique!*" Mozelle exclaimed.

"I don't think you need the highlights. Your own hair color is beautiful on its own. Coo-wee!" Josie fanned herself. "Look at me, talking a customer out of a paying job. I must have sniffed swamp gas."

"Probably all that hairspray I used on Miz Mozelle." Mirna Mae stepped up and smiled approvingly. "Nice work, Josie. Better watch out, Craig'll look twice at this one. Looks like you'll have a bit of competition, after all."

"Really, I'm not interested in Mr. Thibodeaux," Elaine insisted weakly, still shocked at how incredible she looked.

Josie shot a sly grin at Mirna Mae. "I think she doth protest too much."

"She's new in town, give her a break, Josie," Miz Mozelle said.

"So, are you with me or not?" Josie challenged, shooting a glance between her and Mozelle.

"I'm in." Mozelle crossed the room to stand beside her. "Well?"

"Oh, no." Elaine pulled the cape from her shoulders and stood. "I have too much to do."

"Come on." Josie turned her around and grabbed her hands. "You have to show off your hairdo. Lord knows I could use the advertisement. And, you bein' new will be like a man magnet. All the guys will be clammerin' to meet you and maybe some of them will rub off on me."

"No, really, I can't." Elaine searched her brain for the perfect excuse. "I don't feel right borrowing a dress from you. You hardly know me."

"Honeychile, I feel like we're old friends already." Josie pulled her toward the door. "Now get on home and take a long soak in the tub."

"But—"

"No buts. I'll be by at 8:30 with the dress. We'll have a great time. I guar-on-tee it."

The door closed and Elaine stood staring through the glass.

Josie wiggled her fingers, smiled, and then turned back to Mirna Mae, pumping her arm with a sharp downward thrust. Through the glass door, Elaine could hear Josie say, "Yes!"

Steamrolled.

Elaine tried to look at the bright side. Craig was some kind of fancy lawyer. Surely, he wouldn't be caught dead in a rowdy establishment like the Raccoon Saloon. And maybe a night without Craig would help her prove to herself she wasn't interested.

Because she wasn't.

Really.

CHAPTER 16

THROUGHOUT THE DAY, AS CRAIG SLEPT BENEATH THE BED IN FROG FORM, dreams plagued him. In them, his father repeatedly reminded him of his responsibility to carry on the family business. The words "it's your legacy" rang out over and over, until they became more of a chant intermingled with the beat of Voodoo drums.

When Craig felt his brain would explode from the constant barrage, Elaine's voice could be heard as if in the distance, "We have to stop them. We have to do what's right."

Instantly the drums stilled and his father's voice faded. Craig relaxed and fell into a long, deep sleep.

When he awoke, he lay face down on a hardwood floor. Boards pressed against his back and dust bunnies tickled his nose.

Ah-choo! Ah-choo! Ah-choo! He banged his head against the solid object behind his head and swore.

"Craig, is that you back with the human race?" Uncle Joe called from another room.

Craig's eyes flew open and he glanced around. *Where the hell...?* Oh yeah, he'd crawled under the bed to keep from being eaten or stepped on while he slept.

What had been a cavern of space to a frog was now a weight on his shoulders. Craig wriggled his way from beneath the bed, stood up, and brushed the fuzzy stuff from his chest and other body hairs. He flexed his shoulders. The wound from the night before gave him a twinge, but seemed to be healing nicely.

"That scientist lady dropped by before dusk and said she wouldn't be goin' out on the swamp tonight." Uncle Joe stuck his head around the corner, got one glimpse of Craig's naked form and made a face. "You also got a couple friends out on the porch waiting for you. Might want to put on more than dust fuzzies before greetin' them." Uncle Joe chuckled and ducked back into the bait shop.

The pillow Craig lobbed through the air bounced off the doorframe. "Funny. Very funny." Craig grabbed a pair of jeans and a T-shirt from the antique dresser in the corner and slipped into them. Why had Elaine called off the night?

He should be glad. Things were getting too hot and heavy for his liking. Elaine wouldn't understand when he went back to New Orleans and resumed his life as a scumbag attorney.

Whoa, where'd that thought come from? *Scumbag attorney?* The adjective was high-powered, not scumbag. He rubbed a hand over his eyes. The bayou was getting to him. Not a good sign.

All right. So, he didn't have to escort Elaine through the swamp. That left him with a night free to pursue other women in the hopes of finding a cure to his...er...problem. The whole Voodoo thing still had him nervous as hell. "This situation is impossible."

"Then do somethin' about it," Uncle Joe called out.

Craig walked barefoot through the bait shop and out onto the porch overlooking the dock. Night had settled in and flying insects danced around the light fixtures.

Mo lounged against the porch rail while Larry sat on the bench whittling a stick with the knife he kept strapped to his boot.

"Found you a female yet?" Larry asked without looking up.

"No." Craig leaned against a square pole.

"Dat's what we thought." Mo said, pushing away from the rail. "Put on your dancin' shoes. It's ladies' night at de Raccoon Saloon."

Even though he'd been thinking about going out to find a woman to break the spell, when it came right down to it, he really had no desire to carouse. "I don't feel much like dancin'."

Mo crossed his arms over his chest. "We're not takin' no for an answer. I dôn much like havin' a frog for a friend."

"And I enjoy being a frog?" Craig didn't like the way Mo assumed the same position he had a few days earlier when Madame LeBieu had issued her summons.

Larry sheathed his knife and stood. The two men each grabbed an elbow and marched him back through the bait shop.

They can't be serious.

"Come on guys. You don't have to rough me up again." He jetted out a breath. What choice did he have? "I'll go."

When they reached the back room, Mo and Larry dropped his arms and stood with their feet spread, determined looks on their faces.

"We wouldn't be doin' dis if it wasn't for your own good," Larry said.

"Yeah. Just like the other night," Craig muttered, fished his deck shoes from beneath the bed, and slipped into them.

"You'll need a nicer shirt if you want to attract a nice-lookin' woman," Mo said. "Unless you prefer someone like DeeDee Dubois."

"And comb your hair," Larry added.

Dieu. Now he had Mo and Larry telling him how to dress.

Twenty minutes later, the four were on their way to the Raccoon Saloon to get the best table before the band cranked up at nine. Uncle Joe had volunteered to drive. By the amount of cologne his uncle wore, he'd planned on going with or without the younger trio. Craig elected to take his own car to avoid questions and provide a quick escape if the evening turned out even half as depressing as he suspected it would.

As they passed the rental cottage, Craig could see lights on inside. Elaine was home. He'd much rather be with her than out carousing with other women.

Boy, he had it bad. If he didn't watch out, he'd find himself head over heels for the woman.

Good thing he was a confirmed bachelor.

Or else he might really be worried.

* * *

"I CAN'T BELIEVE I let her talk me into this," Elaine muttered. The noise in the Raccoon Saloon was so loud she could have shouted and no one would have heard her. She gave another tug at the miniscule dress she was wearing and groaned.

"Don't you worry, sweetie, you look be-ew-ti-ful. You won't sit down once for all the dancin' you'll be doin'," Miz Mozelle said.

The ramshackle establishment appeared pieced together out of weathered boards, corrugated tin, and aged advertisements. By the size and shape of it, the Raccoon Saloon had probably been an old barn at one time. Cars lined the parking lot and the music blared from beneath the eves.

"Come on. I know one of the band members and if I hurry, I can get in a few requests." Josie rushed ahead, darting through the darkened doorway before Elaine could protest her desertion.

She should have known she was in big trouble when the beautician came by earlier dressed in a hot pink micro-miniskirt and a pink and black polka-dotted Daisy Mae midriff shirt worn off the shoulder.

When she'd tossed an electric blue swatch of stretchy fabric at her, Elaine had caught it in one hand. "This looks like a sleeve, where's the rest of it?"

Josie's mouth had quirked up on one side and waved her hand. "*Ma chère*, that's it. Now run along and pour yourself into it. The band starts at nine o'clock and I want to be there for the first dance."

Now, Elaine felt altogether too conspicuous in her altogether-and-not-much-else. Half a dozen men had already whistled at her, and two'd had the nerve to pinch her fanny. She'd never been subjected to such lewd behavior before in her life.

Appalled at the uncomfortable familiarity, she nevertheless felt a strange sense of power fill her gut and stiffen her spine. She flung back her newly-cut hair and straightened her shoulders. This movement had the added benefit of pushing her chest out a little farther. She hoped the sleeve wouldn't slip down and expose the tight strapless bra Josie had seen fit to provide as well. It was little too snug, pushing her boobs up higher to emphasize her already generous cleavage.

She could imagine the horror of her fellow Tulane professors if they could see her now. They'd have her fired on the spot.

But who knew her here in Bayou Miste? Here, she could be anything she wanted to be and the thought was shockingly exhilarating. That and the new "do" went a long way toward blocking one tall, dark-haired, blue-eyed Cajun from entering her mind.

Much.

The floor was already crowded with people dancing to a mix of Cajun and country-western tunes from the jukebox. Josie beckoned her and Miz Mozelle to the bar, and they perched on stools with a good view.

Not two seconds after they sat, three dark-haired Cajuns sauntered over and asked them to dance. Josie and Miz Mozelle immediately slid off their stools and led their guys to the crowded dance floor.

Feeling suddenly shy, Elaine shook her head. "Not, yet. I'd like to order a drink first." She smiled, hoping the big guy wouldn't push the issue.

Without a word, the man nodded and turned away.

She swung around on the barstool and ordered white wine. "Make that two," she said, on second thought. The false bravado an alcohol buzz could provide was just what she needed.

The first glass of wine she swallowed in one long, steady chug. With the second glass in her hand, she turned back to crowd. The song changed to a slow tune and half the couples left the floor, while the other half swayed to the music. The band milled around on the stage pushing equipment into position.

She gazed longingly at the couples locked in each other's arms as if they were the only ones on the dance floor. She felt envious of them, wishing she had someone to hold her tight and make her feel that way. Little tingles reverberated from her insides to her epidermis. The wine had the effect of giving the bare bulbs hanging sporadically throughout the open room a fuzzy halo effect. She wasn't drunk, just mildly buzzed, and no doubt a tad less inhibited.

The big Cajun from a few minutes earlier appeared in front of her. "You wanna dance, now?" he asked.

Not nearly as inhibited by shyness this time, she nodded and slid from her stool. She remembered the slinky blue dress and tugged the hem down and the neckline up, to ensure the fabric covered all the right places. Then she threw back her shoulders and practiced one of the moves Josie had taught her earlier at the cottage. Swing your hips side to side. If she put one foot in front of the other, the swaying motion would be automatic.

Following the big brut, she pasted a smile on her face and swayed. Catcalls and whistles followed her all the way to the dance floor.

Wow. Who knew Elaine Smith could attract so many admiring wolf-calls? *Brian, eat your heart out.*

Before she had time to bask in the glory of male admiration, the guy pulled her into his arms, snug up to his barrel chest.

Elaine gasped and tried to pull away. "Please, I can't breathe."

"Oh, sorry." He loosened his hold only a little and snuggled his cheek against her hair. The man smelled of woods and tobacco and he held Elaine entirely too close for her comfort.

She was just trying to think up a good reason to excuse herself when the song ended. *Thank goodness.*

But, the man showed no intention of letting her go.

While the jukebox had played, the band completed setup. Couples either split or drifted back to their seats, leaving only Elaine and her bulky captor standing with only a few die-hard couples amid the sawdust. She tugged and tugged, but the guy wouldn't let go of her hand.

"The song is over," she said, since the idiot didn't quite grasp the obvious.

"Ah, come on. Just one more dance," he said, his grip tightening until she felt her bones would crunch.

"There's no music," she insisted.

"*Laissez les bon temps rouler!*" The lead singer shouted into the microphone, drowning out her protests. "Welcome to the Raccoon Saloon. We're the Ragin' Cajuns and the first song for the evening is "Devil with a Blue Dress" a request in honor of one of our guests tonight. Anyone care to give it a guess as to which one?"

Elaine groaned. Just what she needed, more attention and music when she couldn't get rid of the overgrown baboon clutching her hand.

"Really, my foot hurts." And it did from being stepped on several times. "I'm going to sit this one out." When he loosened his hold, Elaine quickly stepped away and glanced around trying to get her bearings.

This evening was clearly turning out to be a huge mistake. How could she gracefully escape back to her safe little cottage?

* * *

CRAIG HAD SAT PEELING the label off his longneck bottle, wondering for the hundredth time what the hell he was doing in the Raccoon Saloon. He hadn't made a single move to find a woman. Every time one came up to ask him to dance, he'd muttered something about not enough beer yet.

Mo, in a clumsy attempt at a two-step, danced by with a brassy redhead, stopping in front of Craig's table. "How 'bout dis one?" he asked.

Craig squelched a cringe.

Larry waltzed by, completely out of step with the music and pumping his partner's arm up and down. The man really had no business being on the dance floor. As he passed Craig, he shouted, "What about her?"

Craig ducked his head and continued peeling paper from the brown glass.

"Ain't gonna get any closer to findin' a cure for your spell by staring at yer beer, boy," Uncle Joe commented from the next chair.

"Leave it, Uncle," Craig growled. His mind wandered back to his uncle's rental cottage. What was Elaine doing right now? Was she reviewing her notes from previous experiments? Or was she on the phone with her ex-fiancé? He tensed and almost left his seat to go find out.

He barely noticed when the song on the jukebox ended and didn't bother to look up when Jacques, the lead singer, called out for everyone's attention.

When the band started playing "Devil with a Blue Dress," he decided he'd had enough. He looked across the dance floor for an escape route. His gaze collided with an electric blue dress and the desperate expression of the one woman who'd been on his mind all evening.

Holy hell.

Escape was no longer an option.

The strains of "Devil with a Blue Dress" registered in his suddenly feeble brain. *Oh, yeah.* She was definitely the devil for plaguing his every thought since he'd woken up. And she looked devilishly hot in that dress.

Before he could engage logic, he was across the floor standing in front of her, eyeing her as if she were an apparition that would disappear if he spoke. "Dance with me."

Elaine didn't protest or question his high-handedness, she just melted into his body.

He crushed her to his chest. *God, she smelled good.* Their bodies fit perfectly together on the dance floor just as they had in bed. Their moves were smooth and natural, a form of foreplay, igniting longing for a more intimate setting. "Why didn't you want to go out on the bayou tonight?" Craig whispered against her ear.

"Mmm... This is much better than swamp water and mosquitoes." She snuggled closer to him.

"*Ça c'est bon.*" He shifted his knee between hers, and pressed his thigh against her pelvis. "I like the dress. I almost didn't recognize you."

"I'm glad you did."

"Me too," he replied. "And here I thought this evening was going to be an incredible bore."

"And now?"

"I'm completely enchanted."

"Big words for a fish boy," she said against his shirt. Her warm breath heated his chest.

"We fish boys have hidden talents that would amaze the untrained skeptic."

She lifted her face to him, the short curling strands of her new hairdo caressing her forehead and cheeks. "Or perhaps you fish boys aren't revealing the whole truth."

He frowned down at her. "What do you mean?" Did she know about his condition?

She stopped dancing. "I know your secret, Craig Thibodeaux."

His heart hammered in his chest. "But how?"

If she knew about the spell, she'd be disqualified to help cure him from Madame LeBieu's trickery. An empty, sick feeling spread through his chest and into his gut. Would he lose the chance to make Elaine love him?

Did he want her to love him?

A sweaty, meaty hand clamped onto his shoulder, pulling him away from her. "What the hell." Craig spun to face his attacker.

A man as broad and solid as a hundred-year-old cypress frowned down at him. Craig didn't consider himself short at six-foot-two, yet this guy towered over him in height and circumference. As with all bullies of gargantuan proportions, Craig followed the rule: never show fear. "Beat it, Gator."

Gator frowned down at him and shot an accusing glance at Elaine. "She said her feet hurt, otherwise, she'd be dancin' wit' me."

"Your feet are much bigger than hers. You've probably been stepping on them," Craig said, in a calm, matter-of-fact tone. With Gator, one had to approach subjects with caution, show him who was boss while remaining calm, and hope you didn't hit on a sore spot.

He was about to congratulate himself on his politically correct form of handling an explosive situation, when Gator's frown deepened. "Are you makin' fun of my big feet?

Damn, he'd done it now. He'd stepped smack-dab in the middle of Gator's sore spot. "No, Gator, I would never make fun of a man's feet."

"Are you sure you weren't makin' fun of my feet? It sure sounded like you were makin' fun."

"No, no, Gator. You have terrific feet."

"You think I have big feet. I don't think I like you, Craig Thibodeaux. I think I'm gonna smash your face."

Craig's heartbeat ratcheted up a notch. Surely the big oaf wouldn't take a swing? Not in a public place.

He was wrong.

A gigantic, meaty fist came out of nowhere and clipped him on the chin, knocking him halfway across the dance floor and flat on his back.

Stars swam before his eyes in bright white, red, and gold. And that was while they were closed. When he opened them, Gator was headed his way.

Elaine yelled and leaped onto the big brute's back, pummeling him with her fists.

Gator's thunderous expression was enough to make a grown man cringe. Craig didn't think even Gator would kick a man while he was down, but Elaine obviously did.

She rode piggyback, with her dress crawling up her thighs revealing way more than she'd want to know. Her screams intensified and she yelled every curse word in the dictionary and some he wasn't sure but thought might be in Latin.

The picture was priceless. He could already see tomorrow's headline: Scientist Gone Mad on the Back of Giant Ape. A chuckle rose up his chest and escaped in a rush. One chuckle led to another and soon his sides were splitting and tears poured from the corners of his eyes.

Gator, with Elaine still on his back, stopped in front of Craig and stared down, confusion written into the frown between his eyes. "You still laughing at my feet, Craig?"

With a quick swipe at his eyes, Craig stood and looked up at Gator. "No, not at all."

"I didn't mean to hit you so hard." Gator waved his hands. "Darn hands. Momma says I don't know my own strength. Guess she's right."

Elaine stopped pummeling and slid from Gator's back, her skirt riding up to reveal lacy white bikini underwear. She rushed to his side. "Are you okay, Craig?"

Craig's laughter ceased as a red-hot surge rifled through his veins to his groin. "I was until I saw that sexy-as-hell lingerie you're wearing."

Elaine's face suffused with color all the way out to her ears. She stood and tugged frantically at the hem of her dress, cursing in a most unladylike fashion. "That's what I get for worrying about you, Craig Thibodeaux. I'm leaving." She spun on her spike heels and took off across the dance floor pushing against anyone standing between her and the door.

Craig shot to his feet and lit out after her. No way in hell was he going to let her get away without exploring those white lacy panties a bit further.

CHAPTER 17

The jerk.

Here Elaine had been upset by Gator's punch and all Craig could do was point out her exposure in front of God and everybody else at the Raccoon Saloon. Well, she could do without his type. She shoved past the same men who'd whistled earlier and shot quelling looks at them when they dared to make crude comments.

Just as she reached the door, Josie caught up with her. The blonde hugged her and smiled. "Congratulations, Elaine. You graduate with honors."

She frowned. "What?" Then she looked back.

Damn. Craig was threading his way through the crowd, gaining ground. If she didn't hurry, he'd catch her before she could make good her escape.

"Hold up, Elaine!" Craig called out.

Panic seized her and she ducked out the door into the night air. Once outside, she realized her mistake. She hadn't brought her car and she didn't have a ride home. Her heels teetered on the gravel in the parking lot and she winced. *Wonderful.* She'd succeeded in cutting off her nose to spite her face.

She turned to go back in and round up Mozelle and Josie, when Craig burst through the door.

"Thank God, I caught you," he said, reaching for her hands.

She pulled away. "You didn't catch me. I don't have a car here. I was on my way back in to get Josie."

"If you want to go home, I can take you," he offered.

"I don't trust you to get me there." Why did he have to look so damn delicious all in black?

His smile curved the corners of his mouth and his eyes sparkled in the few lights shining over the parking lot. "If you can trust me to take you out on the water, you can trust me to get you home."

"I believe I'd be in over my head if I trusted you again."

His face darkened. "What's that supposed to mean?"

"I know your secret."

His body stiffened. "What are you talking about?"

She flung her hand in the air. "You're not a fish boy. You're an attorney."

Craig inhaled deeply and let the breath out, his body relaxing. "Ah. Is that all?"

"You mean there's more?"

"No, of course not," he replied a little too quickly.

She narrowed her eyes. "I don't know what to believe."

"I'm an attorney." He plucked at a leaf stuck to her dress. "So, what's my occupation got to do with us?"

She batted his hand away. "Trust. Don't you get it? I can't trust you to tell me the truth, and I can't trust myself when I'm with you." She clapped her hand over her mouth, feeling her eyes grow round with her slip of the tongue.

Craig's gaze softened, and he closed the gap between them.

All the fight leached out of her body. She didn't put up an iota of resistance when he pulled her into his arms. "Problem is, I can't trust myself when I'm with you, either. For some reason, I can't keep my hands off you." He leaned closer, his mouth hovering over hers. "Nor my lips."

When he still hovered, she reached up behind his neck. "Then kiss me, damn it." She tugged him closer until their mouths touched, and she fell deeper and deeper into an abyss of mindless sensuality.

Her hands roamed over his shoulders and into the front of his shirt, ripping through buttons with a frantic urgency borne of her completely natural chemical reaction. That's all it was. Chemicals.

Yeah, right.

He captured her hands and pulled them away from his skin. "Let's get out of here."

Her glazed eyes cleared and she glanced around the parking lot. Every nerve ending screamed for more of him. If she didn't get him naked in the next five minutes, she'd explode. "Do you have a car?"

"Yes. Thank goodness I insisted on driving separately." He fished around in his pocket and pulled out his keys. With a quick kiss, he pulled her to him and steered her toward a midnight black sports car. Once inside, he started the engine and shifted into reverse. "Where to?"

Feeling a little racy and altogether more uninhibited than she'd felt in her entire life, she answered, "Where did you go to make out as a teenager?"

"Huh?" He stared at her as if she'd lost her mind.

"I've never made out in a car before."

His jaw dropped. "Never?"

"Nope."

"Well then, sweetheart, you're in for a real treat. I promise this night will be unforgettable."

"I'm counting on it." She was more than determined to show him she could be every bit as aggressive and lustful as he was. My, what a new "do" and a racy dress could do for a woman...

Or was it the hot Cajun in the next seat stirring her blood to boiling?

* * *

Craig screeched the car to a halt at the edge of a moonlit lagoon. The half-moon kissed the water with diamonds, a perfect setting to initiate Elaine in the art of car bouncing.

When he shut off the engine, the silence in the interior of the car was only broken by the sound of their breathing—very rapid breathing. He looked around at the cramped interior of the sports car and cursed his poor choice of vehicles. Whatever happened to backseats? A seventies-model Cadillac with a roomy back seat would be handy about now.

His gaze shifted to Elaine.

Her hand reached down to unclip her seat belt.

Oh boy.

The simple motion caused his heart to rev into overdrive. He fumbled for the side levers and slid the seat all the way back, providing a pretty decent amount of space between him and the steering wheel. But would it be enough?

Out of her seat belt, Elaine smiled over at him and shifted in her seat until the hem of her dress rode up, exposing the white lacy panties he'd glimpsed earlier.

He reached across the console to touch her thigh.

Her hand stilled his before he could slide it up her leg to the center of that tempting triangle of material.

"Not yet. I'm experimenting." Her hand slid inside her white panties and proceeded to stroke the very place Craig longed to be.

He swallowed hard.

Suddenly, his jeans were entirely too tight with the strain of his arousal pulsing a tattoo against his zipper. He groaned and looked away, unable to bear another moment of her teasing. "You're killing me, woman."

"Then my experiment is a success."

Craig glanced over at her.

She slid the white panties down her legs and kicked them off her ankles. With a wicked smile, she climbed over the console and planted a knee on either side of his thighs facing him. She leaned forward and levered the seat into a full reclining position before she turned her attention to his zipper.

Was this the shy scientist he'd met only a few short days ago? The one who stumbled over her words as well as her feet? If so, *laissez les bon temps rouler!* Let the good times roll!

* * *

PERHAPS IT WAS THE WINE, perhaps swamp gases. If Elaine were honest with herself, she'd admit she'd sprung free of her inhibitions and was riding a wild hair to the finish line. Damn the microscope and full speed ahead!

With her hands on the metal button holding the waistband of Craig's trousers together, she paused.

"*Ma chère,* don't stop now," he begged.

"I wouldn't dream of it." She slipped the button through the hole and paused again holding his zipper. "You're sure this road is deserted?"

"Absolutely."

"Good." She drove the zipper downward until his erection sprang forward against black briefs, creating a tent. "My, aren't we excited?"

"More than you could ever imagine."

Elaine's blood burned through her veins. She felt capable of conquering the world or, more difficult, her deepest fears—her fear of water, of not fitting in, and most of all, rejection. Tonight, she was on top of the world, and on top of the sexiest Cajun this side of the Mississippi. Now, to show him she had what it took to keep a man's attention.

Excitement churned in her belly, spreading fingers of desire ever downward to pool at her core hovering over his thighs. With her dress hiked up to her hips, she gave him a moonlit view of what she had to offer, and the thought made her even hotter than before.

She leaned back and rubbed her sweet spot against the rough fabric of his black denim-clad thighs. Flames of pleasure leapt through her.

He grasped her buttocks and kneaded the flesh. "I want to be inside you," he said through clenched teeth.

"And so you will," she promised. She leaned forward and ran her hands up the inside of his shirt, threading through the hairs on his chest, tweaking the hard male nipples. With eager fingers, she pulled his shirt from the waistband of his jeans and unbuttoned the last of the remaining buttons. Pushing the garment over his shoulders, she paused. "Does it still hurt?" She eased forward and pressed her lips to the jagged line where the bullet had skinned his shoulder.

"No." His strong hand circled her hip to the front to cup the juncture of her thighs, a finger sliding easily into her warmth. "God, you're so wet." His other hand traveled up her side to fit over her breast. Looping a finger into the stretch fabric of her dress, he pulled it down until the strapless bra was the only thing between her and the night air.

Even the bra was too much. She wanted to be naked, with him inside her. *Now*. She reached behind her back and unclasped the bra, her breasts springing free from the tight confines.

"Glorious," he breathed, wrapping his fingers around her. He massaged first one breast, then the other, pinching the nipples into hardened peaks, until she cried out.

She leaned forward and rubbed her breasts against the mat of hair on his chest, reveling in the coarseness against her tender skin. He was a big, strong man, she was a soft-skinned woman. Such was the way of nature, and nature had outdone itself in Craig.

His erection pressed against her belly, an insistent reminder of his growing need and her burgeoning desire. With smooth precision, she eased her way down his chest to his slim waist. Trailing kisses and tongue flicks all the way to the waistband of his briefs, she gloried in every touch and taste along the way. With a nudge, she parted his legs and slid between his thighs until her knees touched the floorboard. Only then did she unwrap the package. First, she ran her hands up from his balls over the hard shaft beneath the cotton. The heat there warmed her fingers. Then, she grasped the elastic and eased the briefs downward over him until his member was completely exposed.

"Ah geez, Elaine," his fingers dug into her shoulders. "Come up here."

"Uh-uh," she said, her gaze completely focused on his magnificent manhood. "I've only just begun."

Craig moaned in anticipation, and lay back, tucking his hands up behind his head. "I think I've died and gone to heaven."

"You bet your BVDs." Her voice was low and husky, her own desire spinning out of control. "You'll be singing with the angels before I'm done."

"*Mon Dieu*." Craig said to the ceiling of the car and growled low when her hands wrapped around him.

With sure strokes, she massaged his length, up and down. She moved forward and pressed her breasts around him; his hips rose and fell as he slid his shaft between her cleavage.

She hovered over the velvety tip and slid her tongue around the curved edge.

He tensed, his shaft quivering and incredibly hard. "I need to be inside you now, Elaine. I can't take any more of this."

"What about protection?"

"In my wallet, in my back pocket."

They both fumbled for the wallet, rifling through until they found the little foil packet. When Craig went to open it, she held her hand out. "Let me."

She rolled the condom down over him until it fit snugly against the base.

As soon as it was in place, he grabbed her shoulders and pulled her up onto his chest. He nudged her thighs apart and brought her knees up on either side of him.

With her dress nothing more than a belt around her middle, she'd never felt more attractive or alluring. The humid night air kissed her breasts and the man beneath her followed suit.

She eased down over his shaft, her moist opening accepting him without hesitation.

He slid further inside until her buttocks rested against his thighs. He stopped. "Are you all right?"

"Oh, *yes*," she breathed, the flood of sensations pulling her closer to the edge.

"Then let's shake this buggy." He lifted her hips, setting her in motion.

When she pushed upward, he withdrew. When she dropped back onto him, he met her with force enough to shimmy the little car. She rode him hard, meeting him thrust for thrust.

Craig clutched her thigh with one hand while the other probed to find her most sensitive zone.

Already aroused to the point of mindlessness, she toppled over the edge with one flick of Craig's finger. Her body tensed and burst into a kaleidoscope of sensation, rocking her to the very core.

He thrust one last time and joined her orgasm with one of his own. He held her fully sheathing his member, his expression one of utter concentration. Inside her, he pulsed his release.

As one, they relaxed. She dragged in a deep breath and collapsed across his chest, reluctant to sever their connection. "Is it always this good in the front seat of a car?" She buried her face in the crook of his neck and tongued his earlobe.

His chest rose and fell in labored breaths, but he didn't answer.

She leaned up on one elbow, peering into his shadowed face. "Did I do something wrong?" Her heart beat against her ribs as her fear of rejection crept up her chest.

Craig brows angled toward the bridge of his nose. "Don't you have any clue what you do to me?"

She nibbled her lip. "Not really." With a glance down his torso to where they connected, she smiled. "Beyond the obvious chemical reaction, I figure you're used to this." She didn't dare delude herself into thinking she'd touched him on an emotional level.

With gentle hands, he reached up and turned her face toward his. "Don't play this down. What we just shared not only rocked the car, it rattled me, too."

She touched a finger to his lips. "Don't."

He frowned his confusion, kissing the end of her finger.

"Don't say something you don't mean," she continued. "Our time together is limited, so let's not muddy it with false sentiment." If he said something he didn't mean, she'd leave Bayou Miste with a broken heart.

Craig's frown deepened. "You know, for a smart lady, you've got a lot to learn about relationships."

"And you're the expert?" She leaned away from him allowing his flaccid length to slide free. When she glanced up, headlights hit her full in the face. "Oh shit. There's a car coming." She rolled over the console, banging her knee on the shift. "Ouch. I thought you said this road was deserted?"

"It usually is." Craig struggled to get his jeans up, buttoned and zipped. He levered his seat into an upright position.

Red, blue, and gold lights strobed behind the car.

"Damn."

"Cops?" Elaine squealed and fought to shimmy her twisted dress up over her breasts and down over her hips. She'd just covered the important stuff when a flashlight beam pierced the interior of the car.

"Craig, is that you?"

He pulled the edges of his shirt together and glanced over at her. Apparently satisfied she was decent, he rolled the window down. "Hey Billy Ray, whatcha doing way out here on a Tuesday night?"

A man dressed in a dark uniform sporting a polished gold badge peered through the window, shining his light into her eyes and down over her breasts. "Usually find some kids working on increasing the population of the parish. Could happen any night of the week, but especially on ladies night at the Raccoon Saloon." His light panned the interior of the car until it lit on the rearview mirror where Elaine's strapless bra dangled.

If she could have sunk through the floorboard, she would have. Of all the stupid, adolescent stunts to pull...

Her embarrassment faded, pushed out by the elation of having done something she'd missed out on in high school. She'd necked in a car with a boy, and she'd been caught doing something naughty by the police! What an achievement. She only wished she had a girlfriend to share it with over a cup of hot cocoa.

"You okay there, Miss?" Billy Ray asked, practically poking his head into the narrow window. "Craig ain't pullin' a fast one on you is he? I could haul him in, if you want." The officer grinned. "Can't think of anything I'd like better. I'm sure I owe him one or two for all the pranks he pulled on me back when we were kids."

Craig frowned. "She's fine, Billy Ray. Now, could you scram?"

"I didn't hear the lady say she's fine." Billy Ray planted his feet wide and crossed his arms. "Well, are you, miss?"

She struggled to keep a straight face and answered him with all the gravity befitting an officer of the law. "Yes, sir, I'm fine."

The deputy's arms dropped to his sides. "Rats. I could have used a little excitement. You two shouldn't be hangin' out on this old road. Sets a bad example for the teenagers. Now, get on outta here."

"Will do." Craig rolled up the window, revved the engine and spun the car in a circle to head back up the road.

Before they cleared the headlights of the police cruiser, she exploded, laughing so hard she clutched her sides.

"What's so damn funny?" Craig asked, his voice a little on the cranky side.

She gasped for air. "I've never... You should have... I can't believe..." Giggles interrupted every sentence she attempted until she gave up and doubled over.

When she could finally sit up and breathe, she glanced over at him.

His lips quivered and jerked upward on the corners. "You're some kind of nutcase."

She wiped moisture from her eyes. "Why?"

"I'd have thought you'd be mortified beyond belief. Instead, you're bustin' a gut." He reached over and chucked her under the chin, and paused to stroke the side of her cheek.

She leaned into his palm. "It was an experience I've never had." She pressed a kiss to his palm. "I'm glad I got to share it with you."

For a second, she thought she'd destroyed the moment by her words.

Then, in a quiet voice, he answered, "Yeah. Me, too."

For the rest of the short ride to the cottage, they held hands. Neither spoke, nor did she feel they needed to.

When he finally pulled into the gravel driveway of her temporary home, he sat for a few moments staring straight ahead. "Elaine?"

"Mm-hmm?" she murmured drowsily, unwilling for the evening to end.

"Did you leave the door open when you left?"

CHAPTER 18

ELAINE SHOT UP AND FLEW OUT OF THE BMW BEFORE CRAIG COULD stop her.

"Damn it!" Before she could put her foot on the porch, he caught up with her, grasping her arm. "Wait."

"All my equipment is in there!"

"Yeah, and whoever broke in might be, too." No way was she going in there before he'd made sure it was safe. He crossed in front of her, keeping a tight hold on her hand, forcing her behind him. "Go back to the car."

"No. This is my stuff."

He pushed out an exasperated breath. The woman was as stubborn as they came. "Then stay behind me."

"Okay, but don't do anything macho."

He eased forward. "What? You mean you care?" he asked flippantly, his eyes focused fully on the house before him. But his mind was divided between possibly nabbing the bad guy and hearing her answer.

"No more so than you," she shot back.

Boy, that was a non-answer if ever he'd heard one. "Hey, if anyone's in there, I've got a gun the size of a bazooka and I'm not afraid to use it!" he called out.

Elaine whacked him on the arm. "You don't have a gun."

"I know that and you know that, but if there's someone in there, he won't know that. Well, he will now that we've discussed it loud enough for the entire parish to hear."

"I think whoever was here is gone now."

"It pays to be cautious." He crept up to the side of the open door and took a look. The interior was dark and still. A shaft of light shining in from the fractional moon revealed upset furniture and a clutter of items strewn across the floor. "Geez."

"Geez what?" She jerked her hand loose and stepped around him to flip the light switch. "Geez."

The light illuminated the devastation. Craig listened for sounds of movement, but none came from inside.

"Oh, no." Elaine clapped a hand to her mouth. Her eyes filled with tears.

He spotted a spray-painted message on the wall. *Go home, or die!*

For the first time since he'd come face to face with a hungry alligator at the tender age of twelve, Craig knew real, gut-wrenching fear. The threat was written in red paint across the wall of the living room and it was aimed at this scientist he'd come to admire. A person who wanted to help the swamps become a better place. The woman who'd managed to touch him as no other.

He wrapped an arm around her shoulders and pulled her into his side. "Don't worry, sweetheart. We can repaint the walls, and I won't let anything happen to you," he promised, wondering how in hell he could keep that promise when he turned back into a frog in a few hours. "I'm calling the police."

"No, don't. I don't care about the paint." Her voice caught on a sob and with a shaking hand, she pointed to a metal object lying amid the strewn papers and books. "My microscope," she whispered.

Leaving her side, Craig gathered the cold metal from the floor. He looked inside the lens and twisted the viewfinder until the image cleared. "The lens is intact."

"Oh, thank God," she took it from him and stared through the lens.

Then she clutched it to her chest, tears slipping down her cheeks. "My parents gave me this microscope before they died."

"I didn't know your parents weren't alive." Craig frowned. He realized he didn't know a lot about Elaine, and he wanted very much to learn more.

"I was in the last year of my master's program when they were killed in a car wreck."

"How old were you?"

"Twenty."

"Twenty?" Craig did a double-take. "You were twenty finishing your masters?"

"Yes." Elaine's back stiffened and her chin raised a notch higher.

"Damn, were you some kind of brainiac?"

She winced. More tears welled in her eyes and spilled over.

He immediately felt like a clod. He reached out to take her into his arms.

Like an animal avoiding the trap, she jerked his hands loose and backed away. "I guess leopard frogs can't change their spots."

He let his arms fall to his sides. "What are you talking about?"

"Oh what's the use?" She hugged the microscope to her chest and studied the floor. "Even with the provocative dress and haircut, I still don't fit in any more than I did growing up."

"What do you mean 'fit in'?"

She turned and walked a few steps away. "I finished my undergraduate degree when most kids were graduating high school. I never knew what it was like to be a teenager because I was never around kids my own age."

The pain in her voice drew him forward. "So, that's why you've never been out necking." He slipped his arms around her and her microscope and pulled her back against him. He leaned forward and nuzzled her neck. "I would never have guessed. You were fantastic."

Slowly, her body relaxed into his. With a deep sigh, she leaned her head back onto his shoulder, giving his lips full range of her neck. "Do you really think of me as a brainiac?"

The hope in her voice was almost his undoing. Craig turned her in his arms and tipped her chin up, forcing her to look into his eyes. "I'm very much attracted by your intelligence and passion for knowledge. And your bravery to face your deepest fears humbles me. And babe, in that blue dress, *mon Dieu*, you're incredibly hot. But even in khaki slacks at the bottom of a boat, I can't keep my hands off you." He proved it by sliding his hands down her back and over her rounded buttocks.

His movements had the desired effect when the remaining tension in her body eased and she snuggled against him. "You're not just saying this to get me in bed, are you?"

"Will it help?" He grinned.

She backed away enough to look at him warily.

Immediately, he wiped the stupid look from his face. "No really, I'm telling you the truth."

Her creamy breasts pushed up out of the strapless top of her go-to-hell dress, beckoning him.

He leaned down to press his lips to the cleavage before he looked back up into her eyes. "And, if you look like the sexiest devil with that blue dress, that's just icing on the cake."

"It's not even my dress." Her hands slipped around his waist and dropped down to slide into his rear pockets.

He found it difficult to concentrate with her hands in his back pockets. Every movement was an incredible turn on, even without having skin-to-skin contact. "I really should call the police."

"Later," she whispered.

Later he'd be a frog and she'd be unprotected.

She pressed her lips to his neck.

He almost forgot everything but the tingle of sensations. "I should at least call my uncle."

"Will your uncle be upset about the damage to his house?" Her tongue did wicked things to his earlobe.

"Uncle, who?" His hands tangled in her hair and he pulled her head back for better access to her soft lips.

Her eyelids drooped over near-black irises.

"I can't think when I'm with you." He touched his mouth to hers, barely brushing the skin in an erotic, feathery stroke.

"My brain's clouding too," she whispered huskily.

He kissed her again.

"What's my name?" Her hands circled his head and brought him back to her.

"It's Elaine," he answered and claimed her lips, skimming his tongue past her teeth.

The fire in his chest scorched his veins, making a beeline to his groin. His hands circled her waist and he pressed his bulging zipper against her tummy. "I find you far too fascinating for my own good."

"Me too," she whispered.

"And even though tonight wasn't my first time necking—" he could feel her stiffening "—it was the best time I've ever had in a bucket seat. You were so incredibly—" his lips hovered over hers "—hot."

She rose up on her toes to meet his kiss. Her tongue tangled and teased while her hands tugged his shirt from his trousers. Then soft fingers ran up his back and down into the waistline of his jeans. She ground her hips into his, pressing the thin fabric of her dress against the hardened ridge of his desire.

Without pulling away, he said into her mouth, "Woman you're killing me."

She backed up in his arms and did an amazing thing for Elaine. She batted her eyes and smiled teasingly. "I'm sorry, should I stop?"

He had never seen her do this before. "Are you flirting with me?"

Her smile faded, and she blushed a devilish shade of pink. "I've been taking lessons."

"Lessons in flirting?" Craig couldn't believe it. The woman who knew more about science than he'd ever known or wanted to know had to learn how to flirt. For him? "You really did miss out on the finer things in life didn't you?"

"Yes." Again, her chin rose and a little frown wrinkled the skin between her eyes. "But I'm a quick learner."

"And, pray tell, who would be teaching you how to flirt?"

"My new friends, Josie and Miz Mozelle." She braced her hands on his arms to push him away.

"What else did they teach you?" Craig's hold tightened. "Although, I'm afraid to ask."

"Let me go, and I'll show you." Her voice dropped to a husky whisper.

Like a shot, he dropped her arms and practically salivated for her next demonstration. He wasn't disappointed.

She stepped away, turned around, and walked toward the tiny bedroom, her back to him, her hips swaying enticingly with every step. When she reached the threshold, she squared her shoulders. Then she planted a hand on one hip, and swinging a shoulder back where he could view the profile of one breast, shot a come-hither smile in his direction. "Follow me, Cajun."

The blue dress, the come-hither look, and those incredible already-been-kissed lips reached out imaginary fingers, grabbed his manhood and jerked him forward. "Remind me to thank those ladies."

He swept in behind her and pressed his hips to her backside. With a slow, not-so-steady hand, he ran his fingers up the curve of her waist to cup that tantalizing breast. "I never knew school could be so exhilarating."

"*Beb*, you ain't seen nothin' yet."

* * *

CRAIG GLANCED over Elaine's naked shoulder at the clock and stifled a groan. With his body spooning her backside, he wanted nothing more than to lie in bed and make love to her into the light of the early morning. In fact, making love to her could easily become a twenty-four-seven occupation, and he'd be perfectly happy.

Who needed a successful law practice? Especially when it didn't provide nearly as much satisfaction as lying here with Elaine?

He groaned inwardly. Dawn would come and he'd be a frog in a few short minutes. He needed to get to his uncle before he transformed.

With one last, gentle squeeze of her warm breast, he slipped out of the bed and into his clothes.

She rolled onto her back, one arm flung over the pillow next to hers. A small frown wrinkled her brow, but she didn't wake.

He leaned close, drinking in how her naturally dark eyelashes fanned out over her cheekbones and her tangled hair stood out darkly against the white sheets. He pressed a kiss to her lips, then turned and left before he couldn't.

He picked his way through the living room, avoiding broken glass and crinkly paper. The angry red writing on the wall sent a chill through his soul, strengthening his resolve to take the person responsible apart, limb by limb.

A quick glance at the lightening sky forced Craig into a jog to his uncle's house. He needed to warn Uncle Joe to keep an eye on Elaine during the day and not to let her out on the swamp under any circumstances.

He bounded up the last few steps up to the front porch of Uncle Joe's house and pounded on the door. The white clapboard house could have been identical to the one Elaine slept in a few doors down. Another glance at the sky and Craig banged even louder.

From inside the house sounds of furniture crashing to the floor were followed by loud cursing.

"Come on, Uncle Joe!" Craig shouted.

The sun popped up over the horizon. Craig's skin and bones tightened, shrinking and contracting. *Damn.*

The front porch light glared to life, temporarily blinding Craig.

"Who the hell's knockin' on my door at this time of the mornin'?" When Uncle Joe, wearing only black boxer shorts decorated with bright red and pink hearts, opened the front door, the morphing was halfway over.

Craig hunkered in a squatting position, his features half man, half frog. "Uncle Joe," Craig croaked. His words were barely understandable.

"That you, Craig?" Uncle Joe rubbed his eyes and peered closer. "You look a little green around the gills, boy." He chuckled.

Alternating between words and croaking, Craig fought to get his message across before the transformation was complete. "Elaine...trouble...don't—"

Three words. Three lousy words. The transformation complete, he sat with his belly on the floor kicking himself for not getting there earlier.

"What's that, Craig?" Uncle Joe squatted down. "I didn't understand a single word you said." He smiled wryly. "You really need to find you a woman."

Like I don't know that?

"Joe, honey, is there someone at the door?" called a familiar female voice Craig couldn't quite put a name to.

Uncle Joe turned to yell, "No, sweet thang, musta been the wind."

Uncle Joe had a female friend sleeping with him? Interesting. Craig peered around his uncle's leg, but couldn't see anything in the darkened house.

"You gonna make it back to the bait shop all right?"

Craig nodded his froggy head.

"Snookems, you comin' back to bed?" called the voice from inside the darkened house.

His uncle's face turned beet-red in the porch light. "Gotta go."

As the door closed, Craig turned to hop off the porch. He needed to get back to Elaine. Even if he couldn't do anything to protect her, he could at least keep an eye on her.

* * *

THE SUN STREAKED through the window and shone across the bed before Elaine budged from sleep. Without opening her eyes, she indulged in a long stretch in the warmth of the late morning sun. Wouldn't it be nice to make love all day long? Maybe she'd look for Craig today and suggest it.

Her eyes popped open, and she sat up in bed. Was she actually considering propositioning a man in broad daylight? Her? Elaine Smith? Social cripple and egg-head extraordinaire?

Recalling last night's performance, and her major role in initiating it, her lips curled upward and she sank back against the pillows. She'd really done it. She'd seduced a very provoking man. Not once, but twice. And, in the bucket seat of a sports car. *Woo hoo!*

She really was becoming a wild woman, wasn't she? By allowing her sexuality full rein, she'd discovered a sense of power and confidence lacking in her life up until now. Socially inept geek? Not anymore! She could conquer the world.

With a flick of her wrist, she tossed the sheets aside and leapt out of bed. She had work to do and not much time left. After a quick shower, she bravely stepped into the small living room.

I can handle this. I can handle this. She looked around the room assessing the damage. Nothing a broom, a can of paint, and a little elbow grease wouldn't cure. *Remember, I am the new improved Elaine. The Elaine who isn't afraid to go after what she wants.*

Before she touched a thing, however, she called the police.

Half the morning flew by in which Elaine filed a report, and answered the same questions asked separately by each of the three Bayou Miste deputies who'd shown up on her doorstep. When they'd taken all the required pictures, including one of her white lacy undies lying on the floor of her bedroom, the deputies filed out the door, promising to get right on it.

Finally, she could get on with the task of cleaning up the mess. Shoving the sleeves of her white oxford shirt up her arms, she dug in. She had a lot of work to do, to put the place to rights. And maybe afterward, she'd go shopping to replace every pair of khaki slacks in her wardrobe.

Two hours later, she stood back and examined the results of her cleaning spree and inventory. Aside from the paint on the wall, the cottage appeared almost normal. Some of the furniture was a little dented and scarred, and one chair needed a leg glued back on, but nothing major.

Except for her research.

That worried her. Every bit of her research from notes to specimens was gone. Even her dissecting tray with the frog in it she'd kept in the refrigerator and the frozen fish in the freezer had been taken. The anonymous sample she'd received at the university, the catalyst that set this entire effort into motion, was nothing more than a broken jar on the wooden floor of the living room. She'd been so busy doing the research, she hadn't entered it into her laptop or downloaded the information to the university's database. Hell, she wasn't even sure there was an internet connection in Bayou Miste, much less WiFi.

If she wanted to pursue this investigation, she'd have to start over. Did she have the stamina and courage to do that?

Damn right.

But first, she wanted to do a little background investigation. She needed to find out what industries were nearby that could be dumping that much pollution into the swamp. The best place she knew of to get information was from a local who liked to talk a lot.

Hmm. Now, who did she know that fit that description?

"Elaine? You up for visitors?" Mozelle Reneau stood outside the screen door carrying a basket covered with a dishtowel. "I got pipin' hot beignets."

Speak of the devil.

"Please, come in." Elaine hurried to open the door. The sweet smell of hot pastries filled her nostrils, reminding her she hadn't stopped to have breakfast. A glance at the clock made her realize she'd even missed lunch. Her stomach growled.

Dawg sprawled on the porch in front of the door. She had to forcibly push him with the door to get it open enough for Miz Mozelle to get in.

"That's got to be the laziest hound dog this side of the Mississippi," Miz Mozelle muttered, then exclaimed, "*Mon Dieu!*" She stood just inside the living room door, staring at the red paint on the wall. "What happened?"

"Someone paid me a visit while I was out last night at the Raccoon Saloon."

With a sympathetic cluck, Mozelle carried the basket to the kitchen. "I don't know what gets into people to act so rude."

"You and me both."

"*Mais,* don't you worry none. Nothin' a little paint won't cure." She gave Elaine a sympathetic look. "There's just no excuse for threaten' a woman like that."

"Agreed."

"I'll speak to Joe about it today." She smiled a Mona Lisa smile.

"Thank you, Miz Mozelle." The strange smile wasn't lost on Elaine. She wondered what the older woman was up to.

"I noticed you didn't stay long at the Raccoon Saloon," Mozelle said, arranging plates on the table while Elaine measured coffee into the coffee maker.

Not sure how to respond, she asked, "Was that a question or a statement?"

"Just an observation." Mozelle set forks next to the plates, and then turned to face her. "So, did the lessons work?"

Heat crawled up Elaine's neck as she recalled how well the lessons had worked. She couldn't restrain the smile that tugged at her lips. "Oh, yes."

"*Mais*, bless my soul, that makes two." Miz Mozelle grinned and turned back to polish a fork unnecessarily.

Elaine leaned her back against the counter. "Mozelle Reneau, what do you mean by two?"

"Oh, nothing." She waved her hand in the air and remained uncharacteristically evasive for being Bayou Miste's biggest gossip.

"You know you can't throw out a comment like that without filling in the details." Elaine crossed the room and circled Mozelle to get face to face. "From what I've learned about you in the past few days, you have got to be bursting to tell me, so spill it."

Twin flags of color rode high on Miz Mozelle's pale cheeks. She sank onto the bright red vinyl covered chair and smiled up at Elaine. "I asked a man to dance last night."

Having hurdled that barrier herself, Elaine nodded, suspecting that wasn't all Miz Mozelle had done. "Is that all, just one dance?"

Mozelle darted a glance toward the far corner ceiling. "Well, no. We danced several dances." Her face flushed brighter.

"*And...?*" she prompted, drawing out the syllable.

Mozelle stopped staring at the ceiling and looked directly into her eyes. "We danced all night. There, I said it." Her hand fluttered to her throat.

"Does the Raccoon Saloon stay open that late?"

The older woman's forehead wrinkled, her cheeks flushing, and she stared at Elaine as if she were dense. "Uh, no, *chère*. We shared *un p'tit bec* and more." Miz Mozelle huffed. "If I must spell it out. We danced in the sheets."

Elaine sat in the seat across the Formica table from Mozelle, stunned. "Oh!" What did you say to top that? The older woman had scored.

Miz Mozelle popped out of her chair and pulled mugs from the cabinet. Over her shoulder she commented, "I haven't had that good a sex since Mr. Reneau passed away over ten years ago. For that matter, I hadn't had sex at all. I was almost afraid I'd forgotten how."

Elaine cringed and prayed she didn't go into the gory details. She liked the woman, but there was such a thing as too much information. "I'm really happy for you."

With two cups of hot coffee, she returned to the table. "I never thought I'd get Joe to notice me. He's been avoiding me for years."

"Joe? As in Joe Thibodeaux? Craig's uncle?"

"The one and only." Miz Mozelle grinned. "I think the alcohol had something to do with it, but I'm sure in the light of day, he'll realize we were meant to be together."

Elaine clapped a hand to her forehead, scandalized. "Did you get him drunk and take advantage of him?"

Miz Mozelle chuckled. "Of course I did. How else was I gonna get him to dance? The old coot's been pinin' away for Craig's mamma for the past forty years. It was about time he got over it."

"Whoa. Wait a minute. Joe was in love with Craig's mother?" Elaine sat back in her chair. This was an interesting tidbit. "And she didn't love him?"

"I have my suspicions she might have, but Joe didn't get around to askin' a-fore his brother did."

"Wow. And she said yes? How sad." Elaine wondered if Craig knew anything about this. "That had to hurt Joe."

"Yessum." Mozelle smacked her palms on the table. "That's been quite a while back and, like I said, it was about time he got over it. I just gave him a little push. Don't know why I hadn't done it sooner. Must be the new 'do'. Makes a woman feel like she could conquer the world."

Elaine almost groaned. Here she'd been thinking the exact same thing just that morning. Hearing Mozelle say it out loud didn't make her feel all warm and fuzzy like she had earlier. The same words that had empowered her then, now only made her feel uncertain.

Had she coerced Craig into bed last night? Had she taken unfair advantage of him? She closed her eyes and thought through their activities. *Heck, no*. He'd been just as eager as she had. *Whew*.

Still. Maybe she shouldn't get so carried away and over-inflate her opinion of her sexual prowess. Conquering the world was maybe not such a good idea, after all.

Time to change the subject. She opened her eyes. "Miz Mozelle, what are the local industries in this area?"

"Huh?" The abrupt change in topic made Mozelle blink.

"I'm studying the impact of pollutants on the swamps around Bayou Miste. I figure since you've lived here for a good portion of your life, you might know what industries are nearby."

Mozelle waved her hand. "That's easy. There's only one between here and Morgan City. Littington Refineries."

"Littington?" Elaine mentally scratched her head. Where had she heard that name before? Then it hit her. "Does Jason Littington have anything to do with Littington Refineries?"

"He owns it. That place employs most of the people in the three surrounding parishes. Without it, none of us could afford to stay. My husband worked there for thirty years before he retired. You don't suppose that's where the pollutants are comin' from, do you?"

Elaine sure hoped not. "I plan to find out."

Mozelle sipped from her mug. "Be a shame if it causes trouble for the refinery, bein' as how most people depend on it for their livelihood." She focused on the angry red writing on the wall. "You thinkin' someone from the refinery's doin' this to you?"

"It's a possibility. All my specimens and research have been stolen. Whoever did it is trying to keep me from proving the swamp is being polluted."

"And is it?" Miz Mozelle asked.

"Yes."

The older woman's mouth formed a thin line. "It'll be a shame if they close down that refinery."

"I doubt they'd shut it down. Just enforce the current environmental regulations. It would be a bigger shame if everything in the swamp dies due to negligence or turning a blind eye." And a crying shame if she had to stand up in court against Attorney Craig Thibodeaux, who just happened to represent Jason Littington.

"Yes, yes, you're quite right." Miz Mozelle regarded her. "So whatcha gonna do about it?"

"I don't know." Elaine pinched the corner off the powdery end of a beignet, popped it into her mouth and chewed on the sweet pastry and her thoughts. The lump in her chest that used to be her heart hurt with every beat. She couldn't believe Craig hadn't bothered to tell her all this. Had he only helped her collect specimens to keep an eye on the enemy? If so, he was a slimeball who didn't deserve her heartache. "I need to get back out on the swamp and collect more evidence."

Miz Mozelle reached across the table and grasped Elaine's hands. "It could be dangerous."

"I know." All her life Elaine had been safe within her parent's home, safe within the walls of the lab, and safe behind her microscope. But, some efforts demanded that you conquer your fears and leave your safety net behind.

She reread the dire warning on the wall, a chill slipping down her spine. "This is something I have to do."

CHAPTER 19

EXHAUSTED FROM HIS LATE NIGHT ACTIVITIES, CRAIG HAD HOPPED ALL THE way back to Elaine's cottage. Dawg had been waiting there, stretched across the front door as if protecting Elaine from further intrusions.

Craig wanted to pat the dog's head and tell him he was a good boy, but figured it could wait until he was human again. In the early morning hours, he'd hunkered down next to Dawg on Elaine's front porch and slept, waking at every sound, afraid it was someone trying to get to Elaine. He gave up on sleep about the time Old Lady Reneau showed up carrying a basket of what smelled like heaven.

As Miz Mozelle stood on the porch talking to Elaine, the voice clicked in his memory. This was the voice he'd heard earlier that morning at his uncle's cottage! He gaped up at her as if seeing her for the first time. Uncle Joe was sleeping with Mozelle Reneau?

He'd rolled the revelation over and over in his mind. For a woman in her fifties, he guessed she was okay to look at. Although he remembered her as the woman who'd chased the local teenagers out of her peach trees, Miz Mozelle had shared beignets with them on occasion, and darn good ones at that. She'd been alone for the past ten years, since her husband passed. Uncle Joe had never married. Suddenly, Craig wondered why not?

When Elaine had pushed the door open, Craig leapt out of the way to keep from being stepped on by Miz Mozelle or crushed by Dawg. He hadn't hopped fast enough to get inside, but figured it was just as well. The woman could talk the ear off a frog when she had a mind to.

Once the door closed, Dawg had rolled back over and blocked it again. After a few minutes, curiosity got the better of Craig and he thought he might want to hear what was going on in there after all.

He'd hopped down off the porch and around the house trying to get close enough to overhear some of the ladies' conversation. After the success of last night's love lessons, he was anxious to hear if the older woman had more advice for Elaine. He was also curious if Miz Mozelle planned to talk about her visit to Uncle Joe's last night.

Craig had a lot to discuss with his father's brother. He was just beginning to see the black sheep coming out in his uncle.

Unfortunately, no matter where he stood, he couldn't hear the conversation inside the cottage. He hopped back to the front porch and settled in beside Dawg. He would love to have been a fly on the wall. Speaking of flies...He shook himself. *Save the hunger pangs for nighttime. No more flies for this guy.*

What felt like two hours later, Miz Mozelle emerged with an empty basket dangling from her fingertips and a promise to drop by the next day.

"Thanks for the beignets. They were wonderful," Elaine called out.

Miz Mozelle walked away, a smile on her face.

Elaine reached down and patted Dawg's head. "Hey, sweetie. How's my good boy?"

The sound of her voice bathed Craig in the same afterglow from their previous night's foray into foreplay and hot, steamy sex. He wanted nothing more than to take her into his arms and hold her throughout the day. But he couldn't as long as he remained a frog.

"Oh, hi, Todd. I didn't see you out here earlier." Elaine squatted next to him in her khaki slacks and white blouse. She had her satchel and bucket in one hand, and a little powdered sugar on her chin. "Is Dawg taking good care of you?"

Craig stared up at the powdered sugar. If he stretched it, his tongue could reach out and wipe that sugar right off her. But what would that buy him? She'd freak out at being licked by a frog and he'd still be a frog.

Mon Dieu! What the hell had he done to deserve this?

Elaine stood, walked down the steps, and across the street toward the marina.

When Craig could pull himself together and quit thinking about that little speck of powdered sugar, he hopped after her. Where in the heck did she think she was going at this time of day? The sun wouldn't go down for another hour.

Craig hopped faster.

He'd just reached the marina parking lot when she strolled out onto the dock. Uncle Joe was pumping gas into a small outboard tank on a small pirogue.

"Mr. Thibodeaux?" she called out.

"Oh, hello, Dr. Smith. Didn't expect to see you here so early."

So far, even from a distance, Craig could hear everything. He prayed she wasn't there to go out on the swamp.

"I had a break-in at the cottage last night while I was at the Raccoon Saloon. I thought you ought to know about it."

Good. She was just telling Uncle Joe about the trouble at the house.

"Really?" His uncle hung the pump handle and hose on the gas pump and scratched his head. "Never had anything like that happen around here. Any of your equipment missing?"

"No, but all my specimens and research are gone."

"Sorry to hear that."

"Actually, that's why I'm here." She looked around the dock and up at the bait shop. "Is your nephew around?"

Uncle Joe rubbed his chin and nodded. "Likely."

Craig hopped down onto the wooden planks and closer to the pair.

"Do you suppose he could take me out earlier this evening?" she asked.

"Depending on how much earlier."

Craig would have smiled if he could. His uncle had a way of dancing around the issue when he wanted. Must have been all the practice he got as a lawyer thirty years ago.

"I was hoping to go out now. Do you suppose he could he take me?"

With a slow shake of his head, Uncle Joe answered, "Not hardly."

"Maybe I could ask him myself. Is he here?" She glanced back up at the bait shop.

"Maybe he's here, maybe he's not."

Way to be evasive, Uncle Joe. Craig inched closer.

The fine lines of her eyebrows drew together behind her glasses. How long before she got tired of Uncle Joe's riddles and decided to go home?

Soon, Craig hoped.

"Then could you take me out on the swamp?" She implored Uncle Joe with those big green eyes. "Out to your friend Bernie's old fishin' hole?"

Craig might have fallen into those eyes, but not Uncle Joe. "Now, I don't know about that. My eyesight ain't what it used to be at night."

"I really need to get those samples as soon as possible. If we go now, we could be back before dark."

Rubbing his chin, Uncle Joe dipped his head to the side. "You sure you can't wait until Craig can take you?"

"After what happened last night and the other nights we were out on the swamp, I don't feel comfortable going out after dark. But if we're to stop the polluting, I need to get solid evidence to show the EPA."

Joe rubbed his chin again.

Don't do it, Uncle Joe. Craig hopped up and down to get his uncle's attention. *Don't let her coerce you into something dangerous.*

"Well, if you think we can make it back by dark, I guess I could take you."

Oh, Uncle Joe, you caved. Craig croaked his dismay.

"Thank you, Mr. Thibodeaux." Elaine kissed the old man's cheek.

If Craig could have, he would have groaned. Uncle Joe was a goner. The kiss just sealed the deal.

"Could we leave right now?" Elaine insisted.

"Sure. Let me lock up the bait shop. Business has been kinda slow, anyway."

She moved to the side to allow him passage on the boardwalk.

While Joe climbed the steps to the bait shop, Elaine eased over to the skiff and tossed her bucket and satchel in. With careful precision, she placed one foot at a time into the little boat while clinging to the wooden planks on the dock. Finally, she sat on the metal bench and breathed a huge sigh of relief.

Craig admired her spunk, even if he didn't agree with her mission to go out on the bayou. Despite her fears, she'd gotten into the boat all by herself this time.

"I left a note for Craig telling him we'll be at Bernie's old fishin' hole, in case we're late getting back," Uncle Joe called out behind Craig, before he stepped into the boat.

Craig took a flying leap and landed on a pair of rubber hip-waders piled in the front of the little boat. No way he'd let Elaine and Uncle Joe go out in the swamp without him. Too many crazy things had happened in the bayou lately.

He glanced up at the sky. The sun was low, but not quite low enough for Craig to change back into a man. If they ran into trouble out on the water before sundown he couldn't help them, but he'd at least be there to know what was going on.

He had an ominous feeling about going out on the swamp. He felt it all the way to his diminutive frog bones. Maybe the sensations had a little to do with the Voodoo hoodoo curse he was caught up in. But he was absolutely certain something was about to happen, and he wasn't going to like it.

* * *

In deference to Elaine's fear of the water, Craig had driven the boats slow and smooth, easing around twists and turns in the tributaries.

Not Mr. Thibodeaux. He drove like a madman.

Elaine clamped her teeth on her tongue and kept her eyes glued shut most of the way. When they slowed, she looked around to see the overhanging Spanish moss guarding the entrance to what she'd begun to think of as her and Craig's lagoon—a polluted lagoon, but theirs nonetheless.

How strange to be out on the bayou without him. She missed his teasing and his understanding of her fears. Much as she liked Joe, he wasn't Craig, and she didn't have the same comfort level with him.

She pointed. "Could you take me close to that little island?"

Joe aimed for the small outcropping of land. Then he shut off the motor and allowed the craft to drift to a stop with a gentle thump against the bank.

She didn't see a single frog jumping into the water. "Where are all the frogs? And I don't see any dead fish," she mused aloud. "There were at least a half-dozen the last time we were here."

"Maybe someone came in and cleaned up the evidence." Joe dipped a paddle into the water and maneuvered the skiff to another position farther along the island.

At the very least, she could sample the water. Carefully bending over the boat's side, she collected a sample in a tube, labeled it, and slipped it into her satchel.

When they reached the end of the lagoon, Joe dug his paddle deeper into the water to turn the boat around.

Thunk.

She met Joe's gaze.

As one, they peered over the side and into the water. In the shadows cast by the late afternoon sun, they could just make out the curved edge of a barrel below the surface.

"Holy Moses," Joe said.

"No kidding," she responded. "We've found the source of the pollutants."

Joe glanced up at the sound of an engine. "I think we'd better get the heck out of Dodge, or we'll be sittin' ducks in this pond."

"Let's go." She sat up straight, trying to see through the dense foliage and lengthening gloom.

Turning in his seat, Joe pulled the crank rope, and the motor leapt to life.

Thank you, God. Elaine sent a silent prayer to the heavens. Now would not be a good time for the motor to be stubborn. As far as she was concerned, Joe could drive any way he pleased as long as it was fast and furious.

They'd just cleared the low-hanging tree at the entrance, when the same airboat she'd seen before stormed around a bend in the bayou and headed straight for them.

Joe spun the skiff around and gave it all the gas the little motor could take.

The wind whipped her hair out of the neat ponytail, and the strands lashed at her neck. She alternated between watching out for low-hanging branches and glancing over her shoulder. The closer the other boat came, the more she looked back.

"Hang on, I'm gonna turn," Joe yelled.

Already clinging with a death grip, Elaine leaned into the sharp turn. Just as they completed the ninety-degree angle, she looked back. The other boat bore down on them, aiming for the back end of the skiff where Joe sat.

"Look out, Joe!" she yelled.

The force of the collision lifted the smaller boat sideways, launching her from her seat. Joe catapulted into the water several feet away.

Although petrified of the tea-colored water filling her nostrils, she forced herself to be calm. Last time she'd fallen into the bayou, she'd only been in water about chest deep. If she just waited to get her feet under her, everything would be all right. Her lungs burned for a breath of air when her hip finally touched the soft silt at the bottom.

Quickly, she scrambled her feet beneath her and pushed to stand. *Oh, no.* Even standing erect, her head didn't quite clear the surface. Panic surged through her veins, pooling in her gut, threatening to overwhelm her senses. She pushed hard against the slimy bottom, bouncing up to the surface where she gasped for breath before submerging again.

When her head was above the water, she could see dusk had settled over the bayou. Below, fragments of dirt and decomposed vegetation swirled around her, and a bullfrog swam by. *Oh, God.*

She had to get to Joe. He could have been hurt!

* * *

Craig hadn't seen the other boat coming. He'd only seen the terror on Elaine's face seconds before the skiff flipped over. He tried to leap aside, but the heavy rubber of the hip-waders dragged him below the surface. For a few panicky seconds he thought he'd be forever trapped and ultimately drowned beneath the rubber.

Just when he thought he was one dead frog, the rubber waders stopped their downward drift and buoyed upward. He kicked his webbed feet, and swam free. As he reached the surface, the sun plummeted below the horizon, melding shadows together into full darkness.

Before he could locate Elaine and Uncle Joe, the change hit him with the force of a Mack truck. With the strain of bones and skin stretching and growing, the pain dragged him beneath the surface.

With only enough breath in his lungs for a frog to survive, his fully-formed human lungs burned with the need for oxygen. His vision blurred and he fought against the fuzzy haze preceding the black abyss of unconsciousness.

Elaine was in the water somewhere nearby, possibly drowning in her worst nightmare. And who knew how Uncle Joe fared in the collision. The old man meant a lot to him. He'd been the balance in Craig's upbringing. The roots to which he'd clung to in his youth. He couldn't give up, he had to stay conscious and find them.

He pushed through the haze and the darkness, propelling his fully transformed body through the brackish waters to the surface. "Elaine! Uncle Joe!"

His eyes strained against the gloom, and he listened for the slightest sound of splashing.

"Joe!" A gurgling feminine cry rent the air a few yards to Craig's left. He launched himself in that direction. In the meager light still eking its way through the dense canopy overhead, he could see ripples disturbing the water's surface. He dove into the middle of them, his hand connecting with hair. Winding his fingers into the floating tresses, he dragged her up until he could hook his arms beneath hers and lift her to the surface.

Expecting her to kick and scream hysterically, he was surprised when she hung limply in his arms. His heart alternated between racing and standing still. Was she alive? She had to be!

Then her body jerked and she coughed up water. "Joe," she gasped.

"It's me, Craig," he said, swimming her toward a small island, praying the alligators with give them a break this one night.

"Craig? How'd you get here?" she asked. "Where's Joe?"

He concentrated on keeping her head above water until his bare feet touched bottom. He sat her on a large root, grabbed a low-hanging branch, and shoved it into her hands. "Can you hold on until I find him?"

She nodded, tears slipping down her cheeks. "Yes, go."

He threw himself back into the murky water and swam out to the overturned boat. With a deep breath, he dove beneath and resurfaced on the other side. No uncle.

He swam in wider circles bumping along the bottom of the bayou in case his uncle had submerged. In the shadow of a giant bald cypress tree, he found a still form draped over a knobby cypress knee. Uncle Joe!

His face was out of the water but the man wasn't moving. "Uncle Joe?" No response. With his heart in his throat, Craig searched for a pulse. For a moment, he couldn't feel the reassuring beat of the old man's heart. Pain shot through Craig's chest, threatening to shut off his breathing. *Not Uncle Joe. Please, God, not Uncle Joe.*

"Craig? Is that you, boy?" Uncle Joe breathed in a raspy voice.

"Yes, sir. It's me."

"Thought I saw you hop in the boat." Uncle Joe coughed, grimaced and grabbed for his ribs. "Thank God for cypress knees. Kept me from drowning, but I think I busted a rib."

"Don't you worry, I'll have you outta here in no time." Craig glanced around for the boat.

"Where's Elaine?" Joe asked.

"I'm here," she called out from the darkness. "Are you all right?"

"Nothing a little alcohol won't cure," Joe yelled back. He coughed for his troubles. When he got his breath again, he asked, "What about the other boat?"

"Gone," Craig said.

"Good." Uncle Joe inhaled carefully. "Not up to a fight right now."

"No, you're not." Craig didn't remind his uncle they weren't out of hot water yet. With the alligator population up and the fish population down...well now, that made for a bad combination for humans swimming in alligator habitat.

Uncle Joe pushed against the cypress knee, winced and looked around. "What about our boat?"

"I don't know," Craig said. "Hang tight while I check it out."

He swam out to the upside down craft and quickly ran the tips of his fingers along the hull. One corner was dented in six inches, and a gash stretched from the dent up to the rim. He couldn't feel any other holes. Whatever the damage, the skiff was their only option. He had to get Elaine and Uncle Joe out of the water.

Swimming hard, he pulled the boat to the shallows and struggled to flip it onto its belly. The skiff floated, but the motor was waterlogged and completely unserviceable. If they were lucky, they'd make it back to the marina before morning using good old-fashioned elbow grease and a paddle. He just hoped Uncle Joe's injuries weren't life threatening.

With one hand wrapped around the tie-off rope, Craig swam the boat over to Elaine. He helped her over the side onto the cool metal bench.

Her teeth chattered and she clung to him even when she was seated. "I'm glad you found us."

"Me too." He kissed her hard on the lips and peeled her arms from around his neck. "I've got to get Uncle Joe. We're going to be all right." He swam the skiff to where Uncle Joe slouched over the cypress knees. "Need a hand?"

"Yeah, 'fraid I do." Uncle Joe never asked for help. The fact that he would now meant he was in some amount of pain.

"Not a problem." Craig slid his arms under his uncle and eased him over the side of the boat.

The older man grunted, but didn't cry out.

With both of the people Craig had grown to love in the boat, he realized he couldn't get in without a whole lot of questions.

All the while he'd been swimming in the nude. As a frog, he didn't have a need for clothing. As a man, he'd have a tough time explaining his lack of covering. Just as he pondered the dilemma, the rubber hip waders floated to the surface in front of him.

Craig sent a silent thank you to the heavens as he slid them on.

They just might make it through the night intact, both physically and mentally. His jaw tightened. And when he got back to dry land, he planned to nail whoever did this to his family.

CHAPTER 20

ELAINE THOUGHT THEY'D NEVER GET BACK TO THE MARINA. DAMP AND IN a state of semi-shock, her teeth clattered so hard against each other, surely they'd chip.

Without the engine and with only the one paddle Craig wielded, progress was slow.

Cupping her stiff fingers, Elaine baled water out of the bottom of the boat. She wished she could do more to help them along.

Uncle Joe had lapsed into silence facing Craig in the middle of the boat.

Elaine worried he wasn't doing well. She hoped he hadn't punctured a lung with the broken rib. He could also have a concussion, which meant he probably should stay awake.

"Mr. Thibodeaux?" she called out. "Joe."

A few seconds went by before he grunted.

"Are you okay?" she asked.

"Yeah."

He didn't sound okay. She tried to think of something to say that would keep him talking. "How long have you owned the marina?"

"Since I quit law."

Not quite the answer she expected. "I didn't know you were a lawyer. Is everyone in Bayou Miste an attorney and I just didn't know it?"

"No, just the Thibodeauxs," Craig said.

"Why did you get out, Joe?" she asked.

"Had my reasons." His words were clipped, not inviting more digging. The night grew silent with only the sound of the paddle dipping in the water.

She couldn't help herself, she had to ask, "Was it a woman? You don't have to answer. I'm just curious." She rubbed her hands together to get the blood flowing in her cold fingers.

For a long time, Joe was quiet. Then out of the darkness, he said, "Yeah."

Elaine recalled Miz Mozelle's comment about Joe loving Craig's mother, and the pieces fell into place. *Holy Bunsen burners.* She should have kept her big mouth shut. And she would for the rest of the journey back to the marina.

But Joe had more to say. "It was a long time ago. And I still think about her every day of my life. Kinda hard not to."

Elaine persisted, but only because Joe seemed to want to talk about it. "Why? If it was such a long time ago?"

Joe nodded his head in the direction of Craig. "This big doofus keeps coming back to remind me."

Uh-oh. Looked like the Uncle Joe had kept a secret from his nephew and she had just busted it wide open. She wished she could crawl under a rock or slip over the side of the boat. She shrank back on the metal bench hoping she hadn't started a family feud.

"Me?" Craig frowned.

In the light from the half-moon shining down on the bayou, Uncle Joe stared across at Craig. "Yeah, you."

"What do I have to do with your love life?"

What can of worms had she opened with her line of questioning? Elaine had only meant to keep him talking until they could get him back to land and a doctor.

"I fell for the wrong girl back when I was about your age."

"Why was she wrong?" Craig asked.

Elaine thought about her predicament with Craig. She was a scientist, he was an attorney representing a client possibly responsible for polluting the ecosystem of the bayou. How much more wrong could they be for each other?

"She was in love with another man," Uncle Joe said.

Her shoulders stiffened. Waiting for the rest of the story and Craig's reaction was like waiting for a train wreck.

"Did you tell her how you felt?" Craig held the paddle out of the water.

Here it comes. Elaine braced herself, her heart already pinching for Craig.

"Yeah." Uncle Joe's held Craig's. "She married my brother anyway."

* * *

CRAIG'S GAZE bored into his Uncle's for a long minute. "Why didn't you tell me?"

Uncle Joe attempted a shrug, and winced for his effort. "Wouldn't have changed anything. She married your father, I moved to Bayou Miste, and the rest is history."

Craig leaned forward, the paddle dragging in the water. "Why did you run away?"

"I left. Your father wouldn't have wanted me hangin' around like a dadgum fifth wheel."

"You're brothers." Craig dipped the paddle into the water. "Couldn't you have worked things out?"

"No," Uncle Joe said. "For years I couldn't be around her knowing she wasn't mine. And I couldn't forgive myself for betraying my brother."

"For loving my mother?" Craig frankly couldn't see his mother, queen of the New Orleans social scene, with Uncle Joe.

A half smile tilted the corner of his uncle's mouth. "No, for telling her on their wedding day."

"Oh," Craig sat back, the wind sucked out of his sails.

"Yeah, the timin'...how do you say...sucked."

"No kidding," Craig muttered.

"I've kicked myself all my life, wondering if it would have made a difference if I'd told her sooner. When you were old enough to come visit, I pretended you were our son. I probably even wished it. Then you grew up and stayed away from here so long, I thought I'd lost you as well."

Craig ran a hand through his hair. "I didn't know."

"No, you weren't supposed to." Joe shifted on his seat. "When you went on to join the family business, just as your father wanted, I thought you were well on your way to making the same mistakes I did."

"I liked my life," Craig insisted.

"Did you?" Uncle Joe studied him.

Elaine, who'd been sitting quietly in the front of the boat, chose that moment to speak up. "You like representing men like Jason Littington, who very well could be killing Bayou Miste?" At his surprise, she explained, "I heard you were only in town on business and that business was with Littington of Littington Enterprises, the only refinery or major industrial anything between here and Morgan City.

"That's right." Craig felt like he was on the wrong end of a judge, jury, and hangman's noose.

"I'll bet if we pull that barrel we found out of the swamp, we'll find Littington oil at the bottom of it." Elaine glared at him. "And you're proud of representing people like that?"

"I don't judge until I hear both sides of the argument."

"And you tell no more of the truth than absolutely necessary, either." Her voice broke at the end of her words. "Is that one of the first lessons you learned in Law 101?"

"I didn't lie to you, Elaine," he protested.

"You didn't tell me the truth, either." She wrapped her arms around herself to ward off a round of shivers.

"But, I didn't lie," he insisted.

"What else haven't you told me, Craig?" She sniffed, and he suspected the darkness was hiding moisture in her eyes.

"I've told you everything I can. For anything else, you'll just have to trust me."

She huffed. "How can I trust you, when you don't tell me the whole truth? Such as, how did you get out in the swamp and find us? And why are you wearing those...those...rubbery things...instead of clothes?"

He couldn't tell her without ruining his chances to undo the spell. And she would never trust him again if he didn't tell her. Damned if he did, and damned if he didn't. "There're some things I can't tell you right now. Hopefully someday, but not now."

"Can't tell me? Or won't?" Her shoulders rose and fell. "There's no trust."

He stared from her to his uncle, and back again. His heart squeezed tight in his chest. She was slipping away from him and he couldn't do anything to get her back. "I guess that's it then."

"I guess so." Elaine looked away.

"What are you going to do with the information about the swamp?" he asked.

"I'll go to the EPA," she said, her voice low and her head still down.

"Then there's nothing more to say." His heart squeezing in his chest, Craig clamped down hard on his tongue, bound by attorney-client privileges. He'd helped her as much as he could gathering evidence, but he couldn't do anything to inflict harm on his client...until Littington was no longer his client, or he could clear up this mess. *Mon Dieu,* he hoped he could fix this. Craig dug the paddle into the water. The quicker he got back to the marina, the sooner he could get away from her, and those green eyes filled with betrayal.

"Bull feathers!" Uncle Joe shouted, followed immediately by several tentative coughs.

"Stay out of it, Uncle Joe," Craig warned.

"Didn't you hear anything I said to you just now?" Joe whispered in deference to his sore rib.

"Yes, but this is different." He dug the paddle in again, propelling the boat forward and a little to the left. He compensated by dipping in on the opposite side.

"Bull feathers!" Uncle Joe repeated. "You're crazy about this girl. Don't screw it up like I did."

"Uncle," Craig said, his voice low and dangerous. If ever there was a time for the coast guard to show up, now would be good.

The sound of a motor hummed softly in the night.

"Do you think they came back for us?" Elaine asked.

"*Shh.*" Craig tilted his head in the direction of the sound. "Sounds like a trolling motor."

"Larry, you gotta turn de motor off if you wanna gig dose frogs." Mo's voice could be heard before Craig actually saw him.

"But we be getting' there much faster with it dan without," Larry argued.

"Don't do no good for frog giggin' if you scare de frogs all away."

"Why we be giggin', anyway?" Larry asked. "Ain'tcha 'fraid we might catch our good buddy?"

"He ain't a frog at night, *coo-yôn*. An' I got a hankerin' for some fried frog legs."

"Oh, yeah."

Craig turned and stood in the boat, waving his paddle high over his head. "Mo, Larry, over here."

A skiff similar to the one they were in trolled into view.

"Craig, whatcha doin' out here on de bayou? Shouldn't you be findin' you a woman or something?" Mo called out.

He cringed, and quickly said, "Had us a little accident, guys. Think you could give us a tow back to the marina? Uncle Joe could use some medical attention."

"You all right, Mr. Thibodeaux?" Mo pulled the boat alongside the damaged skiff.

"Okay," Joe wheezed. "For an old man with a broken rib, I guess."

"*Coo-wee*! What happened here?" Larry stared at the skiff's damaged corner.

"Had a run-in with an airboat." Craig tossed them the towrope.

Mo whacked Larry in the gut. "I tol' you, der be some powerful bad magic on dis bayou, tonight."

Larry rubbed his belly, frowning. "You didn't tell me dat."

"Well I felt it. I shoulda tol' you."

"You see what I have to put up wit'?" Larry said to Craig. He grabbed the rope and tied it to metal loop at the back of their boat. "Ready?"

"Thanks, guys," Craig said. As usual, his buddies had come through for him.

Mo waved aside his gratitude. "Dat's what friends are for."

Craig smiled, though inside he was in turmoil. Question was, would he come through for them? He had a mess to clean up and it stank just as bad as the polluted barrel at the bottom of the bayou. He had to get to Jason Littington and find out what the hell was going on. And then he had to convince Elaine he was not working for the bad guys. About an hour later, they reached the marina. The bait shop had been closed since Uncle Joe left earlier, but in the parking lot stood a shiny red Mercedes sports coupe.

Uh-oh. Craig's mess had just exploded to gargantuan proportions.

* * *

ONCE MO and Larry tied the skiff to the dock, Elaine hurriedly accepted Mo's beefy hand to pull her to the wooden planks. "Thank you, Mo," she offered, then turned to march up to the bait shop and as fast and as far away from Craig as she could get.

Not until she'd reached the parking lot did she realize she wasn't alone. A woman stepped out of a bright red Mercedes parked under a street lamp, a female like no other Elaine had ever encountered.

She was everything Elaine was not. From her sleek, tailored suit, to her perfectly straight blond hair hanging to an ideal length, not too long, not too short. She was classically beautiful in every way.

With her clothes dripping dry on her body, and her new hairdo in soggy disarray, Elaine felt certain she looked like a reject from the Salvation Army with a Little Orphan Annie hairstyle.

The woman looked down her nose at Elaine and immediately turned her attention to the men coming up behind her. "Craig," she called out and rushed to him, flinging her arms around his neck and pressing her perfectly tailored suit to his hip waders. "I've missed you so much."

"Cassandra, what are you doing here?" Craig's voice was clipped and didn't sound too happy.

"I flew in from France yesterday and found your message on my answering machine. I came because you asked me to, silly."

All of Elaine's righteous indignation about the Littington fiasco paled in comparison to the way her heart hit rock bottom. Apparently, there were other things Craig had failed to tell her, proving he hadn't meant for their relationship to last. He already had a girlfriend, one who could blend into his circles in New Orleans much better than a dweeb scientist who was afraid of the water.

While lover boy was hugging his Cassandra, Elaine slipped away to shower the smell of bayou water from her hair and body. If only she could wash the heartache away with the smell. Exhausted beyond belief, she trudged to her rented cottage, locking the door behind her.

Tonight would be her first night alone since she and Craig had started their steamy affair. She could only stand to be in the bedroom long enough to gather fresh clothing on her way to the bathroom. She'd sleep on the couch and pack her stuff tomorrow. Her stay in Bayou Miste was over. Time to face reality and get back to the university.

So you can resume hiding behind your microscope? a voice inside her head challenged.

No way.

She'd overcome that phase in her life. Damned if she'd let herself backslide.

And her evidence against Littington Industries might have been stolen, but she knew exactly where to find more.

* * *

TWO HOURS at the hospital with Cassandra yammering in one ear, while his uncle read him the riot act in the other, gave Craig a splitting headache. Finally convinced his uncle had no more lasting damage than a broken rib, he dropped him off at his house with a bottle of painkillers and a lecture on taking it easy.

Cassandra was another story entirely. Trying to get rid of her was like a fly trying to shake sticky flypaper. Until she saw his sleeping quarters in the back of...as she put it...the 'worm-infested bait shop,' she'd actually thought she was going to sleep with him. Craig put his foot down and sent her back to Morgan City and the closest Holiday Inn with room service.

Alone.

Finally, he grabbed a phone and dialed Jason Littington. He had some business to conduct with the man. Never mind the clock read three a.m. Craig's life was crashing down around him and he didn't have time for pleasantries.

"Mr. Littington? This is Craig Thibodeaux."

"Craig, why the hell are you calling me at this hour?"

"You got trouble, sir. If you don't want to go to jail, meet me at my uncle's bait shop, A.S.A.P."

"What—"

"Just do it," Craig ordered, his voice firm. "And come alone."

CHAPTER 21

ELAINE BLINKED AT THE SUN STREAKING THROUGH THE COTTAGE WINDOW to her makeshift bed on the couch. Once again, she'd slept the morning away when she should have been working. Didn't she have some frogs to dissect or specimens to investigate beneath her microscope?

She'd tossed and turned on the couch cushions until dawn, before finally drifting off. Her sleep hadn't been any more restful. With Voodoo drums beating and ominous chanting filling her dreams, she felt as though she'd been offered up as a sacrifice in some pagan ritual only to be rejected. Even in her dreams she didn't fit in.

What was it she was supposed to do today? Something big. She sat up and pushed the mass of tangled curls from her face and waited for her fuzzy head to clear. When it did, her empty stomach grumbled.

Or was that her empty heart?

Oh, yeah. The beautiful Cassandra had come to claim Craig, and now Elaine was packing to leave Bayou Miste.

If Cassandra was the type of woman he wanted, no way Elaine Smith could measure up. Nor did she want to. If she'd learned one thing over the past few days, she'd learned she couldn't be who she wasn't. She could improve on herself, but she couldn't and wouldn't change deep down. Hers was a case of 'love me as I am, or don't love me at all.'

Unfortunately, Craig would choose the latter. Hell, he already had. Which was fine. He wasn't the man she'd thought he was.

Why hadn't he told her he was involved with Littington Refineries and trusted her either to understand or to give him a chance to explain? He hadn't done that. Hadn't trusted her. He'd strung her along to further his own interests, just as Brian had.

Well, who needed him, anyway?

You do. The damn voice in her head sounded very much like the chanting she'd heard in her dreams.

A knock sounded at the door. Who could that be at this hour? She looked down at her Tweety-bird T-shirt and flannel boxer shorts. Whatever. With her new 'what you see is what you get' attitude, she opened the door.

Miz Mozelle stood there with her requisite basket full of sweet-smelling pastries and a smile bright enough to light the Chrysler building. "Howdy, neighbor. Thought you could use a little midday snack."

"Oh, hi, Miz Mozelle." Elaine opened the door. With all the enthusiasm of one marching to the guillotine, she turned and padded barefoot into the kitchen to start some go-juice in the coffee maker.

"What's wrong, dear? Are you not feeling well?" Mozelle set the basket on the table and touched her hand to Elaine's forehead. "No fever."

"I'm fine."

If you don't count a broken heart.

"I heard y'all had some trouble out on the swamp last night."

Elaine grimaced. "Good news travels fast around here."

"I was by to see Joe earlier." Mozelle blushed. "Needless to say, I was shocked to find him injured. And you, my dear, were you injured as well?"

"No, I wasn't injured."

Just my heart.

"Joe told me that Cassandra woman showed up lookin' for Craig last night." Mozelle peered closer at Elaine. "Is that what's got your panties in a wad?"

Good news really did travel fast. She forced her tone to be light. "Why should it?"

"I know I'd be upset if I saw the man I was head over heels for huggin' some other woman."

Turning her back to Mozelle, she said, "I'm not head over heels for him. Who said I was?"

"*Chère,* your words say one thing, your face says another."

She raised a hand to her cheek in defeat, and sank to the shiny red vinyl chair. "Oh this is awful. I can't be in love with Craig Thibodeaux."

Mozelle stood next to Elaine, and wrapped an arm around her shoulder. "Sweet Pea, there's nothing awful about lovin' someone. It's a gift."

"A gift if the feeling is returned, a curse if it isn't." She laid her head on the table. "He wouldn't want my love, even if I offered it up with a free sports car."

"How do you know if you don't ask?"

"*Ask?* Miz Mozelle, if you'd seen that woman... Hell, I couldn't compete with her. She's perfect, and I'm..." She glanced down at her faded Tweety T-shirt, lifted a tangled curl. "I'm just me."

"Maybe that's just what Craig wants. He's lived in New Orleans all his life surrounded by everything money has to offer. You have something he can't buy."

"I do?" She looked up hopelessly. "Like what?"

"You have genuine compassion and a heart worth takin' a risk for." Mozelle grabbed her hands and stared into her eyes. "Honey, you're real. From what Joe told me, Cassandra wouldn't know love if it hit her smack-dab in her chemically and surgically enhanced face."

"It's no use, Miz Mozelle, I don't belong here. I need to go back where I do."

"You gonna tuck your tail between your legs and run?" The older woman's lips thinned. "I thought you had more gumption than that. What did I tell you about fighting for your man?"

"He's not my man," Elaine softly wailed. "I don't even know who he is. He knew I wanted to stop the pollution, yet he didn't tell me he represents the man who's causing it! We have nothing in common, nothing." She turned her back to Miz Mozelle, fighting a losing battle to keep the tears from falling. First one slid down her cheek, followed by another, and before too long, a steady stream dripped off her chin.

An arm draped over her shoulder, and the older woman pulled her close. "You got the most important thing in common, sweetie. You got love. Everything else can be worked out."

Steeling herself from the warmth and comfort Miz Mozelle offered, Elaine stiffened and pulled away. "No, we don't, and no it can't."

"That boy loves you. I saw how he looked at you at the Raccoon Saloon the other night."

"That wasn't love." She smacked her palm against the table. "What you saw was an ordinary case of lust."

"Not the way he stuck up for you. I really, truly believe he cares. He just doesn't always know how to show it. Besides, it's just like a man to be stubborn and bullheaded about sharin' his feelin's. You can't expect the impossible. Why, look at me. I've waited the past ten years for Joe to notice I exist. Ten years too long. Sometimes you gotta take matters into yer own hands."

Elaine scrubbed the back of her hand over her eyes. "I can't, Miz Mozelle. I just can't."

The older woman tapped a toe against the wooden floor. "So, that's it? Yer just gonna high-tail it out of here without a goodbye, by yer leave, or kiss my grits?"

"Yes." Elaine grabbed a tissue and blew. "The sooner the better."

"What about the pollution? Who'll make sure they stop?"

"I'll call the EPA and give them the information I know over the phone. Joe can show them where we found the barrel."

Miz Mozelle wrapped her arms around her middle and shuffled to the window, her shoulders hunched, appearing older than she had since Elaine had known her. "What about the friends you made here? Dontcha think we'll miss you?"

"Oh, Miz Mozelle." Elaine crossed the floor and pulled the other woman into a tight hug. "I'm going to miss you, too." She fought against the tears choking her vocal chords. "You can come see me in New Orleans."

"Don't have much call for goin' to the Big Easy. They drive too fast for my likin'."

"You could get Josie to bring you."

"Don't know that I like how fast she drives either," Mozelle said.

"But you'll do it?" Elaine held her at arm's length. The woman's answer meant more to her than she thought possible in the few short days they'd known each other. "Won't you?"

"Sure, *chère*. I'll come see you. But I still think you ought to reconsider and give Craig a chance to explain. You haven't, have you?"

"I can't. I have to go home."

Mozelle hugged her close, patting her back like a child. Then she set her away and lifted her apron to wipe the tears from her eyes. "*Mais*, I guess there's not much else I can do to talk you out of it."

"No, there's not," Elaine said, mist fogging her eyes. "In fact, if I'm to get on the road before dark, I'd better start packing."

Miz Mozelle squeezed her tight once more. "I'm gonna miss you, Elaine Smith. You've been a little ray of sunshine in Bayou Miste. I hate to see you leave."

"Thanks," she said over Miz Mozelle's shoulder, "for being my friend."

Miz Mozelle broke free, scrubbed a hand across her face and looked around. "Is there anything I can do to help?"

"I think I'd rather be alone to pack." If she didn't leave soon, Elaine would be blubbering all over again. Who'd have thought in the little bitty town of Bayou Miste, she'd have found such a good friend in a woman old enough to be her mother?

"If you're sure, I'll just go check on Joe." Mozelle's mouth lifted at the corners. "I think that ornery ol' coot likes playin' sick."

Elaine forced a smile for her friend's happiness. "Go on, he needs you."

She only wished Craig needed her.

After Miz Mozelle left, Elaine dragged boxes out into the living room and tossed in books, papers, and pencils. When she got to her microscope, she hesitated, recalling the night Craig had held her after the house had been ransacked. At the time, she'd felt cherished and cared for. Craig had made love to her all night, his touch gentle, and his passion equal to her own.

Had it all been an act?

She set the microscope on the table and looked around for newspaper to wrap it.

"Leaving?" a feminine voice asked from behind her.

Elaine spun to face the infamous and infinitely beautiful Cassandra. Her empty stomach rumbled loud enough for the other woman to hear, and she tamped down the urge to run screaming from the room.

The other woman wore a finely woven silk skirted suit with dyed-to-match strappy sandals. Every one of her straight blond hairs was pulled back and secured in a neat French chignon. Not a stray tendril dared escape and destroy the perfect symmetry.

Elaine closed her eyes to keep from heaving air from her hollow belly. Tweety-Bird still hung like an old rag from her shoulders over her flannel boxers, the hem of which had given up threads to the washing machine monster years ago. What she wanted to do was crawl under the nearest paper bag and ignore the world.

Unfortunately, hiding was not an option. Elaine opened her eyes and plastered a smile on her face as if Cassandra's visit was no big deal. "Oh, hi. You're Cassandra, aren't you?" Elaine held out her hand.

Cassandra ignored her hand and her question, and let her gaze run the length from Elaine's disastrous hair to her bare feet. "I had to come meet the woman everyone's been talking about."

"Me?" Elaine squeaked.

"Since ten this morning, I've had no less than four visitors and at least two threatening phone calls, warning me to stay away from Craig and someone called Elaine. That is you, isn't it?"

"You have?" Elaine's vocabulary escaped her. What was going on?

"Some man named Mo even threatened to turn his pet alligator loose in my hotel room."

Mo? Elaine barely knew Mo. Why would he be warning Cassandra off Craig? "I don't understand." Elaine ran a hand through her hair.

"I don't either, especially since Craig called me last Saturday, begging me to come all the way from New Orleans to this godforsaken swamp."

Cassandra glanced around the interior of the cottage with distaste. "Craig mentioned he had something important to ask me and he needed me down here as soon as possible." She held up a hand and studied her coral-tipped fingernails.

"And it took you three days to get here?" Elaine could have pulled her tongue out and stomped all over it. Why should she care how long it took Cassandra to come to Bayou Miste after Craig's call?

Had Craig phoned Elaine with a the promise of asking an important question, she sure as hell wouldn't have waited three days to mosey her way down to the bayou. She'd have broken speed limits in every parish from New Orleans to the center of the Atchafalaya Basin.

Elaine's heart sank at what that important question had to be.

"Although Craig came here under the pretext of business, I figured he was here to contemplate the next step in our relationship, and maybe to—" Cassandra's gaze flicked to her, "—sow a few wild oats."

Elaine gasped at the blatant slam. Try as she might, she couldn't halt the flood of heat to her cheeks as she recalled the wild oats they'd, indeed, sown together. Irritation quickly followed embarrassment, and she forced her chin up. "Are you quite finished inspecting the oat fields? If so, I have work to do."

As she studied Elaine, the luscious blonde's eyes narrowed, a considering gleam sparkling in their depths. "You're a bit more intelligent than his usual flings. He has a hit-and-run reputation, but make no mistake, he always comes back to me."

Elaine flinched. Craig had said he wasn't the commitment type. Was Cassandra the reason? "Whatever you say."

A carefully plucked eyebrow quirked over clear gray eyes. "You didn't think he'd stay with you, did you?"

Cassandra's words hit like a punch to the gut. "Look, if you've come to gloat, save your breath. Craig means nothing to me." Elaine swallowed the lump rising in her throat at the lie. "Now, if you don't mind, I really have work to do."

"You're making the right decision to leave. Craig and I have an understanding, and once we're married, I'm sure his little indiscretions will end." The bitch drew in a deep breath and blew it out. Then, with a cardboard smile, she stuck out her hand. "Ellen, it's been...interesting. I'll show myself out."

Staring at the proffered hand, Elaine kept hers at her side. "Don't let the door slam."

Cassandra's smile slipped, she dropped her hand and swung her purse over her shoulder. Her bag caught the microscope perched on the edge of the table and sent it flying to the floor. The device landed with a crash, with the distinct sound of broken glass.

"Damn!" Elaine cried.

The demolition woman responsible for smashing her heart turned and stared down her nose at her cherished microscope. "Did I do that?" She waved her fingers dismissively. "Just send the bill to Craig. He won't mind, we'll have joint accounts soon enough."

Numb and hurting more than she ever thought possible, Elaine moved around the cottage gathering her belongings, stepping around the broken microscope. She'd save that for last. She couldn't bear even to look at the pieces on the floor.

Packing took her longer than she thought. Just before the sun dropped below the tree line, she shoved the last box into the back seat of her sedan and returned to the house for one last look. And to collect her treasured microscope.

The place looked the same as the first day she'd set foot inside the front door, except for the angry red words on the wall.

Go home, or die!

Right now it felt as though she'd be doing both...

Other than the paint, the quaint cottage with its vintage furniture stood ready for the next renter. She walked over to the dinette with the speckled tabletop and bright red vinyl seat cushions. She smiled, running her finger across the surface. Who'd have thought they still had tables like these. She switched the light off in the kitchen and turned toward the bedroom.

She'd left this room for last. The old, white iron bed conjured memories best left behind. Craig lying there in nothing but a smile, stroking the hair from her face, trailing kisses down her neck.

Given Craig's concern for his uncle and his love for the swamp, his representing Littington and his polluting factory just didn't make sense. Why would he jeopardize a place he loved so much?

Elaine could picture a smaller version of Craig, running through the trees of Miz Mozelle's peach orchard. Whether the boy was a younger version of Craig from the past or the possible child he'd bring to Bayou Miste someday, Elaine couldn't tell.

A sob caught in her throat. Why torture herself? They weren't meant to be. Hadn't he said he wasn't one to commit to her?

Now she knew why.

She touched the light switch, setting the room and that chapter of her life in the dark. Now, all she had to do was get her microscope and go.

In just a few short days, she'd connected with Bayou Miste more than all the years she'd spent alone in her house in New Orleans. She stared down at the old microscope lying on its side on the hardwood floor, its gray metal full of memories of her parents, and now Craig.

But, the microscope was a thing, not a warm living, breathing person. If she had a choice between keeping the scope and having a single shot at getting her parents back, she'd toss the scope into the Mississippi in a New Orleans minute, and fight with all her heart to see her parents alive and safe again.

So why wasn't she willing to fight for Craig?

He wasn't married to Cassandra. From the little Elaine had gleaned from their conversation, they weren't even engaged. Basically, she didn't have any real hold on the man. Problem was, Elaine didn't know bupkis about Craig's feelings—for herself or for the perfect Cassandra.

And did she, Elaine Smith, the woman terrified of water, rejection, and serious relationships, love Craig enough to go after him?

Good lord. Was that what she was considering?

A woman used to analyzing scientific phenomena and developing hypothesis, it was clear she hadn't done her work here. She'd observed a change in herself. That change she'd describe as a feeling of completeness when she was with Craig and a corresponding emptiness when she wasn't. The only logical hypothesis she could come up with was...

Love.

But how was she to know if this "love" she was feeling was the real thing if she didn't hang around and experiment? That was the basis of all scientific proof.

What if he doesn't want me? that insidious voice asked.

Was the possibility of rejection so abhorrent she'd refuse to expose her heart? Even if she only had a one in a bazillion probability of Craig returning her love, wasn't even that small possibility worth the risk?

Hell, yes. This time, the voice in her head sounded loud and clear.

Assuming the phenomena was love, how would she feel if he discarded it? Worse than horrible. But at least she would have tried. She'd know for certain one way or the other, and she'd have no regrets for missed opportunities.

That much, she had learned from Miz Mozelle and Uncle Joe.

But what about Craig's dealings with Littington? Could she form a relationship with a man who didn't trust her enough to tell her the truth, no matter how awkward or painful?

She stared down at the microscope. The answer came into focus. As Miz Mozelle had so plainly put it, she needed to fight for her man. If that meant giving him a chance to explain and going toe-to-toe with the intimidating Cassandra, so be it.

She set the remains of the microscope on the table with a thump, and marched out to her car. When she leaned into the back seat to grab a box, a voice sounded behind her.

"Going somewhere?"

"No." Elaine answered before she realized the question had not been internal rhetoric. A chill raced down her spine, and she spun to face the intruder.

With his hip leaning against her car, and his face partially concealed in the shadows, Randall Pratt's eyes glowed with strange intensity.

"What are you doing here?" she demanded.

He pushed away from the car and walked closer, like a snake sidling up to his next meal. "Now, is that any way to greet a friend?"

"You're not my friend." Elaine knew what friends were, now that she'd met Miz Mozelle and Josie.

"*Tsk, tsk.*" He lifted a strand of her hair. "I came to make sure you left town for good."

"I'm not leaving." Elaine planted her feet slightly apart, refusing to back away from his threatening closeness.

"Oh, but I think you will." Randall lifted his hand, pointing a gun at her midsection. "You're coming with me. You've caused more than enough trouble."

Her heart pounding in her chest, Elaine inched backward until her shoulder blades bumped against the cool metal of her car door.

"What have I ever done to you?"

"Don't play stupid. You and the fancy-schmanzy lawyer been nosing around where you don't belong."

Pieces fell in place and lodged in the pit of Elaine's stomach. "*You're* the one dumping the barrels in the bayou."

"Give the lady a prize." Randall jerked the gun toward the door. "Let's go."

"Don't be ridiculous." She infused as much confidence into her voice as she could with a gun pointed at her vital organs. "You might get away with dumping pollutants in the bayou, but you'll never get away with murder."

A swaggering smile slid up one side of his mouth. "I could bury a Mack truck in the bayou and no one would ever find it."

She inhaled a long slow breath and glanced toward Miz Mozelle's empty house.

Randall's gaze followed hers. "Don't even think about screaming. A nine-millimeter bullet may be small, but it leaves a big hole in a person's gut. Makes for a big mess."

Cold metal pressed against her sternum. All the breath left her lungs in a *whoosh.*

"That's more like it," Randall said. "Now, get in the car."

CHAPTER 22

The meeting with Jason Littington had concluded better than Craig had hoped and they had a good idea who was responsible for poisoning the bayou. As the first gray reminders of sunrise lightened the sky, they had a plan in place.

Craig had hurriedly shoved the refinery owner out the bait shop door, locking it behind him. Wouldn't sit well with Littington if he stepped back into the shop and found Craig in the throes of frog metamorphosing.

Unfortunately, Littington's departure had left Craig no time to leave the shop before the change occurred. After shrinking to his bullfrog form, Craig hopped to a quiet corner and slept. The business of staying up all night and changing forms twice a day was exhausting.

His sleep had been intermingled with disturbing dreams of Voodoo ceremonies and an effervescent, full orange moon. When he woke in the late afternoon, an urgent sense of impending doom settled in his gut. What did the night hold in store for this man-frog serving a penance he probably deserved?

Uncle Joe hadn't made it to the shop today, no doubt convalescing with his new sheet shifter, Mozelle Reneau. The marina remained locked throughout the day.

With the "closed" sign still displaying in the front door, customers came, peered in through the windows and left without bait or tackle. Trapped inside, Craig impatiently awaited sunset and his transformation back to human form. He worried about Elaine being alone in her cottage, a target to whatever maniacs had been terrorizing them in the swamp. With Uncle Joe out of commission and Craig locked in the shop, she didn't have anyone to protect her.

The hands on the wall clock crawled through each hour until Craig knew he'd explode with the need for action. Finally, the sun dropped below the horizon. He welcomed the pain of his stretching, growing, and lengthening bones and tissues.

As soon as he could focus, he slipped into jeans and a shirt. Then, he reached for the phone and dialed home. "Hey Mom, this is Craig, let me talk to Dad. Tell him it's urgent."

"Hello, Craig," his father's brisk voice cut across the line. "What's the problem?"

"Dad, I need you to call the EPA and get them down here right away."

"What's this all about?" his father demanded. "Did you seal the deal with Littington?"

Trust his father to be more worried about the Littington deal. "Not exactly."

"You've been down there a week. You should have all the paperwork signed and delivered back to New Orleans by now."

Craig breathed deeply to squelch his rising impatience. "I know, but more important things have come up."

"What could be more important than bringing in new business to the family firm?"

People's lives, the environment, *loving someone.* "Lots, Dad," he answered.

"I sent Cassandra down there to bring you back. She should be there by now."

"She's here." So Cassandra hadn't come because he'd called. She'd come because the boss ordered her to. Figured. "I sent her up to Morgan City. I won't be coming back with her."

"She's an aggressive attorney, son. And a fine woman. You could do worse." His father cleared his throat, his usual prelude to father-son advice. "It's time you started thinking about your future. Maybe even settle down and raise a few kids."

Craig pinched the bridge of his nose, a headache building behind his eyes. "I'm working on it, Dad. Just not with Cassandra."

"Don't tell me you're foolin' around with one of those Cajun swamp gals?"

Craig bit down on his tongue and breathed through his nose several times before he answered. "Dad, I'll choose who I want to spend my life with. If she happens to be a Cajun swamp rat or an Alaskan Eskimo, *I'll* be the one to make that choice, not you."

"Don't take that tone with me, young man. I still control who works for Thibodeaux and Associates."

With a sigh, Craig realized the time had come. "That's true. But not me. I quit."

"Don't be ridiculous." His father huffed. "What's got into you, boy? Did you drink too much swamp water? Has my brother been filling you with crazy ideas?"

"No, Dad." How could he explain to his bottom-line driven father? "I want to do more with my skills and degree. I want to make a difference in the world."

"You make a difference to your clients back here."

"Yeah, a difference as to how much money they get from their fifth divorce in as many years. Or who gets to keep the family pet that cost as much as some people make in a year." This conversation was getting him nowhere. "Dad, I don't have time to discuss this. I appreciate everything you've taught me. Now, it's time for me to get out on own."

Richard Thibodeaux paused as if grasping for something to say to change his mind. "You're making a big mistake," was all he came up with.

"Maybe so, Dad, maybe so. But sometimes you have to go after what you believe in." *Like Elaine Smith.* "Will you call the EPA for me?"

His father hesitated, and then breathed an audible sigh over the line. "I'll call. But don't think we're done with this discussion. When are you coming back to New Orleans?"

"I don't know." Craig ran a hand through his hair.

"Your mother will be upset."

Cheap shot, Dad. "I'm pretty sure Mom will understand." Craig sucked in a deep breath. No matter how he felt about the family firm, he loved his parents very much. "Dad, this may be hard for you to comprehend, but I know this is the right decision for me."

"You should think about it more," his father said. "Take a vacation. Sleep on it."

"I have, Dad." Craig looked out at the darkening sky. "I have to go. Tell Mom I love her."

"Son—"

With a steady hand, Craig set the phone on the hook. *Wow, he'd actually quit.*

All his life, he'd been geared toward following in his father's footsteps, becoming a part of the family business. Now, he didn't have a job. But he had something he hadn't had in a long time—a purpose. He slipped into shoes and headed for the door.

Adrenalin pumped through his veins as he headed across the street and straight for his uncle's rental cottage. Before he launched his mission for the night, he had to be sure Elaine was okay after the previous night's disastrous outcome.

The dark, silent cottage appeared asleep among the row of houses. Elaine's car wasn't in the driveway, and the front door stood ajar.

Craig's heart skipped a beat. Leaping to the porch, he slammed through the doorway into the living room. "Elaine?" His voice echoed through the empty rooms. None of her papers or notebooks lay scattered across the room and every available surface. The little table she'd set up against the wall was gone. He ran into the bedroom and pulled the drawers out on the dresser. *Empty.* The bathroom was clean of any toiletries.

His heart stalled.

Elaine was gone.

She'd packed up and left without a goodbye.

Stricken, he wandered back out into the living room in a numb stupor, the only thought in his head reverberating in incessant repetition.

She's gone. She's gone. She's gone.

The house looked as if Elaine Smith had never been there. Every item of furniture had been moved back to its original location, the room swept, and the dishes cleaned and shelved. Had she been nothing more than a figment of his imagination, another trick played on him courtesy of Madame LeBieu?

Out of the corner of his eye, he saw the microscope standing on the kitchen table.

Thank God. No, she hadn't been only in his imagination. She had been here and left her mark on the town, the swamp, and most of all, him.

A lump lodged in his throat. When he lifted the instrument, a sickening rattle indicated the tool had suffered damage. Elaine loved this microscope. Could she have been mad enough about his betrayal she'd leave behind the last token of her parents' love?

He stared down at the gray hunk of metal as if the cold steel would answer his unspoken question. Had she left it as a message to him that their relationship was over? As broken as this delicate instrument? His hand tightened around the grip.

The clock on the wall bonged. The time had come to catch the polluting perpetrators.

As much as he wanted to follow Elaine and bring her back, he knew any hope he had with her hinged on tonight's activities. His love life would go on hold until he dealt once and for all with the people who dared to dump poison in what he considered his own backyard.

A quick duck into his uncle's house for the new digital video camera he'd gotten him last Christmas, and Craig was off to Littington Refinery.

He backed his car in between a stand of oleanders and magnolias, just past the only open entrance to the plant. With the windows rolled down on his black BMW, he inhaled the moist warmth of the Louisiana night air. The fragrant scent of flowers reminded him of Elaine and of the perfume Madame LeBieu had sprayed in his face.

Craig frowned. Hadn't the Voodoo priestess spoken of a woman who would come into his life? One who'd love him warts and all? Had that woman been Elaine? And fool that he was, he'd thrown her love away through a stupid lack of communication.

With his head tipped up, he prayed to God and the Voodoo Queens of the swamp that he wasn't too late to woo Elaine back into his life.

He'd never met anyone who brought out the best in him as she did. She'd helped him discover the emptiness in his career and the need for more meaningful work. And she'd shown him how important it was to commit to a worthwhile goal and throw your heart into it, no matter how scared or distracted you might become.

He smiled. Elaine was one hell of a woman. And he'd let her get away. With the full moon just days from now, he didn't have time to waste. If Elaine was the woman of Madame LeBieu's spell, he had some serious back-paddling to do in his canoe to make her see him as worthy of her love.

A dingy gray truck lumbered up to the gate, stopped, then passed through. Craig could barely make out the faded letters on the side panel. Acme Chemical Disposal.

Bingo. Let the games begin.

Craig switched his engine on and waited for the truck to come back out with its load of barrels, supposedly headed to a safe disposal site. All he needed was evidence of Pratt and his partner dumping the barrels into the swamp and he'd go straight to the cops, the coast guard, and the EPA with the video.

Littington had agreed to foot the bill for the cleanup. Disturbed by the damage to the environment and by the negative publicity the press would give his company, Jason Littington had embraced the opportunity to offer cleanup. He wanted the bad guys to be caught and put away for a long, long time. He'd insisted he hadn't even been aware of what was going on until the previous day. Acme Chemical Disposal had been the low bidder and all their disposal licenses had been up to date. With no one else collecting the chemicals from Littington for disposal, Acme, or someone in that company, had to be the culprit.

Craig had secretly jumped for joy. He knew how long and expensive litigation would be if the refinery refused to provide the necessary reparations. But thankfully, Jason Littington proved to be open, honest, and concerned, much to his credit—unlike many of Craig's previous clients. Littington still had kids growing up in the parish and he hated the thought of pollution poisoning his home as much as Craig did.

The truck reappeared, slowing to clear the gate. Craig's heart pounded in his chest. He'd never played the role of private detective. He didn't know what to expect from the thugs who'd already shot at him and tried to kill Elaine and Uncle Joe by capsizing their boat. Perhaps he should have gotten a gun from Uncle Joe's collection, but there wasn't time now.

Lights off, he maintained a discreet distance from the lumbering truck, following it to a nearby boat launch.

He parked behind bushes, left the car running and sneaked out with the video camera. Ten barrels stood in the back of the truck. He recognized Randall Pratt and Gator Brouchard as the men rolling the barrels to a boat tied to the pier. Craig was amazed at their gall. They hadn't even attempted to take any of the barrels to the appropriate disposal sites. They'd gone straight from the refinery to the swamp.

With video recorder in hand, Craig caught them on camera rolling the barrels one by one into the boat. Neither man spoke as they worked to move the toxins.

When five of the ten barrels were on board, they returned to the truck. This time when they went in the back, they came out carrying something long and skinny, wrapped in an old blanket. They hauled it on the boat and laid it down on the deck.

Craig frowned. He understood what was in the barrels but what did Randall and Gator have in the blanket? By the shape of it, it could have been a body. Thank goodness Elaine was on her way back to New Orleans. He would rather she was mad at him for the rest of his life, but safe, than be the target for these two thugs of yet another attempt to kill her.

"I didn't sign up for no killing." Gator's voice carried loud enough for the video camera to pick up.

Jesus!

So the lump *was* a body!

A trickle of sweat ran down Craig's back. *What the hell did he do now?*

This was more than he bargained for. If he was smart, he'd get his butt back into his car right this minute and go find the police.

"You're getting paid, aren't you?" Randall tossed a strap to Gator. "Tie those barrels down."

"I said, I didn't sign up for no killing." Gator leaned over and wrapped the strap around a barrel and the deck railing. "You said we were just going to scare people away."

"Look, *coo-yôn*, if the cops get wind of our little disposal operation, not only will the money stop flowing, we'll go to straight to jail. We won't pass go, we won't collect two hundred dollars." Pratt stepped closer, face to face with Gator. "You ever been to jail?"

"No." Gator stepped backward, his legs up against one of the seats.

"Neither have I." Randall poked a finger into Gator's chest. "And I don't plan to. Littington still thinks Acme is a legitimate disposal company, I been feedin' him the fake regulatory docs to keep him and the EPA happy, and as long as he keeps thinkin' that, the money he pays Acme goes right in our pockets. I'm gonna keep that cash flowing. Don't forget this has been the best money you or me ever made. Do you like that big truck you bought?"

"Yeah."

Randall poked Gator's chest again. "And that fancy house you got down in Gulf Shores?"

"Yeah, but—"

Another poke to Gator's chest. "No buts. We keep our mouths shut and take care of the problem." Randall jerked his head in the direction of the body on the deck.

Gator grabbed the finger still pushing against his chest. "All right, I'll do it, but don't poke me again."

Randall's eyes narrowed. But when Gator dropped his finger, he nodded and stepped off the boat. "Time's a-wastin'."

Craig hoped his videocam was picking up everything. As dark as it was, he doubted the visuals would be great. At the least, the voices should be discernible.

Once the boat had been loaded with as many of the heavy barrels as it could hold and remain afloat, Gator stashed the truck in the trees and hurried back to climb aboard. Randall started the engine and pulled slowly away from the ramp.

Damn. How the heck could Craig follow without a boat? Familiar with the swamp in this area, he knew this tributary emptied out where several converged into a large lake area close to his uncle's marina.

If he hurried, he might catch them before they disappeared in the maze of channels. Craig sprinted for his car, and sped along the country road back to Thibodeaux Marina, breaking every speed limit. At the parking lot, he leapt from the car and raced across the dock to a skiff.

One, two, three yanks on the motor's pull start and he was on his way across the swamp. Thank goodness the channels merged close to the marina or he wouldn't stand a snowball's chance of finding the thugs.

As he approached the central lake, he spied the boat headed toward Bayou Black. He followed, praying they wouldn't hear or see him and start shooting.

Several miles out, the larger boat slowed and turned sharply into what Craig guessed was a dense outcropping of overhanging trees and brush.

Instinctively, he killed the engine on his skiff and grabbed a paddle. As he stroked toward the spot where the boat had disappeared, he heard the other engine shut down.

He dipped the oar into the water, silently propelling the small craft forward. A murmur of voices grew louder as he approached. When he drifted within a couple yards of the outcropping, he could see the entrance to a lagoon. He pushed the boat against the muddy banks of an island and stepped out onto land. The foliage was too dense to forge a path through without alerting Randall and Gator.

Keeping an uneasy eye out for alligators, Craig slipped into the inky water, holding the videocam well above the surface, and swam around the trees into the lagoon, hugging the shoreline to hide in deep shadows.

"Hey, watch where you're going! You almost rolled that thing on my toe," Randall complained.

"If you'd get your toes out of the way, I wouldn't roll over them," Gator responded, his voice terse. He grunted and shifted a barrel across the flat deck to the edge and shoved it overboard. The barrel landed with a huge *kerplunk* and sank straight to the bottom.

Craig stood on the silt bottom hidden by a tree branch not five yards from the boat, so far undetected. He held the camcorder up and aimed it at the two men maneuvering another fifty-five gallon barrel to the boat's edge. With a quick flick of his thumb, he pressed the record button.

"Gator, you dumbass. You're tipping it too far my direction. If you're not careful it'll—"

Wonk! The barrel slammed sideways on the deck and rolled toward Randall, knocking him to his butt mere inches from the boat's rim.

"Sorry, Randy, my hands slipped. This one's a little oily."

"I swear, if I didn't need your help, I'd dump your ass over the side along with Littington's barrels."

Craig smiled grimly. He now had video proof of the two dumping barrels into the bayou and the audio was sure to give the police positive identification of the culprits. After the fifth barrel plopped into the water, they turned to the blanketed lump.

Gator nudged the blanket with his toe. "What do you want to do with her?"

Craig's ears perked. Wait.

Her?

Gator had said "her"?

Craig's heart pounded in his chest as the pair unwrapped the lump. When he saw the wild bush of frizzy hair lying against the deck, his heart stopped, lodging in his throat.

Elaine!

All this time he'd thought she was safely on her way to New Orleans. He should have known. The microscope was as clear a message as he could have gotten. She'd never leave without it.

He tossed the camcorder onto the shore, hoping it would stay dry, and swam for the boat, circling around the back to the ladder.

Please don't be dead. Please, God, please.

With blood pounding in his ears, he pulled himself up the ladder, risking a peek over the edge. A loud ripping sound pierced the night.

Elaine's still form jerked and gasped as duct tape was torn from her mouth.

"Get up, girly." Randall reached down and hauled her to her feet. "Cut it, Gator."

Craig braced to leap forward when Gator pulled a long hunting knife from his boot and slipped it between Elaine's wrists. With a quick upward thrust, he cut through the thick gray tape.

She staggered but remained on her feet, peeling the tape from her skin.

"So, what'er we gonna do with her?" Gator asked.

"Shoot 'er and leave 'er as alligator bait." Randall jerked his head toward her.

"No!" Elaine cried out.

Gator and Randall stood sideways to Craig. He feared if he made a lunge for Gator, the big guy would fire the weapon and hit Elaine.

With every ounce of concentration, he willed her to look his way. He'd never believed in magic until Madame LeBieu had put the hex on him. Now he rallied every possible supernatural force in the mysterious swamp, praying for a little Voodoo hoodoo.

Look at me, Elaine.

She glanced up and looked right at him. He pressed a finger to his lips.

With an imperceptible nod, she turned her attention back to Randall and Gator.

"Whatcha waitin' for? Shoot 'er," Randall ordered Gator.

Gator swung toward Randall, gun and all. "Why me? You're always makin' me do the dirty work."

"That's what you're getting paid for. Now, shut up and shoot."

"Don't do it, Gator," Elaine pleaded, backing away from Gator, Randall, and Craig.

The two bad guys turned toward her, their backs now fully to Craig.

Craig smiled, grimly. *Smart girl*. Exactly the reason he loved her.

"You can't give me orders," Gator said. "I'm the one with the gun, not you."

"Yes, you're the one with the gun." she nodded and spoke in a slow, calming tone, but Craig could hear the tremble in her voice. "So far, you've only dumped chemicals in the bayou. Do you really want to go to jail for murder?"

"Don't listen to her, Gator," Randall admonished. "She don't know what she's talkin' about. Besides, who'll ever find her body after the alligators eat it?"

She pointed in Randall's direction. "Don't you see? He wants you to shoot me so *you'll* be the one committing the murder, not him. You'll be the one charged with it—*you'll* be the one facing the death penalty when you're convicted."

Craig eased out of the water, thankful she had the culprits' full attention.

"Here, give me the damn gun. I'll shoot her."

When Randall grabbed for the pistol, Craig lunged.

"What the—" Randall yelled.

Hunkering down like a football player about to sack the quarterback, Craig hit Gator at full throttle, knocking him off his feet.

"Craig, look out!" Elaine yelled.

A loud crack split the air. Sharp, fiery pain glanced off his temple, knocking him backward.

Over the edge of the airboat he flew, hitting the bayou's surface with a huge splash. Water covered his face as consciousness slipped away, and he sank into the cold, black abyss.

CHAPTER 23

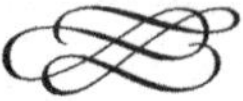

ELAINE SCREAMED. BLIND RAGE AND FEAR FOR THE MAN SHE LOVED turned her vision to scarlet. Acting on pure instinct, she crouched low, balled up her body and steamrolled into Randall's midsection, knocking him sideways. A seat caught the back of his legs and he flipped upside down on the deck. The gun flew from his hand, landing a couple feet from Elaine.

If she went for the gun, she'd probably shoot herself, or Randall would get there first and use it to kill her. She spied a paddle next to her.

As Randall struggled to his feet, she grabbed the paddle and whacked the bastard in the stomach.

"*Oomph!*" He bent double and she whacked him on the back of the head as hard as she could.

He fell to the floor and lay still.

She glanced from one unconscious man to the other to ensure they weren't going anywhere, then she scooped the gun off the floor and slung it as far as she could out into the swamp.

She peered over the boat's edge, squelching the panic before it could rise up and incapacitate her. "Craig?"

No sign of him could be seen in the light from the half-moon. Only a couple of bubbles popped to the surface. The panic she'd held in check burst like a leaky dam.

"No!"

Without giving herself time to think, she threw herself overboard at the spot where she'd seen the bubbles.

Craig couldn't die.

So what if he'd lied, so what if he represented Jason Littington, so what if she couldn't swim? She wasn't going to let the man she loved die.

False bravado lasted as long as it took for her head to sink below the surface, then real fear set in. Just as the terror threatened to overwhelm her, she bumped into something solid with her foot.

Craig.

Reaching below, she grabbed a handful of hair and yanked him up to the surface. The push to get him up sent her down. Her feet touched the silt on the bottom, but her head stayed three feet below the surface.

Her lungs burned for air. What good was she to Craig if she drowned trying to save him? She pushed hard against the bottom of the swamp and sprang to the surface, gulped air, and glanced around for the boat. Then, she sank again, pushing Craig up at the same time she went down.

Her knee bumped hard metal. By the shape of it, she'd found one the barrels Randall and Gator had worked so hard to dump into the swamp. Desperate, she gripped the edge and pulled herself to stand on the barrel, rising above the surface to gasp for breath.

Oh, thank God.

She grabbed for Craig, tugging him toward her. Once she had his head positioned above water, she felt for a pulse. She found it, but he still wasn't breathing. How could she push the water out of his lungs when he was still floating in the swamp? Her only solution was to wrap her arms around his middle from behind and hug with a sharp upward thrust to his diaphragm.

Craig coughed up water and spluttered. When he still didn't start breathing, she hugged again.

This time, he coughed and then inhaled as if he would suck the trees into his lungs, followed by a round of more gut-wrenching coughs.

Thank God, oh, thank God! She held him tight to keep him from going under again.

"Elaine?" he croaked after the worst coughing subsided.

"I'm here," she said softly into his ear, squeezing tighter with her cheek against this back.

"I love it when you hug me," he wheezed, "but could you loosen up a bit?"

Immediately, she let go and Craig sank into the water. She grabbed him before he gulped another gallon of the swamp into his lungs.

"I'm sleepy." His head dropped forward, blood running down her face.

She had to get him on the boat and back to civilization and a doctor immediately.

"Craig." She forced her voice to be strong and commanding.

His head lolled and then came up. "Huh?"

She scooted around the barrel to face him. "Craig, I need to get to the boat."

"Can't swim," he mumbled.

"You don't need to, you just need to stand here."

"Too deep," he said.

"Put your feet down." Elaine quelled the urge to laugh hysterically at her words, an echo of Craig's advice to her just days ago. She braced herself and helped him find his footing on the barrel. When he stood, weak but steady, she kissed him. "I'm going for the boat."

"No, I'll go." He jerked his head as if to clear the haze.

"Don't be silly. You can barely stand in the water."

"You can't swim."

"I'll manage." She gripped his arms and kissed him full on the lips. "Just keep your head above the water." Then she gulped a deep breath and stepped off the barrel in the direction of the boat.

Praying for calm, she sank to the bottom, pushed off the silt and bounced in what she hoped was the right direction. Jumping up, she surfaced to find the boat only two more bounces from her. Repeating the process put her within reasonable dog-paddle distance.

Minus the dignity of a dog, she paddled and kicked until she reached the ladder and clung until she had sufficient breath to climb aboard.

A quick glance behind her proved Craig still stood with his head above the water, but how long could he last before he passed out?

Once on board, she stepped over Randall who stirred and made as if to rise.

Elaine grabbed the paddle from the floor. "Get up and I'll hit you again. Don't piss me off!" Her voice rose, the pitch shrill and past any reasoning.

Randall slumped back to the floor and moaned, muttering, "I should have killed you when I had the chance."

After several attempts at starting the boat, she finally met with success. She eased the lever forward, setting the boat in motion, executing a wide turn in the tiny lagoon. She aimed for Craig, and at the last minute, swerved to miss him, cutting the motor as he had done when they'd gone specimen hunting.

Unfortunately, she cut it too late and the boat propelled forward faster than she would have liked. They were sure to drift by too fast for Craig to grab on.

Elaine leaned over the edge, extending the paddle. "Grab hold!" she yelled.

Craig caught the paddle's edge and hung on until the boat slowed to a stop.

With the paddle firmly in hand and her arms screaming from the strain, she walked it and Craig around the side of the boat to the ladder.

He tried to haul himself on board, but he fell backward into the water.

She leaned over, grabbed his shirt, and pulled while he pushed his way up onto the boat, and then collapsed in a chair.

She switched on a lamp and got her first look at his wound. Blood oozed from a wound slashing across his temple and into his thick, black hair. *So much blood*. "Oh geez, Craig." She swayed, the boat's light blurring around the edges.

"Don't faint on me, now," he said through clenched teeth.

"I'm not." So it was a half-truth. She focused on the light in an attempt to clear her vision.

"Good, 'cause I think I am..." His voice faded and he slid sideways, almost falling out of the chair before she could catch him. Blood seeped from the wound onto her hand at an alarming rate. His face glowed a pale sickly green in the light from the moon.

Without a thought for modesty, Elaine stripped her shirt from her back, ripped off a hunk, wadded it and pressed it against his head. "Don't you die on me, Fish Boy," she ordered, her voice low and tears streaming from her eyes.

He blinked and muttered, "Didn't know you cared."

"I do, damn it. I love you, you big stupid idiot, so dying is not an option! Hear me?"

His head fell back against the seat, a brief smile lifting the corners of his lips. "Love..."

"Don't pass out, now. I don't know my way out of this damn bayou." She tied the wad of fabric around his head with the rest of her shirt. Gator stirred and moaned. Without backup, she couldn't risk leaving them untied. A quick search of the boat produced a roll of fishing line and Gator's knife. Working quickly, she tied the two men's hands and feet. Praying they wouldn't cause any more trouble, she started the engine and steered through the lagoon's entrance.

She slowed the boat, leaned over, and shook Craig. "Honey, wake up. Please, Craig."

"Am I dead?" His head lolled to the side and he opened one eye.

"No, Fish Boy."

"But I see an angel." He almost sounded drunk.

"You're worse than I thought." She smoothed the blood-soaked hair off his brow and pressed a kiss to his uninjured forehead. "You're hallucinating. You probably have a concussion."

"No, really, you're my very own angel, sent by the Voodoo queen."

She gave a nervous laugh. Geez. He really was losing it. "Craig, you've gotta stay with me long enough to get us back to the marina."

"I'm with you, *ma chère*. Wild bullfrogs couldn't drag me away." He lifted his head, squinted in the moonlight and pointed with his good arm. "That way."

* * *

After what seemed like an eternity, the boat glided up to the dock at Thibodeaux marina. Craig floated in and out of consciousness, with Elaine waking him at every fork in the bayou to beg the next round of directions. She'd remained patient with him when he couldn't think straight. Actually, she was looking very tempting in her lacy white bra. Definitely good enough to eat. Too bad he didn't have the energy to reach out and touch her, pull her close, and kiss the rest of her clothes off.

Yup, she was his very own guardian angel. He just hoped he could hold onto her and keep her from leaving him again. He didn't even want to consider her walking away from Bayou Miste without him.

Was it part of his hallucinations, or had she really said she loved him?

Hope soared in his heart. And not just because of the curse.

If she was just trying to make him feel good, it had definitely worked. He wished she'd say it again, though, just to be sure. His heart beat faster when she leaned close enough for him to feel her breath on his ear. Would she tell him the three words he longed to hear?

She lifted his hand and wrapped his fingers around the boat paddle. "Hit them if they give you any problems."

A quick kiss and she jumped out of the boat, like a confident sailor. How unlike the frightened waif of the first night he'd take her out on the bayou.

Too weak to follow, he waited and watched her run across the dock in her jeans and lacy white bra. *Wow*. She could really get his blood running. Unfortunately, it was pumping right out of his body. And his head pounded like the drums the Voodoo queen had employed.

He couldn't quite see up to the bait shop. But he heard a loud crash, the distinctive sound of shattered glass. *Whoa*. She didn't just break a window in the bait shop, did she? Mild-mannered, microscope-junkie Elaine Smith?

He glanced down at the paddle in his hand and the two men bound up in fishing line, glad she was on his side.

He must have passed out again. When he opened his eyes, the dark wasn't quite as dark, and bright lights flashed in the distance up by the bait shop. Someone was talking to him.

"Craig, they're here to take you to the hospital."

He looked up into beautiful green eyes. She wore a white T-shirt sporting a large-mouthed bass and the words "I'd Rather Be Fishing" across her breasts.

"Will you be there?" he asked.

She smiled. "Wild bullfrogs couldn't keep me away." She squeezed his hand and kissed his cheek.

Two men in Emergency Medical Service uniforms helped him out of the boat and onto a stretcher. His legs were no longer useful. He hated being so weak when he needed to be strong for Elaine.

She followed close behind until they reached the parking lot where the ambulance stood, lights flashing, and the entire town was out in force to watch.

When they moved him to the wheeled gurney and pushed him toward the open doors of the ambulance, he stirred enough to say, "Wait."

He stared around at the familiar faces. Maurice was closest to him. "I heard all de commotion. Thought maybe T-Rex was causin' trouble. Glad to see it wasn't." Mo nodded toward a sheriff's car where a deputy was handcuffing Randall and Gator. "Dem's bad ones, dey are. I should have been dere with you, man."

He looked over at Elaine. "It's okay. I had backup."

Larry stepped up beside Mo. "She's a keeper, all right."

Craig's gaze never left Elaine's. "I know."

"So, whatcha gonna do about it?" It was Miz Mozelle. She moved closer, towing Uncle Joe by the hand.

"What do you mean?" He knew what Miz Mozelle alluded to, but he didn't want to declare himself in front of everyone.

Yes, he wanted to tell Elaine he loved her. But he wanted to present her with his declaration accompanied by all the bells and whistles of a romantic evening, planned and choreographed to elicit the desired response from her.

Or was he just scared? He'd lived so long at arm's length from real relationships, could he break old habits?

Uncle Joe stepped up beside him. His white hair stuck straight out, and his T-shirt was on backwards. "She broke the window."

"I'll buy you a new one," Craig said.

"I'm not worried about the damn window." Uncle Joe leaned closer and whispered. "If she'd do that for your rotten carcass, you stand a good chance of breaking that spell."

"I know that, Uncle Joe. I also know I don't deserve her." *Oh, what the hell.* "Elaine? Elaine?" He looked out over the sea of faces and almost panicked when he couldn't find the one he sought.

"I'm here." She slid between him and his circle of friends, and scooped up his hand.

"Did you mean what you said out there on the bayou?"

In the grayish light he could tell the color in her face deepened and she looked away. "Mean what?"

He understood her hesitation. "I worked out a deal with Littington to clean up the contamination." That wasn't exactly a declaration of love, but he was warming up.

"I know. Uncle Joe told me."

"I quit my job with the family firm."

She leaned over and kissed his lips. "Uh-huh."

He was getting a lot warmer. He inhaled deeply and blurted, "I love you, Elaine Smith."

She turned his face to hers. "Are you sure? I thought you were allergic to commitment."

"I was." He reached up and hooked his good arm around her neck, and pulled her down to him. "Until I met a scientist with just the right chemistry for me. I love you because you're smart, passionate, and completely committed to your work. And did I mention passionate?"

She smiled and nodded.

"Look, I know I don't have a job, and I don't really deserve you, but do you think you could love me anyway? Just a little?"

Uncle Joe peered out at the horizon over the bayou. "Guess you'll find out right about...now."

Mo and Larry's gazes followed Uncle Joe's. While they'd been talking, morning had come to the bayou. Bright orange sunlight streamed through the base of the trees, spreading a fiery trail across the black waters.

But Craig focused all his attention on the one woman with the only answers he needed.

She leaned close and whispered against his ear. "I love you more than all the frogs in the bayou, Fish Boy." Then she kissed his very human lips in the red and pink light of dawn.

Since the night he'd fallen victim to the bizarre spell, he never thought he'd say these words, but he sent a silent prayer to the Voodoo hoodoo gods in the bayou. "Thank you, Madame LeBieu, for sending this frog my princess."

* * *

THE END

One Spell...Double the Trouble

VOODOO FOR TWO

A CAJUN MAGIC MYSTERY

VOTE FOR ME

NEW YORK TIMES & USA TODAY BESTSELLING AUTHOR

ELLE JAMES

VOODOO FOR TWO

CAJUN MAGIC MYSTERIES BOOK #2

New York Times & USA Today
Bestselling Author

ELLE JAMES

CHAPTER 1

Bayou Miste, Louisiana

Nothing was blacker than nighttime deep in the swamps. Stars couldn't penetrate the cypress canopy, laden with long tendrils of Spanish moss, dripping down over land and water.

Silence reigned as if all the creatures of the murky waters and dense underbrush held their breaths for something—a cue, a signal, a happening—

A drum thrummed to life, stirring the night air with an ancient rhythm. The gentle sway of a breeze wafted through the gossamer moss, dancing in time to the placid swishing of the breeze through the trees, urging the insects and frogs into song.

"Breathe the air, touch the earth, stir the waters, and play with fire."

Just when Lucie LeBieu thought she couldn't stand still for another moment, the scrape of a match cut across the gentle hum of the night. Bright flame slashed through the darkness, illuminating the faces of three women standing in a circle.

This dark and mysterious place in the midst of the Atchafalaya Basin, on the edge of Bayou Miste, just happened to be home to Lucie, her twin sister Lisa, and her grandmother, the locally infamous Madame LeBieu, Voodoo queen of the surrounding bayous.

"Do you feel de rhythm of de night?" *Mamère* LeBieu's voice caressed the darkness, the sound an extension of the drum's beat.

Lucie shifted, not liking the creepy feeling she always got when her family did these kinds of things. "Gran, this is silly."

"Shh!" The older woman, dressed in a flowing red caftan, set the flame to a fat candle, then an incense stick, and placed them on the ground at the center of the circle. "We must commune wit' nature, become one wit' de power, de energy present in de darkness." Her grandmother's accent was as thick as the humid air and tepid waters of Bayou Miste.

Lisa and Lucie had been raised in New York City for the first eight years of their lives. Any accent they might have acquired in Louisiana since then was out of pure self-preservation, and it wasn't anything to talk about, in their grandmother's book.

"Feel de magick," her grandmother insisted, tipping her face back as if soaking in the moonlight that wasn't visible through the canopy of trees.

"*Mamère,* I never do it right." Lisa tried to shake off the sense of impending doom.

A hand reached out and pinched her arm. "Shut up and listen, Sis," her twin grumbled. "Can't you feel it? It's hot, alive, and sensuous."

"Lisa! Dis is not da time," *Mamère* LeBieu admonished.

Lisa snorted, but kept any further comments to herself.

Lucie stood still, closed her eyes, and tried.

She really tried, but all she got out of the beating drums, the chirping crickets, and the croaking frogs was a healthy case of the heebie-jeebies. "It's no use. I'm not cut out for this Voodoo nonsense."

"It isn't nonsense, Lucie," Lisa said. "I've used it to get guys all hot and bothered on several occasions and it worked great."

"You don't need potions to get guys all hot and bothered, Sis. I'm just not cut out to do this. I mess it up every time." Lucie slumped.

"Den be quiet while I work de magick," her grandmother demanded.

When *Mamère* LeBieu took that tone, Lucie obeyed. The woman didn't get angry often, but when she did, woe be unto whoever roused her ire. The woman had a wicked mean streak. Though Lucie didn't believe in her own version of Voodoo, she'd seen what a dose of *Mamère*'s special powder could produce. Maurice Saulnier had the wickedest itch a man could have for two solid weeks after he'd trampled *Mamère* LeBieu's favorite azalea bush.

She itched just thinking about it.

Mamère closed her eyes and swayed in rhythm with the drum. "Ezili Freda Daome, goddess of love and all dat is beautiful, listen to our prayers, accept our offerings, and enter into our arms, legs, and hearts."

"Here we go," Lucie muttered. "Another spell." She exhaled a long breath. Why couldn't she have been born into a normal family, with normal parents and grandparents?

Her grandmother swayed with the candle's flame.

"Goddess of light and stars from above,
Help dose who lost de way to love.
Grant dem de courage to open de heart
De intelligence dey need to make a new start
De humility to admit when dey been wrong
De determination dey need when dey mus' be strong.
Ezili Freda Daome, goddess of light
Bring dis misguided woman de love tonight."

Lucie backed away from the circle, holding up her hands, anger swirling in her gut. "You did *not* just work a love spell on me. Tell me you didn't, *Gran.*"

"What do you care?" Lisa taunted. "You don't believe all that Voodoo anyway. You said you didn't."

"I don't believe in mine, but *Mamère*'s is a whole different pot of trouble. And it's the principle of it. I don't *want* to fall in love." Lucie crossed her arms over her chest and glared at her grandmother.

The older woman ignored her protest, waved a filmy scarf, and sprayed perfume over the candle's flame.

"You know the story. Been there. Done that. Have the scars to prove it," Lucie mumbled. "For the love of cypress knees, don't mess with my love life." *Or lack thereof.*

"Mouthy tonight, aren't we?" Lisa grinned at her. "That's usually my job. But really, you need to get laid. How long has it been? *Mamère* magick is the best. Let her help you."

"Wow, you make me sound downright pathetic. Has anyone considered what *I* want? Doesn't anyone care?" Lucie spun on her heels and marched back toward the little shack she shared with her grandmother and twin sister. "I'll be at work until two. Hopefully, by the time I return, you two will be in bed and not out here playing Voodoo games."

The drum still beat from the back porch of the faded gray house. "Oh, go home, Remy!" Lucie shouted. "Your drum-thumpin' days are over."

The dark-haired, dark-skinned boy hit the drum hard. "Miss Lucie, you gotta learn ta chill."

"Chill, my fanny." She stomped through the house and up to her old room. There she changed into the miniskirt and grabbed the high heels she'd brought with her from her apartment. Jean Dupree insisted his "girls" dress like Hooters waitresses as part of their jobs at the Raccoon Saloon. Lucie didn't mind too much. When she wore jeans, she didn't get nearly the tips she got when she wore the miniskirt. And Lord knew, they needed the money.

Seemed her grandmother never got ahead of the mortgage payment. Speaking of which, wasn't she due to pay another one soon?

A loud knock echoed up the wooden stairway from the front door, rattling the screen against the doorjamb.

"Keep your shirt on, I'm coming," Lucie called out.

Carrying her high heels, she raced down the stairs, eager to get away from her grandmother's meddling.

Paul Renault, one of the two deputies employed by the parish, stood with his head down, scuffing his muddy black shoes on the faded deck.

"Paul? What are you doing out here at this time of night?" Lucie had gone to high school with Paul. She'd actually turned him down once when he'd asked her to go out. The man was just as shy now as he'd been all those years ago.

She regretted turning him down. How much courage had it taken for him to ask her out? And how long had it taken for him to get up enough courage to ask another woman? The man was still single, for the love of swamps and alligators. What would it have hurt for her to go out on one date with the man? A lot. At the time she'd been head over heels for one low-down, lying swamp rat, Benjamin Franklin Boyette.

"I'm sorry, Miss Lucie. I have a document for Madame LeBieu. I'm real sorry." He didn't meet her gaze, but instead looked over her shoulder. "Is she home?"

"Sure. Why don't you come in while I round her up?"

"No, it wouldn't be right, no." He tapped an envelope against his hand. "I'll just wait here."

"*Mamère!*" She yelled as she turned toward the back of the house.

"You don't have to yell, Lucie. I'm here." Appearing out of nowhere, her grandmother stepped to the door, followed by Lisa, whose face paled, her dark eyes as big as ripe persimmons.

Gran LeBieu opened the door and held out her hand.

"Madame LeBieu, I didn't have anything to do with this, I just want you to know," Deputy Paul blurted. "It's just part of my job. That's all. Please believe me."

What was wrong with Paul? Lucie had never seen him quite this nervous, not even when he'd asked her out. "What is it?"

Paul handed the older woman the envelope, immediately backing away. "Consider yourself served, Madame LeBieu. I'm really sorry." With that, he spun and dove for the police cruiser, peeling out like his pants were on fire.

Her *Mamère* stared down at the envelope.

Lisa slipped an arm around her grandmother in an uncommon show of affection. "What is it, *Mamère*?"

"Somet'ing terrible, I be afeard." Her hand shook as she ripped the envelope open and stared down at the typewritten sheets.

Lucie stared at her grandmother's face, her light mocha skin blanching in the light from the porch. The paper slipped from her fingers, fluttering to the floor. "It can no be." The woman aged ten years in that one moment, her face graying, the wrinkles deepening in her care-lined face. "It can no be."

Her heart hammering in her chest, Lucie snatched the papers from the floor, blinking back tears as she read the legal document.

A sob rose in her throat, and she fought to swallow past it.

"What is it, Lucie?" Lisa snatched for the letter.

"Talk about being up to our ears in hungry alligators," Lucie whispered. "It's a foreclosure notice on the house."

***

"Whaddya gotta do to get a beer around here?" A mountain of a redneck slammed a meaty fist onto the table behind Lucie.

The loud smack made her jump. "Keep your shirt on, LeRoy. I'll be with you in a minute," she shouted over her shoulder. To the ladies at the table she was waiting on, she said, "I've had it. I'm tired of this bar, tired of the bugs and alligators, and tired to death of Bayou Miste." More than anything, she was tired of living from paycheck to paycheck, worrying about money and the possibility of losing everything, including the roof over her head.

The foreclosure notice sealed the deal. She had to do something and do it soon.

"Girlfriend, you want some cheese with that whine?" Alexandra Belle Boyette beckoned with her fingers. "Gimme that beer."

Lucie balanced the heavy tray in one hand and, with the other, set longnecks on the table in front of her two best friends. "Really. No matter how hard I try, I can't make enough money here to pay the bills, much less start fresh somewhere else."

"Good! We don't want you to leave." Calliope Ostelet sipped her beer and then ran her tongue across her lips. "Ummm. Nothing like a tall, dark one to whet the appetite."

Lucie glanced around the Raccoon Saloon. Mounted and stuffed raccoons grinned down at her from shelves lining the bar's faded wooden walls. If she never saw another raccoon again, that would be just fine with her.

She sighed. "I've been wasting my time. There's nothing for me here." As soon as the words left her mouth a pang of guilt followed, pinching her heart. Her sister, grandmother, and the best friends a girl could ever hope to find were in Bayou Miste. But the burden of providing for her little family weighed heavily on her. Lisa was too much like their mother to help. She drifted from dead-end job to dead-end job, rarely contributing to the family coffers. *Mamère*'s income consisted of barter and trade for her services as a Voodoo queen, but rarely did she get paid in cold, hard cash. "No offense, but you know what I mean."

Alex's dark brows dipped together. "You say you have nothing to keep you here. Do you mean nothing or no one?"

With a shrug, she loaded the empty bottles onto her tray. "Same thing."

"You know what your problem is?" Alex set her beer on the table. "You haven't had a decent date since my brother left. Admit it."

Warmth stole up Lucie's neck, and she thanked the poor lighting for disguising the color in her cheeks. "I haven't had a decent date in Bayou Miste, period."

"Hey, Lucie, you gonna flap yer jaw all night? I've been waiting for ten minutes for one lousy beer. You can forget any tip."

She swung around and glared at the man, the empty bottles on her tray teetering dangerously. "LeRoy, you never tip, so what's the difference?"

"Well, if I did, I sure wouldn't leave *you* one." He returned her drop-dead look with one of his own, drumming his stogie-sized fingers on the table.

Lucie raised an eyebrow at Alex and Calliope. "See what I have to choose from?"

"Oh, come on," Alex said. "LeRoy's married. Besides, he isn't the only man in Bayou Miste."

"No, but the rest are just like him—loud, obnoxious, and ugly enough to make a swamp gator look good to me." Lucie lifted a mug of half-foam, half-beer from her tray, walked over to LeRoy's table, and slammed it down hard enough that the foam slopped over the side. "Here's your beer. Now quit yer moanin'."

"I'd rather be moanin' with you beneath me, sweet thang." He leered at her.

"In your dreams, LeRoy." Lucie turned her back, content—well, maybe content was stretching it—to ignore his rude invitation. As if!

A sharp pain zinged her right butt cheek.

"Ouch!" Adrenaline shot through her veins and she spun, fists balled, ready to take on the tank of a louse. "Tell me you didn't just pinch my ass, you bottom-dwelling alligator-turd."

"Lucie, don't lower yourself to his level," Alex warned. "Breathe deeply. Inhale, exhale."

Through a blur of red, Lucie heard her friend's calming words. She inhaled, then blew steam out her nose, repeatedly. When she could see straight, she forced words through her tight lips. "Don't...*ever*...do that again."

"Ah, sweet thang, face it." LeRoy spread his arms wide. "You want me."

"The man really doesn't know when to shut up," Lucie seethed.

"LeRoy, stuff a sock in it." Alex stood, positioning herself between the two, providing a barrier neither dared cross. "Lucie, Jean wants you at the bar. I suggest you go before you do something you'll regret."

She stood her ground. "He deserves to be taught a lesson."

"Be real," Alex said. "He weighs three times what you do."

"Move, Alex." LeRoy licked his lips and rubbed his hands together. "Me and Lucie's gonna have us a little rumble."

But Alex didn't budge. "Go on, Lucie. Jean's waiting."

She glanced from Alex to LeRoy. The idiot was practically drooling, wanting her to respond to his taunts. And she wanted to, with all the bottled anger and disappointment she'd been collecting for over seven years. But Leroy wasn't the problem. "You're right, Alex. He isn't worth the trouble." She turned an icy glare at him. "I'll let you slide this time. But don't touch me again. Or else!"

"Ooooo, I'm scared." LeRoy's laugh implied that he was anything but. "Or else what? You'll give me a lap dance?"

"I'll kick your butt!" She lunged forward. "Then I'll serve your balls as shooters to Mo's alligator."

Alex caught her in a clothesline snag around her shoulders. "Don't go there. LeRoy isn't worth it."

A couple deep breaths, followed by a slow count to thirty, cooled Lucie's temper, and she actually laughed. "Alex, you take all the fun out of waiting tables, do you know that?"

"You gonna be all right?" Alex peered into her eyes.

She still wanted to flatten the bag of hot air, but she had tables to wait and plans to make. With a parting glare at LeRoy, she got back to work.

While she distributed alcohol and snacks throughout the crowded room, worry built into an angry itch, simmering below the surface. What the hell was she still doing in this dead-end town? And how the hell was she going to earn enough money to pay off the mortgage and get the hell out?

Hard work hadn't gotten her anywhere. The factory wasn't hiring and tips were getting more scarce with the economic downturn. She'd have to resort to something she had never considered in her past. Something drastic, life-changing. Something she would never in a million years have considered if things weren't as bad as they were now.

When she'd satisfied her customers for the moment, she returned to Alex and Calliope to pick up where she'd left off. "Okay. I've made a decision. If I can't work my way out of this two-bit town, I'll have to bite the bullet and resort to a little of the V-word."

"V-word?" Calliope's pretty brow wrinkled.

Alex hissed, "Voodoo, dummy!"

"Cool! I love Voodoo." Calliope drank long and deep from her bottle of beer, apparently unconcerned by her friend's rash declaration.

"Maybe Gran LeBieu's Voodoo, but not..." Alex gave Lucie a sheepish grin. "Sorry, honey, but your brand of Voodoo never seems to work out just right. I don't think it's a good idea."

She flung out her hands. "I gotta do something soon, or I'll explode." And *Mamère* would lose the only real home she's ever known.

"Yeah, but..." Alex pinned Lucie with an intense stare. "We've seen your...uh...Voodoo before. You're likely to turn us all into two-headed toads. You may be willing to risk having toads for friends, but I'm not keen on eating flies the rest of my life."

Calliope snorted beer through her nostrils, slammed the bottle back to the table, and choked, her eyes filling with tears. With a big gulp, she managed to gasp and then dissolve into a fit of the giggles. "I've got to agree with Alex on this one. I don't want to end up being a frog like Craig Thibodeaux. Can you imagine hopping around Bayou Miste? If he and Elaine hadn't fallen in love, poor Craig would have been a frog for life. Talk about your wicked Voodoo spell."

Alex reached across the table and pinched Calliope's arm.

"Ouch!" Calliope rubbed the spot, a frown denting her brow. "Why'd you go and do that?"

"Lucie didn't cast that spell," Alex said. "Madame LeBieu did. And she knew what the hell she was doing."

"Oh, yeah." Calliope rubbed her side and nodded across the crowded bar at a couple sitting in the far corner, their heads together and holding hands. "He seems to be just fine now."

"That's exactly my point. Madame LeBieu's the Voodoo queen for a reason. Not so, our Lucie. No offense."

"Alex is right." Calliope smiled at Lucie and patted her arm. "Last time you tried to turn Maurice's alligator into a dog, you only gave the poor beast a bad case of puppy love. T-Rex hasn't been the same since."

She winced. Part of the problem had been and would always be that she really hadn't believed in Voodoo, her own at least, and still wasn't quite sure it would really work. But desperate times and all that...

"Yeah, and Maurice's grandmother has been beside herself trying to keep T-Rex from eating her poodle." Alex squeezed Lucie's hand. "You'd be crazy to try it."

Calliope shook her head. "Poor FeFe."

"FeFe, Schme-fe." She stomped her foot. "That was only one spell gone wacky. Not all of them go wrong."

"Lucie, be serious." Alex set her lips into a straight line.

"Don't give me that look," Lucie warned. "I'm not one of your little brothers or sisters."

"Then don't act like one." Alex crossed her arms over her chest. "Lucie, you can't do it."

Fighting the urge to stomp her foot again, she couldn't stop her words. "I can, and I will."

"Hey, didn't I ask for oyster shooters with my beer?" LeRoy scraped his chair back. "I'm not paying for this beer until I get my shooters."

In unison, all three women yelled at the man. "Shut up!"

"Lucie!" Bartender and owner of the Raccoon Saloon, Jean Dupree, as wide as he was tall and as bald as a cypress knee, slung a towel over his shoulder, grabbed a mug from below the counter, and filled it from the tap. "Quit pissin' off de customers and get back to work." He smacked the heavy drink on the counter, sloshing beer over the side.

She marched back to the bar. "I got the tables covered. LeRoy's just bein' his usual jerk self."

"Well, you missed a table." Jean nodded to a stranger dressed in a leather jacket, seated as far away from the music as possible. "If you have time in yer busy social calendar, could you deliver dis beer to dat table?"

"I don't know, Jean, we swamp debutantes have appearances to keep up." She loaded the heavy mug onto a tray and swung around. "I can't be associating with the riffraff."

"Darlin', we only serve riffraff at de Raccoon Saloon." Jean chuckled behind her. "And I wouldn't be havin' it any other way."

"Someday real soon I'm gonna blow this town and leave you and your precious riffraff behind." As the last word left her mouth, she set the beer on the stranger's table and turned in time to see Eric Littington enter the bar alone.

Lucie's eyes narrowed like a hawk's as it homed in on its prey. Eric Littington, the blond-haired, blue-eyed attorney and son of the richest man in the parish. He and his family had enough money to pay off hundreds of mortgages like *Mamère* LeBieu's. *And* he was running for the U.S. House of Representatives—a position that would take him away from Bayou Miste, away from the parish, and away from Louisiana altogether.

Bingo.

She'd just found her ticket out of all her troubles.

"Oh, and Lucie?" Jean said behind her. "Before you blow town, don't be forgettin' ta give dese shooters to de jerk."

After a long assessing look at her target, she worked her way back to the bar and piled the plate of oyster shooters onto her tray. With growing determination, she lifted the load onto her shoulder and wove her way back toward LeRoy. And just in case Eric should notice, she emphasized the sway of her hips. Wolf calls and shouts followed her through the crowded room.

"Hey, Lucie! If I had a swing like that, I'd put it in my front yard!"

How original. Lucie snorted, but kept a smile plastered to her face. Same old Raccoon Saloon, same old patrons.

Except one.

To hell with financial worries and to hell with this town. I'm getting out.

Laissez les bon temps rouler. Let the good times roll!

CHAPTER 2

BENJAMIN FRANKLIN BOYETTE NOTICED HER THE MOMENT HE SLIPPED into the Raccoon Saloon. That sexy way her midnight-black hair hung down her back to brush across her butt, and the way her hips swayed, made her unforgettable. Damn, how in hell had she gotten even more beautiful in the past seven years?

Ben groaned inwardly. This assignment would be a lot harder than he'd anticipated with Lucie LeBieu around. As much as he'd tried, he hadn't been able to shake her from his mind. And wouldn't, short of a strong dose of Madame LeBieu's Voodoo. Lucie was not an easy woman to forget—all five-foot-three inches of Louisiana hot sauce.

As if in auto-drive, his jeans tightened to the point he had to readjust before he could take another step. Had he known the luscious Lucie would be there, he'd have ignored Alex's advice and suggested another meeting place to conduct his business. He should never have trusted his sister. She'd always had the crazy idea that he and Lucie would end up together.

Didn't she realize that Lucie had been the one to dump *him* seven years ago? When he'd gotten the letter of acceptance from the Louisiana Police Academy, he'd crumbled the paper and tossed it in the trash, telling himself he didn't care anymore. Lucie had agreed to marry him and he was determined to stay in Bayou Miste and spend the rest of his life working to make her happy.

The next day, the world crashed in around his ears when Lucie had given his ring back and said she'd reconsidered. When he'd argued with her, she'd told him flat-out he wasn't good enough for her. She wanted a man who could take care of her, provide for her every need.

He had been willing to try, but apparently trying wasn't enough.

He'd been out of his mind, hurt and angry, saying things he didn't mean. Later, when he'd had time to cool down, he wished he could take back some of those awful things he'd said. But he'd realized the futility. Lucie hadn't wanted him.

His chest tightened at the memory. He'd fallen hard when he'd fallen for Lucie. But he'd had seven years to get over her. Now he was immune to her brand of infection.

That's what he kept telling himself, anyway. Somehow the idea never stuck.

Damned woman. She shouldn't have that kind of hold on him anymore. Not after all this time. Anger surged through him as, with a little more effort than he cared to admit, he pried his gaze from Lucie's swaying hips. Here on business, he didn't have time to reminisce about a flame blown out.

As planned, he'd arrived five minutes after Eric Littington, hoping to give their get-together a look of coincidence versus the planned meeting that it was. He scanned the interior of the bar. Despite being gone for seven years, he recognized just about everyone there. Except the woman in the corner with Craig Thibodeaux and the man in the leather jacket hunkered down in a seat in the shadows by the rear exit. He made a mental note to check out the strange woman and the leather-clad man.

Eventually, his gaze landed on the man he was looking for. Eric smiled as if seeing him for the first time in years, and waved a beckoning hand.

Ben covered the distance to the dark corner in a few easy strides. When he reached the table, he hid a grin.

If Eric planned to blend in at the bar, he'd missed the boat entirely.

His khaki slacks and polo shirt were too sharp of a contrast to the standard jeans and T-shirts the rest of the crowd wore. Somehow, khaki didn't go with zydeco music and oyster shooters.

When they'd been growing up in Bayou Miste, Eric had already stuck out among the other children running barefoot through the bayous. He'd had the best of everything, while Ben had to be satisfied with secondhand clothes and toys. Now Ben shook his head, amazed at how the rich kid and the shrimper's son had become the best of friends. As a teenager he'd envied Eric, until he'd realized that no matter how much Eric had, he'd always been lonely in the small community, isolated by his father's wealth.

Ben wouldn't have traded places with Eric for all the oil money in the swamp. Even with the constant noise and confusion in the cramped four-bedroom house he'd shared with his brothers and sisters, Ben loved his family and had felt sorry for Eric being an only child.

He'd befriended the privileged teen and invited him home to dinner on more than one occasion. He could still picture Eric's face the first time he'd entered the Boyette house. The poor little rich kid must have felt like he was at Mardi Gras, with all the Boyette children gathered around the table.

"Hey, Ben." Eric stood and extended a hand. "Heard you moved back from Baton Rouge." He winked.

"Eric." Ben grabbed the extended hand and pulled him into a hug, like he was family. "It's good to see you." He scooted a chair up to the table opposite Eric, his detective instincts kicking into gear. He studied the fine lines around the other man's eyes. "So what's up?"

His boss had briefed him on the case before he left the Special Criminal Investigation Unit in Baton Rouge, but he wanted to hear the story from Eric himself.

His friend leaned closer. "I need you to be on the lookout for anyone trying to sabotage my campaign for Congress."

"Why? I thought that's how the game's played."

Out of the corner of his eye, Ben saw a flash of long black hair. Lucie bent to pick up a napkin off the floor and all his attention zeroed in on the frayed hem of her shorter-than-short skirt.

He gulped. She made it hard to concentrate.

He returned his attention to his friend. “Eric, you're in politics. You should expect some problems with your campaign.”

“I understand that, but someone broke into my house in Baton Rouge and tapped all my phone lines. Not to mention, someone's been stalking me for the past month. No attempts on my life. But I'd like to know who it is, who hired him and why.”

“And let me guess. You found that hard to figure out in a big city? Too many people, too many possibilities,” Ben finished for him.

"Yeah," Eric said. “I guess that's why your boss thought it would be better if we did this here in Bayou Miste, where you know all the locals. We'll have a better chance of finding the guy if he follows me here.”

With every fiber of his being on Lucie-alert, Ben fought the urge to glance around the bar again, knowing it would be for her, not potential suspects, no matter what he told himself. Instead, he concentrated on his friend. “So, what's your excuse for being here when you should be out campaigning?”

“I'm here on the pretext of a quasi-vacation with my parents for the next two weeks. My campaign manager is setting up a few public speaking engagements while I'm home, complete with television coverage to keep me in the public eye.”

“What about the environmental groups? Aren't you afraid they'll raise a ruckus after the chemical dumping stink in these parts?”

Eric pushed a hand through his blond hair. “My father promised to pay for the cleanup. There might be a protest or two, but I don't expect it to be major. The community knew it wasn't totally the fault of Littington Enterprises.”

“Maybe so, but the tendency is for the media to make an example of the big industries.” Without realizing he'd been looking, Ben spied Lucie and all his attention shifted to her. And she was one hell of a distraction with her thick, dark curls hanging down to her waist and the neckline of her T-shirt dipping low, exposing the full, rounded tops of her breasts—

“The only people who are supposed to know you're here on police work are my father and me." Eric's voice pulled Ben back to the business at hand.

"Beautiful." Ben replied automatically. But his response could just as well have been a commentary on Lucie's breasts or her rounded bottom. A derriere he'd known all too well, a lifetime ago.

"But what about you?" Eric asked. "Won't it seem coincidental that you and I showed up at the same time?"

Lucie swatted a customer's hand when he got too friendly. Just like her to look good enough to eat, but play hard to get.

Get back to business, Ben. She's not interested. Nor are you. Now what was Eric saying? *Oh yeah.* "I've got that covered." Ben grinned. "I applied for a job with Bug Tugsley Extermination. He owed me a favor."

"Do you think the townspeople will buy the story that you're back to start over as a bug exterminator after being a state police detective?" Eric leaned across the table, his voice low enough not to carry to casual eavesdroppers but loud enough to be heard over the music.

"Huh?" He purposely avoided looking at Lucie and forced himself to focus on Eric. "Oh, yeah. All I have to do is tell a few folks that I'd had enough with playing cops and robbers and wanted to get back to family." Which was true in a way. He needed a break from Baton Rouge. After his partner's death, he'd been driving himself too hard. "Word will spread through the grapevine. And what's not to believe? Everyone in Bayou Miste knows the importance we Boyettes place on family."

Then why had it been years since he'd been home?

His gaze drifted to the reason. Lucie.

"That they do." A wistful smile lifted Eric's lips. "Whatever you have to tell them. I just don't want the public to know that you're here to help me. I don't want the other candidates, including the incumbent Richard Gasson, to think I'm getting paranoid. And I don't want whoever's doing this to me to know I'm actively pursuing them."

Ben focused on his friend. "You can count on me."

"Thanks." Eric's gaze swept around the room. "It's good to be back."

"Uh-huh." Coming home had been a bittersweet ordeal. His mother had cried, along with half of his sisters. "Yeah, it's good to be home." He allowed himself another glance around, his gaze zeroing in on the dark-haired Cajun beauty.

With her head cocked at a haughty angle, Lucie swayed through the tables, stopping along the way to drop off full drinks and load the empties. When she reached LeRoy Le Due's table, the man openly leered.

Ben's hackles rose. From what his mother had told him, LeRoy was a married man now. He had no business eyeing Lucie like that.

"Got me my shooters?" LeRoy's voice rose above the crowd and the zydeco band, his gaze on her breasts, not his order of oyster shooters.

Lucie set the plate on his table and shifted the big tray from her shoulder to directly in front of her, two full mugs blocking LeRoy's view of her chest. "Here are your oysters. Now maybe you can be quiet and behave yourself."

"I got anything but behavin' on my mind." The drunkard lunged and grabbed Lucie around the waist.

Thrown off-balance, Lucie's tray tipped. The two full mugs and all the empty bottles slid off, landing with a loud crash on the hardwood floor, splattering beer and shattering glass in a million directions.

But that didn't slow LeRoy down. He hauled Lucie into his lap and ran his pork chop hands over her body.

Lucie struggled to keep the octopus's hands at bay. "Let. Go. Of. Me."

Ben was out of his chair and pushing his way across the crowded room before he could think through his reaction. Adrenaline pumped through his veins, lending fuel to his anger.

"That's it! That tops the charts," Lucie shouted. She breathed deeply several times, but unfortunately the rise and fall of her chest only incited more fondling by the hulking fool. "Your wife doesn't deserve this, LeRoy. Someone's gotta teach you a little respect."

Ben cringed. He'd never known Lucie to back down from a fight, even when the odds were stacked so heavily against her.

Unable to break loose from his roving hands, Lucie dove for the floor, toppling him from his chair.

His grip eased long enough for her to scramble free and shake the beer off her hands.

A high-pitched screech pierced the air behind Ben. He turned in time to avoid being trampled by a crazed woman leaping from table to table to get to the center of the fray. Ben recognized her as Eunice, LeRoy's wife.

Oh, boy. The show was about to get even rowdier. He'd better snag Lucie before Eunice did.

While he shouldered his way through the amassing crowd of betting Cajuns, he lost sight of Lucie for a moment.

Eunice screeched again, followed by what he could only guess was Lucie's yelp.

By the time he managed to get through, Eunice was on Lucie's back, her arm crooked around the Cajun beauty's neck, squeezing the breath out of her until Lucie's face had turned a bright shade of blueberry.

"Stay away from my man, you two-bit hussy! I married him, fair and square, and you got no bidness jumpin' his bones."

"But—" Lucie wheezed around the wiry forearm clutching her throat.

"No buts! I didn't give up the best years of my life with this bastard for no Cajun swamp princess to steal him away in a barroom."

"Now, ladies. I'm sure there's been some misunderstanding." Ben reached over, hooked Eunice by her bony hips and pulled.

Eunice refused to relinquish her hold on Lucie's neck.

Lucie would pass out soon if the other woman didn't let her breathe. She was already going from blue to an alarming shade of purple.

As a cop, Ben had been called out to break up fights every bit as ugly as this one, but not ones involving Lucie. If he didn't do something quick, Eunice could kill her.

He applied his best negotiating voice, honed from years of responding to domestic violence incidents. "Eunice, let go of Lucie. She doesn't want to take LeRoy away from you."

For a moment, the woman's arm loosened.

He seized the opportunity to lift her off Lucie. Before he could set Eunice to the side, she grabbed onto Lucie's hair and yanked her along with her. "This bayou bimbo has got to learn she can't have someone else's husband."

Ben loosened his hold on Eunice to ease the strain on Lucie's hair roots. But she wrapped her legs around Lucie's waist and rode her back, holding onto the hank of hair for all she was worth. "You bitch! I should have known better than to let my man come to this shameful bar with the likes of you workin' here."

"He came on to me," Lucie rasped. "And I'm not a bimbo."

"My LeRoy wouldn't do anything wrong when he's got a wife sittin' at home, wouldja, sweet thang?"

"No, ma'am. I surely wouldn't." LeRoy gasped beneath the weight of the two women.

"So that leaves you lying like the whore you are." Eunice pulled tighter until Ben thought Lucie's hair would fly out in hunks.

"Ladies, this is no way to settle an argument." He tried to pry Eunice's fingers out of Lucie's hair and nearly got an elbow to the groin.

LeRoy scrambled away from the fighting pair and lurched to his feet. He rubbed at his crotch, a grin spreading across his face. "*Whoo-weeee*! Let the good times roll! My money's on you, honey cakes." He pulled out his wallet and started counting bills.

Ben grabbed LeRoy and jerked his arm behind his back, high up between his shoulder blades. "Call her off or I'll tell her the truth."

The smile slipped down the bully's face and then back up again. "Who's she gonna believe, her husband or one of Lucie's ex-squeezes?"

He tightened his hold until sweat popped out on LeRoy's face. "Call her off or I'll do worse than Lucie did to you." Ben lowered his voice to be sure LeRoy got his message. He remembered LeRoy's bullying as a kid, but as an adult, Ben didn't have the time or patience to put up with it.

"Okay, okay," the bigger man squealed.

Ben let up on the pressure.

"Let her go, Eunice," LeRoy said. "She ain't worth it."

Her breath coming in short gasps, Eunice glanced up from beneath Lucie. "You sure? I got her right where I want her."

Lucie reared up, her temples straining against Eunice's hold on her hair. She slammed Eunice back against the floor. "Let me go, you moron! You should be kickin' your husband's butt, not mine."

LeRoy chuckled. “Ain’t never seen her so mad. Kinda like it.”

With a jerk of his arm, Ben reminded the larger man who was in charge.

“Lighten up, will ya?” LeRoy squirmed against the force on his wrist. “Eunice, let the swamp princess go. You and me got better thangs ta do.”

With one last tug, Eunice released Lucie’s hair, shoved her to the side, and stood up as if fighting in a bar were an everyday occurrence for her. “Come on, sweetie. Supper’s ready and waitin’.”

Ben released his hold on LeRoy.

The hulking man wrapped a thick stump of an arm around Eunice’s skinny shoulders and turned her toward the door. “Didja make my favorite?”

Eunice smiled up at him, dwarfed by his bulk. “I sure did. Mudbugs and rice. I caught 'em fresh today in that ditch alongside the road to our place.”

With the fight over, the bar patrons drifted back to their beer, some counting out bills to pay up on their bets. Yup, it was a typical night at the Raccoon Saloon. Ben felt more at home by the minute.

He bent to where Lucie pushed to her hands and knees in a puddle of beer. The color in her cheeks high, she was still so pretty she made his chest hurt. He steeled himself against the onslaught of unwanted emotions and pulled her up into his arms. “Hey, Lucie.”

"Ben?" Lucie blinked, her eyes widening, her face blanching as her fingers curled into his shirt. "You came back," she whispered, then flung her arms around his neck.

He held her close, the scent of her shampoo wrapping around him. This was what he'd been missing in his life. This woman and the feel of her body against his. But it was all an illusion, which would end when Lucie got her bearings. Ben steeled his heart against further pain and forced a chuckle, "Yeah, babe, I'm back, and I can see not much has changed around here. You're still giving the men of Bayou Miste hell."

CHAPTER 3

DESPERATE TIMES CALLED FOR DESPERATE MEASURES.

Lucie LeBieu swallowed the wad of guilt in her throat and stretched up on her tiptoes. When her fingers wrapped around the bottle marked "Tailless Raccoon Spit," she dragged it from the shelf of her grandmother's pantry.

"Need help in there?" Alex called out from the kitchen.

"No. I can handle this myself." *Yeah. Sure.* Just like she handled her love life. And everyone in Bayou Miste knew *that* was nonexistent. But if she was caught with her hand in the proverbial cookie jar, she didn't want her two friends to catch any of the old woman's wrath.

Lucie's grandmother wasn't the normal, run-of-the-mill grandmotherly type. Oh, she had in her kitchen the usual flour, sugar, and everything necessary for a scrumptious batch of chocolate chip cookies, or even yummier Louisiana gumbo. But it didn't stop there—she had many more mysteries stashed away in her cupboards. Tailless Raccoon Spit was only one of the strangely labeled containers Lucie found as she riffled through the pantry.

Her grandmother wasn't an escapee from a mental institution, or a homeopathic healer, per se, although healing did make up the majority of her work. She was none other than the infamous bayou Voodoo queen, Madame LeBieu. And if she knew what Lucie was up to, she'd likely stir up a retribution potion that would give her granddaughter a wicked weeklong itch or something even more dreadful.

But Lucie was madder than a crab in a fishnet, and she wasn't going to let her grandmother's reputation scare her out of doing what she had to do. And her anger was directed toward one red-hot sexy Cajun. "Of all the people to turn up at the Raccoon Saloon, why did it have to be Benjamin Franklin Boyette? Why now? And the rat bastard pretty much accused me of starting that fight with LeRoy." She stomped in and out of the little pantry.

Lucie's friend Calliope opened the container on the counter and dipped a finger into a powdery concoction. "Lucie, you know Madame LeBieu would have a hissy fit if she knew you were messin' with her stash of magic ingredients."

"Stay out of that, Calliope Ostelet." Alex, the more levelheaded of her two friends, swatted at Calliope's hand. "It's liable to turn your skin purple or give you boils."

Lucie ignored the two and walked back into the storage room.

Alex followed, leaning into the doorway to sniff. "What's she got in there, anyway?"

"None of your business, Alexandra Belle Boyette." Lucie emphasized the "Boyette" as if it were a nasty-tasting word. As she pushed past Alex, she redirected her guilt and anger toward her friend. She knew she shouldn't meddle in *Mamère* LeBieu's magic. But now that a foreclosure notice had been served, and worse, Ben was back in town, she had no other choice. "I shouldn't even be talking to you." She stopped on her third trip back to the butcher block in the middle of the cluttered kitchen. "You could have told me *big brother* was back."

A rosy red blush flooded Alex's cheeks. "I would have, but you were too busy waiting tables at the saloon for me to break it to you."

Lucie smacked a tin container on the counter. "Bull."

Alex sighed. "Okay, so I didn't tell you. Shoot, it has been a long time since you'd seen my brother, I wasn't sure how you still felt about him."

"I don't have *any* feelings for him." She marched back to the pantry. "None at all." Then why the hell was there moisture in her eyes, and why was her chest—and strategic points farther south—so tight and achy? She held on to her anger like a shield, praying she didn't break down in front of her friends.

She glanced around the interior of the pantry, blinking to avoid letting a single tear slip down her face. Must be all the potent herbs and cayenne pepper her grandmother kept for cooking up food and the occasional spell. Nope, she wasn't crying over that rat Ben.

"You all right in there?" Calliope peeked into to the dimly lit room.

"I'm fine. I just can't seem to find what I'm lookin' for." *Story of her life*. No matter how hard she tried, she couldn't seem to find her place in Bayou Miste. Especially since Ben left.

But now he was back. After seven long freakin' years! All the more reason to get out. *Fast*.

She spied the last canister she needed and grabbed it. Back in the kitchen, she arranged the various containers in order of the instructions she'd found in the wood-bound book marked "Madame LeBieu's Special Recipes." With the cookbook propped on a stand, she tugged a massive cast-iron stockpot from a bottom cabinet and set it on the propane-powered stove.

Alex's eyes widened and her face paled. "Ah jeez, you weren't kidding, were you? You really are going to use magic. Clear the parish!"

Lucie glared at her former friend.

"Cut the crap, Alex." Her lips pressed together, she leaned over to read the recipe, then snatched up the first container and a measuring cup.

Alex blocked her way to the stove. "Lucie, don't do it. I beg of you."

"Move, Alex."

"Madame LeBieu will be furious," Alex argued.

"Where is she, anyway?" Calliope's gaze darted around the room as if expecting the woman to appear out of thin air. "And where's Lisa?"

"Lisa went to New Orleans and *Mamère* took a poultice to Pete Pasquale on the other side of Bayou Black. He must have been poaching gators, because he got himself bit. She won't be back for half the afternoon." Lucie stared at Alex. "She'll never know I was in her pantry, if you'll move out of my way and let me get on with it."

"Any chance of Lisa dropping in?" Calliope asked.

She cringed. Her twin sister was the last person who needed to know she was attempting magic. As far as twins went, Lucie and Lisa shared looks, but nothing else. Lisa was the yin to her yang, the dark to her light. Her sister was wild, through and through. "No. She left for New Orleans this morning to visit a friend. Thank God."

"Good thing. Maybe she'll stay." With a short, harrumphing snort, Alex stepped around the butcher block and pulled up a stool. "I still think it's wrong, and I don't know what I'm doing here watching, but if this is the way you want to deal with your life, it's your funeral."

"Funeral?" Lucie wanted to laugh at how she'd shied away from the love spell her grandmother had tried to hex her with. And here she was cookin' up one of her own. If they weren't in danger of losing her home, or there was any other way to get rich quick in Bayou Miste, she'd have jumped on it. Snagging Eric Littington was her only hope of saving her grandmother's home and getting herself out of the swamp. "A little love potion isn't that big of a deal."

Alex snorted. "That's what you always say."

"Look, if you're going to watch, at least keep it quiet." Lucie ran her finger down the page, checking off her list of ingredients. "These spells have to be mixed with the appropriate words as well as ingredients, and if someone else talks, I might get things confused."

"We'll be quiet, *right* Calliope?" Alex shot a warning glare across at the redhead.

"My lips are sealed." Calliope drew an imaginary zipper across her lips and grinned, spoiling the effect.

Lucie ignored her friends and concentrated on the recipe book, her stomach knotting automatically. She recalled the last few times she'd tried *Mamère* LeBieu's magic, only to goof up every spell. She couldn't help it if she'd mistaken the Voodoo queen's canister of whole-wheat flour for ground cypress knees. So what if Mo's alligator was in love with Granny Saulnier's poodle? Worse things could happen.

But not today. She was determined to make good her escape from ruin, Bayou Miste, and Benjamin Franklin Boyette.

Ah hell, had she really added *Ben* on to the end of that thought? What did she have to worry about with Ben? Their relationship was no longer an issue—hadn't been for seven long years. A lump rose in her throat and she swallowed determinedly.

Eric was her ticket out of all her troubles and the swamp—not Ben. Besides, Alex had mentioned that Ben was home for good. If that was the case, Lucie had no intention of staying in the bayous. What for?

Because Ben was home, a niggling voice taunted her.

With a vicious twist, Lucie wrapped her thick hair high on the back of her head and clamped it in place to keep it out of the way while she cooked up her future.

"I feel like there should be a drum roll or something." Calliope gave a little giggle. "Well? Isn't every Voodoo spell supposed to be accompanied by drums?"

Alex and Lucie glared at Calliope until she flushed and raised her hands in surrender. "Okay, okay. I won't say another word."

"Good, because I want everything to be perfect for this spell. My future with B—*Eric* depends on it." Her face warmed and she leaned over the potion book, hoping Alex hadn't heard her slip up.

Alex's eyes widened. "Are you sure *Eric's* the guy for you, sweetie?"

Lucie arched her brows at her dark-haired friend. "Let me see...Eric's the son of the richest man in the parish, not to mention he's a United States congressional candidate and the acclaimed golden boy of Louisiana politics. And from what I remember, he was always nice and might have been sweet on me at one time." She tapped a finger to her chin and stared at the ceiling before adding, "Yup, I think he's the right man to get us out of financial ruin and get me out of the swamps." Her attention returned to the book. "Now, if you don't mind, I'd like to cook up a love spell, and you're interrupting."

"Okay. Whatever." Alex shook her head. "Although I didn't hear anything about love in there. Kind of an important ingredient in a marriage, if you ask me."

After a deep breath drawn in through her clenched teeth, Lucie said, "In case you missed it, I did say 'love.' That's why I'm here. Hel-*lo*? Love spell? Voodoo? Jeez. I'm surrounded by amateurs."

"You don't have to be so grumpy," Alex grumbled.

Her face warmed again. Alex was right. She'd been a flaming bitch since she'd run into Ben at the Raccoon Saloon. And she wasn't normally like this. Only where Ben was concerned. With a weak smile at her friend, she muttered a not-so-very-contrite, "Sorry."

"Apology accepted."

Her heart welled with a flood of emotion for her two friends. But she didn't have time for group hugs and a round of "Kumbaya." She had some fancy cooking to do. She turned back to the cookbook. "Start with stump water, dark as night. Two cups of the stuff will be just right."

From the floor, she lifted the brown glass jug marked "Stump Water" and poured it into a measuring cup until the liquid line met the two-cup mark.

"Jeez, that stuff smells like—" Calliope pinched her nostrils together and gagged.

"Stump water?" Lucie finished, then clamped her hand to her mouth. "Shoot, Calliope, you weren't supposed to say anything during the ingredient-mixing."

With hunched shoulders, Calliope pressed her hand to her lips and muttered through her fingers. "Sorry. It won't happen again."

Lucie rolled her eyes toward the ceiling. *As if!* Calliope couldn't shut up for more than thirty seconds at a stretch. She'd likely explode if she did.

Cup in hand, Lucie dumped the contents into the cast-iron stockpot, the smell triggering her own gag reflex. Back at the book, she read the next line out loud. "With the fire set low, add to the soup, a quarter teaspoon of ground alligator tooth."

Lucie twisted the knob on the stove and the acrid scent of propane filled the air. Then, as she'd seen *Mamère* LeBieu do a thousand times, Lucie scraped a match against the rough wooden wall and the head burst into flame. After lighting the burner, she settled the pot over the fire.

Now for the next ingredient. She opened the brown jar marked alligator tooth. The odor from the jar reminded her of her last visit to the dentist—the pungent smell created when drill meets tooth assailed her nostrils. She shoved the measuring spoon inside, retrieving a quarter teaspoon, as the recipe called for.

Careful not to spill or sneeze, she dropped the powder into the water. "Then with a touch, ever so light, add a pair of crawfish eyeballs to sharpen love's sight."

"Ewwww!" Calliope squirmed and shuddered on her stool.

"Shh!" Alex jabbed her elbow into the redhead's rib cage.

A contrite-looking Calliope sat with her hand still over her mouth.

With a warning glower at her friend, Lucie moved on to the next item on the list. "Five drops of spit from a tailless raccoon will ensure the magic lasts until the ten thousandth moon." She unscrewed the cap off a small vial, and dripped five drops of raccoon spit into the stewpot.

Yuck. Some of the ingredients were really disgusting. How did her grandmother work with this stuff day after day?

"I wonder how Madame LeBieu got raccoon spit," Calliope said. "Suppose she bought it off the Internet? Or did she wrestle a tailless raccoon to the ground and knock the spit out of it?" A smile lit her face and she sat up straighter. "Maybe some of the stuffed coons in the Raccoon Saloon are from her spit-gathering."

Alex smothered a giggle.

An answering giggle leaped up in Lucie's throat, but she squelched it before it escaped. She really shouldn't encourage Calliope's interruptions. Instead she sent a withering glance at the two seated women and moved on to the next instruction. "The fragrant blossom of the magnolia tree will enhance the romance, just wait, you'll see." Lucie opened a plastic bag filled with dried flower petals marked "Magnolia Blossoms." She dropped one petal into the pot.

Before Lucie could reseal the bag, Alex jumped up, grabbed it from Lucie and dumped the contents into the pot.

"Hey, the recipe only called for one petal, you just dumped four in there," she said.

"You're long overdue on romance." Alex hugged her and sat back on the stool.

Her vision blurred, Lucie had to blink several times and swallow the lump in her throat before she could go on with her work. God, she loved her friends. When she left Bayou Miste, she'd hate leaving them behind. But she needed a new start away from her past—especially from a past that included Ben. Straightening her shoulders, she got back to business.

"Two tablespoons of cayenne, to top it all off, as all Cajun cooking includes the stuff."

"Um, now you're making me hungry," Calliope whispered.

"Bring to a boil and then count to ten." The handwriting scrawled at the bottom of the page. Lucie had to squint to see the words "turn over" written in tiny letters. She flipped the sheet and read on.

"Turn off the heat and let the brew sit so the potion cools down a bit." As the liquid came to a boil, she counted aloud. "One, two, three, four, five."

Alex and Calliope chimed in, "Six, seven, eight, nine, ten!"

A quick twist extinguished the flame and Lucie fanned the potion, hoping to speed the process.

Alex leaned over the recipe book to read the next set of instructions. "Says here to sprinkle the potion on the wings of a love bug."

"You mean those disgusting bugs that fly around piggy-backed, mating all the time?" Calliope asked.

Alex's lips twisted. "It says love bug. What else could it mean?"

Calliope jumped up from her stool. "I'll go outside and see what I can find. There are usually a bazillion of them making bug-gut glue all over my car."

Before Lucie could utter a word, Calliope rushed out the door. Just as well. Finding the bug would give her something productive to do while they waited for the potion to cool.

Alex bent over the recipe book. "You realize you have to turn this hexed bug loose in the same room with you and your intended target, don't you?"

"I do?" Lucie leaned over Alex's shoulder and read the scribbled words, then grimaced. "That'll be a trick to get me and Eric in a room all by ourselves."

"How are you going to manage that? Sneak into his bedroom at night? I understand they have a pretty impressive security system at the Littington mansion. I don't think you'll get by that."

"Don't worry, I'll think of something." *What,* she didn't know.

Calliope rushed back in, a frown marring her freckled forehead. "What's wrong with this place? Only last week there were hundreds, even thousands of the little creatures."

"What do you mean?"

Calliope grimaced. "No love bugs."

"No love bugs?" Alex and Lucie said in unison.

Lucie's heart sank into her shoes. "All this mixing and angsting for what? Nothing! A big fat goose egg. Great! Just great!"

Calliope held out her hand. "I did find a ladybug. I figure one flying bug is as good as the next. Can you use a ladybug?" Calliope stopped talking long enough to inhale. "Gag!" She clapped a hand over her nose. "That stuff really stinks."

"It's not the smell that counts. It's how well the potion works," Lucie held out her hand. "You couldn't find a single love bug? Jeez, I still have dead ones stuck all over the front of my 'Stang. Why is it you can find them when you don't want them, but as soon as you need one—"

"You can't find one," Alex finished. "Sounds like the story of *my* love life."

Calliope's brow furrowed. "You have guys stuck all over the front of your Jeep?"

"The way my mother keeps throwing them at me you'd think I'd be scrapin' them off my bumper." Alex leaned over the cookbook. "Does it *have* to be a love bug?"

"The recipe says, 'Sprinkle the brew on a love bug's wing and in a loud, sweet voice you must sing, "Fly little bug, fly high up above and make my lovebirds fall in love."'"

"Hey, I thought this was a love spell for people," Calliope said.

Lucie flipped the page back to read the title. "It says 'Love Spell.'"

Alex shrugged. "Whatever. You need a flying bug. All you have available is the blasted ladybug. What can it hurt?"

"Ah, jeez!" Lucie slammed the book shut. "I can see it happening already. Another Voodoo spell gone awry, courtesy of the misfit granddaughter of Madame LeBieu. This time, they might even give me the front page of the *Bayou Miste Herald*."

"Don't sweat it, Lucie." Alex slipped the ladybug out of Lucie's hand into her own. "Maybe the spell wasn't meant to be."

"Yeah." Calliope's face lit up with a huge grin. "And you can stay here in Bayou Miste with us."

With her two best friends, maybe. But top them with a dead-end job, a foreclosure hanging over her grandmother's head, and a nonexistent love life, no way. And to make matters worse, Ben Boyette had come home to stay. Lucie's heart sank into her empty belly like a lead fishing weight.

With the ladybug curled in her fingers, Alex headed for the door. "I'll just let this little guy go while you dump that mess down the sink."

Lucie's mind reviewed the options like a CD disc spinning round and round. *Marriage to a rich man or financial ruin.* Live in a mansion or out on the streets—or in this case, the swamps—of Bayou Miste. Marry Eric Littington and leave, or watch Ben Boyette parade his new girlfriends around town while she ate her heart out.

"Alex, stop!" she shouted.

Alex froze in midstride.

"Give me that damn bug." Her voice echoed in the silent room, calm and surprisingly firm.

Eyes wide, Alex slowly turned back toward her and held out her hand. "Are you sure you want to do this? Seems a bit cold-blooded of you to target poor, unsuspecting Eric with a spell."

A wall of guilt finally broke through her determination and threatened to overwhelm her. She'd never loved Eric. She'd liked him as a friend, but she'd never had any deep emotional attachment to him. Then again, her grandmother couldn't possibly live out on the streets or in the swamps without a roof over her head. Lisa wasn't a reliable source of income. It was up to Lucie to come up with a plan to save her grandmother's home and, so far, this was all she could come up with.

She drew in a deep breath past the lump rising in her throat. "I know it sounds cold-blooded, but don't worry, I'll do right by Eric and make him a good wife. You'll see." Tears welled in her eyes as she thought of

Ben married to someone else. "I have to do this for *Mamère*." And she couldn't stay in Bayou Miste, no matter what. "Alex, please. Give me the bug."

"It's your life, but don't be mad if we say 'we told you so.'" Alex uncurled her fingers, revealing the tiny red and black ladybug.

Lucie scraped the hard-shelled creature onto the wooden cutting board and settled a mason jar over it. Grasping a wooden spoon, she stirred the concoction on the stove one last time for good measure.

With her eyes pressed closed, she chanted to herself, "Please let this work. Please help me find love and happiness." Opening her eyes, she dipped the spoon into the odiferous mix, cupped her hand beneath it, and stepped back to the center island cutting board. Then she inhaled deeply and nodded at Alex. "Will you remove the glass jar?"

Her hand slow and steady, Alex reached out, her fingers hovering over the jar. "You don't have to go through with this, you know."

"Just lift the damned jar, please!" Lucie's arm shook and liquid spilled from the spoon into her hand.

The glass came up, exposing the harbinger of her freedom. The tiny ladybug opened its protective shell and flexed its wings.

Quickly, before the bug could fly away, Lucie dribbled the liquid over the board until one tiny drop touched the ladybug's wing. Then in a clear soprano, she sang, "Fly little bug, fly high up above and make my lovebirds fall in love."

The ladybug flicked its wings several times. A faint greenish glow like that of a firefly lit the tiny insect's wings.

"You did it!" Calliope clapped her hands.

"Yeah, you've done it all right." Alex closed her eyes. "All I have to say is, look out Bayou Miste, we're probably in for a helluva ride."

CHAPTER 4

"I'll need to check for bugs in every room of your office and house." Ben stood inside Eric Littington's office wearing a faded navy-blue coverall and carrying a canister of Bug B Gon.

A giant grin spread across Eric's face, and he rose from the leather chair behind his desk. "Look at you!" He rounded the desk and circled Ben, his gaze running up and down the length of his body. "I got to admit. You look like the real McCoy." Eric leaned closer and sniffed. "You even smell the part."

His lips twisted into a wry smile. "I'd better, if this is going to work."

"So, when you said you need to check for bugs, I assume you mean the mechanical ones?" Eric shoved his hands in his pocket and stepped back.

"Yeah." Ben set the sprayer on the carpet, pulled his bug detector device from his pocket, extended then antenna, switched it to vibrate, and turned it on. Then he walked slowly around the room, searching for all possible locations a wiretap or bug could be hidden. "The downside to my cover is that you'll have to pay to get your home and office sprayed."

"Not to worry. We'll manage." Eric walked to the window. "I'm glad you're the one on this case, after all that's happened in the past couple weeks. This game is starting to get dirty. I want to know who's been tailing me and who hired the dirtbag."

"We can guess at the who-hired-him part." Ben moved a chair beneath the ceiling fan in the center of the room and climbed up to examine the fixture. "Your opposing candidate has to be the one who did the hiring. But your decision to come to Bayou Miste was good. We should have no problems spotting a stranger. Hopefully, we'll have this business wrapped up in a day or two."

Ben's wishful thinking was overriding his patience and good sense. All he could think of was that he wanted out of Bayou Miste as quickly as possible.

Last night at the Raccoon Saloon had been a shock to his system. The sight of Lucie LeBieu waiting tables in her Hooters-style short-shorts and that ridiculously minuscule T-shirt had raised his heart rate to runner's speed. For the first five minutes, he'd thought she was her twin sister, Lisa, until someone shouted her name. Damn, she'd gotten even more beautiful over the past seven years. And every time he recalled those shorts and her incredibly long legs, his blood flowed south in a New Orleans minute, entering places it had no business going. Especially where Lucie LeBieu was concerned. If she didn't want anything to do with him seven years ago, she surely didn't want him now.

But those silky smooth thighs, tinged mocha by her Cajun-Creole heritage, called to him, even now. The chair he stood on wobbled, jerking him back to Eric's office at Littington Enterprises. He shouldn't be thinking about Lucie when he had a job to do. *Concentrate on the task at hand and you'll wipe her clean from your mind.*

"Enough about the case." Eric hooked his thumbs into his belt loops and rocked back on his heels. "How about that waitress last night at the Raccoon Saloon?"

The chair rocked violently. Ben waited until he had it back in control before he answered. "What waitress?" *So much for wiping Lucie from his mind.*

"Don't play dumb with me. You were there, too." Eric stared hard at him. "As I recollect, you couldn't keep your eyes off her."

Schooling his expression into his best poker face, he hopped down off the chair, ignoring Eric's words. He continued his search for hidden devices, feeling around the rim of the large oak desk dominating the room. If his stomach was a little knotted, he didn't need to share that information with Eric. He and Lucie LeBieu were no longer an item.

"Her name's Lucie LeBieu, isn't it?" Eric didn't wait for an answer. "Beautiful, just beautiful. She's one hot latte. I can't get over her."

You and me both, buddy. Hell. Did he say that out loud? Ben looked at Eric. When Eric didn't respond, he breathed a silent sigh.

"Wasn't she the kid who used to tag along behind us in school?" Eric shook his head, staring out the window. "She's grown into quite a woman. And those legs." Eric whistled. "Wow."

Ben's stomach did a flip-flop. Oh yeah, the legs. At times, deep into the night, he could still feel them wrapped around his waist. He circled the desk and dropped onto his back to look underneath. Out of Eric's view, he adjusted his coverall, appalled that the mere thought of Lucie could have him as hard as a cypress tree in no time at all.

"I think," Eric's voice drifted to him, "I'll ask her out."

Ben sat up, whacking his forehead against the underside of the desk. The room dimmed with tiny pinpricks of light squiggling through his vision. He fell onto his back and lay still, willing the miniature glow worms to go away.

"You all right under there?" Eric's face wavered into view.

"Yeah." Ben rubbed the knot forming on the right side of his forehead. "Just knocked my head."

Eric stared at him. "You're going to have a nice-sized goose egg. Want an ice pack?" He lifted a phone. "I could have the on-site clinic bring one up."

"No, I'll be fine." *Stupid, but fine*. As long as Eric didn't mention Lucie again. Ben climbed to his feet and straightened his clothes. Not that he had a hard-on anymore. Nothing like a bump on the head to kill the urge. Maybe he needed to clobber himself every time he thought about Lucie.

"So what do you think about what I said?" Eric asked.

"I think we'll find your rat, no problem."

"No, not about that. About Lucie."

He glanced around the room, looking for a mallet or something. Anything to bop against the growing lump on his forehead. Pain would help him erase her from his brain. He reminded himself that pain was the only thing she'd given him in the past.

His glance swept across Eric. The man was waiting for his response. What could he say? *Go ahead, screw the only woman I ever cared about.* He forced a shrug. "Why not? It doesn't hurt to ask."

"With every eye on my campaign, I've been afraid to ask any woman out." He shoved a hand through his thick blond hair. "Next thing you know, the papers will latch on to the relationship and make it sordid, or have me married before a preacher could say 'dearly beloved.'" Eric sighed. "I guess I'd better not. No use dragging Lucie through the media circus."

Quietly, Ben released the breath he'd been holding. "I'll just check your father's office for bugs."

"Thanks, Ben." Eric's smile was genuine, and a little sad. "I'm glad I can count on you."

"That's what friends are for." He opened the door to Jason Littington's office and stepped in. He stood several seconds, staring off into space, rubbing the lump on his head. *Did I really tell him to go for it?* With a sharp tap on the goose-egg-sized bump on his forehead, he sent pain stabbing through to his stupidity.

Hell. He'd rather poke a finger in his eye than see Lucie with another man.

***

Lucie stepped up to the guard's counter at Littington Enterprises. "Is Eric Littington in his office?"

In his crisp gray and blue uniform, Pascal Pasquale answered without looking up from his X-Men comic book. "Who wants to know?"

"Get real, Pascal." Lucie tugged the hem of her sleeveless powder-blue shirt, regretting her choice of clothing as her overlarge chest stretched the fabric all out of proportion. The matching skirt was too short and tight as well. She'd borrowed the outfit from Lisa's closet, wanting to attract Eric's attention and still look her best when he fell in love with her. "You know who I am. Is he in, or isn't he?"

When she quit fiddling with the shirt, she glanced up.

Pascal's gaze fixed on the disproportionate parts, and his mouth hung open like that of a whale trolling for plankton.

She closed her eyes and counted to five. Then she opened them and lifted Pascal's chin with the tip of her finger until his teeth snapped shut. Pasting on a flirty smile, she leaned over the top of the desk and purred, "Be a sweetie, and see if Eric is up in his office."

"He's up—he's in. Ah, hell, Lisa, why'd ya have to go and bend over like that?"

"I'm Lucie, not Lisa."

"Lucie? But you look like Lisa." Pascal's brows twisted over his nose.

Okay, so dressing like her sister might not have been the best idea.

The phone rang on the desk and Pascal fumbled to answer. "Littington Surprises—I mean Enterprises, may I help you?" He spun his chair, giving Lucie his back.

While Pascal negotiated his way through the phone call and queried Eric's office, Lucie drifted around the lobby. She checked her purse again for the clear pill bottle she'd scraped the ladybug into. The bottle was still there. The ladybug, with its strange, alien-like green glowing backside, climbed around the inside.

"Miss LeBieu."

Lucie spun toward the desk.

Pascal stood at attention, his eyes staring straight ahead, not at her.

He reminded her of one of the guards at the queen's palace in London. All he needed was the fuzzy hat and a red jacket to complete the image. Well, that and a haircut. You could take the Cajun out of the swamp, but you couldn't take the swamp out of the Cajun. "Mr. Littington will see you now. Take the elevators up to the fourth floor. First office on the right." The man had gone all business.

"Thanks." As she walked toward the elevator, Lucie caught Pascal's gaze sliding sideways, following her, his brows drawn together in a confusing mix of anger and longing. What the heck?

She stepped into the elevator, and as the doors closed, she turned to smile at Pascal. Not too much. She didn't want him to think she had any feelings for him other than friendship. In the fifth grade, she'd been nice to him on the playground. Afterward he'd clung to her like a leech. For the entire school year, he'd practically stalked her until her grandmother had threatened to put a hex on him.

No, getting mixed up in a stalker situation with Pascal wouldn't be good for her campaign to snag the bigger fish. Eric was her first-class ticket out of Bayou Miste.

And away from Ben...

As soon as the doors slid open on the fourth floor, butterflies attacked her stomach in a swarm. At the back of the elevator she hesitated. Did she really have the nerve to hex a man to get him to marry her? Had she no shame?

Guilt weighed on her conscience. Her hesitation stretched long enough that the door started sliding closed.

Did she want to stay in Bayou Miste indefinitely? A vision of Ben in the dim lighting of the Raccoon Saloon, smiling across the table at his buddy Eric swam into her head. She could just imagine him smiling across the table from his latest girlfriend, or wife, God forbid.

Her hand shot into the narrowing space between the two doors. The door continued closing, smashing her fingers. With a rush of adrenaline, she gripped the rubber edge with her free hand and pried it open, stepping through to the other side.

Well! A deep, shaky breath, a pat to the treasure in her purse, and she was ready for the next step in her journey. No doubt remained in her mind. This town wasn't big enough for her and Ben.

Her skin twitched at the thought of him moving on with his life without her. She couldn't stand it. No sir. She was better off making a clean break and starting a new life as the wife of a promising young politician on the rise. Imagine the people she'd meet, the galas she'd attend on Eric's arm.

The tight shoes and even tighter smiles she'd have to endure in the name of public appearances.

Her footsteps faltered in sympathetic anticipation of her social obligations and sore feet. If she didn't marry Eric, she'd be forced to leave Bayou Miste penniless and start over anyway—without a single familiar face or friend. Her shoulders straightened.

Her mother, Lynette LeBieu, had been content to move from place to place without money or support. Thank God she'd relented and dropped her and Lisa with her grandmother at the age of six. Otherwise, they would still be scrounging for their next meal, possibly out of a Salvation Army shelter, or worse, a trash can.

Ever since then, she had refused to leap without a net, and Eric Littington would make a terrific net. If she had to become a social icon, she could handle it. She was used to being gawked at. Her looks had garnered more than her fair share of tongue-lolling stares. She'd just have to class up her act a little.

Eric Littington. The letters were engraved in bold letters across the brass nameplate. The matching brass doorknob beckoned to her to open the door. She could hear a muffled voice through the thick oak panels. Maybe she should wait until Eric wasn't busy.

A little devil in the back of her head yelled, "Do it!"

Before she could lose her confidence, or maybe before she could regain her sanity, she knocked.

"Come in."

The brief, commanding words spurred her forward and into the room.

Cell phone to his ear, Eric stood with his back to her, speaking in short, clipped tones. "Yes, I'll be available tomorrow. Noon is fine. Please thank the mayor for me." He turned and glanced at Lucie, his eyebrows rising along with the curve of his lips. "Look, Bryan, I have someone in my office. No, I don't need you here. Take those days off I promised you. Yeah. Catch a big one for me, will ya? I'll be fine. Thanks." Eric hit the off button, shoved the phone into his pocket, and strode toward her. "Lucie, I didn't expect to see you here. To what do I owe the honor of this visit?"

She blinked twice, her mind a complete blank. Her real reason was to snag the eligible bachelor in a marriage merger, but she couldn't say that. As the silence between his question and her answer lengthened, she blurted, "I want to make a contribution to your campaign. But if you're too busy, I'll come back another time." Feet getting colder by the minute, she sensed yet another opportunity for escape, another chance to bow out gracefully before she committed another heinous Voodoo blunder. She backed toward the still-open door.

"No, of course I'm not too busy. However, my campaign manager usually handles the contributions."

"Can I leave my phone number for him?"

"Sure." Eric grabbed a card and pen from his desk and handed it to her.

After she'd jotted her number on the back, she smiled and handed it to Eric. "Call me sometime."

Eric reached out and grabbed her hands. "Please, stay. I've been thinking about you since I saw you at the Raccoon Saloon last night."

Warmth spread up her neck into her cheeks. *Just great*. He'd seen her in her waitress outfit. Not necessarily first lady or congressman's wife material...

She tried a carefree laugh that came out a pathetically nervous giggle. "Oh, that. Contrary to popular belief, I don't dress like that, normally. Nor do I engage in barroom fights on a regular basis." Wow, that sounded really bad. What congressional candidate even spoke to a woman who got into a barroom fight? She mentally kicked herself for succumbing to the need to deck LeRoy last night.

"What a shame." He smiled, his voice melting into her skin like heated butter. "It was the highlight of my evening."

Maybe there was still hope. "You mean you don't think less of me?" Lucie forced a flirty smile she didn't really feel.

With a grin smoothing across his face, he squeezed her hands. "I could never think badly of you." A devilish twinkle lit his eyes. "Not even if you took to the tabletops and stripped."

She matched his grin. "Sorry, not in my repertoire."

She hadn't known Eric well in school. Four years older than she, he'd gone off to a private boarding academy in New Orleans before she had gotten a chance to get to know him. She remembered he used to hang out with Ben at the Boyettes' house, but beyond that, he was a stranger.

His clear blue eyes smiled down at her. "Do I pass?"

For the second time in as many minutes, warmth flooded her cheeks. He was smart, but was he clairvoyant? Could he read her mind? Did he know she was after him as her future husband, the future father of her children? Her one-way ticket out of the swamps?

For once she was at a loss for words. She'd rehearsed her reason for being there, but now with the time at hand, those butterflies had turned into condors beating the insides of her belly with powerful wings. Her grandmother would say her conscience was warring with her.

The silence stretched longer and she still hadn't answered his question. "I'm sorry...what did you ask me?"

"Did I pass?"

"Oh yes! Of course!" Her brain kicked in gear and she coughed, initiating her plan. "I have a tickle in my throat. Do you happen to have some water?" She didn't have to fake the cough much. She'd almost choked on her lie.

Gran LeBieu would wash her mouth with soap if she knew Lucie was lying. Hell, she'd do a lot worse if she found out what her granddaughter was up to.

She knew her grandmother better than anyone else. Gran paraded her gruff, don't-mess-with-me attitude for the masses, but beneath her Voodoo queen persona was a heart of gold. The heart Lucie had grown to love and rely on.

Her grandmother also believed in what was right. And what she was about to do wasn't right. She knew that. But...what option did she have?

She glanced around the office, noting the solid mahogany desk, the smell of furniture polish, leather couches, and oil paintings. Her choices were simple—swamp or luxury.

Swamp. Luxury. Swamp. Luxury.

The tinkle of ice cubes clinking against crystal glass jerked her back to the present situation. With renewed determination, Lucie dug in her purse and removed the pill bottle.

As Eric, with his back to the room, poured water from a glass pitcher, she uncapped the bottle and stared down at her future.

CHAPTER 5

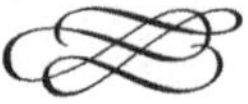

BEN MADE A COMPLETE SWEEP OF JASON LITTINGTON'S OFFICE AND FOUND nothing. No bugs, funky wires, or miniature cameras. On his way back through to speak with his friend, he reached for the doorknob and paused. Was that a feminine voice?

Eric wasn't alone.

And he'd recognize that sound anywhere. Lucie's voice drifted through the slight opening in the doorway between Eric's office and his father's.

What the hell? Ben's first instinct was to charge in and demand to know what she was doing there. Thank God his investigative instincts kicked in. He hovered near the door, out of sight. Wouldn't hurt to know why she was there to see Eric. He considered it part of his job to know who was spending time with the congressional candidate. How better to protect him?

And if he felt a little twinge of jealousy, he wouldn't let it affect his work. No sir. He was a professional. Even where Lucie LeBieu was concerned.

Especially where Lucie was concerned.

He peeked through the doorway.

Eric stood at the bar pouring water into a glass. Lucie had her back to Ben, digging in her purse.

With the barest nudge, he opened the door a little more. The hinge creaked. He ducked out of sight and peered through the narrow slit between the hinges like a young voyeur sneaking a peek into the girl's locker room. Only he was close to thirty. And Lucie stood in the other room, doing who knew what. Though, that outfit was nearly as skimpy as underwear...

Her digging stopped and she glanced back over her shoulder toward Eric, exposing her profile to Ben's view.

One hand shot out, and she shook a small plastic bottle over the massive mahogany desk.

Ben squinted, but couldn't see what, if anything, fell onto the polished wood.

"Here." Eric held out a glass of water to Lucie.

Without missing a beat, she turned and smiled, accepting the glass with one hand, while her other hand dropped the bottle in her purse. "Thank you, Eric." She walked toward the portrait behind the desk and pointed. "Who is that man?"

What the heck was she doing? Her finger pointed at the painting, but she wasn't looking at it. Instead, she scanned the top of the desk and the surrounding floor.

"That's my Grandfather Littington. He built this corporation from the ground up." Eric's shoulders pushed back and his chest swelled. "Despite the ugliness of the chemical spill—"

"Which wasn't your fault," Lucie cut in, a frown dipping between her eyes as she looked around.

"—the Littingtons have always strived to make this business one the community could be proud of."

Ben had heard this line before.

"Hey, you don't have to preach to me." Apparently, Lucie had heard it, too.

Eric cleared his throat and took her hands in his. "Sorry. That is actually part of the speech I'm giving tomorrow in Bayou Miste's town square."

Ben's fists tightened. Did Eric have to hold her hands so...so *much*?

Not that he cared, or anything.

The desk phone buzzed.

Eric sighed and dropped her hands. "I'm sorry, but do you mind if I answer?"

"No, go right ahead." Lucie rubbed her hands on her skirt. "Do you want me to wait out in the hallway?"

"No, stay right where you are." Eric winked, punched the speakerphone button, and stared across at her. "Yes?"

"Mr. Littington, the protesters are back at the gate." The secretary's voice called out over the intercom. "What do you want done? Should I call the police?"

"No, no. They have a right to protest." Eric lifted the receiver to his ear and punched off the speakerphone. He strode to the window and slid open the glass. A faint chant floated in. "So far, they don't appear to be violent. As long as they don't interfere with the employees coming in and out, leave them alone."

Ben didn't envy Eric's life. To deal with campaign opposition shenanigans was enough, but to answer to a swarm of irate environmentalists was double the pain-in-the-neck.

Hidden behind the door, he felt more and more the amateur sleuth than the special investigator. Where was the high-powered detective he was known as in Baton Rouge? Why was he lurking behind a door, spying on Lucie LeBieu when he should be out solving murder cases?

Fed up with himself and his grade-school techniques, he shifted to step around the door.

A movement caught his attention and he froze.

Lucie scooped a small speck off the desk and tossed it into the air over Eric's head. The spec spread its tiny wings and circled around, heading toward her, making an orbit around her head. Brows drawn together, Lucie flapped her hand, shooing the bug back at Eric.

Ben squinted. What kind of bug was it? And why was Lucie intent on directing it at Eric?

His attention still focused on the protest below, Eric remained oblivious to Lucie's erratic movements. "Did you tell him my father left for the day?" Eric said into the phone. He glanced back at Lucie.

She wiggled the fingers on her upraised arm and smiled, then clamped her arm down at her side.

Eric mouthed the word "sorry" before he turned back to the window. "No, he won't be available for comment today." His toe dug into the thick burgundy carpet, and then his foot stilled and his head shot up. "Me?" Another look back at Lucie.

She stood as still as a lurking alligator, a silly, innocent smile pasted on her face. When Eric wasn't looking, her eyes shifted upward, searching for the insect.

What was she up to? He shifted to get a better view of the entire room.

"Okay, okay, I'll be right down." Eric clicked a button on the phone and tossed it onto his desktop. Running a hand through his hair, he stepped up to Lucie. "I'm sorry, Lucie. Since my father isn't here, they want me to come down and say a few words to the demonstrators."

"Is it the group that's been carrying signs all over Bayou Miste?" Lucie asked.

"Yeah. They won't leave unless I talk with the reporter."

"Don't they know Littington Enterprises is paying for the cleanup?"

"Yeah, but any time chemical pollution is mentioned, the environmentalists see it as an opportunity for publicity." He grimaced. "If I don't say something, they could paint an unfavorable picture of my campaign."

"They could make it ugly even if you do say something."

"True, but at least I won't have ignored them." He caught her hands in his. "Will you wait here for me? I really wanted a chance to talk to you."

Her gaze swept the room, her eyes rolling upward until they fixed on the bug circling over her and Eric's heads. A smile spread across her face and she stared back into Eric's eyes. "If you want me to stay, I'll stay."

He squeezed her hands and let go, hurrying out of the office. "I'll only be a few minutes," he called over his shoulder, the elevator's beep ringing out in the hallway.

Ben took the opportunity to breathe deeply.

Good. With Eric out of the room, he had a chance to find out what Lucie was up to.

As soon as the office door swung closed, Ben eased out of the other room.

With her back to him, Lucie swung at the winged creature flying over her head. "Come here, little ladybug," she said in a fierce whisper. "Can't have you getting loose."

The bug altered directions and flew straight at Ben.

He stared at the flying insect. What was all Lucie's fuss about a harmless ladybug?

The woman in question spun on her heel in hot pursuit. When she saw him standing there, she planted both feet in the thick carpet, almost toppling over. "You!"

Her surprise was worth the tedious wait behind the door. A deep-throated laugh rushed up from his throat and almost erupted when the ladybug collided with his forehead. The red and black spotted critter dropped to the rug, almost blending in with the maroon-and-black Persian carpet.

He squatted and scooped the bug into his palm.

"Oh crap, oh crap." Lucie danced around next to him, wringing her hands. Then she shoved her hand beneath his nose. "Give me that."

With her fingers wiggling in his face, he bunched his fist, trapping the ladybug in his palm. Rising slowly to his feet, he studied her wide-eyed, flushed face. "Now, what would you be doing in Eric's office with a ladybug, Lucie LeBieu?"

"I'm here visiting Eric, of course." She shoved her hand out to him again. "I just wanted to catch the bug and take it outside where it belonged, that's all." Bright pink flags of color flew high on her cheekbones.

"Lucie, Lucie, Lucie." Ben shook his head, his hand still firmly clutching the bug. "Your face gives you away. You're lying, aren't you?"

"No!" Dark brows drew downward. "Oh, keep the damned bug. I have to get back to work."

With an exaggerated sigh, he glanced at his watch. "At two o'clock? Raccoon Saloon doesn't open until 7:00 p.m." Ben *tsked* his tongue. "Another lie? And you just promised Eric you'd stay until he got back. That makes three."

"Shove it, Ben Boyette. If you'd just give me the darn bug, I'll be leaving."

Instead of complying with her demand, he circled around her, moving in slow, deliberate steps. "You haven't answered my question. What are you doing in Eric's office?"

"It's none of your business." Lucie crossed her arms over her chest, her chin tilting up at a stubborn angle. "Besides, why should you care?" She reached out and flicked the bright red ant embroidered on his blue uniform. "You're just the exterminator."

Score one for the swamp witch. Direct hit to the ego. "Seems like this was the same argument we had seven years ago."

"Yeah, and what did it buy you? You're back in Bayou Miste. Why didn't you stay gone?"

"Maybe—" He stepped closer until his face was only two inches from hers. Her floral fragrance assailed his senses. How well he remembered that scent. The impact hit him like a football tackle to his knee joints. He shook his head and moved closer.

She threw back her shoulders and lifted her chin. The bayou princess wasn't backing down. He almost grinned. He liked it when she was feisty. She wasn't scared of him or anyone else.

But she *was* bothered. Her breath quickened, as evidenced by the rise and fall of her breasts beneath the light-blue, low-cut shirt.

He smoothed the back of his knuckles along her neck and down to her collarbone. "Maybe I missed you."

For half a second, she stood as if transfixed, her eyes wide, her breathing halted altogether. Then she snorted, a very unladylike sound. "When alligators fly, maybe. Ben Boyette, you're so full of it." She stepped back two paces and held out her hand. "Are you going to give me that bug, or what?"

The back of his hand still tingling, he had to reevaluate his position.

Perhaps it hadn't been such a good idea to touch Lucie. All the images invoked only laid open an old wound he wasn't willing to expose.

Not here. Not now.

He'd spent the better part of the past seven years trying to shake the residual effects of Hurricane Lucie from his life. Touching her, feeling the warmth of her skin against his, was like stoking an eternal flame. How the hell was he going to put it out?

She stood there, her dark brown eyes shining bright, her hair slipping from the clip holding it behind her head. If he tweaked it just once, all that long, glorious black hair would slip free and tumble over her shoulders like so many times before.

"Well?" she demanded, her hand still out, palm upward, her deep brown eyes revealing a little... What? Desperation?

His fingers loosened and he almost caved in. But he stopped himself in time and clenched his hand around his prize.

No. He wouldn't be lured into the eye of the storm again. Having weathered the turbulence once was more than enough for any man. He had to put some space between them. "If you just want to let the bug loose, let me do it for you." Ben strode toward the window. He shoved his hand through the opening, his fist still closed. "Here goes."

"No!" Lucie dove for him, slamming her body against his, grabbing for his hand.

Staggering against her attack, he opened his fingers.

The ladybug slipped free and dropped out of the window, falling...falling...

She lunged for the insect, grasping at air, her body tilting over the window ledge.

He caught her around the middle to keep her from following the bug. Like a punch in the gut, the warmth of her skin and flowery scent of her shampoo bombarded his senses once again. He fought the urge to pull her close and kiss her senseless. Just like old times.

For a moment he let his memories wash over him. Lucie in his arms felt so natural, so right. In a second, his resolve turned to mush, his muscles went slack.

Oh, no. He clenched his teeth. *Not again.* Not Lucie. *She'd* rejected *him,* not the other way around.

Thank goodness all her attention was fixed on the bug's descent. Otherwise she couldn't have missed the blatant evidence of the surge of emotions and testosterone coursing through his body.

She sagged against his arms and tipped her head backward against his chest. "Oh, no," she moaned. "Not again."

CHAPTER 6

ALL HER FRIENDS' WARNINGS PUMMELED AGAINST LUCIE'S CONSCIENCE, with the ultimate mantra, *Don't do it!* reverberating through her skull.

Too late.

The ladybug had delivered its magic to Eric. Now, thanks to Ben, it was loose on the entire town of Bayou Miste.

Ben.

Holy swamp rats, Ben! Her eyes popped open and she glanced down at the arms encircling her waist. Strong, memorable arms. Arms that had held her in passionate embraces on more than one occasion. Arms encased in a bug exterminator's coverall. How ironic. She'd delivered her spell with a bug, and Ben was an exterminator. How fitting.

For a brief moment, she leaned against his chest, savoring the once-familiar warmth she'd enjoyed.

But this was Ben. Ben Boyette. The man who thought she was no better than her sister. A tease.

As if burned, she slapped at Ben's arms, shoving them away. She dashed halfway across the room and stopped, gasping for air from lungs too tight to breathe. "Don't ever touch me again."

His eyes narrowed slightly before he leaned against the window encasement. "Next time, I'll let you jump." He pushed away from the wall and strode toward her. "What were you doing with the bug anyway?"

"Nothing." Her face burned and she looked away from his perceptive gaze. Why couldn't she control her blushes?

"Tsk, tsk." Ben touched a finger to her chin. "Didn't your grandmother tell you lying gives you warts?"

Her breath caught in her throat. His hand against her skin sent fiery sparks straight to the pit of her stomach. "No, it doesn't," she whispered, the warmth of her breath bouncing off his skin to caress her cheek. Her hands rose to push him away. Instead, they rested against the solid wall of muscles.

"Are you willing to take the risk?" Ben leaned closer, his lips a mere inch from hers.

Like a hummingbird drawn to the sweet center of a flower petal, she leaned closer until her lips touched his.

His mouth covered hers, his tongue warring, twisting, tasting, and sliding in and out in a primal imitation of more intimate acts. His hands smoothed down her arms to cup her buttocks, pulling her hips against his.

She gasped into his mouth, the rigid evidence of his desire prodding her belly through the thin fabrics of his coverall and her skirt.

Her blood burned molten hot, coursing through her veins to pool at the juncture of her thighs, moistening her panties. With her heart thundering in her chest and ears, every nerve ending tautened, expectant...ready for more.

Ben broke off the kiss and pressed his lips to her temple, his racing pulse a testament to how the kiss had affected him. After a long pause, he tongued her ear, then whispered, "So, what do you want...with Eric?"

Her red-hot blood froze in midstream. Talk about your alligator pits. What was she doing, kissing *Ben*?

She jerked away and turned her back to him, buying time for her traitorous body to calm. "What's it to you?" she answered flippantly, when she felt anything but flippant. Her brain still wasn't functioning coherently. How could one simple kiss throw her so completely off track?

Who'd he think he was to come strolling in here after seven years? Did he think he could just pick up where they left off? Well, he had another think coming.

Her hands strayed across the surface of Eric's desk and she lifted a paperweight of solid brass, weighing it in her hand. This little gem could put a dent in a man's head the size of Cleveland. Her fingers curled around the cold metal. Oh, the satisfaction of bonking the oaf in the head.

Ben moved a few steps away, as if recognizing the danger of standing within range of the lethal desk ornament. A sly smile quirked the corner of his mouth, as if he knew he'd scored a hit on Lucie's sensitivities.

All the more reason to throw the paperweight at him. The louse deserved a dent in his head for confusing her so badly.

Then, as innocent as could be, he asked again, "Go home, Lucie."

"Look, I have a right to visit anyone I please."

As if ignoring her last outburst, he continued, "You can't possibly represent the protesters outside." He shook his head. "No, they're not really your style."

"Them?" Like he really thought she'd be out in some useless picket line. Ha! But she'd play his game. "Those people don't even live here. Everyone in town knows Littington Enterprises will make good on their promise."

"Then why are you here?"

Back to the original question. With a dramatic down-sweep of eyelashes, a move she'd mastered at the age of three, thanks to her twin sister, Lucie let her lips curl slow and sexy. "Do I have to have a reason to visit Eric, other than, well, he's Eric?" If that kiss had as much impact on him as it had on her, her question would find its mark.

Ben's Adam's apple bobbed once before his mouth settled into a tight line. "Leave him alone."

She'd scored on Ben and she wasn't backing down now. With slow, deliberate steps, one foot in front of the other, designed to take full advantage of feminine hip action, she stalked her prey. The vamp walk was another legacy from her infamous sister, Lisa.

Toe-to-toe, she stood before him and walked her fingers up his chest. Let him suffer a little of his own medicine. "What? Are you jealous of Eric? Afraid he might find me attractive?"

Ben grabbed her hand, squeezing hard.

"Let go." She struggled to free her hand.

He only squeezed tighter. "Stay away from him, do you hear?"

"Why should I?"

Every time she tugged, her chest bumped against Ben's arms. The tips of her breasts pushed out, forming little peaks against the powder-blue shirt she'd specifically chosen for her meeting with Eric. What had been the most subdued outfit in her sister's closet suddenly became a reminder of what she'd always tried so hard to avoid—looking like the swamp trash everyone in Bayou Miste thought she and her sister were.

Well, to hell with them, and to hell with Ben Boyette. *Eric* was her future. Her knight in shining armor, sent to pull her out of the swamp and into the life she wished to become accustomed to. And that damned ladybug better have gotten the point across!

An awful thought suddenly occurred to Lucie. In order for the ladybug to distribute its magic, it had to circle the heads of the spell's victims—er, subjects. In this bug's case, it had circled the heads of Eric, Lucie, *and* Ben. Which meant...

She'd cast a spell on not one, but *two* men. *Double* damn.

She hoped Eric would fall in love with her, but she didn't want anything to do with Ben. Besides, she didn't want his love if it came by way of magic. Wow, she could be in a very deep bayou bog if *both* men fell in love with her.

And the bug was loose on the town!

Ben dropped her hand.

Why did all her spells always end up this way? She should know better by now. But *noooo*. She *had* to try it. And then she had to go and kiss Ben, ruining seven years of attempting to forget him. She beat the heel of her palm against her forehead. "Stupid! Stupid! Stupid!"

Ben grabbed her wrist to keep her from hitting herself yet again. "What is your problem?"

She shoved her palms against his chest. "You! You're my problem." With more force than the last nudge, she shoved him again.

He clasped her hands in his. "What are you talking about?"

Anger at her sorry attempts at magic, anger at her inept attempts to make a life for herself, anger at how he'd never come back for her, all boiled up inside her. She hated that every time she got really mad, she'd do something even stupider—she'd cry.

And sure enough, tears trembled on her eyelashes now. But she refused to give in to them, to let Ben see her upset.

"Why did you have to come back into my life and mess everything up, again? Why?"

A smile quirked the corners of his mouth upward and his eyes twinkled. "Seems to me you're quite capable of messing it up all on your own."

She could fall into those eyes. Just as she had when she was nineteen and gullible. *Get a grip!* She yanked her hands free and grabbed her purse. "Yeah, and sometimes I get a little help from so-called friends. See ya around, bug man."

Without looking back, she raced through the door. She had to catch that ladybug before it spread around more magic. All she needed was for Bayou Miste to be involved in a giant love fest. Wouldn't her grandmother be pleased?

Not!

***

"Hey, what happened in here?" Eric strode into his office, with a backward glance at the elevator door sliding shut behind him.

"I'm not exactly sure." Ben's head spun like he'd been popped by an alligator tail. What had Lucie meant by he'd messed up everything? Again? Hell, *she'd* messed up *his* life seven years ago, not the other way around. She'd toyed with his heart and left it sadly scarred.

"Something must have happened. Lucie blew by me like the building was on fire." Eric frowned at Ben. "Did she say anything? Did you?"

"No." He didn't like lying, but what Lucie had said didn't make much sense, at least not anything worth repeating. "Maybe she had another appointment."

"At least she gave me her phone number." Eric held up a business card. "I'm going to ask her out."

The punch in his gut didn't help the indigestion Ben was working on. "You sure you want to do that?"

"Why not?"

He knew he should stay out of this swamp goo, but he couldn't help himself. Something about Lucie dating Eric bothered him. Bothered him a lot. "She doesn't quite seem the type a congressional candidate would date."

"Oh, you mean her reputation?" Eric waved a hand as if pushing aside the issue. "I'm not worried about that. I think she's smart and spunky. Actually, she's just what a congressman's wife needs to be."

"Aren't you afraid rumors will spread?" Ben persisted when he should have dropped the matter.

"You and I both know how rumors have a way of being blown out of proportion." Eric grinned. "Besides, I like her and want to get to know her better. I still remember her as the skinny little girl from the swamp some eleven years ago. Wow, has she changed, or what? She's pretty amazing."

Amazing was just a part of the picture. Add to her résumé rude, mouthy, and entirely too sexy. Every man in the parish found it hard to keep his hands off her curves. As evidenced by that redneck LeRoy's attempt to grab her at the Raccoon Saloon the previous evening. But Eric wasn't listening. The man was practically drooling.

Ben clenched his teeth to avoid emitting another negative comment about the fair Lucie. If Eric wanted her, let him have her.

Why did that thought roil around in his belly like food poisoning, and make him want to punch something or someone? He needed to get out of the office and into some fresh air before he slammed a fist through the wall. "Whatever. I've made my sweep. No wires or bugs."

"Thanks, Ben." Eric held out his hand. "You don't know how much it means to me to know you're watching my back."

How could he stay mad at the guy? Anger over a woman, especially one as untrustworthy as Lucie, was ludicrous. He took the proffered hand and shook it a little harder than he meant, the lingering sting of Lucie's seven-year-old rejection still festering in his chest. Eric deserved better than Lucie. And Lucie deserved someone who could go toe-to-toe with her and not back down.

Someone like Ben.

Eric strode to the window and stared down. "What the heck is she doing down there?"

"Who?" Ben moved up beside him.

Lucie pushed through the crowd congregated in front of the gates of Littington Enterprises. From the distance, she appeared to be leaping at intervals and swatting at the air.

He suspected she was chasing the bug he'd let loose. Something wasn't right about her obsession with that bug. "I think I'll go down and find out what she's up to."

"Me, too."

"No, really. Don't you have work to do, or don't you need to manage your campaign, or something?"

"Ben Boyette, if I didn't know you better, I'd think you were trying to get rid of me. Do you have a thing for Lucie LeBieu?"

"No." His answer was short, his lips tight around the single word. At one time, his answer would have been entirely different. But not now.

"Are you sure?" Eric's brow furrowed. He stared from the erratic path Lucie followed back to Ben. "I mean, I wouldn't stand in your way, if you wanted to go after her. You probably know her better than I do."

Oh, yeah. He knew her better than he'd ever let Eric know. Besides, Eric was more Lucie's type. He had everything going for him. He'd be "good enough" for Lucie, unlike Ben. That's probably why she'd been in Eric's office to begin with. She'd set her sights on the young politician. "No, I'm sure. You can have her." *She wouldn't have me, anyway*. "You go. I'll stay here and check out a few more things before I leave."

"If you're sure." Eric grabbed the navy blazer neatly hung on the coat rack and raced for the door. "We'll talk later."

***

"Come here, you creepy little bug!" Lucie leaped as high as she could in heels and a short skirt. She'd had to leave her turquoise-blue 1967 Mustang convertible parked in the lot inside the gates of Littington Enterprises in order to chase the spellbound bug on foot.

It flew around the protesters, thank goodness, avoiding the potential for a really messy love fest. She had raced out the gates, charging through the picket line to chase the stupid creature.

And did the love bug head into the swamp like most self-respecting creatures of nature?

No.

The shiny, red, spotted insect with the alien-like greenish glow was headed straight down Highway 9 to Bayou Miste, a stretch of the legs—three miles—from the Littington compound.

A mile and a half down the road, she pulled off her shoes and started throwing them at the bug. "Die, you little beast!" The blister on her big toe and the stone bruise on her left heel slowed her progress to a crawl. Sweat trickled down her forehead into her eyes, blinding her.

The sound of a vehicle approached from behind. She inched off the road into the tall grass, hoping like hell she wasn't stepping off the edge into a muddy ditch, or worse, onto an angry water moccasin. She didn't mind snakes, except when she couldn't see them.

She brushed the perspiration from her stinging eyes and looked up.

A silver BMW sports car rolled to a stop beside her, the passenger window sliding smoothly down.

"Need a ride?"

She leaned over to peer into the dark leather interior of the car to see Eric's smiling face, shining like a ray of hope in the black world of sore feet and hopeless pursuit.

"Oh, yes, please." She melted into the cool leather seat and turned the air vents to blow full blast on her heated skin.

"Where to?"

Oh yeah, the damned bug.

Lucie stopped just short of saying, "Follow that bug!" Instead she nodded calmly, while her insides knotted like a twisted grapevine. "I was headed for town." Her cheeks warmed despite the cool air blowing on them. It was just a little white lie. After all, she was following a bug that was heading for town. Close enough.

With a confused smile, Eric stepped on the gas and the BMW shot forward.

Lucie peered through the windshield, straining to see the ladybug as they blew by. She caught a glimpse of fluorescent green. Good, the bug was still heading for Bayou Miste. If she got ahead of it, maybe she could catch it before it made it all the way into town.

"Why didn't you take your car?" Eric asked.

With an inward curse, Lucie could feel her cheeks burn in anticipation of her next lie. "I was afraid I wouldn't make it through the picket line. Besides, I felt like walking." She grimaced. "Until I went half a mile in these heels. I'll come back to get my 'Stang later."

"The blue Mustang convertible I saw in the parking lot? Nice car."

"Yeah." Lucie loved her little blue car. "My grandmother gave it to me when I learned to drive. It used to be hers."

"Where can I drop you?" Eric asked as they whizzed by the first few houses on the edge of the little community.

Her eye on the rearview mirror, Lucie squirmed around. "Park at the marina, there on the right."

As if landing a spaceship on glass, Eric slowed to a halt on the gravel parking lot outside Thibodeaux Marina.

Before he shifted the powerful sports car into park, she jumped out of the passenger seat, hopping into her high heels, one foot at a time, while lurching back the way they'd come. If she hurried, she could catch the bug before it entered town, spreading misplaced magic on unsuspecting residents.

Boy, Gran LeBieu would have a coronary if she ever found out about her itty-bitty spell.

"Wait!" Eric called out through his opened window. "Where are you going?"

Lucie stopped when she realized how nutty she must look. She turned and pasted a calm smile on the straining muscles of her face. "I see someone I need to talk to. If I don't hurry, I won't catch it—er, him. Call me tonight."

No more time. She had to find that bug. She spun on her heels, sliding a little in the gravel. Then, giving up on a dignified exit, she raced off in a cross between a power-walk and an all-out jog down the rough road leading back out of town.

Not far ahead of her, two carloads of protesters pulled up in front of the Cussin' Cajun, Bayou Miste's only diner. As the young men and women unloaded, signs and all, they stretched across the street, blocking Lucie's path.

A flash of fluorescent green winging past the far side of the diner sent a rush of adrenaline through her flagging body. "Excuse me, pardon me." She pushed her way through the crowd, her gaze focused on the ladybug.

"Hey, Lucie! Where ya goin'?" someone shouted from the steps of the diner.

She struggled to see over the tops of the protesters' signs. Alex and Calliope stood framed in the doorway of the restaurant.

"No time to talk!" she shouted back, dodging around a man pulling a huge sign off the seat of a gas-guzzling, mammoth SUV. She almost choked on a snort when he swung around, nearly clipping her with the sign that read "Down with Oil."

With her head tipped to the side, Calliope called out, "What're you doing?"

"Chasing after George Clooney. What the hell do you think I'm doing?" She didn't slow as the bug flew over the top of the little two-bedroom cottage Maurice Saulnier shared with his grandmother, heading south.

People edged past Calliope and Alex, easing their way into the crowded diner.

"I didn't know George was in town," Calliope called out over the protesters' heads.

"He's not, you idiot," Alex said. "Lucie's probably after the you-know-what."

"What?" Calliope said. "You mean George isn't in town?"

Lucie didn't have time to wait for Alex to explain to Calliope that she was chasing the love bug, nor did she have time to wait for her friends to catch up. Kicking off her high-heeled sandals, she leaped over the low fence beside the Saulnier house.

Piercing yelps erupted next to her, and she almost jumped back over the fence. At the risk of losing sight of the bug, she glanced downward and did a double take. A cotton-candy-pink toy poodle danced around her ankles, yipping at the top of her little lungs.

"Who's that out there?" Ouida Saulnier poked her head around the back screen door. Her normally soft white hair was dyed the same startling pink color as the poodle's.

"It's just me, Granny," Lucie reassured the older woman. Ouida Saulnier wasn't Lucie's grandmother, but everyone in Bayou Miste called her Granny.

"Lisa LeBieu, what are you doing in my backyard?" Granny stepped out on the porch and planted her bony fists on her equally bony hips. "You chasin' after my grandson, Maurice?"

"No, ma'am," Lucie shouted over the deafening noise of the powder puff poodle. "And I'm Lucie, not Lisa."

The bug landed on a white rose next to the porch handrail. If she could just get close enough to snatch it.

"FeFe, hush!" Granny snapped.

Without missing a single beat, FeFe turned her back on Granny and continued yapping.

Lucie inched toward the old woman. "How have you been, Granny? Is your arthritis still givin' you trouble?"

"Quit tryin' to change the subject. You know my arthritis always gives me trouble." Granny leaned forward, her eyes narrowed. "I still wanna know what the fool-darn-heck yer doin' in my backyard."

"I was—" She grasped for a reason that would satisfy Granny when the bug opened the hard casing enclosing its wings and took off past the rose bushes, the hydrangeas, and over the slats of the thigh-high picket fence. "Sorry, I can't stay and chat. Gotta go! By the way, I love the new hair color. Say hi to Mo for me."

With a smile, Granny patted a hand to her pink hair, then her mouth turned downward. "I will not tell Maurice hi for a no-'count floozy. You got no business but bad business, messin' around with Maurice. I've a good mind to tell your *Mamère* what you're up to, I do. No decent girl—"

Lucie whipped through the garden gate and chased off after the bug, leaving Granny, who was in full lecture mode, in her wake. For some reason, Granny couldn't get it through her head that Lisa was Lucie's twin, and Lisa was the troublesome twin. Usually. Although the love bug incident might prove to be equally troublesome, if Lucie didn't get it off the streets.

She rounded the corner of the Saulnier house and spotted the ladybug halfway across the road, heading toward the marina and the open swamp beyond. Between her and the bug stood Eric.

With his back to her, he leaned against his BMW, his cell phone pressed to his ear.

Good. Maybe he wouldn't see her making a complete fool of herself chasing after a stupid bug. She raced across the road, gaining ground on the insect, swatting at the air with her shoe while keeping an eye on Eric.

When the love bug flew out over the docks, she thought for sure she'd lost it. How could she manage to catch a bug in the vastness of the swamp? But the menace landed on a solid wooden post used to tie off the boats Joe Thibodeaux rented out to visiting fisherman.

If she sneaked up on the bug, she had a chance. But how to get past Eric standing in the parking lot?

Crouching close to the corner of a nearby house, Lucie chewed on her thumbnail.

"Boo!"

Lucie jumped straight up and spun around.

Calliope and Alex stood behind her, both sporting huge grins.

"Don't scare me like that," she hissed.

"Why are you hiding behind a house?" Calliope asked in a voice loud enough to raise the dead.

"Shh!" Lucie pressed a hand to her lips and pointed toward Eric. "He probably already thinks I'm a complete flake."

"Where's the bug?" Alex stepped around Calliope.

"Out there on the dock."

"Look, I'll distract Eric. You and Calliope catch the bug." Alex didn't wait for a response. She stepped out from the side of the house and strode across the parking lot toward Eric.

"Eric? Eric Littington? I haven't seen you in a coon's age." Alex strolled across the street, darting a glance backward.

Eric turned toward her, a smile curling up the corners of his mouth. He lifted a finger and mouthed, "One moment." He turned back around and spoke into his phone, then clicked it off and once more turned his baby blues on Alex.

Lucie shook her head. Eric really was a good-looking man. A cross between Matthew McConaughey and John F. Kennedy, he had the kind of looks a girl could swoon over. In fact, any woman would be proud to be his wife.

Alex hooked his arm and managed to turn his back to Lucie and Calliope.

"Come on, let's go." Calliope slipped away from the house and ran toward the dock.

With little else stopping her now, Lucie took off after her. Maybe Calliope should have distracted Eric. She wasn't the most coordinated individual, and she was prone to disaster. Her name really should have been Calamity.

Lucie increased her pace, her bare feet taking a beating on the gravel. She reached the dock an inch before Calliope and pushed ahead toward the post where the bug still rested. As she reached out to snatch the creature, it lifted off and hovered over the water, just off the side of the wood decking.

She leaned out to grab the bug when Calliope caught up, stopping too fast to keep from plowing into her.

All her weight shifting from the dock to teetering over the water, Lucie grabbed for Calliope...and missed. Gravity took over and she fell, hitting the water in a painful belly flop that knocked the wind out of her lungs.

Water closed over her as she plummeted downward among old beer cans, plastic bottles, and a faded tennis shoe. Jeez, maybe the environmentalists had a point... Scrambling to an upright position, she pushed her bare feet into the murky green silt, cringing as muck curled around her toes. When she had her feet firmly beneath her, her lungs burning for air, she pushed off the bottom with enough force to launch her head a foot out of the water. She gasped and inhaled deeply, sucking in as much fresh air as she could before she sank below the oily surface.

When she came up this time, a white flotation ring slapped into the swamp next to her and she hooked her arm around it.

Calliope stood with her hands pressed to her mouth, her eyes wide. "Oops. Sorry!"

With a few swear words poised on her lips, Lucie glared up at her friend, rewriting the old adage, "With friends like Calliope, who needs enemies?"

And to top her humiliation, Eric and Alex pounded across the wooden planks of the dock, grinding to a halt beside Calliope.

Eric squatted on the dock and extended his hand. "Grab hold." In one smooth tug, he hauled her up and out, to stand in the circle of his arms. Strong, virile arms. Arms encased in an oh-so-expensive suit!

She gasped and backed away, her blouse and skirt no longer a smooth powder-blue, but an icky, green-slimed, fishy-smelling mess.

Holy swamp gas! What more could go wrong?

CHAPTER 7

"I CAN'T BELIEVE YOU KNOCKED ME INTO THE SWAMP." LUCIE PLOPPED down in the wooden swing on Alex's back porch. "In front of Eric, no less." In a borrowed terry cloth bathrobe, she stared at the remains of Lisa's best shirt and skirt draped across the railing. She didn't know why she'd bothered rinsing the fishy smell out of them—the fabric was ruined. Lisa would kill her. With renewed vigor, she scrubbed at her hair with the soft white towel. No use poking at a dead crab.

"I said I was sorry." Calliope sat in a folding lawn chair several feet away, her arms crossed over her chest and a frown pushing her auburn eyebrows to a point over her nose. "It's not like I did it on purpose." Her frown disappeared and she jumped from her chair. "You want me to dry your hair for you?"

How could she be mad for long when Calliope meant only the best? The redhead couldn't help that every time she tried to assist, she ended up making things worse. Calliope had always been her friend, even in high school when other girls called Lucie the Bayou Bimbo and refused to talk to her, just because her twin was such a tease.

Lucie slid to the side, making room for Calliope. As loyal a friend as they came. Clumsy, maybe, but loyal. Calliope was a lot like Alex's golden retriever, Sport.

Snatching the towel from her hands, Calliope rubbed at Lucie's long black hair. "Sure smells better than it did before the shower."

"Anything smells better than I did before I showered," she groused, unwilling to let go of her anger.

"So, Lucie, when are you going to tell Gran LeBieu?"

She tensed at Alex's abrupt question. "I'm not."

"Don't tell me you think you can figure your way out of this mess without her." Alex leaned forward, resting her elbows on her knees, a tea glass grasped between her hands, dripping condensation onto the wooden floor. "That bug is still out there somewhere, causing who knows what kind of damage."

"I don't care." She knew she sounded defensive, but the lingering tingle of Ben's kiss just wouldn't go away. And she hated that uncontrollable surge of desire she got every time she thought about him. "I want out of this swamp, and that bug is the only hope I had. Besides, it'll surface again. I just know it."

"Yeah, after it curses half the town. No telling what'll happen." Alex set her iced tea on the table beside her and dangled her hand over the side of her chair, patting the golden retriever panting quietly at her feet. "You really should tell your grandmother."

Lucie sat with her lips pursed shut. What could she say? *I screwed up? Gran LeBieu, please bail me out, again?*

No way.

The cordless phone beside Alex rang, giving Lucie a temporary reprieve from her friend's lecture.

Instead of answering, Alex let it ring four times until the answering machine just inside the door picked up.

"Alex? Pick up the phone. This is your mother."

"As if I couldn't tell by her voice." Alex heaved a giant sigh.

"I know you're there. I saw you and your friends going into your house on my way home from getting my hair done." A pause. "Calliope, honey, pick up the phone since Alex won't."

Dropping the towel on the seat, Calliope rose to honor Mrs. Boyette's command.

Alex leaped from the lounge chair and blocked Calliope's path.

"Don't you dare. You will not answer that phone."

"Why not?" Calliope backed up a couple steps, her eyes widening. "It's your mother, for heaven's sake."

"Exactly. She'll try to foist some poor unsuspecting fool on me again. She never gives up."

"Is she still setting up blind dates for you?" Lucie asked.

"Hell, yeah." Alex leaned her head back against the doorframe, rubbing her temples. "Like I said, she never gives up."

"Just tell her to back off." Calliope took up the towel again and sat beside Lucie.

With a pointed look at Calliope, Alex said, "You know my mother. Until I'm"—she crooked her fingers, making a quote motion—"'safely married,' she won't quit dragging men off the street for me."

Lucie grabbed the towel from Calliope and continued drying her own hair. "Maybe I should have your mother work for me instead of you."

"Believe me, you don't want that." Alex squatted next her golden retriever and ruffled his ears. "Right, Sport? My mamma is the matchmaking queen of the parish. Once she's set her sights on you, you either succumb and marry the latest offering, or kill yourself trying to avoid her other so-called candidates."

Sport's tail thumped against the floor and he reached his foot-long tongue out to lay a big wet kiss on Alex's chin.

Lucie squirmed. She liked dogs, but not in her face. "Have you tried talking to your mother?"

"Till I'm blue in the face." Alex straightened. "But we're not here to talk about me. You've got bigger problems. Since the love bug has hexed two men, one being my unwitting brother, I think you really need to consider calling this whole thing off and undo the spell."

"I can't," Lucie said.

"Why not?" Alex demanded.

"I think the spell is already working." Lucie ducked her head beneath the towel. "Eric seems interested."

"I'd say." Calliope practically bounced on the wooden slats of the swing. "Did you see how he looked at you on the dock? If that isn't love, I don't know what is."

"Hell, he couldn't keep his eyes or his tongue in his head. What red-blooded male could when you could see everything beneath her clothes?" Alex always had a way of bringing Lucie and Calliope back to earth.

Lucie's cheeks heated. "A good thing Eric had the decency to lend me his blazer."

"And providing a good excuse to see him again, huh?" Alex nodded, a conspiratorial smile curving her lips.

"Eric sure is dreamy, isn't he?" Calliope leaned back on the swing, her hands pressed to her chest. "I could go for that one. A regular Adonis, he is."

"Yeah, but Lucie also has that other problem," Alex said.

Lucie's stomach clenched. "Ben." That amazing kiss in Eric's office still hadn't worn off. Even after being tossed in the drink, her lips sizzled. *Damn Ben.* It had taken her seven long years to get over him for a reason, it seemed.

"Oh, yeah, Ben." Calliope tipped her head to the side, her smile soft and dreamy. "You should go for Ben. I've always liked the way that one little lock of hair falls down across his forehead. Mmm. Makes him look dangerous and mega-sexy."

"Ugh!" Alex stuck her tongue out. "You're talking about my brother."

Lucie stared out across Bayou Miste without seeing the houses and streets. Instead she remembered Ben's hair and how she couldn't keep her hands out of it when they were younger and so very in love.

Hold it! Back up, regroup. Not love, but lust. What they'd had could only be classified as lust. Wasn't it?

Considering how quickly he'd left, and how long it'd taken him to come back, it must have been.

Leaping from the swing, Lucie almost flipped Calliope over the back. "No, I'm not going for Ben. What we had seven years ago is long over."

"Yeah, except you forgot one thing." Alex crossed her arms over her chest.

"He thinks I'm pond scum, a bayou bimbo like my sister. What more do I need to remember?"

"Your little bug put a spell on my brother, too. No matter what happened when you were nineteen, Ben's going to fall in love with you, anyway."

"Falling in love won't change his opinion of me." With a moan, Lucie paced across the porch. "I don't need this complication to my plan. Not now."

"You're pretty much stuck with it." Alex plunked her fists on her hips. "You've got two men in love with you—via magic—and it's not fair to either one of them. Shame on you, Lucie LeBieu."

"You sound like *Mamère*." She hung her head for just a moment and then raised it, her chin jutting out. "I'm not ready to call in the big guns. I can handle this by myself."

Alex rolled her eyes. "Yeah, like you did today?"

"So, I fell in the swamp." She tossed the towel on the rail beside her outfit. "No one got hurt."

"You mean, not yet." Alex pointed a finger at Lucie. "And, you still don't have the bug under control."

"No, but I will. I'll go out tomorrow before work and look for it."

"Are there any instructions for undoing this spell?" Alex ran her hand through her dark brown hair, a worried wrinkle in the middle of her forehead replacing her fierce frown.

"I think so." Or at least she hoped so. But only if she decided she needed to reverse the magic.

Alex's eyebrows shot upward. "You mean you don't know how to undo the Voodoo?"

Calliope clapped her hands together and giggled. "Sounds like a song."

"I think it's the same ingredients, only you say all the words backward."

"Do you need the bug?"

Lucie squinched her eyes and hunkered low. "Probably," she whispered. "And I would have had the damned thing if your brother hadn't let it go out the window."

"Good grief." Alex shook her head, opened her mouth to say something, and clamped it shut.

Like an insect under a microscope, Lucie squirmed on the porch seat. "Why do you have to make such a big deal out of this? It's just a little love spell. The world will not come to an end."

"You're playing with my brother's heart, Lucie." Alex spun and paced the deck. "I can't believe you'd toy with him again. I'm not likely to be your friend after all this is said and done."

"But—"

Before she could form a response, the phone rang again.

Calliope was first to move.

"Hold it." Alex flicked her wrist, shoving her palm against Calliope's chest. "Let the answering machine get it."

On the fourth ring, Alex's recorded voice instructed the caller to leave a message at the beep.

"Alexandra, this is Eric Littington. I figured since you're a friend of Lucie's you could answer a few questions for me. Please call me back." He left a phone number and rang off.

Lucie stared at Alex, knowing her friend wasn't happy with what she'd done. But Alex's curiosity had to be just as piqued as hers. Would she return the call and find out what Eric wanted, despite her issues with Lucie's love hex?

Finally, Calliope broke the silence. "Well? What are you going to do?"

"You have to call him back and find out what he wants to know," Lucie said.

Alex's eyes narrowed. "What are your intentions toward my brother?"

"Oh, quit sounding so old-fashioned." She stood. "I have no intentions toward Ben. We were over seven years ago."

"Then why were you so upset the other day when he first came into town?" Alex asked.

"A girl has a right to be prepared for when her ex-boyfriend comes to town. That way I could be sure to avoid his sorry ass."

With a narrow-eyed stare, Alex considered her response. "Do you promise to undo the spell on him?"

Why did Alex have to be such a bulldog? Lucie just wanted to pursue her own path, but her friend wasn't going to let go of the issue. "I'll try," she said, without making an actual promise.

Alex gave her another one of those frowny-faced looks she used on her younger siblings. "You *will*."

"I'll *try*. That's the best you're gonna get." Lucie walked through the door and, lifting the receiver, handed it to Alex. "Are you going to call Eric back?" She held her breath and added. "Please?"

Alex grabbed the phone. "Okay, okay." She replayed the message, jotting down the number. With a long-suffering sigh, she punched it into the phone a little harder than necessary. "Hello, Eric?"

Lucie leaned close. Calliope crowded the other side of Alex.

Missing his first question, Lucie pressed her ear to the hard plastic on the back of the receiver.

"Yes, usually Lucie and I are friends," Alex responded.

Lucie jabbed Alex in the ribs.

"What's Lucie's favorite flower?" she heard Eric ask. "I'm going to ask her out, but I want to do it with flowers."

Lucie mouthed the words *white roses*. Eric was going to ask her out! Her heart should be pounding with giddy excitement. This was what she wanted, wasn't it? Yet she couldn't squelch the I'm-gonna-hurl-because-I'm-a-big-fat-liar feeling in her stomach.

"You know, why don't you ask her yourself?" Alex shoved the phone into her hands and smiled like Garfield the cat after eating the entire lasagna before Odie could get a bite.

Holy cypress knees! She had Eric on the phone. Now what?

"Lucie, are you there?" Eric's asked.

Slamming the headset to her ear, Lucie winced. "Yes, yes, it's me."

"Somehow I lost your number, but I got Alex's from Ben. Figured she'd know how to get hold of you." He stopped for a moment and laughed. "Jeez, I sound like a teenager. The reason I was trying to get you is to invite you to the barbecue my family is hosting at the parish pavilion on Friday night."

"I heard about that. I thought the entire community was invited. Why the special call?"

After a momentary pause, he answered quietly, "I want you to come as my date."

***

Ben stood in front of the window of Jason Littington's spacious study. He'd been all over the house and the grounds conducting a thorough assessment of the security system and checking for bugs. Nothing. Everything was as it should be, tight and operationally sound. Then why was he on edge and ready to jump at the slightest sound?

He refused to consider that his jitters had anything to do with Lucie LeBieu.

Jason Littington sat at his massive desk in the study of the Littington plantation house thrumming his blunt, manicured fingers against the polished surface. "I'm not so sure coming back to Bayou Miste was such a good idea for you, son."

"How else are we going to identify the creep dogging my life?" Eric paced across the Persian carpet, his progress unmarked by sound.

"You were supposed to keep a low profile while you were here, to aid in your campaign." Jason shot Eric a pointed look.

Ben settled comfortably in a brown leather chair, observing the dynamics between father and son.

"And what makes you think I'm not keeping a low profile?" Eric countered.

Jason slid a single sheet of paper across the desk.

His lips pressed into a thin line, Eric snatched up the page and scanned the contents. A smile slid up the sides of Eric's face. "So?" He laid the paper back on the desk.

Ben rose from his chair and strode across to pick up the thin white sheet.

"So," Eric repeated. "I helped pull a woman out of the swamp today. I should think that would help my campaign, not hurt it."

The page had a badly reproduced black-and-white photo of Eric helping a sopping wet woman from the swamp by what looked like the dock at Thibodeaux Marina. Despite her hair hanging limply in her face, Ben would recognize that figure anywhere.

Lucie.

And, obvious to anyone with a pair of eyes and one of these flyers, her blouse wasn't hiding much, if any, of her luscious, fully endowed features. The caption at the bottom of the picture read, "Congressional Candidate Eric Littington in Wet T-shirt Contest With Hometown Hottie."

"You'll be the next Washington scandal if you keep seeing that woman." Not a hint of humor graced Jason Littington's countenance. A little twitch on his left jaw was the only indication of any emotion whatsoever.

"Why shouldn't I see her?" Eric stopped pacing to stand directly in front of his father's desk. "Lucie LeBieu is a very nice young lady."

"With the reputation of being a little on the loose side. She's flirted with every man in the county, and rumor has it she's slept with them all."

The back of Ben's collar heated. Although he and Lucie didn't have a future, he couldn't stand back and let Jason Littington repeat nasty gossip about her. "Lucie has a twin sister, Lisa, who has that unfortunate reputation. Lucie isn't anything like her sister."

"If I can get the rumors confused, the media will make an even bigger mess of the situation." Jason Littington picked up the page and waved it at his son. "Stay away from her if you know what's good for you and your campaign for Congress."

Ben could have predicted Eric's response. He'd seen it at least a dozen times when he'd witnessed Eric go up against his father's demanding presence. Eric always managed to come off looking like the more reasonable of the two. A quality he admired in his friend, and one that made Eric an excellent candidate for government. The man could keep calm in the most unnerving situations and make sound decisions based on facts. When he believed in something, he didn't back down.

And apparently, he believed in Lucie.

Ben remembered a time when he'd believed in Lucie, too. Until she'd shown her true colors. She'd only been interested in status.

Growing up as one of nineteen kids, Ben never much cared for status. Nor did he let the lack of status slow him down.

"Dad, I'm not a teenager anymore, and you can't tell me who I can and can't see." Eric didn't whine, he just stated the facts in a clear and concise manner.

"If you insist on seeing that woman, you'll only ruin your chances of getting elected," the elder Littington persisted.

"Now, wait a minute, Mr. Littington." Ben raised a hand to stop further testimony against his ex-girlfriend. "Lucie isn't a bad person."

"Maybe so, maybe not." Jason flicked his hand toward Ben, although his attention remained on his son. "Eric can't afford to let her bring him down."

"Lucie is a beautiful woman who's smart and determined." *Determined to marry well.* He didn't add that part. He just couldn't stand by and let Jason bad-mouth her. Lucie may have done some rotten things in the past to him, but nothing that deserved such censure.

"It's too late, anyway, Dad." Eric crossed his arms over his chest. "I like her and I want to see her again. I've asked her to be my date for the campaign barbecue Friday night."

Eric's announcement was a punch in the gut Ben hadn't been prepared for. He'd thought for sure Eric would make the right decision and stay clear of Lucie. At least, deep down, Ben had *hoped* his friend would stay clear of Lucie. Not that he wanted to start something up with her again. But, well...

What the heck *did* he want?

Jason shook his head, his mouth in a serious downturn. "Every decision you make will have a profound effect on how your constituency views you. Going out with this Lucie LeBieu woman will only bring scandal and make your voters question your judgment."

"I'll take that chance." Eric's jaw tightened and determination showed in the hard glance he directed at his father. "Lucie's worth it."

Jason stood, the color rising in his tanned cheeks. "Is she worth making her your wife?"

Ben staggered backward. Neither Eric nor Jason paid any attention to him, so wrapped up were they in their little power struggle.

Lucie, Eric's *wife*? Wow, that would be a coup on her part.

She'd turned Ben down flat when he'd asked her seven years ago.

He studied Eric across the room. His blond good looks were a stark contrast to Ben's bayou Cajun dark skin and hair. And Eric dressed for success with every item of clothing he put on, probably down to designer boxers. The man wore his success like a second skin. Hell, it probably came easy to him. Manners and diplomacy had been ingrained in him from birth. And what he hadn't inherited, Jason Littington made sure he'd learned by sending him to the best tutors and universities.

Lucie would do well to marry a man like Eric. Ben could never measure up to someone so classy.

Nor did he want to. He'd leave it to his politician friend to carry that ball and chain. He enjoyed living in the comfort of jeans and well-worn work boots. And tact was something he'd never quite mastered, neither here in Bayou Miste nor on the force in Baton Rouge.

Eric hesitated over his father's bald question. Finally, he looked straight at Jason Littington. "If I fall in love with her, I'd be more than willing to ask her to be my wife."

"It's a good thing. You might want to take a look at the New Orleans *Times-Picayune*." The older man lifted a newspaper off his desk and handed it to his son. "Your opposing candidate is blasting you about not being married, claiming you have no stability in your life and your views."

"My marital status has nothing to do whatsoever with my political views." Eric snapped the paper open and scanned the front page.

"Richard Gasson says it does." Jason tapped the biggest article splashed across the page. "He also capitalizes on his Cajun heritage and your lack of the same."

Ben almost laughed at the irony. For once Eric's money wasn't enough, and he had what Eric never could.

Eric's eyes narrowed slightly. "Not that I put any stock in Gasson's mudslinging, but it just serves to reinforce my stand that Lucie might just be good all around for my campaign."

Ben held his breath, not liking the way this conversation was going.

"How so?" Jason asked.

"If I need a wife, which I don't concede that I do, Lucie would make the ideal one. She's beautiful, she's independent, and she's Cajun. As far as I'm concerned, she's perfect. And I don't care who objects."

Jason glared at his son.

As the quiet stretched into a full minute, Ben shifted on his feet, ready to leave father and son to their argument.

Then a loud crash shattered the silence—and the huge picture window in the study. Ben spun around as the porcelain vase on the end table beside him exploded into a thousand tiny shards. A rock the size of a baseball rolled to a stop on the carpet inches from his big toe, a crumpled piece of paper tied around the middle.

"Good Lord!" Mr. Littington dropped to a crouch near the floor behind his desk.

Eric squatted low, his gaze riveted to the broken window.

All of Ben's police training and a strong dose of adrenaline kicked in to his bloodstream. He ran to the window, flattening his back to the wall beside it, then eased around the frame to stare out into the night.

Across the open lawn, a figure sped past, his legs exposed by accent lights, his face in the shadows of the giant oak trees. The man disappeared into the bushes leading toward the boat ramp where Ben and Eric had played during the summers growing up.

He jerked open the double doors leading out to the garden and leaped over the low porch railing. When his feet hit the grass, he threw every ounce of energy into gaining ground on the vandal.

Before he cleared the bushes blocking the view of the private pier beyond, a motor revved, blasting through the raucous noises of the frogs and insects serenading one another in the still night air.

A few more steps and Ben moved out into the open, charging to the end of the short wooden dock. A small skiff left a V-shaped wake as it disappeared into the dark.

"Damn." He leaped into the nearest high-powered boat and fumbled for the ignition. "Double-damn." No key. How was a person supposed to chase the bad guys when they took the keys out?

His only other choice was a rowboat flipped upside down on the shore. He'd never catch him in that.

Angry for not moving faster to begin with, he walked back to the house and stepped through the double French doors he'd exited moments before.

"Look at this," Jason Littington shoved a crumpled paper into Ben's hands before he cleared the threshold.

As his eyes adjusted to the glare of the lights, he stared down at the block lettering.

"Go away!"

Holding the paper by the corner, he flipped the page over but it was blank on the other side. "That's it?"

A grin spread across Eric's face. "Got to give the guy credit. He's concise in what he wants.

"Unlike, say, a politician?" Ben returned the smile until the elder Littington's creased forehead caught his attention.

"My property has just been attacked and you two are making jokes? I fail to see the humor in the situation."

"Lighten up, Dad." Eric draped an arm around his father's shoulders. "It was just a rock, thrown by someone with a bone to pick."

"A rock today, a bullet tomorrow." Jason strode across to the shattered window. "This time I only lost a window—"

"And a vase." Ben interjected.

"Yes, and an expensive vase." Mr. Littington paused as if to remember where he was in his tirade. "What if this person starts shooting? Lives may be lost."

"Dad, it was only a rock." Eric glanced down at the offending stone. "But you're right. I'd like to know who threw it."

Ben grabbed a tissue from a box on Littington's desk, scooped the rock up with it, and stuffed it into his pocket. "I'll see if I can lift prints off it and the paper."

"Do you suppose it was the man who's been following Eric?" Eric's father asked Ben.

"Could be. Could also be the protesters." Ben frowned. "But since the guy got away clean into the swamp, I'd say he's someone local who knows his way around the tributaries well enough to navigate in the dark."

"Great." Mr. Littington waved his hand in the air. "Campaign crashers, protesters, and local goons. Want to add something else to that list?"

How about a very determined woman intent on marrying your son? Ben added silently to himself. No, he couldn't say that to Mr. Littington. The man was probably an alligator's hair away from running Lucie out of town, as it was. "Look, there's not much we can do tonight. I'll take the paper and see if there's anything I can glean from it. And tomorrow, we'll install additional security cameras that will take in more of the yard. In the meantime, get this window boarded up before you call it a night, if you don't want another one of these crashing through."

Jason and Eric Littington nodded.

"I'll see Mr. Boyette to the door and have the maid clean up this mess." Eric hooked a hand around Ben's elbow and led him out of the study.

He paused at the front entry, dropped his hand away from Ben's arm, and shot a quick glance over his shoulder. "Ben, do you think the message was intended for all Littingtons, or just me?"

"Hard to tell." Careful not to contaminate the evidence, he folded the paper into the tissue and slid it into his back packet. "The message was so short."

"Dad wasn't getting rocks through the window until I showed up." Not a trace of humor graced Eric's face now, only a deep frown.

"Something to be considered."

"I'm worried about my father. He doesn't need this kind of stress." Eric shoved a hand through his blond hair. "Maybe I should leave."

Ben understood family concerns. He loved his mother and every one of his siblings. Eric's apprehension was warranted. "We don't know who did this or whether you or your father, or both, were the object of the warning. Let me do some more digging—maybe something will turn up. In the meantime, keep your eyes open."

Eric's lips twisted into a sardonic half-smile. "Okay. I trust you, man. I know you won't let me down."

As Ben climbed into his exterminator truck, his thoughts ran the gamut of possible suspects. Who the hell threw that rock? Or a better question was, what would he do next?

And if Lucie continued seeing Eric, would she be the next target?

CHAPTER 8

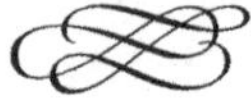

"JEAN, DO YOU THINK I'M A SCREWUP?" LUCIE SLID HER ROUND SERVING tray onto the bar and hiked one butt cheek onto a stool. Business wouldn't pick up for another thirty minutes, and she was feeling pretty bummed and in need of a friend.

He handed her a dry towel and a glass. "No, I don't think you're a screwup. You're the best waitress I got."

Absently polishing the glass, Lucie thought of the mess she'd made of everything. All she'd wanted was to save *Mamère*'s house and get out of Bayou Miste. "Have you ever done something you thought was right at the time, even though your friends told you that you were out of your mind, and despite all their arguments, you did it anyway?"

Jean chuckled. "Yeah, I once ate a hundred goldfish on a dare."

"Ewwww!"

"Half my friends tried to talk me out of it. The other half egged me on. Had a bellyache for a week. These days, I can't even go to the fish store without wantin' to puke."

"That is so disgusting." Her stomach burbled in sympathy. "Did you ever feel right again?"

"No." He took the glass from her and placed it on the shelf behind him. "What I learned from the fish is that I really should have listened to my friends."

"But half of them were telling you to do it and the other half not."

"No. My *real* friends were telling me not to do it."

She sighed. He was right. Her friends had tried to stop her, but she hadn't listened. If Ben hadn't come back she might have backed down on her determination to leave. She might have looked for another way to help out Gran LeBieu. Now she was committed. "Jean, have you ever been in love?"

"Lucie." He shook his head. "You got a customer on table three."

End of conversation. What had she hoped to discover with his answer? Lucie waited the table and when she returned to the counter, Maurice Saulnier had taken up residence on the stool.

Lucie stood next to him and leaned on the counter. Jean had his back to her, pulling beer bottles from cartons, stacking them in the cooler. He glanced back once, but found something else to do that required his attention.

Definitely the end of the conversation with Jean.

"Hi, Lucie," Mo said. He tipped his bottle and swallowed a long gulp. Still in his coveralls with the Littington logo embroidered on the right front pocket, he must have come straight from work.

"Where's Larry?"

"Had to babysit his little sisters tonight. He be makin' a good wife to someone one day." Mo chuckled at his own joke.

"What about you?" If Jean wouldn't answer her question, Lucie may as well poll the only other person within hearing range. "Have you ever been in love?"

"Not Mo. Who gonna love dis big, bad boy?" His words were stated without self-pity, like a man simply asking a rhetorical question.

"Why Mo, any young lady would be happy to have you as her husband." She slid onto the stool next to him.

His shaggy black eyebrows rose an inch. "Would you?"

Gulp. She should have seen that one coming. How to let him down gently? "I'd be proud to be your wife..."

"But. Dey always be buts." Mo shrugged. "No matter, I be happy to live wit' Granny. She cooks, she cleans. What more do I need?"

"Love?"

"Who needs it? It only gives you pain." He clenched his fist over his heart. "Right here."

"Maurice, there's someone out there for everyone. Don't give up." Her heart hurt as if Mo's burly fist had squeezed it. Just as she'd felt when Ben had thrown his harsh words in her face seven years ago. "What if you could come up with a love potion to make someone fall in love with you? Would you use it?"

Maurice tipped his head to one side and squinted as if seeing into a hazy future. "No."

"No?" Was every one of the same opinion about love potions? First Alex and Calliope, and now Maurice. "Why not?"

"She wouldn't love Mo for Mo." He tipped his beer and downed the last bit in one swallow. "I couldn't live wit' de lie."

What could Lucie say to that? Maurice, who didn't have many thoughts crowded into his head, was deeper than she'd imagined. Or the answer was too obvious for even her to see. Love by way of magic was a lie. Plain as Pinocchio's nose—a big, fat lie.

Even if she managed to get Eric to pop the question, would she accept? Could she be happy as his wife knowing she'd orchestrated the outcome?

"Hey, guys. 'Sup?" Alex, with Calliope close behind, stepped up to the bar.

"What's yer poison, ladies?" Jean tossed his bar towel over his shoulder and leaned his elbows on the counter.

"I'll have my usual," Alex said.

"One Miller Lite coming up." Jean yanked a bottle out of the cooler, tipped it under the bottle opener and set it in front of Alex. "What about you, Red?"

Calliope, bless her soul, had a finger touching her chin, and her gaze shot to the far corner.

"Give her the same, Jean, or we'll be here all night," Alex said.

"But I might have wanted something frozen or fruity." Calliope pouted, but smiled when Jean set the beer in front of her. "Thanks, Jean."

"So," Lucie said. "Are you two staking out the bar tonight or do you want me to find you a table?"

"Table, definitely." Alex shot a brief glance around the room. "I'm not man-hunting tonight."

"Honey," Lucie said, "you're never man-hunting. You've got your mother to do that for you."

"You know what they say, don't you?" Calliope lifted her bottle to her lips and swallowed.

Lucie glanced at Alex. "I give up, what do they say?"

A drop of beer trickled out the side of Calliope's mouth and she reached up to wipe it clean. "You'll only find true love when you're not looking."

Again, that little squeezing action attacked Lucie's heart. Maybe she was having a cardio-something. She hadn't been looking for love in a long, long time and certainly not now. Maybe Lucie LeBieu didn't want love—stability was more her goal—but that didn't mean she should dash someone else's hopes.

She leaned back toward the bar and whispered in Mo's ear, "Better be careful. You're not looking for love, so someone's gonna show up and knock your socks off." She kissed his cheek and turned toward her friends. "Come on. Let me find you the perfect table."

After crossing the dance floor, Calliope draped herself across her seat and nodded at Lucie. "So, what's with you and Maurice?"

"Oh, nothin' much." She dusted an imaginary speck off her black tank top to avoid eye contact. Not a chance she'd tell her friends about either one of her earlier conversations. Likely, they'd give her a whopping big, "I told ya so!"

"Someone tell you that you shouldn't have done it, or something?" Alex asked.

Damn her, damn Alex to Hell Bayou. You'd think the girl was psychic, the way she read her mind. Telltale heat crept up her neck to flood into her cheeks, right out to the tips of her ears. "No, that isn't it at all." Her ears were so hot they sizzled.

"Liar."

Busted.

"Who was it? Jean?" Calliope leaned forward. "I love playing the guessing game. I bet five bucks it was Maurice."

"Look, I haven't told anyone else about the love bug." At least that was true. "And I don't plan to."

"Have you done anything yet to reverse the spell?" Alex asked.

She scuffed the toe of her high heel against the wooden flooring. "Not yet."

Alex's lips pressed into a thin line. "Did you even find the bug?"

Lucie paced a tight line in front of the table, her hands waving in the air. "I spent the best part of my day looking all over Bayou Miste for that damned bug. I found dragonflies, beetles, flies, mosquitoes, and other really disgusting bugs, but not once did I see that hexed ladybug. It would be easier to find a needle in a haystack."

"*Coo-wee!*" Calliope sat back her eyes wide. "Do you realize how many bugs there are in the swamp? You could spend your lifetime looking for that one."

She spun toward Calliope. "Exactly!"

While she'd been talking, customers had entered the bar, seating themselves around the room. A lucky break. "I gotta get back to work."

"Don't think you're off my shit list, girlfriend. Until you un-hex my brother, you're mud." Alex's words were harsh but she tempered them with a wink. "We'll talk later."

Lucie hurried to fill orders, barely stopping to chat with anyone for very long. The usual customers had already claimed their favorite tables, and for a Thursday night, the bar was crowded. She recognized a few of the protesters gathered around tables near the door, as if they might have to make a hasty escape from the riled-up locals.

She swerved around a burly Cajun speaking with his hands. As she passed by another table, someone grabbed her arm, pulling her to a stop.

"Lucie, ain't you even gonna say hello?"

In all the bustle, she hadn't seen Pascal Pasquale enter the bar. "I'm sorry, Pascal. What can I get you?"

"I'll have a Bud."

"Anything else? You want some oyster shooters or pretzels to go with that beer?"

"No, thank you."

She swung back toward the bar only to be snagged again. With a pointed glance down at the arm Pascal held in his grip, she asked, "Did you change your mind?"

Pascal held tight, ducking his chin. "Lucie, would you consider going out with me?"

"Huh?" The question was so out of the blue, she hadn't seen it coming. Go out with Pascal? After he'd stalked her in fifth grade?

He looked up, his expression that of a puppy in the pet store. *Choose me! Choose me!*

Always a sucker for the pathetic pooch in the window, Lucie had a hard time coming up with the right words to let Pascal down easy. "No." Okay, so that wasn't so hard. Definitely blunt though, and not the least sugarcoated.

Pascal's puppy-dog plea morphed into an angry Cajun scowl. "Is it that I'm not good enough?"

"No, not at all." She twisted her arm a little trying to dislodge Pascal's hand. "I'm just not interested in going out with you."

"It's Eric, isn't it? Eric Littington. He's good enough for you, isn't he?" Pascal squeezed her arm harder.

"Is there a problem here?" A man's stern tone sounded behind her.

She'd recognize that voice anywhere. How did Ben Boyette always manage to find her in an awkward situation? She refused to turn and see his superior expression. "Thank you, Ben. I can handle this."

"I see that." His words said one thing, his inflection implied, *Like hell you can.*

Lucie bristled and struggled even harder to pry Pascal's fingers off her arm. She'd be damned if she let Ben rescue her yet again. She could get *herself* out of any tangle thrown her way. Her fingers started to cramp. Pascal's grip was like a friggin' vise.

"Pascal, let the girl go." Ben spoke in a quiet, commanding manner. *No, no, no!* She couldn't let Ben be the hero here. It would be one more reason to fall back in love with the bastard, and she wasn't going there. Ever again. It hurt too damned much.

Pascal hesitated a moment and then eased up on his grip.

Lucie yanked loose and stepped out of reach. She could have extricated herself from the situation. Just because Ben stepped in didn't mean she couldn't save herself. He wasn't some tall, dark and handsome hero she'd ever swoon over. Been there, done that, could write a really sappy love song about it. "Thanks," she spit out. To herself, she added, *But that doesn't change a thing.*

***

Ben would bet his paycheck she hated that "thanks." "I only wanted to ask her out," Pascal grumbled. "But no, I'm not good enough. She'd rather go out with that pansy, Eric."

"Know the feeling," Ben muttered beneath his breath.

Lucie darted a fierce look at him. "Ben Boyette, you don't know anything, so shut your trap." With that, she stormed away, tray and all.

Her anger enhanced the sway of her fanny in the cutoff shorts that were paired with that ridiculous black tank top. He drew a hand down his face. Lucie's figure would start a riot before quitting time.

"What did I miss?" Eric walked up to stand beside him. "Ah, I see. Did you two have another spat?"

"No, not at all." Ben pried his gaze from Lucie's bodacious buns and attempted a poker face. "Let's sit."

They found a table in a far corner and both men sat with their backs to the wall. Ben almost laughed out loud. Part of the reason they sat that way was because of the rock through the window the night before. But mostly because of one Cajun swamp siren. From their position, they could easily see Lucie moving between the tables.

"She's a beauty, isn't she?" Eric's question didn't require a response. His gaze followed Lucie's every move to the exclusion of everything else in the bar, including Ben.

"I reviewed the security cameras from the house. As I expected, the vandal was out of camera range when he threw the rock."

"Huh?" Eric turned to face Ben, his eyes glazed. He shook his head and smiled. "Sorry, I can't seem to help myself. She intrigues me."

"She has that effect on most men." Could Eric just shut up about Lucie already? The muscles in Ben's neck were already tight from the Pascal incident. He didn't need more Lucie-related stress. And having other men panting after her didn't help one bit.

"I asked Alex about her favorite flower." Eric's gaze strayed back to Lucie.

"White roses, without those little white filler flowers. Baby's breath, I think." As soon as he said the words, he could have kicked himself. His statement was way more information than Eric needed to know.

"She looks like a roses kind of girl. But why no baby's breath? And while we're on the topic, why do you know all that about her?" Eric finally pulled himself from ogling Lucie and focused on Ben.

Like a worm pinned to the dissecting tray, he fought to keep from squirming. "Lucie and I used to date."

Eric's eyebrows rose. "But you told me you weren't interested."

"I wasn't."

"But you are now?"

"No, I'm not." Ben pushed a hand through his hair and reached for his beer. Oh yeah, Lucie hadn't come by to take their order. "Want a beer? I'll get one from the bar."

"Oh, no, I'm waiting for Lucie to take my order," Eric said. "She should make it over here soon. I'd much prefer her to bring my beer. She's better-looking. No offense."

Ben smacked his palm on the table. "Well, I'm not waiting."

A grin lifted the corner of Eric's mouth. "Ben Boyette, you're avoiding my question."

"Man's got a right." *To avoid a question and to get his own beer.*

With a shrug, the blond man sat back in his chair and crossed his arms over his chest. "Suit yourself. But I suspect there's more to your story than you're letting on."

A lot more. And you're not getting it, buddy. Ben lurched from his chair and stomped toward the bar. As he passed by folks he knew, they raised a hand and smiled in greeting, only to drop the smile and settle for a subdued *Hi.* Ben realized he was scowling like a cranky black bear and forced himself to walk like a normal person, masking his emotions in a friendly Cajun grimace.

Once again, Lucie LeBieu had slipped under his skin and made him itch.

Determined not to stare around the saloon, he kept his eyes on his goal, the bar. He ordered a beer and exchanged a few pleasantries with Jean. A moment later he didn't recall a single word of their conversation.

Longneck in hand, he turned back in time to see Lucie smiling and laughing down at Eric Littington. With her equipment, her tank top should have been declared indecent. And those shorts. Well, Ben's mamma had taught her daughters better than that. Why, every man in the room was staring at her like she was a side of slow-roasted meat. Good enough to salivate over and most definitely good enough to eat.

He groaned. His footsteps slowed and faltered until he barely moved. Every step closer raised his blood pressure another notch and his libido exponentially. What was *wrong* with him? He didn't care about her anymore. He didn't love Lucie as he had seven years ago. She was trouble now, and had been from the get-go.

But he couldn't help himself. And he couldn't stand by and let her flirt with Eric. He had to interfere. Every ounce of testosterone screamed for him to do something about it. She just wasn't right for Eric.

Then who the hell *was* she right for?

Me. The irritating little voice in his head shouted, *Me! Me! Me!*

A bellow from two tables beyond her caught Lucie's attention. She excused herself from Eric and hurried to take another order. But instead of going back to the bar she turned down the corridor to the ladies' room.

Like a hunting dog closing in on the fox, Ben slipped into the shadows of the hallway and waited for her to come out.

As he lurked at the end of the corridor, hidden in the corner, he knew his actions were bizarre and unwarranted, but he couldn't stand by and let her continue to target Eric. He had to show her how wrong she was.

Several women exited the bathroom.

He leaned on the wall and willed his blood to quit pounding against his ears. But as soon as Lucie stepped through the doorway, his heart hammered against the wall of his chest. Quickly, before she could dart out of the hall, he grabbed her from behind and pulled her to him.

She gasped and jabbed her elbow into his ribs.

Sharp pain shot out from the point of contact, but he didn't let go of his grip on her arm.

"Let me go, or I'll scream," she warned.

"Jeez, Lucie, it's just me," he gasped out.

"Ben?" She turned to face him. "What the hell are you doing lurking outside the ladies' restroom?"

"Maybe I was headed for the men's room." He dropped her arm and pressed his fingers to his ribs. "Ouch. I think you broke my rib."

"You deserved it." After a moment, her tight lips softened and she sighed. "Here, let me see." With deft fingers, she unbuttoned his shirt down to where his hand still pressed to his rib cage. "Move."

"Yes, ma'am." Her knuckles brushed his chest, the touch doing crazy things to his erratic heartbeat. But when she reached inside and pressed her fingertips to his skin over the sore spot, he'd had all he could stand. He pinned her to the wall, trapping her hand between them.

"Do you know what you do to me?" His voice was a low growl.

Like a cornered animal, her eyes widened, and her gaze darted to either side of him. "Let me go," she said in a breathy whisper.

His raging body demanded more. He couldn't let her go if his life depended on it. He told himself he would only kiss her once, to prove Eric wasn't the one for her. But the rampaging testosterone in his body told him once would never be enough—not with Lucie.

With one hand caressing her cheek, he slid the backs of his other fingers up her bare arm to trail across her collarbone.

She shivered beneath his touch, goose bumps rising on her creamy arm. "Your skin is just as I remembered it. Smooth and" —he leaned down to inhale her fragrance, his lips lingering near her neck —"smelling of roses."

Her warmth drew him to her and he pressed a light kiss to the pulse beating in her throat. Branding a slow, deliberate path upward, he brushed his lips against her chin and across to claim her mouth. The kiss was everything he'd been fantasizing, and more. Much more.

With a sigh, she leaned into him, ever closer, her hips firmly pressed against his, her arms snaking around his neck. She threaded her fingers into the hair at the back of his neck, pulling him even deeper into the kiss.

He felt as though he'd come home. This was where he belonged, in this woman's arms, kissing her, holding her, loving her like there was no tomorrow and no yesterday. Just here, now. Only the two of them.

His tongue dove deep, twisting and sparring with hers, their kiss taking on a frantic urgency. Her hands slipped inside his shirt, climbing up his chest to feather through the curls there and tweak his nipples.

His blood on fire, he leaned into her, pushing his knee between her legs. He wanted to shove her high up the wall and down over him, taking her right there.

"Ah-*hem*." A feminine voice sounded behind him, but he couldn't focus on anything but Lucie. His head was in a sex-induced fog.

Lucie broke the kiss first. "Ohmigod," she whispered. Then she pushed at him, fighting to be free.

"Next time you two should get a room."

He stepped away from Lucie and turned toward the source of the interruption.

Alex.

"There won't be a next time." Lucie's face was flushed, with a thin sheen of perspiration glowing in the dim light from the ancient fixtures. "This shouldn't have happened. It changes nothing." She poked a finger into his chest. "Ben Boyette, you stay away from me, do you hear? Stay *away* from me." Then she turned and fled back into the crowded barroom.

Were those tears he'd seen shimmering on her eyelashes? Imagine that. Lucie LeBieu never cried. He must really have gotten to her.

A smile curled the edges of his lips.

"I wouldn't be so smug." His sister crossed her arms over her chest and shot him a look that reminded him of their mother.

"She still has feelings for me," he said. The thought exploded in his chest.

"Yeah, but there's seven-year-old baggage that goes with those feelings. Something to do with words said in anger." Alex tapped her chin. "Hmm. Do the words 'You're nothing but a teasing bayou bimbo' ring a bell?"

His brows furrowed. How did she know about those stupid words he'd said all those years ago? "In case you've forgotten, Lucie dumped *me*."

Alex shook her head and turned to leave. "You men are so damn clueless."

He reached out and snagged Alex's arm. "What are you talking about?" Something wasn't right with this entire picture. "Didn't you hear me? Lucie dumped me back then. Why would she do that if she still loves me? It makes no sense."

"Maybe you should ask her." With that parting shot, his sister shook off his hand and left him standing in the darkened hallway, feeling like the clueless man women were always complaining about.

Damn.

Couldn't Alex give him a break and just spell it out?

CHAPTER 9

AH, THIS WAS THE LIFE. LUCIE ARRIVED AT THE PARISH PAVILION IN ERIC'S smooth, sexy BMW. A good-looking man beside her, the smell of leather and luxury filling the air—what more could she want?

Ben Boyette, a little voice whispered in her head.

Shut up! I don't need the man. He didn't care a fig about her, so she had to get him firmly out of her head.

Somehow.

"Something wrong?" Eric asked.

Huh? Oh, yeah. She was with Eric. She sent him a dazzling smile. "No, no. What could possibly be wrong?"

"I don't know, but you looked like you were about to start a fight with your seat belt." He pulled the car into the pavilion's gravel lot, shifted into park, and turned toward her.

She immediately loosened her grip on the silvery safety strap and forced a smile wider on her lips. "I must have been daydreaming."

"Well, I hope you weren't daydreaming about me, then. If I went by the look on your face, I'd be tarred, feathered, and hung out to dry."

Lucie winced. "That bad?"

"Yes." His gentle grin lightened his response.

"If it helps, I wasn't terrorizing you in my dream. I was just thinking of work." That wasn't too far from the truth. She'd been at work when Ben had kissed her.

"Well, tonight you don't have to think about work. Just concentrate on having a good time. With me." He leaned close.

Oh, lord. He was going to kiss her. A sudden surge of panic pressed against her lungs.

He flicked the button and released her seat belt. "I have to warn you, since this shindig was an open invitation to everyone in the parish, there might be reporters here."

"Is that a problem?" Reporters were a norm around Bayou Miste, ever since the big chemical dumping issue. Protesters brought as many as they could into the bayou.

"Well, they do get in the way sometimes and ask a lot of questions," Eric said.

"I should think you would be very good at answering their questions, in your line of work."

"Yes, but since you're with me they'll be asking you questions, too."

"Oh." Why hadn't she thought of that before? Being Eric's date had inherent social obligations. Hmm. "Don't worry." She smiled brightly. "I won't embarrass you." *I hope.*

"I don't think you could ever embarrass me. I just meant for you to be prepared. They may ask some very personal questions." His lips twisted. "Sometimes they aren't very tactful."

"I'll consider myself forewarned."

He climbed out of the sports car and hurried around to open the door for her.

She'd have to thank her friends for helping her shop for the perfect dress for the occasion. The smooth, silk crepe hugged her body from her breasts to her hips where the skirt flared out, swirling down to midcalf. The creamy white fabric complemented her black hair and deep, olive skin tones. Although she was still Lucie LeBieu inside, the clothes definitely gave her the confidence she needed to stand beside Eric.

As she hooked her arm through the congressional candidate's elbow, she fixed her smile on her face and prepared to meet her future.

"Eric, Lucie, good to see you." Ben joined them as soon as they stepped beneath the pavilion. Dressed in scrumptious black jeans accentuating the taut muscles beneath, and topped by a matching long-sleeved black shirt, he looked incredible.

Lucie wanted to stomp her high-heeled foot. Why couldn't Ben just disappear off the face of the earth? He always managed to show up wherever she was and throw off her focus.

On second thought, why should she care?

She glanced up, her gaze meeting his. Warmth spread from her chest downward. Okay, so staring into Ben's eyes wasn't such a good idea. She looked away first. Back to Eric—her future.

"Ben," Eric shook his hand. "How's the bug business?"

"Great." Ben grinned. "Neutralizing as many as I can find."

Was that a wink Eric gave Ben? She must be seeing things. Ben and Eric sure were spending a lot of time together for a potential congressman and an ordinary bug exterminator. Okay, so Ben wasn't so ordinary. But he was a bug exterminator. Not that killing bugs was a bad business to be in, especially in southern Louisiana.

"Please excuse us." Eric gave his smooth politician's smile. "I'd better make my presence known to my father."

"By all means." Ben sketched a mocking bow. A slow, sexy smile spread across his face as his gaze slid up her legs.

Damn Cajun. Didn't he know when to give up? Didn't he know they were finished seven years ago?

Then why did his kiss bother her so much?

"Lucie," Eric was saying, "I'd like you to meet my father, Jason Littington."

Oh yeah, she was with Eric. A man who resembled an older version of her date held out his hand. She had to pull herself together. She'd do well to display her best manners and behavior if she wanted to make a good impression on her future father-in-law. She took the proffered hand. "It's very nice to meet you, Mr. Littington." There, that wasn't so hard. She could do this.

"The pleasure is mine." He half-bowed over her hand in a charming, old-fashioned way. "I've heard so much about you." His suave words were a contradiction to his slightly narrowed eyes.

Instead of feeling flattered, she had a sudden attack of nerves. In the older man's firm, almost painful grip on her hand, she sensed latent animosity. And what did he mean he'd heard so much about her?

She stopped short of defending herself. That would only lend credence to whatever rumors he'd digested as gospel. With as much grace as she could hope for, she pulled her hand free and playfully batted her long lashes at the man. "Oh, don't believe everything you hear, unless it was all good. You can believe that."

Eric's face was a little pale and strained. Apparently, she had been a topic of discussion in the Littington household, and father and son had varying opinions. Interesting. A twinge of guilt rippled through her stomach. She hated to be the object of contention between the men. But if she wanted to attain her goal of saving her grandmother's home and getting the hell out of Bayou Miste, she'd have to suck it up and make it right.

"Mr. Littington, I think it's great what you're doing toward the cleanup effort in the swamp. I know you weren't responsible for the chemical dumping, and think it quite magnanimous of you and Littington Enterprises to fund the effort to remove the toxins."

Wow. She sounded as good as any politician running for office. Butter up the backers, that's how to win a campaign.

"I understand you work at the Raccoon Saloon." The elder Littington completely ignored her eloquence with a statement that wasn't a question. As if he implied her job as a barroom waitress wasn't good enough.

The hairs on the back of her neck bristled and her fighting instincts kicked in. What the heck did he expect? That she could afford to sit at home and learn needlepoint, paint her nails, and eat bonbons all day?

Eric cupped her elbow. "Dad, if you'll excuse us, I believe Miss LeBieu would like a drink, wouldn't you, Lucie?"

Before his father could protest, Eric led her in the direction of the bar.

"You warned me about reporters, but you didn't warn me about your father." She cringed at how waspish she sounded, but her nerves were just a little on the frayed side.

"I'm sorry. My father's behavior was inexcusable. His heart is generally in the right place, but he gets a little nearsighted when it comes to his only son."

"I see." She ground to a stop, pulling her elbow free of his grip. "And I'm not good enough for you?"

"Oh, you're good enough for me." He grinned. "You're great for me."

"But it'll take a little more convincing to win your father's approval." Poor Eric. Up against his father over her.

"What would you like to drink?"

"Sweet tea, please." She figured alcohol, a future father-in-law, and reporters wouldn't mix at this party.

"I'll be right back, don't go away." Eric got in line behind a number of locals intent on making the most of the open bar.

"Did you find the bug yet?" A feminine voice whispered into her ear.

Lucie turned to find Calliope dressed in a wispy floral halter dress. Beside her stood DeeDee Dubois in a very flattering cotton sundress in pastel peach. Her bushy brown hair was combed neatly and pulled back from her face, emphasizing her high cheekbones.

"Ohmigosh, DeeDee." Lucie backed up a step, her gaze sweeping over the other woman. "You look fabulous."

Well, as fabulous as DeeDee could look. Her facial features tended to resemble those of a bulldog, but with the shy smile and a little lipstick, she almost looked pretty.

"Thanks, Lucie." DeeDee blushed and ducked her head. "Calliope made me her science project for the night."

Lucie hugged Calliope, then DeeDee. "I'd say her experiment worked. You look great." She glanced behind them. "Where's Alex?"

Calliope balanced on her toes and spun in a circle. "She's here somewhere. Ah, there she is."

"Where?" Lucie asked.

"Behind the column at the dark end of the pavilion."

"What's she doing there?" DeeDee asked.

Calliope chuckled. "Her mother's here and she's snagged another man for Alex to consider."

Barbara Boyette had Larry Ezelle by the elbow, leading him around like a dog on a very short leash.

"Poor Alex." While Mrs. Boyette wasn't looking her way, Lucie grinned and waved at her friend. "We really need to find her a man before her mother drives her nuts."

"Oh yeah, right. We." Calliope rolled her eyes. "If you get your way, there will be no 'we.' Looks like it'll be totally up to me. You'll be in DC."

"Are you going to Washington, Lucie?" DeeDee asked.

"Er..." Lucie caught Eric's gaze. That was the plan. Although, the excitement just wasn't there. "Maybe someday."

The band started a new set with a lively rendition of "Whatever Boils Your Crawfish."

"That song is one of my favorites. Come on." Calliope grabbed DeeDee's arm, steering her toward the action.

"I'll join you in a bit," Lucie called after them.

But they didn't respond. DeeDee and Calliope had already made it to the bandstand and dance floor that Eric and his father had erected for the occasion. The two women laughed, tapping their toes to the music.

The fiddle player flirted with them, jumping down from the stage to play for the two ladies before he made his way around the dance floor.

A sad smile curved Lucie's lips. She'd miss her friends and the music you could only find here in the Louisiana bayous. Washington, DC would be a lot different.

The song changed to a slow, haunting melody about a woman whose lover never returned from war. A sudden yearning, so overwhelming she could hardly breathe, filled her chest. She glanced toward Eric, still making his way to the front of the drinks line.

He shrugged at her and turned to answer a question from the man standing beside him.

Couples crowded onto the dance floor, moving into tight embraces, swaying to the strains of the song. Craig Thibodeaux drew his new fiancée, Elaine, into his arms.

Poor Craig. Lucie's twin had caused him so much grief when she'd tried to make a play for him. That Lisa was bad news. Seeing Craig and Elaine locked in each other's arms, she was glad her sister's interference hadn't worked. The couple was right together—their love practically oozed from the pores of their skin.

Must be nice.

What would it feel like to be held like that? To be loved so completely you'd sacrifice your life for another? She'd felt that way about Ben. Had sacrificed her needs for him. And for what? Only to be told she was just like her sister—nothing more than a bayou bimbo. That had been his parting shot those seven long years ago.

But before that disastrous day and those hurtful words, Ben had held her close and she had known magic.

"Dance with me." A strong arm circled her waist, the other reaching for her hand.

She melted against Ben, a natural progression from dream to reality. Her hand slipped around his neck and she leaned her cheek against his chest.

Wordlessly, she floated around the dance floor, refusing to allow rational thought to intrude and wake her from this fantasy. She and Ben had always seemed to fit, flowing together as if they'd partnered their entire lives. Her body knew his and responded to his every move in perfect synchrony.

With his chin resting against her temple, Ben dropped her hand and gathered her even closer, his hands sliding down her waist to balance on her hips. With increasing pressure, he pulled her hard against him until the ridge behind his button fly rubbed against her belly.

Liquid mercury coursed through her veins, sending tendrils of fire pulsing lower to the juncture of her thighs. Breathing grew difficult, but she didn't care. Her body rubbing against his sizzled at every contact point. Trembling, her fingers convulsing, she clutched at his hair. She wanted more. She wanted to be naked beneath him, writhing at his touch and immersed in passion only Ben could induce. Skin to skin with nothing more between them than sweat.

"May I cut in?"

Ben jerked to a halt, his head coming up, staring down at her as if asking the ultimate question.

Still dazed by what could only be considered foreplay on the dance floor, she tried to focus on Ben. Then her gaze shifted to Eric.

Holy cypress knees! What had she done?

The fire burning low in her belly extinguished, to be replaced by the warmth stealing up her neck. She glanced around to see how many people had watched her and Ben practically make love to the music. She repressed a groan when Calliope gave her a thumbs-up.

Shit! Shit! Shit!

Warm hands squeezed around her waist and she realized Ben still held her, the music was still playing, and the world, other than Calliope, hadn't stopped to gawk at her humiliation.

She jumped back, brushing her fingers down her dress, schooling her face into an innocent smile.

Ben's eyes narrowed ever so slightly, but then he turned and waved a gracious hand toward her. "Of course you can have her, Eric. I was just warming her up for you."

Anger quickly replaced embarrassment. If she had been wearing sturdier shoes, she'd have aimed one at Ben's shin. The creep! Warming her up, her fanny—setting her on fire was more the case.

With all the haughtiness of a president's wife, she tilted her nose back a bit. "Thank you for the dance." And with as much grace as she could muster, she slid into Eric's arms and danced him away from Ben.

"Hey, isn't it usual for the man to lead?" Eric laughed down at her, holding her lightly in his arms. Unlike Ben's proprietary grip.

She slowed her escape and attempted a laugh that came out sounding more like a choked giggle. "I'm sorry, Eric. Must be the stress of all those reporters lurking on the edges of the crowd."

"If this is too much for you, tell me. I'll have you home before you can say 'Louisiana.'"

"No, no. But I am a little warm." And her discomfort had nothing to do with the air temperature. Dancing with Eric didn't mesh with the aftereffects of Ben's touch still running rampant in her system. "Do you think we could sit this one out?"

"Certainly. I have our drinks on a table nearby. What say we grab them, and you and I can walk along the boardwalk?"

At this point, she would grasp at any method of escaping Ben's presence. "Perfect." She hurried Eric out of the crowd and snatched up the plastic cups filled with half-melted ice and watered-down tea. "Quick, before we're followed." She handed one of the cups to Eric, grabbed his hand, and tugged him through the gate leading to the raised walkway extending out over the swamp.

Once past the noise and crush of the masses, she slowed her pace and relaxed, allowing the monotonous drone of the bayou creatures to soothe her jangled nerves.

At the farthest point of the walkway was an observation deck, large enough to hold ten or more people. Benches allowed visitors to take a break or just to sit and enjoy the sights and sounds unique to the swamp experience. Little plaques bolted to the railing at intervals gave the reader factoids about the local flora and fauna. But in the light of a half moon, the writing was impossible to see.

And apparently Eric wasn't interested in reading, anyway. He leaned his backside against the rail and pulled her into his arms.

Too soon! Too soon! She'd barely gotten her breathing back to normal from her encounter with Ben. How could she go right into another man's arms? Especially when that man seemed intent on kissing her?

"Did you know the parish elementary schools raised the money to have this nature walk built? It took them five years to come up with enough cash," she gushed. "Not only did they raise the money, they also helped with the actual construction, clearing weeds, and cleaning up after the workers."

With a gentle touch, Eric pressed his finger to her lips, stilling her next words.

Uh-oh. He was definitely going to k—

His mouth descended on hers, warm and tender, and incredibly sweet.

The kiss started out as gentle, yet firm against her lips. Not bad, so far. His lips were warm and sensuous, not thin and rock hard.

The pressure increased and his tongue darted out to tease hers.

Okay, so she should let him in to see if his kiss was any better or worse than Ben's. She eased her lips and teeth open.

She returned his kiss, determined to find in him all the passion she'd felt in Ben's kiss the day before. She stood on her tiptoes and laced her arms around Eric's neck, pressing her body against his.

He pulled her close, deepening the pressure, sliding his tongue between her teeth, delving for, and toying with, hers.

Still...

Nothing.

But love could grow, couldn't it? Given time, she'd grow to love Eric more than Ben. At least he'd respect her. Eric made her forget the ugly rumors, the names she'd been called growing up. He'd never call her a bayou bimbo. He'd love her and take care of her. He was just that kind of man.

She pressed harder against him. Why couldn't she feel anything more for him than sincere like? He was a great guy, for heaven's sake!

The more she tried to feel it, the less she did. The kiss was not working.

A click and a flash of light pierced the gloom.

"What the hell?" Eric straightened, his hands dropping to his sides.

She jumped away from him, blinking, her night vision temporarily blinded. "What was that?" In her mind, though, she was glad for the intrusion. She needed time to think, to understand.

"Damned reporter." Eric reached out and cupped her cheek, his thumb rubbing over her bottom lip. "We need to talk."

Unable to think of a coherent response, she nodded. Yes, they needed to talk. Although with thoughts pinging around inside her head like the little metal ball in the pinball machine, she didn't have a clue what she'd say.

"Right now, we'd better get back to the party." He grabbed her hand and pulled her along the boardwalk.

The closer they got to the lights and music, the more she knew she couldn't go back. Not like this. Not after her sensual dance with Ben and her failed kiss with Eric.

Suddenly, a tiny dot of fluorescent green flashed in her peripheral vision.

The love bug!

So much for escaping the crowd, Ben, and Eric. She had to stay and catch the damned bug before it messed up any more lives.

But first she had to ditch Eric. "I sure could use sweet tea."

"Don't move. I'll get you one." He darted off toward the bar. The crowd around the free alcohol had expanded. Poor Eric would be busy for a while. Good.

She spotted the bug just outside the pavilion, not near any people yet but closing in fast on a small group standing at the edge of the platform. Maurice Saulnier stood next to Calliope and DeeDee, all three watching as Mrs. Boyette sailed by with Larry still in her clutches. Mo's deep, rumbling laughter echoed across the open-air pavilion to Lucie.

As if drawn by his amusement, the ladybug altered course and zeroed in on Mo.

Oh, damn. If she didn't hurry, any one of them, or all three, could be hexed.

Running in high heels and dodging partying Cajuns was like negotiating an obstacle course. By the time she'd crossed the pavilion, the bug had made a complete circle around Mo's head.

Still too far to do anything about it, she was blocked by a group of rabble-rousers just starting a conga line. The line was a solid mass, a human barricade. No one would budge from his or her position to allow her to pass through.

"Calliope!" Heads turned at Lucie's shout, but the noise of the music and loud conversations continued.

Calliope stepped away from Mo, closing the distance between her and Lucie. But the conga line had expanded between them.

"The bug!" Lucie shouted and pointed at Mo.

With Calliope out of the picture, the hesitant bug made its decision and plotted an erratic path in DeeDee Dubois's direction.

"Oh, no!" Calliope launched herself at a laughing DeeDee, tackling her to the ground in an unattractive tangle of legs and fancy dresses.

From her position, trapped behind the conga line, Lucie could only shake her head.

Too late. Maurice and DeeDee could be added to the list of tragic victims of her careless meddling.

The bug had made its circle, cast its spell, and was now racing after Larry and Mrs. Boyette.

With Calliope down for the count and a bunch of inebriated, rowdy Cajuns blocking her path, Lucie could only watch, dread swishing around in her belly like stump water.

Mrs. Boyette stopped, with her hand still on Larry's arm, to talk to Elaine Smith. Where the hell was Craig, Elaine's fiancé?

Move, Mrs. Boyette! Move! Elaine scanned the room as if looking for someone and finally pointed at the far corner.

Lucie swung around to see what Elaine had pointed at. Poor unsuspecting Alex stood guzzling a beer and talking with Eric in a darkened corner.

Good. Maybe Mrs. Boyette would get Larry out of there before the bug reached—

Oh crap!

The fluorescent green dot circled Larry's head just as Mrs. Boyette grabbed his arm and marched him away from Elaine.

"No!" Lucie leaped at the conga line. "Let me through!"

Mozelle Reneau made room for her, but only enough to trap her into the dance. Swept into the bouncing, wiggling whip, she twisted to look over her shoulder. She could only watch in utter dismay as the bug rounded Elaine's curly dark hair.

When she finally broke through the line, the love bug had disappeared into the swamp and Elaine stood staring after Larry, a dazed expression on her face.

The sudden awareness of someone standing beside her put Lucie's nerves on alert. The hairs on the back of her neck stood at attention, while a ghost of excitement trickled downward. Only one man had that effect on her.

Ben leaned close, his breath stirring her hair. "What are you up to, Lucie LeBieu?"

CHAPTER 10

LUCIE GROANED. "WHY CAN'T YOU JUST GO AWAY?"

Trouble was, Ben couldn't quite figure out the answer to that very question, either.

And it bugged him.

Every time he was near her, he ached to touch her. Earlier, on the dance floor, he'd completely forgotten where he was—an easy thing to do when she was in his arms.

He was saved from answering her question when Pascal Pasquale broke through the boisterous conga line.

The Cajun security guard's angry scowl, in stark contrast with the smiling faces of the other revelers, triggered his cop instincts.

Pascal marched toward Lucie, his steps on the unsteady side, but his gaze intent, as if he were looking for a fight.

Ben stepped forward, blocking Pascal's path. "Pascal, it's been a long time. What can I do for you?"

"You can get outta my way, for one." Pascal glared up at him. "I wanna talk to Lucie."

"Why don't you let someone drive you home. You've had more than enough liquor for one night."

"I don't need no ex-cop tellin' me what I oughta do." He stood his ground, swaying slightly. "I wanna talk to Lucie."

"Guess you'll have to talk through me, then, 'cause I'm not letting you near her the way you're acting." Ben crossed his arms over his chest.

Pascal clenched his fists and glared at him, hesitating as if he couldn't decide whether to fight or leave.

Lucie touched Ben's arm. "Let him talk. I don't want a fight."

"You heard the woman, let her talk to me." Pascal smirked.

"Are you sure?" He frowned down at her.

"Sure. Pascal and I are old friends, aren't we?"

"Not in our lifetime." Pascal's words were shot at her as if he spat nails. "I saw what you did on the boardwalk."

"Pascal." She darted a glance at Ben. "You know it's not nice to spy on people."

"You've been kissing him." The guard heaved huge amounts of air into his lungs, blowing it out through his nostrils like the cornered beast at a Spanish bullfight. "Pascal Pasquale is never good enough for you—you swamp trash!" Pascal lunged for her.

Ben stepped in the middle of them, grabbing hold of Pascal's arm and wrenching it back and up between the angry man's shoulder blades. "That's enough, Pascal. No one wants a fight here."

"You won't go out with me, but you'll go out with that rich son of a bitch who doesn't deserve you. You know he'll never marry you."

"Shut up, Pascal." Ben jerked the man's arm harder until he gasped and held his tongue. "Now are you going to leave nicely or am I gonna have to call the sheriff over here? I saw him looking this way."

When Pascal refused to answer, Ben pushed his arm up higher.

"Okay, okay, I'll leave."

"What's going on here?" Eric walked up with two plastic cups in his hands.

"We were just having a little discussion, weren't we?" Ben retained his hold on Pascal.

"It's all your fault—you and your father's. You Littingtons take everything from de Pasquales!" Pascal lunged at Eric.

The congressional candidate gracefully dodged the attack, drinks intact.

"Pascal, what you be doin' both'rin' dese nice people?" Pete Pasquale, Pascal's father, stepped through the crowd. "Ain't you got no better manners 'n dat?"

"But Pappa—"

"Don't interrupt me when I be talkin', boy." Pete's reprimand cut through Pascal's protest.

Pascal's angry frown turned sullen, his chin jutting out farther.

"Now what seems to be da problem?" Wearing faded jeans and a fancy cowboy shirt adorned with mother-of-pearl snaps, Pete tapped the shiny toe of his alligator-skin boots and stared across his son's shoulder at Ben. "My boy been causin' a ruckus?"

Ben didn't like the way Pete talked down to Pascal, but he had more pressing problems, like hanging on to one red-hot ragin' Cajun ready to rumble. "He needs to go home and sleep it off."

"I'll take da boy. No need to call da sheriff over here." He smiled and waved at the sheriff standing with a group near the band, and then Pete turned a scowl on his son. "Is dere, boy?"

Pascal's lips thinned into a tight line.

"*Is* dere?" Pete asked again, his voice even more forceful than the last time.

Clearly reluctant to bow to his father's will, Pascal muttered, "No sirruh."

"I can take him from here, Ben," Pete said.

Pascal still shook beneath Ben's hold. The rage radiated heat up through his hands. "Are you going to go peaceful-like?"

"Yes, he will. Woncha, boy?" Pete answered for his son.

With a withering look, Ben said, "I was talking to Pascal." He leaned close to Pascal's ear. "Do I need to call the sheriff over here?"

"Lighten up on da arm," Pascal responded. "I'll come."

By this time, a crowd of reporters had gathered around the three, cameras clicking and flashing, adding to the noise and confusion. Ben shoved Pascal out from beneath the pavilion before he let go of the man's arm.

"What you think you be doin', boy?" Pete whacked Pascal upside the head as he climbed into the rusted-out hull of a pickup, parked nearby.

Pascal's fists clenched. "Don't hit me."

"Ain't never gonna amount to nothin', boy, if you can't make nice with important folks like our very own congressional candidate." Pete smiled back at Eric. "Why can't ya be more like him?"

Pascal collapsed into the passenger seat and slammed the door.

"That boy looks like he done bit into a green persimmon." Mozelle Reneau stood next to Ben.

He responded with a nod.

"What did he mean by the Littingtons taking everything from the Pasquales?" Lucie asked.

"I don't know," Eric said. "He works for Littington Enterprises. I can't understand why he'd turn on me like that."

"Eric," Lucie put a hand on his arm. "It was the alcohol talking tonight. You're not going to fire him, are you?"

"I don't know," Eric shook his head. "He was pretty angry. I'm not sure I can trust him at the complex if he feels like that."

She lowered her voice. "He was only mad because he saw you and me."

Ben's gut tightened. She'd left his arms to go out into the swamp on the boardwalk with Eric. "He was mad because he saw you two kissing." His words came out a lot harsher than he'd intended.

"It was none of his business who I was kissing. He had no right to accost you." Eric set the plastic cups down and grabbed both of her hands.

Ben fought the urge to step between them. *He* wanted to be the one holding her hands and kissing her.

She glanced up from beneath her lush, black eyelashes in what Ben knew was one of her best give-Lucie-what-Lucie-wants looks. "Give him another chance, Eric. I feel like it's all my fault."

"It's not your fault." Eric pressed her fingers to his chest.

The minx bit her bottom lip, staring at her hands intertwined with Eric's. "Maybe not, but I don't like being the cause of a fight."

Ben snorted.

She rewarded him with a glare.

Which only made him smile. He loved getting under her skin. His lower region twitched, reminding him there were other places on her body he'd liked to get to as well.

Apparently, Eric didn't notice their little interaction. He looked up from their combined hands and gazed into her eyes. "You have a good heart, Lucie, to be concerned about Pascal. Must be why I like you so much. I'll think about it."

If Eric got any sweeter with Lucie, Ben wouldn't be held responsible for the contents of his belly. And if he didn't like Eric so much, he'd punch the guy for acting like a lovesick fool.

Lucie smiled so brightly Ben had to squint from the glare. "Thank you, Eric. Pascal's not so bad, he's just had a crush on me since fifth grade. I don't know why he can't get over it."

Ben knew why. Lucie was hard to shove out of your mind. Even a few hundred miles away in Baton Rouge, she'd seemed to sneak into his thoughts at least once or twice a day—and all night long.

Pascal didn't understand what motivated Lucie. She wanted only the best cut. He and Pascal both were hamburger compared to Eric's prime rib. Who'd settle for hamburger when they could have prime rib?

"Why don't we get out of here?" Eric said.

"Yeah," Lucie perched on one foot and ran the other up her leg behind her calf. "I think I've had all the fun my stiletto heels will allow for one night."

Muscles and nerves jerked to attention in Ben's body. That ankle caressing her calf set all kinds of ideas skittering across his overly active libido. *Would they please get the hell out of there before he did something stupid?*

Let Eric have her. Although that ground Ben's gut as effectively as beans in a coffee grinder. Just as Lucie had said about Pascal, Ben would just have to get over it. She wouldn't be with him if he were the last man in Louisiana—unless maybe he owned Louisiana. On a detective's salary, that wasn't likely to happen in his lifetime.

Eric pounded Ben's shoulders. "Ben, it's been fun. You'll stay, won't you? Plenty of alcohol and music." He led Lucie toward the cars.

"Yeah, lots of alcohol and music." He hadn't noticed when "Cotton Eye Joe" had started playing. Normally, it was one of his favorites. He and Lucie used to burn up the dance floor to that particular number. And just because she was leaving with another man shouldn't take the fun out of the song.

About that time the crowd yelled in unison "Bullshit!" in time to the music.

Okay, so maybe he was still hung up on the Cajun beauty, a little.

"Bullshit!" the crowd shouted again.

Okay, maybe a lot.

Eric and Lucie picked their way across the gravel parking lot to Eric's glossy BMW.

Ben had to admit, Lucie looked cool and elegant in her pale dress. No doubt, she could hold her own in a crowd of politicians.

But would she be happy?

***

Hobbling across the gravel, Lucie cursed her shoes. She was just about to lean down and slip them off to run barefoot to the car when Eric hooked her elbow and helped her along. The person who'd designed stilettos must have been a man—one who'd never had to walk across gravel in these stupid excuses for women's footwear.

She could feel Ben's gaze like a slow burn at the base of her neck, yet she refused to turn and look back. Why the hell did he have to come back to Bayou Miste now? After seven years, she'd been certain she was over him. So why did his being here bother her so much? She didn't know, but the sooner she got out of striking distance of his laser vision —and out of these killer shoes—the better.

When they reached the car, her sigh of relief turned to a gasp. "Ohmigod!"

"What the hell?" Eric exclaimed.

Every tire on the little sports car was slashed to shreds, and long scrapes marred the custom finish along the side panels. With only one spare in the trunk, the BMW wasn't going anywhere.

"Who would have done this?" She stood staring at the vandalized vehicle, stunned.

He circled the front and pointed. "Look at this."

Limping to the front, she read the spray-painted words, "Swamp Killer!"

"Good God, Eric. The protesters have gone too far with this. Don't they know you and your father aren't even responsible for the dumping?"

Eric shoved his hands into his pocket. "They may not care who dumped the toxins. Big companies make great targets. But this vandalism can't be tolerated." He pulled his cell phone out of his pocket and clicked on a speed-dial number.

"The sheriff's here, Eric. Who are you calling?"

"The auto club. The vehicle isn't fit to drive."

"I'm sure we can get a lift home from any one of the guests."

"My father left thirty minutes ago, or I'd ask him to take us."

While Eric spoke to the auto club, she balanced first on one aching foot, and then the other.

"Having problems?"

The one leg she was standing on buckled at the knee at the softly spoken words resonating next to her ear. With barely a second to spare, she got the other foot beneath her before she fell into a graceless heap. She inhaled deeply, willing her heart to a more normal pace before turning to level a we-can-handle-this-ourselves stare at Ben Boyette. "Don't you ever go away?"

His smile was smug, his eyebrows inching upward a couple hairs, like Spock's did on the old *Star Trek* reruns.

She wanted to kick his shins. Again.

Eric pressed the end button. "Oh, good. Ben, would you mind giving us a lift home? Seems someone's had a little fun with my car."

What was Eric thinking? Her heart kicked back into overdrive, slamming blood through her veins. *Calm. Just keep calm.* "I'm sure Ben wants to enjoy the party a little longer. Why don't you fetch the sheriff while I talk to Miz Mozelle? I'm sure she wouldn't mind taking us home."

"Not to worry." Ben gave a half smirk. "I was about to leave anyway. I'd be delighted to take the two of you home."

Delighted. Lucie wanted to wipe the smug look off his face with her shoe.

"Great," Eric said. "Let me snag the sheriff first, then we can leave." Before she could protest, he'd jogged off across the gravel to find the sheriff.

Which left her stuck standing next to Ben. Alone. In the dark. Where a person could imagine all kinds of actions she wouldn't even contemplate in the daylight. A tingling sensation shivered across her nerve endings. She turned her back on the object of her confusion.

Alone with Ben Boyette was the last place she wanted to be. Her body didn't know how to respond when he was around. Or rather, her body responded just as it pleased, despite what her head tried to tell it.

"Lucie, we just heard what happened." Alex and Calliope swooped in to the rescue before she was forced into conversation with Ben.

Thank God for nosy friends and neighbors.

Eric and the sheriff were close behind. Soon, a crowd had gathered around the damaged car, insulating her from the Ben Boyette Effect.

Alex pulled her to the fringes of the crowd. "So how's the magic working?"

"Is Eric in love with you?" Calliope asked as only Calliope could, blurting it out, loud enough only a severely deaf person wouldn't have heard what she said.

"Shh!" Lucie's cheeks reddened, but nobody seemed to be paying attention to her, anyway. "I'd rather not everyone hear about my little plan."

"Oh, I'm sorry." Calliope glanced around at the nearby onlookers, making her even more conspicuous. Then she leaned closer. "So? Is he?"

"I think so." Her gaze darted toward Ben. Was the magic working on him, too? Could that explain the close dance of a little while ago?

"Ben's been acting kinda weird all night," Alex said. "I bet the magic is playing hell with him, as well. Although I'm sure the belly-rubbin' you gave him earlier enhanced the affect."

She didn't want to think what would happen if Ben fell in love with her because of a spell. She didn't want his love if she could only get it with magic.

Then why would she settle for Eric's love when it was generated by Voodoo? She mentally smacked her forehead. *Don't get cold feet now, for chrissake.* The magic probably didn't work on a person if he hated her already. Ben couldn't be falling in love with her. No hex was that strong. *Was it?* "Maybe Ben's got an upset stomach," she suggested.

"That's how I felt last time I fell in love." Calliope sighed. "I've never had such a stomachache as when I fell head-over-heels for Rene."

Alex grunted. "That entire box of pralines you consumed didn't help, either."

"I was so in love." Calliope clasped her hands together and stared off into the night.

"And how long did that one last?" Alex asked.

"Two whole months." Calliope's head snapped up and she grinned. "My longest relationship yet."

"Point is, my brother looks like my dog, Sport, when he eats too many sweat socks." Alex propped her hands on her hips. "The guy is an absolute case."

Lucie knew where Alex was going with this conversation, and she hurried to cut her off at the pass. "That's his problem, not mine."

Alex's brows furrowed into a deep crease over her nose. "The way I see it, it is your problem. You set that bug loose, loaded for one bear, and bagged two. You gotta let one of the bears off the hook."

"I'm not undoing the spell." Lucie crossed her arms over her chest. "I have Eric practically where I want him."

"Has he proposed?" Calliope clapped her hands. "I've always wanted to be a bridesmaid."

"Don't eat your cake before you see the shine on the ring, girlfriend." Alex grabbed Lucie's hands. "You can't leave Ben mooning over you like this. It's not right. You and he used to be a thing. What if he really has feelings for you?"

How long had she waited for Ben to come back to Bayou Miste and realize she'd only sent him away for his own good? How long had she waited for him to profess his love and apologize for his hurtful words? *Seven lonely, interminable years.*

"I'm not reversing the spell." She stood firmly on her sore feet. "I'm getting out of Bayou Miste, once and for all."

"What about Mo and DeeDee?" Alex's frown deepened. "And I think the bug zapped Larry and Elaine. What if Elaine tells Craig to shove off? Their wedding is scheduled for a week from yesterday. That's only six days away."

Lucie hunched her shoulders. "We don't even know the spell worked. Why get all worried about something that might not be a problem?"

Another giggle erupted from the swamp. Lucie, Calliope, and Alex all turned to see DeeDee and Mo walking hand-in-hand down the swamp boardwalk.

A stern look on her face, Alex poked a finger at Lucie's chest. "Ben's my brother. Much as I think he's bossy and overbearing, he's still family, and we Boyettes look out for one another. So, if you consider yourself my friend, I suggest you fix it." Alex stomped away, her mouth set in a grim line.

Calliope glanced from Alex's retreating figure to Lucie and back. "I rode with her. I hope she doesn't leave without me." She laid a hand on Lucie's arm. "Are you okay? I mean, Alex was pretty hard on you."

She scuffed her sandal in the gravel. "Yeah, I'm okay. You go on. I don't want you to miss your ride."

"She is mad right now, but you know we love you, don't you?"

"I know, Calliope. I love you, too. Now, hurry."

Calliope scooted across the gravel to the little red Jeep Alex drove. As soon as she climbed in, the vehicle spun out of the parking lot.

Lucie stood on the edge of the crowd wondering what the hell she'd done. She wasn't happy—hadn't been happy since the moment Ben Boyette had shown up in Bayou Miste. Everything she'd tried to do from then on had only made matters worse. And now that she'd started the chain of events, how on earth could she stop it?

CHAPTER 11

Ben opened the screen door and knocked on Miz Mozelle Reneau's front door. He stared down at the straw mat with a bright gold sunflower and the word "welcome" painted across it. He hoped Mozelle was home. His mother said she was as good as they come for town historian or gossip. If you needed to know something, hell, anything, she knew about things as far back as anyone could remember.

And he wanted to know more about Pascal Pasquale's words from last night. What had he meant by the Littingtons taking everything? Ben had grown up in the community and hadn't noticed the Littingtons being anything but gracious and good to the people of the parish.

Mozelle Reneau was his best bet for more information. And the little fact that she happened to be Lucie's landlady had nothing to do with his being on her doorstep. Nothing whatsoever. Besides, he couldn't see the garage apartment from where he stood, anyway.

The haint blue painted door swung open. "Benjamin Franklin Boyette. Why, bless my soul." Miz Mozelle pushed the screen wide open and waved him through. "Come on in and sit a spell. Just powdered a fresh batch of beignets." She leaned close and cupped her hand around her mouth as if she was about to tell a secret in a room full of people.

"Mr. Thibodeaux's favorites." She winked. "I'm sure he wouldn't mind sharin'." Mozelle took a deep breath.

While Mozelle breathed, he took the opportunity to say, "I didn't come to eat Mr. Thibodeaux's beignets. I came—"

"Nonsense." She hooked his arm with a surprisingly strong grip and ushered him into her roomy kitchen. "I always make more than the two of us could possibly eat. That's me, always making more than I need. I should have had a whole house full of children. Alas, my husband, bless his departed soul"—she made the sign of the cross over her chest—"and I weren't blessed with children. So, I give away the leftovers to the neighbors, their children, and sometimes their dogs. For that matter, I've given quite a few to your sister, Alexandra. I think she gives them to her dog, Sport. How else could she stay so slim and trim? Mind you, I'm only guessing. You tell her I don't mind in the least. That's a good dog she has. Minds his manners and doesn't dump in my yard. Occasionally sprays my rose bushes, but so far, I don't see any damage."

"Miz Mozelle," Ben blurted out, his head reeling. How could such a small woman have so much to say? "I wanted to ask you some questions. Do you mind?"

"Have a seat at the table while I get you a cup of coffee." Without stopping, she dashed around the kitchen, pulling mugs from the cabinets and filling them with the thick brown sludge the Cajuns called coffee. "You do drink coffee, don't you? Do you take it black or with cream and sugar? I even have some whipped cream, if you like the fancy kinds."

"Black is fine, thank you." Didn't this woman ever shut up? "About those questions..."

"Why certainly," Mozelle sank into the seat across from him, her eyes wide and her smile bright. "Ask away."

Before Mozelle could slip in another dissertation about beignets or dogs, he said, "Last night at the barbecue, Pascal Pasquale said something to Eric about the Littingtons taking everything from his family. Do you have any idea what he meant by that? I've lived here almost all my life, except the past seven years. Did I miss something?"

Mozelle touched a finger to her chin and stared off into a far corner of the room. “Let me see. Why would Pascal Pasquale say Eric Littington takes everything?”

“That was my question.”

Mozelle’s eyes narrowed. “I don’t recall Eric ever taking anything from Pascal, unless...” The room fell blessedly silent for a few blissful seconds.

He actually managed to breathe two whole breaths, uninterrupted.

Then Mozelle’s eyes widened and she focused on him. “Odette.”

“Odette? As in Odette Littington? Eric’s mother?” He had only met Mrs. Littington once before she died of cancer. He hadn’t known Eric that well at the time. They must have been around fifteen years old when it happened.

Eric had taken his mother’s death hard. He’d missed an entire week of school, and when he came back, he’d been a quiet shell of his former self. “What about Mrs. Littington? I can’t imagine she’d take anything that didn’t belong to her.”

“You don’t know this story?” Mozelle’s smile widened and she leaned forward.

Ben almost expected her to rub her hands together like a child about to eat her favorite dessert.

“Odette was as pretty as a summer day, all golden-haired and full of sunshine. She didn’t have a mean bone in her entire body.” Mozelle’s gaze slipped from Ben’s as she slid into her memories.

"How does Odette have anything to do with Pascal? She died before Pascal could remember her."

"That might be so, but 'Stinky' never let Pascal forget."

"Who's Stinky?" Ben caught himself tapping his fingers on the table. Why couldn't she just get to the point?

Mozelle's brows furrowed. "Odette was nice to everyone, even Pete Pasquale. Everyone called him 'Stinky' back then on account he came straight to school after helping his father prepare the shrimp seines. He always smelled of shrimp and dead fish.

Ben nodded. He'd done his share of shrimping with his father before his dad traded the shrimp boat for a charter fishing rig. But even while his father was shrimping, Ben's work on the shrimp boats was confined to the late evenings, weekends, and summers. Never before school.

"The kids teased Stinky all the time, until, one day, Odette punched a boy in the mouth and told him to lay off."

Ben leaned back. "Mrs. Littington punched someone in the mouth?" He remembered her as a gentle woman with a soft voice and a sweet smile.

"She sure did. Shocked everyone. Especially Stinky."

"I still don't get the connection."

"Hold on to your britches, Ben, I'm getting there." Mozelle jumped to her feet. "Want more coffee? A beignet? I've got some shrimp gumbo if you'd like me to warm some for you."

He inhaled and counted to ten. Mozelle was only trying to be nice. "No, thank you."

Mozelle topped off Ben's coffee mug with a steamy brew. "When Stinky saw Odette punch the other fella in the mouth, he took her defense as a sign of love. That silly man thought Odette loved him."

"And did she?"

"No, of course not." Mozelle pushed a beignet in front of Ben and sat down across from him. "She was already dating Jason Littington, who'd gone off to college that year. Pete followed her around like a lost puppy for weeks. Poor girl couldn't get rid of him. After one of Jason's visits back to Bayou Miste, Odette disappeared. Her family was pert near frantic with worry. She showed up a day later with Jason. They'd done eloped and she had a shiny new ring on her finger."

"I'm still not seeing the connection. Odette didn't belong to Pete."

"No, she didn't. But Pete thought she'd been forced into marriage with Jason. He even tried to kidnap her and take her into the swamps."

Ben leaned forward in his seat. He couldn't even picture the elegant Mrs. Littington being dragged through the swamps by Stinky Pasquale. "What happened?"

"Jason found Stinky before he could get his boat started. Punched him out and threatened to have him thrown in jail if he ever so much as spoke to Odette again."

"So what does that have to do with Pascal?"

"Pete ended up marrying Frenchie Champeau, whether out of spite or what, no one knows. If it was spite, the darn fool boy only cut off his nose to spite his face. Made himself and Frenchie miserable. Frenchie got pregnant with Pascal at the same time Odette was pregnant with Eric. You'd have thought a child of his own would settle Pete Pasquale down. Instead, he compared Pascal to Eric at every turn."

Ben finished for Mozelle, "And Pascal could never live up to Eric."

"Nope." Mozelle shook her frizzy, brassy head. "Every time Eric excelled in something, Pete was sure to tell Pascal that should have been him."

"Damn." Ben had more than a little empathy for Pascal. He'd witnessed how Pete had belittled him in front of the town last night. "No wonder Pascal hates Eric."

"Yessuh." Mozelle pleated a napkin between her fingers. "Now, I worry about Pascal falling into the same trap as his pappa."

"How so?"

"Didn't you see how Pascal was about Lucie last night?" Mozelle fixed a penetrating gaze on him. "Pantin' after her like a rabid dog, he was."

Why was Mozelle staring at him like he was just as guilty? Suddenly feeling like a rat cornered by a hungry alligator, he squirmed in his chair. Had he been just as obviously smitten as Pascal? "You think Pascal is angry enough at Eric to cause trouble?" Nothing like asking a question about someone else to deflect the scrutiny off oneself. He mentally patted himself on the back, although that squirmy feeling persisted.

"He caused a little trouble last night, didn't he?" Mozelle asked.

"Yeah, but it could have been the alcohol." Ben's job was to discover anybody interfering in Eric's campaign for Congress. Was Pascal Pasquale a threat? Would his obsession with Lucie cause problems?

Damn. He sat up straight. Would Pascal try to kidnap Lucie to keep her from seeing Eric?

"I'm not sure Pascal had the time to trash Eric's car, but he sure has a hankerin' for that Lucie." Mozelle stared hard at him again, then looked down at the napkin she'd shredded. "What happened to you and Lucie? I thought you two were in love way back when."

"That's ancient history." He didn't want to discuss Lucie with Miz Mozelle. She obviously already saw more than he'd intended.

"You two were pretty thick back before you left for the police academy in Baton Rouge. Weren't you engaged?"

"Yeah, for about two days."

"What happened?"

"I got a letter of acceptance to the police academy and she dumped me." The old pain of her rejection turned like a knife in his gut.

"Why didn't you take Lucie with you?"

For some idiotic reason, his mouth opened and answered for him, because surely he wouldn't be telling the queen of gossip about his sorry excuse for a love life. "Couldn't afford to at the time. She told me to go without her—that I wasn't good enough for her."

"Is that what happened?" Mozelle shook her head. "Huh. After you left, she moped around town for weeks as if her favorite puppy had died. Doesn't make sense."

"Did to me. She wised up. Why would she want to marry a cop? I'd never make the kind of money she wanted to marry." Ben stood. "Anyway, she wants Eric. He fits her criteria—rich and influential. As far as I'm concerned, he can have her."

A sad smile tipped the corners of Mozelle's mouth. "Still have feelins for the gal, do you?"

"Hell, no." *Liar.* He turned away from those older, knowing eyes and shook his head to clear the devil whispering in his ear. He *didn't* have feelings for Lucie. She'd dumped him. Why would he ever want to get involved with her again?

And why did he still long to hold her in his arms...?

"Sometimes people have good reasons for pushing the ones they love away. If you still have feelings for her, you ought to ask her why she sent you away."

"Seven years is a long time. I'm not going there again."

Mozelle stood up beside him and laid a hand on his shoulder. "Hurt pretty bad the first time, huh?"

"Something like that."

"Would have been hard to cart a wife around, goin' through the academy and those first few years as a rookie cop, I suppose." Mozelle wrapped two beignets in a napkin and handed them to him.

He took the warm pastries without seeing them. Memories of those last few days with Lucie crowded into his mind. She hadn't changed a bit. Lucie was still beautiful and soft and smelled of roses.

"I see you got some thinking to do. And I got a fella to go visit. Mr. Thibodeaux and I take coffee at this time of the morning." She ushered him to the door. "If you don't eat those beignets, give them to one of your brothers or sisters. And Ben?"

"Yes, ma'am?"

"You should ask Lucie why she really sent you away. A woman's mind can work in mysterious ways."

He stepped out onto the sunflower mat, his head clouded with memories. Why *had* Lucie pushed him away? And why had she moped around after he'd gone? Could his angry words have hurt her? At the time, he hadn't thought so. She'd been pretty harsh with him, blind-siding him with her rejection.

Hell, nothing made sense when it came to women.

Why couldn't women be more straightforward, like men?

***

"*Mamère*!" Lucie stood with her door open and her mouth hanging slack. "What are you doing here?"

"Don't an old woman have de right to visit her favorite grand-daughter?"

Her eyes narrowed. "Since when do you come visit me? You usually send a command for me to visit you. And grandmothers aren't supposed to have favorites."

"Be dat as it may, don't be rude and keep dese ol' bones standin' on de steps."

"I'm sorry." Lucie stepped aside, allowing the swamp's most infamous Voodoo queen access to the inner sanctum of her one-bedroom garage apartment. She followed at a distance, wary and ready for anything. *Mamère* never paid her a visit. "If this has anything to do with the fight at the barbecue last night, I didn't start it."

Gran LeBieu worked her way through the apartment to the minuscule kitchen where she rummaged until she located Lucie's stash of tea bags. "Can't a body visit family wit'out de second degree?"

Eyes narrowed, Lucie propped a fist on one hip. "I've never known you to just go visit. Fess up. Why'd you come?"

With a teacup full of water in her hand, her grandmother fumbled with the door of the microwave, trying to pry it open. "Newfangled gadgets, can't open dem to save my life."

Lucie opened the door, stuck the cup inside, and turned the oven on. Then she leaned against the counter, her arms crossed over her chest. "*Mamère*, you're stalling."

The old woman stared straight into her eyes, her gaze direct and unflinching. "Let me get my tea, den we be settin' for a come-to-Jesus talk."

A lead weight sank to the bottom of Lucie's stomach. She felt as she had when she'd gotten caught stealing a watermelon from Charlie Hughes's watermelon patch. Had her grandmother found out about the spell? If so, who'd spilled the beans? Alex? Calliope? They were the only ones that knew. Now, here she was quaking in her slippers, fixin' to have an inch or two skinned from her hide.

The microwave binged. With a teabag in one hand and the cup of hot water in the other, the most sought-after and feared Voodoo queen in the Atchafalaya Basin made herself at home on Lucie's couch. "Come. Sit."

"I can explain," Lucie blurted.

The older woman held up a thick finger. "Don't you be talkin'. Let me tell you a thing or two." Her grandmother dipped the tea bag into the steaming water several times, dragging out the agony until Lucie thought she'd scream. "I don't know what you be up to, and maybe I don't want to know."

"You don't?" She sagged against the arm of the couch, relief filling her stomach like a cool drink of water.

Gran LeBieu gave her one of those stares that might as well have been attached to a curse.

Lucie stiffened and straightened away from the couch, her stomach churning again.

"Is dere something you be wantin' to tell your ol' *Mamère?*"

A flood of heat filled her face. "No, there's nothing out of the ordinary going on, nothing at all."

Liar, liar, pants on fire, a wicked voice called out in her head. How could she sit there and tell her grandmother a bald-faced lie? This woman had taken her in when her own mother had abandoned her.

Lucie dropped to her knees in front of the old woman, tears welling in her eyes. "Oh, Gran, I can't lie to you. My life is so screwed up, I don't know what's up from down."

Gran LeBieu patted her hands. "Everyt'ing is going to be fine. Jes you wait and see."

Lucie buried her face in her grandmother's bright-red muumuu. "Have you ever done something you wished you hadn't, but you can't undo it without hurting others?"

"You be talkin' in riddles, girl." Gran LeBieu's forehead wrinkled.

With a sigh, Lucie pushed to her feet and turned away. She really should tell her grandmother everything, starting with— "You know Eric Littington, don't you?"

"Jason Littington's boy?"

"Yes." She spun to face her grandmother. "He's handsome, smart, and going places in his political career."

"Nice young man, if I recall." The old woman's brows wrinkled. "What's your point?"

Cold feet set in, and Lucie's good intentions froze. She forced a casual shrug. "No point, I was just making a comment."

"What about dat Benjamin Boyette?"

Her heart flip-flopped. Now why would Gran LeBieu bring him up? She couldn't remember saying anything regarding Ben since her grandmother walked through the door. "What about him?"

The older woman slid a sideways glance at her. "He's handsome, smart, and going places."

"Gran, he's a bug exterminator."

The old woman's lips thinned. "It's an honest livin'."

"Besides, why should I care?" Her nonchalance had cost her with that pesky little voice inside telling her she was fibbing. She still cared.

Her grandmother's brows rose on her dark forehead. "Why, indeed?"

She fought not to squirm under her grandmother's scrutiny. "It's not like it was before he left, if that's what you're thinking."

"I wasn't thinkin' anything."

"He never loved me."

Gran LeBieu shook her head, a sad frown creasing her forehead. "You sent him away."

"It was something he'd wanted all his life. If I had married him, he would never have gone." The seven-year-old loss still hit her square in the gut. "And what do I get for my sacrifice? He called me a bayou bimbo!"

"He was hurt and angry."

"What was I? Chopped sushi?" Lucie wrapped her arms around her middle, fighting tears. She refused to shed another over that man. "Gran, he didn't come back."

"Would you? If I be recallin' rightly, you threw his love back in his face."

"He didn't come back." She repeated, her voice fading off as a damned tear spilled from the corner of her eye.

"Have you told da boy you still love him?"

"I *don't* love him. He's rude and overbearing, and couldn't care less about me. Besides, I'm going to marry Eric Littington."

Every line in Gran LeBieu's face spelled disapproval. "Do you love Eric?"

The question was the crux of all the arguments she'd had with herself and her friends. But she'd gone into this plan with her eyes wide open, and she wasn't ready to back down. "What does it matter? Lots of marriages are based on respect. Love is too hard and...messy."

"Can't have the satisfaction of making a mud pie if you don't get your hands in the mud."

Lucie pouted as she had when she was a child. "What if I don't like mud?"

"Mud is good for the swamp girl."

"That's just it, I'm tired of living in the swamp. Eric is my ticket out."

"Marriage shouldn't be a ticket, it should be all about the love between a man and a woman."

With her heart still aching from a years-old wound, Lucie couldn't hear her grandmother. Didn't want to. "Love hurts too much."

The older woman nodded once. "Sometimes. Nothing be worthwhile if you don't work hard for it."

"Love has to be equal on both sides."

"'Xactly. Think of what you be sayin', girl. Eric is a good man. Does *he* deserve to be one side to an empty equation? Dat don't add up, Lucie."

"I have thought about it." She threw her shoulders back and stood with her feet slightly apart. "I'm going to marry Eric and we'll live happily ever after, just like a friggin' fairy tale." Her bold statement had lost its effect with the big tears that chose that moment to pop over the edge of her eyelids and slide down her cheeks.

"Then why aren't you happy, now? Don't you want to know the joy of loving and being loved?"

Her mouth moved but nothing came out. Why wasn't she happy? Wasn't Eric falling in love with her just as she'd planned? *Hell.* "I don't care if I ever fall in love again."

"Love has a way of finding you." Her grandmother touched a finger to Lucie's chin and tipped it up. "You jes got to be patient and be ready for it when it comes."

"I was patient for seven years. I can't be patient anymore." She scrubbed the tears from her cheek. "That's why I've done something stupid. Gran, I—"

Her grandmother laid a chubby finger over Lucie's mouth. "You don't have to tell me everything right now. When you be good and ready, come see me."

She smiled through her watery eyes. "You're right, Gran. I made this mess, I need to try to fix it first before I call in the big guns."

"Remember, yer ol' *Mamère* is only a boat ride away. If you be needin' me, I be dere." The old woman swallowed one more sip of tea and stood. "Now, I got a handsome young man waitin' to take me back to de swamp where I belong."

She leaned forward and kissed her grandmother's cheek. "Thanks for coming to see me, Gran."

"Don't wait too long to call on the big guns, *ma petite*." Gran LeBieu kissed her on the cheek and let herself out the door and down the steps.

Lucie leaned against the doorframe and resisted the urge to follow the older woman out into the swamps where she could hide from all her mistakes.

Her grandmother climbed up into a rusty old pickup with Maurice Saulnier. After a few chugs and coughs, the ancient chariot lurched to life and out of the driveway.

As the truck disappeared down the narrow street, Alex's bright-red Jeep fishtailed around the corner, honking and burning rubber as if a maniac were at the wheel.

What the hell?

Lucie waited until Alex's Jeep screeched to a complete stop before she descended the stairs. No sense putting herself up as a target to the crazed driver.

Before the engine shut off, Alex and Calliope flung the doors open and leaped out.

"Did you see the front page?" Alex asked.

"Oh my God, Lucie," Calliope interjected. "It's all over the parish and clear down to N'Awlins."

"What is?" Lucie asked.

"The picture of you kissing the most eligible bachelor in the state of Louisiana." Alex ducked back into the Jeep and pulled the New Orleans *Times-Picayune* from the seat.

Lucie swallowed the wad of guilt lodged in her throat only to have it hit rock bottom in the pit of her stomach. There, occupying half of the front page, was a picture of her in a lip-lock with Eric Littington.

CHAPTER 12

"So, Miss I-Can-Fix-Everything-With-Magic, what are you going to do about this?" Alex tapped her finger against the picture of Lucie kissing Eric.

Lucie cringed. "Nothing."

"Nothing?" Alex folded the paper and whacked it against her palm. "You can't do *nothing*. What about Ben?"

"What about him?" She feigned indifference. But she wondered if he'd read the article, and, if so, did he give a rat's ass?

A plain four-door sedan slid up against the curb, followed by another and another, like a rental-car parade.

"What the heck's going on?" Lucie asked.

Out of the first car leaped a reporter in jeans and a tan sports jacket, camera in hand. *Snap!*

The flash blinded her and she staggered backward, suddenly all too aware of the cutoffs, tank top, and house shoes she wore. Had she even combed her hair this morning?

"Miss LeBieu, what are Eric Littington's intentions toward you?" the reporter asked.

The second car parked and another reporter dressed similar to the first leaped out, pad and pencil poised. "Miss LeBieu, does Mr.

Littington pay you for your favors?"

"What!" She stood in stunned silence as cars filled the street, and more reporters shouted questions.

"Come on," Alex grabbed her elbow, spun her around and hustled her up the stairs.

Calliope followed at a slower pace, her eyes rounded.

Lucie pushed through her doorway into the safety of her apartment, away from the shouting reporters.

"No, Eric hasn't made his intentions known that I know of," Calliope was saying at the top of the stairs.

Alex snagged Calliope's arm and yanked her through the door. Then she leaned out and shouted, "Miss LeBieu has no comments to make at this time. Please, go away."

Just inside the front door, Lucie peeked out at the crowd gathering in the driveway below. Her head spun and her stomach felt like the inside of a coffee grinder. "Where did they all come from?"

Alex shut the door, leaned her back against it, and crossed her arms over her chest. "From all over Louisiana."

Lucie pushed a hand through her tangled hair. "Why such a big deal over a little kiss?"

With an exaggerated roll of her eyes, Alex stomped into the living room. "Honey, if you haven't figured it out yet, you've been sniffing too many swamp fumes. Eric's running for high government office. Any little scandal means big news."

"Um, I like the guy with the brown hair in the denim shirt." Calliope stood next to the window and was staring out of it. "Do you think I could get him to go out with me?"

"If you promised him the scoop on Lola LeBieu here," Alex said.

Calliope turned to look at Alex, a small frown creasing her forehead. "Who's Lola?"

"Lucie, you yutz!" Alex raised her hands to the ceiling. "I was talking about Lucie!"

Lucie couldn't help the little grin that sneaked out. Calliope could be so clueless at times.

"And what are you smiling about? You could ruin Eric's entire campaign." Alex paced across the room and spun to face her. "And what about Ben?"

"Could you please leave Ben out of this?" she asked in frustration.

"I can't. He's my brother. How do you think he'll feel when he sees this?" She shook the paper at Lucie.

Why did Alex have to be so pushy about Ben? "Why would he even care? He's been away for years and hasn't spoken word one to me. Besides, we don't have a clue whether or not the spell worked."

"I sure as hell hope it didn't." Alex twisted her hair in the back and clamped it in place. "That bug flew over DeeDee Dubois and Mo Saulnier, as well as Larry Ezelle and Elaine Smith. Now wouldn't they all make fine couples?"

"Ooh, there's one with blond hair and blue eyes. *Yoo-hoo!*" Calliope yelled through the window, fluttering her fingers. Then in a conversational voice she said, "I heard Elaine left town in a hurry this morning."

Lucie's heart flip-flopped and bounced up into her throat. "She what?"

Calliope turned toward Alex and Lucie. "She left town."

"How do you know?"

"I thought everyone knew." Calliope's attention strayed back to the window.

"Apparently not." Alex walked to Calliope and grabbed her shoulders. "Focus, Calliope. How do you know about Elaine?"

"Hey, you don't have to hold on so tight." The redhead shook Alex's grip loose and brushed her hands over her arms. "Miz Mozelle called Mirna Mae, who told Josie Ezelle, who called me."

Lucie paced in front of the couch, her head spinning with this new development. "Why did she leave?"

"Josie said something about postponing the wedding. Oh, I don't know. You know I have this short-term memory problem. I can't remember all the details. All I know is that she left town this morning."

"Did Craig go with her?" Lucie held her breath, waiting for the answer. *Please, let Craig have gone with her.*

"No. I do remember her saying Craig didn't go."

Alex glared at Lucie.

She held up her hands. "Now, don't go putting one and one together to come up with five-hundred and fifty-seven thousand, Alexandra Belle Boyette. There's bound to be a perfectly good explanation for Elaine leaving town."

"You saw the way Maurice was mooning over DeeDee last night. Eric's been all over you since bug-day, and Ben's moping around like he lost his best friend. And now Elaine's gone." Alex propped her hands on her hips. "How many lives do you have to wreck before you fix this problem?"

Her chest hurt and her eyes stung. "Oh, I don't know!" How had everything gotten so messed up? "I barely make enough money at the Raccoon Saloon to pay my own rent. How am I supposed to help *Mamère* with her mortgage? And it's been such a long time… I just wanted someone to fall in love with me and get me out of this hellhole. Is that so bad?" Tears spilled over and trickled down her cheeks. She dashed them away and turned her back on Alex's accusing face.

"Oh, Lucie." Alex's voice softened and she moved to put her arms around her. "Wanting to be loved isn't the problem. It's how you're going about it. You can't *make* a person fall in love with you by using magic."

"Magic works for Gran LeBieu." She shook off Alex's hands and walked away. "Why not me?"

Alex followed. "Do you really want to be with someone the rest of your life knowing you tricked him into marrying you?"

That thought had occurred to Lucie. Often enough to keep her belly in knots. "Eric is so nice. I think he really cares about me."

"Is it the magic or does he truly love you?"

"I don't know."

Alex could be relentless. "And how do you feel about Ben? Do you still love him?"

"How can I respond when I don't know the answer myself?" Why couldn't Alex leave her alone?

"Well, I suggest you find out." Alex strode to the door and paused. "Come on, Calliope."

"Oh, good. Let's hurry before the blond gets away."

"Good grief," Alex muttered. "You'd think you'd gone a whole day without a man in your life."

"I'll have you know," Calliope said, "I haven't been out since a week ago last Saturday."

"Wait a minute." Alex frowned. "You went out with me."

Calliope flipped her long, red hair over her shoulder and smiled as she stepped up to the door. She had that feral look in her eyes she got when she was on the hunt for a man. "That doesn't count."

"Figures." Alex stared over at Lucie. "Think about it, Lucie. I'll call tomorrow." She turned to Calliope, her hand hovering over the doorknob. "On the count of three."

"What?"

"We're going to rush through the door, down the steps, and out to the Jeep."

Her smile turned upside down. "You mean I can't stop and say hi to the nice man with the blond hair and blue eyes?"

"No, Calliope," Alex said.

With a heavy sigh, Calliope's lower lip jutted out. "Darn. Oh, well. Toodles, Lucie. Or should I call you Lola?"

"One. Two. Three!" Alex yanked open the door and shoved Calliope out.

The mob of reporters all yelled at once and camera flashes blinked like fireflies on steroids. Lucie slammed the door shut and leaned against it.

What had she gotten herself into? Did she really want to be the center of attention for the paparazzi and have her entire life laid open to the media?

Bang! Bang! Bang!

She jumped away from the door.

"Miss LeBieu, just a few questions," a reporter called through the solid wood.

With her hands pressed to her ears, she shouted, "No comment."

"Please, Miss LeBieu, we'll only take a moment of your time."

"Go away or I'll call the police."

Silence.

She breathed a sigh and pressed her fingers to her temples. Everything was happening so fast her head hurt.

Wow. The spell must really be working. How could she doubt it? The attraction between Maurice and DeeDee couldn't be explained any other way. And Eric would never consider going out with her and risking his campaign.

Holy swamp fungus! She had a date with Eric today! She glanced at the clock. In exactly twenty minutes. With a fleeting look down at her shorts and tank top, she yelped.

Bang! Bang! Bang!

"Don't you ever give up?" she yelled. "Go away!"

"Lucie, it's me, Ben. Let me in."

Ben? Her heart lurched into overtime. What was Ben doing here? She didn't want to talk to him. Every time she did, she got more confused. Maybe if she didn't answer, he'd go away.

"Lucie, I'm not going away, so you might as well let me in."

She groaned. What was he, her punishment for crimes involving magic? She unlocked the door and walked back into the living room.

Space, she needed space.

The door opened and Ben stepped in. The tiny apartment seemed to shrink with the addition of his broad shoulders.

She couldn't breathe. Had he stolen the air as well as the space?

Ben's hair was mussed as if he'd run his hands through it several times. He used to do that when he was upset about something. Not that she remembered every little detail about him. Such as how he tapped his fingers on the steering wheel to the beat of his favorite Garth Brooks song. Or how he'd stop and stare at the sunset on the bayou. Or how he'd twirl her hair around his finger when he wasn't thinking about anything at all. Her stomach knotted into a sharp pain. No, she didn't remember every little detail. "Why are you here?"

***

"You know why I'm here." Ben took in the view of Lucie in her short shorts and bright-pink tank top and had to remind himself why he was here. *To warn Lucie off Eric.* Perhaps he was overstepping his authority, but he felt partially responsible for the success of Eric's campaign.

Lucie's shoulders slumped. "No, I don't know why you're here. You made yourself clear last time I saw you."

He ignored her words and stalked toward her. "Just tell me one thing." He stared into her eyes. "Do you love him?"

Say no.

"By him, I assume you mean Eric?" She looked away, refusing to meet his gaze. She was stalling. If she really loved Eric, she wouldn't hesitate with her answer. Would she?

He stopped in front of her. "Do you love him?" *Uh-oh, he'd gotten too close.* Now he could smell her perfume, a soft blend of roses. The same scent she'd used seven years ago. Some women never changed. The memories invoked threatened to overwhelm him, and he swayed toward her. If he raised his hand he could brush his fingers against her breasts.

The same breasts that were rising and falling in an erratic rhythm.

What was he thinking? This was Lucie, his ex-fiancée. The woman who hadn't loved him enough to marry him seven years ago.

Lucie stepped back, and inhaled. "I don't know why everyone is making such a big deal over a little kiss."

"Was that all it was?"

"Yeah, just a kiss." She tipped her head back and met his gaze square-on, as if challenging him to argue with her.

"If I had kissed you, you wouldn't say that."

Her lips parted in a silent gasp, her eyes opening wide, before they narrowed. "You think pretty highly of your talents, Mr. Boyette."

"Do you doubt me?" He stepped closer.

She inched backward and pushed a stray hair behind her ear. "You flatter yourself. I'm not the least bit interested in you." Her gaze darted to the far corner of the room, avoiding his.

"That's not the impression I got day before yesterday." That kiss had been crazy good.

She made a face. "Temporary insanity."

He reached out and turned her face back to his. "Are you afraid of me, Lucie?"

Her chin rose out of his grip. "No, I'm not."

When he closed the distance again, her breath caught but this time she remained in position, her shoulders stiffening as if bracing for impact. She pushed her hair behind her ear again. *Ah-ha*. She had to be only a step away from all-out panic.

He almost smiled. He liked to make her uncomfortable. She sure as hell made him uncomfortable, from the twitch next to his eye all the way down to his— Well, everywhere. "Does he make you moan like I used to?" he whispered.

She stared at his mouth, her tongue swiping nervously across her lips. "Past tense. Ancient history," she said, her voice breathy.

"Are you sure?" He ran his palm along her jawline and into the hair at the nape of her neck. God, she felt all silky and feminine. His groin tightened.

She tipped her head backward, but she didn't move away. "I'm immune to you, Ben. You're old news."

He drew her closer until his lips were only a sigh away. "Does he make you shiver in anticipation?"

Her body quivered beneath his hand as if directed by his suggestion.

All teasing forgotten, he sealed her lips with his. He'd come to prove a point. Admittedly, at that exact moment, he couldn't remember what the point was. All he knew were the touch, the feel, and the incredible scent of her. Like an erotic addiction, destined to scorch his soul.

When her lips parted on a gasp, he dove in, tasting and teasing, his tongue against hers. His hand swept down her back to cup her cutoff-clad derriere, hauling her belly against the stiff ridge of his denim fly.

She leaned against him, her fingers clutching at his shirt instead of pushing away. Her hands slid up his chest to circle his neck and she pressed her breasts to him.

His heart racing, his veins pumped blood so fast through his body he had a head rush. Which must account for *his* temporary insanity. Hell, for seven years, he'd worked hard to forget this woman. What was he thinking, kissing her?

Thinking was no longer an option. All he could do was feel. The softly frayed edges of her shorts tickled his fingers and he inched his hands lower to slide across the rounded swells of her bottom.

Her skin was silky-smooth and warm. When she drew away to fill her lungs, he didn't relinquish his hold or allow her a chance to remember it was him kissing her, not Eric.

With the ease of someone who knows the way, he trailed kisses from her lips along the side of her cheek to the sensitive spot behind her ear.

Another shiver shimmied across her frame and she moaned deep in her throat.

"Ah, Lucie," he said against her hair. "How could you say you love someone else when you make love to me like this?" He kissed her hair and sucked her earlobe into his mouth.

But her body was no longer melting softly against his. Her back had stiffened and she sure wasn't moaning any more. She removed her hands from around his neck and shoved against his chest. "Benjamin Franklin Boyette, you're about as low as a scum-sucking catfish."

He leaned back and forced a carefree grin while his heart hammered crazily inside. "Why, because I proved a point?"

Her eyes narrowed. "And what point might that be?"

"You don't love Eric."

With a quick downward sweep, she knocked his hands from around her hips. "I'm going to marry Eric Littington and there's nothing you can do to stop me."

He steeled himself from reeling backward, trying to ignore the kick in the gut he experienced from her words. So, she wanted to marry Eric. "What, is he rich enough for you, Lucie? Is he successful enough to make you finally want to tie the knot?"

With her soft, sensuous lips forming a hard line, she met his gaze with a hard-ass stare. "At least he isn't a cop dropout bug exterminator." With a quick sidestep, she ducked around him and practically ran for the door. "Leave, Ben. You're good at that."

"And you're good at throwing me out, aren't you?" The heat of desire he'd felt only moments ago surged hotter in his anger. "Well, Lucie, if a loveless marriage is what you want, I hope you get what you deserve."

She opened the door and waved her hand like Vanna White motioned toward the letters on *Wheel of Fortune*. Turning her back to him, she stared out at the street below.

If that was the way she wanted it, then to hell with her. He marched toward the door.

Just as he reached her, Lucie said, "Omigod!" and slammed the door.

His momentum carried him forward and he had to put his hands up to keep from crashing nose-first into the solid wood paneling. "Jesus, Lucie! First you want me to leave, and now you—"

"Shut up and let me think." Her gaze darted around the tiny room, and she wrung her hands. "There!"

Huh?

She pointed at the coat closet next to the door. "Get in there." Before he could move, she hooked her arm through his elbow and dragged him to the side.

"No way." Ben planted his feet in the carpet. "Do you mind telling me what the hell's going on?"

***

Lucie shot a quick glance out the window, still stinging from Ben's kiss and follow-up comments. But she refused to let him get the better of her. Did he think he could waltz in, kiss her, and make her forget about all her dreams and plans? Okay, so she forgot everything in the world when Ben kissed her. As if all the lonely years had been stripped away, she fit right into his arms. How did he do that? For heaven's sake, he'd been gone for *so* long.

A sleek white limousine pulled up next to the curb outside. The only person she knew who could and would drive around Bayou Miste in a limo was Eric. The chauffeur climbed out and opened the back door. Eric emerged dressed in a sexy black tuxedo.

Lucie wondered how he'd gotten away without a swarm of reporters following him but talk about a knight in shining armor charging in to rescue her on his trusty steed—okay, limo. Eric was everything a girl dreams about—sophisticated, charming, incredibly handsome, and loaded. Everything Lucie needed to be happy.

Except love, whispered that pesky voice in the back of her conscience.

So, she'd grow to love him, and he would love her. She had the spell to thank for that.

Like eating raw persimmons, her success wasn't sitting so well with her. Eric was such a nice man. Didn't he deserve more?

The man in question leaned into the car and pulled out an embarrassingly large bouquet of white roses.

And he was romantic. Definitely Prince Charming to her Cinderella. Only she was feeling a little more like one of the wicked, conniving stepsisters than the sweet-tempered soon-to-be-princess.

Ben leaned over her shoulder. "Oh, so that's how the cookie crumbles."

Drat the man. Why did he have to come back to Bayou Miste and confuse her so? Well, she just had to shove a little steel into her backbone and do what she'd set out to do. Ben no longer had a place in her future.

Then how could she explain how unraveled she'd gotten over one kiss?

Ben was smiling all superior-like.

She'd show him. "Yeah, I told you I'm going to marry Eric Littington, and I don't need you messing things up for me. Now, are you going to hide in the closet, or am I going to have to scream?"

"You wouldn't."

She sucked in a deep breath and opened her mouth to scream.

Ben clapped a hand over her lips and glanced out the window. "Okay, okay. I'll get in the closet."

"Good." She held the door for him. If only she had a key to lock the big oaf in. It would serve him right.

Just as he stepped inside, a knock sounded on the door. "You better get that, you don't want to keep your future waiting."

She slammed the door, narrowly missing his nose.

With a smile plastered on her face she didn't really feel, Lucie opened her front door to what could only be described as a bush full of lovely white roses.

"Eric, what a surprise." She stood blocking the doorway. "I must have lost track of the time."

"I'm sorry. Should I have called ahead?"

Add considerate to his list of attributes. Unlike the jerk in the closet.

"No, no, I should have remembered. Could you give me a few minutes to change into something more appropriate?"

"Certainly, take all the time you need."

Lucie started to close the door in his face.

But Eric stuck his hand out. "Do you mind if I wait inside?" He grinned. "I've had a group of reporters on my tail all day. I put some diversionary tactics in place before I left the house. I don't know how long that will last."

"Oh, yeah. Come on in." She spoke loud enough to get the message across to Ben in the closet. Double drats! How was she going to get rid of Eric so that she could shove her unwanted closet guest out the door? "I guess you saw the papers."

"I think everyone in Louisiana saw the papers." His gaze scanned the interior of her little apartment. "Do you have a vase to put these in?"

"No, but I have a glass I think would work just fine. Why don't you have a seat on the couch?" She raced for the kitchen and found the biggest plastic cup she could and filled it half-full of water. With the cup balanced in her hand, she ran back to the living room, all five steps, and held out the cup. "Could you put the roses in this while I go change?"

"Sure."

She set the cup on the table and made a dash for her bedroom. Her nerves were screaming by the time she shut the door between them.

"So what do you think we should do about the picture?" Lucie asked through the door panel.

She riffled through her clothes until she found a figure-hugging, strapless red dress. She called it her go-to-hell red dress because when she wore it she felt like she could rule the world and everyone else could go to hell if they didn't like it. The dress gave her a sense of power. And right now she could use an infusion of confidence. Especially when she felt as if her entire world was in the midst of crashing down around her ears.

And if Ben just happened to see her in it, maybe he'd regret what he'd left behind so many years ago.

"I've been thinking about what to do," Eric's muffled voice drifted through to her as she stripped out of her cutoffs, tank top, and bra. "I've come up with a plan."

"Yeah?" She slipped the slinky red dress up over her hips and zipped the back. Then she slid on her black stilettos, fluffed her hair, and feeling very go-to-hell, threw open the door to her bedroom. "And what plan is that?"

Eric turned toward her, his mouth opened to say something but his jaw dropped to his chest instead.

Lucie basked in the self-satisfying moment of silence, congratulating herself on her choice of dresses.

"Wow, Lucie." Eric's head swayed from side to side. "Wow."

Anxious to get out of the apartment and away from Ben, she grabbed her purse and headed for the door. "I'm ready to go. You can tell me about your plan on the way to the limo." She raised her volume as she stood next to the closet.

"Oh, the plan's simple." Eric opened the front door and held it for her.

Just another reason to love Eric over Ben. Eric knew what chivalry meant. The bug man probably couldn't even spell it. "How sweet of you to open my door for me." Again she spoke a little louder than necessary.

"I'd crawl to the ends of the earth for you, Lucie." He lifted her hand to his lips and pressed a kiss to her knuckles. "Which brings me to my plan."

Her heart did little flip-flops. Not many men had ever kissed her knuckles. The sensation was not unpleasant. With time, she was sure she could grow to love Eric. And to hell with Ben! As Eric lingered over her hand, she started feeling a little uncomfortable. "You said you had a plan?"

"The plan? Oh, yes. I think we should announce our engagement."

"What?" She staggered backward at the same time as a loud *whomp* could be heard from the vicinity of the closet.

"What was that?" Eric peered over her shoulder at the closet.

"Nothing. Aren't we late for dinner? We should be going." She hooked her arm through Eric's and dragged him through the door.

"No, I'm sure I heard a sound coming from that closet."

"It's b-bugs. I have a serious bug problem. I've been fighting them for years."

He frowned, resisting her tugs on his arm. "Then maybe we should call in an exterminator to take care of the job? I know one you might use."

She almost laughed hysterically. "I definitely don't need an exterminator to fix my problem. He'd probably only make it worse. Really, come on. I'm finished here."

"Okay, if you're sure." He opened the door a crack. "Coast is clear of reporters, let's go."

When they'd settled in the backseat of the luxurious limousine, Lucie heaved a huge sigh. Juggling two men was absolutely exhausting. Perhaps she should consider breaking the spell, after all. She was beginning to think men were too much trouble.

CHAPTER 13

Engagement!

Ben stumbled out of the closet into Lucie's empty living room. His head smarted where he'd banged it on the hanging bar, but it didn't feel nearly as pained as his heart.

Eric and Lucie were not right for each other—he barely knew her. He didn't know that when she slept she snored softly. What kind of politician's wife snored? Eric would drag her all over the country and leave her alone often as his schedule demanded. Lucie didn't do alone very well. Ever since her mother dropped her and her sister Lisa on her *Mamère* LeBieu, she'd done everything in her power to always be with someone. She belonged in the swamp with people who knew and understood her. People like Alex and Calliope.

And me?

Ah, hell. He'd sworn he wouldn't get involved with her again and here he was all eaten up by Lucie and Eric's engagement. He ought to be happy for her. She always wanted financial security and a real family.

She could have had all that with him. Okay, so maybe the financial security hadn't been there seven years ago, but he had it now. As a detective for the state police, he made decent money and he'd even managed to put away a little nest egg.

He pushed his hand through his hair and winced. So what? Lucie wouldn't marry him—hell, she'd rejected him once. Why risk a second rejection? Besides, she'd made it perfectly clear what she wanted. Or rather, whom she wanted. And he wasn't in that picture.

He strode for the door and paused with his hand on the knob.

The taste of Lucie still lingered on his lips. Her soft curves had fit perfectly against him when he'd held her. What happened all those years ago to make her go from hot to cold and break off their engagement? Maybe Mozelle was right—he should ask Lucie. At least he'd know the real reason and could put the issue to bed.

He groaned. Bed was exactly where he wanted to be with Lucie. But she was out with Eric, possibly getting engaged and making a commitment to another man when she couldn't make that same commitment with Ben.

Give it up, Ben Boyette.

As he jerked the door open and strode out, his cell phone chirped.

He hit the talk button. "This is Ben."

"Ben. Jason Littington. Could you get over here right now? I believe Eric's campaign has reached a crisis point."

"Sure. Do you want me to bring Eric?"

"No. He's part of the problem. So, can you make it?" His words were clipped and angry, as they used to get when Eric was in trouble as a kid.

Ben wondered what else could go wrong. "I'll be there in five minutes."

Click.

As promised, five minutes later, he entered Jason's home office.

Mr. Littington stopped drumming his fingers against the solid mahogany desk and rose to greet him. "Thank God you're working to protect Eric and his campaign. I didn't know who else to turn to."

"What's the problem? And why isn't Eric here to discuss it with us?"

Jason tossed the front page of the *Times-Picayune* across the desk to land in front of him.

The kick in his gut was only slightly less painful than the first time he'd seen the picture of Eric and Lucie kissing. "Is this what you called me over to discuss?"

Jason's brows rose. "Did I underestimate you, Ben? Do you not see the potential this LeBieu woman has to ruin Eric's run for Congress?"

He bristled at Jason's reference to "this LeBieu woman." "What's wrong with Eric seeing Lucie?"

"She's not the kind of woman a congressman marries." Jason strode across the floor and stood at the window staring out at the night. "I knew she was trouble when he brought her to the barbecue. Now he's taking her out to one of the more exclusive restaurants in Morgan City."

"So?"

"So? The public will have them married before the first constituent casts a vote. I knew he should have married a respectable woman before he started this campaign. Single candidates have too much stacked against them. The public wants to know the candidate is stable and ready to assume responsibility. Not gallivanting around the swamps with a bayou bimbo."

Ben counted to ten to keep from blasting Jason. But the ten count didn't help. "Lucie isn't a bayou bimbo." He couldn't ignore the irony of his defense. Hadn't he used those very same words in anger on Lucie when they'd broken up?

Mr. Littington snorted. "She works as a waitress in a bar wearing skimpy outfits that show more than they cover. What else would you call it?"

"A living." Littington was usually so tolerant of the people of Bayou Miste and would gladly sink money into the community to keep it alive. But when it came down to his son, Jason lost all perspective.

"My son cannot marry a bar waitress. It'll ruin him."

"Being a waitress isn't a bad thing." Why was he sticking up for Lucie and Eric? He didn't want Lucie to marry Eric any more than Jason did.

Jason smacked his palm on the desktop. "You have to stop Eric from making a huge mistake."

His head jerked up. "*Me?*"

"Yes, you. Sources say you and this Lucie woman used to be an item."

"That's history. Old history."

Jason strode across the room and stood directly in front of him. "I'll pay you double what you make on the force to make your affair with Lucie current news."

"I can't do that to Eric or Lucie."

"I'll pay you triple."

Triple was a lot of money. "No, I can't. For one, it's against my ethics. And if Lucie and Eric really love each other, more power to them."

"Then I'll pay you to convince them they aren't in love." Jason spun and paced across the Oriental carpet. "The polls indicate that Eric stands a real chance of winning against the incumbent, Gasson. A scandal could blow this opportunity. Ben, they've only known each other for a few days. How could they possibly be in love?"

He pondered Jason's statement. If Eric and Lucie weren't in love, he'd be doing them a favor by breaking it up before they made the ultimate mistake of getting married. "If I decide to test them, and they prove they are really in love, will you step back and let Eric and Lucie make their own choices about marriage?"

Jason chewed on Ben's question, his brows drawing together into a straight line over his eyes. "I don't believe Lucie is the right woman for my son."

"That wasn't the answer I was looking for." Ben stuck out his hand. "It's been nice talking to you, Mr. Littington. I'll show myself out." When Jason didn't take the proffered hand, he shrugged and turned toward the door.

"Wait!" Littington grabbed his arm.

He stared down at the hand, then back over his shoulder at his friend's father. "Yes, sir."

"Okay, I'll step back. But you have to make an effort to interfere with their romance. A real effort to come between them."

"I can do that." He wanted to know whether Lucie really loved Eric anyway. "And I don't want your money for this job. I'll do this on my own. If they end up getting married, I'll consider it my wedding present."

Jason opened his mouth to protest.

Ben held up a finger. "If they aren't meant to be together, hopefully Eric will understand I did it to save him from a future divorce."

The older man nodded. "Fair enough."

"Now, if that's all you needed from me, I'll get back to work."

Ben's thoughts were already miles away at a fancy restaurant in Morgan City. He had a few ideas on how to "test" Lucie and Eric's love for each other. He couldn't wait to put the ideas in motion.

***

Lucie sat in back of the limousine with Eric's arm draped over her shoulder. They'd been to the perfect restaurant, eating steak and lobster cooked to perfection, drinking the perfect wine for the meal, and Eric had been perfectly romantic the entire evening. Then why the hell was she thinking of Ben's kiss?

"A penny for your thoughts?" Eric squeezed her arm, his thumb brushing against her breast.

Lucie turned so that he couldn't quite reach the front of her dress and forced a laugh. "You'd be wasting your penny."

"Is there something troubling you? Was the food not to your liking? Have I said anything to upset you?"

"No, not at all. Everything about tonight was"—she struggled to hide a grimace—"perfect."

"Lucie, being with you has made me so happy. It's as if you've brought the magic back in my life."

A lump of cold guilt settled in the pit of her stomach. Why did he have to go and mention magic?

He hugged her close against him. "Lucie, I've felt pretty lousy all evening about my earlier suggestion."

A sudden weight lifted off her chest and she smiled up at Eric. "You, too?"

He grinned. "Yeah, I realize how badly I handled it."

She laughed. "Oh, thank goodness. I thought you were serious."

The limousine pulled up in front of her apartment, effectively ending their conversation while the chauffeur climbed out and opened the door for them.

She slid out first and turned to Eric, who'd straightened behind her. "Thank you for a wonderful evening. It couldn't have been nicer." *Now will you please go so I can think?*

"I'll walk you to your door. You can never be too careful." He snatched her hand in his with a surprisingly strong grip.

"Aren't you afraid the press will see us together?" She glanced around, realizing for the first time she hadn't seen any the entire evening. "Speaking of which. I haven't seen a single one all evening."

Eric's chest puffed out. "I made reservations in Morgan City and tipped off the reporters so that we could go the opposite direction. I wanted time alone with you. Now, let me escort you to your door."

"Okay." But only to the door, then she'd go in alone. She led the way to the top of the stairs of the white clapboard garage apartment. When she reached the top, she faced Eric. "Thank you again for a wonderful evening." *Now please, please, please, please go.*

Instead, he raised her hand to his lips and pressed a kiss to her fingers. "Lucie, I was serious about my earlier suggestion. It was the delivery I regret."

Oh, no. Her heart tightened in her chest. *Please just go home.*

"I think I've loved you, Lucie, from the very first moment I saw you in the Raccoon Saloon. I would be so honored if you would marry me."

Like a movie where the sound was out of sync with the video, Eric's lips moved and his words sank in a second later. And a full speechless half-minute later, her brain engaged. "Eric, we've only known each other for three days. How can you be so sure?"

He laughed and pressed her hand to his chest. "I don't know. All I know is the enchantment I feel being in your company, and I don't want to lose that."

Her heart did a sliding plunge to the bottom of her belly. "Are you sure? Marriage is a huge step. One you should make with the person you want to spend the rest of your life with." *Like I wanted to do with Ben.*

"I've never been more sure of anything before in my life."

"What about your campaign? Will this make things worse for you?" She grimaced. "I don't have the right credentials to be a politician's wife."

"I don't care." His brows furrowed. "Would you be terribly disappointed if I didn't get elected?"

"No, of course not."

"I wouldn't care as long as I had you."

Oh man, had that bug's magic worked, or what? Eric had it bad.

"Eric, I think you're smart, sweet, and so romantic." She fought for the right words. Hell, she fought for *any* words. What did she want to say to him? Here he was presenting her with exactly what she'd schemed to win—a marriage proposal from the most eligible bachelor in the bayou. And all she wanted was for him to disappear.

"I feel a 'but' coming on." He lifted both of her hands and kissed them. "Please don't say no. Give it some thought. I'll wait. I know this is sudden, and, like you said, we've only known each other for a few days. Just promise me you'll think about it?"

Eric was offering her everything she dreamed of—financial security, a lavish lifestyle, and his unconditional love. Why couldn't she say yes? "Okay. I'll think about it."

He blew out a long breath, as if he'd been holding it, waiting for her answer. "Great. Then I'll leave you to your thoughts."

Finally. She had a lot to think about, and the sooner he left the sooner she could get started thinking. She tugged on her hands.

He didn't let go. His blue eyes shone bright in the soft glow of her yellow porch light. He stepped closer until her hands were crushed between their chests. Then he dropped them and pulled her into his arms.

She braced herself, knowing a kiss was expected after a marriage proposal. And maybe, if she kissed Eric, it would shake the taste of Ben's earlier kiss from her mind. The Cajun bug man shouldn't have any bearing on her decision whether or not to marry Eric. She closed her eyes and tipped her lips upward to meet Eric's.

Eric skimmed the edges of her teeth and dove in deeper, his hand sliding from the small of her back to cup her rump, snuggling her closer. The hard ridge of his zipper pressed against her go-to-hell red dress. The man had it *seriously* bad.

She leaned into the kiss, dancing her tongue against his, trying to capture the "magic" he said he felt.

After several rounds of dueling tongues, she sighed. The magic just wasn't there for her. Had the bug only worked on Eric and not her? Or had the magic only worked for her on Ben, since he was the last one the bug had circled? Whatever the case, she had to extricate herself from this embrace as gracefully as possible.

She tipped her head away.

Eric leaned closer, nibbling her lower lip. "Oh, Lucie, I can't believe I found you." He trailed kisses down her neck, his hands siding up her sides to cup her breasts.

How in hell did she get out of this? She couldn't shove him away and risk his falling down the steep steps. She needed some way to distract him.

Bang!

The porch light over their heads exploded into a zillion shards of paper-thin glass, showering down over them.

"What the hell?" Eric clapped his hand on her head and shoved her to the wooden planks of the landing.

"Ouch!" Tiny slivers of glass were embedded in her hands and knees. "Why the hell did you do that?" She tried to rise, but Eric held her down, crouching next to her.

Bang!

Her heart leaped into high gear. The first bang she'd attributed to the glass exploding, but the second one had nothing to do with a faulty lightbulb. "What was that?"

"Gunfire. Give me your key."

"I can't."

"Why?"

"My purse fell down there," she pointed to the ground ten feet below. "Damn, and this was my best dress." She tugged at her skirt to keep her butt cheeks from lighting the evening sky. Then she reached up to pull the top securely over her breasts to keep them from falling out.

So much for her go-to-hell red dress. She'd hate to die all exposed. Why didn't they make sexy dresses for dodging bullets? She should design an all-purpose dress for today's woman. Built to last under the worst conditions, rain, snow, bullets—

"Gerald? You okay down there?" Eric called out to the chauffeur below.

"Yes, sir," he responded from somewhere beneath the stretch limousine.

Eric fumbled in his pocket for his cell phone and punched 9-1-1. "This is Eric Littington. Someone is shooting at us. We're at Lucie LeBieu's apartment. You know the place? Fifteen minutes? That long? Yes, we'll stay low." He hit the end button and looked sideways at Lucie. "Stay low? We're perched on a friggin' deer stand, prime targets for anyone with half an aim. Are you okay? Not hurt, or anything?"

Lucie's lips twisted in a wry grin. "Nothing but my pride." And her dress.

He smoothed her hair out of her face. "Sit tight, I'm going to find out who was shooting."

Her hand reached out to hold his. "Don't, Eric, it's dangerous."

"I can't just stay here and wait. The guy might get away before the police get here."

"Is that such a bad thing?"

"Are you kidding?" Eric grabbed her shoulders and held her away from him, his knitted brows a big indication of his concern. "You could have been killed!"

"And you could be killed."

He shoved his cell phone at her. "Hit 5 and the talk button. I'm going after the guy."

"But—" Eric ran down the stairs and across the narrow driveway to the bushes on the other side. "Come on, Gerald. Let's catch us a prankster."

"Yes, sir." The chauffeur rolled from beneath the car and raced after him.

"Eric!" Lucie climbed to her knees and stared after his disappearing figure.

Bang!

Down on her stomach again, Lucie remembered Eric's instructions and dialed 5.

After barely an entire ring, a curt male voice answered. "Boyette."

"Ben? Oh, thank God!" A sudden sense of relief washed over her, quickly followed by confusion. "Why does Eric have you on speed dial?"

CHAPTER 14

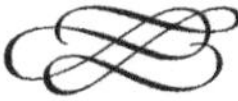

BEN SLOWED HIS EXTERMINATOR TRUCK, PRESSING THE CELL PHONE TO HIS ear. He'd been halfway back from the restaurant in Morgan City, kicking himself for missing Lucie and Eric, and consumed by thoughts of the two together. Had he been so entrenched in images of Lucie in Eric's arms that he'd conjured this call? He held the device away to glance at the phone number. Eric's name was written in digital letters across the white screen. "Lucie? Why are you dialing from Eric's cell?"

"Because he's off in the bushes chasing after some nutcase with a gun." Was that a sniffle? "You didn't answer my question."

Ben's heart thumped against his rib cage, his cop instincts and adrenaline kicking into overdrive. "What do you mean, a nutcase with a gun?"

"Just what I said. Someone took a couple potshots at us, and I ruined my best dress ducking the bullets."

The kick in his gut made him pull his foot off the accelerator. "Holy shit! Lucie, where are you?"

"At my apartment."

He jammed the accelerator to the floorboard. "Stay put. I'll be right there."

"Tell me you're not going to take fifteen minutes like the sheriff?" Despite her complaints about ruining her dress, her voice shook.

"Make it two, sweetheart." He was still four miles from Bayou Miste, but the fear in her voice spurred him to go faster.

She sighed into his ear. "That's more like it. Now, hurry, before Eric gets hurt."

"Don't hang up, darlin'."

"Are you kidding? You're stuck with me."

His heart surfaced from his apprehension for her safety to let her words wash over him. *You're stuck with me.*

If only she meant for life...

As he skidded into her driveway, his heart lodged in his throat. Other than Eric's limo, the driveway was dark and appeared deserted. He leaped from his bug exterminator truck and shouted, "Lucie!"

"Ben?" A shaky voice sounded from the top of her landing and her dark head peered out from between the railings.

"*Merci Dieu*." He released the breath he'd been holding and raced up the stairs.

Lucie eased up to her knees, tears glistening in the moonlight like the shards of glass littering the landing.

Without a thought for Eric, he pulled her into his arms and held her close. Her warmth dispelled the cold, sick feeling he'd had in his helter-skelter race to get here. He smoothed his hand over her hair and down to her bare shoulders. Her skin against his made the old flame in his heart burn even higher. *Lucie, Lucie. Why did you send me away?* his heart cried out. But his mouth remained mute, pressed to her temple.

When her body shuddered against him, he set her away and pushed the hair from her eyes. "You have glass in your hair."

She smiled shakily up at him, tears pooling in her eyes. "That's not the only place I have glass." She held up her hands, where tiny slivers had cut into her tender skin. Blood oozed from the miniature wounds.

His stomach clenched. He was used to seeing blood from more extensive and sometimes mortal wounds. But not on her. He pulled her hand close and stared down at it. "We need more light."

"My hands can wait, I'm more concerned about Eric and the chauffeur."

His tender thoughts exploded in a rush of apprehension. Oh yeah, Eric. His responsibility and his friend. How could he forget? "I'll find them. You go inside."

She frowned and hesitated.

"For once, don't argue, Lucie." His fingers tightened on hers. "I can't go after Eric until I know you're safe."

Her frown disappeared. "I wasn't going to argue. It's just that I can't get in. I dropped my purse below the steps when the light exploded."

He kissed her forehead. "I'll find it. You stay here. But stay down."

Without protest, Lucie crouched in her red dress, her eyes going round again as she peered into the darkness.

He took the steps two at a time, and scrambled among the gravel and weeds until he spotted a thin black shadow that proved to be an evening bag.

Ten seconds later, he had her door open and Lucie escorted into the apartment. He pressed a brief kiss to her lips when he would rather have folded her in his arms and drowned in her. "I'll be back as soon as I find Eric."

"Someone looking for me?" Eric's voice called out from the bottom of the steps.

Lucie stared up at Ben for a moment, her lips poised as if for another kiss. Then she blinked and her face flushed a rosy pink. The moment was gone.

"Eric!" She rushed out the doorway and met Eric halfway down the stairs, hugging him tight as if he were the only person she could ever love.

Ben stood at the top of the stairs telling himself the sight of Lucie in another man's arms didn't bother him. But it did. "Ah-hem. Think you two can knock it off enough to tell me what happened?"

Eric circled Lucie's waist with his arm and walked her up the stairs. "Sorry, Ben. Shall we go inside where I can fill you in while we wait for the sheriff?"

"Only if you get your hands off my girl," Ben wanted to say, but

couldn't. Lucie wasn't his girl anymore. Hadn't been for a long time. And by the looks of it, she was Eric's girl now. But that didn't stop the surge of possessiveness flooding through his body. He needed to hit something, preferably his friend Eric.

As Eric and Lucie climbed the steps, Ben heard a siren in the distance. Eric paused with his foot on the last step and shook his head. "*Now* they come."

The wailing increased until a sheriff's sedan slid sideways into Lucie's driveway.

Lights went on in windows of the nearby houses. Mozelle Reneau opened her front door. "Lucie, what the fool-darn-heck is going on?"

"Don't worry, Miz Mozelle, I'll fill you in tomorrow," Lucie called down to her landlady.

Mozelle squinted. "That you, Ben?"

"Yes, ma'am."

The deputy leaped from his squad car, weapon drawn. "I'm here, everyone just stay calm."

"I'd be a heap happier if you'd point that pistol at something besides me, Billy Ray," Mozelle called out.

"It's okay, deputy," Eric said. "Whoever did the shooting is long gone."

"And how do I know *you* didn't do the shooting?" the deputy asked, turning his pistol to point at Eric.

"Because he was the one being shot at!" Lucie stomped her foot. "Put the gun away before someone gets hurt, Billy Ray."

As if disappointed he didn't get to shoot anyone, the deputy dropped the muzzle of his Glock. "You sure he's gone?"

"Yes. I chased him past the marina before I lost him."

"Damn. I always wanted to apprehend a perp." Billy Ray shoved his weapon into its leather holster.

"Maybe next time," Ben said from the top of the stairs.

Billy Ray took a deep breath and blew it out on a huge sigh. "Someone want to tell me what happened here?"

Eric looked up at Lucie, standing on the landing. "Will you be all right?"

Lucie nodded.

Eric turned and descended the narrow steps. "I'll fill you in."

"You'll need to come down to the sheriff's office to fill out a report."

Eric looked back at Ben. "Could you take care of Lucie while I follow the good deputy to file my report?"

"Don't worry," he said, his night suddenly looking less grim, "I'll take care of her."

"Lucie, I'm sorry the evening turned out this way. I'd planned it to be very special, really unforgettable."

Lucie laughed uneasily. "Mission accomplished. I guarantee I'll never forget tonight."

"See you tomorrow?" Eric gazed up at her with that lovesick-cow plea in his blue eyes.

Ben wanted to puke.

Especially when Lucie nodded.

Eric turned back to the deputy. "Let's get this over with." Then he climbed into the rear of the limo, Gerald assuming the driver's position. After the deputy backed out of the driveway, the limousine followed.

"You two sure you're okay?" Mozelle asked again, hope in her voice. "I got some beignets I can warm up in a jiffy."

"No thanks, Miz Mozelle." Lucie pushed her hair out of her face with the back of her hand. "I'm so tired I can't see straight."

"Thanks, but I think we'll pass, Miz Mozelle. Good night," he said with added emphasis.

Mozelle disappeared behind her door, leaving him and Lucie alone on the landing.

"Come on, let's clean you up." He hooked Lucie's elbow and guided her back into the garage apartment, wondering how the evening had ended up in his favor yet again. Hell, why was he looking a gift horse in the mouth? Eric had asked him to take care of Lucie. Ben had every intention of doing just that.

***

"Damn, damn, damn," Lucie muttered. Her world was knocked askew from earlier that day when she'd known what her goal was and had pursued it relentlessly. Eric was her future, Ben was her past.

Past, past, past.

Why did Eric have to be so nice and trusting? How could he not have a clue about Ben and his impact on her resistance?

Didn't he have even an inkling of how hard she was trying not to feel it? She wanted to marry Eric, not Ben. Then why the hell did she feel more secure and at the same time completely off-balance when around Ben?

And now, just when she was most vulnerable, she was stuck with the jerk.

The jerk smiled. Not an I-got-you-cornered-smile, but a gentle one. Why? Why? Why did he have to go and get all kind and sweet? She was doomed. *Doomed!*

She felt her walls crumbling. But she had to make an effort to forestall the inevitable. "Look, Ben, I can handle it from here. You don't have to stay."

"I made a promise to Littington. I keep my promises."

Ouch. She cringed. That barb hurt more than the glass shards in her hands. She knew he was referring to their broken engagement. But hell, she'd had reasons to break it off. Damned good reasons. But he still hadn't gotten it, and he probably never would. No use rehashing ancient history. "If I ask you to leave, would you?"

He shook his head. His smoldering gaze bore into hers, sending tiny warning signals to her melting brain cells. *Make him leave, before it's too late.*

Then he took her hands in his and raised them palms upward. "Come on, I'll help you pick the glass out of your hands and anywhere else you may have gotten splinters."

The low voice and tender look was her undoing.

He led, and she followed like a lamb to the slaughter. She hadn't been able to resist him in the past—what made her think she could now?

All thoughts of Eric receded into the back of her mind, and all she could think of or feel was Ben. He led her to her little bedroom and sat her on the edge of the bed.

"Where do you keep your first aid kit?"

Too overwhelmed by images of what she and Ben could do beneath the sheets, and keyed up from her near-death experience, she had to remind herself to breathe. "In the medicine cabinet behind the mirror."

He ducked into the bathroom.

She could have jumped up from her questionable perch on the mattress and strolled back into the living room—putting distance between her and the bed. But she didn't. She waited for him to return, and he came back with the first aid kit, cotton balls, and a wet washcloth in hand.

He paused for a moment and gazed at her as if he'd never seen her before. Seven years earlier he'd seen every inch of her, including a few nooks and crannies she'd blushed about.

"What?" She reached up to brush her hair from her face and winced when a shard of glass pressed deeper into her flesh.

He shook his head and hurried forward, laying the items he'd collected on the nightstand. "Nothing. Let me see those hands." He pulled a pair of tweezers from his pocket and sat next to her on the bed. "Let's get those bad boys out of there before your hands get infected."

She sat in numb silence, inhaling the scent that was so very Ben. "You still wear the same cologne." Her eyes suddenly widened. "Did I say that out loud?"

He chuckled. "Yes, you did, and yes, I do. A gorgeous young woman gave it to me a long time ago and I haven't found anything I like better."

Her heart skipped a beat. Was he talking about fragrances, or did he mean he hadn't found another love as great as hers in all these years? "That's a long time stuck with the same-ole-same-ole."

"Some things are good enough to keep for life." He removed one shard of glass at a time until all the little pieces were fished out of her palms. Then he looked up. "Any other places?"

She gulped and gazed longingly into his eyes. She started to shake her head, but she nodded instead, and held out her leg. Her short red dress crept up her thigh, exposing a considerable amount of skin.

A sharp intake of breath indicated that he wasn't as unaffected as he pretended. As his gaze swept the length of her leg from hip to toe, he dropped to one knee. "This—" His voice broke. He cleared his throat and started again. "This won't hurt a bit."

"Promises, promises," she muttered. Getting over him had hurt more than anything. Was she up to getting over him a second time?

His hand circled her ankle and slid up the back of her calf.

No, definitely not. Based on the explosion of her senses at his slightest touch, she wasn't up to washing Ben from her mind. She was a mere mortal, not prone to acts of selflessness, or able to hold up under the pressure of masochistic torture.

When his fingers connected with the sensitive zone at the back of her knee, she moaned.

He darted a worried frown up at her. "Hurt that bad?"

"Oh, yes." He had no idea what he was doing to her or the repercussions that would reverberate through her life afterward. *She* did, yet she still did nothing to stop him. Oh, no, our little swamp girl didn't even try.

His frown deepened. "I'll kill the bastard." With the tips of the tweezers, he eased the slivers of glass from her knees, one at time. His gentle touch, combined with the little prickle of pain, fired her nerves to a screaming pitch.

"That's all of them." He pressed a cotton ball to the mouth of the bottle of rubbing alcohol and tipped it upside down. "This may sting a little."

She was already clamping down hard on her tongue trying to hold back her desire to moan aloud. Or was it to hold back her desire? She'd lost track.

When he pressed the sopping cotton ball to her knee, she jerked forward, pain jolting her temporarily back to her senses.

He blew gently on her knee to ease the fire, only to create a far more destructive burn in her lower abdomen. He pressed a kiss to her knee and another to her inner thigh.

Without conscious thought, she spread her legs ever so slightly, allowing him greater access—to that wet, delicious place.

Ben glanced up at her, as if gauging her resistance.

She should call a halt right here. He was giving her the opportunity. But she couldn't begin to stop the inevitable, and frankly, she didn't want to. Her knees dropped apart, her dress riding higher until the thin line of her black string bikini panties peeked from beneath.

Light flared in Ben's eyes. He leaned forward and, with feathery flicks, glided his tongue in a lazy trail up her thigh, alternating between tonguing and nipping until he was wedged between her legs, his broad shoulders pressing them wider. With a pause, he glanced up at her, his brown eyes reflecting the light from her nightstand, intensifying the gleam in them.

She laced her hands through his curling black hair, urging him closer. "Oh God, Ben, don't stop now."

"As you wish, baby. You're calling the shots." As he spoke, his breath blew against her inner thigh, already highly sensitive to his touch. He backed away enough to close her legs, hook his fingers into the lacy black elastic of her panties, and slide them down her legs. With a flirty flick, he slung the scrap of lace to the far corner.

As cool air hit the moist area between her legs, she tried to spread her legs again.

"Not yet." He held her legs together, then rose from his kneeling position, pulling her off the bed to stand in front of him. "I want to see you."

A warm shiver rippled across her skin and she reached behind her back, lowering the zipper of her strapless red dress until it slid off her breasts and down over her hips to pool at her ankles.

Naked, exposed to the man she'd never stopped loving, she felt no shame in her own skin, just a deep longing.

The fire in Ben's eyes enveloped her, clothing her in the moment.

"Your turn." Lucie stepped forward until her bared breasts rubbed against his jumpsuit, the uniform of his newly chosen profession. So he wasn't a cop anymore. His choice of jobs didn't make him any less of a man. A very desirable one, at that. "I love a man in uniform," she said, "but I like it even better when he's out of uniform." With her fingers firmly wrapped around the pull-tab, she ran the zipper down to the bulging point between his legs.

Ben gasped, his head falling back, his body tensing. "You're killing me."

"Oh, baby, I've only just begun." Her hands dipped inside the open edges of the jumpsuit, settling on the taut muscles of his midsection. Waves of excitement pulsed through her body, diving southward. Liquid oozed from her, making her moist, ready for him to enter her. But she still had work to do.

With her fingers weaving their way through the wiry curls on his chest, she ran her hands up to his shoulders. Then she pushed the fabric over and off, exposing a darkly tanned wall of rippling sinew.

"*Ooo-la-la*. Let me taste you." Her distended nipples rubbed across his chest as she rose up on her tiptoes and pressed her lips against the vein in his neck—the vein pumping warm blood through his body at an alarming speed. She sucked the salt from his skin, liking the taste and texture, perhaps a little too much. When her mouth came away, the light purple evidence of a love bite remained.

Her lips curved. She'd marked him as hers. Now it was his turn to mark her.

She stepped away, dropped her eyelids to half-mast and crooked her finger. In her most seductive voice, she asked, "Are you just going to stand there? Or are you going to make love to me?"

She turned her back and climbed into the bed, knowing full well her bottom was exposed to his view, her moistened cleft practically begging him to take her.

The rustle of clothing, the thump of a shoe, followed by another, were all the indication she needed that he would follow. She lay full out on her stomach, her legs slightly apart, waiting for him to join her.

Which he did, in less than thirty seconds.

She knew, because she'd counted as she held her breath. That small niggle of doubt had crept back in, only to be swept away when he straddled her, draping his body over hers. "I thought you'd never come," she whispered.

"I thought I'd never get here," he breathed into the back of her neck. He kissed her nape and worked his way downward, tickling her spine with the tip of his tongue until he reached the crease of her buttocks.

He slid off the end of the bed, spread her legs, and pressed his cock between them, his hands palming her rounded cheeks, massaging the muscles, moving downward to the line between buttocks and thigh. With a gentle glide, he traced that line inward to her aching center.

She hunched upward, trying to make that connection between her swollen nether lips and his long, work-hardened fingers. She wanted to feel the sexy abrasion of his rough skin inside her. More than that, she wanted him filling her to full, completing her. Her bottom hiked higher, pressing backward.

Ben's finger found her center, and dipped inside.

All the Voodoo magic in the world couldn't conjure the explosion within. This was more than magic, more than anything she could have dreamed. Tension built in every muscle and nerve ending, begging for release. "Oh, Ben, you're killing me!"

"Honey, I've only just begun," he said, echoing her own words. Then his finger slid out and his tongue slid in.

She practically jumped off the bed, the feelings so intense she thought she'd die of pleasure.

She pressed her face into the comforter to muffle her screams. Every flick he inflicted on her clitoris rent another scream until she writhed in the sheets. "Please, oh God, Ben. Come inside me, now."

The exquisite torture ceased, leaving her teetering on the precipice of orgasm.

He grabbed her hips and pulled her against him, nudging his cock against the opening of her swollen entrance. But he hesitated. "What about protection?"

"Damn." How could she have forgotten?

She climbed to her hands and knees and reached inside her nightstand, groping for a foil package she was sure was there. Her little bit of hope stashed away for, how long was it—two, maybe three, years? About the time she'd given up on Ben ever coming back. But he was here now and she couldn't wait.

Her fingers closed around a stiff square. "Oh, thank God!" She twisted and collapsed on her back in the middle of the mattress holding up her prize. "Quick!"

Ben snatched the treasure from her hand and ripped it open.

She stole it back and eased it down over his magnificent cock. "Oh yeah, baby. I remember you." She lay back, her knees dropping wide.

A wicked glitter in his gaze, he leaned over her and pressed his lips to her opening, darting his tongue inside. His head lifted and he grinned naughtily. "Just testing."

"Oh, I'm more than ready." She'd been ready for this moment for a very long time.

One agonizing kiss at a time, he slid up her body until he lay over her, his penis pressed to her core.

"Ben!" she squealed. "Hurry!"

"I'm coming, I'm coming," he reassured, smoothing the back of his hand along her chin. Then he drove home, filling her in one hard thrust.

With a gasp, she curled her legs around his waist and clenched, holding him close as she absorbed him, stretching to accommodate his size and length.

Then he pulled away until the velvety smooth tip was a breath away from falling free of her.

She flexed her legs, drawing him back in. "Please, don't tease me." Were those tears in her voice? Was she that desperate for him she'd cry? Did she still care that much? Man, she was going to be in big trouble. "Do it, Ben. Do it, like before."

"Ah, Lucie. I've missed you so damn much." He pressed a kiss to her lips and rammed home. In and out, he rode her hard.

She met him thrust for thrust, planting her feet on the bed to give her added lift. She climbed that precipice and toppled over the edge, exploding into a million glittering fragments of light.

He jerked to a halt, his body rigid, his cock pulsing. His lips pulled back over his teeth in a groan with the strain of his release. Then he collapsed on top of her, squashing the air from her lungs.

She didn't care. Ben was with her—inside her—as she'd dreamed of for so long. Everything would be all right. Tomorrow she'd wake up and all would be right with the world.

He shifted to his side and lay down next to her, pulling her into the circle of his arms. "Ah, Lucie. You feel like heaven." He smoothed a hand over her naked skin.

She basked in the afterglow of being loved by him. Surely, after what they'd just shared, he loved her. She snuggled closer, pressing a kiss to his bare chest.

"See?" Ben whispered into her ear, teasing her lobe with his tongue. "You can't possibly marry Eric. Besides, you'd never be happy as a congressman's wife. You belong here, in the swamp.

CHAPTER 15

"LUCIE! OHMIGOD!" BURSTING THROUGH THE DOORS OF THE SHEAR Safari Beauty Salon, Calliope, with DeeDee Dubois in tow, made a beeline for Lucie's chair. "We're so glad you're here."

Josie Ezelle, the young beautician wearing the salon's skintight leopard-print uniform skirt, dropped the strand of Lucie's hair she'd been cutting and stepped back. "Hi, ladies."

Lucie cringed and forced a casual smile to her lips. "Hey. I didn't realize you two had appointments today." Otherwise she would have rescheduled. She didn't feel up to the inquisition, no matter how well-intentioned.

She sure as hell didn't want to discuss the lapse of sanity that caused her to sleep with Ben. After last night's faux pas she had a lot to think about, and couldn't possibly complete an entire thought with Calliope's incessant chatter blasting through her brain cells.

Whatever. Her life was already so screwed up, what more could go wrong?

"I'm giving up my appointment for DeeDee, if that's okay with you, Josie?" Calliope hugged the cosmetologist.

"Fine by me." Josie held her scissors far from her body to keep from poking the effervescent redhead. "What's it gonna be? Cut, highlights, facial?" Josie turned back to Lucie and snipped another lock of dark hair.

"The works!" Calliope threw her hands in the air, smiling ear to ear. "DeeDee has a date."

"That's wonderful news." Josie's hand paused and then continued combing through Lucie's hair. "Who's the lucky guy?"

Lucie cringed for the second time in one morning. She knew the answer.

DeeDee blushed, the fiery red burning a mottled trail up her neck into her cheeks. She giggled and whispered. "Maurice Saulnier."

Josie leaned closer. "Who?"

"Mo," Lucie interjected, her tone flat, her happiness for DeeDee decidedly absent.

DeeDee's little brown eyes rounded. "Do you think it's crazy? I know Mo is much too handsome for a girl like me, but he did ask me out, and"—she nibbled her lip—"I want so much to go."

Immediately, guilt set in and Lucie softened her response. "Oh, DeeDee, of course I'm happy for you. Maurice is a really nice guy and so are you. Girl, I mean. You're a nice girl."

DeeDee's smile returned, lighting up an otherwise doggish countenance. The poor girl's face was too long, her eyes closely set and beady, and her nose big enough to be considered manly. DeeDee had been born with the title of "Dog-Faced DeeDee" through no fault of her own. But she did have pretty hair, the deep brown of a chocolate lab. And her glow of happiness softened all her harsh features to almost pretty.

Lucie's own natural optimism became more and more elusive, to the point she felt downright depressed. Because of one simple spell, she'd caused this transformation in DeeDee. That was the upside. The downside was that the unfortunate woman would be absolutely heartbroken if she reversed the magic.

Calliope herded DeeDee into the chair beside Lucie. "DeeDee wants a mani, pedi, facial, cut, and style for her date. Don't you, DeeDee?"

DeeDee nodded.

"Mirna Mae?" Josie called out.

A chair scraped in a back room and a diminutive older woman wearing a leopard-print skirt and bony-rib-hugging tank top matching Josie's appeared in a doorway. "Whatcha need?"

"Could you do a manicure while I finish up Lucie?" Josie asked.

"Guess I could. Got nothin' better to do than eat Mozelle's beignets and drink coffee. Come on, girl, let's skin this alligator."

DeeDee frowned at Calliope and hesitated. "You aren't gonna skin my hands are you?"

"I will"—Mirna Mae raised an eyebrow— "if you don't get yer buns in my chair afore I count to three."

Lucie smiled at DeeDee. "Mirna's bark is much worse than her bite. And she does a fabulous job on fingernails. Go on. We want you perfect for your date."

Her frown disappearing, DeeDee scooted into the little chair across the table from Mirna Mae.

"Well, well, DeeDee," Mirna Mae arranged bottles of polish and nail files. "Since when are you and Maurice an item?"

Lucie stared in the mirror, trying not to be too obvious about her interest in the woman's answer.

The same mottled flush stained DeeDee's cheeks. "Oh, we're not an item." She ducked her head and murmured, "Yet."

"Yet, huh? So when did the boy ask you out?"

DeeDee sighed, all but melting in her chair, a smile lifting the corners of her lips. "At the barbecue. I tell you, it was like magic."

Lucie's gaze darted to Calliope and she frowned a warning.

But Calliope wasn't the sharpest tool in the shed. "Yeah, Lucie's bug—"

Lucie kicked out hard, the pointed toe of her high-heeled shoe connecting with Calliope's shin.

"Ouch!" Calliope reached down to rub her injured leg, while shooting an accusing frown at Lucie. "What did you do that for?"

"I'm sorry," she smiled at Calliope and shook her head. "My foot must have slipped." She made a slashing motion across her neck and pressed a finger to her lips. "Ixnay on the ugbay."

"Ixnay?" Still rubbing her shin, Calliope's brows drew together, then her eyes widened and a grin spread across her face. "Oh, yeah. Gotcha."

Apparently oblivious to Lucie and Calliope's charades, DeeDee continued, "If it hadn't been for Calliope knocking me down, none of this would have happened."

Calliope beamed proudly. "That's me all over for ya. Chalk it up to these clumsy feet." She winked at Lucie.

Lucie groaned and struggled not to roll her eyes. *Lord, save me from my friends*. Keeping secrets was not one of Calliope's strengths.

Josie leaned close to Lucie's ear. "I get the feeling there's a lot more to the story. Wanna spill?"

Her gaze met Josie's in the mirror. Man did she need someone she could talk to, but... "No, there's nothing more to say. As far as I could see, it was just as Calliope said."

Josie's lips tightened briefly, then she asked over her shoulder. "So how did Calliope's knocking you to the ground bring you and Mo together?"

"It was like a complete fairy tale." DeeDee sighed again. "He helped me to my feet, and when Calliope got up, she knocked me into Mo's arms." She stared dreamily out the window. "It was so romantic and thrilling. Next thing I knew, we were walking out on the boardwalk and he was asking me out. Me!"

As Josie snipped away at her hair, Lucie's heart sank further and further into her belly. What a mess she'd made. DeeDee would be devastated. The first guy to pay any attention to the woman, and all because of a little Voodoo snafu on her part. Not to mention the mess she'd made of her own situation. She was supposed to marry Eric, but she'd slept with Ben.

"There." Josie set her scissors on the counter and fluffed Lucie's hair. "You're all done. Take a look."

She peered at her reflection without seeing the glorious black tresses falling in luxurious waves. How the heck was she going to undo the disaster she'd created? "It looks great, Josie. Too bad you can't fix problems as nicely as you fix hair."

Fists on her hips, Josie gave her a narrow-eyed look. "Girlfriend, I can't fix what I can't see."

The back door burst open and Alex skidded in, gasping for breath. "Lucie!" She pressed a hand to her chest. "You gotta get out of here, quick!"

Her heart bouncing from the pit of her belly into her throat, she leaped from the chair, cape and all, and ran to her friend. "What's wrong, Alex?"

Alex laid a hand on her arm and panted as if she had been running. "The press, the demonstrators, all hell's broken loose." She stepped aside and motioned to the glass doors and windows at the front of the Shear Safari salon.

Outside, she could see cars pulling up in the few parking spaces lining the busy streets of Morgan City. A news van with a rotating satellite antenna on top of it double-parked, blocking Lucie's and Calliope's cars.

"I thought the press was in Bayou Miste clambering around the Littington estate." Lucie's stomach knotted. "What are they doing here in Morgan City?"

"That's what I was trying to tell you." Alex grabbed her arm and ushered her to the back of the salon. "Someone got wind that Eric Littington is here at the local jewelry store having a family ring fitted for a certain young lady he hopes to marry."

Lucie planted her feet and stood firm against Alex, stalling. "Wait just a minute. And why do you think this has anything to do with *me*?"

Alex gave her *the look*. "Don't play dumb with me, Lucie LeBieu. This is just what you wanted, what you planned. Hell, what you cooked up!"

She winced. "Okay, so it is, but that doesn't necessarily mean I said yes."

Alex's eyes widened. "So he *did* ask you?"

That icky feeling crept across her skin. The same feeling she'd had when she'd lied about stealing from Charlie Hughes's watermelon patch. She'd gotten away with it then because Charlie'd had a soft spot for the Voodoo queen's granddaughter. Or maybe he'd been afraid of what Lucie's grandmother might do to him if he pressed charges.

Calliope and Josie crowded around Lucie, blocking her escape through the front door. Was it just her, or was the air getting scarcer in the little shop? She couldn't lie her way out of this tight spot. These girls weren't Charlie. Lucie sighed. "Yes, he did ask me to marry him."

"Ohmigod! Lucie!" Calliope grabbed her hands and jumped up and down. "I'm so happy for you. It worked! It worked!"

"What worked?" DeeDee asked from her position at the manicure table with Mirna Mae. "What's going on? Tell us, please."

"Yes, tell all. My ears must be getting old," Mirna Mae groused. "I only heard about every fifth word. Gotta get a dad-blasted hearing aid so I can keep up with my eavesdropping."

"Nothing worked." Lucie pushed through the suffocating group of women.

"Eric Littington asked Lucie to marry her." Calliope clapped her hands together.

"Congratulations, Lucie," DeeDee said, her face wreathed in smiles. "I'm so happy for you."

"That's wonderful, Lucie." Josie hugged her close.

"Good catch, if you ask me," Mirna Mae said, without looking up from the fingernail she was filing. "Man's got money and political aspirations. Probably the most eligible bachelor in the parish."

The only person who didn't congratulate her was Alex. Her face was set in a deep frown. "What about Ben?"

The knot in Lucie's gut clenched until she felt like she'd toss her meager breakfast all over the shiny linoleum floor.

"Ooh, that's right." Josie's eyebrows rose. "Weren't you and Ben a thing some years back?"

"*Were*. Past tense. Back before he left for the academy," she said. If only he was still a part of her distant history. But his role in her life was all too fresh. Why did he have to be so sexy, and why did she have to be such a pushover and sleep with the man?

"That's what I thought." Josie ducked to glance at her own reflection in the mirror and run a comb through her hair. "Geez, with Craig Thibodeaux and Eric Littington snatched up, that's two less eligible bachelors for us poor girls of Bayou Miste."

"There's still Ben, Larry, and Maurice," Calliope offered.

DeeDee's stricken gaze darted toward the group.

"DeeDee here seems to have snagged Mo, not that I'm interested." Josie smiled over her shoulder at DeeDee. "He and my brother, Larry, have been friends for so long, I can't think of him as anything but another brother. Good thing you're marrying Eric, and Ben's free and back in town, Lucie. I'm thinking about going after him myself."

Lucie's heart flipped over and landed with a thud in her gut. Holy swamp muck! Josie was a pretty girl with big blond hair and pale, creamy skin. Completely opposite of her own dark haired, dark-skinned looks. Ben was bound to find her more attractive. The thought made her feel like the nails on her fingers should lengthen into claws. She had a sudden urge to scratch Josie's eyes out. "I haven't agreed to marry Eric."

"No?" Calliope's brows shot upward.

"No?" Alex's frown deepened.

"No?" Josie grinned.

"Why not?" Mirna Mae asked.

"Yeah, why not?" DeeDee echoed.

Good question. She wished she could answer it.

A reporter, followed by a cameraman, stepped through the front door. "Is there a Miss LeBieu in here?"

Josie tossed her comb to the counter and strode toward the reporter. "Sir, do you have an appointment?"

"No, I just want a word with Miss LeBieu." The reporter pressed a handheld digital recorder to his mouth. "I'm inside the beauty salon where Miss LeBieu has her hair done. Miss LeBieu, is it true congressional candidate Eric Littington proposed to you last night?"

Dread washed through her intestines like a moldy milkshake. How the hell was she going to undo this fiasco? The whole world knew. Or at least all of Louisiana would know Eric had proposed by the time the five o'clock news aired. Would they also know she'd slept with Ben Boyette the same night Eric had proposed? Where was Saint Jude, the patron saint of lost causes, when you needed him? Who else had the power to bail her out of this mess?

"Don't answer," Alex said.

"Don't worry, I'm not about to." Feeling like a big fat fraud and totally unworthy of her friends, Lucie shifted to make sure Alex stood directly between her and the cameraman.

"Miss LeBieu, is it also true you make your living as a waitress and a stripper?"

Rage burst through her veins and she tried to shove Alex aside so she could get to the reporter and punch him in the teeth. "No, that is not true!"

"Leave it, Lucie." Alex, with Calliope's help, restrained her and kept her from making a bigger scene.

"Sir, if you don't have an appointment," Josie stepped in front of the cameraman and held her hand over his lens, "you'll have to leave."

"In that case," the bigmouthed reporter said, "I'd like to make an appointment for right now."

The unflappable Josie, stood her ground. "The only opening I have is for bikini waxing. If you'll just step into the back room and drop your drawers, we can get to work."

The reporter's eyes widened. "Uh...I don't think so."

Lucie smothered a giggle at the man's horrified expression. Served him right. She'd like to wax his body for his rude insinuation.

"Then you and your shutterbug friend here better leave before I call the police." With the threat of being waxed hanging over them, the two men didn't resist. Josie, as smooth as you please, ushered them out of the shop and locked the door with an exaggerated *click*.

Alex and Calliope loosened their hold on Lucie and stepped away.

"Thanks, guys." She rubbed her hands over her bare arms. "I don't know what I'd do without you."

"Yeah. That's what friends are for." Alex gave her a twisted smile and glanced out the window, where a growing crowd of reporters swarmed around the salon. "I'm afraid this may be one mess we can't get you out of. Only you can do that. And by the looks of that mob, it ain't gonna be easy."

***

Ben paced the sidewalk across the street from the jewelry store Eric had entered thirty minutes earlier. Who'd tipped the reporters off about Eric's proposal? And why the hell was Eric already having a ring fitted? Lucie hadn't said yes. At least that's what she'd told him. Had she lied?

Last night had nearly put him in the grave with a heart attack. Or was that with a broken heart? When he'd responded to Lucie's frantic call, he'd been hit with a double whammy.

Someone had taken a potshot at Lucie and Eric. His stomach still flip-flopped when he thought of the possibility of Lucie lying in a pool of blood because of some fanatic with a gun.

He had a sinking suspicion he'd screwed up last night. Why couldn't he keep his big foot out of his mouth when he was with her? By sleeping with her, he'd really thought he'd convinced her not to marry Eric. Then he'd gone and opened his stupid mouth and made her madder than a wet hen.

She'd kicked his ass out of her apartment so fast she'd had to throw his clothes out with him. Thank goodness Miz Mozelle hadn't come out to witness his humiliation.

Now, with Eric on the verge of making the biggest mistake of Ben's life, he couldn't even begin to think straight. Tough, nothing-but-focused Benjamin Franklin Boyette was in a tailspin and he couldn't pull out. All he knew was that he had to stall this business with the ring. And he had to get Eric out of town before the reporters converged on him, and his friend made some stupid announcement about his intentions to marry Lucie.

But how could he stall him without looking like a jealous ex-lover, which he was feeling more like with each passing step?

"There's his car!" a man shouted.

Ben recognized him as one of the protestors from Bayou Miste. Apparently, they'd followed the reporters to Morgan City. A mob of people dressed in white T-shirts with green lettering and cartoon pictures of dead frogs and fish scattered all over them moved en masse toward the jewelry store.

Ben crossed the street and ducked in before the crowd got there.

"Eric, you got trouble brewing." He glanced over his shoulder and pulled the door closed.

"What's this?" The sales clerk blinked twice behind his owlish glasses before straightening. "Sir, you can't hold that door, this is a place of business."

"Ah, Ben." Eric turned and smiled across at him. "I'm glad you're here. I need your opinion."

"No time for that." He braced himself for the first protester, who reached for the doorknob. "You need to go through the back door if you want to avoid the mob outside."

"What mob?" Eric squinted and then his brows rose. "More demonstrators?"

"That and reporters." He leaned back, his hand gripping the knob as the man on the other side of the door attempted to pull it open.

"Don't worry about them. They have just as much a right to shop here as I do." Eric continued smiling, much to his annoyance. "Let them in, Ben."

"They aren't here to shop, Eric, and you know it." He didn't relinquish his hold.

Other demonstrators knocked on the windows, their muffled yells falling on Eric's deaf ears. The man was completely befuddled. Ben recognized the Lucie effect. Hell, he had it himself. Problem was, he didn't know how long he could hold out against the growing crowd. His hands were starting to sweat.

"Do you think Lucie would like my mother's engagement ring or a new one all her own?"

Ben groaned. He had to stop Eric from getting a ring and keep him safe all at once. How the hell could he do that when Eric was floating on cloud nine? "Why don't you wait until the woman says yes?"

Eric leaned against the counter and sighed. "I hope she says yes." Then he frowned at Ben. "Can you think of any reason she wouldn't?"

Because she doesn't love you, she loves me! He bit hard on his tongue to keep from saying what was in his heart. Hell, he didn't know what she was thinking. Never had. But Eric was an honorable man and she couldn't find a better one to marry. As rough of a life as she'd had, she deserved someone like Eric to wrap her in silk and diamonds. "No, I can't think of any reason for her to say no."

How could he hope to compete with Eric? His heart sank to a new low, pretty much at bottom-clinging pond silt. Especially after what he and Lucie had been up to the night before. Eric was his friend, yet here he was betraying him by omission—and by deed last night.

"I think she'd like one of her own." Eric leaned over the counter and pointed at the glass. "I'll take that one in a size six."

Damn, Eric even knew her ring size. Ben remembered it from all that time ago, when he'd asked Lucie to marry him. He still had the ring tucked away in a drawer at his mother's house.

The door shook as yet another protestor struggled to open it. *Get a grip, man. She's not yours, never has been.* Last night had meant nothing to her.

But the world to him.

"I'll have to have it sized," the clerk said, glancing nervously at Ben. "Really, sir, you should step away from the door."

"How long will it take?" Eric asked, completely oblivious to Ben's struggles or the clerk's distress.

The man behind the counter shot a desperate look toward Ben. "It could be ready by tomorrow."

"That's good." Eric smiled. "I have just the place I want to take her." Eric handed the clerk his credit card.

Just as the congressional Romeo was signing the credit slip, Ben's hands slipped off the knob. "Ah, hell. Look out, here they come."

Eric tucked the receipt in his pocket and turned as half a dozen people in frog T-shirts spilled into the store, carrying signs and chanting, "Clean the swamps!"

They were followed by reporters armed with cameras and microphones.

Ben edged in front of Eric, creating a physical barrier between the demonstrators and the candidate.

With a hand on his shoulder, Eric spoke softly into his ear. "Ben, you can't keep them away, let me handle this."

Fine. He stepped aside. It was Eric's funeral.

As he shifted, he noticed a man standing among the demonstrators, dressed in a white T-shirt with "I Love LA" written in green letters. Ben wouldn't have noticed, except he didn't quite fit with the others. He didn't have the "I want to save the world one seal pup at a time" look about him. He was older and he sported deep frown lines around his narrowed eyes.

Ben recognized the man as the leather-jacketed stranger in the bar the first night he'd met with Eric. As this realization struck, the frowning man reached into a satchel.

Was he going for a gun?

Ben tensed. Before he could react, the man removed his hand from the bag and lobbed a bright green balloon through the air, straight for Eric.

"Get down!" Ben yelled so loud the demonstrators around him ducked. Without thinking, he reached out to catch the balloon. When rubber met flesh, the balloon burst, splattering thick paint the color of shamrocks all over his hand and down his arm.

"What the hell?" Eric said.

Ben spun toward his friend and the reason he'd been assigned this mission.

With a puzzled frown denting his forehead, Eric rubbed at the paint on his cheeks. He looked like a victim of an alien massacre with green blood spatter from the waistband of his wrinkle-free khaki slacks up to the top of his neatly combed hair.

A collective gasp rose from the demonstrators gathered around Eric. Cameras flashed like so many strobe lights, temporarily blinding Ben.

Then a single voice shouted, "Save the frogs!"

A moment later the roof shook with the combined voices of a dozen demonstrators chanting, "Save the frogs!"

Ben grabbed Eric's elbow and ushered him to the back of the store where the nervous salesman stood rubbing his hands together as if working up a lather. "Oh dear, oh dear." His gaze locked on Eric's shirt.

"Where's the back door?" Ben asked.

The salesman threw his hands in the air. "In the back. Where else?"

He pushed Eric around the counter toward the rear of the small building.

The worried clerk surfaced from his stupor long enough to protest, "Sir, you're not allowed in the stockroom!"

Ignoring the man, Ben led Eric through the maze of boxes and jeweler's worktables to the back door.

"Come on, let's get out of here." He took off at a trot down the alley behind the store, listening for Eric's footsteps behind him.

After passing several buildings, he slowed and looked around.

Eric caught up and grinned. "This campaign is getting more interesting by the minute. How are we supposed to get to our cars?"

Ben was just trying to figure that out when he noticed the bright-red Jeep parked in the alley a few buildings down from where they stood. "Alex."

"Alex? As in your sister, Alex?" Eric asked.

"Yeah. I think we have a ride back to Bayou Miste."

Just as they reached the Jeep, Alex burst through the back door, followed by Lucie.

His stomach clenched. She looked stunningly beautiful, her long black hair falling in shiny waves around her shoulders, framing her face.

"Ben! What are you two doing here?" Alex asked.

Eric strode straight up to Lucie and grabbed both hands. "Lucie, my dear. You're gorgeous."

Her gaze darting from Eric to Ben, her cheeks flushed, then her eyes widened as she focused on the green splatters. "Good Lord, Eric, what happened?"

Eric held up his hands. "It's okay. A few overzealous protestors and a balloon full of paint. Nothing a new shirt and shampoo won't take care of."

"But that's awful!" She dropped one of Eric's hands to reach up and wipe a spot of paint from his brow. She darted a look at Ben, her lips tightening around the edges.

If he'd thought she'd gotten over her anger from last night, he was sadly mistaken. Yet his gut tightened as she tenderly caressed Eric's cheek. She obviously cared about the guy. *But how much?* And how could she love another man when she'd made such passionate love to him last night?

He pulled his keys from his pocket and tossed them to Alex, then held out his hand. "Let me have your keys. You can take my car. It's parked in front of the jewelry store a couple blocks down."

"But you're covered in paint!" Alex wailed.

"Don't worry, I'll have your seats professionally cleaned," Eric reassured her.

"But— But..." Alex's brows met over her nose and she looked ready to cry. "My Jeep's my baby."

"We'll be careful. Now quit blubbering and hand over the keys." Ben held his hand palm upward, crooking his fingers impatiently.

Calliope stuck her head out the back door of the hair salon. "Hey Lucie, Alex, you better hurry, they're going around— " she stopped midsentence and stared at Ben and Eric. "Hello guys, where's the party?"

"Hi, Calliope." Eric grinned. "The party is down the street, only I don't recommend the decorations." He slid into the passenger seat as if he were sliding into a limousine.

Calliope giggled. "Me, neither. Although I do look good in green, I don't fancy that particular shade."

Ben climbed into the Jeep and tapped his fingers on the steering wheel. "If you two are through discussing color choices, maybe we could get the hell out of here?"

"Testy, aren't we, Mr. Boyette?" Lucie turned to Calliope. "What were you saying when you came out?"

"I was saying something?" Calliope scrunched her eyebrows together. "Oh, yeah. That crowd is leaving the front door as we speak. I suspect they might be headed around here to the back to catch you."

"Get in, Lucie," Ben ordered.

"Yeah, come with us," Eric reached out and caught her hand.

"Damn," Lucie muttered.

Ben figured the last place she wanted to be was anywhere near him. But the rising hum of a dozen voices spurred her into action. She yanked open the back door of the Jeep and hopped in.

He fought to keep from busting out with a smile, and his heartbeat sped up in anticipation. After he dropped Eric off at his house, he could pick up where he left off last night with Lucie.

If he could get her to forget about what he'd said...

After what they'd shared, Lucie couldn't be serious about marrying Eric. And he fully intended to remind her why.

CHAPTER 16

Lucie hunkered down in the back of Alex's Jeep, as much as a person could with her knees jammed into the back of the seat in front of her. *Ben's seat.* For every bump, she banged her knees into Ben's back through the cushion. Deliberately? Maybe. She held onto the roll bar and set her teeth against the jolting ride—mad because she'd been chased out by reporters, madder because she had to leave her Mustang, and maddest because she'd had to ride in the same car as Ben.

Holy swamp goo! What the hell was she doing in the same vehicle as the man she'd made love to *and* the man she planned to marry? Sadly, they weren't the same person. Guilt wadded in the back of her throat like an old sock.

Could her life be any more difficult?

Eric craned around to look at her, his boy-next-door face and sincere smile making her feel more like a heel by the minute. "Darling, would you like to join me for lunch?"

Panic filled her belly with butterflies. She couldn't be in the same room alone with Eric. Not after last night. Surely her face would give her away, or she'd say something equally revealing. No. She couldn't. Not yet. Eric was too nice a guy to lie to. She had to find a way to fess up before the hole in her gut turned into a genuine ulcer. Eric deserved better than two-timing swamp trash.

She wanted to sink through the floor and disappear. *My God.* She'd become her mother and her sister! Sleeping with any man who'd call her pretty.

She shot dagger looks into Ben's back. And prayed he could feel them. Oh, for a Voodoo doll to stick full of pins!

Just as she was projecting daggers into him, he looked up into the mirror and smiled at her. That smirky, I-know-what-you're-thinking look. She kicked her foot under his seat hard enough to make him jump, causing him to swerve onto the shoulder.

Eric grabbed the dash. "What's wrong?"

Ben's brows lowered, practically connecting over his nose. "Thought I saw a skunk."

"Great. All I need to top off the paint on my shirt is to smell like a skunk. Not candidate material, if you ask me. You sure it was a skunk?"

Lucie couldn't resist. "Takes one to know one, huh, Ben?"

Eric laughed and jabbed his elbow into Ben's rib. "I believe she just called you a skunk. Are you going to take that from her?"

"I've taken a lot more than that." Ben glanced back at her. "Would you care to expand on that, Lucie?"

He wouldn't dare kiss and tell. She narrowed her gaze at him. *Would he?*

"What has my friend Ben taken from you that you didn't willingly give?" Eric asked, still oblivious.

"See, that's just it." Ben slowed to take a corner. "I only took what she more than willingly gave me."

"Sounds mysterious." His teasing tone belied his serious look. "And here I thought you two weren't even close after your breakup so long ago. What else don't I know about you, Lucie, darling?"

She gulped and choked on her own spit, bursting into a fit of coughing.

"Are you okay?" Eric turned in his seat, all teasing gone. "Ben, perhaps you should pull over. I think she can't breathe."

She coughed and coughed, tears running down her cheeks, her face burning with the effort to breathe. Between fits, she choked out, "No need to stop. Just take me home." She swallowed in spasms and finally got her throat under control. Whew! She couldn't have timed that any better. With all her sputtering, Eric hadn't noticed she never answered his question.

A musical jingle sounded from the front seat.

Good, maybe Eric would get involved in a long conversation on his cell phone and not ask her any more revealing questions that would make her spill her guts like an eviscerated pig. No, that wouldn't do. She still hadn't made up her mind whether to say yes or no to Eric's proposal. But she knew she'd have to come to grips with sleeping with Ben. And probably confess.

Oh, man, oh, man. What had she *done*?

"Hey Neal, what's up?" He listened for a moment. "At the house? Now? I'm in no condition to meet with a contributor. Okay, okay. I'll sneak in the back door. Stall him until I can duck into the shower and get the paint out of my hair. Aren't you going to ask me what paint? Oh, you've heard?" He shook his head. "Great."

Finally, she was getting a break, Eric had an appointment to keep. Yay! That could buy her a little time to figure out her dilemma.

And her future.

Eric turned around in his seat, a crooked smile lifting one side of his mouth. "Lucie, I must apologize. My campaign manager insists I speak immediately with one of the chief contributors to my campaign fund. Apparently the paint incident has made it around and I need to show my game face." He laughed out loud. "*Without* the paint. Could we reschedule lunch to dinner?"

Another break! Thanks to heaven and cypress knees. "I'm sorry, Eric, I have to work tonight."

His blond brows furrowed momentarily, then shot upward. "Even better. We can go out tomorrow night. There's something I have to pick up in Morgan City, anyway." A secretive smile curled his lips.

What was that look for? "I'm sorry, Eric, I have to work tomorrow night, too." Could she be lucky enough to avoid him for another entire night? She held her breath.

"Then I'll pick you up from work."

Her breath shot out in a whoosh. "But that's two o'clock in the morning!"

"All the more reason to see you home." His smile widened. "We can go to Morgan City for breakfast."

Wait. Breakfast? Or *breakfast*?

Damn!

Okay, so she'd have a little more than thirty-six hours to make up her mind. That was doable. Wasn't it? Deciding whether or not to marry Eric should be easy enough in that amount of time.

His grin was so infectious, she couldn't say no—at least to the date. Nor would she give Ben the satisfaction of thinking he had anything to do with her reluctance to go out with Eric. She pasted a happy smile on her face and met Ben's gaze in the rearview mirror. "Sounds wonderful."

Ben's brows furrowed and the Jeep lurched forward.

Ha. Let the man stew. He didn't own her or have any right to tell her whom she could or couldn't marry. Or have breakfast with.

When she glanced out the window, she was surprised to see the sweeping driveway leading to the Littington estate. The trip from Morgan City she'd thought would be endless was almost over.

"Pull around back, if you would." Eric ducked low in his seat as they passed a black Lincoln Navigator.

As soon as the vehicle came to a halt, Eric jumped out and reached in to assist Lucie to the ground so she could switch seats. For a moment he held both her hands in his and gazed lovingly down at her.

Guilt washed over her in waves. Eric was so nice. Perfect husband material. And by the look in his eyes, he was smitten. She'd gotten what she wanted; all she had to do was to reach out and take it. Why was that so damn hard? Why wasn't she the least bit happy?

"Do you realize how much your hair glistens in the sunlight? You're beautiful, Lucie. And every moment away from you is an eternity."

She tugged against his grip, uncomfortable with his pretty speech. How strange, when she'd always dreamed of a man saying such things to her. "Don't, Eric."

He chuckled. "What? Am I embarrassing you?" He turned to Ben. "I can't believe I'm embarrassing a woman who can hold her own at the Raccoon Saloon."

Ben snorted. "Yeah, hard to believe." His words were for Eric, but his enigmatic gaze rested on her.

Eric stared down into her eyes. "I'm sorry you got dragged into what's turning out to be a dirty campaign, but I'm not sorry I met you."

"Eric—"

He pressed a finger to her lips. "Sadly, I have to go. But I will see you tomorrow when we can have a nice, long talk. There's so much I want to say." He kissed her knuckles. "Until then." He helped her into the front seat and stepped back with a bow.

Ben revved the engine and pulled away—a little faster than she thought was necessary.

Eric stood for a moment, waving, then disappeared into the house. Poor, poor Eric. What had she done to make him so besotted?

Oh, wait. The love bug.

"Very touching." Sarcasm dripped from Ben's two words.

"At least he isn't rude and degrading, like some people I know."

"Namely me?"

She glared at him. "That's where I would start the list."

"What do you want with Eric? The man's in the middle of a heated campaign. He doesn't need distractions."

"So, now I'm just a distraction?"

"You've always been a distraction, Lucie." The soft look he shot her way tempered his harsh words. "You're hard to forget."

She crossed her arms over her chest and stared out the window, willing the sudden tears not to spill from the corners of her eyes. After having cried an ocean of tears over this man, she didn't need to shed another. Especially in front of the oaf. No sirree, not one.

"Not for *some* people," she gritted out.

Warm liquid made a trail down the cheek closest to the window. *Oh no*. Why now? After seven years, she should be well over Ben. She reached up on the pretext of pushing her hair from her eyes, scrubbing at the tear before it made it to the bottom of her cheek.

He would *not* see her cry.

***

Ben knew what she was doing, had seen the glistening tears pooled in her eyes, and his heart cracked a little more. "What's wrong with us, Lucie?"

"Nothin'. Because there isn't any 'us.'"

Well, that pretty much put him in his place. He pulled into her drive and shifted into park.

Lucie grabbed the door handle.

Before she could open it and jump out of his life again, he placed a restraining hand on her shoulder. "Sweetheart, we need to talk."

She stared down at the hand on her arm and then up into his eyes, her frown expressing her anger, her watery eyes the hurt. "You should have thought of that seven years ago. Let go of me, Ben."

"Let go of you, as in your arm? Or let you marry Eric?"

"Both." Her face was set, but her bottom lip trembled. "Why did you come back to Bayou Miste, Ben? You don't belong here anymore than I do."

"I came back for the job."

Lucie snorted and flicked the collar of his bug exterminator uniform. "Yeah, right. And I'm the queen of England." She shrugged out of his grip and slid from the Jeep. "Leave me alone."

As she walked away from him, he called out his window, "Do you love him?"

Her footsteps halted and for a moment she stood with her back to him. Then she turned. "If I told you I did, would you leave me alone?"

Not quite the answer he wanted. He let all the air out of his lungs like a deflating tire. "If you really love Eric, as he seems to love you, I'll step aside."

"Then step aside." One eyebrow rose in challenge.

"You didn't answer my question."

"I feel under no obligation to answer any question from you, Benjamin Franklin Boyette." She spun, her hair flipping over her shoulder as emphasis, and walked away.

He sat for a moment, watching her hips twitch side to side as she climbed the steps to her garage apartment.

She hadn't said she loved Eric. In fact, she'd deliberately avoided the question.

The lump of a heart that had been parked in his chest for seven long years suddenly felt lighter. His blood flowed freely through his veins after having been clogged for way too long. Clogged with unanswered questions, and a love long lost. The blood flowed so freely, he almost felt light-headed.

Lucie had not admitted to loving Eric.

Another thought slowed his dizzy brain. Even so, that didn't mean he stood a chance with her. She'd shown him the door once; why did he think he could win her over a second time around?

He slammed his hand against the steering wheel. Why did women have to be so damn complicated?

###

"Why do women have to be so damn complicated, Jean?"

Ben sat across the bar from Jean Dupree, the bartender. He'd gone about the business of protecting Eric all day when he would rather have been shaking a few answers out of Lucie's head. He couldn't get her off his mind, not for a single moment, and he was sick to death of being rattled by a woman.

"Do you think if I had the answer, I'd be tending bar in Bayou Miste?" Jean dried a mug and set it on the shelf behind him. "Take that one," he nodded at Lucie. She was weaving her way through the crowd, a smile on her face, her skimpy T-shirt showing enough belly to keep the predominantly male customers happy and horny. "She's worked for me the last seven years and she's still not married. Every other waitress got married. Some several times. But not my Lucie."

She hadn't made it back to the bar since Ben came in. He was looking forward to her reaction, while at the same time dreading it. How many times did she have to tell him to get lost before he got the hint? Still, after last night, he couldn't help but have hope. She couldn't have faked her abandon during their lovemaking. Hell, she wouldn't have let him do what he'd done if she didn't care a little.

Would she?

Perhaps all the sly comments of some of her customers were true and she'd become a slut like her sister Lisa since he'd left town. He shook his head. No. He knew better. Lucie's flirty act was a cover for a sad, lonely young woman whose promiscuous mother had dumped her and her sister when they were little girls. You didn't get over something like that. Not ever.

Only Ben and maybe a few of her closest friends knew her background. She was so afraid of ending up like her mother, she flirted but never followed through.

Except with him.

Then why the hell hadn't she married him, as she'd promised?

He downed his second beer and swiveled to face the room. "I just don't understand women."

"Me, neither." Pascal Pasquale claimed the seat next to Ben.

"Want the usual?" Jean Dupree asked.

Pascal shook his head. "No, I need something to numb the senses. Make it a whiskey."

"Hey, Pascal, sorry I had to get rough with you the other night." Ben stuck out his hand.

Pascal took it and shook. "I deserved it. I acted like a damned fool."

Jean set a glass of whiskey in front of Pascal. "Love has a way of making us humble."

"Yeah," Ben and Pascal said at the same time.

Ben stared down into his beer. "Doesn't help, either, when the competition looks better than anything you got to offer."

"No shit." Pascal tossed the whiskey back and swiveled on his seat to stare out into the crowd. "Makes you wish the competition would just go away."

"Yeah," Ben said. "But even without any competition you don't always get what you want." As well he knew. He hadn't had any competition seven years ago, and Lucie had still pushed him away. "Having the competition out of the picture doesn't always mean the lady will fall for you."

Pascal frowned. "Gives you more of a chance, though."

"Only if there are feelings there to begin with." So, if Eric were out of the picture, would Lucie reconsider being with him—Benjamin Franklin Boyette, bug exterminator?

Hell, she'd told him he wasn't good enough once, why would she think any more highly of him now?

Because they'd had great sex last night. Wasn't that enough to convince her he was the only man for her?

Although he'd changed out of the uniform of his undercover profession, as far as the lovely Lucie knew, he was still nothing more than a bug man hanging around pesticides. It stank. If she'd ever loved him, she'd be able to look past that and love him for who he was inside, regardless of the outer shell of a navy blue uniform with a giant ant on the front.

But then again, Eric had everything going for him, especially with his classic good looks—not that Ben considered himself a slacker. Eric was rich—however, money didn't buy everything, as Eric himself could tell you from his childhood experiences. But to top it all off, Eric was well known and climbing the political ladder. Hell, he could be president someday—the leader of the friggin' nation.

That sinking feeling hit Ben's belly like sour beer. *Damn.*

Pascal banged his empty glass on the counter. "Hell, some folks get all de breaks!"

"Whatcha bellyachin' about now, Pascal?" Lucie walked around Ben to the other side of Pascal and laid her tray on the counter. "I need a Coors, two Bud Lights, and a rum and coke."

Jean slid a mug full of beer her way and stuck another under the tap. "Gotcha."

"Ah, Lucie," Pascal said. "If you'd just marry me, I wouldn't have such a bellyache."

"Pascal, I told you back in the fifth grade, I like you, but I just don't love you. Can't we be friends and call it a day?"

She hadn't said two words to Ben yet. But he knew she was aware of his presence by the way she completely avoided making eye contact. And the way she was flirting with Pascal as if tossing her avoidance in his face.

"I love you, Lucie." Pascal grabbed her hand. "Always have, always will."

Now, there was a sentiment Ben could relate to.

"No, you don't." She tugged her hand loose. "It's just a crush. You'll find someone who curls your toes, and you'll forget all about me." Her words were gentle, her smile genuine.

He had to admire Pascal. The guy had a lot of balls to up and spit it out so publicly.

Ben scratched his head. Hmm. He hadn't tried that tactic. But based on her response to Pascal, he wasn't so keen on the technique. Unlike the redneck Cajun, public humiliation wasn't his style.

Well, at least he wasn't alone in the boat called *Lucie's Conquests*. But the old saying "Misery loves company" was as empty as his life.

Tired of her cold shoulder, he straightened and smacked his hands together. He preferred anger to indifference. Perhaps he could stir her up a little. "What are you going for, Lucie, a record of notches on your bedpost for all the hearts you've left broken in your wake? Chalk up another for Hurricane Lucie!"

She didn't respond with words, but if her glare had been a fillet knife, she'd have sliced clean through him in one long, painful stroke.

He smiled. *Now we're getting somewhere.* At least she'd acknowledged his existence.

"Give it up, Pascal." He patted the Cajun on the shoulder. "She's not interested in the likes of us. We're just homegrown swamp gators and she has bigger fish to fry. Besides, she's in love with someone else."

Having thrown the gauntlet, he awaited her response. Now maybe she'd answer his question.

"What do you know about love, Ben Boyette?" she snapped. "I bet you wouldn't know love if it slapped you in the face." She didn't wait for a response, just lifted her tray and flounced off. Her cutoff shorts showed a whole lot of leg to the rest of the world, as evidenced by the appreciative whistles of the patrons of the Raccoon Saloon.

"Try me, honey," he called after her, although she'd already gone out of earshot.

Pascal emitted a low whistle.

He turned to face the other man and noted how he, along with everyone else in the room, watched Lucie's progress across the crowded floor.

Ben was appalled. Did *he* look like that? With the sad, kicked-puppy eyes and mouth so far down he could have passed for a basset hound? *Holy shit.* Was there no cure for the woman?

He spun back to Jean. "I'll take a whiskey, too."

Jean handed him a glass of amber liquid and stared at him through the smoky haze. "You feeling all right, Ben?"

"Not really."

Pascal turned to Jean as well. "Give me the same."

"Pascal don't look any better," Jean said. "Must be something goin' around."

"Of that, you can be sure." Ben tossed the drink back, searching for that numbing feeling Pascal had spoken of earlier. Maybe he should take his own advice and give up.

Why should she be interested in mudbugs when she could have lobster?

***

The night had been interminable. Lucie had smiled and flirted with the customers as always, but her heart wasn't in the light banter and careless conversation, and her tips showed it.

How was she supposed to come to a decision about Eric when Ben kept showing up and confusing her even more?

She'd breathed a huge sigh when the bane of her existence finally left the bar. Now she could concentrate on her work and getting through the night without collapsing into a sniveling crybaby. Pascal still sat at the bar, his sullen gaze following her around until well after midnight, when he also gave up and left.

Every muscle in her body flagged and she counted the minutes until the bar closed at 2:00 a.m. She swept, filled napkin holders, and scrubbed tables until the last waitress left and only she and Jean remained. She was exhausted, emotionally and physically. All she wanted was a hot shower and cool sheets. When the routine cleanup was complete, she looked around for the bartender. "Jean?"

No answer.

Her heart scudded to a groaning low. "Jean? You better not have left without me!"

"I told him I'd lock up." Ben stepped out of the shadowy doorway that led to the back stockroom.

"But my Mustang is still in Morgan City. He was my ride," she wailed, very near bursting into tears.

"Now I'm your ride."

"And that's supposed to make me feel better?" She threw her hands up into the air. "I'd rather walk."

"It's two miles to your apartment. Are your feet up to the task after you've just spent the past six hours on them?"

His raised eyebrows nearly got him a flyby with the napkin holder she still held.

"So are you going to swallow your pride and ride with me or not?"

Her feet really did hurt and she didn't have the strength to walk. "Damn you, Ben."

He grinned. "I'll take that as a yes."

CHAPTER 17

"If you're going to try to talk me out of marrying Eric, save your breath. That particular topic is not up for discussion." Lucie climbed into the front seat of the bug exterminator truck and let her head drop back against the headrest. All she wanted was a hot bath and bed.

Alone.

"We don't have to discuss anything if you don't want to."

"Good, because I don't."

He shifted into reverse and backed out. "Fair enough."

"Then why did you offer to take me home?"

"Because I couldn't get you off my mind."

She emitted a very unladylike snort. "Like I buy that."

"No, really. I'm having a really hard time concentrating on my work since I got back to town. All because of one dark-haired Cajun hottie. I think your grandmother must have put some kind of hex on me."

Every previously relaxed muscle in her body tensed to alert. *Had he guessed?* Did he know about her unfortunate spell? Her heart did flip-flops in the pit of her stomach, threatening to upend the bowl of Jean's famous gumbo she'd eaten four hours ago.

With a stolen look at Ben's calm profile, she shook her head. No. No way. Her friends were all sworn to secrecy. But what about Calliope? Had she inadvertently let it slip?

Only one way to catch a fish—go fishing. With a deep, steadying breath she asked, "What makes you think magic was involved?"

"Why else would I be completely distracted?"

Her laugh sounded forced even to her own ears. "How much concentration does it take to spray houses for bugs?"

A smile quirked at the edge of his lips. "You have a point. But I wouldn't want to miss and spray Granny Saulnier's prized poodle or Mo's alligator. Even though Granny Saulnier wouldn't mind T-Rex out of the picture, she's kinda attached to FeFe. By the way, what color is she today?"

"Granny Saulnier's hair or FeFe?"

"Both."

"Lilac." Lucie laughed despite her previous fear of being caught in her little stint at playing Voodoo queen. Ben's teasing comments about FeFe and T-Rex defused her worries and had her leaning back against the seat again, her lids drifting shut.

Although her eyes were closed, her other senses were at full alert. Despite the chemical odor of the truck, she could smell the sandalwood and whiskey on him. She could hear every breath he took, and hear the rustle of his button-down chambray shirt as he maneuvered the narrow streets of Bayou Miste. If she let the last seven years of loneliness slip from her mind, she could almost imagine she and Ben were still together out on a date. He was even driving at a slug's pace to prolong their time together, just as he had when they were young and in love.

Just like old times.

But that was a long time ago. Too long.

"This reminds me of the good old times." Ben's voice covered her like a liquid blanket, warming her in places she'd only dreamed about until last night.

"Some of them were." She'd give him a little leeway without getting snippy.

He chuckled.

She peeped through one eye. "The comment wasn't meant to make you laugh."

"Sorry. I was recalling the time we rode the Ferris wheel twenty times at the Shrimp and Petroleum Festival in Morgan City. We wanted to break Craig Thibodeaux's record of most minutes spent kissing on a Ferris wheel."

"Yeah, I had motion sickness for a week." She smacked his arm. "To this day, I can't ride on a Ferris wheel without getting queasy."

"I forgot about that." His brows dipped for a few moments, then his face brightened. "Do you remember the time I brought you water lilies from the bayou? I spent five hours beating off the mosquitoes and alligators to get them."

"Yeah, I remember. I was so excited until I stuck my nose in one of the flowers and a red wasp stung me. My nose swelled up like a baseball and I ended up in the Morgan City ER overnight. And that was the same week as my senior class pictures. I thought I'd never live it down. Come to think of it, I still get comments from old classmates."

"Oh, yeah." The truck was crawling now. At this rate of speed, she wouldn't get to her home, shower, or bed for a week. Yet she didn't protest. Reminiscing, although sadly nostalgic, was fun.

"I know," Ben burst out. "How about the time we went skinny-dipping in Bayou Black. You gotta admit that was a blast."

"Until the alligator ate my clothes." A smile sneaked up on her and for a moment she forgot all her worries. "I had a helluva time explaining to Gran LeBieu why I was wearing your shirt and nothing else. Next thing I knew she was handing me a box of condoms. 'Use them!' she said."

"Think that alligator choked on your swimsuit?"

"At the time, I sincerely wished he had. That was my favorite bikini." She sighed. "I guess that was my punishment for being stupid."

"A pretty small sacrifice if you ask me. Could have been your skin he bit into." Ben shuddered. "Scared the crayfish out of me."

"Ben Boyette, now I know you're lying. Nothing ever scared you. You were always running around with your hair on fire, driving too fast, pulling dangerous stunts—except when you were with me. You couldn't have been scared of a little ol' alligator."

"Little, hell! He was twelve feet long and only ten feet away from where you stood in the water."

Warmth filled her at his admission. "So, why were you scared, Ben?"

***

Ben's heart mimicked the pace it had beat when Lucie had stood naked before him, the water swirling around her hips. Rivulets gleaming in the moonlight had trickled off her hair and down over breasts bathed blue by the moonbeams. He'd been so entranced, he hadn't seen the alligator until it was almost too late.

He sucked in air and blew it out through clenched teeth. "I was an idiot to let you talk me into swimming in the bayou to begin with. Especially Bayou Black." He gripped the steering wheel until his fingers turned white. "I could have lost you forever."

He'd been so upset at the thought, he'd asked her to marry him the next day.

And she'd accepted. How happy he'd been, imagining himself in love and Lucie loving him, too.

His elation had lasted all of two days, until Lucie dumped him.

"Why did you quit detective work?" Lucie asked.

He stiffened, surfacing from the mire of his past. "Why do you want to know?"

She glanced down at her hands. "Just curious. When you left Bayou Miste, you were hell-bent on a career in law enforcement. What changed your mind?"

He didn't answer right away. What could he say without telling her the truth? He was undercover and no one was supposed to know the real reason he was in Bayou Miste. The only thing he could think of was an incident that had almost made him resign from the force. "On a routine stakeout, I made a mistake. A bad one."

"Did you get fired over it?"

"No." He hoped his clipped response would put off her natural curiosity and make her too uncomfortable to dig deeper. Years had passed since he'd talked about his partner, Skeeter.

But she wasn't willing to drop the matter yet. "I've never known a Boyette to give up on anything. Why did you leave?"

"The mistake cost my partner his life." All the old pain and guilt rushed over him, making him relive the horrible moment he'd held Skeeter's lifeless body in his arms.

"I'm sorry."

"I didn't have the stomach for law enforcement after that. I didn't want the responsibility of another person's life in my hands." If not for his lieutenant's support and confidence in him, he would have quit three years ago when it happened.

She sat in silence, her face reflecting the meager light from a half moon shining through the truck window.

He pressed his foot to the accelerator, uncomfortable with spilling his guts to her. The rest of the short trip to her apartment flew by. As he turned into her driveway, he slammed on the brakes before he hit the car already there. Or rather, the ancient boat.

The license plate was from California.

Lucie stiffened beside him. "Don't even park, Ben."

"Why? What's wrong?" He stared at the car in front of them, his hands clenching into fists, ready to take on anyone who dared to hurt her. "Does this car belong to someone you know?"

"No!" Lucie inhaled sharply and blew it out, her eyes glistening in the light from her porch. "Yes! I think... Hell, could you take me to Alex's house, please? I can't go in there. I just can't." Her voice broke on the last word and she buried her face in her hands, her shoulders shaking with silent sobs.

Although he'd much rather stay and face whoever had made her cry, he shoved the shift into reverse and pulled out of the driveway.

Her hand shot out, touching his arm. "Wait."

"What do you want to do, Lucie?" He pulled against the curb, put the truck into park, and turned to face her. "Do you want me to go with you to face this person? Are you scared? Is he dangerous? Tell me!"

She hung her head, gulping hard, making a valiant attempt to stem the flow of tears. "No, not dangerous. And no, I don't need you to protect me. This is something I have to do myself." She reached for the door handle and swung the truck door open.

"Wait! Are you sure?" He frowned. He was about to insist on accompanying her to her apartment, when she looked up and gave him a watery smile. A very unconvincing smile.

"Yes, I'm sure. You can go home. No one is going to hurt me. Not anymore. Really, I'll be okay." She gave him the same shaky smile. "Thanks, Ben." After stepping down from the truck and closing the door, she strode across the driveway and stood at the bottom of the steps for a moment, as if gathering her chaotic thoughts.

He waited at the curb, uncertain whether to wait in the truck or ignore her protests and go after her.

As he sat in frustrated indecision, she trudged up the steps and entered her apartment.

He sat a moment longer, wishing he'd gone with her.

Who the hell could it be, who had her so panicky one moment and so depressed the next?

CHAPTER 18

THE WOMAN LYING ON THE COUCH COULD BE NO ONE ELSE BUT LUCIE'S mother, Lynette.

Lynette pushed up to a sitting position, shoved the shoulder-length black hair from her face, and blinked several times. Then her eyes widened, and a smile spilled across her face. "Lucie? Omigod, Lucie!" She leaped to her feet and ran forward, her arms outstretched. "Look at you, you're all grown up."

Lucie raised her hands in a defensive block and stepped backward before her mother could throw her arms around her. After schooling her face into an unreadable mask, she asked, "How'd you get in?"

The older version of herself came to a halt two feet in front of her. Her mother's shoulders sagged and the light in her eyes faded. "Miz Mozelle let me in."

After waiting all her life to see her mother again, she just couldn't see past the years of loneliness and heartache she'd been forced to live through because of her.

This was the woman who'd abandoned her.

"Why are you here?" She didn't soften her question. All twenty years of pain and anguish pushed her words out in a harsh rasp.

"I wanted to see my girls." Her mother's eyes filled with tears.

After twenty years? *Give me a freaking break.*

"Lisa's in New Orleans, why don't you go there?"

"I missed you." Lynette hung her head. "I wanted to tell you I'm sorry."

Lucie spun away, laughing to keep from crying. Yet she didn't quite succeed. She choked back an unwilling sob, swallowing hard. "After twenty years," she whispered.

"I know. There's no excuse for what I've done to you. I'm not here to give you excuses."

"Don't bother." Furious, she turned toward the woman who gave birth to her. "Nothing you say now can give me the mother I didn't have growing up."

Tears welled out of eyes rimmed with wrinkles. "I don't deserve it, but would like you to hear me out."

"I'm tired, Lynette. And I really don't have the energy to deal with this." Hell, she had problems enough, without having more turn up on her doorstep.

"I know you're angry." She put her hands up when Lucie would have jumped in. "And you have every right to be. What kind of mother would leave her child?"

"The worst kind."

"Yeah, you're right. The worst." She nodded, swiping away traces of tears from her cheek. "I know. I made so many mistakes, I gave up counting."

After all this time, Lucie would have thought she was immune to a kick in the gut from the one person who could have made a real difference in her life, but had chosen not to. But the kick found its mark. Whether it was intentional or not, Lucie didn't care.

"And I was one of your mistakes." She straightened her shoulders and leveled a look as devoid of emotion as she could muster at her biological mother. "You've said you're sorry, now leave. You're good at that. Good-bye, Lynette. Maybe we can do this again in another twenty years."

Her mother stared at her for a moment and nodded. "I deserve that, and I can respect your desire to kick me out. I'd really like a chance to talk, but I can see you're not ready. I'll be around for a while, in case you change your mind. I'm staying at Mamma's."

"Thanks for the warning." Lucie walked to the door and yanked it open. "I'll be sure to avoid it."

Lynette gathered her purse and closed the distance between them. She paused in the doorway and glanced into Lucie's eyes, her own filled with tears, again. "I didn't want to leave you and your sister. But I loved you so much, I had no other choice." She reached up to touch her cheek.

Lucie jerked away as if stung.

Her mother's hand fell to her side. "I'm very sorry I hurt you." She turned and left.

With a hefty shove, Lucie slammed the door after her, the ceiling rattling with the force of the impact.

In a numb stupor, she found her way to her small bedroom and fell flat on her back across the bed, clothes and all. She didn't have the strength to deal with all this, much less to breathe. She was tired of trying to make the right decisions, tired of making mistakes, and tired of trying to find love in a world filled with pain. All she wanted to do was crawl under a rock and hide until it all went away.

With one hand grasping the comforter, she rolled into a fetal position, dragging the blanket over her. Naturally, the bed linens still held Ben's scent.

God, she couldn't get away from that man! And now her mother had come back to Bayou Miste. What the hell was she going to do?

Blessed exhaustion claimed her and dragged her into a dream-filled sleep where Voodoo drums beat a haunting echo in her head and Gran LeBieu stood over her, shaking her head.

***

Ben knocked on Miz Mozelle's blue door the following morning, hoping like hell Lucie wasn't up and moving about where she could see him. He'd parked his bug truck a block away and walked, just to make sure. What he was about to ask Mozelle Reneau was none of his business, but he needed to know more about the visitor who was at Lucie's last night.

Miz Mozelle opened the door, and a smile lit her finely wrinkled face. Her bright, unnaturally red curls were a riot of color against her pale skin. "Why Benjamin Boyette, it's a pleasure to see you. Come in. Come in!" She stepped aside and held the door wide.

The sweet smell of freshly fried beignets wafted through the opening, wrapping around his empty stomach and yanking him across the threshold. "Miz Mozelle, your kitchen smells great! Are you making beignets again?"

"Sure as shootin'! Get your heinie in here and sit a spell, while I fry up the last batch." She moved ahead of him to the homey kitchen filled with early-morning sunlight. "What brings you along so early this morning, Benjamin?"

How did he broach the subject without sounding like a jealous lover? "Frankly, I was curious about Lucie's visitor."

"Ah, yes." She paused to concentrate on her task. With the expertise of many years of experience, she attacked a ball of pastry dough with a rolling pin, leveling it in a few efficient strokes to an eighth of an inch thick. "That would be Lynette."

"Lynette? As in Lynette LeBieu? Lucie's mother?" Ben rose halfway from his chair. "Damn! When did she come back to Bayou Miste?"

"Yesterday." With a butter knife in hand, she sliced the thin dough into two-and-a-half-inch squares.

Ben sank into his chair at Mozelle's dinette set and shook his head, trying to picture how Lucie might have reacted to her mother showing up after a twenty-year absence. "Man, Lucie's not going to be happy."

"Maybe not, but she needs closure, as my shrink would have said." Miz Mozelle looked up. "I let her in to wait for Lucie last night."

Ben leaned to the left to glance out the back window to see if the Cadillac was still there.

As if reading his mind, Mozelle said, "Oh, she left shortly after Lucie got home. By the way, I saw that you dropped her off. What happened to her car? Break down or something?"

He shook his head. "No, it's in Morgan City at Josie's shop. Long story." One he didn't want to get into. "Any idea what went on over there?"

Mozelle glanced over the pot of bubbling oil as she dropped a thin wafer of dough in. The hot liquid hissed and spit as eruptions of oil popped out of the pot and landed on the stovetop. Within a few short minutes she fished a golden brown beignet out of the vat and laid it on a paper towel. She sprinkled it with powdered sugar, scooped it onto a sandwich plate, and handed it to Ben.

"None whatsoever. But I had a nice long chat with Lynette yesterday evening while she was waiting for Lucie to get off work."

The delicious, sweet scent of the beignet filled his senses, calling out to him, reminding him he hadn't eaten breakfast. Without waiting a reasonable amount of time for the confection to cool, he gingerly lifted it by the corners, burning his fingers in the process. But he didn't let go. Instead, he blew on one side and bit into the featherlight pastry. A dusting of the powdered sugar drifted onto the front of his shirt, but he didn't care. "Miz Mozelle," he moaned. "This is heaven."

She beamed. "Thank you kindly. My Joe thinks I'm trying to fatten him up. Gained fifteen pounds since we started going out."

"I can feel my arteries clogging as we speak. But if I drop dead of a heart attack, I'd die a happy man."

"That's pretty much how Mr. Thibodeaux puts it." She laughed and pulled another fluffy treat from the hot grease. "So, when are you going to marry Lucie?"

Blindsided, Ben inhaled sharply, dragging powder sugar into his lungs. He burst into a fit of coughing, thanking his lucky stars he was choking so he didn't have to answer Mozelle's question.

She shoved a glass of water into his hand and thumped his back with surprising strength. "Got yer breath back now?"

He gulped water until he'd emptied the glass and set it on the table. When his breathing was pretty well back to normal, he polished off the rest of the beignet and started to get up.

"You got so busy coughing, you never answered my question." Miz Mozelle planted her hands on her hips. "When are you going to marry Lucie?"

Ben cursed silently. "I told you, she turned me down last time I asked."

"You talkin' about that mess when you were kids?" The older woman clucked her tongue. "Remember the ol' saying, 'That was then, this is now.'"

"She told me I wasn't good enough for her. As far as she knows, I'm nothin' more than a bug man."

"What do you mean?" Mozelle's brows sank low over her nose and she stared into Ben's eyes. "Is there more to your return to Bayou Miste than yer lettin' on?"

He realized his mistake and answered the best he could. "Even if there was, I wouldn't be at liberty to say."

"I knew you couldn't have come back with yer tail tucked between yer legs like some kicked dog." She grinned and smacked him on the back again.

"Is that what people are saying?"

"No, but it sounded good, didn't it?"

"You're a case, Miz Mozelle."

"Damn straight, and I don't apologize for nothin'." She squinted her eyes. "Well, maybe if it's important, I do. Speakin' of which, did you ever ask Lucie why she dumped you?"

Mozelle could shift so quickly in midstream she created a whirlpool effect, sucking him under. He shook his head. "I didn't need to. She'd already told me once I wasn't good enough."

"And you believed her, I suppose." Mozelle rolled her eyes. "I keep forgettin' how downright thickheaded men are."

"Thanks a lot." He stepped into the living room. "It doesn't matter anyway. She's going to marry Eric Littington. And he's a much better choice for her."

"How do you figure?"

"He's not bad-looking, he's loaded, and he's a rising star on the political scene. What more could a woman want?"

"Ben, I usta think you were a smart man. Now, I'm not so sure." She heaved a big sigh. "What about love?"

Love. That elusive emotion he thought he had experienced just once, only to have it slip away. "Eric's got that covered. He's so hung up on her, he's practically losing sight of his campaign."

"That's Eric." Mozelle retrieved another beignet from the sizzling oil. "What about Lucie?"

He walked through the living room and leaned against the back of a bright floral-print couch. "I don't know. He proposed two days ago. She hasn't given him an answer, but he's bought the ring."

"Stall them!" Mozelle exclaimed.

He swung toward her. "How can I? He has a date with her tonight after she gets off work. He's expecting an answer."

"What do you think she'll say?"

His chest tightening at the thought, he shoved his hands in his pockets and stared at his shoes. "I don't know."

"So what are you waiting for? Go find out!"

"How?" He glanced up at the older woman.

"Le'ssee... Ask her?"

"She'd tell me to go jump in the swamp."

"Men!" She wiped powdered sugar off her hands with a dish towel. "If you want something done, get a woman to do it. Hell, I'd ask her myself, but I promised Joseph I'd go fishin' with him today." She dug around in a duffel bag of a purse and pulled out a cell phone. "What did we do before these little jewels?" She punched the keys.

"Who're you calling?"

She held up a finger. "Hello, Alex?"

"Alex?" His frown cleared and he smiled. "Damn. Why didn't I think of that?"

Mozelle's raised brows told him clearly. *Because he was only a man.* "Alex, your brother needs to know if Lucie's going to say yes to Eric's proposal tonight."

Mozelle listened for a moment, and frowned at Ben. "He's a man. Do I need to say more?"

As an ex-cop, then a detective, and now a member of the elite Criminal Investigator task force, Ben thought of himself as a pretty tough guy. Miz Mozelle was making him out to be a lightweight wimp next to his sister.

"So you'll do it and report back to your brother?" She paused, listening.

Ben leaned closer. Despite his disgust with himself, he wanted to know if Alex would get the information from Lucie.

"What condition is that?" Mozelle asked.

"Condition?" he wanted to yell into the phone. *"Alex, for God's sake, don't be stubborn!"* But he held his tongue.

Mozelle laughed. "You got it. I'll send him over with two beignets just for Sport. Thanks, Alex. See ya in church Sunday." She ended the call and winked at him. "Be nice to your sister. She's doin' you a favor."

"I don't need favors from you or my sister. I can ask Lucie the question myself."

"And she'd tell you?" One of Mozelle's eyebrows crept upward. "Sometimes you ain't got the sense God gave a gnat." She patted his cheek. "But I love ya anyway. Now get on outta here. I have a date."

He headed for the door, stopped, and looked back at the amazing Miz Mozelle. "Thanks."

"Thank me when you have a ring on that girl's finger, not a minute sooner."

He stepped outside and inhaled the heady scent of honeysuckle and magnolia blossoms. If he could convince Lucie not to marry Eric, could he convince her to marry him, instead? His batting average wasn't so good with oh-for-one. Did he have the fortitude to step up to the plate again with the possibility of being struck out a second time?

Did he love her enough to risk going through all that pain again?

Hell, yes!

Then why not start now? He didn't have to wait for Alex. He could do some snooping into Lucie's psyche all by himself. Besides, she could probably use a shoulder to lean on about now, what with her mother returning after a twenty-year absence.

No time like the present. He marched around Miz Mozelle's house and up the steps to the garage apartment. He knocked and waited.

Nothing.

He knocked again, this time louder.

Still no answer.

Damn! How had he missed her again?

***

About the time Lucie pulled her pillow over her head to block out the banging on the door, her phone rang on the bedside table.

She let it ring five times before she reached out lifted it and slammed it back on the receiver. "I'm not home! Not to Eric, not to Ben, and especially not to mommy dearest!" She pulled the comforter up to her chin and her pillow back over her head, pressing it into her face until she couldn't breathe. Maybe she could smother herself out of this pickle.

When her lungs began to burn and panic set in, she flung the pillow aside and gasped.

Jeez. Well, she could rule out that method of suicide. Sleeping pills were out of the question as she didn't have any, nor had she had a need for them, until now. She didn't own a gun, and knives were too messy. Carbon monoxide poisoning was out of the question since every appliance in her apartment, including the water heater, air conditioner, and heater, ran on electricity.

Damn. She'd just have to live through another day.

CHAPTER 19

Lucie's head and feet hurt, but most of all her heart hurt.

Time was running out.

She'd avoided the phone, company, and any contact from human beings all day long. Finally, she'd unplugged the telephone and buried her head beneath her pillows once again.

When she'd tried to call in sick, Jean told her Brandy had beaten her to it. He was counting on her as the only waitress at the Raccoon Saloon that night. She couldn't call in sick or she'd be fired.

Great.

With a heavy heart she slipped into the "uniform" that would make any Hooters waitress proud, and hitched a ride to work with Maurice's grandmother and her poodle. Her mood reflected the color *du jour* of Granny and FeFe's matching hair. Blueberry, Granny informed her. To Lucie, it was blue funk.

"Hey, Lucie, what's gotcha so down?" Jean set two frothy mugs on her tray and went back to the tap for two more.

"Nothin'."

Everything.

Her whole damn life!

"Well, try smilin' a bit. You're scarin' the customers."

"Right. Smile." With her teeth bared at the bartender, she lifted the tray to her shoulders and set off in the direction of the beer-drinking customers. As she snaked her way through the usual crowd of rowdy Cajuns, she plunked the beers on the table so hard golden liquid slopped over the sides.

"Hey, watch it!" A lumberjack of a Cajun scooted back and cursed at the damp spot on his lap.

"Oh, Amos, I'm sorry." She dabbed at his jeans with a bar towel. How much worse could it get? Her life was in the crapper and she couldn't even do her job right.

"*Coo-wee,* baby! Spill some of dat on me." The man next to Amos waved her forward.

Heat suffused her cheeks when she realized what she was doing, dabbing at the man's crotch. "Oh hell! I'm sorry, Amos. This one's on me."

"Oh please, Lucie." The man next to him pressed his palms together in prayer. "I don't mind wearing a little beer if it means you'll wipe it off." He sat back from the table and spread his arms wide. "I'm all yours, honey, spill away."

Despite the weight of her worries, Lucie managed a smile. "Keep your shirt on, Marcus. I'm not gonna spill beer on you."

With his hands clutched to his chest, he heaved a big sigh. "My heart's broken."

"Get in line, buddy." Luc whacked him in the belly with a back-handed swing. "You and every guy in this joint are heartbroken."

Lucie tipped her head, frowning. "Why?"

"Rumor has it you're marrying Littington," Marcus said.

"Rumor, hell!" Amos picked up a copy of the *Times-Picayune* and smacked it against the table. "Says so in the paper."

"And you believe everything you read in the newspaper?" She snorted and placed empty bottles on her tray.

Amos grabbed her free hand. "You mean it isn't true?"

Marcus dropped to his knees on the floor. "Bless my soul! There is a God!"

"Get up, Marcus." She swiped her rag over the table and straightened. "I didn't say I *wasn't* marryin' him."

"Then what did you say?" A low voice asked behind her.

Lucie's heart turned a complete cartwheel and landed with a thunk against her rib cage.

"Ben!" she swung around, tray and all, and bumped into his chest. Empty bottles teetered and toppled over side. She reached out with her free hand to grab for the bottles, upsetting the others. Before she could utter an ugly curse word, five bottles had crashed to wooden floor, four of them bouncing, and one, unfortunately, shattering. "Damn!"

Ben's warm hand on her bare arm stopped her from stepping backward. "Don't move."

"Let go of me." His fingers seared through her skin, creating havoc with her heart rate. "I have to clean up this mess."

"No, the glass could go right through those crazy high-heeled shoes you're wearing. Let me."

"No way, Ben." She yanked her arm free. "This is my job. I'll do it myself."

"If you'd stop being so damn hardheaded for just one damn moment, you could see straight. You're not wearing proper shoes, any idiot can see that."

"So now I'm an idiot?" She lifted the tray in front of her like a shield. "You're one to be talking—a man who couldn't see the nose on his own face!"

Ben's brows twisted into a frown. "What's that supposed to mean?"

"If you ever bothered to look past it, maybe you'd know. Now, move!"

"Lucie, you're talking in riddles and I'm not in the mood to figure them out."

Before she could emit another scathing retort, Ben scooped her up into his arms and marched across the floor to the bar, plunking her down on an empty seat. "Stay, or else."

She started to push off the stool only to bump into his chest. "Or else what? You'll turn me into a toad?"

He leaned close and whispered loud enough for only her to hear, "Stay, or I'll kiss you in front of God and everybody."

Her breath caught and she almost choked on how much she wanted just that. Until she realized he'd only meant it as a threat. But she didn't want to tempt him. No telling how she'd respond. And wouldn't that be a pretty sight. Kissing Ben when she was supposed to marry Eric —not good.

She shut up and let him clean up the glass. That was the least he could do for rattling her. Besides, if he hadn't sneaked up on her, she wouldn't have dropped the bottles in the first place.

If she were honest with herself, she'd admit she was a little on edge. Had been all day. And who wouldn't be, with the kinds of decisions she had to make?

Alex and Calliope showed up out of nowhere and slid into the seats on either side of her. Ganging up on her, no doubt.

"Hey, girlfriend," Calliope said. "Takin' a break?"

Lucie harrumphed her answer.

Alex squinted through the smoky haze. "Is that my big brother cleaning the floor? I'll be damned. Never saw him do that at home."

"Damn right," she answered.

"Isn't that your job?" Calliope asked.

"Up until a minute or two ago, I'd have agreed." Lucie turned her back to the room. "Jean, I'm on break for the next five minutes. Could you hand me a Miller Lite?"

"You know I don't like my girls to drink while they're on duty."

"I'm on break, so technically I'm not on duty. Are you going to give me that beer, or am I gonna have to crawl across the counter and get it myself?" Her voice rose with each word she uttered until she sounded like a nagging housewife.

"Okay, okay. You don't have to bite my head off." Jean slammed a mug frothing with foam on the counter.

"My, my. Aren't we the growly bitch tonight?" Alex said.

"I'm not in the mood, Alex." She downed half the contents of her mug in one long swallow.

"I noticed." Alex gave her a long, penetrating look. "Along with practically everyone else in the bar."

"If you're here to promote your brother's cause, save it." She tipped her mug and poured the rest of the icy liquid down her throat. "I don't need another person questioning my decisions tonight."

"Jean, Miller Lite, please." When Jean set the mug in front of her, Alex lifted it and turned toward Lucie, a sly smile slipping across her face. "And have you made any?"

"Any what?" Lucie eyed her empty mug and pushed it away, almost sending it over the opposite edge of the bar.

"Decisions?"

She closed her eyes and tilted her head back. "If you were my friend, you wouldn't ask."

"I am your friend," Alex said. "And as your friend, I'm worried about you."

"Don't be. I can take care of myself."

"I'm not so sure lately." Alex laid a hand on her arm. "You're really tense, you've got circles under your eyes, and you're as cross as a trapped ringtail."

"Yeah," Calliope said. "You haven't been as much fun to hang around lately." She smiled and patted Lucie's arm. "But I'll hang around you no matter how bitchy you get. That's what friends are for."

Lucie looked from Calliope to Alex, then groaned. "Am I getting that bad?" She dropped her forehead to the edge of the bar and banged it twice. "I'm so confused, and feeling guilty and, well, I don't know what to do!"

Alex pulled her into her arms and hugged her tight. Calliope hugged her from behind.

"We love, you sweetie." Alex smoothed her hand over Lucie's hair. "Everything will be okay."

"First there was Ben, then Eric, and...and that damned bug!" She sobbed into Alex's shirt.

"I know, sweetie." Alex pushed Lucie's hair out of her face. "Shh. It's okay."

"And now, my mother's moved back to Bayou Miste!" She leaned back and stared into Alex's eyes, her own filling with tears. "What am I supposed to do?"

"Dry your eyes, honey. You're a tough ol' bird. God never gives us more than we can handle. You'll see." She pulled a tissue from her purse and dabbed at Lucie's eyes, then handed her the tissue.

"I'm not handling this very well." She blew her nose and straightened.

"No, you're not."

With a pout, Lucie said, "Hey, you're supposed to be supportive."

"I am, when I think it's right. And some of the stuff you've been doing lately just isn't right."

She crossed her arms over her chest, bracing herself. "All right. Go ahead, say it."

"Say what?" Calliope asked.

"I told you so," Lucie said. "I can tell Alex is dying to."

"I'm not going to rub your nose in your big, fat mistake. I love you, Lucie. I want you to be happy. I just don't think you've gone about it the right way."

"And you would have done it better?" she asked, some of her hurt pushing her to add, "And how long has it been since you've had a decent date?"

Alex stiffened. "That's hitting below the belt."

"Do you like your mother picking your men for you?" She felt compelled to go there.

"No. But we weren't talking about me, were we?" Alex poked a finger to her chest. "We were talking about *you*, Lucie. *You* got this ball rolling. Or should I say, bug flying? Now, *you* have to make the big decisions."

"Wait, whoa!" She raised her hand. "Did anyone ever tell you you're a freakin' bulldozer, Alex?"

Alex had the grace to blush. "Well, yeah, but—"

"No 'buts.' However, you're right. I got this bug flying. I have to make the tough decisions."

"Lucie, are you going to marry Eric?" Calliope asked.

"I don't know!" Overwhelmed, Lucie jumped off the stool. "Jean, my break's over. If you need me, I'll be waiting tables." Without another word to her friends, she snatched up her tray and dove into the crowd.

Avoiding Ben and the bottle mess, she headed toward the entrance, debating a quick escape, yet knowing she couldn't leave Jean without a waitress. Just when she thought she might catch her breath, a strikingly beautiful older woman stepped through the doorway.

Holy swamp gas, her world was blowing up in her face! Of all nights, why did her mother have to go and show up at the Raccoon Saloon?

***

Ben scraped fragments of glass into the dustpan Jean had provided, keeping one eye on Lucie and the other on the guy in the dark corner. If he wasn't mistaken, the man in the back was the same one who'd tossed paint on him and Eric in the jewelry store in Morgan City.

What was he doing here? And why was he watching Lucie?

His blood boiled on high heat. He was used to all the guys in Bayou Miste ogling the swamp princess. Not that he liked it. But a complete stranger had better keep his distance. After the man's performance the other day, he deserved close scrutiny. The man had been arrested, but must have been let out on bail.

As he carried the broken bottles to the trash can, Ben glanced at the clock over the bar. Midnight. The place didn't close till two, and the crowd looked as though they were settling in for the long haul. Smoke hung heavy and stale in the air, the music and laughter loud enough to damage eardrums.

Half a dozen guys stood around the bar, shouting for beer. As the only waitress on duty, Lucie couldn't be expected to keep up with everyone.

She looked dead tired.

He wished he could whisk her away from the smell of spilled alcohol and cigarettes. Out into the fresh night air to hold her under the moonlight. Maybe if he kissed her, and this time told her he loved her, she'd tell Eric to get lost.

When he noticed a woman, who could have been Lucie's clone, step through the door, his heart squeezed hard in his chest. She was older, but every bit as beautiful as her daughter.

Lucie's face blanched and her mouth tightened, but she didn't so much as acknowledge her mother.

She had to be hurting. He could have wrung Lynette's pretty neck for waiting all these years and then having the gall to show up and expect Lucie to welcome her home.

He wanted to go to Lucie and hold her in his arms, kiss away her heartache. With that in mind, he stepped toward her, only to stop when another person entered the bar.

Eric Littington.

Too late. He should have stolen her away earlier. Now he was obligated to let her make up her own mind about his friend. Damn! Once again, his timing was off. He'd do well to keep his focus on the stranger and make sure he didn't pull another stupid stunt with Eric. His desire to make things right for Lucie would have to wait.

"Ben!" Eric strode across the room and settled into the chair opposite him. He was all smiles and in a good mood.

Ben wanted to snarl his greeting. Instead, he stuck out his hand. "Hey, Eric."

"Didn't expect to see you here." He glanced around the room, his gaze following Lucie's every move.

The blood in Ben's veins moved like molten lava on a slow crawl. He wanted to hate Eric for everything he had, for everything he was. But he couldn't hate him. He'd been his friend for years. Yet how much was a guy supposed to suck up before he exploded?

"So, tonight's the big night, huh?" It took every ounce of his determination to speak the words out loud. He held his breath waiting for Eric's answer, hoping by some stroke of fate, Eric had changed his mind.

"Yes, sir!" Eric patted his trouser pocket. "Made it back to the jewelry store in Morgan City today to pick up the ring. I'm ready."

"The question is, is she?" His gaze drifted to Lucie. Even tired and worried, she was beautiful. He'd give his left nut to be with her as he had the other night. The raw knot of guilt flared in his belly and he glanced back at Eric.

Obviously, Lucie hadn't shared their secret with him. Otherwise, he wouldn't be sitting so happily next to the man who'd screwed his potential fiancée. He had mixed feelings about Lucie telling Eric about their stolen night together. If Lucie chose to marry Eric, the confession would only ruin their chance at a happy future. On the other hand, maybe if Eric knew, he wouldn't marry Lucie. She'd be free to marry him.

Ben sat forward, his heart thudding against his chest, the temptation to tell driving his mouth open.

Eric chose that time to wave at Lucie, a joyful smile on his face.

With a sickening realization, Ben sank back in his seat. He couldn't ruin Lucie's opportunity for happiness. She deserved a chance at the good life.

His biggest regret was that she hadn't chosen him. Marriage to Lucie would never have been peaceful, but he was sure it would have been a helluva ride. She'd have kept him young into his old age.

"You're getting a terrific woman," he said.

With a laugh, Eric ran a shaky hand through his hair. "She hasn't said yes, yet. God, I hope she does."

On the outside, Ben nodded and agreed with his friend, while on the inside, he prayed she'd say no.

Please, God, let her say no.

CHAPTER 20

By the time Jean escorted the last customer from the bar, Lucie was as jumpy as a flea on a dog, her stomach tied in one huge, nervous knot. With Alex, Calliope, Ben, Eric, and Lynette all staring at her for the last two hours, she felt like raw steak in a room full of hungry vultures.

Sheesh!

At least Eric had offered to wait out in the car while she switched from her "uniform" to decent clothes. Jean would lock up, so all she had to do was change into the shirt and slacks she'd brought along for her breakfast date with Eric.

The two-hour effort to ignore her friends, ex-fiancé, potential fiancé, and long-lost mother had taken its toll. She was balancing on her last nerve and in no mood to go out. What she wanted was a long hot bath and an even longer night's sleep.

Would Eric understand if she asked him to take her home?

One look at his handsome, eager face, and she'd known she couldn't put him off another night. Somehow, in the next hour or so she had to make a decision whether or not to marry Eric.

As she slipped into her slacks, she weighed Eric's pros for the hundredth time in the past few days. He was handsome, wealthy, a political climber, completely in love with her, and incredibly nice—and don't forget romantic.

Tugging a ribbed-knit coral T-shirt over her head, she had to give the cons equal consideration. *Okay, so list the cons already!*

She stood for a moment, staring at her reflection in the mirror. "Come on, girl, Eric has to have some cons."

He wasn't Ben.

The longer she thought, the more frustrated she became. Eric didn't have any cons? Holy crab cakes—the man was perfect.

So what are you waiting for? Go get him.

An image of Ben lying next to her in her bed popped into her mind. "Because you haven't told him about Ben—and the teensy little fact that you slept with him the night Eric proposed," she said to her guilt-ridden face in the mirror.

She'd been looking at it all wrong. She'd been thinking only about what *she'd* get out of marrying Eric. What would *Eric* get out of this marriage?

She stepped into her high-heeled sandals, one at a time.

He'd get *me.*

She thought about that for a moment. She wasn't so sure that was a pro for him. More likely, it was a huge con in the scheme of all that had transpired in the past week. She'd resorted to magic to lure him in. Kinda like a black widow luring her ill-fated mate in for the kill. Her natural aversion to eight-legged beasts had her shivering in the heat. Then, after he'd proposed to her, she'd slept with his friend...and hadn't had the decency to enlighten him.

And she came with baggage. Loads of it! And her biggest bit of baggage had just moved back to Bayou Miste with *her* baggage, wanting to work her way back into her daughter's life. Like that was going to happen. *Not!*

A knock at the door made her jump.

"Lucie?" Jean's voice called out. "You coming out or do you want me to lock you in?"

Jean's comment was too close to the truth. She glanced at her watch.

Shit! She'd been in the bathroom for fifteen minutes! Eric would be getting worried.

"No, Jean, I'm coming out." Her hands shaking, Lucie left the safety of the bathroom and the stale smoke of the bar, and stepped out into the night.

With a deep, cleansing breath of humid swamp air, she marched across the parking lot to meet her fate, still without a clue what it was going to be. If only everyone hadn't ganged up on her, showing up in force to keep her mind in a jumble.

She needed to focus. *Remember, Eric is perfect and Ben is not an option.*

The perfect man stepped out of his BMW and met her halfway. "Lucie." One word. Spoken like a parched man holding out his hand for life-giving water. Eric wrapped her in his arms and hugged her close. Then he steered her to the passenger seat and held the door open as she climbed in.

Perfect. The man was absolutely perfect.

She had no idea why the repetitive thought was making her less happy by the minute.

"I thought you might be too tired to go all the way to Morgan City, so I packed a snack. I have a special place I'd like to take you that's a little closer and a lot more private, if that's okay with you?"

She leaned back against the leather seat and closed her eyes, willing herself to relax. *You're not going before a firing squad.* "That would be...perfect."

The engine hummed to life with barely a sound. Wrapped in the quiet cocoon of the car's interior, her numb ears reveled in the stillness. She loved Cajun music, but hearing the blaring noise night after night got old, and her ears would probably pay the price. For the moment, she was content to let the silence lull her to calmness.

Like the calm in the eye of a hurricane.

***

Ben had left the bar a few steps behind the man in the leather jacket. As much as he wanted to follow Eric and Lucie, he needed to learn more about this stranger who'd tossed paint on him and Eric. If he was the one sabotaging Eric's campaign, he had to catch him.

Leather Man climbed into a navy-blue Ford Taurus and pulled out of the parking lot.

With the car in his peripheral vision, Ben sauntered casually to his Audi, which he'd left in the parking lot earlier. After all, it was considerably less conspicuous than the exterminator truck. Once in the car, he jotted down the license number.

When the man's rental car turned onto the highway, Ben jammed the Audi into drive and spun out after him. He didn't have far to go. The Taurus had backed into an overgrown side road, just a few yards past the entrance to the bar's lot. He would have missed it if he hadn't seen the brake lights flash once before blinking out.

Okay, what are you up to? He drove past and around a curve in the road. Once out of sight, he executed a U-turn, switched his lights off, and sneaked around the corner at a snail's pace. He found his own hidey-hole in the bushes a tenth of a mile from his quarry. Two could play this game.

Now, they'd wait—Leather Man for Eric—probably—and Ben for Leather Man. And waiting gave him way too much time to think.

His mind drifted to Eric and Lucie and what he knew was going to take place this evening. He wanted to stop it. But only Lucie could do that. She had to decide whether Eric was the man for her, or if he, after a seven-year absence, still had a place in her life and heart.

Then a sickening thought occurred to him. *He hadn't offered her a different choice.* He hadn't offered her anything, because he was afraid she'd reject him as she had so long ago. Hell, she was going to make a decision based on only one offer.

Damn! He'd screwed it up again.

Cursing his own stupidity, he pulled out his cell phone and punched one of the autodial numbers. Might as well do some work, since that might be all he had left after tonight.

"Hey, P.J., this is Boyette."

"Boyette! Long time no see! Wassup in the swamps?"

"Same ole, same ole. Loads of fish, too many bugs to count, and a few alligators to wrestle."

"Boring, huh? Sure could use you back at the department."

"How's the new guy working out?"

"Okay, but he's not you."

"He'll get the hang of it. And I'll be back before you know it." Ben stared out at the dark shadow tucked in the bushes ahead of him. "Hey, P.J., need your help."

"Shoot."

"Need a license check on a rental." Ben gave P.J. the license plate number, a description of the vehicle, and his cell phone number so P.J could call him back.

"Got it. I'll get back with you when I have something. You take care. When you get back to Baton Rouge, the wife wants you to come by for some jambalaya."

"Will do. Thanks, P.J." He clicked the phone off and settled back to wait. Such was the life of a detective. Hurry up and wait. Sometimes he'd wait all night long outside a residence and nothing would happen. Other cases were more interesting. The trick to investigation was to keep a low profile and observe.

A stream of cars and pickup trucks paraded in both directions away from Raccoon Saloon. The bar was closing. Jean and Lucie would be the last to leave, Lucie in Eric's car. He waited to see what Leather Man's next move would be.

The moonlight gave him an added advantage. He could see the occasional glint off the shiny metallic finish. Five minutes passed, then ten. His cop instincts kicked into heightened alert. Not long now. Fifteen minutes after the last customer left, lights speared the darkened road as Eric's BMW pulled onto the highway, heading away from him and Leather Man.

Just as he anticipated, Leather Man pulled onto the highway behind Eric and Lucie. *Lights off.* The navy Taurus was a shadow tailing the unsuspecting congressional candidate. If not for the occasional brake lights, Ben might not have seen the car at all.

As he slid onto the road behind Leather Man, his pulse increased. Not because he was a predator on the prowl, but because he didn't know if this was the same guy who'd taken a shot at Eric and Lucie a few nights earlier. If he was, they could be in trouble tonight.

He closed the distance to within a hundred yards, afraid to get too far behind in case he lost them. The moonlight helped, but tall trees crowding the roadsides cast inky shadows over the pavement for long stretches.

When Eric turned off the main highway onto another smaller road, Ben knew exactly where he was going. His heart bottomed out. Eric was taking Lucie to one of Ben and Lucie's old haunts. *Jesus*. The place he and Lucie had made love for the first time. Would she remember?

Even more disturbing, Leather Man was right behind them. This was a particularly lonely stretch of road. Nobody lived out here and only the occasional teenagers came out here to drink or make out. He hoped some of those teenagers were out here tonight. Perhaps that would discourage Eric and Lucie from staying. If the place was deserted, Eric would propose to Lucie—and Leather Man might pull some stupid stunt.

Great! Should he turn his headlights on and let Leather Man know he was back here? Perhaps the Taurus would turn around and leave if he did. But then Lucie would see his car and wonder what the hell he was doing following her. She might even think he was there to ruin her chances with Eric.

Eric parked his BMW at Make-Out Point on the edge of Bayou Black. The lights blinked out.

A few car lengths behind Eric, the Ford Taurus had come to a halt, its brake lights glaring red beneath the canopy of trees overhanging his position.

What was the guy doing?

Ben shoved his Audi into park, turned his interior light switch to the off position, and climbed out. Hell, maybe he'd just ask. But he'd keep it quiet so as not to interrupt Eric's little talk with Lucie.

As he approached the rear of the Taurus, the red taillights blinked off and the car spun out, spitting gravel into his eyes.

He blinked the dust from his vision in time to see the car heading straight for the BMW.

Good God.

"Lucie!"

***

Eric had been gracious enough to remain silent throughout the short drive. The reprieve from the storm of mindless inner chatter had lulled Lucie into a state of near calm. Until the car halted and the engine switched off.

She opened her eyes. Before her, moonlight spread over the bayou like a silvery cloak. Although she hadn't been here in a while, she instantly recognized this place and her stomach turned a flip.

Talk about an unwanted jaunt down memory lane.

He'd brought her to freaking Make-Out Point? The point was a small pullout area where tourists could come to see the swamp during daylight hours. The kids used it at night for necking. She and Ben had made out here on more than one hot, steamy night. One particularly beautiful moonlit evening with Ben, she'd lost her virginity.

Not a good reminder, considering Eric's intention. How could she say yes to Eric when they were in a place filled with such amazing memories of Ben? Jeez! All her calm flew out the window.

She turned to Eric to ask if they could go somewhere else, but he was staring at her as if she'd hung the moon over the swamp. "I found this place today while I was out driving around, and I knew it was perfect for what I want to say to you."

There went that word again. Perfect!

Her pulse quickened and her chest tightened to the point she felt as though someone was sitting on it, squeezing the air from her lungs. Well on her way to a full-scale panic attack, she wasn't ready for Eric's next words.

Eric's eyes widened as he stared into his rearview mirror. "What the hell?"

Huh?

"Lucie!" A shout outside the vehicle alerted her they were not alone.

She glanced into the mirror on her door. Headlights flared to life, blinding her.

Wham!

The BMW lurched over the low earthen rise, throwing Lucie forward. Her seat belt tightened, catching her in time to save her head from smacking the dash. Eric wasn't so lucky. His head whacked the steering wheel with a dull *wonk*.

As if in a B horror movie, Lucie saw bushes and small trees race by the window as the BMW plunged toward the murky waters of the bayou.

Helpless to stop the forward momentum, she willed herself to be calm. They were going in. She prayed to God and her grandmother's Voodoo magic the water wasn't deep.

The front of the BMW dived beneath the surface and jammed into the soft silt of the bayou bottom. Water spilled in through the floorboard, rising fast to her knees. She fumbled to release her safety belt.

"Eric!" She felt next to her for Eric. Slumped over the steering wheel, he didn't respond when she shook him. The water was rising at an alarming rate.

She had to get him out! With her hand on his seat belt, she followed it to the safety catch and pressed the button. The lock didn't release. She jammed her thumb on it, shaking and tearing at the metal clasp. Water was up to her chest now, if she didn't hurry, they'd both drown. "Eric, wake up! Please, wake up!"

With barely enough time to take a deep breath, the fetid smell of the murky swamp water, now rising to her neck, pressed against her senses. Eric would die if she didn't get him out. She tipped his head back to keep his nose from submerging.

She pushed away from him, sucked in air, and dived for the door handle. Her hand smoothed across the door until her fingers closed around the little lever. She tugged. It was locked. She tugged again and the locking mechanism released, but the door wouldn't open. She tried to pound her fist against the window, but her hand bounced back like dandelion fluff in the wind. She surfaced inside the car and gulped in precious air. Then she dived down again, braced her feet on the console, her shoulder against the door, and shoved. *Move, damn it!*

***

When the Taurus hit the back of the BMW, Ben was fifty yards away. His heart stopped for a split second before it raced to fill his veins with adrenaline.

The bastard was trying to kill Eric and Lucie! Ben raced forward, ready to rip Leather Man apart.

When he reached the Taurus, the white reverse lights lit the night. He didn't have enough time to move out of the way. The car backed right into him. He flung himself over the top of the trunk, crashing against the back windshield. He hit with enough force that the windshield cracked into a million pieces, the safety glass the only reason he didn't fly through into the backseat.

When the car slammed to a stop, he slid off the trunk onto the gravel, rolling to the side, out of the tires' reach.

Before he could catch his wind, the Taurus skidded out of the parking area and disappeared into the night.

Head spinning, he lurched to his feet. Pain shot through his shoulder, and his lungs hurt when he breathed. But he didn't care. Lucie and Eric were in the BMW and he couldn't see it anymore. With a hand pressed to his side, he limped to the edge of the bayou.

The rear end of the BMW was barely above the surface. Steam and bubbles percolated from where the engine had submerged. No sign of Eric or Lucie.

His breath hitched. *Oh God. Please let Lucie be all right.* He kicked off his shoes and plunged into the swamp. He had to get them out before they drowned. He no longer cared if Lucie married him or Eric. He just wanted her alive.

His hands skimmed the passenger side of the car until he reached the door. The water was five feet deep at this point. He tugged on the door handle. The heavy metal door didn't budge. The force of the water on the outside of the car wasn't equalized with the interior. Which meant the inside wasn't completely full yet. Until the pressure equalized, the door would be impossible to budge. But he couldn't wait—they could be drowning.

With his foot braced on the back door, he grabbed the front door handle and pulled as hard as he could. The door opened enough to let a flood of water race in.

"Help!" Lucie's voice cried out once, right before the water filled the rest of the interior.

He wrestled the door open, reached in, and grasped her slim hand flailing in the water. He pulled until she surfaced, sputtering and coughing. She clung to him, her legs wrapping around his waist.

"You can stand in the water here," he said into her ear.

"Omigod. Eric!" She dropped her feet to the bottom and pushed off Ben and moved to dive back into the car.

"No." He caught her before her head disappeared beneath the murky water. "You get to the shore. I'll get Eric."

"But—" She tugged against him, her gaze sweeping the water's surface.

"Just do it! You're wasting time and we don't know if there are alligators out here."

She darted a quick look around. "Okay, but he's unconscious. Hurry!"

"I'll get him. Now go." He didn't wait to see if she followed his orders. He dragged in a deep breath and slipped beneath the surface, feeling his way across the passenger seat to the driver.

Eric was slumped over the steering wheel, held in place by his seat belt.

Ben worked at the belt's clasp until he realized he was wasting his time. With one hand holding the steering wheel, he dug in his own pocket, his lungs burning with the effort to stay submerged. He realized he couldn't stay down a moment longer, and he backed out of the vehicle, surfacing to catch his breath. While he inhaled another breath, he dug in his pocket again until he found his pocketknife. Thank God. No Cajun worth his salt would be without one.

Back in the swirling, murky water, he pulled himself over to Eric, sliced through the constricting belt, and freed Eric's arms. The unconscious man floated toward the ceiling.

With a hand full of Eric's shirt, he pushed backward toward the passenger door, dragging his friend with him. He surfaced, immediately bringing Eric's head above the water.

But Eric wasn't breathing. His lungs had to be full of water given the amount of time he'd been under.

Ben dragged him to the shore and pulled his body out of the swamp enough to work on him. He flipped him onto his stomach and straddled his hips. With both hands, he pushed against Eric's ribs, forcing the water up and out of his lungs.

He leaned into Eric's back. "Come on, buddy! Out with the old, in with the new. Breathe!"

***

Heart in her stomach, Lucie dropped to her knees next to the still man. "Spit it out, Eric!"

Ben pushed again.

This time, water erupted from Eric's mouth and he coughed.

"Eric, oh my God, Eric!" She pushed the hair off Eric's forehead. "He's breathing!" She smiled up at Ben in the moonlight.

But Ben's face was an unreadable mask in his own shadow. "Help me turn him over, will ya?"

Together they rolled Eric onto his back. "Lucie?" he said, his voice a hoarse whisper.

Ben got to his feet. "I'm going for my cell phone." He paused for a moment. "You gonna be okay?"

"Yeah." Eric coughed and gave a weak excuse for a smile. "Really. And thanks."

Ben turned and loped to his car.

Eric's eyes drifted shut, and he lay still.

Heart still thundering, she leaned close to listen for the steady rhythm of air moving in and out of his lungs.

"Lucie?"

She jumped. "I'm here, Eric."

"Scared for"—he coughed—"you."

She laughed and lifted his hand to her face. "I'm the Voodoo queen's granddaughter, what could possibly happen to me?"

He smiled and curled his hand around her cheek. "Did I ask you?"

"Ask me what?" she asked, before she could think. *Oh yeah.* Her heart leaped from her belly to her throat. *Don't do it, Eric,* she cried inside.

"Will you marry me?" He gripped her hand.

As she stared down at him, wondering what she could say, the hair on the back of her neck stood up. Ben stood behind her. He had to have heard Eric's question.

Eric's hand slipped back into hers. "I love you, Lucie."

With the word “no” poised on her lips, she felt weak pressure on her fingers.

“Don't say no,” he whispered. “Please.”

How could she say no? The man could be dying, for all she knew. She inhaled air to the bottom of her lungs, squeezed her eyes shut, and answered, "Yes, Eric."

Behind her, she heard a sharp intake of breath. Though Lucie's heart cried out for him to protest, Ben didn't say a thing. He didn't plead with her to change her mind. No protestations of love or offers to sweep her off her feet.

What did she expect? He'd offered for her once. A man wasn't likely to risk getting burned twice by the same fire.

For a girl who'd finally gotten exactly what she'd wanted, why was she so miserable?

What a mess.

And Eric wouldn't have asked her in the first place if it hadn't been for her magical spell and one tiny bug. She was a complete fraud, a louse, a low-life Voodoo queen wannabe without compassion and love for anyone but herself. She'd never be truly loved by anyone.

In the meantime, she sat with Eric's head in her lap, afraid to face the only man she'd ever really loved for fear of witnessing his disappointment—or worse, his contempt.

Fifteen minutes seemed like forever, waiting for the emergency medical service to arrive.

With a smile curving his lips, Eric drifted in and out of consciousness.

She wished she could drift out with him. With Ben's car the only other available transportation not under five feet of water, she was glad when Eric surfaced long enough to ask, "Will you ride with me in the ambulance?"

When the EMS arrived, she climbed in beside Eric and played the dutiful fiancée all the way to the hospital.

The press must have been listening to their scanners, because when the ambulance arrived at the small hospital in Morgan City, they were mobbed.

Thanks to the state police who'd followed along as an escort, they made it inside with minimal delay. She found herself scanning the crowds for Ben. He'd said he'd follow them. Had he changed his mind?

Eric's father met them at the ER entrance and followed them inside, demanding a private room and any specialist money could buy to ensure Eric's survival.

Once Eric was diagnosed with a small concussion, bruised ribs, and fluid on the lungs, they settled him into a room and loaded him with antibiotics and painkillers.

Finally, able to get close enough to speak to Eric again, Lucie leaned over him and said, "If you don't need me anymore, I'm going home."

Eric grasped her hand. "Did you have the doctors look you over?"

"Yeah, no harm done, other than a broken nail."

"Dad?" Eric leaned back, his eyelids drifting closed over drug-glazed eyes.

Jason Littington moved to the head of the other side of the bed. "Yes, son."

"Lucie and I are engaged. Be nice to her, will you?"

The elder Littington stared across his son at her. Instead of contempt or snobbery, he gave her a gentle smile. "Welcome to the Littington family, my dear. I'm sure I'll love you like the daughter I never had."

She would rather have had his contempt. With Jason Littington being so cordial when his son's fiancée had tricked him into falling in love with her, she felt lower than a scum-sucking snail.

She wanted to crawl beneath the rock she'd slithered out from under. Her chest tightened, her heartbeat fluttered like a skittish cat, teasing her system into thinking it was delivering life-giving blood to her body. But her pulse was so shallow it made her light-headed. She had to get outside. Now!

Eric was out cold; he wouldn't miss her.

After some lame-ass excuse to his father, she practically ran out of the hospital room.

She stopped at the nurse's station and asked for a pen and a sheet of paper. She scribbled a note and handed it to the nurse, knowing it was cowardly, but it had to be done. "Could you please give this to Jason Littington before he leaves?"

Without waiting for a response, Lucie hurried out of the hospital. She stood on the concrete sidewalk and inhaled deep breaths of thick, humid Louisiana air, trying to tamp down the rising panic. When she'd regained a tentative level of calm, her brain engaged and she realized she didn't have a ride home.

She was about to turn and reenter the hospital to find a telephone, when a silver Audi slid to a stop in front of her.

Her stomach knotted and all her hard-won calm skittered down the sewer drain. She'd rather face an entire firing squad of reporters armed with cameras than the one man with the ability to break her heart.

Ben.

CHAPTER 21

WHY HE COULDN'T LEAVE WELL ENOUGH ALONE, BEN HADN'T A CLUE. HE tried to rationalize that Lucie would need a ride home after the ambulance had delivered Eric to the hospital.

Deep inside, he knew he wanted to ask her, "Why?" Why had she pushed him away all those years ago; why did she say yes to Eric and not to him?

She stood looking at the car, her face strained as if she were afraid of him.

"Get in," he said, a little more brusquely than he'd intended.

When Lucie climbed into his car, he fought to keep from pulling her into his arms and shaking her to within an inch of her life. How could she marry Eric? Didn't she know she was supposed to love *him*?

Oh, yeah. She'd told him he wasn't good enough for her.

"If we're going home, it helps to put the shift in drive," she murmured.

Heat filled his cheeks. He'd been so buried in his misery he hadn't realized the car was still idling in the hospital parking lot. He jammed the shift in drive and floored the accelerator.

Lucie gasped, a hand fluttering over her heart.

He shot a glance her way and immediately let off the gas. Her face had drained of color.

"Sorry." *What was wrong with him?* Hadn't she been through enough without him scaring her by driving like a sulky teen?

Her laugh was more a breathy sob. "No. I'm a bit jumpy."

Damn! He should have known she was fragile. Hell, she'd almost drowned! His blood ran cold. *Lucie had almost drowned in that car.*

His lips pulling into a tight line, he concentrated on the road back to Bayou Miste, keeping his speed to five miles an hour under the posted limit. Hunkered in her corner of the front seat, she stared out the window into the inky black night. The moon had disappeared behind clouds.

They drove in silence until he pulled into her driveway. He expected her to leap out and race up to her apartment.

Instead, she sat staring up the stairs, a shimmer of tears reflecting light from the brand-new bulb glowing over her door.

The man who loved Lucie more than life itself screamed inside him, urging him to action. *Say something! Tell her you still love her. Tell her you don't want her to marry Eric. Do something!*

Then the logical man who'd regulated his life for the past seven years overruled him.

Lucie had made her choice. She would marry Eric. He would go back to Baton Rouge and that would be the end of any stupid dreams he may have conjured while at home in the swamps.

Why the hell wasn't she getting out of the car?

Finally, she fumbled for the door handle. After her second attempt, he sighed and stepped out. By the time he got around to open her door, she had pushed it wide and stood up.

When he grabbed her elbow, he felt the tremors. She was shaking so hard her teeth rattled as she collapsed against him.

Ah jeez! She was going into shock. He should have recognized it when she wasn't talking. Lucie always had something to say.

He scooped his arm under her legs and lifted her as easily as if she were a child. But her luscious curves were anything but childlike. As the side of her breast rested against his chest, he sucked in air.

A sob escaped her lips and she pressed her face into his damp shirt, wrapping her arms around his neck. He had to put her down quickly—before he couldn't let her go at all. He strode to the steps and took them like he was in a race for his life. He was in a battle to retain his sanity. With Lucie clutched against his body, his gray matter scrambled. He couldn't think beyond the next step until he reached her door.

A giggle erupted from her, ending in a sob. "I don't have my key."

"Where is it?"

"In the swamp?" She sniffed and stared up at him.

"Think you can stand?"

She nodded. He dropped her legs, still holding her around her middle.

When her knees buckled, he held tight to keep her from falling. "Yeah, sure you can stand." One hand holding her, he reached into his pocket and pulled out his trusty pocketknife. He unfolded the blade and jammed it between the door and the frame, jimmying the door handle with the knife until the door swung open.

"I can take it from here," she said, not even frowning at his handiwork.

Beneath his hands, he could still feel her tremors. She needed someone, and the only person immediately available was Ben Boyette.

Sucker. How could he maintain control when she was so soft and sweet? How could he respect her choice and his friend's trust, when she clung to him as though he was her lifeline?

As soon as he pulled her into his embrace, lifted her off her feet, and moved across the threshold, all his control crumbled.

"Don't leave me, Ben." she leaned her face into his chest.

He inhaled and blew his breath out slowly, fighting the rising surge of desire flooding his veins. "I can't stay."

"Please."

"What about Eric?" he ground out.

Her fingers clenched against his chest. "I was going to say no."

"But you didn't." And she'd broken his heart as he stood watching her promise herself to another man.

"I couldn't." Her head hung low. "He was hurt."

"You chose *him,* Lucie."

"I want *you.*" Her voice was the barest whisper he had to lean closer to hear.

"But I'm not good enough, am I?" The old hurts bubbled up and he stepped away.

She swayed, her brows furrowing. "This has nothing to do with what happened seven years ago."

"It has everything to do with what happened."

"Tell me." She dragged in a deep breath. "Would you have gone to the academy if I hadn't made you leave?"

"Hell no, I wouldn't!"

"Exactly. It was your dream, Ben. Ever since we were kids playing in the bayous." She shook her head. "I couldn't take away your dream."

He blinked, her words taking a long moment to sink in.

"I don't believe this." He turned his back on her, his gut clenching at her revelation. "You're lying. You told me you'd always wanted to marry up. Had you married me, we'd have been poor. You couldn't stand that, could you?" He spun toward her, wanting to hurt her as she'd hurt him all those years ago. "*Could you?*"

All the color drained from her face and her shoulders sagged. "What's the use, Ben? You don't want the truth. So why are we discussing history? Just go away."

"Yeah, I should." He pushed his hand through his hair, but he didn't make a move for the door. He strode toward her until they stood nose to nose. "I should, but I can't."

She gazed up at him, her eyes widening.

When her bottom lip trembled, he lost control and crushed his lips to hers. He plundered her mouth, his tongue pushing past her teeth. The warmth of her beneath his hands fired his soul, a soul he'd long thought dead.

Lucie belonged to him!

And her response matched his, passion for passion.

When he finally broke the endless kiss, he grabbed her arms and shoved her back. Her eyelids drooped, her lips were swollen with his kiss.

"Does he make you feel like this? Does he make you come alive in his arms?"

"No."

Triumph swelled briefly in his chest.

Everything he felt was so right and so wrong at the same time, his gut tightened into a knot. Lucie was the woman he loved, yet she'd promised to marry his friend. How could he betray his friend by kissing his fiancée? What had started as a means to comfort her after her frightening experience had snowballed into something he wasn't sure he could stop.

Just then, her hand slipped up the front of his chest to rest against his heart. "I know it's wrong, but I don't want to be alone tonight." Her hand circled his neck and she pulled his lips back to hers. She kissed him, claiming his mouth, his heart, and his soul. With one hand entwined in his hair, her other hand slid beneath his shirt, lacing through the hairs on his torso.

She shivered, and he realized they both still had on the wet clothing they'd worn in the swamp. He broke off the kiss and stepped back.

Her hair hanging limp around her shoulders, her shirt clinging to her body in damp places, she very much resembled a drowned rat. But her eyes shone bright, and she was still the most beautiful woman he'd ever known.

Once again, he lifted her from her feet and carried her, through the tiny bedroom to the attached bathroom. When he set her down to lean in and turn the shower water to hot, she clung to him.

"I'm going to regret this later." He tipped her face up to his. "But I can't stop myself now." With a frustrated sigh, he tugged her shirt up over her head, tossing it to the linoleum floor. His hands on her waistband, he slowly unzipped her slacks, then slid them—well, maybe yanked—until they dropped to the floor in a sodden heap. In nothing but a lacy black bra and bright-red string bikini panties, her hair hanging like dreadlocks around her face, Lucie was stunning. Her deep olive complexion complemented the midnight black of her hair and her root-beer-colored eyes.

Then a shiver shook her from shoulders to hips. Goose bumps stood out on her arms, while steam filled the small bathroom. "Have you ever gone swimming fully clothed in the swamp at night before tonight, Ben Boyette?" She trembled again and crossed her arms over her breasts. "I don't recommend it. Especially if you're trapped in a sinking car." She laughed, her voice shaky, uncertain.

He pulled her to him, bent, and caught her beneath her thighs, wrapping her legs around his fully clothed waist. Then he pushed the shower curtain aside and stepped beneath the spray, clothes and all.

"But you'll get your clothes wet!"

"Hey, I was swimming in that swamp, too. Besides, I don't care." Her breasts bobbed beneath his nose and he gave in to temptation, smoothing his cheeks between the tawny mounds pushed high by her bra.

She threaded her fingers into his hair and pressed his face against her skin.

Blood rushed from his limbs to his groin in a mad race. He stiffened against the tight confines of denim, groaning at the sweet pain.

"Not fair." She pressed a kiss to his temple. When he bit through the lacy material of her bra, she arched her back and moaned. Apparently frustrated by his slow progress, she reached behind her and unsnapped the hooks, her straps sliding down over her shoulders, the cups falling forward.

He nuzzled the black lace aside and sucked in a full, round areola, tonguing, laving, and suckling until it beaded into a hardened tip. He gave equal attention to the other until she squirmed against the hard ridge of his cock.

Water ran down her back and over his shirt and jeans, quickly making him hot and sticky, and entirely overdressed for the shower.

He set her on her feet and pulled his black T-shirt over his head, flinging it behind him. It landed with a splat on the side of the tub.

Before he could work on the rest, she ran her hands from his shoulders downward through the thick hairs on his chest. Her lips followed her hands, teasing and tasting both of his hard brown nipples.

He couldn't strip out of his jeans fast enough. Tangled in the soggy mess, he hopped on one foot and almost fell on the slippery surface of the porcelain tub.

While he maneuvered out of his jeans, she slid her red panties over her hips and kicked them off.

When they finally stood naked in the spray of the shower nozzle, they came together like ravenous creatures, too long starved of each other's bodies.

He reveled in the silky smoothness of her skin rubbing against his. He soaped his hands and ran them over her full, jutting breasts, tempting the nipples to matching peaks. She leaned back to allow water to run over her shoulders and down through the suds. Narrow streams dripped off the tips of her breasts and slid down the corridor of her cleavage to disappear into the curly mound of dark, springy hair.

His hands following the trail of soap, he cupped the juncture of her thighs, opening her nether lips like a flower to pluck at the petal within. She arched against him and moaned. Her fingers trailed down his arm to the hand tempting her to the edge. She pressed him deeper. One, then two fingers slid inside her and back out to trace her creamy essence over her most sensitive spot.

With his hardened cock pressed to her hip, he inhaled the soapy, fresh scent of her, and swooped in to claim her lips.

The more he stroked, the more tense she became until she grabbed his hand.

"Stop!" She gasped, her shoulders stiff, her eyes squeezed shut. Then she pressed his hand over her mons and rocked against him. "Oh, God, Ben." Her cream wept onto his fingers. "I need you. Now!"

Her hands circled his neck and she climbed up him to wrap her legs around his waist. He steadied her to keep her from sliding off, their bodies slick with soap and water. Then he lowered her, sheathing his shaft completely in the warm, pulsing center of her. *God, she felt good.*

With her legs locked behind him, he turned her to press her back against the cool tiles. Then in a primitive, natural rhythm, he slid in and out of her. The rising tension that had been building all along burst in a fiery explosion of sensations. He sank into her and held steady as wave upon wave of mind-blowing orgasm consumed him, sucking the very soul from his heart and breath from his lungs, shooting him into clouds of pleasure he'd only dreamed of.

When he fell back to earth, he leaned his body against her, crushing her between him and the shower walls. "I swear I just had a near-death experience." He groaned and nuzzled her neck.

She lay against him, her head drooping on his shoulder. "If that's what death feels like, I should have died a long time ago."

***

Lucie slipped from Ben's arms early the next morning. After a short, dream-filled night plagued with ghosts of ancient Voodoo queens, she gave up any pretense of sleep. Awakening before Ben had its advantages. She could fill her heart and memory with the sight of him resting peacefully in her bed. Lying on his side, his broad shoulder loomed over her, beckoning her to smooth her hand over the muscled planes.

The sheet had slipped below his waist, allowing her a glimpse of his magnificent cock, slack now in slumber. How she'd ridden him through the night, climbing the peak to bliss more than once, only to fall back into his arms. He caught her every time and snuggled against her, spooning her in his embrace, his shaft pressed to her bottom only to rise for another round of beautiful sex.

She ached to touch him, awaken him tenderly with a gentle caress, a kiss, her hand sliding down his body to grasp him.

Her own body quickened and oozed liquid desire. She wanted him again, and again—to wake beside him for the rest of her life. But she couldn't, knowing she had unfinished business to take care of, a spell to undo, and apologies to make to her almost-fiancé.

With costly determination, she remained hands-off, choosing to admire without disturbing his sleep. Dark shadows smudged the skin beneath his eyes. He hadn't been asleep long. Their unwanted swim in the swamp and their to-die-for mattress calisthenics had taken their toll on his body as well as hers.

With the gray light of dawn squeezing through the cracks in the blinds, the room lightened.

If she planned to make a break for it, she'd have to go soon. He was likely to wake at the slightest sound and expect to find her lying beside him.

She padded barefoot and naked across the room to her dresser. Easing drawers open, she selected the appropriate undergarments, jeans, and shirt, and quietly made her way into the living room. After dressing in record time, she ran a brush through her tangled mop, tied her tennis shoes, and peeked one last time at the man she'd always loved, wishing things had turned out differently.

He slept on, blissfully unaware of her stealthy escape. Next time she saw him, he'd no doubt wonder why the hell he'd slept with her in the first place.

Unable to live another day with the lie she'd created, she knew she had to find a way to break the spell. Eric deserved to find someone he really loved. As nice as he was and as much as she liked him, she didn't love him.

And as much as she *did* love Ben, she couldn't continue a relationship with him, knowing he might only return her love because of a selfish spell she'd concocted. If she couldn't have him with his love given freely, she didn't deserve to have him at all.

Having screwed up her own chances, she prayed she wasn't going to ruin Maurice and DeeDee's chances at love and a happy life together.

Either way, Lucie had to break the spell. But first, before her guilt overwhelmed her and the reporters got wind, she had to officially break off her engagement.

CHAPTER 22

"You put out an APB on the guy?" Ben wanted to get his hands on the bastard who'd tried to kill Lucie last night and almost killed Eric and him.

"We did. I'll let you know as soon as we have him in custody."

"Good." He scrubbed a hand through his hair. "Get Ron to conduct the interrogation. I bet he'll spill his guts in fifteen minutes flat."

P.J. laughed into the phone. "I bet he doesn't last ten."

"You're on for twenty bucks."

"Get anything back from forensics on that slug you found at the girl's apartment?"

"Not yet. I'll give them a call this afternoon.

"Let us know. If the two incidents are related, we'll have more evidence to nail the guy with in court."

"You bet." He would use every talent in his arsenal of detective skills to catch the guy from last night and whomever he worked for.

Ben clicked off his cell phone just as he pulled into the hospital parking lot. He felt as if he had a wad of swamp silt sitting at the bottom of his belly. How could he face Eric when he'd slept with his fiancée last night?

How could he not? He'd been assigned to protect Eric, and report on what little he'd found out about the murder attempt.

But if he could slip in a little plug for Eric to reconsider his engagement, more power to him. Although, how he'd bring up the subject, he didn't have a clue.

But more than anything, he wanted to bust up the engagement and take Lucie for himself. He just wished he didn't like Eric so much. If it were anyone else, he could just punch him out and tell him to get the hell away from his girl!

Eric was sitting up in bed, his ear pressed to a cell phone, when Ben walked in. "Yeah, I think the doctor would have released me this morning, but my father insisted I stay around for additional observation. I think he wanted the press to have time to cool their heels and me to get my strength back before I'm bombarded with questions."

He listened for a moment and grinned. "Yeah, he's probably right. After swallowing a bayou full of swamp water, I didn't feel like facing a media swarm. I should be right as rain by tomorrow, so don't cancel my Daughters of the American Revolution speech. They've been real good to me and I'd hate to let the ladies down. Look, Neal, I got company." He nodded at Ben. "We'll talk later."

"Sorry to interrupt." Ben hesitated in the doorway. He'd never liked the antiseptic smell of hospitals. That, and the huge amount of guilt he had weighing him down, made for a nasty combination in his gut.

"Not at all." Eric waved him in. "We'd been at it for fifteen minutes. I was getting cauliflower ear." He rubbed at the ear he'd had plugged into the cell phone. "I don't know which is worse, being on the phone for hours, or having to wear a hospital gown that doesn't quite cover my ass." He tugged at the strings behind his back, but soon gave up and leaned back against the pillow.

Ben forced a smile. "The gown, definitely."

"Noticed you had some of the local cops guarding my door. What's up with that?"

"After last night's attempted murder, I didn't want to take any chances." He leaned against the wall, just inside the door.

Eric nodded. "That's what I figured. Thanks."

With a nod, he dismissed Eric's gratitude. He didn't deserve it. "Ever heard of a guy named Robert Davis?"

"No." Eric shook his head. "The name doesn't ring a bell. Why?"

"The car that bumped you into the swamp last night was rented by a man named Robert Davis."

"I haven't heard of him, but maybe my campaign manager has." Eric lifted his cell phone. "Want me call him back and try the name out on him?"

"In a minute." Ben strode across the room and stared out the window, struggling with how to broach the subject of Eric's engagement.

"Lucie left a few minutes before Neal called."

Ben swung back to face Eric. "She did?" *Dilemma solved*. Since Eric had brought her up, he might as well plunge in and get it over with. *Okay, smartie, how?*

Eric's eyes narrowed slightly. If Ben hadn't glanced up right when he did, he wouldn't have noticed.

"Ben, are you still in love with her?"

When he should have felt a rush of relief for the opening, his throat clogged. He wanted to shout, Yes! Yes, he still loved her, more than life itself.

But the frown on Eric's face brought him back to reality. As far as Ben knew, Lucie still planned to marry Eric.

"You don't have to answer my question." Eric looked away. "It's just that you get tense every time she's around or I mention her."

"Yes, I still love her." Ben turned his back to Eric and stared out the window, without seeing the parking lot below. "I don't think I ever stopped."

"She kinda gets under your skin, doesn't she?"

"Yeah. I let her get away once and I've regretted it ever since." He spun toward Eric. "If you love her half as much as I do, you'll hold on as tight as you can. Don't let her get away. Because if you don't snap her up, I'm going after her. And this time, I won't let her go."

Eric's lips twisted into a wry half smile. "Yeah. She's pretty special."

Images of Lucie's naked body flittered through his thoughts. Her teasing smile and gentle touch still tingled along his nerve endings. "You don't know the half of it."

"I just wonder if she can handle being a congressman's wife." Eric scratched his chin and slid a glance up at him.

Lucie? A congressman's wife? Although he'd told her differently, he knew she could do anything she set her mind to, and do it well. "Lucie's tough, she can handle anything, and she'll make a beautiful addition to your campaign and life."

Had he really told her she wasn't cut out to be a congressman's wife? No wonder she'd been so mad. It ranked right up there with his stupid, angry words of seven years ago, when he'd called her a bayou bimbo. He'd said that to draw blood. To match the blood she'd drawn when she'd given him his ring back and told him he wasn't good enough for her. She'd struck him right through the middle of his heart.

"I don't know." Eric rubbed his chin.

His heart leaped. "Are you having second thoughts?" *Please say yes!* He held his breath.

Eric shook his head. "I love her, and I'd marry her in a heartbeat."

"But?"

"But nothing." Eric crossed his arms over his chest and grinned. "She's terrific."

"Yeah, she is." Ben sighed. *So, it was over.* Lucie was going to marry Eric, and he would go back to Baton Rouge and try to piece his life together for the second time. "Congratulations."

"Don't congratulate me yet," Eric said. "I haven't gotten her to the altar. Who knows, she may change her mind, like she did with you."

Ben could only hope.

***

"Bless my wrinkled ol' soul! I swear I be seein' de ghost of my granddaughter, Lucie." Gran LeBieu clutched her ample breast and staggered backward.

"Gran, I'm in trouble, and I need your help." Lucie stepped past her grandmother and strode through the door that hadn't seen paint since 1957.

Despite the shabbiness of the furniture and the curling paper with the roosters and hens on the kitchen wall, Lucie loved this house. It had always been her safe haven, her home when no one else wanted her. She and Lisa had come here as little girls and grown up with the bayou as their playground. When she'd sent Ben away, she'd retreated to her grandmother's house to grieve her loss. And God bless her wise old soul, Gran LeBieu hadn't pressed her for details, but let her tell her story when she was ready.

She ducked her head into the small guest bedroom, searching. "Where is she?"

"Who?"

"Lynette."

"Your mama was very upset the night before last."

"She's not my mama, and I'm not responsible for her happiness. She never felt responsible for mine." She stood facing her grandmother with her fists propped on her hips. "Is she here?"

"Dere be many things you don't know about your mama."

"I don't want to know her. She didn't bother to get to know me." Although she'd come for her grandmother's help, she couldn't stand the thought of facing her biological mother. The pain was still too fresh.

Gran LeBieu rested a hand on her shoulder. "She had her reasons for staying away."

"There's no reason good enough for a mother to dump her daughters and not come back for twenty years." She jerked away and searched the other room.

"Did you bother to ask her?"

She chose to ignore her grandmother's question. "She's not here."

"She took de boat to Bayou Miste for a few groceries. She won't be back for an hour."

“Good, 'cause I need your help.” Lucie let out a sigh and let her hands fall to her sides. She might as well jump in. "Gran, I've done something stupid."

"And you think stupidity belongs only to the young?"

"No. I believe it belongs only to me."

"Come sit, girl." Her grandmother grabbed her hand and led her to the threadbare sofa and sat, motioning for Lucie to sit beside her. "Unburden your soul with ol' Gran LeBieu."

"I really need *Madame* LeBieu's help."

"Dat bad?"

She hung her head, bracing herself for her grandmother's wrath. "Worse."

"And what could be so bad you are afraid of your *Mamère?*" She held Lucie's hand in her chubby brown fingers, stroking her in a gentle, soothing rhythm.

Lucie took a deep breath and held it. "I cast a spell." She squeezed her eyes shut and waited.

The older woman's hand stopped in midstroke. She didn't say anything for a few moments—long enough that Lucie risked a peek from beneath her eyelids.

Gran LeBieu sat with her lips pressed together and turned downward in a slight frown. When she met her gaze, she shook her head. "You know how I feel about you practicing de magic."

Her grandmother's disappointed tones were more lethal than her wrath. Lucie's eyes clouded and tears spilled down her cheeks. "I'm sorry, Gran. I know I shouldn't have done it. But I couldn't stay in Bayou Miste. Especially when he came back."

"Ben?"

"Yes, Ben." Her tears trailed down to her chin and dropped into her lap. She scrubbed at them, but they wouldn't stop.

Her grandmother lifted her chin, forcing her to look her in the eye. "Voodoo be powerful magic, something not to be taken in vain or for selfish reasons."

"I know." She pressed her cheek against her grandmother's hand. "I was so wrong, and I couldn't have made a bigger mess if I'd tried."

Gran LeBieu pulled her into her arms and hugged her close. "Tell me."

Between sobs, she poured out all the sordid details of her magical mess. Her grandmother kept her supplied with tissues until her story and her tears ended.

The Voodoo queen sat in silence for several moments, her forehead creased in a frown. When she looked up, her potent gaze seared into Lucie's most secret thoughts. "Who do you love?"

"Oh Gran, I don't know who I should love." She wrapped her arms around her belly and rocked back and forth. "Eric is everything a girl could want for a husband."

"But you don't want him." Her words were a statement, not a question.

"No, I don't." She sighed. "I've tried, but I can't love him."

Her grandmother's gaze had the same effect as pinning her to a wall. "You can't because you still love Ben."

Lucie buried her face in her hands and cried tears she didn't think she had left. "I do."

"Then why do you think you have to undo this spell? If Ben loves you, you have what you be wantin'."

She looked up. "I'd thought about that, but I can't leave the spell in place."

"Why?"

"I have to let Eric go to live his life and find a woman to love. One who is more deserving than me."

"But if you undo the spell, Ben may or may not be in love wit' you anymore."

Lucie pushed off the couch and walked to the window where sunlight and warmth spilled through. Closing her eyes, she soaked in the rays, hoping to thaw the chill in her heart. "I know." She turned to her grandmother. "I can't have Ben if he doesn't love me of his own free will. If he only loves me because of a spell, I won't find the happiness I've always wanted."

"Looks to me like you have all de answers den." Gran LeBieu stood. "You have to undo de spell."

Lucie nodded. "That's why I came."

"You want Madame LeBieu to fix what's broke?"

Hope and dread filled her chest. "Could you?"

Mamère crossed her brown arms over her chest. "No, I cannot."

Her heart thumped around in her chest, then fell to her stomach. "You can't or you won't?"

"Both."

All Lucie's hopes crashed around her ears. Her grandmother had always helped her through tight spots. Why not now? "Then what am I to do?"

"You have to find de bug."

"I've tried, but it's been all over the place."

The old woman smiled. "That's where I might be able to help."

"Oh thank you, Gran." She hugged her grandmother. "How? How will you help?"

"I have just de potion you need to catch de bug."

"You do?" She clapped her hands together. "How soon can I have it?"

Her smile faded to a stern line. "As soon as you make me a promise."

"I promise not to play in Voodoo without your permission from now on."

"Dat's not de promise."

She frowned. "What do you mean?"

"I want you to promise me you'll talk with your mother and actually be listenin' dis time."

Her gut clenched as if she'd been sucker punched. "I can't."

Her grandmother cocked an eyebrow at her. "Can't or won't?"

"Both."

"No talk, no potion." Gran LeBieu turned her back on Lucie.

How could her grandmother ask her to do this? "She left me," she said in a hoarse whisper. "Twenty years ago."

Gran LeBieu turned back to her, one eyebrow raised. "Is it a deal, or not?"

Lucie pushed a hand through her hair. She didn't know which was harder, forgiving her mother or losing Ben. But she knew she couldn't live her life regretting the choices she made.

She reluctantly stuck her hand out. "It's a deal."

***

"What are we doing out in Alligator Alley in the middle of the night?" Alex asked. "What's the big secret?"

Lucie reached beneath the pirogue's seat and pulled out the antique glass perfume atomizer her grandmother had given her earlier that day. "Gran said the potion would only work when exposed to moonlight."

"The moon shines in my backyard just as well as it does out here," Calliope grumbled.

"I know, but the reporters have been swarming all over the parish." She held up the bottle and prepared to spray. "I didn't want them to see what I'm about to do."

"And just what are you about to do?" Alex pulled the paddle out of the water and rested it across her lap.

"I'll bet you five dollars, she's frog-giggin' for a man." Calliope giggled at her own joke.

Lucie glared at her in the light from the half moon. "Look, I appreciate both of you coming out to help me." She drew in a deep breath and blew it out slowly. "I'm going to catch the love bug."

Both women gasped.

"So you're finally going to do it?" Alex clapped her hands together. "You're going to undo the spell?"

"Oh, Lucie. Are you sure?" Calliope clutched her arm. "But DeeDee and Maurice are sooo in love!"

"I know, I know." She hated hurting the new lovebirds. "But it can't be helped. The magic was wrong." She raised her palm to Alex. "I know. You told me so. Maurice and DeeDee will have to take their chances. I can't leave the spell in place."

"But DeeDee will be devastated. And we just had her hair straightened." Calliope's pale face shone sad in the moonlight. "She's never been happier."

The lead weight of her heart slowed to a morbid beat. She was going to remove a spell that had quite a few people in Bayou Miste living a lie. "And what if the bug contaminated Elaine and Larry? Elaine's supposed to marry Craig in just two days. Has anyone seen Elaine?"

"No." Calliope's shoulders slumped.

"Your sister would have been happy to bust them up a couple months ago," Alex said.

"She was wrong and had no business interfering in their lives. They love each other and deserve to be together. And I don't deserve to marry a man who can only love me because of a spell."

"Omigod!" Alex threw her hands in the air. "Lucie's growing up!" She plunked her fists on her hips and frowned. "Frankly, sweetie, it's about time!"

"Alex, you're getting on my last nerve." Lucie glared at her. "I'm not *that* heartless."

Alex snorted. "You've sure been acting like it lately."

"Well, I mean to change that." She handed Calliope and Alex each a butterfly net, then raised the bottle and wrapped her fingers around the bulb. "I'm not exactly sure what'll happen when I spray this stuff. But Gran LeBieu said it would help me catch the bug."

"Do you have to say anything, a spell or incantation?" Alex asked.

"Oh please, don't!" Calliope held her net in front of her. "I don't relish the idea of being a bug."

"I'm not chanting any spells or changing either of you into bugs, so get a grip." Lucie raised the atomizer higher, into the air above her head. "Ready?"

Both Alex and Calliope squinted and hunkered low in their seats.

With a determined pinch, Lucie squeezed the bulb of the atomizer, sending a spray of what smelled like sleazy French perfume into the night air.

Calliope covered her nose. "Ewww! I smelled it." She glanced at her arms. "I'm not turning into a bug, am I?"

"No, silly," Alex said, but she glanced at her arms in the light from the moon. "Actually, it smells like the cheap perfume my great-aunt Rachel used to wear."

Lucie ignored them and squinted into the night. Where was that darn bug?

"I wonder how long it takes to work?" Calliope held her net up and scanned the sky.

A mosquito landed on Lucie's arm and sank its greedy little pointy thing into her. She smacked it and another that landed not two inches away.

"Hey, I'm being attacked here." Calliope swatted at her arms and neck.

"Me too," Alex said. "And it ain't by a love bug."

Lucie scrambled for the can of bug spray that was kept beneath the seat of the boat and sprayed herself then tossed the can to Alex. What was taking the love bug so long?

A bright light bumped into her forehead and dropped into her lap. Her heart jumped. Was this it? She stared at the bug in her lap.

"Did you find it?" Alex leaned close.

"No. It's just a firefly." Lucie lifted the bug and tossed it high. It circled and bumped into her again. "What's wrong with you?" She *shooshed* it away only for it to return again, followed by another and another.

"Oh! Oh! I have a ladybug on me!" Calliope bounced up and down on her seat. "Is it the one? Is it?"

Lucie and Alex peered at the bug.

"No." Lucie shook her head, disappointment filling her belly. "The love bug had a kinda greenish glow."

"Suppose it faded?" Calliope swung at half a dozen bugs flying around her face.

What did Lucie know about magical bugs? "I don't think so."

"Hey, I've got one." Alex's voice shouted into the night. But when she stared down at the ladybug on her arm, she sagged. "No glow."

Within seconds, ladybugs, mosquitoes, june bugs, fireflies, and every bug known to southern Louisiana swarmed them.

"Holy bug bath!" Lucie swatted the creatures away. "This stuff must have called the entire population of bugs in the swamp!" A bug flew into her mouth. *Bluh*! She spit it out, coughed, and sputtered. With her eyes squinted as closed as she could get them and still see, Lucie cried out, "See it yet?"

"Not a damn thing," Alex muttered through clenched lips.

"There it is. *Bluck*! I swallowed a firefly!" Calliope gagged. "*Ewww*!"

"Don't just sit there, catch it!" Lucie dove for the ladybug with the greenish glow. Without a net, she couldn't quite reach it and almost tipped the boat.

"Let me." Alex leaned out and batted at the air with her net. "I caught something!"

"Let me see." Lucie grabbed Alex's hand and pulled the net close. Inside were two-dozen bugs of varying species, including a handful of ladybugs. But no greenish glow.

Alex shook the net free of her catch and all three women squinted at the sky again.

Bugs coated their clothing, bare arms, and hair.

"*Ewww*! I have bugs everywhere. I can feel them crawling around." Calliope tossed her net to the floor and flipped her red hair from side to side, combing her fingers through to shake the bugs loose. "*Ewww*!"

"There it is." Alex pointed above Lucie.

She dove for Calliope's abandoned net and spun to look at where Alex still pointed. About five feet above her head, the hexed ladybug circled in an erratic pattern.

Lucie stood straight up and swung her net through the myriad bugs whizzing around her and buzzing her ears.

Unfortunately, Alex stood and swung at the same time. The little pirogue tilted one way. When Lucie leaned the other to compensate, so did Alex. Their combined weight flipped the boat, Calliope, and all.

Lucie plunged into the swamp and sank beneath the surface. At first, she panicked. The last time she'd been in the swamp, she was trapped inside a car. When her feet touched the bottom, she scrambled to stand. Within seconds, she was standing in water a little over four feet deep. And she still had her net in her hand.

A quick scan of the contents sent her heart racing. "I caught it!"

"At least we know where your priorities are." Alex waded over to where she stood.

Calliope joined them. "Thanks, you two. If I'd known we were going for a swim, I'd have worn my swimsuit instead of my favorite pair of Gap khakis." She grabbed Lucie's hand. "Let me see."

Jumbled among twenty or so other wet bugs lay a ladybug, glowing a faint greenish color, its hard red shell closed tight.

A small amount of weight lifted from Lucie's shoulders. At least she had the bug now. It couldn't do any more damage.

"Quick, do the spell before you lose it again," Calliope said.

Despite being up to her neck—well, maybe her chest—in swamp water, Lucie thought back over the words her grandmother had her memorize.

"Come little creature, 'tis time to be free
Let go of your past and then you will see
Life can go on as fate did intend
Love given freely finds you in the end
Reverse the bad magic that led you to be
With a green shiny heinie for all who can see
All will be well by the mystic Voodoo
When those who know not, bow to those who do."

"That's one funky spell." Alex inhaled and blew it out. "Well, let's hope it works."

All three women leaned over the wet net full of creepy-crawlies and stared down at the one brightly glowing ladybug.

"Look!" Calliope hopped up and down, splashing water in their faces. "The green glow is going away."

Just as she said, the ladybug's aura dimmed until they could no longer distinguish it from the other ladybugs caught in the net.

The rest of the worry hanging over Lucie lifted. *The spell was reversed!* Eric could get on with his life, and Craig and Elaine would get married. The little bit of elation was quickly followed by a deep sense of sadness. DeeDee and Maurice would be devastated. Not to mention her own little problem—she was totally, head-over-heels, hook-line-and-sinker in love with Ben.

And ending the spell would have erased any chances of Ben loving her back.

CHAPTER 23

THE MORE BEN THOUGHT ABOUT IT, THE MORE HE WASN'T OKAY WITH standing by and watching Lucie marry a man she probably didn't love. How could she love Eric when she'd slept with him? Not once but *twice* in the past week. He could still feel her moving beneath him, crying out his name in the heat of passion.

The images haunted him. Haunted him so much he'd do anything to win her back.

Thus, the trip to Madame LeBieu.

He'd caught Joe Thibodeaux as he was closing up shop at Thibodeaux Marina, and rented a boat. With darkness quickly cloaking the bayou, he'd taken the twisting channels to the old woman's house in the swamps. He could have found it in the dark, as many times as he'd visited it when he and Lucie were dating. Now as he stood on the porch, his hand raised to knock, he didn't know if he could go through with his plan.

The door swung open before he could change his mind.

"Benjamin Franklin Boyette! What you be doin' on my porch at dis time of de night?" Madame LeBieu's deep Cajun accent fascinated him and gave him the chills at the same time.

He'd heard a rumor that she'd changed his old buddy Craig Thibodeaux into a frog a few months back. How much truth there was to the rumor, he didn't know. Craig had been at the bar several nights ago getting close to a nice-looking lady. He hadn't noticed anything green or froggish about him. Still... The woman knew things about Voodoo that kept most sane people away.

But times were desperate, calling for desperate measures. If he wanted to win Lucie back, he had to do it before she up and married Eric.

"Madame LeBieu, I need your help."

Her eyes narrowed. "You have no called me Madame LeBieu since you and Lucie dated. Are you here for de Voodoo?"

He took a deep breath and sighed. "Yes, ma'am."

She stepped back into the house and opened the door wide. "Come in, boy."

Once inside, he stopped short. A woman, the spitting image of Lucie, rose from the couch. For a moment his heart leaped into high gear. Upon closer review, fine lines around her eyes and mouth gave her away.

"Nice to see you again, Lynette." He stuck out his hand.

"Ah, Ben." She smiled, Lucie's smile. "Good to see you, too. I've heard a lot about you."

Ben's heart warmed to this woman before he remembered her history of having left Lucie to be raised by her grandmother. He dropped her hand abruptly. "I'm sorry, I haven't heard much about you." He didn't disguise the contempt in his voice. This woman had hurt his Lucie. A deep scarring wound she might never overcome.

"You've heard enough to condemn me, I see."

"You left your children. What do you expect?"

She shrugged. "I didn't expect anything. But I'd hoped I could at least tell my daughter why. Look, you've obviously got business with my mother. I'll go to my room." Lynette LeBieu disappeared into a small bedroom and softly closed the door behind her.

Alone with the formidable Madame LeBieu, he didn't know how to begin. He'd been so determined when he'd marched up her steps. But having met Lynette reminded him of Lucie's reasons for wanting to leave Bayou Miste, and why she deserved a better life than the one she'd been given growing up. Suddenly, his own desires and needs seemed selfish. Unwarranted. He turned to Madame LeBieu. "I shouldn't have come."

"Let me be de judge of dat." She pointed to the couch. "Sit."

Like an obedient dog, he did as he was told and perched on the edge of the worn floral cushion, elbows propped on his knees, fingers threaded together in front of him.

The Voodoo queen, in her bright-red muumuu, sat beside him, her broad bottom taking up half the seating area. "Now, what be de problem?"

"Lucie."

"Dat pretty much narrows it down. Could you be more to de point?"

He ran his hand through his hair, standing it on end. "I love her."

The old woman's head tipped back and she stared down her nose at him. "Ahh. My lovely granddaughter."

"Lovely, and frustrating, and completely insane." He leaned back and waved his hand in the air. "Yeah, Lucie."

"Why did it take you so long to come back to my Lucie?"

Ben pushed to his feet and strode across the floor. "I didn't think she wanted me. Hell, she told me I wasn't good enough for her!"

"Up until dat moment, did she give you any reason to doubt her love?"

He paused in midstride and thought back through seven years of hurt pride and pain. He'd thought Lucie loved him as much as he loved her. "I'd have given up everything to make her happy. I thought she would have done the same."

Madame LeBieu raised her eyebrow. "And didn't she?"

Ben stared at her, trying to comprehend that look and knowing he wasn't getting it. "I don't understand. You'll have to spell it out for me."

The old Voodoo queen rolled her eyes. "Men can be so foolish and blind." She took his hands in hers. "Lucie gave up everything because she loved you more dan you deserved. She gave up her happiness for you to follow your dreams."

Ben reeled. Madame LeBieu's words echoed Lucie's, only he hadn't listened when Lucie had said them. Hell, he'd thrown them back in her face.

Could they be true? Could she really have done that...for him?

And for all this time, because of his stupid pride, he hadn't seen what was painfully clear now. She'd sent him away to allow him the chance to follow his dreams.

And he hadn't come back for her.

No wonder she was so pissed. She'd sacrificed her happiness for him to have the life she couldn't give him. And he hadn't even given her the opportunity to explain. He'd let pride get in the way a second time, and he could well have lost her for good.

No.

That's why he'd come out to the old witch's house tonight. "I've made too many mistakes to deserve her, but I love Lucie more than my own life." His grip tightened in Madame LeBieu's hands. "I can't lose her again. I need a love potion to help her change her mind about marrying Eric. I want her to marry me."

The old woman tipped her head to one side. "Have you bothered to ask her?"

"She'd laugh in my face. She wouldn't believe me. Why should she? I've been too stupid to believe her." He never thought he'd do it, but Ben dropped to one knee in front of Lucie's grandmother. "Madame LeBieu, I want to marry your granddaughter. Will you help me win her back? Will you give me a love potion or something to make her love me as much as I love her? Please?"

Okay, so he was begging. Sometimes a man had to do what a man had to do.

"After such a very pretty speech, how can dis ol' woman not help?" Madame LeBieu dropped his hand and disappeared into the other bedroom. Within seconds, she returned and handed him a fancy perfume bottle with a bulb at the end of a tube. "Be careful with dis potion. Spray a little on you before you see Lucie. Don't talk to any other female first. It must be Lucie."

Hope filled his chest. "Will it make her love me?"

"If she doesn't love you after dis," Madame LeBieu raised her right hand, "I'll give up making de Voodoo."

Whew! That was an endorsement, if he wasn't mistaken. "Thank you, Gran LeBieu." He leaned over and kissed the old woman's cheek. "You're the best Voodoo queen in the bayou."

"Damn right! I be de only Voodoo queen."

Ben didn't wait. He was out the door and into the johnboat before the screen door could slap closed behind him.

He couldn't wait to try the potion on Lucie. The sooner she realized she loved him, the sooner he could return to sanity.

***

After a fitful night's sleep, Lucie climbed into her car and drove the short distance to the agreed-upon location. Though she was already twenty minutes late, her thoughts were so centered on what impact the reversal spell would have, she almost missed her turn.

Alex and Calliope stood outside the Cussin' Cajun, waving like fans at a celebrity. She was past them before her brain engaged and she realized they were waving at her. Without thinking, she slammed on her brakes and the rear end of her car skidded sideways and stopped two inches from Granny Saulnier's prized poodle, FeFe.

The little dog yelped and all three pounds of bright-orange fluff leaped straight up in the air.

Seemingly out of nowhere, Maurice and DeeDee rushed to grab the dog. DeeDee got there first and snatched FeFe into her arms, shooting a glare at her. "You should drive more carefully, Lucie LeBieu." She cooed at the little dog. "It's okay, FeFe. I won't let that meano Lucie hurt you."

Maurice stepped up behind DeeDee and slid his arm around her waist, nuzzling her neck.

"Sorry!" she called out the window. She completed her U-turn and crept to a parking place next to Alex and Calliope.

"Lucie, you're late." Alex rushed to the driver's door and yanked it open. "We're so glad you got here, though. I tried calling your cell phone, but you didn't answer."

Lucie dragged her body out of the car and stood rolling the kinks out of her tense shoulders. "It's at the bottom of the swamp in my purse."

"Oh, yeah. I forgot." Alex nodded toward the happy couple and the orange poodle. "You saw Maurice and DeeDee?"

"Yeah." She sighed, staring at them, their happiness making her queasy. "I guess the spell didn't work on them. Have you heard anything from the Elaine-Larry-Craig front?" Lucie hoped at least one of the problems would be cleared up.

"Yeah," Alex said. "I talked with Joe Thibodeaux. He said Craig and Elaine had some big argument and decided not to get married."

"Oh, no!" Lucie's queasy stomach dipped and roiled. "Did he say what it was about?"

"No, he just said they decided not to get married." Alex said. "Read into it what you will. The man was too busy with customers."

Lucie sank to sit on the curb, and buried her head in her hands. "This is all such a mess. Do you think there's any chance it could have worked for some and not others?"

Calliope grabbed her arm and pulled her back to her feet. "Only one way to find out."

"I know, I know." A dull throbbing beat against her temples. Too much swamp water and worry. "I better get it over with."

"Don't you want breakfast first?" Calliope asked.

Her dipping, roiling, burbling belly rebelled. "No way! I'd rather face the music on an empty stomach. Girls, wish me luck."

***

"I'm sorry to say that since the night you were bumped in the swamp, the police haven't seen hide nor hair of one Mr. Robert Davis," Ben said.

"I don't like it," Eric strode across the room to the liquor and water decanters. "The man tried to kill me once, maybe twice, if you count the shot-out lightbulb. Both times, Lucie was with me. She could have been killed."

"I know." Ben's gut had been in a permanent knot since the swamp-swim incident. "No one wants to nail this guy more than I do. Unfortunately, he's disappeared for the moment. I've got the local sheriff's department, state police, and a few of my buddies in the FBI looking for him."

"Damn it!" Eric slammed his fist against the counter, rattling the crystal glasses. "What do you think I should do? I can't put Lucie at risk." He turned to face Ben. "Maybe I should withdraw from the congressional race."

"No. You can't. That's exactly what this guy wants."

"I can't let my running for Congress endanger those I love. And who's to say he won't target Lucie to get to me?" Eric jammed his hands in his pocket. "I have too many speeches and dinners to attend to keep an adequate eye on Lucie."

"So what are you suggesting we do to protect her?" Ben asked.

Eric swung toward the window and stared down, silent for a moment. Then his shoulders stiffened. "Ben, I want you to be Lucie's bodyguard."

Eric might as well have punched him in the gut.

The congressional candidate faced him. "You're the only one I trust to protect her."

"I think you should hire a professional bodyguard for that one. I've been tasked to protect you."

"I can take care of myself." Eric strode toward him. "I'm more concerned about Lucie."

"I am, too, but—"

"You're the perfect choice. You already know her and no one would think you were a bodyguard."

"But—" He couldn't be around Eric's fiancée and not touch her. Torture like that would either unman him or make him insane.

"Do it, Ben—for our friendship." Eric held out his hand. "For Lucie."

As if reaching for a snake, he placed his hand in Eric's. "Okay. But only until I can get someone we both can trust in place. In the meantime, I'll have Billy Ray tag along with you."

"Deal."

They shook hands.

"Now I have work to do. I'd really like you to check out Dad's office again. I'm worried that someone might have it bugged."

"Sure." Ben spun toward the door connecting Eric's office and Jason Littington's. Before he stepped through, he turned back. "Eric, I'll take care of her."

"I know." Eric nodded, his mouth twisted in an ironic grin. "I know."

CHAPTER 24

"PASCAL, COULD YOU PLEASE RING ERIC'S OFFICE AND ASK IF HE HAS TIME to see me?" Lucie tapped her high heels on the smooth granite floor, her nerves screaming to get this over with.

Pascal jumped to his feet, knocking over a cup of pens and pencils. "Lucie, you can't marry Eric. You should marry me and be my wife."

"I don't love you, Pascal." She gathered the spilled items and placed them on the counter. She didn't love Eric, either, and she hoped he didn't love her. That's why she'd come to see him at his office. She'd have gone to his home, but she'd been told he'd already returned to work.

"I won't let you marry him," Pascal said.

"Get over it, Pascal, you don't have a chance with me. I thought I made myself clear back in fifth grade." Why did men have to be so dense?

"You were nice to me then." He reached across the counter and grasped her hand in his. "You have to have feelings for me."

"I do. I feel like you could be a friend—nothing more." Her heart squeezed tight in her chest, hating the hurt look in Pascal's eyes, knowing the feeling of loving and not having that love returned. But she was tired of the same argument. With a yank, she pulled her hand free.

“What do I have to do to get through to you? Now, will you get Eric or do I have get him myself?"

"Are you looking for me?"

Lucie spun toward the deep voice.

In his business suit, Eric looked elegant, incredibly handsome, and every bit the congressional candidate. The light-gray silk-and-wool-blend suit complemented his blond hair and blue eyes. He was as close to a Greek god as Lucie had ever come to marrying, and she'd given him up.

What kind of stupid had she become?

"Could we go to your office?" she squeaked.

"No! I will not let you take my Lucie." Pascal came out from behind the front desk and cocked his fists at Eric.

To his credit, Eric didn't show fear, he pressed his fingers to his temples and sighed. "Pascal, it's okay. She already called off the engagement. Now, put your fists down before I have to fire you. Your threats are starting to get on my nerves."

"You aren't going to marry him?" Pascal looked to Lucie for confirmation.

She shook her head. "I'm not marrying Eric."

“Then you can marry me!”

“No, I'm not going to marry you, Pascal. Not now, or ever.” She wanted to reach across and wring his idiot neck. She hooked her arm in Eric's and pulled him toward the elevator. “Come on, before I inflict violence upon him.”

Eric chuckled. “Remind me not to make you mad.”

“I will.”

Once in his office, she didn't know how best to ask Eric if he still loved her. He might answer yes to keep from upsetting her.

With a quick look toward his father's office, Eric strode across and pulled the door closed, leaving a slight gap. “So, what brings you here today, Lucie?”

She could think of only one way to prove whether or not the potion had worked for him. She dragged in a deep breath and turned to face him. “Eric, kiss me.”

"Huh?"

She waved him forward. She didn't have time to play around. "Kiss me."

"I thought we were through. You said you didn't want to marry me."

She stomped her foot, frustration building by the moment. She had to know if the spell worked. "Humor me, just this once."

Eric frowned but moved forward until he stood directly in front of her—within kissing range. "I don't get it."

"Just shut up and kiss me." She grabbed the lapels of his tailored suit and yanked him toward her, her lips crashing against his.

Without hesitation, his hands circled her waist and pulled her against him.

To Lucie's dismay, Eric deepened the kiss, until his tongue pushed past the barrier of her teeth and tangled with hers.

He didn't push her back, didn't stop the kiss until a full two minutes later. When he did come up for air, he rested his cheek against her hair and held her in his embrace. "Nothing?"

Tears welled in Lucie's eyes. "Nothing. As much as I wanted to, I can't love you like you deserve." She kissed his lips gently. "I think you're a special man and deserve someone who loves you with all her heart."

"Well, thank you for your honesty." Eric smiled down at her.

"You'll be okay?" Lucie asked.

"I'll be fine." Patting his chest, he winked. "It'll mend."

"Thanks, Mr. Littington, I'll just check Eric's office—" The voice came from the connecting door Eric had closed only moments before. "Oh, excuse me."

She jumped out of Eric's arms and spun to face the intruder. She stopped short of smacking her forehead. Of all the people to witness her in Eric's embrace, her luck would make sure it was Ben.

"Sorry to interrupt. I didn't realize you had company." With his hands shoved in his pockets, Ben stared at her, although his words were directed at Eric.

"Not at all." Eric grinned. "We were through, weren't we Lucie?"

Only she would know Eric's crooked smile was a strained attempt at looking normal. Her gut twisted. Damn! Why hadn't the spell worked?

Then another thought occurred to her and she stared at Ben. Had it worked on him?

One thing was certain. She couldn't conduct the "kiss test" on him here. Not in front of a heartbroken Eric. She may be stupid, but she wasn't totally insensitive.

She touched Eric's arm and smiled gently. "I'll go." Without a backward glance, she dashed for the elevator and punched the down button, praying the doors would open and swallow her before Ben or Eric could join her. Already embarrassed at being caught kissing, she didn't have the heart to "test" Ben yet.

Or was she chicken? Did she really want the love spell to be broken for Ben? Had the spell worked for Ben, but not Eric? It hadn't worked to undo Maurice and DeeDee's match, nor Elaine and Craig's problem with Larry. She just had to know about Ben, and the sooner she found out the better.

But not now.

The elevator slid open and she stepped in, collapsing with her back against the far wall.

A hand shot in when the doors were only inches from closing, forcing them open again. In stepped Ben, and all Lucie's troubles seemed to multiply in intensity to screaming-meemie level.

They rode down in silence and stepped out of the building through the glass double doors.

When she should have been testing whether the undo spell had worked, she'd stood tongue-tied in the elevator. Instead of asking Ben if he still loved her, she'd walked outside. His bug truck stood next to her Mustang in the parking lot. It was now or never.

"Lucie."

"Ben."

They both spoke at once.

"Go ahead," Ben told her.

"The other night." She paused, her gut clenching in a painful knot. "When you stayed with me," she gazed up at him, her eyes narrowing, "you never said you loved me. Do you?"

Ben pulled her into his arms and crushed her to his chest. "Oh Lucie,

I thought I could love you no matter what. But I can't. Not now, not with the situation the way it is."

Lucie almost wept. The undo spell hadn't worked for Eric, but had for Ben. Why? Was this fate's way of fixing her mistakes by making her pay for them for the rest of her life?

For a moment she reveled in his embrace, loving the feel of his arms around her, breathing in the smell of him. She sniffed. What was that? Cheap perfume? Kinda reminded her of the stuff she'd used last night to attract every bug in the swamp. Why did Ben smell like perfume?

She pushed away from him.

"I can't live this lie," he said. "I can't love you, knowing it's wrong."

Huh? "Why is it wrong?"

He turned away and shoved a hand through his hair. "Lucie, you have to make the decision about what's important in life. Whether it's money, position, love, or forgiving your mother—you have to do it. No one else can." He spun to face her, his gaze boring into hers. "If you can straighten out your life and still have room left in it, come see me. Until then, I can't love you."

An emptiness so vast she couldn't put her arms around it filled Lucie. Ben was telling her he didn't love her. Or as he put it, couldn't love her.

Well, that was that. The undo spell had worked for one out of the four hexlings.

She fought the tingling prelude to tears welling in her eyes. "Thanks, Ben. I understand."

"Lucie—"

"No, Ben. You're right. I have to fix my life." With a forced smile, she climbed into her car and shut the door.

Ben stood where she'd left him, his gaze never leaving her as she cranked her engine. Couldn't he get into his bug truck and out of her sight? He was done with her, why did he have to linger? Was it some grotesque kind of punishment?

Her entire body shook as if she'd been tortured. With her hand on the gearshift, she shoved it into reverse and slammed her foot onto the accelerator. She couldn't get away fast enough. Unfortunately, she didn't look in her rearview mirror in time to stop herself from slamming into Eric's BMW.

Kaboom!

An explosion, of greater magnitude than merely bumping a car in the parking lot, rocked Lucie's Mustang, throwing her against the steering wheel. Pain stabbed through her head before blackness darkened her vision.

***

The blast knocked Ben to the ground, the concussion reverberating through his ears. After several seconds, his mind reengaged. What the hell happened?

Flames leaped from the crumpled remains of Eric Littington's BMW. In front of it stood Lucie's little turquoise Mustang convertible pockmarked with shrapnel from the explosion.

"Lucie!" He shouted, and raced to pull her from the wreckage before the flames from the BMW could consume the Mustang.

Adrenaline kicked in as he lifted Lucie in his arms and carried her back into the building.

"Call 911!" he shouted at Pascal. "We need an ambulance."

The Cajun stood there with his mouth open, staring at Lucie, making no move to do as Ben had told him.

"Do it!" he shouted.

The sharp order broke through Pascal's shock and he fumbled through the call, before he hung up and joined Ben.

Gently, he laid her on a couch in the lobby, bending close to feel for her soft breath against his cheek.

Thank God, she was breathing. With a cursory glance all over her, he noted a few cuts and bruises, but nothing life-threatening. What he couldn't see worried him more. She'd been unconscious now for several minutes and he couldn't tell whether or not she had internal injuries.

He wanted to gather her close to him, but he was afraid of causing more injury. If not for the fire, he'd have left her in the car for the emergency medical technicians to handle. If she'd suffered spinal injuries, he could have exacerbated them.

"Wake up, Lucie," he called out to her, pressing a kiss to her ear. "Wake up, sweetheart."

"Oh my God!" Eric cried out from across the room. "What happened?" He strode across the granite tiles in the lobby, followed by his father.

"She backed into your car and it exploded," Ben said, his voice flat, the gravity of what had happened not at all lost on him.

Eric sank into a chair across from the couch and dropped his face into his hands. "Oh, sweet Jesus. Lucie, what have I done to you? That explosion was meant for me."

"I didn't do it!" Pascal cried out, his eyes wide, his face pale beneath his Cajun swarthiness. "I only wanted Eric to leave Lucie alone. I never tried to kill him."

"What are you talking about, Pascal?" Eric asked. "No one is blaming you for the explosion."

"I didn't do it." Pascal dropped to his knees in front of Lucie. "I never meant to hurt anyone."

Eric started to say something, but Ben put a hand out to stop him.

"Tell us about it, Pascal," he said softly, when he'd rather reach out and wring a few answers out of the distraught man.

Pascal sobbed into his hands. "I threw the rock through the window, and I shot the light out when Eric was kissing Lucie. But only because I wanted him to leave." He looked up, his face wet with tears. "I never wanted to hurt him and I definitely wouldn't hurt Lucie." He stared down at her, his face softening into a weak smile. "I love Lucie."

"Seems like quite a few of us do," Ben muttered.

Pascal's brow furrowed and he stood. "I may not like Eric Littington," he said, his mouth twisting into a snarl. "But I didn't blow up his car."

Ben stared up at Eric. "You need to have security sweep the compound. I'll bet Davis is out there somewhere. He must have planted the bomb after you arrived this morning."

Jason pressed a hand to Eric's shoulder. "I'll take care of it." He strode to the communication console and radioed security. "Get everyone out there. I want that man caught."

Not as much as Ben did. The man had hurt Lucie. Anger burned deep in his veins. If he could, he'd tear the bastard apart limb from limb. But first, he had to know Lucie would be all right.

Sirens could be heard through the thick glass windows, and moments later, emergency medical technicians rushed in, some carrying medical kits, others pushing a stretcher.

"Over here!" Ben shouted. He moved aside to let the professionals take care of Lucie. But he didn't let her out of his sight for a second. He would be by her side no matter what. That's where he belonged, not Eric. He looked across at his friend and noted a reflection of the anguish he felt himself. Eric really loved Lucie. But they weren't married, yet.

Ben's lips tightened. As much as he liked Eric, he wasn't going to give up on Lucie without a fight. He loved Lucie enough to make the ultimate sacrifice. He wouldn't be wearing that stinky love potion Madame LeBieu gave him for any other reason.

CHAPTER 25

"I don't know why I have to stay here when I feel just fine." Lucie hated lying in bed and liked it even less in a backless nightgown.

"My, aren't we the fusspot." Alex slid down in the vinyl-covered seat next to Lucie's bed and flicked the television remote. "Wonder if the news is on." She flipped through the channels until she found the local newscast.

"That's Eric!" Lucie leaned forward. "Turn it up!"

"In today's news, congressional candidate Eric Littington is in New Orleans to speak with the Daughters of the American Revolution. Mr. Littington, tell us about the car bomb that exploded at the family refinery in Bayou Miste, yesterday.

"The bomber was taken into custody by the Louisiana State Police."

"Thank God," Lucie said.

The report continued, "Rumor has it the bomber was hired by your opponent, Richard Gasson. Do you have any comments on that?"

Eric chuckled. "Only that it's a heck of a way to run a campaign. In most states, they let the constituents decide elections."

"Sir, we heard your fiancée was hurt in the explosion."

"Yes, she was." The smile slipped from Eric's face. "Only she's no longer my fiancée."

"What?" The reporter stepped back a moment as if shocked by the news. "Would you care to elaborate?"

"Miss LeBieu is doing much better, but we've decided not to get married after all." His smile returned. "Which leaves me more time to handle the issues of the state."

"Did she break it off, or did you?" the pesky reporter asked.

Eric's lips thinned, but he never lost his very charming smile. "That's up to the lady to tell. Now, if you'll excuse me, I have a speech to give."

Alex turned to Lucie, a frown between her brows. "I thought he was going to wait until after the election to announce your canceled engagement?"

Lucie sighed. "That's just the great kinda guy he is. He'd sacrifice his chance to win to release me from the engagement."

"You should have married him," Calliope said. "I bet five bucks he'll win anyway. Who wouldn't vote for him? He's so damned sexy."

Alex tipped her head to the side. "Wonder what Ben will think about that."

"Probably nothing," Lucie said. "I told you, he said he didn't love me."

"*Couldn't* love you," Alex corrected. "There's a difference."

"Yeah." Lucie lay back against the pillows. "Whatever."

"I bet you five bucks you didn't know he was here all last night sitting where Alex is, holding your hand." Calliope rocked back on her heels, a smirk on her face.

Alex kicked her foot at Calliope's shin. "Enough with the betting. Besides, you weren't supposed to say anything."

Lucie's heart kicked into high speed. Ben spent the night here? Why hadn't he said anything, woken her up, kissed her? Anything!

The redhead wrinkled her nose. "You know how well I keep secrets."

"Yeah, not at all," Alex grumbled.

Calliope took the remote from her and flipped through the channels. "Hey, I haven't seen *I Love Lucy* reruns since I was in grade school." She sat forward from her perch on the windowsill.

"Who cares?" Lucie smacked the sheets and blew out a huffy breath. She couldn't get on with her life from a hospital bed. "I really need to see my grandmother."

"And you will," said a voice from the doorway. Lynette LeBieu stepped through, a little hesitantly. "Do you mind if I see you first?"

Alex popped out of her chair. "Here, you can have my seat. Come on, Calliope, we have giant-sized coffees with our names on them somewhere in this Popsicle joint."

Calliope gave her a confused look. "Alex, you know I don't drink coffee."

Before Lucie could protest their desertion, Alex grabbed Calliope and they were out the door, leaving her stuck with the woman who'd ditched her twenty years ago.

Somehow, all the hurt and anger wasn't quite as intense as the first time she had seen her mother. After all that had happened and the mistakes she herself had made, she wasn't nearly as resentful. People made mistakes. Some bigger than others.

For a few awkward minutes, neither woman spoke.

Lucie grabbed for the remote and punched the mute button, silencing Desi Arnaz in the middle of "Lucy, you got some 'splainin' to do!"

"How appropriate." Lynette snorted softly. "That's exactly how I feel. I have some 'splainin' to do. I don't suppose you'd listen while I do it?" Hope shone from her eyes.

With a shrug, Lucie stared at the television without seeing it. "Might as well. I'm a captive audience until they give me my clothes and marching orders."

Lynette's smile slipped from her face and she laughed one of those laughs that conveyed little humor, but a lot of pain. "Now that I'm here, I don't know where to start."

"Try twenty years ago when you dumped me and Lisa on Gran LeBieu." Her words were delivered with slightly less of the anger she'd felt a few days ago.

Her mother winced. "I'd rather go back a little further than that."

"Suit yourself." Lucie was listening, but she wasn't feeling charitable enough to make it easier for the woman.

"I was seventeen when I met your father. He was eighteen. But we fell in love so deeply, we knew we had to be together, no matter what."

Despite her reluctance to hear her mother out, Lucie wanted to know more about the mystery man who'd been her father. "So what happened to him?"

"We were on the way home from a football game when a drunk driver ran us off the road. We crashed into a tree. I was thrown from the car, and Richard was killed instantly." Lynette looked away, but not before Lucie saw the tears trembling on her lashes.

"It was all so horrible," she continued. "One minute we were planning a wedding for after graduation, the next I was going to his funeral." She stared out the window, her gaze far away from the parking lot below. "I remember that day like yesterday. It rained. Not a surprise for southern Louisiana. I was so sad, I threw up on the way home." She wiped a tear from her cheek and turned back to grimace at Lucie. "I didn't know until later that I was pregnant.

"Your grandmother was wonderful. She helped me all along the way, even came with me into the delivery room. But I couldn't get over your father's death.

"I couldn't go back to my old life. Everywhere I turned, I could see Richard there. I dropped out of high school and went to work to support you and Lisa. I didn't want my mother to be burdened by me and twins. So I moved away, hoping it would make me stronger. I'd wanted to stand on my own two feet. We went to Texas, where I worked as a waitress in a bar. It was the only place I could make enough to support us and pay for a sitter."

Lucie didn't want to feel empathy for this woman who'd left her for so long. But her heart ached for the young mother desperately trying to make a life for herself and her children.

"I couldn't make it on my own. Babysitting costs were too high, and I missed your father so much it hurt all the time. I started drinking to numb the pain. One drink led to another, and another, until I couldn't climb out of the bottle long enough to care for the little girls I loved more than life itself."

Tears welled in Lucie's eyes as she remembered the little six-year-old she'd been, lapping up any crumb of attention her mother would throw her way.

Lynette kept talking as if the floodgates had finally opened. "One day, I was driving somewhere, I don't remember where. You and Lisa were in the car with me. I was half-stoned from the liquor I drank at all hours. I didn't see the car until too late. I broadsided it, killing the driver." Lynette doubled over as if the pain was fresh. "She was just a teenager and I killed her! And I almost killed you."

"Oh, God." Her hand sneaked out and she touched her mother's arm. Here she'd been feeling sorry for herself because Ben didn't love her. How awful to know you'd killed someone out of your own carelessness and couldn't give that person her life back.

"You and Lucie went to live with your grandmother on that day. I was charged with vehicular manslaughter and spent six years in jail. I had time to dry up, but the guilt never went away."

A deep well of sadness opened up and Lucie fell in. "Why didn't you come back after you'd done your time in prison?"

"I couldn't forgive myself for what I did. I didn't want you and your sister to know what a horrible person I was. Believe me, I didn't want to kill that girl. If I could, I'd give my life to bring her back." Tears ran freely down Lynette's face and silent sobs shook her frame. "I couldn't face you two knowing what I'd done. I was better off dead." Her voice faded away into a whisper.

Lucie remembered looking out at the swamp, hoping beyond hope her mama would come for her. All those years other girls had their mothers to love and be loved by. Not Lucie and Lisa. If not for Gran LeBieu, she would have died of loneliness. "Why now?"

Again, her mother laughed, more of a hiccupping sound of self-derision. "I needed so badly to see you, to tell you I was sorry, and that I never stopped loving you. I had to tell you...before the cancer takes me." Her voice faded off into a room gone completely silent.

Lucie sat stunned, unable to utter a word. She'd just gotten her mother back. How could God take her away again?

"Look, I've said what I wanted to say. More than anything, I'd like to get to know you, but that's completely up to you." Lynette stood and slid her purse over her shoulder. "Your grandmother is waiting out in the hallway. I'm sure she'd like to see that you're all right."

With a numb nod, she stared after her mother as she slipped through the doorway.

Holy swamp turtle. She wished she could crawl under a rock. Her emotions threatened to overwhelm her. After twenty years, her mother had come back to die. How unfair was that?

Gran LeBieu stepped into the room, her eyes filled with the pain Lucie was only beginning to feel.

"Oh, Gran!" she cried.

The old woman sank onto the side of the bed and gathered Lucie in her arms and together they wept.

"Why, Gran? Why?" Lucie sobbed into her shoulder.

"De magick works its own agenda, my girl." She squeezed her hard and then set her away.

Gran LeBieu yanked a tissue from the box on the nightstand and dabbed at Lucie's cheeks and her own. "Aren't we a pair?"

Lucie laughed and the tears welled up again. "And I thought *my* life was a mess."

"Sometimes it takes other's troubles to show us de way with our own."

Which brought Lucie back to her love spell dilemma. "Gran, the undo spell didn't work."

Her grandmother frowned. "Did not de ladybug stop glowing?"

Lucie nodded. "Yes, but Eric still loves me, Maurice still loves DeeDee, and Craig and Elaine broke up. The only one it worked on was Ben." Her chin dropped. "He doesn't love me, Gran."

Her grandmother stared at her for a long time. "What did you learn about castin' Voodoo spells?"

Lucie snorted. "Like you said in your spell, leave it to the pros."

The old woman propped a fist on her hip. "What else?"

"You can't make someone love you with a spell. If they don't love you without the spell, it's not real love and it's not yours to keep."

Gran LeBieu nodded. "Very good. Dat's all you needed to know."

"But what can I do to make the spell go away?"

With an upturned hand, Gran LeBieu smiled. "What spell?"

"The love spell I used on the love bug?"

"Oh, dat one." Gran stood and straightened her muumuu. "Not to worry. It did not work in de first place."

"What do you mean?" Her head reeled as if she were about to pass out.

"Jus' what I say. It did not work." Gran grinned. "You used de wrong bug. Every good Voodoo queen knows you have to follow all de directions or de spell doesn't work."

Lucie flopped back against her pillow. "You mean I didn't have anything to do with Elaine and Craig splitting up?"

"Nope."

"And the love bug didn't make Maurice and DeeDee fall in love?" All this worry, all this time she'd thought she's screwed up so many lives.

"Nope, again."

"*Wooweee*! So Maurice and DeeDee found each other on their own." She'd been lifted up by joy after all the sadness she'd been feeling, only to crash to the earth again. "Then Eric really does love me."

"Dat's right."

"And Ben doesn't and never did." She sank even lower in the mire of anguish.

"Oh, I wouldn't say dat." Her grandmother smiled her wickedly mysterious smile that left people guessing.

Her eyes narrowed. "What do you know, Gran?"

The old Voodoo queen drew herself up to her full height and stared down her nose at her granddaughter. "What is told to Madame LeBieu in confidence, stays in confidence." She winked. "But I know someone dat came lookin' for a love potion of his own."

Lucie's eyes widened and her heart tripped several times before settling into a speedy pitter-patter. "Ben?"

Her grandmother crossed her arms over her chest. "I'm not sayin' one way or de other. But you best get yer heinie out of de bed. De doctor said you could go."

She flung the sheets aside, jumped up and threw her arms around the old woman. "Thank you, Gran. Thank you!"

"Don't be thankin' me yet." She handed Lucie a bag of clothes and *shooshed* her toward the bathroom. "Hurry up, dis ol' lady and your mama will be waitin' outside for you."

CHAPTER 26

"YOU CAN'T MAKE ME GO TO WORK. I'M CALLING IN SICK." LUCIE PLOPPED on the couch and refused to budge.

Calliope and Alex ganged up on her and, each grabbing an arm, hefted her off the couch and into her bedroom.

"Get your clothes on," Alex said, "you're going to work!"

"Yeah, how else will I get a free beer if you're not there serving?" Calliope smiled. "It's one of the perks of having a friend working at the Raccoon Saloon."

"And we're not letting you louse it up," Alex planted both fists on her hips and stood with her legs apart, blocking the door out of the bedroom. "Now move it."

Lucie popped a salute. "Yes, ma'am!" She trudged to her dresser and pulled out a shirt and skimpy shorts. "But I'm warning you...payback's a mother."

"Yeah, yeah," Alex said. "Big talk for a woman who hasn't been outside her apartment for two days."

"We thought you were going to grow mushrooms under your toenails or something," Calliope flopped onto the bed and frowned at the black T-shirt and frayed shorts Lucie flung onto the comforter. "You're not wearing that, are you?"

"Yeah." She strode into the bathroom, squirted toothpaste on her toothbrush, and made a loud production of brushing her teeth to avoid any attempts at conversation with her so-called friends. Didn't they know she no longer had the will to live, and all she wanted to do was wallow in her own self-pity?

She spit, rinsed her mouth, and spit again.

"All right already, enough with the spitting." Alex appeared in the doorway. "Get your fanny out here and get dressed. We're not going to get our usual table if you make us late."

Lucie snarled at her nemesis. "I'm beginning to see why your mother wants you married. You need someone else to boss around besides your siblings and friends."

"And you need to get over whatever bug crawled up your ass." Alex's harsh words were tempered by a huge grin. "Oh, come on. It won't kill you to go back to work. You'll feel better before the night's over, I promise."

"And if I don't?" How could she? Ben hadn't been by to see her, despite what her grandmother had said. Which went back to Lucie's original hypothesis—Ben didn't love her. Now she knew how her mother felt when she'd lost the love of her life. Pretty much like sucking scum off the bottom of a pond.

When she dragged herself back into the bedroom, Calliope had a silly, sneaky smirk on her face. What the hell was she up to? Lucie bent to pick up her shorts and ratty T-shirt only to find her favorite floral skirt and matching coral sleeveless blouse in their place. "I can't wear that to work. Where'd you put my shorts?"

Alex gave her another sneaky smile. "I hid them."

"Fine, I have more." Lucie turned back to her dresser, only to find her shorts drawer empty.

Calliope held out her hand to Alex. "You owe me five bucks."

"Fine," Alex said. "The first round's on me."

"Fair enough," Calliope responded.

"Hey, what the hell's going on?" Lucie stood in her panties and bra, getting madder by the minute.

"I bet Alex you'd go right back for more shorts," Calliope said. "I was right."

"I'm not wearing that skirt or shirt, so cough up my shorts."

Alex and Calliope stood with their arms crossed.

Surrounded and not up to a fight, she gave in. "Fine!" She grabbed the skirt and jammed her legs into it, pulling it up over her hips. The shirt went on just as fast. "Let's go."

"What about your hair?" Calliope dashed into the bathroom and returned with her hairbrush and proceeded to yank every knot and tangle out by the root.

"Ouch! Give me that before I'm bald!" She snatched the brush from Calliope and dragged it through her hair until it hung springy and shiny. She glanced at her reflection in the mirror. "What's the use? I'm still in Bayou Miste and I'm destined to die an old maid."

"Not after— *Yeeouch*!" Calliope jumped away from Alex, clutching her arm. "Why'd you go and pinch me, you freaktoid?"

"Look, blabbermouth, shut up." Alex turned to Lucie. "Quit whining and let's go."

Lucie stared from Calliope to Alex and back. "Okay, what gives?"

"Nothing." Alex glared at Calliope. "Right, Calliope?"

A guilty blush spread across Calliope's cheeks. "Uh, right. Nothing." She shot for the door. "Let's go before we're late."

Alex followed Calliope.

"Before we're late for what?" She retrieved her purse from the kitchen counter and trotted to keep up with the other two girls.

"Since your 'stang is still in the shop, you can ride with us."

"But you two never stay until closing. How am I supposed to get a ride home? I really should stay home." She turned toward the stairs. "I'm calling in sick."

"We'll stay until you close. All right? Satisfied?" Alex hopped into her Jeep, turned the ignition, and revved the engine to maximum rpms. "Sheesh! What does it take to get you to work?"

"I don't want to work. If I did, I'd get myself there." She climbed into the backseat and stared up at her apartment, wishing she could go back inside and bury her head under a few dozen pillows.

All the way to the bar, she couldn't shake the nagging suspicion that

Calliope and Alex were up to something. "If you're planning on fixing me up with some loser, forget it. I'm not interested in dating."

"Not to worry. We couldn't care less whether you ever date again," Alex said.

Calliope giggled.

They were definitely up to something. But what, Lucie hadn't a clue. How unlike Calliope to keep a secret for more than five seconds. Must be a whopper. Lucie hoped at least it didn't involve her. She settled into the backseat and lost herself in her own morbid musings.

Ben hadn't called, hadn't stopped by, and hadn't breathed a word to her since her little incident with the car bomb. Was he truly finished with her?

The acids in her belly burbled, a reminder she hadn't eaten in a while. She thought back. Hell, she hadn't eaten anything since lunch yesterday! Whoever said love didn't kill you didn't have her stomach.

The parking lot was still fairly empty, as the big crowd never arrived before nine. The regulars would already have taken up their favorite seats and eaten their way through several giant bags of pretzels, popcorn, and peanuts.

Same ole, same ole. She sighed. Did nothing ever change in this Podunk town? Was she destined to be a wrinkled old waitress and die at forty because she'd tripped on some Cajun's big feet? She climbed out of the Jeep and straightened her skirt and shoulders. She was in the dumps, but there was no use having everyone else join her. With a job to do, she might as well do it right.

"Lucie!" Jean rushed out from behind the counter to greet her with a bear hug that took her breath away. In shock, and not exactly sure how to handle Jean's unnatural exuberance, she patted his back.

"It's okay, Jean. I've only been gone two days." When he let her go, she put a few feet of space between them.

Jean lifted his bar towel and dabbed at his eyes. "I'm just so happy you're back and you're okay. Excuse me." His face bright red, he took up his position behind the bar, head down to the task of polishing glasses that didn't need polishing.

What was up with him? Something was way off about tonight, but she couldn't quite put her finger on it.

Brandy was already hard at work when Lucie arrived, and soon people filled the room to overflowing. And it wasn't even nine-thirty! Lucie had to hustle to keep up with the drink orders. When the crowd kept growing, her nerves clenched and she doubled her effort to stay on top of the work. Jean had hired a new waitress while she was gone. Her name was Toni-with-an-I, and she was from Morgan City. Even with all the assistance, Lucie couldn't help the rising sense of panic.

"I'm not up to this," she admitted to Alex and Calliope when she stopped by their table to drop off two longneck Miller Lights.

"Oh, you can handle it, just hang on a little longer." Alex peered toward the door.

"Who are you looking for?" Lucie shook her head. "Oh, who cares, I don't have time to think, much less ogle men." She spun toward the bar, trying to remember if she was supposed to get a Guinness or a Bud Light.

That's when she heard the sirens. What the hell?

"Jean? Are we in violation of something?" She leaned her back against the bar, a prickle of fear creeping across her skin in a trail of major goose bumps.

More sirens joined the first. The band trailed off to the electronic screech of a microphone too close to the speakers.

"Uh, Jean?"

"Yeah, Lucie?"

"What's going on?" She stared around the room at the crowd that had suddenly gone silent, all eyes riveted on the door.

"You're about to find out," Jean said.

The door burst open and a Louisiana State Trooper in full uniform, including his mirrored sunglasses, stepped in. He marched halfway across the floor and stopped, planting his hands on his hips, looking tough enough to toss alligators.

A chill snaked down her spine. She'd hate to be on the wrong side of this cop.

Behind him streamed in no less than a dozen more troopers and the entire local sheriff's department. Even Billy Ray stood staring straight ahead, a serious-as-sin look on his face.

Numero uno cop cleared his throat. "Is there a Lucie LeBieu on the premises?"

Her breath caught in her throat. "Me?" she squeaked.

"Are you Lucie LeBieu?" The trooper turned toward her.

What had she done? Her gaze darted around the room.

Jean's mouth twitched at the corners. Was that humor or fear?

Whatever. Jean was no help. She squared her shoulders and faced the officer. "Yes, sir. I'm Lucie."

"Ma'am, please come with me." He marched up to her. "You can come along quietly or I can handcuff and frisk you."

"I'm for frisking." LeRoy Le Due yelled out. "Let me."

"Shut up, LeRoy," Lucie yelled into the crowd, then to the trooper she asked, "What am I being charged with?"

"Tampering, ma'am," he said in his deep monotone voice.

"Tampering with what?" Her heart thumped wildly against her chest.

"You have the right to remain silent," the officer's hand circled her elbow and he pulled her toward the door.

Holy cypress knees! What had she done? Was she being charged with bombing Eric's car? "I didn't do it!"

"Yes, ma'am, we have it from a reliable witness that says you did."

"Did what?" she cried.

The crowd fell in behind her as the trooper led her through the entrance out into the parking lot.

Lights from a dozen squad cars blinded her and she raised her hand to cover her eyes. Once outside, the state trooper dropped his hold on her elbow and stepped away.

An electronic squealing noise ripped through the air followed by someone talking through a loudspeaker. "Is it on? It is? Oh. Okay."

"Can someone tell me what's going on?" Lucie cried.

"Lucie LeBieu, step away from the bar!" The disembodied voice sounded over a loudspeaker.

"What am I being charged with?" Her empty stomach was no match for the flock of butterflies beating inside. She had no desire to go to jail. Especially when she didn't understand why.

"You're being charged with tampering with a man's heart." The giant voice, laced with static, was familiar.

A strange tingling battled with the butterflies in her belly. "And whose heart would that be?"

"Isn't it enough to know you tampered and you're going to be held accountable? What have you got to say in your defense?"

Her heart sang. *Yes!* She knew that voice. It was the voice that plagued her dreams, day and night. "I plead guilty. Am I allowed to have a lawyer?" She squinted against the lights. Where was he?

"No, you won't be allowed a lawyer."

"So you're to be the judge, jury, and executioner?"

"That's the idea. Miss LeBieu, by your own admission, you've been found guilty of tampering with a man's heart. You're being sentenced to life."

"Life?" She stepped forward, a smile lifting her lips. "Isn't that a bit harsh?"

"Possibly. If you consider it harsh to be sentenced to a life with me." Ben stepped forward, dropping a bullhorn to his side.

She closed the distance between them. "I'd consider it a pleasure to be sentenced to life married to the bug exterminator."

He cocked his head to the side. "You mean you'd consider me good enough even as a bug exterminator?"

"I'd take you even if you were the honey hut cleaner." She gazed up at the man she'd dreamed of for seven long years. The man she'd never stopped loving and never thought she'd ever see again. "On one condition."

Ben's eyebrows rose. "Since when is the accused allowed to make deals?"

"Consider it a plea bargain." She walked her finger up his chest.

Ben held the bullhorn out to the side. "Somebody take this. I think I'm going to have my hands full."

She gave him her sexiest smile. "You can count on it."

Billy Ray ran up to take the bullhorn. "Does she need convincing, sir?"

"No," Ben said without looking up from Lucie's gaze. "I think we've put the screws to her. She's talking."

"If you say so, sir." Billy Ray ran back to join the circle of people surrounding her and Ben.

"Well, I'm sorry to say, you don't have the choice of honey hut man *or* bug exterminator."

Her heart dropped like a lead ball into the pit of her empty belly. "You don't want me?"

"Oh, I want you, all right, but I'm not a bug man or the honey hut man." He shook his head, his lips thinning into a straight line.

"Then what kind of man are you?"

"Let me introduce myself." He held out his hand. "Benjamin Franklin Boyette, criminal investigator with the Louisiana State Police."

"You're with the state police? You're living your dream?" Her chest swelled with pride.

"Yes, ma'am." He tipped his head in a nod. "And I'm living my dream in Baton Rouge, but if you want to stay here in Bayou Miste, I'm sure I could work it out."

"I don't care where I go or stay, as long as I'm with you." She wrapped her arms around his waist and pressed her cheek against his chest.

But Ben pushed her back. "Wait, I'm not done." He turned around in a circle. "Can I have a little intro, please?"

Sirens roared to life, blasting every eardrum for miles around, animal or human. When Ben sliced his hand across his throat, they all silenced.

He turned, a grin spilling across his face. "Love the sirens."

Her brows furrowed. "Intro for what?"

"This." He dropped to one knee and took Lucie's hand in his. "Lucie LeBieu, will you marry me?"

Her heart exploded with joy and she almost did a Snoopy dance there in front of half the Louisiana State Police force. But she tamped down the smile threatening to break through. "Ben, you haven't met my condition."

"Oh yeah, you did mention a condition." He held his arms wide. "You name it."

"Hand over the love potion my grandmother gave you."

"Love potion?" His innocent look was a bit too innocent.

"Don't play dumb with me, Benjamin Boyette. I've got your number."

He pressed a kiss to her hand. "Honey, you've got my heart."

"And you have mine." Her eyes narrowed. "I just want to make sure I don't have any competition."

"Hey Lucie, my beer's getting cold," Alex yelled from the doorway to the Raccoon Saloon. "What's it going to be? You gonna marry that baboon of a big brother of mine or not? He's been driving everyone nuts."

"Have not!" Ben retorted.

"Have too!" The crowd disagreed in unison.

Ben had the grace to look sheepish.

"Well, Lucie?" Calliope asked.

"Yes!" She yelled loud enough for everyone to hear. "Yes, I'll marry him."

As Ben wrapped her in his arms and swung her around, a cheer rose higher than the treetops, echoing across the waters of Bayou Miste.

The sound carried to a cabin deep in the swamp where a wise Voodoo queen stood in her bright-red muumuu.

A lone ladybug buzzed past her nose in an erratic pattern until it landed on the porch rails, folding its wings beneath its hard shell.

Madame LeBieu winked at the tiny creature. "And dat, my little love bug, is de way it's done."

THE END

Careful what you wish for...

DEJA VOODOO

A CAJUN MAGIC MYSTERY

BAYOU MISTE

NAWLINS

Hotlanta

NEW YORK TIMES & USA TODAY BESTSELLING AUTHOR

ELLE JAMES

DÉJÀ VOODOO

CAJUN MAGIC MYSTERIES BOOK #3

New York Times & USA Today
Bestselling Author

ELLE JAMES

CHAPTER 1

Bayou Miste, Louisiana

"Boyette, I hope this idea works." Edouard François Marceau scrunched his smartphone between his ear and shoulder as he sat on the bench by the back door of the rental cottage. With his hands free, he pulled off a muddy boot and dropped it to the porch planks. "If it doesn't, we may have us one dead witness on our hands, and that bastard Primeaux will get away with murder."

"Don't worry, it'll work," Ben Boyette, his partner in the Special Criminal Investigations Unit in Baton Rouge, reassured him. "Did you have any trouble finding the old trapper shack?"

"Did anyone ever tell you GPS devices work best on roadways, not waterways? Still, we managed with a few dead ends and switch-backs. If I lose this thing, I'll have to hire a tracking dog with gills to find them. Holy Jesus, that swamp is a freakin' maze! Marcus and I counted no less than nine alligators while we were out there. And those were the ones we could *see*."

"Did you point them out to our witness?"

"You bet." Ed shifted the phone to the other ear and attacked the laces on his left boot. "That ought to make even *her* stay put."

"You think? After the drug-running, backstabbing, mafia thugs she's been shacking up with, the alligators probably looked tame."

"Good point." One-handed, he tugged at the remaining muddy boot. The phone slipped, and he grabbed for it. "Tell me again why we're playing babysitter to a witness and why you didn't take this assignment?"

"Number one, I don't trust anyone else to get our witness to the courthouse alive. I suspect we have a mole in the force. And I'd have done it, but I'm up to my neck in trials over the serial rapist case." Ben sighed. "Since I did all the legwork, I'm the one in court. God, I hate courtrooms. But, we have to nail this guy so it sticks. Otherwise, I'd be there in a heartbeat. Oh, and I have a pregnant wife at home."

"Oh, yeah. That. Guess you're right. Although, I'd switch with you in a second. You're the one with all the experience wrestling alligators."

"You'll survive. Hopefully, the only alligator you have to wrestle is my moth—" Ben stopped in mid-sentence as if he changed his mind about what he was going to say next. "By the way, how are your digs? Mom buy your story?"

"Yeah." Ed padded through the small cottage, appreciating the homey feel of it. This was the kind of house he'd always pictured belonging to his grandmother. If he'd ever known her. "I hate lying to your mom, though."

"She'll get over it. Did my share of fibbing to get out of doing the lawn a couple times growing up." He chuckled. "Come to think of it, I can still taste the soap. That woman could see right through every lie. She always caught me. But she loved me anyway."

"Yeah. She had to love you, you're her son." And Boyette was damned lucky to have her.

"I'm sure your mom did the same."

"Don't bet on it. Never knew her." His voice was a little harsher than he'd intended. A twinge of longing flickered across his subconscious, which he quickly squelched. No use pining after something he never had.

After all these years, he hadn't realized how much he missed having a mother until he'd met Ben's. Barbara Boyette was the consummate maternal figure. Care and concern written in every smile, wrinkle, and gray hair.

Ben cleared his throat. "Oh, by the way, do you like kids?"

Ed pushed his boots to the side and stood. Did he like kids? "Never thought about it. Why?"

"No reason. Did mom invite you to dinner already?" Ben asked.

"Nope."

Ben laughed. "Don't worry, she will."

"Is that bad?"

"Uh, no, not at all." Ben's answer was a little too swift for his comfort. "She moves quickly with single men."

"I'm not single, I'm divorced. There's a difference. Is there something you're not telling me?" He tamped down a sudden urge to get out of town. Fast.

"No, no. Nothing at all." Now Ben's voice sounded entirely too cheerful.

He should definitely run from this small town stuff as fast as his Nikes could take him.

"Mom's a great cook. She just sometimes cooks up more than her guests are ready to swallow."

Now he knew for sure Ben was keeping something from him. "What the hell do you mean by that?"

"Okay, so you're all set, then." Ben ignored his question. "Lay low and go fishing enough to keep Marcus and our girl fed and happy."

"Gotcha." He looked around the tiny cottage, the walls closing in on him already. "One question."

"What's that?"

"What the hell am I supposed to do with my time for the next few days?"

"Keep an eye open for suspicious characters. Otherwise, make like a vacation, and relax."

"I don't think I've ever taken a vacation." He scratched his head and thought back. No, he'd hung out at the office even on annual leave. All that use-or-lose vacation time got lost each year. "What do you do on a vacation?"

"Sleep until noon, girl-watch, you know, the usual thing."

"Maybe on Cocoa Beach, but in Bayou Miste? I'd go so far as to say the alligators outnumber the people. I don't think I've seen one live human besides your mother and the marina owner. Tell me, Ben, do they count the alligators in the census?"

Ben's outright laughter blasted Ed's ear. "Bayou Miste isn't that bad. Think about it, you arrived in the middle of the day, right?"

"Yeah. So?"

"School and work should be getting out by now." Ben chuckled again. "Just wait."

He didn't like the sound of his partner's laugh, it had a devilish quality. "Wait for what?"

"To meet the family. You're gonna love them."

"I thought it was just you and your mother."

Ben snorted. "Oh, no. I have eighteen brothers and sisters."

He fumbled the phone and almost dropped it. "Holy hell!"

"Yeah, that's what it's like around my house after school."

The introverted halls of Monti-Ed-zuma crashed around his ears.

Nineteen children in one family? What were his parents thinking? Obviously, they hadn't been thinking, they'd been—

"What have you gotten me into, Boyette?"

"You're a tough guy, you can handle it."

* * *

AS THE TUNE TO "When the Saints Go Marching In" played on Alexandra Belle Boyette's phone for the sixth time in thirty minutes, she lay down on the couch and crammed a pillow over her ears. "Please leave me alone."

"Why don't you answer it and get it over with?" Calliope sat across from her, scraping the silver coating from a scratch-off lottery ticket, her long, wild, light red hair fanning across her shoulders like a cape. She wore a halter top and an ankle-length, tie-died peasant skirt, her legs tucked under her. No matter the circumstances, she always looked relaxed and carefree.

"No way." Alex sat up and leaned her face in her hands. "She'll ask me again if I've been seeing anyone, or she'll invite me to dinner at the house and drag some poor slob to the table with the family."

"So? What's wrong with that?"

"Even if I liked the guy, one look at my family and he'll run screaming into the bayou."

“Damn.” Calliope frowned at the lottery ticket and tossed it onto the table. Then she looked across at Alex with a smile. "Your family's wonderful."

"Yeah, all nineteen of them." She rolled her eyes. "In this day and age, who in their right minds would have nineteen children?"

Calliope grinned "Your parents."

"Yeah, and what did it buy them?” She sat up. “An early grave for my father and insanity for my mother." Despite her flippant words, she still felt the pain of loss. Her father had been the rock in their lives and she missed him terribly, even two years after his passing.

"Alex, your mother loves every one of you and only wants to see you happy."

"I wish she could love me a little less."

"You don't mean that."

"Yes, I do. She won't leave me alone about love and relationships. I'm happy with the way things are. I have my own business, I'm in the best shape of my life. I have this great house. What more does she want?"

"Grandchildren?"

She snorted. "Big Brother Ben has that market nailed. She'll have her first grandbaby in three months. Lucie's getting as big as the bayou."

"Speaking of Lucie, I saw her yesterday when I was in Baton Rouge. And you’re right. She *is* getting big.” Calliope smiled. “She looks great. Pregnancy must agree with her.”

“Yeah, and Ben’s over the moon. His chest is swelling so much, I doubt they can find shirts to fit him.” Alex was happy for her brother. At the same time, a stab of intense longing hit her right in the gut. She had to suck in air to relieve the pressure.

"Oh, I almost forgot." Calliope jumped from her seat on the couch. "Lucie asked me to give you something."

She cringed. "Oh God, what now?"

Calliope fished in her pocket and dug out a small red velvet drawstring bag.

When Alex peered inside, she almost gagged. It smelled like something the cat dragged in from the swamp. "What is this stuff?"

"She didn't say. I bet five bucks it's some Voodoo remedy."

"Egad!" She dropped the bag on the end table. "You remember the last time she dabbled in Voodoo she almost had the entire town of Bayou Miste under her wacky love spell."

"But it all worked out in the end. Lucie married Ben, Maurice and DeeDee scheduled a Christmas wedding and Elaine and Craig eloped. The whole magic thing couldn't have turned out better. And, she's been taking lessons from her grandmother."

"Maybe that spell worked out all right, after a considerable amount of bad luck and a few murder attempts. But the one she put on Mo's pet alligator gave the poor beast a bad case of puppy love for Granny Saulnier's poodle. T-Rex still hasn't gotten over it."

"I don't know what it is. She asked me to give it to you the next time I saw you. I did and now my duty is done." Calliope blinked, all innocence. "Maybe it's a sachet you're supposed to put in your drawer to make your clothes smell good."

She wrinkled her nose "Not this stuff. It could make a grown man weep. I swear it has that rank odor of stump water." She shoved the bag toward her friend. "Take it back to her. I don't want to risk getting caught up in one of her crazy spells."

"Oh, no." Calliope held up her hands. "I'm not carrying that thing around. It might give me hair in places I have no business growing hair. Or worse, maybe it'll make me lose hair that I shouldn't. No, if you want her to have it back, you'll have to give it back yourself."

"Fine, I will. Next time I'm in Baton Rouge." She frowned at the sachet bag. "In the meantime, I have to put up with it. I hope it isn't anything dangerous."

The phone sang again and she flopped down on the couch pulling the pillow back over her head. "Why couldn't I have had Lisa and Lucie's mother, who stays gone for twenty years at a time?"

Calliope stood at the sound of the third ring. "Because your mother loves you, and you should be nicer to her." She reached for the phone.

"Don't do it, Calliope," She warned. "If you value our friendship, you won't touch that phone."

Calliope cocked an eyebrow and punched the talk button. "Hello?" She listened. "Yes, Mrs. Boyette, Alex is right next to me. Sure. I'd be happy to relay the message. Seven o'clock? I'm sure that would be fine. Me, too? That would be nice. Good to talk to you, too, Mrs. Boyette. Bye, now."

"What did she want?"

"You and I are invited to dinner at her house at seven tomorrow night. Oh, and put on that slinky red dress you wore to Lucie's bachelorette party."

"My mother said that?"

"Well, most of it." Calliope grinned. "I added the part about the dress."

"Thanks, Calliope. Don't know what I'd do without you." She dripped sarcasm. "But I'm willing to try it."

Her friend dropped into the chair and tucked her legs underneath her. "I heard Lucie's Grand-mère LeBieu has been coaching her on Voodoo, again."

She punched her pillow and set it against the arm of the couch. "Should we consider moving to another state?"

The redhead tipped her head to the side as if considering her jest. "Possibly."

"Geesh. I just got the gym operating in the black, I hate to sell and start somewhere else."

Calliope's eyes lit up. "We could move to Biloxi."

With a very unladylike "Ha!" Alex stood and paced around the room. "That's the last place you need to move."

"Why?"

"Don't play dumb with me." She stopped in front of Calliope, planting her hands on her hips. "Biloxi would be entirely too much temptation for you. What, with a casino on every corner, it would be like navigating a minefield."

"I'm not that hooked on gambling. Besides, I could get a job in one of the casinos." Calliope's eyes twinkled and an excited grin spread across her face. "The pay and tips would beat what I get at the Raccoon Saloon."

"You should be happy you landed Lucie's old job. She got great tips."

"I guess moving is out of the question." Calliope's smile turned downward and she heaved a sigh. "I miss Lucie."

"Me, too," Alex said. "Why do things have to change?"

"Yeah," Calliope sighed again. "Why do people have to get married and move away?"

"Although, Lucie seems very happy." She could still picture Lucie's glowing face at the wedding. How had she lucked into finding the love of her life here in Bayou Miste?

Calliope's eyes got all dreamy. "Do you think we'll ever find someone to love as much as Lucie loves Ben?"

"Not me. I only date the guys from hell."

"Like Theo?"

Alex rolled her eyes. "Why can't that bonehead take the hint?"

"Still botherin' you?"

As if to prove her point, her phone sang the theme for Jaws, the da dum, da dum sound grating on every last one of her nerves. She launched herself across the coffee table, snatched the phone, and cocked her arm to throw.

Calliope grabbed the device from her hand before she could let go. "Hey, don't ruin a perfectly good cell phone because of a guy."

She drew in a long breath and let out the tension with her exhale. "You're right. You're right. I'd miss my phone more than Theo."

"Not all guys are like Theo, you know," Calliope pointed out.

She snorted. "You haven't seen the ones my mom keeps throwing at me." She settled back on the couch and hugged a pillow to her chest. "I don't know where she gets them, but they've all had major 'me' hang-ups."

"What do you mean?"

"It's all about the guy." She wandered around her tastefully decorated living room where everything had a place and everything was in it. "Why can't I find a guy who thinks *I* hung the moon? A partner who will love me even when I'm majorly PMSing. Someone who will love me unconditionally, no matter how bad a day he's had."

As if he sensed how upset she was, Sport, Alex's golden retriever, trotted across the room and sat at her feet, his tail sweeping the floor in a steady rhythm. He stared up at her, mouth hanging open like he was smiling at her, his eyes pleading, "pet me".

She reached down and scratched behind his ears. "I don't think I'll ever find someone to love me like that."

"Sport loves you like that." Calliope giggled.

She laughed. "You know, Calliope, you're right. I need a guy like Sport. One who will greet me at the door, always happy to see me. Someone who can forgive me for forgetting his birthday. Someone who's happy no matter what I feed him or how fat I get." She squatted next to Sport and hugged him around his neck.

"Wouldn't it be neat if Sport were a man?"

"Yeah." She loved the silky feel of Sport's coat against her cheek. He loved her no matter what. "I wish he were a man. Then maybe my mother would quit trying to set me up."

"Hey, Sport." Calliope snapped her fingers. "Come here."

The dog laid a long wet tongue across Alex's cheek and wiggled loose to go to Calliope.

"How would you like to be a man?" The redhead rubbed her hand in his thick fur. "I bet you'd be really sexy, huh, boy?"

Alex stood and brushed the dog hair off her workout pants. "I have to get ready for work. Would you mind taking Sport out for a walk?"

"I'd love to." Calliope leaped from her chair. "Wanna go outside, boy?" She reached for the leash hanging on a hook inside the coat closet.

"Just don't let him whiz on Miz Mozelle's rose bushes. She never says anything, but I'm sure she doesn't appreciate it. I don't know what it is about her rose bushes that inspires him to grace them."

"We'll steer clear." Calliope snapped the lead on Sport's collar.

"And watch out for Granny Saulnier's poodle."

"FeFe?"

"Yeah. Sport has a thing for her. If you're not careful, he'll yank your arm out of its socket going after her."

"I'll be careful." Calliope paused with her hand on the front doorknob and looked back with her eyebrows raised. "Anything else before we go for a nice walk?"

"Get out of here." Alex lobbed a pillow at Calliope as she and Sport exited.

* * *

LATER THAT NIGHT, Alex lay in her bed, Lucie's Voodoo pouch lying on the pillow beside her. She'd had a particularly tough aerobics session at the gym and her muscles ached.

She lifted her cell phone and dialed.

"Hello?" Lucie's sleepy voice answered.

"Did I catch you doing something I only dream about?" she asked.

"Sleeping?"

"Never mind." She stroked the red velvet bag. "Is Ben home?"

"No, he's putting in a late day with the prosecuting attorney. You know, his criminal investigation stuff."

"What, and leaving his pregnant wife to fend for herself? Who's going to make the run to the convenience store for your latest cravings of sardines and pickles?"

"He's got orders to pick some up on the way home. How are you, Alex?"

"Great. I'm in the best shape I've been in a long time, I'm healthy, my business is booming and I've never been happier." Geez, she sounded like a broken record. A pathetic broken record, at that.

"Lonely, huh?"

That empty feeling gripped her belly and she automatically reached over the side of her bed to pat Sport's head. His wet nose nuzzled her hand. Was she lonely? Was that why she'd called Lucie in the first place? "Yeah, a little."

"Consider yourself hugged."

"Thanks." But a real hug would have been much warmer. From a real man—even better.

"Did Calliope give you the present?"

"Yeah. Actually, that's why I called." Alex lifted the pouch in her hand. "What is it?"

"A little Voodoo good luck for one of my best friends."

She grimaced. "Uh, gee thanks, Lucie. I can't tell you how happy it makes me."

"Relax, Alex." Lucie laughed into her ear. "You won't wake up as a frog or anything. My grandmother helped me with it, so don't worry."

"I can't tell you how relieved I am." Only slightly. Madame LeBieu knew her stuff. As the well-renowned Voodoo queen of the bayou, her spells always worked the way she intended. Unlike Lucie's.

"I can tell you're not thrilled." Lucie laughed. "Gran watched me every step of the way. She loves you like another granddaughter. Why would she propose something that would hurt you?"

"Let me remind you, she turned Craig Thibodeaux into a frog," she said, her voice flat.

"Yeah, but it all worked out in the end, didn't it?" Lucie sighed. "I love you, Alex. I just want you to be happy."

"I'm happy." Her hand tightened on the phone. "Why can't everyone figure that out?"

"Maybe you protest too much?"

"I'm not protesting." Alex realized, as she said it, she was doing just that. Her lips clamped shut.

"Is it a crime to want all my friends to be as happy as I am?" Lucie's voice drifted off.

She could imagine Lucie patting her swelling belly, and a sudden surge of maternal longing struck her right between the breasts. Why was she mooning over having a baby? Hell, she'd helped raise all her younger brothers and sisters. "I'm happy. Really." Even to her own ears, her voice wasn't very convincing.

"Give the Voodoo charm a chance, Alex. That's all I ask."

Lucie's voice cut through her ill temper and she relented. "Assuming I give it a chance, what is it supposed to do?"

A long pause met her question. Not a good sign. "I'm not exactly sure. Gran LeBieu said it would bring you good luck."

"In terms of what?" A chill swept down Alex's spine.

A whimpering sound rose from the floor beside her. Sport must have sensed her unease.

"It's okay, really. Gran LeBieu wouldn't give you anything that would hurt you."

"I'm shaking in my sheets here."

"Look, if you don't want it, bring it back with you the next time you're in Baton Rouge."

"I will."

"And when will that be?" Lucie demanded.

"As soon as I can break free from the gym." She knew that was an excuse. The thought of visiting Lucie in all her happy, pregnant glory made her own life look boring, lackluster, and downright sad.

"You're working too hard, Alex. Let Harry take over for a weekend. You need some down time."

She straightened her shoulders, refusing to give into downheartedness. "No, I like being busy."

"And you like going home alone?"

"Yes."

"Alex, it'll happen for you," Lucie said. "When you least expect it, love will knock you over."

"Like it happened with you?" She snorted. "I don't want to fall in love because of a Voodoo love potion. I want a man who loves me for me."

"Much as I'd like to take credit, my love spell never worked. Gran LeBieu confirmed, it had to be cast by a love bug, not a lady bug. If you remember, we couldn't find any love bugs, so we used a ladybug. She let me think it worked to teach me a lesson."

"What?" She shook her head. "You mean my dumb brother didn't need a kick in the pants to tell you he loved you?"

"Maybe he needed that kick in the pants, but he didn't need the love spell."

"I knew that," Alex said. She didn't know whether Lucie's news was good or bad. If the love spell didn't work, what were her chances at love? She fingered the velvet bag. "So, Lucie, what is this bag, really?"

"Gran LeBieu said it would help make your wishes come true."

Alex shuddered. "Kinda like my genie in a bottle?"

"I'm not entirely sure. I just thought you needed a little push, a boost to get you started."

"Look, Lucie, just because you're in love and that makes you happy, doesn't mean I have to be in love to be happy." But she had been pretty lonely since Lucie left. And she hadn't had a decent date in...When her visual memories started dating back to high school and she couldn't name a single unforgettable—happily they'd been forgettable—date, she grimaced. "Okay, I'll keep your gift for now, but I'm still not convinced I need it."

"Which makes me all the more convinced you do."

"I have my own business, my own home and a wonderful, if a little meddling, family. I don't need a love interest."

"Oh, Alex. You're my best friend in the world and I only wish you could feel how I feel."

"That's you, honey. And I'm happy for you." She didn't add, and I miss you like crazy. Why mar Lucie's happiness?

"Oh, Ben just walked in," Lucie said. "Hey, *mon cher,* anything you want to say to your baby sister?"

The distinct sound of smacking noises carried across the line and Lucie giggled. "Beeennn, I'm on the phone with your sister." Another giggle.

A pang of longing twisted in her gut. Again. What the hell was going on?

"Alex? That you?" Ben's voice blasted into Alex's ear.

"Yeah, bro."

"Lucie's gotta go now."

More giggling erupted in the background and an indignant, "Ben! What about the baby?"

"Look, I have some ironing to do," she said. Suddenly, she couldn't stand listening to their playful antics on the phone.

"Yeah, okay," Ben said, obviously distracted.

"Tell Lucie I'll call tomorrow."

"Gotcha—damn..." A loud clunk was followed by dead air of being disconnected.

Alex plugged the phone into the charger on the nightstand and turned off the light.

She fought the strange pressure in her chest. What was wrong with her? She was happy. She sniffed. Was she coming down with a cold? Were her glands swelling in her throat, choking off her air?

A tear slid down her cheek. *Oh hell.* She didn't need this. Self-pity was for weenies, not for black belts in karate or really kick-ass business owners.

She flung her hand out, bouncing it off the empty pillow beside her. The velvet pouch bumped against her fingers.

"Sport?"

After a brief pause, a cold, wet nose poked up over the side of the bed.

"I'm so lucky to have you." She ran her hand over his velvety snout. A long tongue snaked out and licked her fingers.

Sport was always there for her without being annoying or obsessive. Alex shivered. She'd had her share of boyfriends and stalkers. She'd rather remain celibate than go through that again.

But deep down, she ached for that closeness. And hell, she hadn't had sex in so long she wondered if she remembered how. Was she going to die one of those frigid old maids destined to read erotic romance novels to get her jollies?

I'm Pathetic.

And her mother would drive her stark-raving mad if she didn't quit shoving fresh meat at her every chance she got.

"Oh Sport, I wish you were a man. That would solve all my problems." She settled against her pillow and closed her eyes. "It would take a lot of magic to get my mother to back off. I'm not even sure having my own choice of a boyfriend will satisfy the woman." She yawned and snuggled in, pulling the comforter up to her chin to ward off the chill of the air conditioner.

As she drifted into a half-awake, half-asleep state, the bed sank down on the far side. Sport had leapt up beside her.

Too tired to tell him to get down, she gave up and let go.

A thrumming sound filled her dreams, building into a full bass echo of drums. Somewhere in the back of her sleep-numbed mind, she recognized the drums as those played at the Voodoo ceremonies Madame LeBieu conducted on those rare occasions when a little extra umph was needed to initiate one of her spells.

Just as she succumbed to oblivion, an eerie chant echoed through her head, "Wishes come true. Wishes come true. Wishes come true."

Alex sighed and gave in to the magic.

If only wishes really came true.

CHAPTER 2

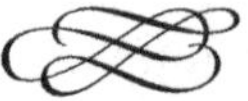

THE DARK-HAIRED STRANGER LAY WARM AGAINST ALEX'S BACK, THE FUR on his chest tickling her arms. A sexy tongue teased at her ear, sending tingles across her skin. Ummmmm. That felt good. She knew it was a dream, and she didn't want to wake to an empty bed, so she forced her eyes to stay closed so that she could enjoy the fantasy until her alarm blasted her awake.

She snuggled deeper in her sheets, imagining the heated skin of her dream man pressing against the back of her thighs. How long had it been since she'd slept with someone—well besides one of her siblings in her crowded family home?

Her man whimpered softly and the errant tongue traced the side of her neck.

She scooted back to snuggle against the man in her dreams only for him to drape a heavy arm across her waist and lick her cheek

Ew! Some dream man. Who ever heard of a full throttle tongue-swipe across the cheek as being even remotely sexy? Maybe it was time to wake from this dream and kick Mr. No-more-manners-than-a-dog out of her dream and bed. Through the thick haze of slumber, she had an oh-duh moment.

Sport.

Sport had sneaked into her bed right as she'd fallen to sleep. He usually did whenever they had a thunderstorm or if he sensed her loneliness.

Eyes still closed, she raised her hand to her cheek. Yup. It was wet, all right. Double ew. Dog slobber. That's when she opened her eyes to the gray light of dawn sneaking around the blinds shuttering her window.

She rolled to her side and faced the culprit. Where her ninety-pound fraidy-cat of a dog should have been, lay a full-sized man with a startling resemblance to a young Brendan Frazier. And he was naked from the top of his broad shoulders down past the limp—well she tried not to look—to his toenails.

A shocked moment passed before her sleep-fogged brain engaged and then registered with a blinding flash of *intruder alert, intruder alert!*

Screaming at the top of her lungs, Alex leaped out of the bed with her feet still tangled in the sheets. Instead of hitting the ground running for the door, she hit the hardwood floors face-first, cursing her brother for talking her into removing the carpets.

Before she could disentangle her legs, a thump sounded on the other side of the four-poster bed.

Oh crap, oh crap. He was coming after her.

Frantic now, visions of being raped raced through her head as she was being trapped by her Laura Ashley sheets. She peered beneath the bed wishing she could see through the clutter of boxes to the other side.

Then a whimper sounded from the floor between the bed and the outside wall. "Sport?" Where was her dog? "You better leave my dog alone, you son of a bitch!"

With the determination of a mother wolf guarding her cub, Alex finally shed the constricting sheet, leaped to her feet and grabbed for something to clobber the man threatening her dog. The only item she could find was her color-coordinated pillow that resembled a light blue giant tootsie roll. Like she could beat a man to death with a pillow. Oh well, she only had to hold him off long enough to free Sport and make a run for the door.

Another whimper sounded from the other side of the bed, spurring

Alex into action. "I said, leave my dog alone." She inched around the post and braced herself for attack.

Pushing up to his hands and knees was a man with light cinnamon hair and soft brown eyes. And yes, she hadn't been seeing things—he was completely naked.

When she screamed, the man yelped and pressed his face to the floor, cowering like a whipped dog, with his hands covering his head.

While the man crouched, staring up at her with wide, nervous eyes, she committed his features to memory. A girl never knew when she'd have to identify a man in a police line-up. His hair was the same soft reddish-brown color of Sport's and his eyes threatened to melt her when they rounded all scared-like. Sport had that same look when he was hiding in a closet because of a booming thunder storm.

Get a grip, woman. This is a naked man. In your house. And he had his arm around you, in your bed! "Holy Jesus! Get out, or I'll call the police."

The man trembled all over but backed into the corner instead of fighting his way out.

Great. Out of all the houses—okay so there weren't that many in Bayou Miste—why did this crazy man have to crawl naked into hers?

Because you live alone—vulnerable to any bare-skinned man's sex-fetish whim.

Her heart beat so fast, she couldn't hear past her pulse pounding in her ears. No wait, that was pounding on the door.

"Out! Get out!" she yelled, pointing her fiber-filled weapon toward the bedroom door.

The man glanced past her, his gaze nervous as if he was afraid of her. Alex, all five feet, six inches of damned tough, angry girl. Good, he was afraid, as well he should be.

"Out!"

The banging carried through from her living room to her bedroom. Oh, thank God. For once, Calliope was on time for their morning jog.

Alex backed toward the door holding her pillow in front of her like a weapon. "I'm going into the living room and I *will* call the police. Unless you want to go to jail, you'd better leave."

"Alex, what's going on?" Calliope called through the thick wood paneling. "Was that you screaming?"

The man's head shot up and he rose onto his knees, peering over the top of the bed, his eyes wide, his face intent on the doorway.

Then before she could do anything but stand there like a lunk, the man leaped over the bed and loped for the living room.

Oh, no! Calliope had a key to the front door. She prayed this once she wouldn't use it, or psycho-man might hurt her.

Alex raced after the intruder, chasing him down the hallway. She nearly wiped out on the loose throw rug at the corner.

A few steps ahead of her, the man sped through the kitchen and dove for the doggie-door. He yelped when he hit the floor, and struggled to squeeze through anyway. But the door was built for a medium-sized golden retriever, not for a broad-shouldered man. He backed out and stood, his gaze darting right and left.

The crashing sound of the front door banging against the wall indicated that Calliope had used her spare key.

At the sound, the man's head perked to the side and he sniffed. Then he charged through the other entrance to the kitchen heading for the front door.

"Look out, Calliope!" she cried.

A scream ripped through the air, followed by complete silence.

"Calliope? Oh, God. Calliope!" She ran through the kitchen, her heart in her throat. "That bastard better not have touched—" She screeched to a halt.

Her redheaded friend stared at the open doorway, her mouth hanging wide open.

"Calliope?" Alex frowned when she didn't respond. "Did you see him?" She began to wonder if the naked man was all part of her pathetic spinster imaginings.

"Did I see him?" Calliope held a hand to her chest. "I saw every glorious inch of him."

Too late, she realized it wasn't shock registering on Calliope's face, it was full-fledged gaw-gaw. "Holy shit, Calliope, you're drooling over a naked intruder."

"Yes, ma'am, until I run out of spit." Her mouth still hung slack. "He was gooorrrrgeous."

"That man is guilty of breaking and entering and you're ready to jump his bones?" She slammed the door and turned to face her friend. "Are you that desperate?"

"Yes, oh yes. Did you see those muscles, sinews, and organs? Ah yes, organs..." Calliope walked toward the door as if in a trance.

"Hellloooo!" She waved a hand in front of Calliope's face. "Are you missing the part about breaking and entering? The man might have hurt —" Alex's eyes widened and she squealed. "Sport. Ohmigod! Sport!" She spun on the same small throw rug almost shooting it out from under her and charged down the hall back to the original scene of the crime. "What has that son-of-a-bitch done with my dog?" she wailed.

As soon as she entered the room, her eyes scanned the space end to end, while her heart pounded against her eardrums. Neither hide nor hair of the dog could be seen. She leaped up on the bed and peered over the other side where she'd heard whimpering earlier. Nothing.

"Where's Sport?" Calliope appeared in the doorway, a worried frown marring her freckled forehead. "Sport? Here boy?" Her voice trailed off as she stared into Alex's eyes. "Where is he?"

She climbed off the bed and checked the window. Locked. "He couldn't have gotten out this way. And the man couldn't have gotten in."

"If Sport is outside, he wouldn't have gone far. He always comes home," Calliope said, her hopeful tone choking the air out of Alex's lungs.

"That bastard." Tears welled in her eyes and she sank onto the side of the bed and then jumped up. "My bedroom has been violated by a strange man. And where is Sport? If that jerk—"

"Why would he take Sport's collar off?" Calliope's words cut through her fog of pain. She fingered the bright read nylon band lying among the sheets. "And why would he take the time to reconnect the clasp?"

The man's eyes flashed in her memory. They were the same deep brown as Sport's.

Why the thought of her Voodoo dream sprang into her thoughts, she didn't know. The lingering reverberation of thrumming drums and magical chants sent a lone chill slithering across her skin, raising gooseflesh.

She hopped up from the bed and ran through the house. "Sport! Sport!"

"He's not in here, Alex." Calliope hurried to the front door and threw it wide. "Sport? Sport! Come here, Sport!"

Alex joined her and they stepped out on the porch calling out in unison, "Sport!"

A bush on the corner of the house shook and whimpered.

She looked at Calliope. "Did that bush just whimper?"

Calliope's eyebrows rose. "Sport hides in that bush when he's scared." She nudged Alex with her elbow. "Why don't you go check it out?"

"Me? Why me?" She shrank back. A naked stranger accosting her once in her lifetime was enough. She didn't feel like risking a second flashing. "Sport." Her voice dropped an octave and she did her best I'm-the-big-sister-threatening-your-life voice she could muster. "Come here. Right now."

The bush shook again. But a hairy head pushed out and half of the body emerged.

The naked man.

Alex grabbed Calliope and shoved her behind her. "Go away!"

The man's gaze darted from side to side and he whimpered like an abused animal.

"Don't be so hasty." Calliope tried to push her away. "Let me handle this."

"No, Calliope. The guy is obviously a pervert."

Although the bush covered the man from the waist down, Alex could still see enough to know the guy was still without clothes.

"How do you know? He could be someone who got lost from a nudist colony." With a determined shove, Calliope manhandled Alex out of the way and held out her hand. "Hi, I'm Calliope. And you are?"

"Woof!"

She stepped back. "Did that man just bark? Tell me he didn't just bark."

Calliope laughed. "I believe he did."

A scary thought wiggled its way into her subconscious, growing into a crazy, outlandish, completely idiotic idea. "You don't suppose...I mean..." She shook her head. "No, that's ridiculous...Lucie wouldn't... Hell, she's not trained in that kind of thing."

Without taking her gaze from the man standing so hesitantly in the bush, Calliope said, "What are you talking about? You think this man is Lucie's Voodoo gift?"

"Could it be?" She peered closer.

"If so, I say don't look a gift horse in the mouth. There are much better places to stare at a horse." Calliope vamp-walked across the porch and down the stairs. "Come on, *bebe*!"

The man frowned and crouched lower in the bush, darting glances at Alex as if pleading with her to save him from the fiery redhead stalking him.

"If this is Lucie's so-called gift, what happened to Sport?" she asked.

As soon as she said the name Sport, the man's head jerked toward her and he stood taller.

Huh?

She stared hard at the soft brown eyes and reddish brown hair. "Sport?"

The man's eyes widened and he opened his mouth, "Woof!"

She screamed, and Calliope jumped back and screamed, too.

The naked man shot out of the bush and bare-footed it as fast as he could across the gravel drive and out into the street.

Her friend turned toward her with a hand on her hip. "Don't scare me like that!"

Alex's shocked brain reengaged and she yelled, "Ohmigod. Calliope, we have to catch that man."

Calliope grinned and rubbed her hands together. "Now, you're talking."

CHAPTER 3

Ed peeked out a window at the house next door. Still early on a Saturday morning, he might escape before his neighbors spied him. He liked a solitary morning jog to clear the sleep from his brain. And he wasn't so sure he was up to Barbara Boyette's unrelenting cheerfulness this early in the day. Ben's mom was terrific...in small doses.

As far as he could tell, the coast was clear. He could make a hasty escape if he left now.

He had to hurry, before the masses of Boyettes caught him and reeled him in for the inquisition.

He ducked out the back door, turned to stick the key in the lock. By the time he swung back around, two identically beautiful young women stood facing him. Each wore their thick, black hair pinned at the back of their heads with long loose ringlets trailing down over their exposed shoulders. But it was their dresses that made him think he'd taken a step back in time. They wore beautiful peach-colored ball gowns that looked as if they walked straight out of the late eighteen hundreds.

"Hi," they said in unison.

He slapped a hand over one eye and refocused. No he wasn't seeing double. There were two of them. Damn, Ben had mentioned the bayou was said to be magical. But time travel and seeing double?

"Let me guess," he said, "your last name is Boyette."

"Yes!" Again, both girls answered in unison, their smiles practically blinding him.

One of them stepped forward. "I'm Dolley, and this," she pointed at her replica, "is Madison."

He frowned, glancing from one to the other. "You're kidding right?"

Both dark heads tipped to the right. And Thing One—was she Dolley—said "About what?"

"Your names." He smiled when they continued to look confused, and added, "You mean you're really Dolley and Madison?"

"Oh yes!" both said, the stereo frighteningly in tune.

"Okay, I'll buy that. Now, if you'll excuse me..." he moved past them.

"Wait, Mr. Marceau," Dolley said.

Madison finished with, "Mom wanted us to invite you to dinner tonight."

Dinner with eighteen kids? Did she think he was insane? "Please tell her thank you, but I have plans."

"Mom told us not to take no for an answer." Thing Two—Madison—or was she Dolley—smiled and stepped in front of him.

The other twin grinned. "And we'd like you to come, too."

"Yes, we would," Madison chime in.

Pre-jog, pre-coffee, Ed wasn't up to handling the combined enthusiasm and he was feeling just a little outnumbered by sunny faces. He was not a morning person and he couldn't stomach those who were irritatingly cheerful before nine o'clock.

"So? Can we expect you?" Dolley-Madison asked in unison.

He inhaled and prepared to say a firm "No."

But they turned some incredibly bright smiles on him. "Please?"

His opened his mouth, and knew he couldn't disappoint this early in the morning. "Okay."

Two bouncing cheerleaders in ball gowns hopped up and down, clapping their hands, their dresses ballooning out with each movement.

His temples throbbed. If he didn't get away soon, his head would spontaneously combust. "If you'll excuse me, I'm going for a jog."

"See you at seven?" they asked.

He forced a smile. "Seven it is." Then he made his escape, taking off at an all-out run designed to put as much distance between him and the southern belle twins as possible. Holy hell! What had he agreed to?

He rounded the end of the block, glancing back to make sure the girls weren't following him. Thank God! He'd left them behind.

When he turned to face front, he ran into a brick wall, head first. Wham!

He staggered backward, his head reeling. When his vision cleared, he realized the wall hadn't been a wall at all, but a man.

A naked man.

"What the fu—"

The other guy was still flat on his naked ass, shaking his head like a dog shakes the water off his fur.

"Hey, buddy, you all right?" He reached out a hand to help the man up, and cringed. What kind of pervert ran around in the nude in a small town? Did he have some funky disease that would rub off on contact? Or had he escaped an awkward tryst with a married woman?

Ed needn't have worried. The man completely ignored his outstretched hand.

Out of the corner of his eyes, a flash of powdery pink flashed past his ankles. He ripped his gaze from the naked pervert to follow a ball of pink fluff skittering down the sidewalk.

He looked closer to determine the cotton candy was in actual fact a toy poodle dyed an outlandish shade of pink.

The man in front of him leaped to his bare feet and chased after the animated powder puff, shouting, "Woof!"

Ed shook his head. He must be hearing things. Had that man woofed?

"Sport!" a female voice called out.

"Sport!" yet another feminine entreaty split his eardrums.

The yelling voices preceded the appearance of two women from the end of the street. One was wearing skin-tight biker shorts and a sports bra, and had her fiery red hair caught up in a ponytail. The other...

Holy hell.

His jaw dropped. The collision must have hit him harder than he'd thought. Suddenly he couldn't breathe and was seeing things.

Her hair was as black as his brand new Mustang convertible parked in the garage at his apartment building. Her eyes were bright blue and she had smooth, creamy skin that reminded him of a cup of pale, milky mocha. And boy was there a lot of skin showing. She wore a frothy blue baby-doll nightie. The gown did nothing to cover the black, lacy string bikini panties peeking out with every step as she raced down the street barefooted. And oh, those luscious breasts bobbed unfettered beneath the filmy fabric.

The jogging beauties slid to a stop in front of him. Apparently, they were real, not just a figment of his imagination.

The redhead spoke first. "Did you see a do—" she didn't get the chance to finish her sentence when the black-haired beauty jammed her elbow into her gut.

"Man. Did you see a man run by?" demanded the woman in the blue baby-doll nightie.

Interesting. Even without his usual five-mile jog and gallon of coffee, his senses were now on full alert.

Standing this close to that short, sheer, blue gown was doing crazy things to his gray matter and other parts of his body.

The women looked flustered. But then one of them had a reason. Hell, she was running around in an outfit that couldn't be licensed for public consumption in the free world.

He loved seeing her worry her full, ruby mouth and made it a point to worry it more. "Can you describe this man?" he stalled.

The dark one squirmed. Wow, she even squirmed beautifully. If he weren't careful, he'd be making a tent of his jogging shorts.

The redhead jumped into the silence. "He has reddish-brown hair, brown eyes, and a body to die for." She paused and added, "Oh, and did I say he was naked?"

He let an eyebrow inch upward. "Naked?" He asked the dark-haired one. "Any particular reason a man is running around the town naked?"

The black-haired beauty's eyes flashed, but she didn't answer.

"We scared him," the redhead supplied.

Since she'd stopped in front of him, the dark one hadn't uttered a word.

He considered it a challenge. "Do you always run around Bayou Miste in your...black string bikini underwear?" He trailed his gaze down her front to the dark shadow of her underwear barely visible beneath the filmy skirt of her nightgown.

A blush started in the vicinity of her cleavage and traveled up her neck into her cheeks. Score! "Come on, Calliope, this man doesn't know anything." The dark-haired one grabbed the redhead's arm and tried to drag her away.

"But Alex, I'm enjoying the show." She smiled a wicked smile and eyed the front of his shorts.

Too late, he'd been too intent on making Miss Naughty Nightie squirm, he'd forgotten about his own arousing reaction to her delights.

She glanced down, color brightening in her cheeks. But her mouth curved on the ends. "I take it by show, you mean comedy?" A thin, dark brow winged upward. "I've had my laugh. Ha, ha. Now, come on, Calliope. We have to catch Sport."

His ego flagging, Ed couldn't help tossing a parting shot. "What, is this some kind of kinky game you're playing?"

"And if we are, did you want to be invited?" the one called Calliope asked, her grin widening.

"Maybe." He answered the redhead, his gaze fixed on Alex.

"Too bad." Blue nightie actually tsked her tongue. "We're a little more selective of our playthings." With a dismissive sweep of her gaze from his head to his feet, she put him firmly in his place.

Then she was racing down the street, her firm buttocks even more interesting in the black lace bikini.

Ed turned to jog after her. He had to know who she was. More important, he wanted to get to know those lace panties more intimately. After two steps, he had to pause and adjust. Nope, he wasn't jogging in the next five minutes. Not in his...uh...condition. Later. In a town as small as Bayou Miste, he'd easily find her.

Then he thought of his busybody neighbor. Perhaps Mrs. Boyette would know who the dark-haired babe was.

WOW. Who was the hunk of macho male? Alex fought to keep from looking back at the man who'd been eyeing her favorite sexy underwear. If she was going to be caught running around half-clothed in Bayou Miste, at least she had on her best. Somehow, she didn't think the present situation was what her mother had in mind when she told her to "always wear good underwear...you never know."

In her jogging shoes, Calliope was making better time at catching up with the naked man. Alex hobbled along as fast as she could, her bare feet taking a beating on the gravel.

If by some freaky quirk of fate and Voodoo hexes, Naked-Man wasn't a man at all but her dog transformed into a man, she had a huge problem on her hands.

How the hell was she going to keep him under wraps until she could get Lucie back to Bayou Miste to undo the spell? She couldn't even catch the man...er...dog.

Poor Sport. He must be terrified.

Calliope disappeared around the next corner. Alex hoped she'd catch Sport before he did something to hurt himself.

Before she neared the street they'd turned on, she could hear shouting and high-pitched barking.

With little regard to her bruised feet, she picked up the pace and rounded the corner in a gut-splitting sprint. Then she had to dig her sore heels into the pavement to keep from tripping over an eight-foot alligator stretched across the middle of the road.

Pandemonium would have been less crazy than what was going on.

At the business end of the alligator, the one with the jagged teeth and lethal jaws, stood Granny Saulnier's toy poodle, FeFe, yapping her little head off with as much ferocity as a five-pound, pink powder-puff could muster. At the other end of the alligator was Naked-Man, woofing at the top of his human voice.

She recognized the alligator as Maurice Saulnier's pet, T-Rex. He was probably coming to woo FeFe when Naked-Man interrupted.

Calliope stood near where Alex had come to a halt, shouting, "Shoo,

T-Rex! Shoo!" She flapped her hands trying to scare the alligator away from the dog and the man. *As if!*

"Calliope," she called out over the commotion.

"Stop that alligator." Calliope grabbed Alex's hand and pulled her up beside her. "You have to stop him before he hurts our gorgeous man."

"He's not our gorgeous man, and T-Rex isn't a bad dog to be shooed away."

"Well, I want that man, and T-Rex thinks he's a dog. Please get him to leave, before something important gets hurt."

The poodle continued yapping non-stop, her high-pitched staccato voice grinding on every last one of her nerves. "Oh, T-Rex, eat the damned poodle, already."

"Alex Boyette, I heard that. How dare you tell that darned-fool alligator to eat my poor little FeFe." Granny Saulnier tottered out onto her porch shaking a broom. When she spied Naked-Man, her squinty little eyes went as round as shiny new dimes. "Pre-vert!" For a four-foot eleven package of spindly bones and bright pink hair, she moved fast. Down off the porch she came like a whirling pink dervish whacking at the air with her straw broom. "Get some clothes on, you pre-vert."

T-Rex got one look at the broom and scrambled backward, away from the crazy woman wielding it. Naked-man's eyes rounded and he whimpered.

When T-Rex backed right into him, Naked-man yelped and jumped straight in the air, his feet churning before they hit the ground. He leaped across the alligator's tail and raced straight for her and Calliope.

Before they could move, he ploughed through the middle of them, knocking Calliope flat on her butt and spinning Alex around.

"Alex Boyette, I don't know what you're up to, but I'm telling your mother about this." With one hand, Granny Saulnier scooped up the yapping pink poodle from in front of the gaping jaws of T-Rex. With the other hand, she applied the stick end of the broom to the alligator's head. "And you! Go back to the swamp where you belong." With that, she turned and marched back to her sunny yellow house.

Alex shook her head for a moment, too overwhelmed by the events to react. Then she grabbed Calliope's hand, hauling her to her feet. "Come on, we gotta catch him before he gets into any more trouble."

Which meant going back the same way they'd come and possibly passing the he-man-macho guy in the tented shorts. Warmth surged throughout Alex's body, her nipples tightening into pointy headlights, poking out of the diaphanous fabric like twin pencil erasers. Wow. All that for a stranger whose name she didn't even know. She wondered if he'd be in town long and, if so, if they would run into each other again.

She and Calliope resumed their hunt of Naked-Man. Hopefully, he was headed back to Alex's little cottage.

Disappointment hit her like a wet blanket in the face when she didn't see her handsome stranger again. Oh, well. She didn't have time to stop, and he probably thought she was wacky anyway, chasing after a naked man while wearing nothing more than her skimpiest nightgown.

The people of Bayou Miste were used to crazy things happening, what with their very own Voodoo queen a mere hop-skip-and-jump away on the bayou.

She slowed to a walk, her tender feet having had enough of the gravel and already warming pavement. If Naked-Man, whom she suspected might be her dog, wasn't back at the house, she would definitely get dressed before she ventured any farther afield in her search.

"Sport!" Calliope called out ahead.

Alex trailed behind, convinced she lived in the twilight zone of jokes and wondered when the punch line would hit her in the face.

When her house came in view, she heaved a sigh of relief. Calliope was talking to the bush in low, soothing tones.

Naked-Man shook the bush with every quiver of his large body crouched beneath.

"*Mon Dieu,* Alex." Calliope turned, her face beaming. "I think you're right. I think that's Sport."

She shoved a hand through her hair. "What did I do to deserve this?"

"I don't know, but when you figure it out, I want to do it, too." Calliope stared back at the shaking bush. "Then whenever I needed a date, all I'd have to do is visit the local humane society."

"Don't go making plans yet. We don't even know if this is Sport."

"It is. I just know it."

Alex stepped closer to the bush and held out her hand like she did when she was trying to coax Sport out of the closet on a stormy night. "Sport? Come here, boy."

The man with sad-puppy eyes rose just enough so his head was clear of the azalea blossoms, then he whimpered.

"Come on, boy." She couldn't believe she was standing in her front yard in her baby-doll nightgown coaxing a naked man out of her bush. "I'm soooo going to have words with Lucie."

The man crouched back down.

"It's okay, boy," she said in the soft singsong voice she used when she wanted Sport to drop the sparrow he'd been chewing on. "I'm not mad at you. I'm just mad at that sorry excuse for an amateur Voodoo priestess."

Her soft words and gentle tones were doing the trick, because the man inched out from behind the bush and walked toward her.

Her heart rate jumped to what it was after a particularly tough session at the gym. What was she thinking? This guy was a man, not a dog.

He was tall and muscular, not short and furry. And all that naked skin was... well...intimidating in full sunlight.

She took a step backward with her hand held out, inching up the steps to the front door. "Want a biscuit, boy? Want a treat?"

The man's eyes widened.

When she opened the door, he shoved past her and ran for the kitchen, the same way Sport did when he knew he was getting a special dog yummy.

Alex groaned and stared at her friend. "I'm going to kill Lucie."

Calliope's eyes glowed. "Did you see those gorgeous glutes?"

CHAPTER 4

Ed jogged to the end of town on one side of the canal, crossed over a bridge and jogged back on the other side. He took his time studying the clapboard houses, some on stilts, others hugging the ground, daring to take on another storm surge like they'd experienced in Katrina and even more recently during torrential rains that had afflicted the bayous. Everywhere there was old metal, there was rust, and paint seemed to be in a constant state of mildewing or peeling.

He might have found it rather depressing if not for the optimism of the azalea bushes and flowers planted in front of every other house. With the constant humidity and abundant rain, flowers bloomed in wild abandon.

Though he studied the town for potential dark, shadowy areas and henchmen hideouts, his mind couldn't help but drift back to his strange encounter of the naked and near-naked kind earlier. After bumping into the sexy lingerie kitten that morning, he'd had to wait a good ten minutes for his hard-on to subside before he could resume his morning workout. That didn't keep him from looking around every corner in hope of catching another glimpse of the naughty nightie. Alas, no luck. At least the town was quiet and so far there was not a threat to be found.

A cool shower helped wash away the sweat and residual attraction to the sex kitten in blue. Once he'd slipped into a white polo shirt and jeans, he decided he'd better get what he needed to establish his cover. Having grown up in Baton Rouge, he should know everything there was about fishing. Yet none of his foster parents had ever taken him.

Lucky for Ben, his father had been a shrimper. His father no doubt had taught him all there was to know about shrimping and fishing in the bayou and along the coast. Apparently, his dad had passed away a couple years ago.

The single good thing about losing his parents at a young age was that Ed didn't still mourn their loss. He'd barely known them.

He could see the sorrow in Ben's eyes whenever he spoke of his father. They'd been close. Well, as close as a man with nineteen children could get. Holy hell, had they really had nineteen children?

As he stepped out the front door of the cottage he'd rented from Mrs. Boyette, he felt the vibration of his phone in his pocket. He dug it out and hit the talk key. "Marceau."

"Ed, how was your night?" Ben said in his usual too-cheerful-in-the-morning tone. Must be a Boyette trait.

"Great."

"Mom get around to inviting you to dinner?"

"Hey, I'm supposed to be keeping a low profile here. How am I supposed to do that having dinner with the biggest family in town?"

"You'll be one of the family by the end of the meal. The better to blend in with the locals."

"Yeah, yeah."

"So, who'd she send?"

"Huh?"

"Which one of my brothers or sisters came to deliver the invitation?"

"A couple of southern belles in old-fashioned dresses, talking in stereo."

Ben chuckled. "That would Dolley and Madison, home early for summer vacation from Tulane University. Probably on their way to work at the Beauregard Plantation. They lead tours through the old plantation house during the summer. Make an impression on you, did they?"

"They don't take no for an answer," Ed groused. "And way too cheerful before nine in the morning."

"They get that from Mom. Have you had a chance to look around town?"

"Yeah. Took me fifteen minutes." He slid into the nondescript, gray Jeep they'd rented for the mission and closed the door before continuing. "Not much to the town."

"It's usually pretty quiet, but we do get tourists coming in to do a little fishing and the occasional bayou tour."

"I'll be on the lookout for the strange-looking tourists then." Ed twisted his key in the ignition. "Speaking of strange, is streaking a part of the norm in Bayou Miste?"

"Streaking?" Ben paused. "What do you mean?"

"As in men running naked down the street followed by women in their night clothes."

Ben laughed. "I have no idea what you're talking about."

"Never mind. I'm on my way to Morgan City for a fishing pole and whatever it is I need to look like I'm going fishing."

"You could get that stuff at Thibodeaux's Marina right there in Bayou Miste."

"I want to at least appear to look like I know what I'm doing." He backed out of the driveway and headed north. "And that I own my own gear."

"Wait a minute," Ben said. "You mean you've never been fishing? Ever?"

"I tried to tell you, this bayou vacation isn't my thing."

"You're in for a treat. Make sure you hook up with Joe Thibodeaux. He'll take you out and show you what fun real fishin' in the bayou can be."

"I'm here on a mission, not to have fun."

"Man, you have really got to lighten up. You're an old man at what...thirty?"

"Thirty-two. Same as you, man." He drove out of town and headed up the highway toward Morgan City. "Anything new on Leon Primeaux?"

"Still sittin' pretty behind bars."

"Anyone been in to visit?" Ed asked. "Are they monitoring his calls?"

"So far he's been quiet."

"I don't like it. That man has so many minions scattered over the state of Louisiana and beyond, I'll bet he's already contacted one of them to put a hit on our witness."

"Exactly the reason why we have her in such a remote location. Keep your eyes open. Could be just about anyone after her. Or more than one. It's easy to hide a body in the bayou and there are plenty of people willing to do just about anything for a buck."

"That's why I'm here running interference for a witness, instead of investigating murders and corporate espionage."

"Got you out of the office, didn't it?"

"I'd rather be investigating a double homicide in the seedier side of Baton Rouge. At least then I'd know what I was looking for."

"Look, Ed, I gotta go. I'm appearing in court in a few minutes," Ben said. "Let me know how dinner at the Boyette house goes."

"Yeah, if I survive. Somehow, I get the feeling I'm the main course to be served up."

"You don't know how true that might be."

"Wait, what do you mean?"

"Out, here." The line went dead.

Ed dropped his smartphone on the seat beside him as a speed limit sign flashed by. Hell, he'd been speeding. All he needed was to get hauled into jail for reckless driving and his cover would be blown. He eased his foot off the accelerator and reminded himself he was supposedly on vacation. A mile out of Bayou Miste, he noted a dingy, rundown shack of a barn with a sign perched precariously over the entrance. *Raccoon Saloon*. Since when did raccoons drink beer?

It had a well-worn gravel parking lot with fresh trash scattered around the building. Probably the local watering hole. At least he'd find some entertainment there. If it was a popular gathering place, he might have a chance to study the people, maybe look for those that looked as if they didn't belong.

Hell, by the time he finished dinner with the Boyettes that evening, he'd be ready to toss back a beer or two.

In Morgan City, he purchased hooks, a bag of plastic worms, and a cheap tackle box. Although he went for the least expensive of the accessories, he sprang for the nicer rod and reel. Hell, he'd never owned a fishing pole.

He juggled his purchases as he clicked the button to release the locks on the Jeep.

"Dat dere's a nice pole ya got, mista." A tall, burly man with dark curly hair and brown-black eyes climbed out of an old pickup. He wore a coverall with Littington Refineries embroidered on the front and a matching baseball cap rimmed with greasy fingerprints.

"Thanks," he said, lifting the hatch.

The young man stuck out his massive paw. "Name's Theo Ledet."

He shifted his fishing pole to his other hand with the tackle box and clasped the man's hand. "Ed Marceau."

Theo crushed his fingers in a bone-crunching grip. "Goin' fishin'?"

No, I'm going snipe hunting. "That's right." He pulled his fingers free and shook blood back into them. What did they feed these bayou bumpkins?

"Hear dose largemouth bass be bitin' in Bayou Black." Theo leaned against his truck, as if settling in to chat for a while. "Where ya be takin' out at?"

Not exactly sure what the guy was asking, Ed answered with his canned response, "I'm vacationing in Bayou Miste."

"Dat so? Where you from?"

"New Orleans," he responded, also part of the lie, since he lived in Baton Rouge.

"Bayou Black's just a hop, skip, and a jump from Thibodeaux's Marina." Theo shoved his cap to the back of his head. "Tell, ol' Joe, Theo said hey, will ya?"

"Will do." He shoved the tackle box into the rear of the Jeep. "Thanks for the tip."

"Who ya rentin' from in Bayou Miste?"

"Renting a cottage from Ms. Boyette." Not that it was any business of Theo's.

"Mighty fine woman." Theo pushed his hat to the back of his head. "Dat be my gal's mamma."

"Really?" Ed glanced up. Best to know who to stay away from. Theo looked like he would be the winner of any barroom fight. Ed had no intention of poaching on the big lug's territory. Again, not that he was interested in dating any of the bayou princesses. An image of a dark-haired beauty in a baby-blue nightie popped into his head. Well, it wouldn't hurt to talk to one. Might help establish his cover better. "Which one is your gal—girl?"

"Alex. She and I been goin' out fo' a couple months, now."

"That's nice." He slid his pole into the back of his vehicle, leaning the end over the back seat, then he shut the hatch, hoping the man would get the hint and leave.

"It's dolla beer night at de Raccoon Saloon tomorra night, if ya got a hankrin'."

"Just might." He edged toward the driver's door. "If you'll excuse me, there's a largemouth bass with my name on it out there."

The man scratched his head. "You shore 'bout dat?"

Ed shook his head. The man was a few fries short of a Happy Meal. "Just a saying. Nice talking with you." He dropped into his seat and shut the door before Theo could say another word. With a wave, he backed out of the parking space and headed back to Bayou Miste, praying Mr. Ledet wasn't going to show up for dinner at the Boyettes that night. Dinner with eighteen kids and their boyfriends would be like eating at a school cafeteria with all the noise and food fights he'd found annoying when he was a kid himself. He wondered if he could bow out of the invitation without incurring another visit from Dolley and Madison of the perpetually synchronized variety of twins.

"How'd it go, today?" Alex called out as she strode into her house. Exhausted from leading two aerobics sessions, one kick-boxing, and one black belt karate class, she'd done nothing but worry about what was going on back at her house with Sport and Calliope. Thank God, Calliope was off that day from her job at the Raccoon Saloon. Alex wouldn't have known what to do with Sport while she ran her business in Morgan City. Her sister Harry helped out at the gym, but she had her own classes to lead and the bookkeeping to attend.

"We're in the kitchen," Calliope called out.

Before she could set her purse on the hall table, the man she'd chased through town that morning burst through the doorway to the kitchen and ran full-out at her.

Alex backed away, her hands held up. "Down, Sport."

Unfortunately, Sport had never learned any manners, and he hit her square on, planting his hands on her shoulders.

She bumped against the door and squinched her eyes shut as Sport licked her cheeks, his entire body shaking.

"Ew! Stop." She braced her hands on his shoulders and pushed him away. "Damn it, stop!"

Calliope laughed. "We'll have to work on that." She leaned against the wall, smiling. "He catches on quickly, if you work with him."

"I'm sure." When Alex had Sport at arm's length, she scrubbed a hand across her wet face and looked at her dog...er man.

He wore baggy jeans, cinched at the waist with a thick black belt, an equally baggy shirt half-tucked into the jeans and nothing on his feet.

"Where'd you find the clothes?"

"In a bag marked 'dirt bag' in the hall closet." Calliope grinned. "I assumed they were some of Theo's."

She nodded. "Yeah, I meant to give them back weeks ago, but I didn't want to get into another argument with him. I can't believe I went out with him in the first place. What was I thinking?"

"You were drunk and thinking you hadn't been laid in a year."

Alex's lips twisted. "Thanks for the reminder." She shrugged. "He wasn't even that good."

"So why'd you dump him?"

"What do you mean?" Alex glared. "We weren't exactly going together."

"He thinks you were."

"One night in the sack and he thought we were practically married. I'm mean really. He left extra clothes at my house like he was moving in. After one night." She pulled the ponytail out of her hair and ran her fingers through the curls. "Shit, I'll never, ever get that drunk again." She reached up and pushed a hank of hair out of Sport's eyes and got her hand licked for the effort. "No."

Sport frowned, his shoulders sagging.

"Your mom called to remind you about dinner tonight," Calliope said.

Alex rolled her eyes. "You told her we couldn't make, right?"

"She wouldn't hear of it. Said she had a surprise for you."

With a groan, Alex flopped onto the recliner in the living room, extending the leg-rest to raise her aching feet. "I'm too tired to deal with family tonight. Besides, what are we going to do with Sport? We can't leave him alone until we find a way to undo the spell."

"Any luck getting hold of Lucie?" Calliope circled the recliner and stood in front of her.

Alex sighed. "I called no less than twenty times. She wasn't answering her phone."

"We could make a trip out to Madame LeBieu's place."

"Since you didn't cancel on Mom, we can't until after dinner." She pinched the bridge of her nose to ward off the headache threatening to explode there.

"Then I guess we're stuck." Calliope sat on the other end of the couch.

Sport dropped to the floor beside her and laid his head on her knee.

She patted his hair, smoothing her fingers through the reddish gold strands.

"So how did it go today?" Alex asked again.

Calliope grinned broadly. "We made progress."

"What do you mean, progress?"

Still petting Sport's head, she continued, "Since Sport is physically a man, I've been teaching him how to act like one." She sat forward and patted the seat beside her. "Sport, sit."

Sport glanced up, his dark eyes gleaming. He pushed up to his hands and knees and stood, then plopped on the couch, like a sloppy teen.

"Good, boy." Calliope pulled something out of her pocket, unwrapped it and popped it into his mouth.

As Sport chewed, his eyelids drooped and he leaned into Calliope with a sigh.

"What did you give him?" she asked.

"Chocolate." Calliope dug another out of her pocket and tossed it to her.

She caught it with one hand. "You're not supposed to feed dogs chocolate."

"But he's not a dog." Calliope jumped up, grabbed Sport's hand and pulled him to his feet. "And come see what else we've been working on."

Convinced she was living in some really bizarre nightmare, Alex dragged herself out of the lounge chair and followed her friend to the kitchen table.

"Look what Sport can do." Calliope handed the man a fork and stuck a plate of spaghetti in front of him.

"Are those my leftovers from Salianos? I was going to take them for lunch today and completely forgot."

"Shh. Let him show you his new trick." Calliope stood beside Sport. "Eat."

He glanced up at Calliope and down at the plate. His hand shook and the fork tilted sideways as he dug into the spaghetti and then lifted it to his face. Some of the spaghetti made it into his mouth, some landed on his lap. But he smiled as he chewed.

"Good, boy." Calliope patted his head and brushed a napkin across his cheek. "And he can talk."

"You're kidding me."

"No, listen." Calliope took the fork from him and laid it on the table. "What's your name?"

"Woof!"

Alex shook her head. "I don't know why you're bothering."

"No really, he can do it." Calliope faced Sport and bent to get at eye-level with him. "What's your name?"

Sport stared from Calliope to Alex.

"It's okay," Alex said.

He turned to Calliope and puckered his lips. "Sport!" The sound was more like a bark, but he'd done it. He'd said his name.

Alex's brows shot up. "Wow. For a dog that just became a man last night, I'd say he's making progress. Can he say anything else?"

"He knows six words." Calliope waved a hand at her. "You try. Say Hi to him."

Feeling a little silly, as if she was talking to a child when the figure before her was clearly a man, she said, "Hi."

"Hi!" Sport said in immediate response and so forcefully, Alex jerked back and laughed.

"Very good, boy." She reached out and caught herself before she patted his head.

"He can say bye, please, thank you, and good."

"I am impressed. All in one day?"

"Just think what he could do in a week."

She shook her head. "He's not going to be human for a week. Not if I can get hold of Madame LeBieu or Lucie."

Calliope's smile faded. "Ah, but I like Sport like this."

"You liked him as a dog."

"But this way I have a man to hang around with." She smiled again. "And he's pretty darned good-looking for a man, don't you think?"

Sport smiled, baring shiny white teeth.

"Still, it's not fair to Sport to be stuck in a man's body. He's not cut out to live as a human and we don't know how long the spell will last. If you teach him how to be human, how will he feel when he goes back to being a dog?"

Calliope pouted. "Ah, Alex, you take all the fun out of things."

She pulled Calliope into a hug. "I'm sorry. It's the practical side of me. The one that took care of a dozen siblings for years."

"And here you are trying to take care of me." Calliope sighed and stared down at Sport sitting so naturally at the table. "And Sport."

"I'll give my mother a call and see if I can talk our way out of dinner with the family."

"Good idea. Maybe you'll have better luck than I did. I can't say no to your mother."

"I think she's got a little Voodoo magic in her." Alex headed back to her purse in the hallway, calling over her shoulder, "No one can say no to her." She dug her phone out of the bottom and hit the speed dial for 'Mom,' noting all the missed calls she'd had from her and Theo.

Why couldn't he get it through his thick head she wasn't interested?

"Hello," a bright female voice answered.

"Let me speak to Mom," she demanded.

"Nice. I'm home for one day and my big sis doesn't even say hello. I see how it is."

Alex prided herself on recognizing each of her sibling's voices over the phone. As the oldest daughter, she was always the one calling to remind them of someone's birthday. "Sorry, Amelia. When did you get in?"

"I drove up from New Orleans this morning. I'll be here a few days."

"Good. Why don't you come by the gym while you're in town?"

"I will. I could use a good work out."

"Is Mom around?"

"No."

"No? Where is she?" Her hope of getting out of dinner dwindling, she stared across the room at Calliope and Sport.

"She should be back any minute. Had to run a pot of soup to Mrs. Badeaux. Apparently she's laid up with the gout."

"Tell her to call me when she gets back, please."

"Why don't you talk to her when you come to dinner?"

Because I don't want to come to dinner. Alex bit down on her tongue. She hadn't seen Amelia for several months.

"Oh, wait." Her sister laughed. "You don't *want* to come to dinner, do you?"

She sighed. "How'd you guess?"

"Dolley and Madison told me about the man Mom's got lined up for you."

"So it *is* another match-making attempt. I knew it."

Amelia chuckled softly. "Dolley and Madison were all excited. They said he's really cute. Even I'm looking forward to meeting him."

"Good. You can have him. I'm perfectly happy single."

"Honey, you're preaching to the choir. But Mom means well."

"I know. I've just had something come up and well..." How did she explain over the phone about her dog becoming a man? No one would believe it.

"The only way you're going to get Mom off your back is to bring a guy home."

As if a light bulb went off in her head, she stood with the phone in her hand, staring straight ahead, ideas exploding within.

"Alex? Did I say something wrong?"

"No. No, you didn't. In fact, you said something so right, I can't believe I didn't see it for myself."

"What did I say?"

"Nothing. Just tell Mom I'll be there for dinner."

"I'm taking it that it's not on my account, although I'll be happy enough to see you."

"Of course I'm coming for you, sweetie." *And to parade a man in front of Mom to show her I'm capable of getting one on my own.* Perhaps Lucie's Voodoo was exactly what she'd sold it as, the answer to her prayers, her dreams come true. "And tell her to set an extra plate at the table."

Finally, she'd get her mother off her back.

She clicked the cell phone off and called out, "Calliope, we've got work to do if we're going to dinner at Mom's house."

CHAPTER 5

ED STEPPED INTO THE MARINA BEFORE FIVE O'CLOCK IN THE EVENING, hoping to catch Joe Thibodeaux before he called it a day.

A white-haired man stood behind the counter, digging through a box of what looked like junk to him.

"Mr. Thibodeaux?" he called out.

"Ain't no mister here," the older man grumbled and jerked his hand out of the box, a hook buried in his thumb. "Name's Joe."

"Joe." Ed closed the distance. "Need help getting that out?"

"Got it." Joe jerked the hook out and stuck the bleeding thumb into his mouth. "What can I do for ya?"

"I need a fishing guide."

"*Mais,* now maybe I can help you out." Joe studied him. "What kind of fish are you hopin' to catch?"

Thinking back to his encounter with Theo Ledet, he answered, "Largemouth bass."

"Been bitin' pretty good back in Bayou Black." Joe rubbed his thumb on his jeans. "Wanna go with a group or solo?"

Being in a group would advertise his inexperience. "Solo."

Joe set the box on the floor and straightened. "When you figurin' on going out?"

Ben had said something about the locals knowing the optimal times to fish, and Joe was supposed to be one of the best guides around. "I understand you're the expert in these parts. What time is good for you?"

"Anytime's good time for me. But if you wanna catch largemouth bass, the water levels will be right in the early morning or late at night. Gotcha some spinners or buzz bait?"

He had no idea what the man was talking about, but didn't want to let on. "Not yet. I have my pole but hoped to get bait here." He glanced around the dingy interior of the marina. Racks of every kind of lure, hook, line, and bait stretched before him in a daunting array. "You've been fishing these bayous, Joe, I trust your knowledge. What works for you?" With a quick glance at the older man, he let go of the breath he'd been holding throughout the whole bait question.

Joe led him down the aisle and picked out several spinners and buzz bait combinations. "These oughta work. And if you plan on catching flathead catfish while we're out, you'll want some of these." He pulled a plastic container from the glass-front refrigerator on the side wall, opened it, and grabbed a couple of balls of something nasty looking.

The stench nearly knocked him to his knees. Eyes watering, he pulled his shirt up over his nose. "What the hell is that?"

"Best stink bait in south Louisiana." Joe's leaned his nose over the container and sniffed. "My own recipe. Stinks like hell. Just the way catfish like it."

A recipe Ed had no intention of ever using. "I'll stick to bass for now, thank you."

Joe shrugged. "Missing out on some good catfishing. Mozelle Reneau has a mighty fine recipe for fried catfish and okra. Might even get her to fix up a mess, if you get a hankerin' while you're here."

"Thanks, but I'm just here to fish." He didn't think he could ever eat catfish again, knowing what these people used for bait. "Bass fishing, if it's all the same to you."

Joe sealed the lid on the stink bait container and placed it back in the refrigerator. "So when do you want to head out?"

"How early is early morning?"

"We'd leave at five. Gotta be here by four-forty-five to stow your gear."

He was really wishing he'd been volunteered for any other job but this one about now. "Then I guess I'll see you at four-forty-five tomorrow morning."

When he walked out of the marina with his purchases, Joe walked out with him, locking the door behind him. "Speaking of fried catfish..." The marina owner tipped his nose into the air.

He did the same and the scent of fried fish made his stomach turn over.

"That would be my dinner callin' me," Joe said.

A four-door Ford Fusion pulled up to a house two doors down from the marina. A gray-haired man got out, reached into the back seat and pulled out a small suitcase.

"Another tourist?" Ed asked, trying for casual curiosity.

"Yup. Called this mornin' looking for a cottage to rent. Just lucky I had a cancellation or he'd be out of luck."

"Is he from around here?"

"Said he's from New Orleans. We get a lot of folks out from New Orleans. They like to get away from the hustle and bustle." Joe's lips twisted. "I certainly understand that. Usta live there myself."

"You did?" He faced the older man, sure he was pulling his leg. He acted as if he was part of the bayou, born and bred.

"You'd never know it by looking at me, but I was a high-fallutin' lawyer back in the day."

"And you gave it up for this?"

"Damn right I did." Joe scratched his scraggly beard. "Ain't never looked back."

"Why?"

"You know what lawyers are like." Joe hitched his jeans. "It just wasn't me."

Having gone up against some of the slimiest attorneys Louisiana had to offer, Ed nodded. But then he wasn't sure he got the lure of the bayou. Not yet. So far it was hot, steamy, and full of insects and other less savory creatures. The sooner Leon Primeaux went to trial, the sooner the Ragsdale woman could leave the swamp, and him with her.

"The man say why he's here?" Ed asked.

Joe rocked back on his heels, digging his hands into the back pockets of his faded, ragged jeans. "Same as you."

He did a double-take before he realized what Joe was talking about. "Avid fisherman, huh?"

"*Mais*, he said he was looking for some good fishing." Joe's mouth twisted. "Not sure about avid. Have ta wait and see."

"Has he hired a guide yet?"

"I asked him, but he said he just needed a boat, no guide." Joe's brows dipped. "Don't like renting my boats until I know whoever's taking it knows his way around the swamp. Mr. Mills said he can get around on his own. Hope I don't have to go lookin' for him."

Interesting. A tourist wanting to get out on the bayou by himself. He made a note to keep an eye on the man. "Mills, huh? A common enough name."

"First name's not so common."

"Oh, yeah?"

"Oscar." Ed shook his head. "Reminds me of one of those kids' puppet shows on TV." Joe hitched up his pants. "I better get going. Don't want to be late to Miz Mozelle's dinner table. See you in the morning."

Ed glanced at his watch. He had just enough time before dinner to get back to his cottage and make a call to Ben.

He made it back to the rental without being accosted by alligators or Boyettes. As soon as he entered, he placed a call to Ben, leaving a message for him to run a search on Oscar Mills, assuming that was his real name.

With thirty minutes left to kill, he thought he might use it to figure out what the hell all this stuff was he was expected to use at the butt-frickin' crack of dawn.

He sat on the front porch and spread out the equipment he'd purchased. "This can't be all that difficult." Hell, if those folks on the reality shows could fish in the bayous, an educated man from Baton Rouge ought to be able to do it. He pulled his computer tablet out and cursed at the lack of WiFi. Okay, so he was on his own. With a half hour to go before the dinner gauntlet at the Boyette cafeteria, he was determined to make it work.

He started by trying to let out a little line from the rod and reel combo. After several attempts, he leaned back with no more line out than he'd started with. Short of tearing the reel apart, he didn't have a clue.

"You have to press the lever on the side to loosen the line," a small voice said from beside him.

He jumped and nearly decked a boy with black curly hair and bright blue eyes.

Beside him stood a girl with softer features but of the same height and with the same blue eyes.

"Let me guess," Ed said. "Boyettes?"

They nodded in unison.

"Do you all come in pairs?"

Again, in unison, they shook their heads.

"Do you have names?" he asked.

"I'm Teddy," said the girl and she pointed at the boy. "He's Roosevelt, but everyone calls him Rosie."

The boy's eyes narrowed and his fists clenched. "Only if they want a fat lip."

Ed raised his hands in surrender. "Okay. I'm not looking for a fight. Roosevelt it is."

The two sat on the porch at his feet and stripped the lures from their packaging.

"I take it you've done this before," he stated.

"Our oldest sister's been taking us fishing since we were little," Teddy offered. She released the line from the reel with practiced ease and threaded it through the rings along the length of the pole.

Since the twins couldn't be more than six or seven themselves, that meant their sister had been taking them fishing since they were toddlers, barely out of diapers. "She must be pretty good at it."

"She is," Rosie said. "Knows all the good places to go." He tied a lure to the end of the line and hooked it to one of the rings.

"Does she guide fishing tours?"

Teddy reeled the line in until it grew taut, the hook on the ring anchoring the line so that it didn't fly around. "No, she owns a gym in Morgan City."

Ed made mental notes about the kids' handling of the rod and reel so that he could do that later without looking completely inept. "She owns her own gym?"

"Yes, sir." Rosie arranged the other hooks, lures and spinners in the tackle box. "We go there for Karate lessons."

"Sounds like she's looking out for you," Ed observed. He hadn't had any older siblings to look out for him. Since his own parents had died when he was four, he'd been pretty much on his own to figure out important things like tying his shoes, let alone lures on fishing lines. Some things he'd mastered on his own, others he apparently had to learn from seven-year-old strangers.

"You're coming to dinner aren't you?" Teddy stood and brushed the dust from her cutoffs.

"Yes, ma'am," he said.

She nodded, all serious. "Good, 'cause we came to get you."

He put the pole and tackle box inside the door and locked the cottage before setting off across the yard to the Boyette house, Teddy's little hand in his and Rosie marching alongside, too much of a man to hold his hand. He marveled at how small and yet trusting Teddy was and how good it felt to have a child's hand in his. Made him feel big and somehow more responsible. He shook off the unwelcome idea and concentrated on what lay ahead. Kids...who thought they'd be...well...not so annoying? Or was it only in small doses?

Having an escort reminded him of the nightmare of what he was in for that night. Dinner with an army of children who all looked and sounded alike. So much for escapes. The Boyettes had him surrounded. He'd have to wring Ben's neck next time he saw him. This place...this family...should have come with a warning label.

* * *

"WITH THE NEW CLOTHES, shoes, and haircut, it'll work," Calliope said. "Trust me."

Her stomach churning, Alex slowed the closer they got to her mother's house. "I don't know. It seemed like a good idea two hours ago, but now I'm getting cold feet."

Sport walked upright between them, his gaze darting around at every movement, his feet still clumsy in the over-sized shoes they'd borrowed from Maurice Saulnier. Once, Calliope had to jerk him back from going after a cat. Alex had to hold him steady when a squirrel raced up a tree in front of Miz Mozelle's house.

This is a really bad idea. She almost turned and ran back to her house at least half a dozen times in the few blocks they'd gone. "He has the attention span of a..."

"Golden retriever. Give him time, he's been human for less than a day." Calliope hugged Sport's arm. "You're a good boy, Sport."

"He *is* a good boy. Poor, baby." She could imagine the dog's confusion after waking up a man and then having her wave a decorative pillow at him when he'd done nothing wrong. She hugged his other arm, partly out of love for her dog, and partly to keep him from seeing Granny Saulnier's pink poodle out of the corner of his eye.

They'd come all the way across town without any major incidents. They could make it through one meal at the Boyette house. It wasn't new territory for Sport, just a new perspective. Armed with the training they'd given him throughout the early evening, he should be able to handle one evening with the family. With so many people at the table, Sport wouldn't be required to say much.

Unless...

"God, I hope Mom doesn't go all Inquisition on Sport." Her cold feet got colder. "If she starts giving him the third degree and he answers with woof, I'm sunk."

"Why don't you just tell your mother what really happened?" Calliope leaned around the man in the middle. "She might be of help getting Sport back to where he belongs."

Torn between lying and dealing with yet another dud her mother dragged off the streets, Alex was ready to try anything. "I really hope by bringing Sport over as my manfriend that I can put the kibosh on Mom's matchmaking."

"You could have done that with Theo," Calliope said.

She shuddered. "I didn't want Theo at the dinner table with my family. I care more about by family than to subject them to that creep."

"Point taken, but you and I both know that if your mom doesn't like Sport as your *manfriend*, she'll keep pushing men at you."

"I have to do something. She's making me crazy." Alex held tight to Sport as a bird flew down in front of them, snatched a bug off the road, and flew away. Maybe it wasn't the best idea to use Sport for this lie. She had never been good at lying to her mother. The woman was psychic or something. She could see right through her and every one of her children. The taste of soap in her mouth lingered in her memories of the times she'd been caught telling lies.

As they approached her childhood home, Calliope whispered, "Last chance to back out."

On the verge of performing an about-face, she ground to a stop.

From the opposite direction, Teddy and Rosie led the tall, dark and handsome man she and Calliope had run into early that morning when they'd been chasing Sport through the streets.

"Oh, my God," Alex muttered. "Of all the people she could be trying to set me up with..."

"The man from this morning." Calliope giggled. "I can't wait to hear the conversation at the dinner table."

"Mom will be mortified if she finds out I was out chasing a naked man through the streets in my nightgown." She tried to turn, dragging Sport with her. "Turn around before he sees us. Quick!"

Sport tensed and refused to go the other way. Apparently he recognized the twins and wanted to greet them as always.

"Uh-oh. We accounted for Sport being comfortable at your mother's house, we didn't take into account that he'd want to jump all over your siblings, like he usually does." Calliope strained to hold the man back as Alex dug her feet into the ground.

"Holy hell. Heel, Sport," she said as quietly and firmly as she could.

Sport's body trembled from head to foot, but he heeled.

"Think that man will recognize us from earlier today?" Calliope asked.

"Pray he doesn't."

With the strength of his one-hundred-seventy-pound body in his favor, Sport dragged the women to the door of the Boyette home, arriving at the same time as Teddy, Rosie, and the stranger.

"Alex!" Teddy dropped the man's hand and rushed forward, hugging her around the middle.

Rosie, with a little more restraint, hurried to hug her as well, leaving the man standing alone by the steps.

Teddy remembered her manners first. "Come meet Mr. Marceau."

So the man had a name.

She glanced across at him, guarding her expression. "Mr. Marceau."

"Call me Ed." His gaze locked on hers, a smile tugging at the corners of his lips. "So we meet again...Alex, is it?"

"Alex Boyette," she said in a rush, her nerves compromised by his devastating half smile. She wondered how much more disturbing a full smile would be. The widening grin let her know he remembered her from that morning. So much for going unnoticed in a small town. She held out her hand. "Nice to meet you."

"Nice to put a name to a...face." His warm tone and the strength of his fingers curling around hers sent a rush of electric current washing over her. She yanked her hand free and turned to Calliope. "These are my good friends, Calliope and Sport."

Ed shook Calliope's hand and reached out to shake Sport's.

Sport stared at the hand.

She nudged him in the side and whispered, "Shake!"

Sport's brows furrowed and he lifted a limp hand.

Ed shook it and let go.

One more hurdle passed. She let out a breath and turned toward the house. "Let's go in," she said, her voice high, strained. "This was a really bad idea," she muttered beneath her breath.

Ed climbed the stairs beside her, "Did you say something, Ms. Boyette?"

"No, no." Her cheeks burned. She was a terrible liar. "I just can't wait to see what Mom has fixed for dinner."

Inside offered no relief from outside. Hugging Sport close to her, she led the way through the hallway and into the large dining room where it looked, to the untrained eye, like the Boyettes were having a family reunion. The only one missing was Ben. And her father. A pang of sorrow pulled at her heart. Frank Boyette had loved every one of his nineteen children and made it a point to talk to and hug each of them at least once each day.

A tiny hand slipped into hers. "Alex, sit by me, please."

She smiled down at the littlest of the Boyette brood. "Hey, Molly." She lifted her five-year-old sister in her arms and hugged her close. "How's my sweet baby girl?" Her mother constantly reminded her that she could have had children Molly's age by now. Even Teddy and Rosie's age, if she'd started having kids right after finishing college.

"You look so natural holding a child, Alex. You need some of your own." Barbara Boyette sailed into the room, carrying a large platter of fried catfish, setting it down in the middle of the oversized table her husband had made out of an antique door he'd found in a building they'd been tearing down in Morgan City. He had prided himself in making something out of nothing and never lost an opportunity to instill in his children a sense of thrift and ingenuity.

God, she missed him. She could have moved to a larger city where she would have made more money and put her marketing degree to better use. But she had a lot of reasons to hang around and help her mother. Eighteen reasons to be exact.

Her mother swooped in to nab Ed. "Oh, you did make it. Good." She hooked her arm through his and led him to the seat next to her usual spot and pushed him into it. "You'll sit, here." She glanced at Alex. "Alex, honey, put your sister down and come introduce yourself to Mr. Marceau. I believe you two are closest in age."

Holding Molly like a shield, she shook her head. "Mom—"

"Doesn't she look like she'd make a great mother? She's single, you know." Her mother rested a hand on Ed's shoulder and smiled across at her. "Hurry and sit, dear, the fish is getting cold."

Barbara rounded the table and hugged Calliope. "Oh, dear, it is so good to see you." Every time she saw Calliope, her mother embraced her like a long lost relative. Even though she'd seen her two days earlier. "And who do we have here?"

Calliope smiled, her lips tight. "What's your name?" she said to Sport.

Sport's eyes grew wide and he barked, "Sport!"

Her mother laughed, "Well, then Sport, nice to meet you. I'm so glad you could come to dinner with Calliope." She squeezed Calliope's arm. "Nice to see you dating again."

Calliope shook her head. "I'm not—"

"You two can sit across from Mr. Marceau and Alex."

Alex swallowed a moan as her mother sat her friend and Sport across the wide table from where she was expected to eat.

"Ed, Sport, meet the family." Her mother pointed as she went. "Ben's the oldest, and he's not here right now, but you know him already. Alexandra Belle is next, then Harry and Truman, Amelia, Abraham, George Washington, Dolley, Madison, John Kennedy, Thomas, Edison, Paul Revere, Susan B, Woodrow, Eleanor, Teddy, Roosevelt and Molly B." She breathed in and sighed. "Did I leave anyone out?"

"No, Mom," Alex said. "That about covers it." This was always the point at which any halfway interesting man her mother coerced to the dinner table got that glazed look and found a convenient excuse to escape as quickly as possible.

Her mother shooed some of her siblings into the kitchen to fetch the rest of the meal.

She studied Ed. His eyes weren't glazed and he didn't have that deer-in-the-headlights look. In fact, his lips were twitching with what looked like the beginning of a smile. He wasn't bad-looking. Some women would find him very attractive. Ah, hell, who was she kidding? He was sexy, handsome, and had a great smile.

Alex's biggest problem with him was that her mother had set her up, once again, and she wasn't interested in a relationship. Not now when she barely had time to run her business. Between the deal she was working to provide hospital employees access to her gym and now Lucie's hex, she was booked. No time for love or dating. Still...he was nice-looking and his grip had been firm, not limp like that of some of the men Alex had met. Never mind the electric current that had zipped up her arm at his touch.

"Is there something I can do to help?" she asked, rather than take her designated seat beside the man who'd seen her practically naked in the street that morning.

"No, no, Truman and Amelia are—well, bless my soul, there they are now with the fixin's."

Truman and Amelia entered through the swinging kitchen door, carrying heaping bowls of red beans and rice. They were followed by Dolley, struggling under the weight of a platter spilling over with hush-puppies, Madison with a bowl of green tomato relish, and JK carrying two pitchers of iced tea.

As Amelia passed Alex, she whispered, "He is a hunk, isn't he? Wouldn't mind waking up to him every morning."

She groaned. Even her sister was in on her mother's plot to marry her off.

"Please, everyone have a seat." Barbara Boyette lifted her hands like a conductor and everyone scrambled for their seats. She was no exception. Old habits died hard in this family. She pulled out her chair in time for her mother's hands to fall, and sat, as cued, her shoulder brushing Ed's.

She scooted away, glancing down at Molly who had managed to squeeze into the chair beside her. For the first fifteen minutes, most of the conversation centered on passing trays of food and comments praising the chef. She waited for her mother's usual lead-in to her oldest daughter's availability.

Calliope cut Sport's catfish and Sport managed to spear the bites with his fork, cleaning his plate faster than anyone else. He always did like Mom's fried catfish when he was lucky enough to get the leftovers.

Throughout the meal, Alex barely touched her food, her heart lodged in her throat, waiting for Sport to do something that would make her mother ask more than her usual amount of questions.

When everyone filled their plates and eaten a good portion of the food, her mother started the conversation. "Mr. Marceau is a friend of Ben's, up from New Orleans for vacation."

"Please, Mrs. Boyette, call me Ed," he said.

She shoved a forkful of catfish into her mouth with the hope her mother wouldn't ask her a question she'd be expected to answer.

"Are you single, Ed?" her mother didn't waste time.

Alex fumbled with her fork and it fell to the floor between her and Ed.

They both reached for it at once, knocking heads.

Ignoring the pain, she whispered, "Please don't mention this morning."

Ed stared across at her and winked.

"Sorry." She grabbed her fork and sat up quickly, ignoring the scent of Ed's cologne. He smelled really nice. She hoped he was as nice as he smelled and honored her plea.

"Yes, ma'am, I'm single," Ed answered. "I was married once."

"Widowed or divorced?" The matriarch popped a bite of food into her mouth.

"Mom," Alex warned. "You're grilling your guest."

"Not at all." her mother waved her hand. "I'm getting to know him."

Ed's lips twitched. "My wife left me, claiming I was never home. And no, we didn't have any kids."

Alex prayed her mother would end her inquisition. Unfortunately, it was not to be.

"Are you in law enforcement, like my son?" Alex's mom asked.

"No, ma'am." Ed tugged at the collar of his shirt before answering. "I'm a trained mediator." The tips of his ears turned a little red.

Alex studied him in her peripheral vision. Interesting. Her own ears heated and turned red every time she told a lie. Was Mr. Marceau lying to her mother? "What exactly does a mediator do...Ed?" She hesitated over his name as if by saying the name it brought them even closer than side by side at the dinner table.

Again, his ears reddened. "A mediator is someone people go to in order to help them settle disputes out of court." He turned to her.

"Teddy and Roosevelt tell me you own a gym in Morgan City. What does a gym owner do?"

Before she could open her mouth, her mother jumped in. "She helps old ladies like me stay in shape, don't you, honey?"

"Yes, Mom, thank you."

"I bet you work out a lot," he commented. "I like to jog, myself." He popped a bit of catfish in his mouth and chewed.

Alex stewed, waiting for him to out her with her mother.

"The best time to jog around here is early in the mornings," Dolley said. "Right, Alex?"

The tips of her ears burning, she replied. "I wouldn't know. I save my energy for the gym... for the most part." *When I'm not chasing a naked man through the streets.*

"I prefer jogging in the morning." Ed looked up with a challenging smile. "You never know what you might see."

She nudged Ed with her knee and regretted it when a shot of awareness sped through her system at the simple touch.

"Sport, we're so glad you could join us this evening." The consummate host, her mother turned to Sport and Calliope and saved her from the conversation leading to the reveal of her early morning antics.

She clenched her fork and shifted her anxiety from one issue to another, praying for divine intervention.

Her mother smiled. "Sport's an odd name for a man. Alex has a dog named Sport."

"We all had a good laugh over it, didn't we, Alex?" Calliope smiled brightly. "Sport and Alex went to Tulane together."

"You did?" her mom queried politely.

Calliope whispered into Sport's ear and he barked, "Yes!"

"Are you staying in Bayou Miste, Sport?" she asked.

Calliope whispered again and Sport barked, "Yes!"

Alex saw it coming and waited for the next question.

"Really?" her mother asked. "Where?"

Calliope stared pointedly across the table at Alex.

She couldn't let her friend bear all the burden of the charade and jumped in with, "Actually, Mom, he's staying at my house."

"Oh." Her mother looked from Sport to her and back. "Are you two...you know...?" her gaze panned the table of young people. "Maybe we should discuss this later." Her lips pressed together.

"We're friends, Mom," she provided. "And yes, discussing it later would be best."

"Ed, Ben tells me you're an avid fisherman." Her mother drew attention back to her choice of men for Alex.

"I'm hoping to spend my vacation doing a little fishing. I've scheduled a guide for early tomorrow morning."

"Oh, that's too bad. Alex is very familiar with the bayous and knows all the best places to fish, don't you, dear? Perhaps she can take you out in the evenings after she finishes up at the gym."

"Mom, Mr. Marceau would probably rather go with his guide. Besides, I have Sport visiting."

"I could watch Sport while you take Ed out on the bayou," Calliope offered. "I mean, I could keep him company."

She glared at her friend.

Before she could back out of it gracefully, Ed sealed the deal with a smile and, "I'd like that."

The younger children finished their dinners before their older siblings. To avoid further questioning, she jumped up to help Molly, Teddy, Rosie, and Eleanor clear their plates. By the time they ran off to play, the adults had finished. Dolley and Madison gathered the rest of the empty plates and started in on the dishes.

"I'll help," Alex offered.

"No, *ma chère*." Her mother headed her off before she could duck into the kitchen and disappear. "Why don't you give Mr. Marceau a tour of the garden? *C'est magnifique* in the starlight."

She pulled her mother to the side. "Mom, stop playing matchmaker. I know you care about me, but I don't need help finding a man. Besides, like I said, I have Sport staying with me for a little while. Men aren't going to want to go out with me while I have a man staying at my house." There, that lie slipped off her lips a lot easier than the last. And it wasn't totally a lie. Sport *was* a man...for the time being.

Alex's mom touched her arm, her forehead lined with worry. "Sport seems nice and all, though kind of quiet. Are you sure you want to have a man stay with you, alone in your house?"

"I'm twenty-nine, Mom, not nineteen." She patted her mother's hand. "I know what I'm doing."

"Mr. Marceau is such a nice gentleman."

"Yes, I'm sure he is."

Her mother patted her arm again. "Then show him around the garden, and I promise not to bother you anymore."

She knew better than to believe her. "I can't leave Sport alone."

"I don't know why. He and Calliope seemed to have hit it off." Her mother smiled toward her friend and her man-dog. "She's quite taken with him. I saw her whispering to him all through the meal."

Calliope chose that moment to wave at her and called out, "Sport and I are headed back to your house."

"I'm coming," she said.

"Alex, please," her mother begged.

God, she hated it when her mother begged. Since her father had passed, she hadn't been able to say no to her mother.

"Stay and visit," Calliope offered. "I can manage Sport by myself."

"See?" Her mother beamed. "All taken care of."

This is not happening. All the effort to parade Sport in front of her mother as her boyfriend had somehow backfired. Now her mother had it in her head that Sport was Calliope's main man. *If only she knew.* If she had been a good daughter, she'd have been honest with her mother at the start. The opportunity to tell her the truth had come and gone about the time she introduced Sport in the first place.

"Fine." She waved her friend off and turned to find Ed. "One spin around the garden and I'm out of here." She didn't look forward to spending time alone with the man, not when his touch made her skin tingle and his semi-smiles brought on an attacks of butterflies in her belly and a strange ache between her legs. But if it would get her mother off her back, she'd do it and get back to her real issue—finding a way to turn Sport back into a dog.

CHAPTER 6

Dolley and Madison had Ed cornered in the living room, refusing to give him the opportunity to escape through the door and out of the Boyette house. They'd filled him in on their summer job duties of guiding tourists through the Beauregard Sugar Plantation House. Then they'd gone into a discussion of the different classes they were taking toward degrees in Marine Biology at Tulane. Listening to the pretty young girls in stereo was giving him a headache. He glanced around for help getting away and spotted Alex headed toward him.

"Mom said she promised you a tour of the garden. Come on." She grabbed his arm and practically marched him toward the rear of the house.

As they stepped out into the warm, humid night, he breathed in the thick bayou air and let it out.

Alex didn't give him time to absorb the ambience, though, jerking him down the steps of the back porch and onto the lush green lawn.

"In a hurry?" he asked.

"A night tour of the garden won't take long in the dark and you'll be free to go," she said, her tone short, clipped. Something had her panties in a twist.

Remembering a pair of black, lace panties, he wanted to know what had her riled. If it was him, even better. He purposely slowed.

Because she had hold of his arm, she was forced to match his pace or let go. "Do you always run around with your hair on fire?" he asked.

Alex's lips tightened and she glanced across at him, letting go of his arm. "I'm sorry. My mother makes me nuts."

"She obviously cares about her children."

"I know." Alex sighed and walked to the edge of the bayou canal. "Sometimes too much. Thanks for keeping this morning's incident to yourself. I'd never hear the end of it, if my mother found out."

"You're welcome." Ed leaned against a cypress tree and crossed his arms. "I have to admit, I've seen some crazy stuff, but never a man streaking through town followed by a woman in a sexy nightgown." He chuckled, the image still fresh in his mind and equally as tantalizing.

Alex's cheeks grew a deeper shade of pink and her lips twitched into a smile. "Must have seemed pretty strange."

"I was warned they did some crazy things down in the bayous, but what exactly was your friend Sport doing running around town in the altogether?"

"He was..." Alex glanced in all directions and finally stammered, "...he was getting some air." She shrugged as if streakers were an everyday occurrence in Bayou Miste. "Sport is a bit of a free spirit. A nature-lover."

"Are you in love with Sport?"

"We've known each other for a while and I love him dearly...as a friend." Alex blinked. "Not *that* kind of friend. I mean, we're not doing anything. Although he did sleep in my bed last night, but that was before I knew—" She stopped, clapping a hand over her mouth. "I'm sorry. I must sound crazy. It's been a helluva day and I'm having difficulty processing it all."

"You seem to be popular in these parts. Your mother says you're single, but I ran into a guy in Morgan City who said his girlfriend was an Alex Boyette. Is there more than one of you?"

Alex moaned. "For the record, I don't have a boyfriend. I don't want a boyfriend, and the man you met—"

"Theo," Ed offered.

"—is on the verge of being slapped with a restraining order." Alex dropped onto a nearby stone bench and buried her head in her hands. "All I want to do is run my business and be left alone. Why can't my mother understand?"

He sat on the bench beside her and stared out at the canal in front of him. "You're lucky to have a family who cares."

"I know." She sat back and stared out at the water, too. "My life is too complicated right now."

For a few minutes he said nothing, enjoying the peace of the bayou as the cicadas began their song and frogs croaked. "I take it you're the sister who taught Teddy and Roosevelt all they know about fishing?"

Alex snorted. "It doesn't even touch what my dad taught me, but I'm trying to fill the space."

"When did he pass?"

"Two years ago." She sniffed and touched a finger to the corner of her eye. "I miss him," she whispered, her voice catching.

He slipped an arm around her.

When she stiffened. He assured her, "Don't worry, I'm not interested in a relationship either. I'm here for a short time, then I'm gone."

After a moment, she leaned into him.

He marveled at how natural and warm and good it felt, her body nestled into his. "Whose idea was it to name all of you after famous people?"

"Dad's." She laughed. "He thought it would be easier to remember our names."

"He had a point," Ed said. The stars laid a blanket of diamonds across the water and the big blossoming flowers all around them gave off a soft, pleasing scent. He could almost see the attraction one might have to bayou living.

But the longer he sat with Alex curled into the crook of his arm, the more uncomfortable he became. His groin tightened, his body heated, and those damned black lace panties flashed through his mind like a persistent neon sign. Finally, he removed his arm and stood. "Well, that should satisfy your mother. I'll just duck in and tell her thank you and be on my way back to my cottage."

Alex stood and laid a hand on his arm. "Ed?"

Her touch lit his blood on fire and it was all he could do not to pull her into his arms. "Yes, Alex?"

"Thanks for not saying anything about...well, you know."

"It'll be our little secret."

Then she leaned up on her toes and pressed a kiss to his lips.

Before she could get away, he captured her around the waist and deepened what was probably meant as a chaste, thank-you kiss into a damn-you-and-your-black-lace-panties bruising kiss that left him breathless.

When he set her back on her feet, he wondered who was more surprised by the kiss, he or she. "In case your mother was watching," he lied and beat a hasty retreat, afraid if he stayed, he'd be in a lot more trouble than he already was.

Now would be a good time to get out on the bayou and check out how his witness was faring. Things had gotten far too dangerous in town.

* * *

ALEX HURRIED BACK to her house on the other end of Bayou Miste, her head in a whirl, a deep ache building at her core. All because of one little ol' soul-defining-curl-a-girl's-toes kiss. What was supposed to have been a quick walk in the garden had turned into something a lot different.

Ed.

What woman in her right mind fell for a guy named Ed? "Not that I'm falling," she muttered aloud. "Not in a million years. I have a house of my own, a business in Morgan City, a family who needs me and a dog..." She clutched her hair, ready to rip it out. "Oh, my God, I have a dog who needs to be returned to his rightful body." She knew she didn't have time in her busy schedule for a romance, no matter how badly she now wanted to get laid. Relationships required time—a commodity she didn't have a lot of. Besides, Ed would be leaving town at the end of his vacation to return to New Orleans.

From what she had observed of friends with long-distance relationships, they didn't work.

Besides, her business and her family were here and took up all of her time. *Get it through your thick head!*

Alex jumped back and screamed as a large, male figure stepped in front of her.

"Hello, Alex."

Pressing a hand to her thundering heart, she funneled all her frustration into the one person she had no desire to see... "Theo Ledet, you scared the begeesus out of me."

"Sorry, I just wanted to see you."

"By slinking around in the dark?" She planted her fists on her hips. "What the hell are you doing in Bayou Miste? I told you, I don't want anything to do with you. That one night at the Raccoon Saloon was a mistake."

"I thought you loved me."

"Read my lips, Theo. I. Don't. Love. You." She'd tried letting him down softly, but nothing had gotten through to him. Not talking to him, not yelling at him. "I had too much to drink. I wasn't thinking clearly. What happened was a *huge* mistake."

"But I want to marry you. Make an honest woman out of you."

She stared at him, realizing she was talking to a very dense brick wall. "Tomorrow, I'm going to march down to the county courthouse and file for a restraining order. Do you know what that is?"

He nodded. "Uh-huh."

"It will mean that if you get anywhere near me, you will be violating the law and they will throw your sorry ass in jail." She inhaled and let it out slowly, trying to bring her pulse rate down. "Theo, leave me alone. Please."

She didn't give him the opportunity to respond. Instead, she pushed past him and jogged the rest of the way home. The entire way she felt as if she was being watched. Twice she almost tripped over her own feet looking back to see if Theo had followed her. The street was clear, but the feeling continued all the way to her house.

The door was locked and she had to knock; a creepy sensation like a spider web floating over the back of her neck made her knock again, louder than she'd meant to.

Calliope yanked open the door. "What's wrong? Where's the emergency? Between you and Sport, you'd think the bayou was on fire."

She fell through the door and slammed it behind her, shooting the bolt home.

Sport stood beside the door, his eyes narrowed, his lips pulled back over his teeth, a rumble building in his chest.

"Is he growling?" she asked.

Calliope stroked Sport's arm. "It was the weirdest thing. Just before you started banging, he rushed to the door and did his human version of barking, then growled. What's out there?"

"Theo, for one."

"That jerk-wad. What did he want?"

"What do you think he wanted?" She pushed the spooky sensation to the back of her mind and kicked off her shoes.

"To marry you and give you a dozen children just as dumb as he is?"

"You got it."

"Well, you said you wanted someone who would love you no matter what."

"Yes, but I also want him to be able to string more than two words together in a sentence and sound halfway intelligent."

Calliope's lips twitched up on the corners. "Like Ed Marceau?"

"I don't know what you're talking about." Her ears burned.

"Ha! So you two did more than smell the roses as you walked through the garden, didn't you?" Calliope pointed a finger in her face. "Don't lie. Your ears are turning red. Fess up. You have the hots for the mediator."

"He's here on vacation. When he leaves, he's gone."

"So?" Calliope spread her arms wide. "What's it hurt to have a little fling? Who knows, you might end up tossing your dirty sweatshirt in the ring and moving to the Big Easy."

"I'm not moving to the Big Easy. My business and my family are here."

"You aren't responsible for raising your siblings. Your mother has a good handle on that and they're growing up."

"Yeah, but they don't have Dad around anymore to teach them the things they need to know that Mom doesn't have the time or inclination to teach."

"Like what?"

"Fishing, karate, self-defense. How to tie a slip knot."

"Honey, they can join the Boy Scouts."

"My love-life is not what's in question at the moment." She stared at Sport curling up on the couch, yawning. "We have to get Sport back to normal." She squared her shoulders and pulled on her mud boots. "Can you stay with him while I pay a visit to Madame LeBieu?"

"At night?" Calliope shivered. "In the dark? Aren't you afraid of getting lost?"

"I know my way around the bayou day or night. Besides there's a sky full of stars and a nearly-full moon rising. Plenty of light to get around. I shouldn't be gone for long."

"Promise me you'll be careful."

"I know the risks." Yeah, but she didn't know why she'd been so spooked minutes earlier. She shrugged it off as a residual effect of her encounter with Theo. "Don't stay up."

"Where do you want Sport to sleep?"

"He seems comfortable where he is. You can have my bed or the futon in the spare bedroom."

"I'll take the lounge chair, just in case Sports wakes in the night."

"Thanks for helping."

"I'm glad I had the night off. Remember, tomorrow night I have to work."

"Oh, yeah. And Mom volunteered me to take Ed out fishing at night. I hope Madame LeBieu has an answer to our Sport problem by then." Alex grabbed a flashlight and let herself out the front door. She glanced right then left, peering into every shadow, that creepy sense of being watched still as strong as when she'd entered.

Theo must have scared her more than she originally thought. Bayou Miste was a quiet little corner of the bayou, free of crime and bad guys. Well, for the most part. There was the time when Ben had come to flush out the man responsible for the attacks on congressional candidate Jason Littington. And the guys who'd tried to kill Craig Thibodeaux's fiancée, Elaine, when she'd discovered them dumping pollutants in the bayou.

Okay, so it wasn't as quiet and safe as she liked to think. But, damn it, she had to get to Madame LeBieu and undo the damage to Sport. She'd be careful and keep her eyes and ears open for bad guys and alligators.

She set off across the road and down the bank to the canal where she kept her skiff tied off to a cypress tree. She stepped in and, with her paddle, pushed away from the bank and pulled the rope to crank the motor. It chugged, spit out a cloud of smoke and engaged. With her hand on the till, she spun the little boat around and skimmed along the still surface of the canal. As she passed the marina, a movement caught her attention and she turned to look back, studying the shadows at the corners. Nothing moved, no one stepped out. Yet, that sense of being watched persisted until she reached a fork in the channel and headed out into the bayou where Madame LeBieu's shack had stood for as long as Alex could remember.

She could find her way with her eyes closed, as many times as she'd visited Lisa and Lucie LeBieu growing up. It still felt strange to know that Lucie wouldn't be there. Having married Ben, they'd moved to Baton Rouge over a year ago. Lisa, her twin, was in and out between her life in Atlanta and her home here in Bayou Miste.

As she skimmed across the water, she let the events of the day slip from her shoulders. To many, the bayou at night might appear spooky, filled with deadly creatures and magic. To Alex, it was the time she remembered her father most. He'd bring her out to fish under the stars. She and Ben had been the oldest and spent more time with him on the occasional weekend he took off from his business of shrimp fishing in the gulf. They'd sit in silence for the most part, hooks in the water, waiting for a nibble. They had been good times that brought back even better memories.

Alex slid into the little dock in front of Madame LeBieu's house, tied off, and stepped up onto the rickety wooden planks. Before she reached the front porch of the weathered structure with the peeling paint, the old woman flung open the door and filled the entrance. She wore a bright pink, red, and yellow muumuu and a flamboyant red scarf tied around her head and knotted in a big bow. Her light mocha skin glowed in the moonlight, her dark eyes sparkling like the stars above. "Alexandra Belle Boyette, what you be doin' in de bayou dis late at night?"

"Hi, Gran LeBieu." She climbed the steps and hugged the woman who was as much a grandmother to her as she was to her own granddaughters. She'd spent many nights in Lisa and Lucie's room with Calliope going over teen magazines and talking about the boys at school. "I came to see my favorite Voodoo priestess."

The old woman waved her toward the door. "Come in, come in. I have chicory abrewin'."

"Thank you, but I can't stay long." As Alex followed Madame LeBieu into her ancient kitchen, memories washed over her, making her long for the simpler times when her dad was still around, and she and her girlfriends only worried about what to wear and who to gossip about. She ran her hand along the edge of the antique stove where Lucie had concocted a love spell that seemed to have turned the town of Bayou Miste upside down.

"Tinkin' 'bout ol' times?" Madame LeBieu pulled a ceramic mug off a shelf and poured the fragrant chicory-flavored coffee from an old metal pot. "Tell dis ol' woman what be troublin' you."

Alex plopped onto a stool, leaned her elbows on the big butcher block at the center of the kitchen and buried her face in her hands. "Oh, Gran LeBieu, everything's a mess."

"Did not de *gris* help wit' de wishes?" she asked.

Alex dropped her hands and stared across at the Voodoo queen. "That's what I'm talking about. The pouch you helped Lucie make, what kind of magic was in it?"

"A little o' dis, a little o' dat." The woman shrugged. "Did your wishes come true?"

"No!" Alex stood and paced across the room. "That little *gris* bag turned my dog into a man. Mom finally came up with a decent matchmaking candidate who kisses like nobody's business, and I have a man-dog living with me who pees on rose bushes and chases Granny Saulnier's pink poodle. I don't recall wishing for any of that." She flung her hands in the air and faced the Voodoo queen. "Help!"

"Drink." Madame LeBieu filled another cup with chicory-flavored coffee and sipped from hers. "All will be well, if you give de magic time."

"But I don't have time! Poor Sport doesn't have a clue what's happened. Calliope is teaching him how to be a man. What happens when the spell wears off and he goes back to being a dog? He'll be so confused. And I don't have time to keep him out of trouble. He's learning how to open doors and talk, but he's still a dog."

"Dis dog is much smarta dan you tink." Madame LeBieu set her cup on the butcher block and smiled at her. "He learn what he need to know because he loves you. In time, you will be glad o' dat."

"Can you see the future?" She grabbed the old woman's hands and squeezed. "Will this mess clear up before I go insane? Before I have to own up to the whopping lie I told my mother about Sport? I don't know how much more of this I can handle."

Madame LeBieu squeezed her hands. "You be fine, my sweet Alex. All will be well in time."

"Can't you give me something to put things back like they were? A potion. An anti-spell *gris gris* pouch. Anything. I need my life back in order."

"Was you life so great?"

"Yes! I have my own business, I'm close to family. I was happy."

"And alone."

Oh, no. Not Gran LeBieu, too. "I like being alone!"

"Do you?" Madame LeBieu's intense gaze brooked no lies.

"Mostly." She did miss male companionship. Her lips still tingled from that kiss she'd experienced with Ed, leaving her with a whole lot more longing than she'd started the day with. "Okay, so it's been a little lonely lately."

"And you not be gettin' younger."

"Oh, please. You sound like my mother." She pulled her hands free of the old woman's. "Twenty-nine is not over the hill."

"No, but you have so much more love to give, for a man, for children."

"I have enough children in my life."

Madame LeBieu shook her head. "Not you own."

"I don't even have a man in my life, how can I even think of children?" She pushed her shoulders back. "I take it you don't have anything in your bag of tricks to help me out of this colossal mess."

The woman spread her arms wide. "De magic mus' run its course."

Tears welled in Alex's eyes—of frustration and anger. Not so much directed at the Voodoo queen. She couldn't find it in her heart to be mad at this woman who had the best interests of her community at heart. She was angry at her own dissatisfaction that led to her rash wish, and her inability to alter the resulting events. "Thank you anyway." She rounded the butcher block and hugged the woman close, inhaling the scent of perfume that reminded her of her friend. "I miss Lucie."

"She, too, misses you, *ma chère*." Gran LeBieu patted her back. "Give de magic time."

"You don't have a spell that will make me more patient do you?" She leaned back and stared into the woman's dark brown eyes, almost black with her magic.

"Maybe, der is someting dat will help." She shifted Alex away from her, and went to her pantry where she kept everything from sugar and flour to the spit of a tailless raccoon. When she returned, she held something in her hand. "Close you eyes," she commanded.

Alex closed them, laughing nervously. "You aren't going to turn me into a frog, like you did Craig Thibodeaux, are you?"

"No, *ma chère*. Shush and listen to you heart."

Something like powder touched her face. She flinched but kept her eyes closed tight. For a moment, Alex almost wished she'd kept her mouth shut. Madame LeBieu's spells always worked out, but the process sometimes proved tricky.

"Ezili Freda Daome, Goddess of love and all dat is beautiful, listen to our prayers, accept our offerings, and enter into our arms, legs, and hearts."

Alex listened as a soft rumbling like the drums of the ancients thrummed in her head. Her senses sharpened, her thoughts cleared, and her focus centered on the Voodoo queen's softly spoken words.

"Mistress of love, hear my plea,
help dis woman's eyes to see
As troubled times mus' be unfold
to loose de bonds of past dat hold
and know de course when darkness reign
and sacrifice tho gives her pain
help her to embrace de right
for only love will win de fight.
Ezili Freda Daome, Goddess of love and all dat is beautiful, hear me now."

With a soft touch on her arm, Madame LeBieu broke her trance. "Go, *ma chère*. De hour grows late."

She blinked her eyes open and stumbled toward the door and out to the dock. As she steered her skiff back home, she went over what the Voodoo queen had said, analyzing every word of the old woman's *cunja*. What did she mean troubled times unfolding? Hadn't they already unfolded with Sport turning into a man?

Around the bend in the channel, she went. Where the water had been smooth as glass from the route she'd come, she noticed the residual waves of a recent disturbance, headed out the opposite direction. Alex spun on her seat and studied the wake in the moonlight until another bend in the path blocked her view.

A chill slithered down the back of her shirt and she revved the throttle, sending her little boat skimming toward the little town of Bayou Miste and home, telling herself that whoever was traversing the swamp this late at night was probably out frog gigging or fishing. Uh-huh. Then why did she hear the sound of drums echoing in her head like a recent memory?

CHAPTER 7

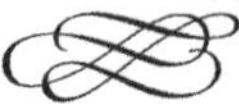

Ed held his GPS in front of him as he inched along the waterway, praying he could find the way at night as easily as he had during the day. The bends and forks in the liquid back roads weren't as clear as they'd been before and he wasn't sure, but he thought he'd heard another engine. He'd killed his motor immediately and listened.

Yes, it had been another motor. By the way it gave off a high-pitched, fading whine, it was a small one, headed the opposite direction. When it faded into the distance, Ed restarted his own engine and continued his trek through the bayou for several miles until he came upon what appeared to be an abandoned shack jutting out of the marsh on stilts, tucked into a stand of cypress trees on a rare knoll of land.

He tied off on the ramshackle jetty and climbed out of his boat.

Nothing stirred. No lights shone from the window. As it should be. The Ragsdale woman and her guard were given strict instructions to remain at the rear of the cabin at all times. The windows in the back had been spray painted black to block any light from shining through.

When he pushed the front door open, he waited for someone to challenge him.

Not a sound. His senses on alert, he pulled his Glock from the case on his belt and eased through the door

The cold nose of a rifle pressed into his side.

"You better be Ed," a deep, deadly voice stated, "or you're dead."

"Relax. It's me." Ed pushed the nose of the weapon away, cleared the doorway and closed it behind him before flipping on his flashlight with the red lens cover.

"Well, damn. I'd hoped to get to shoot someone." Marcus Caldwell led the way to the back of the house.

Ed chuckled. "That bad?"

"Worse," he stated. "It's been one of those days. One lousy day and she's already bored and ready to return to Baton Rouge, hit men be damned."

"I feel your pain." He thought he had it bad in town. It was nothing compared to being stuck in the bayou with a demanding, pain-in-the-ass mob informant. "Any movement?"

"A couple of guys came by in a pirogue rigged with a trolling motor right at sunset." Marcus snorted. "Thought I might get to shoot someone then. Turns out they were frog giggin'."

"Did they nose around or see anything?"

"Nope. It was if they never even saw the old house back here."

"Good. I know you'd rather be where the action's at, but the less people who know anyone's out here, the better."

"Yeah, yeah." Marcus paused in front of a closed door. "Anything going on in the real world?"

"I wouldn't know. I wouldn't consider Bayou Miste the real world."

"Gotta be better than spending time with the informant from hell."

Ed clapped a hand on Marcus's back. "I spoke to Ben earlier. He said Leon isn't talking and from the calls they've monitored, they've gotten nothing."

"So we don't know when he'll have his people make their move."

"No." Ed smiled in the faint glow of the flashlight. "Cheer up. It won't be long. The trial is in three days. Primeaux's thugs have to be looking for their star witness."

Marcus patted his rifle. "I'll be ready." Then he opened the door to the kitchen area at the back of the house.

"About time you got back." Phyllis Ragsdale sat in a folding chair at the collapsible camp table they'd set up in the empty kitchen. She wore shorts and a tank top that didn't quite cover her ample, surgeon-supplied breasts. With her brassy, bleach-blond hair piled on top of her head, she leaned back and propped her bare feet on the ice chest, fresh blue polish gleaming in the light from the Coleman lantern. "Did you bring me the chocolates I asked for?"

Ed reached into the backpack he'd carried up from the boat, pulled out a bag full of every kind of chocolate bar Morgan City's dollar store had to offer and tossed it on the table in front of her.

"Oh, there is a god." She dug into the bag and ripped into the first bar, sinking her teeth into the chocolate caramel and peanuts. "I might survive after all," she said, chewing and talking with her mouth open. "That good fer nothin' louse get fucked in the slammer yet?"

"No, Phyllis," Ed replied. "He's waiting in his very own jail cell until the trial."

"I hope someone jacks him up." She took another bite of gooey chocolate. "He ain't done nothin' but slap me around from the day we met."

"You didn't have to stay with him," Marcus pointed out.

She snorted. "Yeah and I lived in a bed of fuckin' roses? Once ya know somethin', you know somethin'. If he hadn't got caught with his hand in that senator's cookie jar, he'd still be knockin' me around. Between me and the senator, we'll put the bastard away." She smiled up at Ed, chocolate clinging to her teeth. "Then I'll have more time for the likes of you, Eddy."

He hated it when people called him Eddy, especially trash-mouthed women like Phyllis. She'd called him Eddy from the time he'd loaded her into the SUV to the time he'd dropped her off at this Cajun-bubba version of a safe house. If he hadn't needed her testimony so badly, he'd have thrown her to the alligators on the trip out.

"I'd better get back," Ed said. "I have to be fishing out on the bayou early in the morning."

"I don't want to hear your hard luck story, Marceau. While you're sleeping like a baby on a real bed, I get to spend the night in a folding chair, watching over Ms. Pottymouth."

"Oh, you can't leave yet." Phyllis lurched out of her chair and waddled her way over to him, walking on her heels with her wet toenails in the air. "Dontcha wanna stay and play cards? I play a mean strip poker." She draped an arm over his shoulder and ran her fingers along the V of his polo shirt. "Really, I lose, every time," she purred, pressing her boobs against his chest.

He grabbed her wrist and removed her other hand from his shoulder. "I'd rather poke my eyeballs out. But thanks for the offer." He stepped away before she could get her octopus arms around him again. "Why don't you play a hand with Marcus?"

"Thanks, man." Marcus glared at him. "I might just shoot you anyway."

Phyllis pouted. "He's no fun. He keeps threatening to shoot me."

"Yeah, he's like that." Ed chuckled and slipped the straps of his backpack over his shoulders. "He's a trigger-happy son of a gun." He leaned close to Marcus as he passed him on the way to the door and said in a tone loud enough for Phyllis to overhear. "If she gives you any trouble, shoot her in the knee. It'll keep her from moving around and she'll still be able to testify."

"Hey!" Phyllis cried. "I'm not deaf."

"Give the dog a bone." He nodded to Marcus. "If you have any troubles, send up a flare."

"They don't pay me enough for this gig," Marcus groused.

"No, they don't." He opened the door and clicked on his flashlight. "You don't have to walk me out."

"Please. I can use the fresh air after all the nail polish fumes." Marcus walked him to the front door and they stood in the shadows as they scanned the bayou below for movement.

After several long moments Ed whispered, "All clear. See you tomorrow night. Can I bring you anything?"

"A gag for her mouth?"

"You got it." He left, dropping down into the boat and turning on his GPS to get him back. He'd be glad when this assignment ended and Leon Primeaux was safely tucked away in a federal prison for life. He could get back to civilization, away from the bayou and the temptation of kissing a certain bayou princess.

Hell, why did he have to go and think of Alex? Even after visiting the woman from hell, his libido jacked up every time he thought of Alexandra Belle Boyette and that kiss.

That *damn* kiss.

* * *

ALEX BENT TO tie her tennis shoe. As it neared the end of her day at the gym, she was so tired, she could barely see straight. She had struggled throughout to keep up with, much less lead, her aerobics classes and had taken a nasty kick to the jaw in her black belt karate class.

That's what lack of sleep got you. She'd tossed and turned after her trip to visit the Voodoo queen. When she did drift into a troubled sleep, she'd dreamed she was running through town in her nightgown. Ed was at the end of the street, waiting for her, his arms open wide.

Joy filled her heart and she tried to run faster, but her feet sank into mud, the suction pulling her back. The sound of Voodoo drums filled her head and a dark presence stared out at her from the shadows of Bayou Miste. Suddenly she was alone on a tuft of land in the deepest, darkest part of the bayou, surrounded by cypress trees whose branches were draped in long swaths of Spanish moss, sweeping low to the ground like arms reaching out to her.

A dark silhouette disengaged from the shadows, stalking her, his eyes glowing red in the moonless night.

She tried to scream but no sound came out of her. As the fiend steadily advanced on her little island amidst the stagnant water, she saw the flash of a light-colored animal headed her way. It was Sport. Not the man he'd become, but the dog she knew and loved.

Right when the man reached his hands out to clutch her throat, Sport leaped into the air.

"Earth to Alex."

She shook her head and looked up, taking a moment for her eyes and mind to focus on her twenty-seven-year-old sister, Harry. "What's up?"

"You have ten minutes until your next aerobics class. Do you want me to take this one? You look beat."

Alex dropped onto a metal folding chair and sighed. "Would you? I don't know what's wrong with me. I don't have it in me today."

"Could it be you were up all night dreaming?"

"Yes. As a matter of fact, I was."

"About a certain hunky man?" Harry grinned.

Boy did Harry have it wrong, but then if she explained her dream, she'd probably end up spilling her guts about Sport, the Voodoo hex, and her late night trip into the bayou. What was easier, confessing to the insanity or letting her sister believe she'd stayed up all night mooning over a very sexy man and a kiss she wouldn't soon forget?

"I saw you kissing him in the garden. So did Mom and everyone else. Did she finally strike gold and find you a keeper?"

Alex refused to meet Harry's knowing gaze. "He's all right."

"All right. You were playing tonsil tag long enough that he had to be more than all right."

"Please, Harry. Ed's in Bayou Miste on vacation. When he leaves, he's out of my life. Why get attached?" Alex heaved herself out of the chair and walked over to the punching bag, giving it a light cuff with her fist.

"Because he's nice, good-looking, and apparently a good kisser." Harry grabbed the bag and held it steady.

Alex bounced up on her toes and swung at the bag like a boxer. "So?"

"So? So why don't you see where it goes? He'll be here at least a week. That's plenty of time to find whether or not he's a possibility."

"Harry, he lives in New Orleans. That's two hours from Bayou Miste. He has a job; I have a business. Do the math. It wouldn't work, even if I wanted it to. Long distance relationships don't last."'

"You don't have to stay in Bayou Miste, you know."

"It's my home."

"So, come home to visit every once in a while. What would it hurt for you to get out in the big wide world and see more than the stinkin' bayou?"

"Says the one who lives in Morgan City. I never wanted to leave, you did. Speaking of which, why haven't you?"

Harry shrugged. "I don't know. I guess I was waiting for you to go first."

"You'll be waiting a long time."

"Hey, wait a minute. This discussion isn't about me. It's about you and the very distinct possibility of you finding someone to love."

"In Ed?" She chuckled. "The best I can hope for is a quick fling. I'm not moving, and we're back to 'where does he live?'" She bounced again on her toes and threw a side kick at the punching bag. "It won't work."

"But Mom thinks you—"

She kicked the bag again hard enough that Harry staggered back. "Why is it Mom worries about me, when you're just two years younger and don't have a boyfriend?"

"Probably because you're closing in on thirty and your biological clock is ticking." Harry grinned and stepped away from the punching bag as Alex slammed it again with another kick. "How about I take that class for you?" Her sister backed away and made a run for the dance room where the aerobics class was held.

"Did you kick all your frustrations out, or should we go away and come back later?" Calliope led Sport into the gym, keeping out of range of the swinging punching bag.

"It's okay, I don't think I could kick again without falling on my ass."

"Ass," Sport repeated and grinned at Alex.

"No, Sport," Alex said, reaching out to touch his arm. "That's a bad word."

He tipped his head. "Why?"

Alex looked from him to Calliope. "This is new."

"We've been watching TV all day. He's a childlike sponge. You wouldn't believe all he's learned today. He's actually stringing together sentences. Go ahead, ask him something?"

She stared at Sport. "How are you, Sport?"

"Fine, thank you," he said, his words stilted but clear and understandable, not barked like those of the night before. "How are you?"

Alex laughed and clapped her hands. "Very good, thank you." She hugged him and hugged Calliope. "Amazing."

"Yeah, I know. And I hate to leave him, but I have to work tonight and I need to go home and change first."

"Right. You don't know how much I appreciate your staying with him all day."

"It was a pleasure, really. Sport's such a nice guy. A girl could fall for someone like him."

"Calliope..."Alex frowned. "He's a dog. Don't forget it."

She sighed. "I know." Then she stood on her toes and pecked Sport's cheek with a kiss. "But I love him as a man or a dog. Gotta go!" She turned and ran for the door, her eyes suspiciously moist. Before she reached it she stopped and turned. "Oh, and your kitchen sink has a leak. I put a bucket under it and called your mom." Then Calliope was gone.

"Why she leave?" Sport asked.

Alex studied Sport, still shocked that he was speaking so well within such a short amount of time. "She has to work."

"Why?"

"Because she has to make money."

"Why?"

"You need money to pay for things like food and a place to live."

"Do you work?"

She laughed. "Yes, Sport, I do. But right now, we can go home. Harry is taking my last class for the day."

"Calli..." Sport's lips twisted and he started over. "Callipuppy loves Sport?"

"Yes, Sport. Calliope loves you." With a gentle smile, she hooked Sport's arm and led him toward the door. "I love you, too."

"Sport hungry."

"Then let's get you something to eat and get home to see what's going on with my kitchen sink."

They stopped at a barbeque restaurant and got two brisket sandwiches to go. By the time they reached Bayou Miste, Sport had eaten his way through both and was begging for more.

She parked the car in the driveway. Before she switched the engine off, Sport bounded out and ran up the porch steps and into the house.

"Sport, wait!" Had Calliope left her front door unlocked? She hurried after the man-dog. Noises from the kitchen drew her there.

Sport stood by a figure lying on the floor. "What are you doing?"

The man with his head tucked under the kitchen cabinet, answered, "Trying to fix a leak. Where's Alex?"

"Hello?" she called out from the hallway.

"Oh, Alex." The man's head came up fast, banging into the pipe above him.

"Ed?" She entered the room. "What are you doing in my kitchen?"

"Your mother asked if I'd ever fixed a leaky pipe in kitchen sink." He scooted out from under the sink and sat up, rubbing the back of his head. "I didn't know then that she meant *your* sink. She gave me a key and sent me down the street to this house."

Alex crossed her arms. "I'll have a word with my mother. You're on vacation, not here to be her handyman."

"I never was much of a handyman, but I have fixed a leaky kitchen sink before. And I looked it up on the internet." He stood, the width of his shoulders making Alex's kitchen seem much smaller than before.

Her heartbeat stuttered then beat faster, slamming blood through her veins. This man had been in her dreams, in her thoughts, and in her head all day long. Having him in her kitchen was...well...overwhelming.

"Are you done?" she asked, her voice a little breathy, to her dismay.

He wiped his hands on a dishtowel, nodding. "Try it out for yourself."

Alex would rather have stayed across the room from him. Not that she thought he would attack her or anything. More because she didn't want to be attracted to him or risk being close enough to kiss. But he waited for her to test his handiwork.

She eased past him, the scent of his aftershave playing havoc with her senses.

With her attention on him instead of her faucet, she reached for the handle blindly and turned it.

Water poured out of the drain below the sink and sprayed her legs. She jumped back and ran right into his chest.

"Damn." Ed reached around her and turned off the faucet. "Guess I need to try again. Give me a minute, and I'll have it fixed." He dropped down on the floor and slid under the cabinet again, soaking his shirt. "Could you hand me that pipe wrench on the floor beside you?"

She scooped the wet wrench from the puddle of water and handed it to Ed. "Righty tighty, leftie loosey," she said from memory. Her father had taught her that saying, while helping her work on her first car when she was sixteen.

"I knew that." Ed twisted the wrench to the right. "Try it now."

"You sure you don't want me to check it out first?" she asked.

"Well, actually, you might want to."

She dropped to her haunches and ducked into the cabinet, her chest pressing against his. "What seems to be the problem?"

"This pipe connection is old and had come loose." He pointed to the pipe. "I thought I was tightening it, but I guess I loosened it instead."

She had stopped listening as soon as Ed started talking, the vibrations of his chest rumbling against her breasts, causing her entire body to tingle.

"You want to tighten it yourself?" he asked. When she didn't respond, he said. "Or not." His gaze captured hers. "Maybe we should leave it to a plumber."

Alex straightened and backed away so fast her foot slipped in the water and she fell on her ass beside him.

Ed scooted out from under the cabinet and pulled Alex into his arms. His fingers skimmed along her arms and down her back, sending mini shockwaves into her skin everywhere he touched. "Are you okay? Anything hurt?"

"Only my pride." She moved and winced. "And my tailbone."

"Does that mean our fishing night is off?"

"I don't think I could sit comfortably in a boat after that." What a great excuse to get out of a night alone with Ed.

"Alex?" Calliope's voice called to her from the front of the house. "Why's the front door open?"

"In here." She struggled to stand.

Ed straightened and helped her to her feet as Calliope burst through the door.

"There you are." She stared from Ed to Alex. "Oh, you have company."

"No, I don't." Alex's cheeks heated. "Ed was here fixing my leaky sink." She turned the handle as if to prove it, and the pipe held. "See?" Then she remembered. "I thought you had to work tonight."

"One of the other girls asked to take my place tonight since it's cheap beer night. I thought I'd come back here and hang out. Maybe take Sport for a walk or something."

"Yes, please." Sport pushed through the kitchen door and headed for the front of the house.

"Are you sure you want to?" she asked. "I mean, there are all kinds of distractions."

"It would do us both good after being cooped up in the house all day. Be back in a little while." Calliope ran after Sport, catching up as he darted outside, the door slamming in their wake. With Calliope and Sport gone, she stood in the kitchen, alone with Ed.

Her pulse pounded through her veins as she turned to face him. "Well, how much do I owe you for your work?"

Ed gripped her elbow in his hand and pulled her against him. "One kiss," he said, his tone deep, rich, and as smooth as melted chocolate dripping over her body.

She pressed her hands against his chest, her gaze slipping from his eyes to his lips. "Just one?"

His mouth crashed down over hers, stealing her breath away. Arms like iron bands clamped around her middle, molding her body against his.

Unable to resist, she sank into him, her arms slipping around his neck, urging him deeper, her teeth parting to allow his tongue access to hers. Her leg slipped around his, the position pressing her aching center to his muscular thigh.

The kiss was so intense, she didn't register that it was her phone jangling until the sixth ring, and it was in the purse she still had hanging on her shoulder.

"You might want to answer that," Ed said, his lips skimming across her cheek and down the long column of her throat.

Fumbling blindly in the jumble of her purse, her hand curled around her cell phone and yanked it out as Ed's fingers slid the strap of her tank top off one shoulder and down her arm. She jammed her finger on the talk button. "What?" her breath caught and held as Ed's lips trailed to the swell of her breasts.

"Alex?"

Even the jarring sound of her mother's voice didn't yank Alex out of the spell Ed's hands and lips were weaving over her body. "Uh-huh."

"Are you home?"

Big, warm fingers hooked the hem of her shirt and dragged it up over her head, forcing her to take the phone away from her ear before replacing it and replying, "Uh huh."

"I asked Ed to fix your leaky sink. Is he still there?

At that moment Ed flicked the catch on her bra and her breasts spilled free. "Oh, yeah."

"Let me talk to him, please."

Past cognitive thought, she handed Ed the phone and reached for the hem of his shirt.

CHAPTER 8

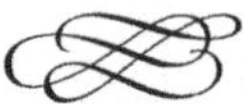

ED HELD HIS ARMS UP AS ALEX SLID HIS WET SHIRT UP OVER HIS HEAD AND tossed it across the room. Then he pressed the phone to his ear. "Ed speaking." He bent to take one lush nipple between his lips and pulled it into his mouth.

Alex moaned softly, her fingers threading through his hair.

"Oh, Ed, how'd it go?" Mrs. Boyette asked. "Did you fix the leak?"

Letting the breast slide out of his mouth, he nipped the tip before answering, "It's fixed."

He brushed his lips across the other nipple and it beaded into a tight little, tasty bud.

"Thank you so much for doing that for her," Mrs. Boyette droned on.

"You're welcome." He nipped the bud and rolled it across his tongue.

Alex's leg slid up the back of his calf and she straddled his thigh, rubbing her crotch against him.

Molten heat shot to his groin and he nearly came.

"Now, make sure my daughter thanks you properly."

"Oh, she is. Sorry, Mrs. Boyette, gotta go." He hit the end call button and tossed the phone onto the counter. When he turned his attention back to Alex, a frown was pressing her brows together.

"Maybe we shouldn't..."

"Oh, I know we shouldn't." He growled low in his chest, the most primal instinct urging him on. "If you want to stop, say so now, otherwise..." Ed cupped her bottom and lifted her, shoving her up against the wall.

She wrapped her legs around his waist and pressed her full, luscious breasts against his naked chest. "What if Calliope and Sport return?"

"Then we'll make this quick."

She breathed in and then let out a long stream of warm air that brushed across his neck. Leaning forward, she whispered, "Then hurry."

He didn't need a second invitation. Ed bent to claim her lips, thrusting his tongue between her teeth, stroking hers in a sensual dance.

When he broke off for air, he lifted her. "Which way?"

"Down the hall, first door on the left," she said, her words clipped, her breathing coming in short gasps.

His dick swelled against the confines of his jeans, aching to be free. Blinded by lust, he marched down the hall and kicked the door to her bedroom open, carried her through, and shut it with his foot.

Though her bedroom was a study in femininity with a pink and yellow floral comforter and light cherry furniture, all he could see was the bed.

"Put me down," Alex said. Her legs slid to the ground and she stood in front of him, ripped the buckle loose on his belt, and stopped. "Are you packing?" She pointed to the holster attached to his belt where he kept his Glock.

He shrugged. "I hear there are really big alligators in these parts." He tweaked her nipple, rolling it between his thumbs. "Does it bother you?"

"No, my brother carries." She reached for the button on his jeans. "Besides it makes you seem more dangerous." When she couldn't get the button free, she slid her fingers into his waistband.

"Dangerous, huh?" He brushed her hands aside and yanked her bicycle shorts down to her ankles, where he noted her bright pink toenail polish gleaming up at him.

She stepped free of the garment and kicked it to the side.

He groaned.

Instead of black lace panties, she wore a neon green thong, the tiny patch of fabric covering the apex of her thighs and nothing else. With a grin, she hooked the thin elastic band and slipped them off.

Quicker than he could say *orgasm*, he pulled his wallet from his back pocket, and fished out a small foil packet. He tossed it to her and she caught it. While she tore it open, he kicked off his shoes and peeled his wet jeans off, laying them, gun and all, across a chair. "Last chance to change your mind."

Her gaze slid over him, catching on his erection. "No way you're backing out now. Show me what this handyman can do." She slid the condom over his cock and circled her hand around him, leading him by his staff toward the bed.

"Just so you know," she said as she scooted her butt onto the mattress and spread her legs wide. "I'm not interested in a long-term relationship."

"How long is long?" He captured her face between his palms and tipped her head back. "I'm here for a week. Two tops."

"I like my independence." She wrapped her legs around his middle and pressed her heels into his buttocks.

"I hope that's not all you like." He slid into her slick entrance and her channel tightened around him, drawing him deeper.

Alex fell back against the mattress, her head tipped back, her fingers pinching her nipples as he drove into her again and again.

Long, black hair worked free of her loose braid and spread across the pale pink and yellow comforter. Her gorgeous curves made him want to bury himself inside her. Her heels dug into him, urging him faster, deeper, harder until he was hammering, the intensity of his thrusts driving him to the edge far sooner than he'd expected.

One last time and he pulled free and dropped to his knees between her legs.

Alex leaned up on her elbows, her face flushed, her eyes glazed. "Why did you stop?"

"I want you to feel it, too."

"Oh, hon, I am."

"Not like you're going to." He spread her thighs and kissed a path up to her damp core and thrust his tongue into her.

"Okay. I'm beginning to see what you mean." She dropped to her back her fingers clutching his hair. "Please, continue."

He chuckled and parted her folds, moving in to take the sweet spot by storm.

One flick and she moaned. Another and her back arched off the bed, her fingernails digging into his scalp.

His cock swelled even more as he sucked her clit between his lips and pulled hard.

"Oh, my, don't."

He let go and blew a warm stream of air over her heated sex. "Want me to stop?"

"Oh, my, don't...stop!" She dragged him by the hair back to where he'd been. "Please!"

He swiped his tongue over her in a long steady stroke, then flicked the tip, again and again until her body tensed, her hips rising, pumping. When he had her where he wanted her, he stood and scooted her up on the mattress and climbed between her legs.

In one long forceful thrust, he drove into her as deep as he could and held for a moment to gather himself. He leaned over her and captured her mouth with his as he withdrew and slid back into her, settling into a steady rhythm, the pace increasing with the pressure inside him. He held tight to his control for a full minute then let go, allowing the sensations to catapult him into the heavens. Buried deep inside her, he dropped down onto her, breathing hard.

When he could think again, he rolled to his side, taking her with him.

Alex wrapped her arms around his neck and pressed her face into his neck. She didn't say a word.

He brushed the hair out of her face and tipped her chin up. "Are you okay?"

For a long moment, her face remained pressed to his neck and she didn't speak, then she slapped her hand on his chest and pushed up. "No. I'm not all right." Alex glared at him and rolled off the bed.

"I'm sorry. How did I hurt you?"

"Damn it." She stood in front of him, her hair curling around her naked breasts, her shoulders back and fire flashing from her eyes. She was so beautiful it took his breath away.

Alex pointed to her door. "Get out."

"I must have misunderstood." He eased off the bed. "When you said please continue..."

"Just leave." Her voice caught and if he wasn't mistaken, those were tears trembling on her lashes.

He pulled up his damp jeans and zipped.

Her bottom lip trembled and one lonely tear made a shiny trail down her face.

Up to that point he had been ready to leave. But this...

"Oh, hell, Alex." He reached out and yanked her into his arms, crushing her to him.

Her body shook against him, her tears wetting his chest. "It wasn't supposed to be like that."

"If you'd tell me what it was supposed to be like, maybe I could do better." He tipped her chin up and stared into blue eyes swimming with tears.

"You don't understand." She shook her head, more tears slipping down her cheeks. "You're supposed to be a fling. I'm not supposed to be that impressed. You're leaving!" She flung her hand in the air, catching him on the chin.

He flinched and drew back without loosening his hold around her middle.

Alex's eyes rounded. "Oh, Ed, I'm sorry. I didn't mean to hit you." She leaned up and pressed a kiss to the spot she'd hit him. Her mouth moved along his jaw line to his lips where she seared her mark on him.

His hands slipped down to the swell of her bottom and he tightened his hold as heat flowed south, swelling his cock yet again, where it nestled against her belly. When she broke off the kiss, she leaned her forehead against his chest. "This was a mistake."

"Didn't feel like one to me." He tugged her closer, rubbing the ridge of his jeans into her soft skin. "Let me get this straight. You're disappointed because you weren't disappointed?"

"Yes!" She palmed his chest, the sound like a slap. "Now I need you to go and never come back."

He chuckled. "Problem is, I'm having a hard time leaving." Again, he pulled her into his arms and held her, enjoying the feel of her breasts, the taut muscles beneath satiny-smooth skin, and the curve of her narrow waist right before the sensuous flair of her hips. "Yeah, a really hard time."

Alex pushed away and sighed. "Thanks anyway, but we can't do that again." She turned and gathered her clothes, slipping into her stretchy bicycle shorts and grabbing a baggy T-shirt from a drawer. When she had pulled the shirt over her head, she faced Ed.

He frowned and slid his feet into his shoes. "That's it?"

"I told you. I don't believe in long-term relationships, especially long-distance relationships.

Why he felt the need to argue, he didn't know. But when he opened his mouth to tell her he wanted to see her again, he didn't get the chance.

"Alex, we're home!" Calliope's voice cut through the tension-thick air.

Alex's eyes widened and she ran for her bedroom door. "Stay here until I get your shirt. And don't say a word."

"Why?" Then a thought hit him. "Hey, you and Sport aren't together, are you?"

"Huh? He's my—" She clamped her lips shut and stared at him then turned toward the door. "Just stay."

Before she could sneak out, her door flew open and two faces peered in.

"Alex?" Calliope's eyes grew as wide as saucers and her mouth dropped open.

Sport's eyes narrowed, his lip curled back in a snarl, and he actually growled.

"I think that's my cue." Ed eased past the pair, ducked into the kitchen, grabbed his shirt, and escaped through the back door. Instead of walking straight back to his cottage where he stood a chance of running into more of the nutty Boyette clan, he pulled on his shirt and headed the opposite direction, passing by the marina.

The sun was well on its way to the horizon, painting the sky in brilliant shades of orange, purple, and mauve. He couldn't see past the anger simmering just beneath the surface.

His phone vibrated in his pocket and he yanked it out. The caller ID indicated yet another Boyette to torment him. One he was obligated to answer. "What?"

"Ed?"

"Yeah, who did you think it was?"

"What's wrong?"

I just screwed your sister, she threw me out, and I'm not sure why, although I have my suspicions. "Nothing."

"Good, got something for you. Not much to go on, but thought I'd pass it on." He paused. "You sure you're all right?"

"Just spit it out, will ya?"

"Okay, okay. Although I'd like to know what's got your shorts in knot."

I really don't think you do, buddy.

"Word on the street is that Leon's put a bounty on our girl's head."

"We figured he'd hire a hit man, but a bounty?" He stopped walking, a heavy weight settling in his gut. "Damn. If that gets advertised far and wide, we'll have every thug in the lower forty-eight gunning for her."

"Yeah. It's a rumor we can't substantiate, but I thought it was worth warning you."

"Thanks."

"Anything I can do for you?"

"Got an army of bodyguards you can spare? If the rumor is true, my job here just got a whole lot more complicated." *Even above and beyond your sister.*

"You, me, and Marcus are the only ones who know where we've stashed the witness. Not even Gordon Dean knows where she is," Ben said. "Every so often he tests me by asking, but I haven't told him or anyone else. We have to keep it that way."

"Understood." He didn't much care for Gordon. As his supervisor, he had to take orders from the guy, but he didn't have to like him. Tall and cocky, he thought a lot of himself. Ed always walked the other way when he spotted his boss's shock of neatly combed white hair headed his way. The man was annoying, flashy, and too politically oriented for his tastes.

"Ed, remember, it's important for you to blend in with the locals, let them know you're really there on vacation. We can't have someone poking around asking questions about you and watching your every move. The more believable you are as a tourist, the less likely they'll follow you out to the safe house. Have you met some of the residents yet?"

"Your family seems to comprise eighty percent of the population of Bayou Miste."

Ben chuckled. "Seems that way, doesn't it? Has Mom tried to set you up with one of my sisters?"

"Oh, yeah. First night at dinner."

"Which one? Alex?"

"You got it."

"Take it all with a grain of salt. My mom is determined to get her married off before she's thirty and Alex is equally determined to retain her independence."

"I've noticed that. Besides, she'd got a man living with her." *And he growled at me when he caught me in your sister's bedroom.*

"What?"

"I take it that's news to you."

"Yeah. And here I thought she was a confirmed bachelorette. She must really care about this guy to let him move in with her. I'll have to call Mom for the scoop. In the meantime, keep your head low."

"Will do."

"Hey, Ed, if you want all the latest gossip on the comings and goings in Bayou Miste, pay a visit to Mozelle Reneau, or spend some time talking with my mother or Joe Thibodeaux."

"Got it. How's that trial going? Are you gonna free up anytime soon to help out down here?"

"Doesn't look like it. I've had some of the guys here volunteer to help babysit our witness, even Dean."

"He'd lower himself to play bodyguard to our diva?"

"I think he wants a piece of the limelight when we bring her in to testify."

Ed snorted. "I could do without that kind of help."

"Exactly the reason I chose you for the job."

"Thanks. Send the city dude to the bayou to wrestle the alligators. I see how it is."

Ben laughed. "You can handle it, as long as you don't take the plunge. Alligators love things that make a big splash."

Nice. He pocketed his smartphone and continued his stroll along the streets of Bayou Miste, keeping a close eye out for two-legged snakes and four-legged alligators. A desk job was looking better every minute.

* * *

"I CAN'T BELIEVE you did the nasty with Ed." Calliope kneeled in front of Alex, holding her ankles while she did a set of fifty crunches on a mat.

Some local businessmen played a game of three-on-three on the basketball court at the other end of the building. Sport sat on a pile of mats nearby, watching as the men played, ready to jump up and chase the ball every time it rolled his direction.

Alex had pushed herself and her aerobics classes hard today and she couldn't let up now. Every time she gave herself downtime, she thought of Ed and she couldn't afford to dwell on what couldn't be. Her abs burned with each repetition until she fell back against the mat. "It was a mistake. Can we not talk about it?"

"Are you kidding me?" Calliope let go of her ankles and rolled back on her heels. "I want all the details."

"Your turn."

"I'm not the one needing to burn off my sexual frustrations."

Alex rose to a kneeling position and pointed to the mat. "Get down and give me at least thirty."

Calliope dropped onto her back, bending her knees. "You don't have to be bitchy."

"If you're doing sit-ups," she grabbed her friend's ankles and leaned into them, "you won't have the breath to grill me with questions."

"You used to be fun." Calliope groused and, huffing and puffing, gave her a half-hearted attempt at crunches. After twenty-five reps, she collapsed against the mat. "So how was he?"

Alex sat back and drew her heels in, dropping her knees to the side and bent over until her forehead touched the floor. "Freakin' incredible."

Calliope jumped to her feet. "What did you say?"

"Freakin' incredible. He was freakin' incredible." She looked up, her heart pinching in her chest. "I told you, I didn't want to get involved with someone who wasn't going to stick around. I'm not cut out for long-distance relationships, and my life is here." Alex rose and folded the mat, stacking it in the pile beside Sport. "It's just as well. He's not into long-term relationships, either."

Calliope darted in front of her. "He said so?"

"No, but he didn't protest when I told him I wasn't into them." She dodged around Calliope and headed for the room she'd set aside for karate classes. "Come, Sport."

Sport hopped off the mats and followed.

Running to keep up, Calliope pointed out, "Those are two entirely different things. He might be looking for his perfect match. And that could be you, *couyon*."

"I'm not stupid. Don't you and Sport need to go for a walk, or something?"

Sport grinned and grabbed Calliope's hand. "Callipuppy take Sport for walk."

Calliope frowned at her. "Fine. But don't think you're getting out of talking this easily." She slipped her arm around Sport and stared into his eyes. "You're so cute. I can't resist."

Alex frowned. "Calliope."

"Don't think you can give me advice on love. *You're* the one who's all messed up." She turned and marched Sport out of the room, calling out over her shoulder, "I'll bring Sport home later."

With a sigh, Alex bowed, stepped onto the mat, braced her feet slightly apart, and bent her knees. She balled her fist and struck out at the air, pulling her arm back sharply.

"This where you take out all your frustrations?"

She spun and dropped into a defensive position, her arms drawn into her sides, ready to strike.

Ed leaned against the door, no hint of a smile tugging at the corners of his lips, his face poker-straight, his brown eyes near black with intensity.

"How did you find me?" She shook her head. "No, don't tell me. Mom." She turned away and resumed her stance, this time throwing a double punch. "Why are you here?"

He slipped out of his shoes, bowed, then advanced on her, closing the distance until he stood so close she could smell his aftershave. "What happened last night?"

She shook her head. "Nothing." Her stomach clenched. She balanced on one foot and kicked the air as if she could kick her emotions into outer space. Damn this man for coming into her world and making her question her life. "I told you it was a mistake."

"No, it wasn't. Look at me and tell me it was a mistake."

When she didn't, he laid a hand on her arm. "Alex."

Something snapped inside, and she swept out her leg, planted her palm on Ed's chest and shoved.

Ed landed on his back and she came down on him, pressing her knee into his chest. "Why can't you leave me alone?"

He lay there for a moment, staring up into her eyes. "Because I can't." Then he erupted beneath her, flipped her onto her back, and pinned her to the mat with the full length of his body, trapping her wrists above her head. "Your words are telling me one thing, but your body language has an entirely different story."

"I told you, I don't want to see you anymore."

He shook his head. "Now, see? There you go again." He leaned close, his lips hovering over hers. "Look into my eyes and tell me you don't want to kiss me."

She struggled beneath him, refusing to face him. When she couldn't break his hold on her, she made the error of locking gazes with him. All the fight seeped out of her.

"Tell me," he repeated.

"I don't..." She bit her lip, her body burning everywhere his touched hers and she wanted his lips to claim hers so badly she could taste it. "Damn you." Glaring up at him, she whispered, "Kiss me, already."

His mouth came down on hers, crushingly possessive.

When he released her hands, she threaded her fingers through his hair and dragged him closer, deepening their connection, her tongue thrusting through to slide along his.

Time seemed to suspend as they lay on the mat, locked in a kiss that rocked her world and scattered all her well-laid plans for her life and future to the four winds.

At last, Ed raised his head, his eyes glazed, his cock nudging against her. "Told you."

"Why did you come here, today?"

"I needed a work out."

"Alex?" A voice sounded outside the room.

She squirmed beneath him. "Let me up."

Ed rolled to the side and she jumped to her feet as Harry ducked through the door.

"Oh, there you are—" Harry's gaze bounced from her to Ed, who was rising from the floor, straightening his shirt. "Sorry, did I interrupt something?" She grinned. "I can come back later."

"No. You didn't interrupt anything. Ed was just leaving."

"Actually, I came to see if I could get in some time on the weights." He turned the full wattage of his killer smile onto Harry.

Alex groaned, her tummy tightened, and her core ached. How was she supposed to concentrate on her business with Ed in the building?

Harry fell for Ed's charm. "Of course. I can show you the weight room, if you like." She darted a glance at Alex. "Unless you'd rather have Alex show you."

She waved her hand. "No, please. Show him. I have errands to run, then I'm headed back to Bayou Miste. Can you take my afternoon classes?" She didn't really have anything pressing, but she had to get out of the same room with Ed to regain some sense of self-control. Every time she was around him, she couldn't think straight. Her structured existence fell to pieces.

"You could use a little time off, sis. You've been tense the past couple days. Why don't you go out for lunch, go shopping, or get a manicure? I'll cover for you." Harry hooked Ed's elbow and led him away, smiling up at him.

She loved her sister, but at that moment, she wanted to scratch her eyes out.

Ed is mine.

Whoa. Where had that thought come from? Ed was no more hers than the moon. He was temporary. She was firmly rooted in her life here in the bayou, near a family who needed her.

With a blunt reality check, she reminded herself that Ed hadn't made any declarations with his kiss or making love the previous evening. He'd bought into the short-term quickie idea and probably wanted to add it to his list of vacation activities to be enjoyed while in Bayou Miste.

She slapped a hand to her forehead. Of course. He only wanted the fling she'd offered in the beginning. Except, where she'd wanted to end it after one amazing hop in the sack, he wanted to take it through the rest of his stay.

Then what?

Then life would return to normal. The spell on Sport would wear off and Alex's structured, predictable life would resume.

She tugged her shirt in place, bowed at the corner of the mat, and left the karate room, realizing she was deluding herself. Never again would she look at those mats the same way.

Crap. Why did Ed Marceau have to pick Bayou Miste as his choice for a vacation in the first place?

CHAPTER 9

ED REALLY HADN'T HAD TIME TO WORK OUT THAT MORNING AND HE wasn't exactly sure why he'd headed for Morgan City when his job was to keep his eyes open in Bayou Miste. But after his early fishing date with Joe, he'd made a pass through town in his Jeep and headed to Morgan City.

What he'd hoped to accomplish with that kiss was another mystery.

Alex Boyette wasn't part of his plan. Bayou Miste was a detour on his road to a promotion in the Criminal Investigations Division of the Louisiana State Police Department. He knew what life as an officer of the law did to marriages. His ex-wife had left him after three years of sitting at home alone more nights than he'd been there.

Then why had he gone back for more, when Alex had told him to get out and stay out of her life?

Because she was beautiful.

No, that wasn't all. She cared about others, not just herself, and she wouldn't abandon family.

But she had a man living with her. One she'd admitted caring for.

After a quick tour of the weight room with Harry, he made his excuses and headed back to Bayou Miste and back to work. With a bounty on Phyllis Ragsdale's head, he didn't have time to play with the locals, no matter how tempting.

As he cruised through Bayou Miste, his stomach rumbled. The town was so small, it couldn't justify the usual fast-food chains. His choices were limited to the Pancake House and the Cajun Kettle. He pulled into the Cajun Kettle's lot and parked.

The outside of the building didn't inspire great confidence in what lay within. Weathered white paint peeled from the sides, mildew gave the entire building a greenish tinge, and the wrought iron tables and chairs sitting on a concrete pad had long since lost their umbrellas meant to shade customers from the hot Louisiana sun.

He pushed through the screen door and a bell jingled over his head. Inside the lighting was dim and it took a moment for his eyesight to adjust. Red and white checkered vinyl tablecloths covered the mishmash of tables and booths in the interior. The black and white linoleum tiles shouted the fifties and probably dated back to then based on their worn appearance. The order counter was so old, it looked gnawed-on by local wildlife. But the Cajun seasonings scenting the room promised better fare than ambience and made his stomach rumble even louder.

An older woman with coppery red hair and gray roots collected a paper bag from the counter and turned. When she spotted him, she smiled. "You must be Mr. Marceau. Joe's been tellin' me all about you."

"I'm sorry, should I know you?" He held out his hand.

"Mozelle Reneau, but you can call me Mozelle or Miz Mozelle." She turned to the chalkboard listing the menu items. "Clovis makes the best shrimp-okra gumbo in the parish. It is *très bon,* and the blackened catfish is fresh. Joe caught them this morning. But you know that."

Knowing what Joe used to catch the catfish, he opted for the gumbo. He placed his order with the big man behind the counter, who would better fit the role of a bouncer at the Raccoon Saloon.

While he waited, Mozelle continued to talk.

"We don't get too many folks come to visit in Bayou Miste. Seems like we've had more than our share just this week."

His ears perked. "Is that right? I thought I was the only visitor."

"Oh, no." She laid her hand on his arm. "A retired gentleman rented

Joe's cottage the same day as you rented Barb Boyette's. Funny, you two coming in the same day." She shifted her bag of food to her other hand. "Interesting man, Mr. Mills. Goes out every day in his boat for hours and comes back without any fish. Wonder what he does out there all day long." Mozelle stared into the distance then shrugged. "Who knows? We've had stranger visitors than that. Take the *couyon* who came in this morning, asking about airboat rentals. *Dis-moi la verité!* No one rents their airboats. Anyone who's been out in the bayou knows you have to have experience handling one of them and they aren't cheap."

"Did he give you his name?"

Mozelle's brows wrinkled. "No, as a matter of fact, he didn't." The bell over the door jangled and Mozelle started. "*Coo Wee!* Look at the time. I promised I'd be back in ten minutes. Joe's bound to be growlin' for his lunch. Nice to talk with you, *ma chère*. Stop by after fishin' for some beignets tomorrow morning. I make a fresh batch every other day." She scooted out the door, leaving blessed silence in her wake.

Ed took a seat by the window where he could watch the town's main street. Before long, the burly man emerged from the kitchen carrying a huge, steaming bowl of gumbo and a plate of crackers. The scent of shrimp and spices wafted up, making his stomach rumble in anticipation. As he dug his spoon into the thick liquid, the bell over the door rang again and Alex sailed in.

"My usual, Clovis, please." Alex turned to find a seat, spotted him, and rolled her eyes. "Are you following me?"

"Seems I was here first." He lifted his spoon. "Look, you might as well join me. I promise not to attack you or your food."

She frowned at him.

"Come on, Alex. Relax. What's having lunch with me going to hurt?"

"*Mais, oui*. I guess it won't." Her feet dragging, she walked across the floor and dropped into the seat across from him, letting out a huge sigh. "How long did you say you'd be in town?"

"Counting the days already?" His lips twisted. "A week, maybe two. Then I'll be gone and you won't have to bump into me anymore." That thought made a hard knot twist in the pit of his belly. Having only known Alex for a whole day, he found he liked her company and might miss it when he left.

Clovis set a bowl of gumbo in front Alex with the requisite plate of crackers.

"Thanks, Clovis." She lifted her spoon and nodded. "*Bon Appetit.*"

They ate in silence until most of the food in their bowls had all but disappeared.

"I'm glad you're not one of those women who picks at her food." Ed set his spoon in the bowl and leaned back.

"I own a gym, teaching several aerobics classes every day. I burn calories."

"Have you always been in this great of shape?" His gaze raked over her, admiring the curves, clearly defined by the skin-tight exercise outfit she wore.

Her cheeks reddened. "No. I grew up chubby. In case you didn't notice, Cajun food can be fattening. When I went to college, I learned how to control my diet."

"And your life?"

"Yes."

"So you went to college to learn how to become a control freak, huh?"

Her lips thinned. "If that's what you want to call it. I like structure. So sue me."

"And relationships are too messy?" He lifted a cracker and broke it in half, dunking it into the remaining soup at the bottom of his bowl.

"I didn't say that."

"I consider it implied."

She scraped the last bit of rice from her bowl with her spoon and stuck it in her mouth, then sat back, her eyes narrowing. "You're a mediator. I bet you have to deal with a lot of divorce cases, don't you?"

He nodded, on edge to give the right answers that fit with his cover.

"With all those divorces, I'd think you'd be the last one to believe in long-term relationships." She leveled a direct stare at him. "Have you ever been married?"

Ed's chest tightened, that knot in his gut growing. "Yes."

Alex's eyes widened and she sat up straighter. "Oh, please tell me we didn't...I didn't...with a married man."

He raised his hands. "No. I'm not married anymore. Divorced three years ago."

"Why?" This time she raised her hands. "Sorry, that's personal. You don't have to answer."

For a long moment he didn't. "It's okay. My job was too demanding. She wanted more...of me...of my time." As soon as the words were out of his mouth, her brows wrinkled into a frown and Ed realized his mistake.

"Your job? I didn't think a mediator's job was that demanding. Isn't it strictly an eight to five commitment?"

He tossed the other half of his cracker in the bowl. "The point is, she needed me around more, and I wasn't there."

Alex sat across from him for an extended, silent moment, then asked, "Did you love her?"

Ed looked down at his empty bowl. "I don't know. I've never been sure what love is, or if I've ever loved anyone before."

"I know it's a different kind of love, but what about your parents?"

"Died when I was four," he stated, his voice flat.

Alex leaned forward "Your adoptive parents?"

"Foster homes." The more she questioned, the more the gumbo in his gut churned.

When her brows furrowed and she reached out to lay a hand on his arm, he jerked away. "Look, I don't need anyone's pity. You don't miss what you don't have."

Alex shook her head. "I can't imagine having grown up without the love of my parents. Even now, I miss my dad so badly, it hurts every time I think of him."

"That's the beauty of never having loved your parents." He snorted. "I never knew mine. I feel no pain." He pushed to his feet. "Look. I don't need you or anyone else. What happened last night was nothing more than good sex."

"And that's why you came looking for me today?" she asked.

"Yes." He walked to the door without looking back into Alex's sad eyes.

Anger, he could stomach. Pity? Never.

He stepped out into the bright sunshine, dragging his shades from his pocket.

"Ed!" Calliope waved from across the street.

"Ed!" Sport echoed and waved as well.

"Wait up." Calliope glanced both ways and waited for traffic to pass.

In no mood to talk, but not wanting to be rude, he waited for Calliope and Sport.

A tractor-trailer rig rumbled past from one direction. As it passed, Calliope and Sport stepped into the road.

With their attention on the big rig, they didn't hear or see the dark, four-door sedan racing down the middle of the street from the opposite direction.

Ed edged out into the street, his hand up. "Wait," he called out to Calliope and Sport.

The car swerved toward him and accelerated.

He didn't have time to get out of the way and braced himself for the impact.

At the last moment, Sport leaped across the road and pushed him out of the way. He fell back against the curb and rolled out of range of the car's tires.

Sport wasn't so lucky. The car clipped him in the side, sending him flying into the outdoor tables and chairs in front of the Cajun Kettle.

Ed rolled to his feet, but not in time to catch the license plate. The vehicle had peeled out, leaving a trail of smoke.

Behind him, a scream rent the air and the door to the restaurant slammed open. Alex rushed forward, dropping to her knees beside Sport.

The man whimpered, a gash in the side of his face, bleeding onto the concrete.

Ed jerked his phone out of his pocket and tossed it to Calliope. "Call 9-1-1." Then he bent over the man who'd saved his life. The man Alex loved.

* * *

SPORT LAY SPRAWLED across Alex's bed, sound asleep after swallowing three pain killers and a tall glass of water. The trauma of being hit by a car had taken its toll on him, and his old canine habit of sleeping the day away kicked in.

Alex stood on one side of the bed holding his hand. "I should never have wished him to be a man."

Calliope sat in a chair on the other side, petting his arm. "He could have as easily been hit by a car as a dog, and might not have survived." She lifted his hand to her cheek, a tear trailing down her cheek. "He's been so good about everything that's happened to him so far."

"Poor Sport." Alex rubbed the masculine arm. Damn the Voodoo magic that put him in that position. "I want my dog back."

"I want Sport to be okay."

She stared across at her friend. "Oh, Calliope, you can't fall in love with Sport. You don't know how long he'll be a man."

"It's too late, Alex." Calliope brushed the hair from his forehead, careful not to disturb the bandage on his cheek. "He's gentle, he's kind, and he's everything a man should be."

"He is, isn't he? He's like another member of my family." She thought of Ed, her heart aching even more for a man who'd never known the love of a family. He'd even admitted he wasn't sure he'd loved his wife. How sad.

At that moment a knock sounded on the door.

She didn't have the heart to get up and answer it.

After a moment the front door squeaked open and footsteps echoed down the hallway.

Ed poked his head into her bedroom, then entered, carrying a box of chocolates. He laid it on the table beside the bed. "Calliope told me Sport likes chocolate. How's he doing?"

"Better."

"I still think we should have called 9-1-1. He could have internal injuries."

She had done her best with butterfly bandages, pulling the edges of the gash on Sport's cheek together. She too would rather have taken him to the hospital in Morgan City, but Calliope had reminded her he had no insurance and worse, no name to give the administration at the regional hospital in St. Mary Parish. Ed had helped them get him back to her house and into her bed where he'd promptly fallen to sleep.

"I owe him my life," Ed said simply. "Chocolates seem inadequate thanks for taking a hit for me."

"I'm sure he'll love them." Calliope sniffed. "He loves chocolate."

Not for the first time, frustration led Alex to pace. She left her bedroom and crossed the hall to the living room where she marched from end to end, going over and over in her mind the events of the day.

"You're going to wear a hole in the carpet," Ed said from the entrance to the living room.

"I can't stand around and do nothing. I saw what happened through the window of the Kettle. That driver was purposely trying to hit you." She stopped in front of Ed. "Are you sure you didn't get a license plate? Not even a part of it? Can't they run a plate with a partial?"

"The police can, but I got nothing. By the time I pulled myself out of the gutter, it was gone."

"Damn." She ran her hand over his chest, reliving the horror of what she'd witnessed. "What if Sport hadn't been there? What if that car had hit you?" Her hand stopped and she gazed up into his eyes through the mist of tears in her own. "That could be you banged up, or worse."

His mouth quirked upward on one side and he captured her hand in his. "Feeling sorry for me again?" He shook his head. "Don't. I can take care of myself."

"I nearly had a heart attack." She leaned her forehead against him. "That car coming so fast. You standing in its path." She wrapped her arms around his middle and buried her face in his shirt. "And then Sport, throwing himself in front of the car."

Ed stiffened beneath her. "You love him, don't you?"

"Sport?" She sniffed into his shirt. "Of course, I love him, and he loves me. He's been a part of my life for the past eight years. He helped me through the death of my father. I don't know what I'd do without him."

"Was he upset about last night?"

Alex sniffed again and looked up. "Upset? Why?" As his question sank in, her eyes widened. "Oh, you mean about us?"

"Well, yes." He set her at arm's length. "If you love him, why did you fool around with me?"

With the truth poised on the tip of her tongue, she hesitated. As good as it felt to have Ed's arms around her after what she'd witnessed, she couldn't continue down this path—no matter how wonderfully solid and warm he was against her. Until she resolved her issues with Sport, she couldn't consider any kind of relationship at all. Long-distance or short-distance. And Ed would be leaving soon. She'd be smart to end it now. Although she hadn't been too smart lately.

"Sport is very special to me," she said at last. "He understands me."

Ed's arms fell to his sides.

Cold that had nothing to do with the AC unit blasting in the window washed over Alex.

He backed away until his legs bumped into the couch. "Tell him thank you for saving my life."

When Ed turned to walk away, she caught something in his expression that made her chest tighten. Was that hurt in his eyes?

She raised her hand to stop him, and let it fall. It would be best for both of them to stop this craziness before it went any further.

Before he reached the door, Ed spun back, stalked across the floor, and grabbed her arm, yanking her against his chest. His lips crashed down over hers in a breath-stealing kiss, slanting over her mouth, his tongue diving in to claim hers.

She melted into Ed, her hands sliding around his neck, urging him closer, knowing she shouldn't.

He backed her against the wall and scooped his hands beneath her thighs, wrapping her legs around his waist. When his lips left hers, he seared a path down her neck. "Does he make you feel like this?" he asked.

She couldn't lie. "No." Her body was on fire, blood raging through her veins. A deep, wrenching ache built at her core, spreading outward. She wanted him more than anyone she'd ever wanted in her life.

Then he untangled her legs from his waist and let her legs drop to the ground before he stepped back, his eyes cold. "Think of that when you're with him."

Her heart pounding, tears welling in her eyes, she watched as Ed left her house, the screen door slamming closed behind him.

She walked back to her bedroom to find Sport wide awake and perky.

Calliope sat on the bed with him, a deck of cards laid out across the sheets. "Sport woke up and seems to be feeling fine." Calliope leaned over and pointed at his cards. "That's a pair. See? Two queens. "

Alex scrubbed a hand across her face and sank into the chair beside the bed. "Tell me you're not teaching Sport to play poker."

"Of course, I am. He's learning fast. He already plays better than you."

"Great."

Calliope scooted off the bed. "What's wrong?"

"Ed left."

"Is he coming back?"

"Probably not."

"Alex." Calliope shook her head. "What did you say to him?"

"He thinks I'm in love with Sport."

"Why would he think that?"

"Because I implied as much."

Calliope rolled her eyes. "Why do you push men away?"

"The timing is not right for me to be in any relationship. I'm finally getting my business off the ground—"

Her friend pressed her fingers to her ears. "Blah, blah, blah. You sound like a broken record. You really need to get over yourself and live a little."

Her cell phone rang and she pulled it out of her pocket, glad, for once, to see her mother's picture in the display screen. Anything to avoid another lecture from Calliope. "Hello, Mom."

"Dinner will be at six tonight. Don't be late."

"Mom, I can't make dinner. I have Calliope and Sport at my house."

Calliope snatched the phone from her. "Mrs. Boyette, Alex can make it to dinner, after all."

She groaned and reached for the phone, but her friend danced out of reach.

"No, no, don't worry about us," she was saying. "I'm taking Sport out for dinner in Morgan City. I'll take a rain check on that gumbo though. You know how I love it. Yes, we should be back in time for the festival. Yes, it was good talking to you, too. Bye now, *ma chère*." Calliope clicked the phone off and tossed it back to Alex.

"Thanks a lot." She nodded toward Sport. "You shouldn't take Sport out after being hit by a car earlier today, he needs rest."

Sport rose from the bed, stretched, and winced, pressing his fingers to the bandage on his face. "Sport okay." He smiled and winced again. "Ow."

"He'll feel better after we stop at his favorite barbeque place." Calliope slipped an arm around Sport's waist. "Right, Sport?"

"Right. Want barbeque."

"I'd rather go with you two than to my mother's house. You know she's going to throw Ed at me again."

"Is that so bad?"

"The way he left out of here? Yes."

"You have got to learn to loosen up." Calliope ducked around her. "I'll be back in a few minutes. I need to run to my house and freshen up." She pointed at Sport. "Stay. I'll be back shortly."

"Sport stay."

After Calliope left, Alex straightened the bed and stacked the deck of cards on the nightstand.

Sport's gaze followed her around the room. As a dog, that didn't bother her. As a man, it made her more self-conscious.

"What wrong, Alex?"

"Nothing you would understand, unfortunately." She sighed and left the bedroom to straighten the living room. She had to keep moving. Whenever she slowed down, she thought. About Ed. *Damn it.*

"Ed love Alex?"

She spun to face Sport. "Where did you get that idea. From Calliope?"

He shook his head like a dog shakes his coat and sniffed. "Sport smell it."

"You can smell love?"

Her man-dog nodded. "Alex love Ed."

Her laugh caught on a sob. "I barely know Ed. I met him yesterday. You can't fall in love in a day."

Sport tipped his head. "Why?"

"You just can't." She ran past Sport and into her bathroom where she stripped out of her clothes and ducked beneath the cold spray of her shower, hoping it would shock her back into reality.

All it did was make her wet and cold.

As she toweled dry and slipped into a clean cotton sun dress and sandals, Sport's question echoed in her mind. *Why?*

Why can't you fall in love in a day? At the ripe old age of twenty-nine, had she discovered for the first time that love at first sight actually existed?

CHAPTER 10

Ed sat on the porch steps, replacing the spinner with the buzz bait on his fishing line. Joe hadn't judged him when he'd first thrown his line out in the bayou and immediately snagged a cypress knee.

The older man had untangled the snag and retied his line before casting his own line, thus showing him the proper technique. The two mornings he'd been on the bayou had been the most peaceful times he'd ever experienced. Even when an alligator drifted by, he'd been calm, accepting that the bayou might be serene and beautiful, but it held its own dangers. Being aware of his surroundings was key.

When he finished tying the lure, Ed sat back and stared out across the small town of Bayou Miste. Through the late afternoon, residents could be seen stringing lights on their houses and fences, draping colorful beads on the bushes, and hanging garish flags in the yard. A small carnival had moved in the night before and set up in the community park. Carnie music drifted toward him, bringing back memories of the few times his foster families had taken him to the fair in Baton Rouge. He could almost smell the funnel cakes from where he sat.

He'd been cornered by Barbara Boyette an hour ago and coerced into coming to dinner at the Boyette house, yet again. Not looking forward to it, but realizing how much more difficult it would be to say no to the woman, he'd agreed, praying Alex wouldn't be there. Knowing Barbara Boyette, she would play her hand at matchmaking again.

Ed chuckled.

"Whatcha laughing about?" a tiny voice asked from beside him.

He spun toward the sound and shook his head at the smallest of the Boyette brood, Molly B. "I'm laughing at how funny people can be."

"What people?"

"Everyone." He gazed down at the pretty little girl with the dark ringlets hanging down from her two ponytails perched high on her head. "How are you today, Miz Molly B.?"

"Fine, thank you," she responded politely.

"What does the B stand for?"

"Brown," she answered promptly. Her chest swelled out and she tipped her chin up. "I'm unsinkable."

"Well, Miz Molly Brown Boyette, what can I do for you today?"

"Mamma sent me to get you." She held out her hand with all the trust of the five-year-old child she was.

Ed wondered how anyone could let their small child wander so far from their own front door with so many pedophiles stalking the streets, looking for their next victim. That had been only one of his reasons he'd never wanted children. And the fact his own childhood had been less than wonderful and he wouldn't wish that on a kid.

He glanced toward the Boyette house and could see Mrs. Boyette, peering through the window. Okay, so Molly B wasn't alone, but being watched over by a loving mother.

He lifted a hand in greeting and Mrs. Boyette waved back.

"Guess that's our cue." He stepped down off the porch, Molly B.'s hand in his. A warm feeling tugged at his heart. Maybe if he'd been inclined to have children, his wife wouldn't have left him. Hell, he'd heard she'd already had one baby with her new husband and had a second on the way.

Maybe kids weren't such a bad idea, with the right parents. If he could have kids like Molly B., Teddy and Rosie, it couldn't be too bad. They'd grown on him.

Inside, the Boyette house was every bit as chaotic as it was the night before. Children of all ages and a few of the grown ones crisscrossed each other's paths setting the table, icing the glasses, and carrying trays of food into the dining room.

A dozen "Hello, Mr. Marceaus" crossed with a few "Hi, Eds" made him feel welcome and wanted there.

Mrs. Boyette backed through the swinging kitchen door, carrying a heaping plate of dirty rice.

"Oh, there you are Mr. Marceau. We're so happy you could make it."

"Here, let me." He grabbed the heavy platter from her and set it in the middle of the table, marveling at how strong she was. "I'm renting your cottage, you don't have to feed me, too, you know."

She laughed. "*Mais, oui*. But what's one more mouth when you have so many? Sit, Mr. Marceau."

He obeyed the command with a smile. "Yes, ma'am. Please, call me Ed."

"I do feel as if you're too young to be called Mr. Marceau. You're the same age as my son, Ben, I believe."

The family gathered around the table, a few missing from the night before. Ed couldn't remember which ones, but he only counted fourteen of the siblings.

As if in answer to his unspoken question, Mrs. Boyette said, "Harry and Truman had other plans tonight, Amelia had to head back to New Orleans sooner than she'd expected, and Alex—ah, there she is." Barbara Boyette smiled as her oldest daughter stepped into the room.

His hand tightened on the napkin in his lap.

Alex wore a dress for the first time since he'd met her, the soft cotton molding to her shapely figure like a glove. Her legs were bare and she had strappy sandals on her feet that displayed her pretty little toes with the bright pink polish he'd admired last night as he'd stripped her bicycle shorts down her legs.

His groin tightened and he reined in his thoughts. Now was not the time to think of Alex naked. Not in a room full of Boyettes. He nodded. "Alex."

She gave him a cool nod in return. "Mr. Marceau."

So it was *Mr. Marceau,* now. He supposed it was appropriate, given they weren't going to see each other anywhere but at her mother's dinner table.

He'd like to think he choked down the shrimp *etouffee* and dirty rice Mrs. Boyette had prepared, but it slid right down his throat, despite the heavy tension brewing between him and Alex. "Mrs. Boyette, you could open your own restaurant." He sat back and patted his belly. "Best *etouffee* I've ever eaten."

Barbara Boyette smiled and blushed. "Thank you, but I have ulterior motives. I'm just buttering you up."

He sat forward. "Need a sink fixed? You got it."

"Better off hiring a plumber," Alex muttered.

Her mother scowled at her and shined a smile at him. "As a matter of fact, I do have a favor to ask of you, Ed."

"Name it." He'd figure out whatever mechanical puzzle she had for him, just to prove to Alex he was up for the challenge.

"Tonight is the local Crawfish Festival, and I'm too tired to take the children. Would you and Alex be dears and take them?"

A cacophony of cheers rose from the younger Boyettes.

"We'll help," Dolley and Madison volunteered, in unison.

"George and I had plans to hit a movie in Morgan City, but we can cancel if you need us to," Abe offered.

Their mother waved them off. "No need. Between Ed, Alex, Dolley, and Madison they'll have it covered. You two go on."

He almost laughed out loud at the stricken expression on Alex's face. It was that look that made him say, "Alex and I would be happy to help. Wouldn't we?" He raised his brows in challenge.

Alex's jaw twitched, but she managed a nod. "We'd love to," she said through clenched teeth.

"Since that's settled, you better get going. Molly B. won't last too long and she's been looking forward to going all week. She even saved her allowance for cotton candy."

"*Pink* cotton candy," Molly piped up.

"Then pink cotton candy it will be." He pushed back from the table and helped carry dishes to the sink.

Alex caught him coming out the swinging door as she was going in. "What are you trying to prove?"

He held the door for her. "Nothing. Your mother has been kind enough to feed me and I want to return the favor." He leaned close. "Not everything is about you, Ms. Boyette." He let go of the swinging door and it smacked Alex in the butt.

Her voice carried through the wood paneling. "Oh! That man!"

The children gathered in the hallway, Teddy, Rosie, and Molly hopping up and down, too excited to stand still. Woodrow and Susan B. grinned and laughed, but refrained from the exuberance shown by their younger siblings while Paul, Thomas, Edison, and JK waited outside, teenagers and therefore too cool to be associated with the rest.

Alex counted heads. "There are fourteen of us. Dolley and Madison, you take the teens. Mr. Marceau and I will take the subteens."

Molly tugged on his finger. "Am I a subteen, Mr. Ed?"

He scooped her up in his arms. "Yes, ma'am, you are."

"Can I ride piggy back?" she asked, crawling across his arm and onto his back like a monkey.

"I can do better than that." He hiked her up, settling her little legs around his neck and ducked low as they headed out the door for the four-block walk to the park.

Alex wondered how she'd been conned into spending another evening with the man whose kisses made her forget everything she'd worked so hard to build.

And damned if he didn't look right surrounded by the often overwhelming Boyette family. She would never have guessed he'd grown up a foster child. And damned if he wasn't the first man that hadn't run screaming from her raucous gaggle of siblings.

He'd make a great father.

Mon Dieu! She had to quit thinking that way. It would merely lead to heartache.

Ed was good at his word, keeping a close eye on the little ones, attentive to their every need, even taking the boys to the portable potties when they'd had too much soda. He marched Molly over to the stand selling pink cotton candy, and held it for her when she rode the spinning rides.

Teddy and Rosie squealed with delight when Ed made three basketball tosses in a row, winning a pretty purple unicorn, which he promptly handed over to Teddy.

Calliope and Sport found them in front of the shooting stall where Paul, J.K., Thomas, and Edison went up against Ed for the grand prize of a toy Daisy BB gun. It took five rounds of games before Ed worked his way up to the grand prize. He insisted on carrying it home to present to their mother for her approval first.

Rosie tapped Ed's arm and the big man bent toward him. When he straightened he headed toward Alex, Rosie beside him. "We're going to make a quick trip to the bathroom. Can you handle them while we're gone?"

She nodded, admiring Ed's trim waist and narrow hips as he walked away. The man made jeans look sexy.

"Nice ass." Calliope leaned close to her. "And he's so good with the kids."

"Yeah," she said, wiping all enthusiasm from her voice, not wanting to encourage Calliope to continue.

Her friend swatted her shoulder. "Don't be so grumpy. How often do you find a man who fits in with your family?"

Never. "I have too much going on in my life right now. I can't even think about this...this...thing."

"That *thing* is feelings."

Ed returned with a smiling Rosie, running alongside him.

They looked so natural together, smiling and laughing. Alex's heart squeezed. The man needed a family of his own.

Calliope stood back as Sport watched Ed helping Teddy and Rosie toss rings over the necks of bottles. "He's perfect for you. Sometimes you have to take a chance."

"I told him I didn't want a relationship." Alex raised her hands. "And I have a man living with me."

"Speaking of whom." Calliope turned to Alex. "I'd like to take Sport over to my house. I promised we'd watch all the *Homeward Bound* movies together."

Alex captured Calliope's hands. "At the risk of sounding like a broken record, don't fall in love with Sport. The spell might not last."

Calliope cast a soft glance at the man-dog trying his hand at throwing rings. "I'll try not to, but I'm afraid it's far too late. Besides, I'll take all the love I can get, as long as it lasts."

Her friend had a point. When you had a chance to love, you had to go for it. How did the old saying go? *Better to have loved and lost than to never have loved.* "I guess it's okay." Unfortunately, that would leave her alone and being alone wasn't all that great anymore, not when she'd sampled what being with someone felt like. "What time are you bringing him home?"

"Rather than wake you, he can sleep on my couch." She raised her hand. "Honest. Just sleep."

"Okay," she agreed, reluctantly. Her friend was grabbing for every minute she could spend with the man she was falling in love with, knowing it probably wouldn't last. Being in love with a man who turned back into a dog was a much bigger hurdle to overcome than being in love with a man who lived in a different city. So what was her problem?

* * *

THROUGHOUT THE EVENING, Ed remained attentive to the children, not letting the little ones out of his sight for a moment. At the same time, he looked around for unfamiliar faces. The entire time he was at the festival, he felt as if someone was watching him. With the trial date approaching, paranoia was bound to surface, not to mention Leon Primeaux's hired hit men.

Twice he thought he'd seen someone lurking in between tents. One tall man wore a hoodie that obscured his face. Ed never got a close look at him before he turned away and disappeared behind a booth. Molly chose that time to trip and fall. He couldn't excuse himself and go after the man without leaving the kids or Alex alone for a few minutes. When he'd taken Rosie to the portable bathrooms on the edge of the border of the carnival and the parking lot, he could have sworn they'd been followed, but when he turned around, no one was behind them.

Alex and Calliope had their backs to him and were talking with two strangers when Ed glanced away from the kids playing games. Both men were big and tall. One wore overalls and a faded T-shirt that had a five-year-old advertisement for the crawfish festival.

The other man was a little bigger and wore old army camouflage pants and a ripped black T-shirt with the words *I'm with stupid* written in bold white letters. "She got away from Granny 'bout thirty minutes ago. Cain't find her nowhere."

"I haven't seen FeFe since earlier this afternoon," Alex was saying.

"Sport and I just walked up from my house a little while ago and didn't see her along the way," Calliope said.

"*Mais*, if you do, give ol' Mo a call." The man backhanded the other guy in the gut. "Come on, Larry."

Larry stuck his hands in his pockets and rocked back on his mud boots. "Maybe T-Rex done her in, or she got runned over by some *couyon* what ain't got a lick 'o sense runnin' ova a pink poodle."

"Shut jo mout' ya ol' coonass. Granny'd be bawlin' her eyes out iffn' someting happens to dat danged mutt."

"Something wrong?" Ed interrupted.

Alex turned to him. "Ed Marceau, this is Maurice Saulnier and Larry Ezelle, friends of ours. They're looking for Mo's grandmother's poodle, FeFe. She went missing a little while ago."

"She be pink today," Larry took his hands out of his pocket and shook Ed's hand.

Mo shook Ed's hand next, his brows furrowed. "You de fella fishin' in the mornin' with Joe?"

He nodded. "That would be me."

"Catch anyting?" Mo asked.

"Joe caught a couple of catfish. I'm angling for bass, but no luck so far."

"Bayou Black's good for de largemouth bass," Larry offered.

"Iffn' you're inta frog giggin', de swamp over by de ol' trapper shack is chalk full of dem. But ya gotta go at night to get de bigguns."

He tensed. The trapper shack was where they'd hidden the witness. "Do many people go giggin' at night?"

"Mostly me 'n Larry," Mo said. "But der be some mo' boats out late at night in de past coupla days. Not sure what dey be after, but dey be movin' too fast to gig frogs."

Was someone searching the swamps for something more than frogs and fish? He needed to get out to the shack and make sure Marcus was ready, in case whoever it was meant to hunt stool pigeons. He'd have to go later, when no one was around to see him head down the canal. He couldn't risk being followed.

Mo backhanded Larry in the gut again. "We best be goin'."

Mo and Larry lumbered off, muttering as they went about pink poodles and alligators.

Molly B. tugged on Ed's shirt and raised her arms.

He lifted her and laid her head on his shoulder, where she went right to sleep.

"I think it's time to head home." Alex patted her sister's back and gathered the others.

The walk back was a combination of bursts of laughter and tired silence, the night proclaimed great fun by all. Except for Alex, who looked none too thrilled to be in his company.

* * *

ALEX HAD TRIED to be mad at Ed for his earlier parting kiss and for volunteering them to take the little ones to the festival, but couldn't stay that way. He'd displayed a side of himself that she found hard to resist. A softer, caring side that raised him up several notches in her estimation.

Well, damn. If he wasn't from New Orleans and planning on returning there soon, she could fall for guy like Ed.

As they arrived in front of the Boyette house, Calliope and Sport said their goodbyes and continued on to Calliope's house, hand in hand.

She shook her head, but what could she do? For the time being, Sport was a man.

Once inside, Ed and Alex tucked Molly B. in bed, each pressing a kiss to her soft forehead. Alex moved down the hallway giving each of her siblings a goodnight hug and kiss, working her way back to the front door where she watched as the little ones all hugged Ed and the teens shook his hand.

He bent to return their hugs and laughed at J.K.'s attempt at a joke.

How did he do it? He'd charmed his way into their lives. He even kissed her mother's cheek and thanked her for letting him take the kids to the festival.

She ducked out the front door, intent on making her escape before she fell for the man all over again. She was halfway down the driveway when the front screen door slammed.

"Alex, wait."

She pretended she hadn't heard him, ducked her head, and walked faster.

Footsteps sounded behind her, coming fast.

She wasn't ready to be alone with Ed again. She increased her pace until she was running. A block from her house, he caught up to her, grabbed her arm and spun her around.

"Damn it, Alex. I just wanted to give you this." He lifted her hand and placed a miniature version of the stuffed unicorn he'd given Teddy into her palm.

Her pulse pounded and her heart squeezed hard in her chest as Alex stared at the stupid little purple unicorn. Tears welled in her eyes and slid down her cheeks. "Damn you."

"I thought you could use some cheering up since Calliope and Sport took off without you." He tipped her chin up and brushed the tears from her cheeks. "Hey. What's this?"

"Why do you have to be you?" She flung her arms around his neck, leaned up on her toes and kissed him hard on the mouth.

His hand slid around her waist and he pulled her against him, drawing away from her mouth to whisper, "I don't understand you."

"I don't understand me either." She laughed and kissed him again.

His hands slipped down over her bottom and he lifted her, wrapping her bare legs around him.

"Not here," she said and sucked his bottom lip into her mouth, then let go to press kisses to his cheek, his ear.

"Your place." Ed carried her toward her little house, refusing to put her down.

"Go around back, I have noisy neighbors that report to my mother."

Ed crossed a yard and slipped around the house to her back door where he set her on her feet. She pulled the key from the pocket of her sundress and slid it into the lock. Past caring what she was doing, she shoved the door open and they fell through. All she wanted was to feel.

Ed grabbed the hem of her dress, ripped it up over her head, and groaned, staring down at her with an expression so hot it made her knees melt.

Then he hooked the thin strap of her string bikini panties and slid them slowly down her legs, his knuckles skimming her skin all the way to her ankles.

Naked and on fire, she combed her fingers through his thick brown hair and backed up until her bottom bumped into the kitchen dinette table. Then she hoisted herself onto the edge and parted her thighs, already wet and ready for him. "Come here."

His hands rose to his belt buckle and he hesitated. "What about Sport?"

"We have an understanding."

"What if I'm not comfortable with that understanding?"

"You're not staying. Why should you care?"

He stepped between her legs, still fully dressed, his hands cupping her cheeks. "Because, despite what you might think, I do care." Then he kissed her again, the caress a connection that seared a path all the way to her heart. "I care too damned much."

"It's not meant to be anything beyond tonight," she whispered against his lips.

"Then let's make tonight count." His fingers wove through her hair, tugging until her head dropped back, exposing her throat to his lips, his teeth, and his tongue. He branded her with his heat as he pressed his lips to the pulse beating wildly at the base of her throat. He moved to the ridge of her collarbone and downward to capture one puckered nipple between his teeth.

"*Mon Dieu,* I'm on fire." She reached for his shirt, tugging it up over his head and dropping it to the floor.

He unbuckled his belt and flicked the button to his jeans open.

Alex ran the zipper down, freed his erection into her palm and guided him to her entrance.

His body stiffened and he held back, the velvety tip of his cock nudging, but not entering her. "I have protection in my wallet."

Alex reached around him, removing his wallet from his back pocket.

He snatched it from her and held it out of her reach. "I'll do that."

A little shaken by the force with which he'd grabbed for the wallet, her lust cooled. "I only wanted to help."

"I know." After a quick kiss to the tip of her nose, he held the wallet away from her, opened it just wide enough to remove a foil package, then slid it into his back pocket. He tore the packet open and rolled the condom down over his cock before curling his fingers around the back of her neck. "Did I tell you how pretty you were in the dress you wore tonight?"

"The one you threw across the room?" She tried to hold onto her irritation at his handling of the condom, but the way his fingers kneaded the back of her neck, she was quickly becoming putty in his hands.

"You should wear dresses more often. They show off your legs."

She warmed to his compliment. "It's not practical to work out in a dress."

"It's a shame." He skimmed her lips with his, sliding his tongue in to stroke the length of hers. "You really have great legs."

She shrugged off her misgivings as he started the assault on her senses all over, this time taking one breast into his mouth and sucking hard enough her body responded with an answering tug at her center. She wrapped her legs around his hips, wanting him inside her.

He held back, unlocking her ankles from behind him and dropping to his knees in front of her, kissing her belly and moving lower. His big hands spread her thighs wider, skimming fingers along the sensitive skin, angling closer to that aching place, begging for consummation.

She leaned back on her hands, caught in the magic of his touch, eager for what came next as his thumbs parted her folds, exposing her to him.

He flicked her with his tongue, moistening the little bundle of nerves and flesh.

Alex's breathing grew ragged and she her body tensed. "Please."

He tongued her again, this time in a long, sensuous glide, circling back to do it again. He slid a finger into her channel, then two, then three, swirling around the juices, while his mouth worked that nubbin of intense desire.

"*Mon Dieu!*" Her hips rocked, pressing closer to the wonder of his tongue, his hands, his mouth. "You make me come undone," she gasped.

He chuckled and rose to his feet. "That was the plan. Now," He wrapped her legs around his waist, pressing the tip of his cock to her entrance. "Make magic with me." With one, swift thrust, he entered her, sliding all the way in.

She cried out and clutched his shoulders, digging her nails into his skin.

He pulled halfway out. "Am I hurting you?"

"No! Do it again." Her inner muscles tightened, refusing to release him. "Faster."

He pumped in and out of her, hard and swift, his face tense as he held her hips.

As the sensations intensified, her legs tightened around him and she flew over the edge in a fire burst. Tingling started at her core and flooded her body, spreading outward all the way to her toes.

Ed slammed in one more time, his body stiffening as he held her hips, pressing deep inside, the width and depth of his member filling her completely. When his hold loosened, he gathered her in his arms. "You are incredible."

"You're not so bad yourself." Replete, yet exhausted, she leaned into him her face nestling against his muscular chest. "What is it you didn't want me to see in your wallet? A picture of an old girlfriend?"

"No." He tipped her head back and gazed into her eyes, still connected to her in the most intimate way. "There are no other women in my life." He didn't say it, but she could swear the words *Only You* lingered in the air. With his thumb, he skimmed her bottom lip, then followed it with a gentle kiss.

She sighed and wrapped her arms around him. "What is it about you that keeps me coming back for more?"

He chuckled. "My magnetic personality?"

Though his words were true, she snorted. "Nah. Must be the incredible sex."

He leaned back and brushed the hair from her cheek. "What's next?"

A loud crash saved Alex from answering as a rock sailed through her kitchen window.

Ed ducked, dragging her with him, but not fast enough.

The rock clipped her chin and she fell off the table into Ed's arms.

Silence settled over them.

Ed tilted her face and studied the gash in her chin. "Are you okay?"

"Yes, but what happened?" She pressed her fingers to the wound and felt warm, sticky liquid. "*Mon Dieu,* I'm bleeding."

"It doesn't look bad. Just—"

"A flesh wound." She glanced around. "Still have that gun on you?"

"Yes, why?"

"Can I borrow it? I'm going after that son of a bitch who broke my window."

"If it's all the same to you and you're sure you're all right, I'll go." He winked at her, his gaze skimming across her naked body. "You're not exactly dressed for the occasion."

"Fine. You go." She gave him a shove, then grabbed his sleeve and yanked him back and kissed him full on the mouth. "But zip it and be careful."

CHAPTER 11

ANGER SENT ED THROUGH THE DOOR LIKE A ROCKET BLASTING OFF THE launch pad. Based on the trajectory of the rock, whoever had thrown it had been standing in Alex's backyard. He peered into the darkness broken only by moonlight filtering through the overhanging trees. Nothing moved but the branches of the trees swaying in the breeze, no silhouette shifted in the gloom, lurking, waiting to pick a fight.

Gun drawn, he ducked low and slipped into the shadows, listening for the sound of footsteps running away. Who the hell would have targeted Alex's house? Had someone figured out he was part of the detail protecting the Ragsdale woman? Hell, he hadn't been doing much of a job by jumping Alex's bones every chance he got.

Granted, the festival had been a great opportunity for strangers to mix and mingle with the locals. If anyone had spotted Marcus and Phyllis at the old shack in the bayou, they might run off at the mouth without realizing they were giving away the location of a protected witness.

He had enjoyed his time with the Boyette children, all the while keeping an eye open for strangers. He'd spotted the retiree, Oscar Mills, wandering amongst the crowd. Alone.

They'd sized each other up from a distance, but moved on.

Other than that one encounter, he hadn't gotten any vibes from any of the other passersby. But that didn't mean someone wasn't watching him, waiting for him to make his next visit to the witness.

He searched through backyards and then headed out to the main road.

Mo and Larry were headed his way, Mo carrying a puff of pink.

Larry raised a hand. "We found FeFe."

"Glad to hear it," Ed said.

"She be scarfin' up hotdogs de kids done dropped at de festival." Mo shook his head. "Gonna have her one helluva bellyache."

The pink poodle was nestled in the crook of the man's arm, listless, her head hanging low.

"Did you two happen to pass anyone on the street a few moments ago?"

Larry and Mo both shook their heads.

Mo shifted the poodle to his other arm. "Dint see no one runnin' but saw a car take off."

"Which way was it headed?"

"Toward Morgan City, I be guessin'." Mo patted the dog. "Better get FeFe home before Granny calls out de National Guard." The two men went on their way.

Ed continued the search of a two-block radius from Alex's cottage, finally admitting defeat. Whoever had thrown the rock had gotten clean away, probably in the car Mo had mentioned, headed for Morgan City.

Two attacks in one day and the common denominator seemed to be him. The rock would have hit him in the head had he not ducked. Alex had been hit instead.

The reckless driver on the street today had made a determined attempt to run him over, not Sport. Sport had taken the brunt of that attack.

Perhaps Alex was right. Their relationship would end badly, but not for the reasons she'd listed.

With his gun still held in the palm of his hand, he headed back to Alex.

She met him at the back door, pushing it open with one hand, while holding a dish towel to her chin with the other.

"He got away."

"I'm glad." Dressed in a T-shirt and shorts, she hugged him around the middle. "I was worried you'd be hurt. I bet it was some random teen getting a little rowdy after the fair."

He disengaged her arms and made a circle around her kitchen, lowering the blinds over the windows. When he finished, he crossed to her and pulled out a chair at the dinette. "Sit."

Alex smiled crookedly at him. "Giving orders now?"

"Damn right." He softened his words with, "Let me see." Gently, he pulled the dish towel away from her face and studied the damage the rock had made.

"I think it'll bruise more than anything." She smiled up at him. "It just ticks me off that someone broke my window."

"I'm more worried about you than a damned window." He carried the towel to the sink and ran clean, cold water over it, returning to dab the blood away. "Do you have a first aid kit?"

"In the bathroom cabinet." She started to rise, but he laid a hand on her shoulder.

"Stay here. I'll get it." He hurried into the bathroom and rifled through the well-organized contents of the cabinet until he found a small plastic container with First Aid written on the outside.

"It's not that bad, just a bruise, really," Alex called out.

Ed returned and dabbed antibiotic ointment on the cut, then spread a bandage over it. When he was done, he kissed her lips. "Come on, you can shower while I clean up the glass."

She frowned. "I can do this."

"I know. You take care of everybody else, and you're capable of taking care of yourself." He lifted her hands and squeezed them. "But this once, let me." Before she could protest further, he scooped her up and carried her to her bedroom, setting her on her feet with a pat on her behind. "Now go."

"Will you still be here when I'm done?" she asked.

"I'm staying." His jaw clenched. "At least until you go to sleep. You really should get a dog."

"I know." Her eyes glazed with unshed tears and she turned away.

Hadn't her mother said something about her having one called Sport? Probably named after the man she lived with.

He wondered if the dog had run away, thus the reason for the sudden tears.

After sweeping up the broken glass, he made a pass around the exterior of the cottage and reentered as Alex emerged from her bedroom, dressed in the baby-doll nightgown she'd worn the first morning he'd seen her running through Bayou Miste.

Had it only been two days ago?

Her eyelids dropped to half-mast and she smiled. "You can sleep in here."

"I'll sleep on the couch." If he lay down with her, he'd once again lose focus on why the hell he'd come to town in the first place.

"Really?" She glanced down at her nightgown. "I don't tempt you in the least?"

He closed his eyes and drew in a deep breath to slow his pulse and tamp down his libido. "Darlin', you'd tempt the devil to sell his soul. But it's best if I don't get too close to you. There's only one way it could end."

She twirled the end of her long, black hair, hanging in loose, damp ringlets around her face. "Is that a bad thing?"

"Got to bed, Alex."

She huffed and turned, the hem of her nightgown flouncing, revealing a pair of black lace panties.

He groaned and turned his back on her, his hands clenched in fists and shoved into his pockets to keep from reaching out and grabbing her. He strode to the window and peered out on the street where a light shined down from the lampposts at the corner of each block. Nothing moved except the cars and trucks headed away from the festival. Soon even those thinned to a trickle.

After much bed-squeaking and sheet-rustling, the house grew silent.

He crept into Alex's room.

She'd gone to sleep with her back to the door, her arm around the spare pillow, and clutched in her fingers, the little purple unicorn. A frown dimpled her forehead and he wondered what she was dreaming about. Was it him, her attacker, or maybe Sport and Calliope? She was keeping something from him about Sport. He couldn't believe for a moment that they had an open relationship. Alex wasn't the kind of woman who tolerated a mess. Open relationships smelled of disorder. The bandage on her chin stood out in the dim light shining from the hallway. The more Ed stared at it, the angrier he grew. After one last trip around the house, securing windows and checking the locks on the doors, he dialed Ben.

"Ed?" a groggy Ben answered. "Anything wrong?"

"I'm not sure." He paced the kitchen keeping his voice to a low whisper.

"Talk to me," Ben's voice snapped like a whip across the line.

He filled him in on the hit-and-run and the rock through Alex's window while he'd been there, but skipped the part about the great sex with his sister.

"You're right to be worried. I wonder if we need to bring her in early. Sounds like having her there could make it dangerous for the people of Bayou Miste."

"That's what I'm afraid of." Ed's chest tightened. The folks around here might end up being collateral damage in an all-out war between Primeaux's army and the Louisiana State Police. "I'm headed out to check on our pigeon and make sure everything's still good out there. I'll let you know."

"I think it's time for me to pay a visit."

"No," he said, a little too forcefully. "If anyone links you to Ragsdale, they'll follow you here."

"Okay, no visit."

"Anything on Oscar Mills?" he asked.

"Nothing yet. But then I've been busy at the courthouse. I'll check in the morning. We're still on board to bring Ragsdale in day after tomorrow. Wait, that would be tomorrow since it's already today. Are you and Marcus up to it? Need me to send reinforcements?"

"We can play it by ear today and see what unfolds. If I think it's risky, I'll give you a shout."

"I'm concerned about using my cell phone to talk to you. I might call you on one of those burner phones next time I call."

"Understood."

Ed hung up, checked once more on Alex, then slipped out the back, locking the door behind him.

Time to get serious. The clock was ticking, Leon Primeaux's trial would begin the following day. If someone was after him to get the location of Phyllis Ragsdale, he had to stay on his toes. No more playing around with the local attraction.

He laid a hand on her shoulder and shook her. "Alex."

She yawned and stretched, her eyes opening, a smile curving her lips. "Hey."

"I have to go, now, but I don't want to leave you alone."

"I'll be fine."

"I'd feel better if you went to your mother's house and stayed there until I get back."

"Where are you going?"

"I have some things to check on. Please, go to your mother's house."

"Okay. But don't be gone long." Her hand slipped across his face and she pressed a kiss to his lips.

He wanted to slide under the sheets and continue where they'd left off before she'd fallen to sleep. But he had work to do. He kissed her one last time and left, slipping out the backdoor, praying she'd do as he'd asked and go to the Boyette house.

* * *

After Ed left, Alex climbed out of bed and padded barefoot through the house to the kitchen and peered around the corner of the blinds out into the darkness of night. She would have missed him, had he not slipped from the corner of her house to the shadow of a tree at that moment. A thrill of fear skittered over her until she recognized the way he moved and his dark profile briefly illuminated by the stars.

Why would Ed sneak around like a crook or spy in the night rather than walk down the street? The incident of him snatching his wallet from her hands popped up in her mind and she wondered again, what was he hiding? Was he really there on vacation? Sure, he'd been fishing with Joe every morning, but what else was he doing while she was in Morgan City working? Something wasn't right and his surreptitious behavior didn't appear to be the kind to keep the neighbors from talking. Not when he carried the kind of gun he did.

Alex smacked a palm to her forehead when she thought of how she'd bought his line about carrying a gun in the bayou because of the alligators. Granted, she'd been surprised on more than one occasion by Maurice Saulnier's pet alligator, T-Rex. The creature stretched to over eight feet long now. He needed to transfer him to an alligator farm before he hurt someone or ate his grandmother's poodle.

In the meantime, Alex had a dilemma. She was falling for a guy who probably wasn't being truthful with her, while she hadn't been completely honest with him. Then again, how did one tell the guy she'd made love to twice that the man living with her was really a dog?

If Madame LeBieu wasn't going to help her, she'd have to make a run to Baton Rouge and get Lucie to undo the magic that made Sport a man.

Damn. Tomorrow she had an important meeting with the administrator from the hospital at Morgan City dropping by to negotiate a contract to provide services to their employees. And it would have to be late in the afternoon. That wouldn't leave time for her to make it to Baton Rouge before rush hour and would put her back later than she liked.

Alex watched for a little while longer, but didn't catch sight of Ed again, though the shadows near the corner of her house seemed to shift several times. She shivered and crossed her arms. Without Sport in the house as a dog, she didn't have that same comfort level living alone. And she didn't own a gun like Ed's. She scrounged through her kitchen drawers and unearthed her favorite butcher knife and carried it to her bedroom, laying it on the nightstand before settling beneath the sheets. How much nicer would it have been had Ed stayed. With his arms around her, holding her cocooned against his body and his gun lying on the nightstand instead of the butcher knife, she'd have slept a whole lot better. Or not.

With a groan, Alex rolled over, tucking the spare pillow against her. It wasn't a muscular chest by far, but it was better than the emptiness of being totally alone. Ah, hell, who was she kidding? Nothing was better than a muscular chest attached to a warm body.

She wondered how Calliope and Sport were doing. Had they watched the movies and then gone to sleep...in separate locations? Deep down, she suspected those two were headed for heartbreak, and she was well on her way there herself.

* * *

KEEPING TO THE SHADOWS, Ed slipped away from Alex's house, hugging the edge of the bayou, moving from bush to tree to boathouse until he made his way back to the little boat he'd rented from Mrs. Boyette. The GPS was hidden in the leg of an old pair of hip wader boots that had seen much better days.

Ed crouched low to the ground in the shadows and waited, listening for any sounds of movement. After a while, the crickets, cicadas, and frogs sang again, the dissonant sound blocking out everything but the rumble of trucks on the highway or the occasional bark of a lonely dog.

With the stealth of a ghost in the night, Ed slipped over the rim of the boat and pushed away from the bank, using the wooden oar. For the first fifty yards, he paddled the small craft through the mirror-smooth water until he came to the first fork in the bayou that would lead him away from the canal that paralleled the highway and out into the maze of the bayou. When he'd rounded a bend and the town disappeared from sight, he cranked the engine and guided the skiff to the little shack in the bayou where Marcus and the Ragsdale woman waited for news from the outside world.

Rather than tie off to the rickety dock, he ran the boat up into the shore beneath the overhanging Spanish moss. Halfway up the bank to the back porch of the shack, he tripped over a line, landing on his hands and knees, cursing to the rattle of tin cans. He grinned and stayed down until a figure emerged from the back of the shack and slipped silently toward him.

"I know, I better be Ed, or I'll be dead." Ed called out when Marcus came within range of his whispered call. "I like the early warning system."

"I put The Mouth to work stringing cans. Kept her busy for most of the afternoon."

"Good thinkin'." Ed stood and brushed the moss from his hands and jeans.

"She wanted to help me string them out there. Threatened to shoot her if she stepped one foot out of the building."

"That trigger finger gettin' itchier?" Ed led the way up the hill. Marcus followed, walking backward, his automatic rifle aimed toward the bayou.

"Been more traffic today than the past two."

Ed's head jerked toward him. "Anyone suspicious?"'

Marcus snorted. "Hard to say. They all look the same. Most of them had fishing poles. One boat came by with a man in it that didn't have a fishing pole. He did have a camera and was takin' pictures."

"Of the shack?" Ed climbed the steps of the back porch, his hand on the doorknob.

"Yeah."

"Not good."

"You tellin' me. I had him in my sights."

"I'm surprised you didn't shoot him."

"I coulda," Marcus said. "Alligators round here would have cleaned him up. Counted two in the lagoon across the channel. Don't think the water's quite deep enough here to have hidden their boat for long, though."

"You scare me the way you think, you know that?" Ed chuckled and pushed the door open.

"Not much to do out here, but think."

"No shit." Phyllis Ragsdale sat at the card table, a mirror propped between cans of beans, the Coleman lantern beside the mirror as she plucked her eyebrows. "I won't have any brows by the time we leave this shithole."

"Nice to see you too, Ms. Ragsdale."

"Fuck you."

"Had to put up with that all day." Marcus thumbed the safety on his rifle as if he'd like to put a bullet in the witness and end everyone's misery.

Ed really had it easy in town compared to what Marcus was dealing with.

"What do you hear on the outside?" Marcus asked.

"Need to maintain your nonexistence here in the bayou. I think things are heating up in Bayou Miste." He filled them in on the two attacks.

"What, no bullets?" Marcus kicked a chair out into the middle of the floor and sat, then pulled the magazine from his weapon and ejected the round from the bolt. In less time than it took to say *laissez les bon temps rouler,* he'd stripped the weapon down, laying the parts on the floor in front of him. "Wouldn't mind someone trying to make a run at this place. Beats the boredom and spending time with The Mouth."

"Yeah, maybe someone will shoot your dumb ass," Phyllis said, shifting her plucking from her eyebrows to the whiskers on her chin.

"Being on high ground, you're in a better position to defend, if you see them coming." Ed glanced around at the gaudy, peeling wall paper that had probably been glued back in the sixties. "Another thing to consider is that this shack is a prime candidate for a Molotov cocktail, served hot and wet. As old as the wood is, it would burn before you got your painted toenails out."

"That's one thing Trigger Happy Marcus and I agree on. We're ready for a little action."

"Well, you're going to get it tomorrow. We're making a trip to Baton Rouge for the first day of the trial."

Marcus looked up from cleaning his weapon. "About time."

"Thank God," Phyllis said. "I could do with a real night's sleep in a real bed."

"Sorry. It might only be a preliminary hearing and you'll be back here by the end of the night."

"Shit." She threw her tweezers on the table. "Tell me something I *want* to hear."

"You're still alive and Leon's still in jail," Ed said.

"Big fuckin' whoop." She stood and stretched, the tube top she wore sliding dangerously down over her huge breasts while her shorter than short shorts rose up displaying more than Ed ever wanted to see of her ass.

"I'm usually good for a piece of ass," Marcus said, squirting oil onto a cotton rag. "But not that."

"Oh shut up, you know you want it." Phyllis plumped her boobs, then refocused her attention on Ed. "Did you bring me chocolate today?"

"I brought you enough to last a week, the day before yesterday."

"I got bored." She shrugged. "I'll take that as a no. No chocolate, no TV, not even a radio in this godforsaken rat trap."

"Sorry. It was this or risk being nailed by one of your ex-boyfriend's mercenaries."

The woman snorted. "I'm beginning to think I should have taken my chances."

"I better go. I'm due to go fishing in a little under an hour. The diehards will be stirring."

"You wouldn't want to take her with you, would you?" Marcus slid the bolt in place, reassembled the rest of the weapon, and stood. "This place would be a whole lot nicer without her mouth."

"Hang tight. It won't be much longer." He rested a hand on Marcus's shoulder.

"I'll walk you out."

He stepped out on the back porch, followed by Marcus. "Stay here. I can find my way back without your help."

"Watch out for the—"

"Booby trap? I think I can find it this time."

"You managed to step over the first one. Look out for it as well."

"Will do." He nodded toward the shack. "Try not to kill her, even if she deserves it."

"I'll do my best." Marcus stood on the corner of the porch as Ed stepped off into the brush. Before Marcus had pointed out there were two alligators in the area, he hadn't considered that he might run into one there. Now he was on the lookout for them. Between the alligators, mad drivers, rock launchers, and the bitchy witness, and making love to a beautiful woman and then leaving her to defend herself—guilt formed a knot in his chest—he wasn't getting much sleep.

But then he could sleep when this was over. Or when he was dead.

CHAPTER 12

ALEX DIDN'T SEE ED ALL DAY. HE DIDN'T SHOW UP AT THE GYM AND HE hadn't called. After the first two nights of great sex, she'd practically come to expect more.

The meeting with the Hospital Administrator netted a contract that would put her in the black and make her a tidy profit she could use to reinvest in additional equipment and resources. But a successful business coup didn't have the same thrill as it had a week ago. Not when all she could think about was Ed and how great he'd been with the kids the night before, not to mention how incredible it had been making love on her kitchen table. She'd never eat another meal there without thinking about it.

"Wow, you really have it bad." Harry waved a hand in front of her face. "I've been talking to you for two whole minutes and you haven't heard a word I've said."

"Sorry." She pulled her ponytail out and ran her fingers through her hair. "I guess I'm tired."

"Late night with Mr. Marceau?" Harry's grin was sly. "Did you get that bruise performing mattress gymnastics?"

"Harry!"

Harry laughed, then her smile faded. "You haven't told me how you got that bruise. Did he hit you? Because if he did, he'll have me and the rest of our family to answer to."

Alex smiled, touching her chin. "No, he didn't hit me. Some teen lobbed a rock through my window. I just happened to catch it with my chin."

"*Coo Wee!* The little jerk-wad." Harry tipped her face to the light. "What's with kids these days? Mom made note of the fact Ed didn't return to his cabin all night. Was he staying to protect you from the creep?"

"Great. The woman's too nosey for her own good. Mom's going to get her hopes all built up and for what?" She rolled her eyes. "A big fat nothing. He's only into me for a vacation fling. And I'm not interested in anything more than that."

"So you keep saying. But are you sure? You've been more distracted than I've ever seen you since he showed up."

"It's this hospital deal. I've been keyed up over it."

"Yeah, right. You didn't even stutter or hesitate when you gave your pitch. I was so proud of you."

"I internalized the nerves." In fact, her head had barely been in the game. If she hadn't had the gym in top shape with the help of her team, they might have walked away.

"No, you were thinking about Ed." Harry raised a hand. "Don't try to feed me another line."

"Are we eating lines, now? Is it some kind of new diet? I could use one, I've put on a pound or two in the last couple of days."

Calliope entered the gym office, Sport in tow. "Leapin' lily pads, what happened to you?"

With a sigh, Alex touched her chin. "It's a long story. The bigger question is where the heck have you two been?" She glared at her friend. "Have you decided to move Sport into your place permanently?"

"I would, if you'd let me." Calliope grinned and hugged Sport's arm. "We had the best time watching movies into the wee hours." She yawned. "I'll be worthless at work. Speaking of which, I promised Sport you'd bring him to the Raccoon Saloon tonight."

She groaned. "Why did you do that? I'm too tired to think, much less go out."

"Please." Calliope grabbed Alex's hand. "Sport's never been there and we don't know when or if he'll get another chance. He isn't going to be in town for long." She hoped.

Sport looked at her with a hint of the sad dog look in his brown eyes. "Please."

"Guess who's going out tonight?" Harry laughed and headed for the door.

"Oh, no you don't. If I have to go, you're coming with me!" Alex called out.

"I'll dust off my cowboy boots." Harry waved without turning back.

Calliope pressed a kiss to Sport's cheek before heading out to go home and get ready for work.

Alex had promised her mother she'd bring pizza home for the family. She placed her order and picked it up before leaving Morgan City. Looking forward to a quiet drive back to Bayou Miste, Alex was instead bombarded with one question after another. It seemed Sport wanted to know everything as fast as he could think to ask.

"What is blue? How do cars work? Where do babies come from?"

By the time they pulled up in front of her mother's house, Alex's patience had been exhausted.

Her mother opened the front door for her and Sport. "Oh, Alex, thank you for bringing dinner. The kids were about ready to gnaw on the furniture."

Alex carried in four large boxes while Sport carried the other four, and they set them in the middle of the table.

"Who's not coming?" Alex asked after counting the number of settings at the table. Harry had called her before she'd gotten to Bayou Miste and said she'd had to take the late shift at the gym for a sick employee. Truman had his own place in Morgan City and didn't come to dinner often.

"Abe and GW called and said they had other plans and Dolley and Madison are staying late at the plantation for a special event."

"Will Ed be eating with us?" Teddy asked, saving Alex from letting her mother know she cared.

"No, *ma chère*," she patted her young daughter's hair. "He said he had plans, but thanks anyway."

"I wonder what plans he had," Alex said absently.

"Interested?" Her mother smiled. When she frowned in return, her mother went on to say, "He mentioned something about heading to Baton Rouge tomorrow and needing to take care of some business before going." Her mother sighed. "It's too bad, I was getting used to having him at the dinner table, and the kids like him, too." She glanced across the table at her. "You two didn't have a fight, did you?"

"Why would we have a fight? It's not like we're dating or anything." She didn't look her mother in the eye and her ears burned. *Mais, it was the truth.* They weren't dating. You couldn't call a night of plumbing and taking a herd of kids to the festival anything like a date.

"Oh, Alex, you did, didn't you?"

"No, Mom. We didn't argue." She glanced at her watch. "I have to go. Calliope made me promise to take Sport out to the Saloon tonight. I want to get there before the crowd to get a seat."

Her mother kissed her cheek. "Ed's a good guy. You should give him a chance, honey."

She sighed and hugged her mother. "I know. But he's not here tonight and I have to go."

"At least you're not saying no. *Mais,* have a good time, *ma chère*." Before she left the room, her mother had pizza on the plates of the youngest Boyettes and was taking her seat. The woman could have run an army, she was so efficient.

As she stepped out the door, Granny Saulnier's poodle, FeFe, ran by, the hot pink supplanted by day-glo orange.

Sport tensed and leaped off the porch after the poodle.

"Sport!" Alex ran after him and waited until she'd gotten out of hearing range of her mother's house before yelling, "Sport! Heel!"

He ground to a halt, his entire body quivering.

"Come," she said, using all the commands her mother had taught by example.

Sport's head dipped and he turned toward her. "Sport bad?"

"Yes," she said, but couldn't stay mad at him. Not when he looked so forlorn with those sad, puppy dog eyes. "What are we going to do with you, *mon cher*?"

"Sport like FeFe."

"I know." She hooked his arm with hers. "Do you miss being a dog?"

"Sport love Callipuppy."

"Oh, dear. No, Sport, you can't. Even though you're a man now, you'll go back to being a dog when the spell wears off."

He tipped his head. "Sport not understand."

"Never mind. Let's go have some fun. It might be the first and last time you get to go to a saloon."

He perked up. "Callipuppy there?"

Alex could almost imagine his floppy reddish-brown ears rising. Her heart wrenched. She missed having her golden retriever greet her when she arrived home, all happy and excited, begging for a treat.

She led Sport back to her car and drove to her house, where she unloaded a medium-sized pizza she'd bought to put in the freezer and eat the next day. Since she hadn't had the heart to sit at her mother's dinner table without Ed being there, she opened the box, pulled out two plates, and ate with Sport.

When they were finished, she changed, straightened her hair, applied a bit of makeup to her bare face, and helped Sport choose from a selection of three outfits Calliope had bought for him to wear out that night.

They arrived at the Raccoon Saloon a little after nine o'clock. Music vibrated through the building, into the night.

Sport was bobbing his head to the beat like he'd done as dog. Even then, he'd enjoyed music. She grabbed his arm and pasted a smile on her face. Tomorrow she'd head into Baton Rouge if she had to in order to get Lucie to undo the spell. Sport might as well have fun on his last night as a human.

The place was hopping with a Zydeco Band playing traditional Cajun music, upbeat and crazy. She tried to get in the mood, but fell short.

Sport spotted Calliope as she carried a tray of empty beer mugs. She was as beautiful as ever, wearing a pretty pink halter top and a long floral skirt, with her wild red curls pulled over one shoulder in a loose ponytail.

Breaking free of Alex's hold, Sport made a beeline for her. She dropped her tray on the counter and wrapped her arms around his neck as he hugged her around the middle and swung her around.

Alex sighed. She wished she could find that carefree exuberance that Calliope and Sport seemed to own. Their happiness to see each other made her want to go back home and crawl into a gallon of Rocky Road ice cream.

Calliope guided Sport to an empty stool at the bar and set a beer mug in front of him.

Alex groaned, wondering what reaction his new man-body would have to alcohol. She hoped he wouldn't turn out to be an angry drunk. She glanced around as the bar filled with locals stopping by for a little beer and fun after a hard day's work. Most of the men worked at Littington Industries and still wore their work overalls with Littington embroidered on the chest.

She half-hoped she'd see Ed there amongst the familiar faces. But then her mother had said he had business to take care of before he headed to Baton Rouge the following day. Hadn't he said he was from New Orleans? What business would have in Baton Rouge? Unless he'd been called in to mediate a special case. But in the middle of his vacation?

She still couldn't help but think that some things about Ed Marceau didn't add up. Next time she saw him—if there was a next time—she'd try to get her questions answered. Like why did a mediator need to carry a gun? And last night, why had he slipped away from her house like a special agent in a spy movie?

She slid onto the stool beside Sport and lifted the long-neck beer Calliope set on the counter in front of her. "What if I'd wanted draft tonight?"

Calliope shook her head. "You always get the long-neck. Face it, Alex, you're predictable."

Predictable? "You say that like it's a bad thing." She couldn't help being defensive. She prided herself on her orderly existence. It had earned her a degree in marketing, a business, and a house she was paying for, all by herself. "Predictable gets results."

Calliope rolled her eyes. "Haven't you ever wanted to do something rash? Something you hadn't thought through completely?"

Like making love to Ed? "I have. A couple times." *Lately.*

"I'll bet you thought it to death afterward and talked yourself out of doing it again." Calliope flipped her long, loose ponytail over her other shoulder and smiled. "You really need to let go and go with the flow. Let your spirit guide you. Listen to what's inside your heart, not your head."

"And fall in love with a dog?" She snorted.

Calliope frowned. "At least I *let* myself fall in love." She flicked her skirt with as much anger as her happy spirit could muster, grabbed a full tray of drinks, and went back to work.

"Why you make Callipuppy mad?"

Already regretting her words, Alex lifted her beer to her lips. "I know I shouldn't be ugly. Calliope's my friend. *You're* my friend. I should be happy you two have found each other." She turned around on her stool and stared out at the crowd.

"Alex sad?"

"Maybe."

"Why?"

"I don't know."

"Alex love Ed?"

She turned to Sport. "Why would you say that?" she raised her finger. "And don't tell me you smelled it."

Sport's brows wrinkled and he tipped his head like he did when he was trying to figure something out. "Alex and Ed are like Callipuppy and Sport." He smiled, his open, how-easy-is-this grin. "Love."

"It isn't that simple."

"Why?"

"Alex can't have Ed." She shook her head. Now she was talking like Sport. "When he leaves, he won't come back."

"Why?"

"He doesn't live in Bayou Miste."

"Then be with Ed where Ed lives."

"I can't." Alex sighed. "I live here."

"Why?"

Why indeed?

Calliope sailed over to the bar, her cheerful face glowing brighter every time she looked at Sport. "I'm on break." She set her tray down and grabbed Sport's hand. "Come dance with me."

Sport let her drag him to the dance floor where she taught him how to two-step. The band took a break and the jukebox took over. Within five minutes they were circling the floor to a country song. They looked like they belonged together. Happy and in love.

Another sigh escaped her, and as much as it hurt to witness their happiness, she couldn't drag her gaze away. The music slowed and Calliope wrapped her arms around Sport's neck and leaned her cheek against his chest. He held her around her middle and rested his face against the side of her hair, closing his eyes. When the song ended, Calliope leaned up on her toes, cupped Sport's face and kissed him. From where she sat, it appeared Sport was kissing her back. Another song started up and the couple resumed swaying, oblivious to everyone else dancing by them in a flowing waltz.

"Dance wit' me, Alex," a voice said next to her. "Or be you too good for ol' Theo?"

A chunk of lead hit the pit of her belly. She turned to stare up into Theo's eyes. The man reeked of too much alcohol and sweat.

Way to put the kibosh on dreams of love and happiness.

"Go away, Theo." She turned away from the dance floor and lifted her bottle to her lips.

* * *

Ed spent the afternoon preparing for the next day's transportation of the witness to the courthouse in Baton Rouge. He cleaned his rifle and handgun, filled the rental car's gas tank, checked the tires, and charged his smartphone. He even went to Morgan City to purchase a burner phone in case he needed an untraceable number, should the mission go south.

The plan was to move the Ragsdale woman under the cover of night, late enough that everyone would be in bed asleep. Until then he had to cool his heels and wait. He'd declined Mrs. Boyette's dinner invitation, claiming he had things to do. Truth was, he didn't want to see Alex when all he wanted to do was hold her and kiss her and...well, lose sight of the reason he was there. If the rock through her window last night was meant for him, he might already have put her and her family in danger.

At nine that evening, darkness had settled over the bayou, but it was still too early to make his move. He'd paced the length of the house and back a hundred times, working through every scenario he could imagine and his potential response. Between him and Marcus, they had to get Phyllis out alive and deliver her to the courthouse without incident.

His phone vibrated in his pocket and he jerked it out. Caller ID indicated a blocked number. He pressed the talk button. "Yeah."

"Ed, it's Ben."

"You on a burner?"'

"Yes. As close as we are to D-day, I didn't want to risk your phone being traced from mine."

"Great minds think alike." He gave him the number of the burner he'd purchased earlier. "What's happening on your end?"

"Primeaux has had someone observing him twenty-four-seven and he hasn't seemed to make a move to have our witness terminated."

"What are the chances he'll let her live to testify against him?"

"Everyone at this end is betting a hundred to one."

"Right."

"Tomorrow's going to be hectic. Have her wear a bullet-proof vest, you and Marcus, too. If he really has a bounty out on her, you know there will be bullets flying." Ben heaved a tense breath. "Any other attacks on your end?"

"Not today, but then I haven't been outside much, other than to jog this morning and once this afternoon."

"Oh, I did get something on Oscar Mills."

He tensed. "Shoot."

"Retired DEA sharpshooter."

"Retired DEA sharpshooter?" He shook his head. "What's a guy like that doing here in the bayou?" Unless he was hired by Leon. "Anything in his background show he's gone dirty? Any foreclosures? Owe a ton of money? Default on his loans or taxes? Cousins in the Primeaux family? Anything?"

"No. The man was highly decorated in the DEA, retired early after twenty-five years of service. He's only forty-three."

"Hell, he could be on his second career as Leon's hit man." Ed ran a hand through his hair. "I don't like it."

"You have a couple hours to kill. Sorry, poor choice of words." Ben chuckled. "You have a couple hours before the extraction—get out there and get a bead on Mills."

"Will do."

"And Ed?"

"Yeah."

"Be careful."

"I think I'll be more in danger of crossfire from Marcus shooting at Ragsdale than anything else. Have you heard the mouth on that woman?"

Ben hung up, laughing.

He tucked his weapons into their cases, locked them, and shoved them under the bed. With his keys in hand, he locked up, jumped in his car, and drove slowly along the main street through town, checking out any movement. Before he reached the cabin where Oscar Mills was staying, the Ford Fusion Mills had been driving pulled out of his drive and headed north.

Falling in behind him, but keeping a reasonable distance back, Ed followed the retired sharpshooter, all the way to the Raccoon Saloon. Was he stopping there for a drink or to meet with one of Primeaux's men?

Only one way to find out.

He passed the saloon and gave Mills enough time to park and enter, before he made a U-turn on the highway and returned to the bar, parking in the rear.

He slipped in through the back door the employees used. With no one there to question him, he managed to enter the saloon unnoticed, emerging near the hallway leading to the bathrooms. For the next few minutes, he panned the interior of the saloon, until he found Oscar Mills sitting at one end of the bar, nursing a beer, by himself, while staring out at the room full of natives line dancing or drinking pitchers of beer and downing oyster shooters.

At the other end of the bar, closest to Ed, a big man stood with his back to him. By the breadth of his shoulders and the way he stood, he guessed it was Theo Ledet.

The man swayed and spoke loud enough that Ed could hear his words over the music. "What, are you too good ta dance wit' me now dat you got de hot shot from Naw-lins to screw?" The man leaned into whoever he was talking to, swaying.

The woman to whom he spoke reached up a slim hand and slapped the crap out of him.

He staggered a step backward and braced his feet. "You shoulda not done dat." He reached out and grabbed her.

A flurry of movement and flying arms resulted, and, within seconds, Alex Boyette had Theo Ledet face down on the sticky barroom floor with his arm twisted up behind him. She stepped into the middle of his back and said, loud enough for everyone in the joint to hear, "Theo Ledet, for the last time. Leave. Me. Alone."

Ed chuckled. She hadn't been kidding when she said she knew karate. Then again, the man had been stone drunk.

Alex stepped over the guy and started toward the dance floor. She'd only gone two steps when the dumbass on the floor grabbed her ankle. She toppled like a statue, hit the ground hard and lay there stunned long enough for Theo to haul himself to his feet and grab her by her hair.

Every protective instinct inside him erupted into bottled-up rocket fuel and Ed launched himself across the room, plowing over chairs, legs, and people scrambling to get out of his way.

As Theo pulled Alex up by the hair, he flung a right hook into the side of his face.

Theo barely recoiled, but he did let go of Alex's hair and turn the full force of his inebriated anger on him.

"Back off, Ed, I've got this," Alex said as she rolled over and staggered to her feet, pushing her hair out of her face. "The man has a jaw of iron; you won't faze him—"

Theo threw a punch aimed at his nose.

Ed dodged to the side, but wasn't fast enough to miss the second swing. He took it in the jaw and jerked back, pain radiating through his head.

The next punch, he was ready for. He dodged, hooked Theo's arm, and yanked it up behind his back between his shoulder blades. "You gonna act nice or am I gonna break it?" he demanded.

Theo whimpered. "I'll be nice. Promise."

"You gonna quit following Miz Alex and leave her alone?"

"Yes sir, I be leavin' dat gal alone."

Alex focused on the bartender. "Call the sheriff, this man needs help getting home." Once he had Theo loaded into a patrol car, Ed returned to the saloon. Oscar still sat at the end of the bar. His gaze met Ed's, a smile curling the corners of his lips. He tipped his mug at him and nodded.

When he looked around, Ed noted Calliope and Sport locked in an embrace on the dance floor, but Alex was gone.

Face it, buddy, you have to move on. Mills didn't appear to be a threat, and looked like he'd be at the saloon for a while.

Having already wasted enough time in town, it was time to get out to the bayou and collect the package to be delivered.

CHAPTER 13

THE EXTRACTION WENT SMOOTHLY. MARCUS AND ED GOT PHYLLIS OUT OF the swamp with no problem other than trying to keep the harpy quiet when they'd reached Bayou Miste. Marcus looked ready to pull the trigger. If not on her, then on himself.

After spending four days with the witch, he was certain Marcus would get off on an insanity plea.

To burn time, they sat in the car on a deserted road west of Baton Rouge for a couple hours. They weren't expected to arrive at the courthouse until nine in the morning. He and Ben had planned a circuitous route so they could throw a tail or see if anyone was following them.

Phyllis whined and complained about wearing the bulletproof vest, claiming it wasn't her color and it made her look fat. In the end she put it on for fear Marcus would be the one to shoot her.

On the drive through Baton Rouge, the occupants of the Jeep grew tense. Even Phyllis shut up as they got closer to the courthouse where she was to testify against one of the most ruthless mobsters south of the Mason Dixon line.

Twice Marcus thought he'd spotted a tail. Twice Ed rerouted and took another turn to confuse any would-be hit man. As the clock neared nine, they rolled up to the steps of the courthouse. Marcus got out first, his hand on his gun inside his suit jacket, and held the door for Phyllis to alight.

Ben met them with two other plainclothes cops. Ed circled the car and blocked the view as Phyllis stepped out.

Some members of the press, who'd gathered around the prosecuting attorney at the top of the steps of the East Baton Rouge Parish Courthouse, spied the vehicle and moved as one to get an interview with the next arrival from the trial of the century.

As Phyllis stepped up on the sidewalk, her heel caught on the curb and she lurched forward.

One of the plainclothes cops jerked backward and landed on his ass on the concrete, groaning.

"Gunshot fired!" Ed yelled, planted his hand on Phyllis's head and shoved her into the back seat on the floorboard, folded her legs in after her, and slammed the door. "Get in!" he shouted to Marcus.

The back windshield exploded in a spray of glass fragments.

While he ran around to the driver's side, reporters screamed and uniforms herded bystanders into the courthouse. Marcus dove into the passenger seat and Ed gunned the accelerator, sending the damaged rental flying away from the crime scene.

He tossed the burner to Marcus. "Call Ben, tell him we're going to stash the loot and wait for an all-clear before we attempt this again."

"What the fuck?" Phyllis raged from the back floorboard. "I'll sue the state of Louisiana on assault charges. Did you have to be so goddamn rough? Shit, I broke a nail!"

As planned, if the transfer got botched, they ditched the Jeep in a parking garage and picked up the replacement and headed back to the bayou, taking a long route to make sure no one followed. They'd decided the bayou was the best location since they could see danger coming, and if it came to an all-out war, fewer people would be hurt in the crossfire, than if they hid her in town.

Frankly, he couldn't wait to get back. Number one, to get rid of the witness from hell whose mouth should be exiled to a deserted island. Although he wouldn't wish that on the fish and the palm trees.

Number two, he wanted to see Alex and make sure she was all right. Hell, and to admit to her that he was falling for her.

* * *

ALEX HAD CALLED in sick to her gym for the first time in the three years she'd owned it. After seeing Ed last night take a hit for her, she'd wanted to go to him, melt into his arms, and tell him she loved him. But the feelings were so raw and uncontrolled, she'd run from them, from Ed, from what she really wanted. Once she'd gotten into her car, she realized her mistake. She should have gone back in and told Ed how she felt. Instead, she'd gone home in a funk so blue she couldn't focus.

Sport had spent the night at Calliope's again. Which meant Alex had been alone throughout the night. She'd tossed and turned, her body alternating between cold and lonely and raging heat from memories of what she and Ed had shared in her bed, on her kitchen table, and all the places they hadn't had the opportunity to try out.

Sometime during the night, she'd fallen into a deep, dreamless sleep and slept past her alarm. When she finally woke, it was past nine o'clock and the sun peeked through her blinds. Too wound up to focus on work, she'd called Harry and asked her to pull a double, taking the early and the late shift that day. With energy to burn, she pulled on her jogging shorts, sport bra and sneakers, and hit the road.

Joe Thibodeaux was out in front of the marina painting the exterior wall as high up as he could reach without a ladder.

Too curious to pass him by, she slowed to jog in place. "What happened to your morning fishing buddy?"

"Cancelled. Said he had business to take care of today."

She jogged a few more steps in place. "Did he say when he'd be back?"

"Nope. Said not to expect him back in. He'd call if he wanted to schedule another morning." Joe shook his head. "He was comin' along pretty good for a man who'd never put a hook in the water."

Alex stopped jogging. He'd said he'd come to Bayou Miste to get some fishing in on vacation. "He'd never been fishing?"

"Couldn't have. Not the way he handled the rod." Joe scratched his beard, smearing white paint on his face. "What he lacked in experience, though, he made up for in enthusiasm."

Interesting. A man on vacation in a bayou town who'd never been fishing. "Have a nice day, Joe."

"You, too."

She jogged past her mother's house, almost tripping over her own feet as she passed the little rental cottage where Ed stayed, craning her neck to see if he was home. Disappointment flooded her. His car was gone and the place looked empty. If he never came back, that's how it would remain.

A lump the size of a wadded up tube sock lodged in her throat and she had to blink to clear her vision. Pushing harder, she ran faster and faster, until she was a mile out of town and feeling no better. She turned and headed back, passing her home once again.

"Alex!" Her mother waved at her from her porch. "Care for a cup of coffee?"

Tired and sweating, she shook her head. "No, thanks, Mom. But I'll take a glass of iced tea if you have some."

Her mother smiled. "I even have some fresh beignets—Miz Mozelle brought them by this morning. She wanted to give them to Ed, but he hasn't been home all night. I thought he wasn't heading into Baton Rouge until this morning, but I guess he left under the cover of darkness." She shrugged. "Our benefit. We get the beignets."

Alex bypassed the large dining room table, opting for the dinette that seated six in the Boyette kitchen. "Kids off to school?"

"Left a couple hours ago." Her mother poured two glasses of iced tea and set them on the table, sinking into the seat. "This is one of my favorite times of the day."

"Morning calm?"

"Umhmm." She sipped from her glass and smiled. "My other favorite time of day is dinner when everyone's here and talking at once."

“Don’t you get lonely?”

“Oh, no, *ma chère*. I like my time alone. Much as I love my children, I look forward to the day when I can leave Bayou Miste.”

Her heart skipped several beats and then hammered away. "What?"

Her mother patted her hand. "To travel, *ma chère*. This will always be my home, but when I was young, before I met your father, I used to dream of seeing other places, other countries. I still have those dreams." The light in her mother's eyes made her appear younger, more vibrant.

She could almost visualize the young woman she'd once been, before nineteen children had tied her down. "Why did I never know that about you?"

Her mother smiled. "Your father loved Bayou Miste, it was his home and he never wanted to leave. I was happy with that, as long as I had him or my children." Her eyes glazed with tears. "But once my work is done raising all of you, I want to spread my wings, before I get too old to do it."

Alex swallowed on the knot in her throat that the memories of her father always brought. "Did you ever regret having so many of us?"

She smiled, shaking her head. "Never. I can't imagine life without every one of you." Her mother reached out and caressed her cheek. "My one regret was that you had to grow up too soon. Now, I'm afraid you feel responsible for all of us, and that's not at all what I wished for you, my first daughter. I dreamed of you spreading your wings, getting out of Bayou Miste, and experiencing the world."

"And here I am." A tear pushed out of the corner of her eye and slipped down her cheek. "I couldn't leave you to handle everything by yourself."

Her mother smiled. "I'm pretty tough. I can handle things." She leaned forward as if imparting a secret. "And in case you didn't notice...I'm not all by myself. Your brothers and sisters are quite capable of helping out, just like you did growing up. It builds character." She covered Alex's hand with hers. "If there's another life you want to lead or were afraid to dream, don't let it pass you by. Reach out, run toward it. You have my blessing. Not that you need it."

"Oh, yes, I do." More tears trickled down Alex's face and she squeezed her mother's hands.

"If that young man comes back, don't you push him away like you always do. Give him a chance."

"What if he doesn't want me?"

Her mother shook her head. "Who wouldn't want you?"

She laughed, the sound catching on a sob. "From Mom's mouth to God's ears."

"Now go to work. The day will pass much more quickly."

She left her mother's house, her heart much lighter, her feet barely touching the ground.

When she entered her house, she shed her workout clothes, grabbed a towel, and headed for the bathroom while dialing Lucie's number.

"Alex, did you hear?" Lucie asked, her voice shaking.

She had reached to turn on the shower, but paused. "Hear what?"

"About the shooting." Lucie sobbed into the phone. "At the courthouse. Someone tried to kill the witness in the case against the mobster, Leon Primeaux. One of the cops escorting her was hit."

She gripped the phone, her heart clenching so tightly she could barely breathe. "Where's Ben? Was he there? Is he all right?"

"He was there!" Lisa cried some more while Alex held her breath. "But he's okay. He wasn't hurt."

The air rushed out of Alex's lungs and she sagged against the sink. "Don't scare me like that!"

"I'm sorry. I was shaking so badly, I thought I'd miscarry this baby. I'd heard it over the news and I tried to get Ben on the phone and...and...I was so scared, Alex. I'm not cut out to be the wife of a cop."

"Yes you are. You know you love him." She did her best to soothe her friend when her own hands were shaking. "Can you imagine being with anyone else?"

"No. But if something should happen to him, I couldn't stand the idea of living without him."

She envied Lucie. She'd found someone she cared about so much she would sacrifice everything to be with him, even her life. And she couldn't be with a better man than Ben. "*Ma chère,* we never know how much time we have with the ones we love. Be thankful for every day you have with him."

"I know. I know. I'm being hormonal, but I love him so much."

"Honey, he's okay. You're going to be okay. Take a deep breath and pull yourself together. The baby needs you to be strong."

After a few sniffles and a loud snort as if Lucie was blowing her nose, she said, "Thanks, Alex, I needed to hear that. Now, I *know* you didn't call for me to have a nervous breakdown in your ear. Why *did* you call?"

Figuring it would take Lucie's mind off Ben's near-miss, she drew in a deep breath and launched into the reason for her call. "Is the Voodoo that made Sport human permanent?"

"Oh, Alex, I have no idea. Whatever Gran LeBieu put in that *gris gris* bag had to have been some powerful stuff to have done what it did."

"I need to know if it will stick."

"*Mais,* the spell she put on Craig Thibodeaux lasted over a week. I'm not even sure my grandmother knows how long her spells will last. She always says something like *they'll last as long as they're needed* or something vague like that. Why? Are things pretty bad down there?"

Alex sighed. "No. But I wonder if it's possible for the spell to be made permanent."

"You'll have to run that by my grandmother." Lucie paused. "Are you falling in love with Sport as a man?"

She laughed and then sobered. "No, I'm not falling for Sport, but Calliope is. And he's in love with her."

"*Coo wee!* I can't say I miss the craziness of Bayou Miste." Lucie clucked her tongue. "That's so like Calliope. She has such a big heart."

"I know, and I'd hate to see it broken."

"Wish I could help."

"You can help by taking care of yourself, my godchild, and my big brother."

"I'll do my best. What about you, Alex?" Lucie asked. "Is there someone special in your life? I always dreamed we'd have babies at the same time so that our children could grow up together. Anything on that front?"

She cringed when she heard the sound of her biological clock ticking for the first time. Immediately Ed's face appeared in her mind. "No, nothing yet."

"I'll burn a red candle for you," Lucie offered. "Maybe it will bring you luck on the love front."

"Thanks, but don't burn the house down doing it." She hung up, jumped in the shower, and got ready for work, after all. Staying home left her way too much time to think. She needed the day to go by quickly like her mother had promised. Her heart beat faster in anticipation of seeing Ed that evening. *Please let him come back.*

* * *

"I'M sick and tired of being in this car. I'm hot, I'm thirsty, and I have to pee like nobody's goddamn business."

Marcus and Ed chimed together, "Shut up!"

Phyllis Ragsdale sniffed. "I'm the one being shot at. You could be a little more sympathetic to the lady present."

Marcus glared at the woman in the back seat. "You are no lady. You're a—"

"As soon as it's dark," Ed cut in, "we'll take you back out to the bayou and you can stretch, drink, and pee to your heart's content."

"I don't want to go back to the bayou. It's dirty, buggy and...and...unairconditioned!"

"And you might stay alive a day longer there than in the city," Ed said, his voice a little less strained. The sun was setting and they had been driving down back roads with grass growing up so close to the edges, the roads appeared as if they hadn't been used in decades. Every once in a while, they stopped in a pullout or overgrown driveway to cool the engine and find a bush to urinate behind. The last stop had been over an hour ago, and even he was ready to get the hell out of the car.

As the sun set and the stars started popping out against the black backdrop of sky, he turned the car toward Bayou Miste, slipped onto the first side street, and parked behind an empty building. "Tighten your vests."

Phyllis shrank against the back seat, showing the first signs of fear since leaving Baton Rouge. "You think they'll be gunnin' for me here?"

"We don't know, but there's only one way to find out." Marcus climbed out and held the door for her. "Let's go."

Ed and Marcus flanked her as they hurried across the street and down the bank of the canal to where they'd tied off the pirogue.

The trip back to the shack in the swamp passed without incident and very little talking. Phyllis insisted on sitting at the bottom of the boat, as low to the water as she could get without getting wet. When they arrived at the shack, Marcus took the lead and cleared the building before they stepped one foot inside.

By the time Ed returned to Bayou Miste, collected the car, and drove to the rental cottage beside the Boyette house, he was tired and ready to hit the sack for some much-needed rest. He glanced down the street, wishing he could see all the way to Alex's house. Was she awake? Would she let him in, if he were to knock on her door? After all that had happened that day, all he wanted was to feel her in his arms.

He climbed out of his car and headed for the little house that had become more of a home to him than his apartment back in Baton Rouge.

A movement on the porch made him reach for his gun, setting his senses on alert.

"Is that a gun in your hand, or are you happy to see me?" Alex's chuckle drifted to him on the warm, moist night air, wrapping around him like the scent of honeysuckle.

"What are you doing here, sitting alone in the dark?"

"Waiting for you to come back."

"What if I hadn't?"

"I guess I'd have gone home." She rose from the steps and waited for him to close the distance. "You look tired."

"It's been a rough day."

"Wanna tell me about it?"

"No, I want to know why you left the saloon last night without saying anything to me."

"I wished I hadn't as soon as I did. Too many things hit me all at once and...and..." she shrugged, "I ran."

"What things?"

"Things like realizing I was beginning to care too much about you." She smiled, tears trembling on her lashes. "I was scared."

"That would make two of us, then." He stood in front of her wanting to take her into his arms, but realized that if she was scared of her feelings, she had to make the first move.

Alex held her arms open.

He walked into them and hugged her for a long time. Her body melted against his, fitting perfectly. He would have stayed that way much longer, but the events of the day kept coming back to him, like a car's factory-installed warning light that couldn't be turned off. "Let's go inside."

She didn't resist, taking his hand as they climbed the steps. "I know we haven't known each other that long, but I missed you today."

Ed unlocked the door, pulled her through, and locked it behind her, then pressed her against the door and kissed her.

Her hands locked behind his head and she leaned into him, opening to the thrust of his tongue, sliding her leg alongside his.

When he had to come up for air, he peppered tiny kisses along her cheekbone to her ear and down the side of her neck. He couldn't get enough.

She laughed and feathered her fingers through his hair. "I've wanted to do this all day long. I'd been counting the minutes until you came back."

He leaned back and gazed into her blue eyes. "After you left the saloon last night without saying anything, I thought you were done with me. What made you change your mind?"

"A very wise woman told me not to let life pass me by out of some mistaken sense of duty." Alex shrugged. "I decided it was time to start living for me."

"And how do I fit in this picture?"

Her face shined up at him. "I feel alive when I'm with you. More alive than I've felt in a long time."

He cupped her cheeks, his heart melting at what the sparkle in her eyes. "You don't know me."

"But I want to." Alex turned her face to his palm and kissed it.

"What if you don't like me when you *do* get to know who I am?"

"I'll take that risk."

"That's pretty bold for someone who craves structure in her life."

"I'm turning over a new leaf. I even rearranged the towels in my bathroom so that nothing is stacked according to the color."

"Big step for a control freak."

"Hey." She slapped him on the shoulder, playfully. "It is, for me."

Ed leaned his forehead against hers. "Like I said, this has been a rough day."

Alex stiffened beneath him. "If you'd rather I left and let you get some rest, I will."

"No. Please, stay and let me finish." He brushed his thumb across her cheek, loving how soft and silky her skin was. "Even during the worst parts of my day, I couldn't stop thinking about you."

Alex's brows wrinkled. "In a good way or a bad way?"

He chuckled. "Definitely in a good way." His smile faded. "The problem is that right now, I can't afford to think about you."

"What do you mean?" She gazed into his eyes, her light blue ones darkening to gray. "What aren't you telling me?"

"There are things you don't know about me and I can't tell you right now."

"I was right." She pushed against him. "You're married."

"No. I'm single. In fact, some, including your brother, would call me a confirmed bachelor."

She stopped struggling and rested her palms against his chest. "And are you? Confirmed?"

"Until I met you." He kissed the tip of her nose and she stood on her toes to kiss his lips.

He returned the kiss then gripped her arms and set her at arm's length. "Give me time. I have something to take care of before I can think of us."

"If you told me what it was, maybe I could help."

"No." He wanted to tell her the truth, but the more she knew the more she would become a target of Leon's band of murderers. "I can't. You have to trust me."

She sucked in a breath and let it out slowly. "Okay. We'll do this your way." Her fingers tightened in his shirt and she pulled him close until they were nose to nose. "But know this—When I want something badly enough, I don't give up easily."

He laughed and brushed his lips across her full, sensuous mouth. "Baby, I'm counting on it."

This time when they kissed, he let himself believe there would be another time for them. After the trial. After his job here was done.

Tires squealed outside and a loud crash put his senses on alert. He shoved Alex to the floor and crouched there with her.

"What the hell was that?" Alex cried.

The scent of gasoline filled the air and then smoke filtered in with it. "Fire." Ed leaped to his feet and ran into the living room of the little house. The front window had a gaping, jagged hole and the old sofa was drenched in gasoline and fire. And the fire was spreading quickly. He grabbed a throw pillow and beat at the flames, but the gasoline had soaked into the cushions and no amount of beating was going to stop the fire from spreading. It swept to the filmy curtains beside the window and licked at the ancient wallpaper.

"Leave it." Alex grabbed his arm and dragged him toward the door.

He couldn't let her go out the front for fear it was a trap and someone could be out there waiting to shoot at them as they made a run for it. He turned her toward the rear of the house and ran for the back-door as smoke filled the interior.

As they fell through the back door, Ed tucked Alex into the curve of his arm and ran with her to her mother's house.

Barbara Boyette met them at the back door, her phone in her hand, the children gathered behind her, eyes wide and scared. "I called nine-one-one, they're sending a fire truck from Morgan city. They'll be here as soon as they can."

Ed shoved Alex into her mother's arms. "Keep her here and stay inside until I come back. Don't follow me. Do you understand? "

Alex and her mother nodded.

He made a wide circle around the two houses, checking all the shadowy bushes and dark corners of buildings for anyone lurking, ready to take a shot at him or anyone else. When he felt comfortably sure whoever had thrown the homemade fire bomb at the house had gone, he ran into the Boyette house. "It's okay, whoever did it is gone. But if that fire spreads to the trees, it could put your house in danger. We need to gather all the hoses you have."

Alex led him to the burning house and located the hoses on the outside, while Mrs. Boyette put her army of children to work collecting buckets and hoses around her house.

They sprayed the exterior of the Boyette house and fought back any burning embers that strayed in their direction. Calliope and Sport joined them.

"We were awake, watching old reruns when we saw that the sky light up." Calliope swept a hand out, taking in the disaster. "*Coo wee!* We never thought it was your mom's house. We came to help." She and Sport started a bucket brigade. Joe Thibodeaux, Mozelle Reneau and Oscar Mills, the retired DEA agent, joined the fight, along with other neighbors. It seemed as if the inhabitants of Bayou Miste all teamed up to save the Boyette house from destruction.

By the time the fire engine arrived, the rental cottage was too far gone to save, but the Boyette house stood as strong and intact as ever. Firefighters hooked up giant hoses to the hydrants and sprayed a steady stream of water at the core of the fire, pumping hundreds of gallons of water onto the flames.

Alex and her mother herded the children away from both houses, maintaining a strict headcount throughout. Friends and neighbors stood by, watching as the house burned and the firemen fought the blaze.

Ed glanced around at the throng, knowing that arsonists like to lurk on the fringes and witness the destruction. It gave them a sense of power. He scanned the faces in the crowd of neighbors and onlookers, searching for anyone who looked different. It was then that he spotted someone he recognized that didn't fit in with the other residents of Bayou Miste. "Alex," he whispered into her ear and laid a hand on her shoulder. "Is that Theo Ledet standing in the shadow of the house down the street?"

Alex turned the way he directed and scanned the street. "Yes, it is."

"If I remember correctly, he doesn't live in Bayou Miste, does he?"

"No, but he likes to come down from Morgan City to the Raccoon Saloon." She stiffened. "You think he did this?"

His hand dropped to his side. "I don't know, but I'm going to find out." He slipped behind the crowd and walked along the other side of the street that paralleled the bayou until he was across from the house where Theo hid.

As he crossed the street, Theo spotted him, his eyes widened, and he ran.

Ed took off after him. In his peripheral vision, he saw Oscar Mills leap from the front porch of his rental, and run straight for Theo.

Theo dodged the former agent and Ed tackled the younger man to the ground, yanked his arm up behind him, and pinned it between his shoulder blades.

"You got him?" Mills asked.

"Got 'em," he answered. "Thanks."

"Good, 'cause I couldn't have done much more than that." Mills bent over his knees and sucked air into his lungs. "Damn, I'm out of shape."

Alex caught up with them, breathing fast. She stood with her fists on her hips, looking like a warrior ready to rip into the man on the ground. With her eyes burning bright and twin flashes of color in her cheeks, she was so beautiful, Ed almost let go of his captive to kiss her.

"Theo Ledet, did you burn my mamma's rent house down?"

"No." Theo grunted as Ed pushed his arm up higher. "No, I didn't."

"If you didn't do it, why the hell did you run?" Alex crossed her arms. "Stinks like guilt to me."

Ed pushed the arm even higher. "Tell the truth. They can pull prints off the bottle you threw. You won't get away with it."

The man strained beneath him, his face streaked with sweat. "Okay, okay. I did it."

He jerked the man's arm, anger burning in his gut. That fire could have killed Alex. It could have spread to her family's home, maybe injured one of her siblings, like Teddy or Molly. "I told you to leave Alex alone."

"I was a gonna, but dat man paid me damn good money to do it."

His heart skipped a beat and he leaned closer to Theo. "What man?"

"The one at the Raccoon Saloon. He paid me to start de fi-yuh."

"What'd he look like?" Ed demanded.

"Like a business man, wearing pressed pants and de polo shirt. Older. White hair." Theo groaned. "Let up on de arm and I'll tell ya more."

He eased the man's arm down a fraction. "Talk."

"He wanted me to distract you."

"Why?"

"I dôn know. He asked 'bout airboats and guides to get out in de bayou."

"What did you tell him?" Ed demanded, his hand tightening on the man's arm.

"I tol' him 'bout Thibodeaux. He wanted a different guide, someone not from Bayou Miste. So I tol' him 'bout my cousin what live up de road toward Morgan City. He dôn have no airboat, but knows someone what do."

"When did you tell him this?"

"Afore I come to set de fire. Couple hours ago."

Alex glared down at Theo. "You almost burned my family home to the ground."

"I dint want dat. Only to get rid of de man what took my gal."

Alex leaned toward Theo. "When are you going to get it through your thick head. I'm not your girl, never was and never...I repeat...*never* will be."

"You wit' dis man now?" Theo jerked his head toward Ed.

"As far as you're concerned, yes." She challenged Ed with a glare that made his heart kick over and warmed his insides. "Now, if you'll excuse me, I'm going to get the sheriff."

She was back in moments, dragging the sheriff and two of his deputies who'd come to help direct traffic around the emergency personnel handling the fire.

They loaded Theo into their vehicle and took him to Morgan City's jail house on suspicion of arson.

By the time they finished with Theo and returned to the fire and the diminishing crowd, the firemen declared it safe to go back to their homes. It was nearing morning, and the first streaks of gray lit the eastern sky. Joe and Miz Mozelle had helped Mrs. Boyette and the older children get the younger ones inside and put to bed.

Then Miz Mozelle, Joe, and Oscar Mills stood outside with Mrs. Boyette, overlooking the smoldering hulk of the rental. Once the last fire engines had left along with all the emergency personnel, quiet finally descended on Bayou Miste.

Ed approached an exhausted Mrs. Boyette and took her hands in his. "I'm sorry."

"*Mon cher,* what have you to be sorry about?" She gave him a weak smile, the wrinkles around her eyes deeper, and the shadows beneath her eyes darker. She had enough to worry about without him being there.

"I'm afraid my being here has put your family in danger."

"Don't be silly." Mrs. Boyette hugged his arm. "How could that be?"

"I can't say now, but I won't be staying in Bayou Miste much longer." He met Alex's gaze over her mother's head.

Confusion warred with hurt in her expression. "Do you want to stay at my house until you have to leave?"

"No." Every moment he spent with this family put them deeper and deeper in the danger that was Leon Primeaux's doing. "I have to go."

Before he'd taken two steps away from Alex and her family, he paused to listen to the sound of a speeding vehicle, headed their way.

The car raced down the street and skidded into the driveway, spewing gravel.

He reached for his gun. "Stay back."

Mrs. Boyette leaned around him, peering at the car in the driveway. "It's Ben and Lucie!" She pushed past him and ran toward the driver emerging from the car, landing in her oldest son's strong embrace.

Alex and Calliope followed, pulling Lucie into a group hug.

"Oh, Lucie, why are you two here, when you should be home with your feet up?" Alex asked.

"I came with Ben." Lucie rubbed her hand over the mound of her belly. "He said he needed to get to Bayou Miste ASAP, but he wouldn't tell me why and I wouldn't let him leave me. Not after today's shooting at the courthouse." She wrinkled her nose and glanced at the damp, smoking remains of the rental. "I'd say we're a little late."

Ben shook his head "I hope not." His gaze caught Ed's over the top of his mother's head. "Heard from or street informant. Word's out. They know she's here."

CHAPTER 14

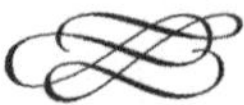

ALEX GLANCED FROM HER BROTHER TO ED. "WHAT ARE YOU TALKING about?"

Ed's focus remained on Ben, his face tense, his hand still resting on the gun attached to his belt. "How? No one else should know."

"You two work together?" Alex touched Ed's arm.

"Yes," Ed answered, the word clipped, not inviting more questions from her.

She refused to be ignored. "You weren't here on vacation to fish?"

"No." His lips twisted. "Although I did fish as part of my cover."

"Which would explain why you didn't know how." Anger burned inside, and disappointment. He'd lied to her from day one.

Ben's mouth tightened. "There's a mole on the force. Someone must have leaked it that you and I were hiding her. A person on the inside could have put a trace on my cell phone usage or contacted the phone company for a records search. Whatever happened, Primeaux's thugs know she's in the area."

"She who?" Lucie's face had gone white. "The witness who was shot at this morning?" She gripped Ben's arm. "Tell me she's not here—she's not in Bayou Miste."

"Sorry, darlin'. But Phyllis Ragsdale, the key witness in Leon

Primeaux's trial has been hiding out on the bayou for the past three days."

Her chest tightened. No wonder Ed had come to Bayou Miste. And that would explain why he'd disappeared on occasion.

"Ed's been undercover watching for signs of Primeaux's hit squad, while Marcus, our other man, has been babysitting the Ragsdale woman out in the bayou."

"I'm sorry I had to lie to you," Ed said to Mrs. Boyette, his gaze shifting to Alex. "I couldn't say anything to anyone. We didn't know who to trust and couldn't risk word getting out."

"Now that they know she's here, all hell's gonna break lose." Ben's jaw tightened. "Ed and I have to get out there and make sure she survives the day." He turned to his mother. "Keep Lucie inside and safe."

Their mother nodded, her face tired, but determined. "I will."

"If you have a gun, get it out and use it if anyone approaches any member of your family," Ed said.

Alex swallowed her anger. "If they're hiring someone to drive an airboat, you'll need something faster that will go where an airboat goes and get you there before them."

Ben's head dipped as if he was thinking hard. "If they could get someone out this early without a reservation, it would still take time to travel the distance along the canals and tributaries. We need an airboat."

"Sorry, we've been getting by with your mother's jon boat." Ed shook his head. "Top speed is about twenty knots."

Oscar Mills stepped forward, his face smeared with soot from helping with the fire. "Joe's got one."

Joe grinned. "That's right. I do."

Ben and Ed faced the man and spoke simultaneously. "Since when?"

Joe's grin widened. "Yesterday. Had it in the shop, rebuildin' the engine. Was about to start advertising bayou tours. Oscar, here, was gonna be my first customer."

"What are we waiting for?" Ben headed for the marina.

"Wait," Ed called out. "If we go out on the bayou now, and they see us, the chances of getting back unharmed are slim. We need a plan."

Oscar Mills raised his hand. "I'd like to help."

"I don't know you." Ben frowned. "How do I know you're not one of Leon's men?"

"I spent twenty-five years as a DEA agent before I was medically retired."

"Seems kinda strange, you showing up at the same time I did," Ed said.

"That was pure coincidence." Mills's smile faded.

"Joe says you've been out on the bayou every day and that you weren't taking any fishing gear."

Oscar shot a glance at Joe. "I didn't come to the bayou to fish."

Ed and Ben crossed their arms across their chests at the same time.

"Then why did you come?" Ed asked.

"I came to see Madame LeBieu." Mills ducked his head. "I heard she was a good healer."

Lucie giggled. "Seems my grandmother has a following that extends beyond Bayou Miste. What did you need healing for?"

Mills's back straightened and he held his head high. "I was diagnosed with brain cancer."

Alex gasped, a band tightening around her chest. "Brain cancer? Isn't that terminal?"

The agent nodded. "All the doctors gave up on me. I was ready to try anything, even Voodoo."

For the first time since she'd met the man, Alex noted how deep the lines were around his eyes and how pale his face was. "How long did the doctors give you to live?"

"Anywhere from four months to two years."

Silence fell on the folks gathered. She couldn't think of anything to say that wouldn't sound trite. Her heart went out to the man who'd been desperate enough to seek help from a bayou legend.

Oscar raised his hands. "It's okay. Whatever Madame LeBieu has been giving me is working. The tumor has been shrinking. My doctors are calling it a miracle."

"Can you still shoot straight?" Ed asked.

Mills nodded. "I have my own guns, too."

"Ammo?" Ben asked.

"Two magazines each," Mills responded.

"You can ride with Ben in the jon boat," Ed said. He turned to Alex. "Sorry, babe. Duty calls. Stay with your mother until we know Bayou Miste is safe." He cupped her face, brushing a thumb along her cheek. "We'll talk when this blows over."

Her heart pounding against her ribs, she stared up into his eyes. "Promise?"

"You bet." Then he kissed her. Although brief and hard, it left her feeling as if it wouldn't be the last, should he survive the day.

Joe kissed Miz Mozelle and Ben kissed Lucie and his mother then the men were gone, headed toward the marina.

Alex stood with Calliope and Lucie, but her heart and her mind went with the guys.

"I want to go. Okay?" Sport's gaze followed the men. "Maybe help?"

Trust Sport to voice exactly what she had been thinking. She'd give anything to be out there, helping make sure no one got killed.

Calliope held his hand. "No, Sport. They have training."

"Sport—I have training." His chest puffed out, his brows dipping low and menacing.

Alex laughed and said softly, "Obedience school isn't enough, sweetie."

"I want to help." Sport stared after the men, his face tense.

She patted his arm. "You can, by helping protect the family."

Her mother stepped up beside her. "I should have known Ed was a cop or something. He had that look about him."

"What look is that, Mom?" She could have kicked herself for not seeing it sooner.

"That need to protect look." She winked. "He's pretty sexy when he takes charge, don't you think?"

"Oh, yeah," Alex whispered. "He's sexy all right. I just hope he comes back alive so I can tell him what I think about all the lies he fed us."

"*Ma chère*, he had reason."

"Yeah, Alex," Lucie said. "Cut him a little slack. It's part of the job and part of yours as a significant other to be supportive."

"Who said I was his significant other?" she demanded, wishing it could be true.

"You really are blind, you know." Calliope grinned and spun to face Lucie. "We've been so caught up, I haven't had a chance to admire your baby bump."

Lucie smiled. "I'd wondered when you were going to say something."

Alex forced her attention away from the marina and the fear running through her that everything was not all right and wouldn't be until Ed returned unharmed.

It had been three months since she had been to Baton Rouge to have lunch with Lucie and she looked so different, it brought tears to her eyes, along with a twinge of envy. "You look wonderful."

Lucie's lips twisted. "Fat is more like it."

"No. You're radiant and more beautiful than I've ever seen you."

Calliope hugged Lucie, "Pregnancy suits you."

"Yes, it does." Mrs. Boyette took her arm. "And I'm sure you haven't slept all night. Let's get you inside and your feet up."

Alex hung back. "Mom, I'm going to head home for a shower and change of clothes."

Mrs. Boyette stopped on her way into the house. "You heard Ed, he wanted you to stay with us until they were sure all was clear."

"I'll only be little while. I don't have clothes here and I need to check on...on...my dog."

"Don't be long, or I'll worry," her mother called out.

"We'll come with you." Calliope grabbed Sport's arm. "Won't we?"

"Yes, we will," Sport said, sounding more and more like a man than a child learning to talk for the first time.

Alex prayed for Calliope and Sport's sake the Voodoo spell would last. Sport made a wonderful man and Calliope deserved to be loved so unconditionally.

The three of them walked to her house as the sun popped up over the horizon in glorious shades of mauve, orange, and yellow. Birds sang, flowers bloomed, and nature continued unimpeded by the danger looming in the bayou. Alex didn't let it fool her for one moment.

* * *

ED AND JOE took the airboat, while Ben and Oscar followed behind in the jon boat, moving much slower and staying low and as close to the vegetation as possible to avoid detection. Loud and rising high above the water, the airboat was the decoy to draw attention to them and away from the small boat.

They made it to the shack without spotting another vessel.

Marcus rose from the grass, his AR15 pointed squarely at Ed's chest. "You here of your own free will, or is that man holding a gun on you?"

Joe chuckled. "I'm the chauffeur. No weapons on me? See?" He held up his arms, then his shirt, displaying a rounded white belly and beltless jeans. Then he patted his pockets and was about to pat his legs.

Ed interrupted, "He's with me and we've got trouble."

The little jon boat putted in behind the airboat.

He hurried down and helped Ben and Mills out, then he jumped in and pulled the little boat beneath the cypress tree with the thick overhang of Spanish moss. He stepped ashore, climbed up the hill and looked back. The boat was completely concealed from the hill and from the water.

Ben nodded. "Good thinking."

"You and Mills will escort the witness while Marcus, Joe and I provide a distraction."

"Does that mean I get to shoot someone?" Marcus grinned. "About damned time. I was ready to put a bullet through my head as soon as you left last night."

"That bad?" he asked, hurrying toward the shack.

"Worse." Marcus got there before they did and flung open the door. "Get off your ass, we're movin' out."

"Thank gawd." Phyllis Ragsdale leaned out the door, blinking at the sunlight. "I'll be glad to see the last of this shit hole. I hope you're taking me to a hotel where I can get a shower and a fuckin' massage."

Ben's brows rose. "Is she kidding me?"

Ed and Marcus shook their heads. "You have no idea the trash that comes out of this woman's mouth."

Ben grinned. "We might have a cure for that." He held out his hand. "Ms. Ragsdale, if you'll come with me, we'll get you to safety."

"That's more like it." She shot a glare at Ed and Marcus. "At least *he's* a gentleman." She picked her way down the bank and stared at the airboat. "And that is more like the transportation I expect."

"Sorry, Ms. Ragsdale. We're not going in that." Ben led her toward the curtain of Spanish moss.

"You're kidding me, right?" She ducked beneath the moss. "Well, goddamn. You can't expect me to get in that toy boat those two baboons have been haulin' me around in. I'm not goin'."

The whine of engines in the distance alerted Ed to trouble. "Get her quiet and keep low until we're out and away from here," he called out as he jumped onto the airboat.

Joe followed. "Hope this damned thing starts," he muttered as he cranked the engine. It fired up the first time.

Marcus, loaded with every weapon he could sling across his shoulders or clip to his bullet-proof vest, leaped aboard as Joe pulled out into the channel and spun around. He handed Joe a similar vest. "Put it on."

Ed held the helm while Joe shrugged into the vest. "Gonna get crazy out here?"

"You want me to drive?" Ed asked.

"Oh, hell no. I'm game, just watch my back while I drive this baby."

"You got it. And keep as low as you can." He took one side of the airboat and Marcus hung off the other, a smile on his face as the wind blew the last four days of babysitting Ragsdale out of his hair.

As they turned onto the main channel leading away from Bayou Miste, another airboat skimmed up over a man-made earthen berm and splashed into the water a hundred yards behind them.

"Here we go!" Joe hit the throttle and the airboat sped across the water, the fan blowing air out the back at upwards of two hundred miles an hour, the sound loud enough to blow Ed's eardrums.

Marcus lifted a set of binoculars to his eyes, leaned out as far as he could, and studied the boat behind them. "They're loaded for bear!" he shouted above the noise. "Get ready!" He hooked his arm around a metal handrail, slung his high-powered rifle up to ready position, and waited for the first shot to be fired.

He didn't have to wait long. Soon bullets spit water up beside the boat and pinged against the giant fan blade.

Joe headed straight for a cypress forest, gunning the engine. "Hold on!" he shouted.

At the last moment he turned left, the boat skidding sideways across the water and shooting forward.

Ed had the side toward the oncoming boat and let loose with all thirty rounds in his magazine, zeroing in on at the men aiming at him. One jerked back and fell out of the boat. The other hunkered lower and kept firing. Ed hit the magazine release, dropped the empty, and slid another in place. Shifting his aim to the driver of the other craft, he did his best, the swaying of the boat making it more of a challenge. In the second five-round burst, he hit the driver and the vessel swerved to the right, the gunmen up front, scrambling to hang on.

Joe shouted, "Going airborne!"

Ed gripped the handrail and bent his knees.

Thibodeaux hit the throttle hard and sent the airboat over a mound of dirt and crashing into another area of the swamp covered in giant lily pads.

The boat behind them flew over the mound and landed with a huge splash.

Joe swerved to the right, giving Marcus a clear shot of the slowed boat, and headed for a stand of cypress.

Marcus fired off a burst of bullets, hitting two of the four men left on the trailing boat. The attackers swerved left.

Joe cocked the craft to the left and Ed opened fire.

The approaching boat dropped back and turned around.

"Joe!" Ed yelled, and waved at the Joe to get his attention, then pointed behind them.

They'd figured out the witness was not aboard their boat and were headed back the way they'd come.

Joe spun the airboat to follow them, pushing the vehicle as fast as it would go. Slowly, they gained on the other craft cutting through a stand of tall marsh grass, until they pulled alongside it. Marcus fired on the remaining gunmen, wounding one. The other threw himself overboard. The driver maintained his speed, and glanced over at their boat. He pulled a hand gun and aimed it at Joe.

Joe swerved at the last moment, missing an alligator nesting mound.

The other boat hit it on one side, tipping the craft enough that the driver lost control and crashed into a cypress tree.

Joe kept going. "Where to?"

Ed scanned the bayou. No other boats could be seen anywhere around them. "Rendezvous point."

Joe nodded and turned, taking them into a darker, denser part of the bayou, where cypress trees towered over the water, Spanish moss hung low enough to touch the surface, and sunlight barely reached within.

Ed shivered, wondering what he'd gotten himself into. He had to trust in Joe to get them where they needed to go and hope Ben and his boat had arrived safely at their destination. And he prayed they bad guys didn't head back to Bayou Miste and cause more trouble for Alex and her family.

CHAPTER 15

ALEX EMERGED FROM HER BATHROOM, WEARING CLEAN JEANS, A BABY BLUE tank top, and her hair pulled back in a ponytail, too impatient to blow it dry and straighten the curls. Her heartbeat hadn't slowed since Ed and the guys had headed out into the swamp. She needed to jog, sprint, or work out to burn off the nervous energy, but didn't want to get too far from home in case they came back soon. "Heard anything?"

"Nothing." Calliope sat with Sport on the couch, his arm over her shoulder, holding her close.

"You two look good together," Alex admitted.

"I love Calliope," Sport said.

Calliope squeezed his hand. "I love you, too."

Alex didn't comment on their mushy comments, but instead wished she and Ed were sitting there saying the same things. "You're getting the hang of talking normally, Sport. I thought it would take you longer."

"Television is great." He grinned and stood, extending a hand to Calliope. "We go back to Alex Mamma's house?"

Calliope let him pull her to her feet. "You bet."

"When this is all over, we should take Lucie and Sport out to see Madame LeBieu," Alex said.

"No!" Calliope stepped in front of Sport. "You can't turn him back into a dog."

She smiled. "Relax, I want to ask her for something to make him a human permanently."

Her friend's shoulders relaxed. "Well, then I'm all for it."

"Are you sure you want to stay human, Sport?" Alex gazed at his soft brown eyes. "I have to admit, I miss my dog, but it's been great getting to know you as a person."

Sport reached out and touched her face. "I miss you, too. And sometimes I miss chasing FeFe." He grinned. "But not T-Rex."

She laughed at the memories of Sport chasing FeFe only to be brought up short by Maurice Saulnier's pet alligator. "I hope Madame LeBieu can help."

"Me, too." Calliope slipped an arm around Sport's waist and leaned into him. "He's everything a girl could ask for."

"We should get going. Mom will be worrying if we take much longer." She led the way to the door. Heeding Ed's warning, she checked outside for any suspicious movements, then held the door for the two lovebirds. As she fit her key into the lock, she remembered her cell phone on her nightstand. "Looks safe enough. You guys go on ahead. I need to place a call to the gym and make sure my staff opened it on time."

"Don't be long," Calliope called out, already halfway down the driveway, her hand in Sport's.

"I won't. Tell Mom I'll be there in fifteen minutes, tops."

"Will do."

Alex entered the house, went straight for her bedroom, and snatched up her cell phone. As she paged down through her contacts, the front door creaked.

"Did you decide to wait for me?" she called out, her hand poised over the number to the gym as she stepped into the hallway.

Instead of Calliope, a tall man wearing a ski mask stood in her hall with a wicked looking handgun pointed at her chest. "Alexandra Belle Boyette?"

Her heart nearly leapt out of her chest, and all her karate training scrambled in her brain. "W-who wants to know?" she answered, her thumb pressing the number on her phone, praying whoever was on the other end would answer immediately instead of letting it ring ten times like usual.

"We're going for a walk." The man motioned toward the rear of the house.

"Wow, you've got a gun. Where are we going?" She spoke in a loud, clear voice. If someone was on the other end of the line, hopefully they'd hear and call the police. Her gaze darted from the man in her hall toward the front door, praying Calliope and Sport would return. But at the same time she prayed they wouldn't or they'd be in danger, too.

"Turn around and walk. Make a sound and I'll shoot you."

"Please don't shoot me," she said as loud as she could without being too obvious. Willing her mind to calm, she weighed her options. Turn the way he'd indicated or take a bullet. Now wasn't the time to be a fool.

When she turned away from him, he slipped up behind her and pressed the gun into her side. Then he grabbed her cell phone, threw it to the floor, and stomped on it, killing any chance of someone finding her by tracing her phone.

Before she could drop into a ready stance and use her training in karate, the man clamped her arms to her sides and stepped in close enough that she could smell his cologne. What murderer wore cologne to a killing?

Then he jerked her wrist up between her shoulder blades.

Pain shot down her arm, bringing tears to her eyes. She rose up on her toes to alleviate it, but he pushed harder. Then she felt a thin strap of plastic rub against her wrist, and he pulled her other arm behind her and zip-tied her wrists together.

Again, he brought her close enough so that she couldn't kick out. With her hands tied behind her back, she was in a heap of trouble with no way to fight free. She opened her mouth to scream, but he shoved a wadded up sock into it. Big enough to fill her mouth and absorb all her spit, but small enough not to be noticed by someone from a distance. Clever on his part. Really bad on hers.

"Move." He pushed her to the back of the house and through the rear exit into the back yard. His hand left her side for a moment as he yanked his ski mask off his head and tossed it to the ground. "Keep walking."

Like she had a choice. All her self-defense classes had taught her to fight no matter what. Even if her attacker shot or stabbed her. Most attackers killed their victims anyway.

He crossed to the street behind hers, cutting through the yards, working his way to the far edges of town where some of the houses had been abandoned, their owners relocating to the city to find work. The farther away they got from her house, the deeper she sank into despair.

No one was expecting her for another ten minutes. Plenty of time for this man to kill her or shove her into a car and leave town undetected and then dump her body in the bayou. No one would know where to look. No one would find her before the alligators stripped her bones.

Her pulse pounding, her eyes shifting left and right, Alex had to make a move before she ran out of options.

He shoved her toward an abandoned mechanic's shop on the farthest edge of town. No one ever came back here and what few yards they'd passed through, the owners had already left for work or school.

If she wanted to get out of this mess, she had to do something soon. She threw herself to the ground, landing hard on her arm. She twisted around, caught her attacker's legs in a sweep and brought him down.

"Damn!" he muttered, hitting the ground hard, his gun flying from his hand.

Struggling to stand without the use of her hands and arms, she lurched to her feet and ran as fast as she could. She'd gone less than a block when she was hit from behind in a flying tackle. With no way to brace for her fall, her head hit the curb. Pain blinded her, then everything went black.

* * *

JOE PULLED the airboat up to the dock at the marina and shut down the engine. Ed leaped out and pulled out his burner phone, punched in the number to Ben's, and waited for it to ring, hoping they had reception where they were in the bayou.

"We made it," Ben's voice came across.

"I'm calling in the local sheriff to get out there and clean up the mess."

"Do that. We're good for the time being, although our witness is in a flap. If Madame LeBieu doesn't have something to cure her trash mouth, I might shoot her before Marcus gets the chance."

Ed grinned. Hang tight. We'll be out to pick you up as soon as we're sure we got them all."

"Will do."

Joe stepped onto the dock. "Don't look now, but here comes trouble."

He glanced down the street. The entire Boyette clan was moving his way en masse. He scanned the faces and didn't see the one he wanted to see the most. His heart thumping hard against his ribs, he ran to meet them. "Where's Alex?"

Calliope spoke first, tears streaming from her eyes. "She went back for her cell phone. We went ahead of her. We'd only been gone fifteen minutes. When she didn't show up, Sport and I went back looking for her. She wasn't there and all we found was this." Calliope held up a broken cell phone.

He gripped Calliope's arms and forced her to look at him. "Where did you find that? How long ago?"

"In her house, on the floor. She's been gone twenty minutes." Calliope crumpled into sobs.

Mrs. Boyette touched his arm, her face pale, her tired blue eyes gray with worry. "There's more." She glanced back at the little ones, already crying in their older siblings' arms, and lowered her voice, "I received a call before we left to come looking for Alex. The man on the phone said he'd kill Alex if we didn't bring him the witness." Her fingers dug into his arm. "Please, help me bring my baby back." Her eyes shimmered with tears. Her eyes were older, but Alex's looked so much like hers, it hurt Ed to stare down into them.

"I'll bring her back, Mrs. Boyette," he swore.

"Alive," she whispered.

He nodded, praying he could. He glanced around at the Boyettes. "Go home and call the sheriff. Then get on the phone with every one of your neighbors and ask if they saw anything. Cars, strangers, anything out of the ordinary. Tell them to watch for strange cars, any cars and write down the license plates and the direction they're heading."

Dolley stepped forward. "We've been watching the road and the canal for signs of your return."

Madison finished, "Not a single car has passed in twenty minutes."

"Good, that means he might have taken her on foot." Ed glanced around. "Anyone know of a tracking dog in this area?"

Sport's eyes widened and he stepped forward. "Yes."

Calliope put a hand on his arm, her eyes rounding, filling with moisture. "No."

He stepped up to the man who'd lived with Alex. "If you know of a tracking dog, get it out here. The sooner the better so that he can pick up the trail."

Sport nodded, patted Calliope's hand and said softly. "I have to do this."

Calliope threw her arms around his neck and sobbed into his shirt. "I love you, Sport. Don't do this."

Ed turned to Mrs. Boyette, every instinct telling him they were running out of time. "Go, make those calls."

The Boyette family turned as one and ran back to their house.

He turned to Joe. "Top off the fuel in the airboat. We're going to need it."

Joe nodded and jogged back to the marina.

He gripped Calliope's arm and dragged her free of Sport's embrace. "We don't have much time. Show me where you found the phone."

She swiped an arm across her damp face and ran toward Alex's little cottage, bursting through the open front door.

He followed, stepping into Alex's empty house, his heart squeezing tightly in his chest. He had to bring her back. This sunny little cottage wasn't the same without Alex's determined, vibrant personality filling it.

"There." Calliope pointed to the floor in the hallway where pieces of hard plastic had been scattered.

Ed searched every room, working his way toward the back of the house where the back door stood open, the screen door not firmly latched. "They went out this way." He ran out in the backyard and found a ski mask lying on the grass. He lifted it, sniffed it, and wished he had the abilities of a tracking dog himself. By the time they got one there, Alex's kidnapper could have taken her away from Bayou Miste.

"Ed." Sport emerged from the house, Calliope clinging to his arm. He clutched a small pouch in his hand. "I know of a dog, but I will need help from Madame LeBieu."

Ed's head jerked up, his gaze narrowing on the man standing before him. "The Voodoo queen?" Why?"

"She can help. Trust me. She might be our only hope." Tears streamed from Calliope's eyes. "Take Sport. It's what he wants. With Madame LeBieu's help, he can find Alex."

Desperate and running out of time, he nodded toward the other man. "Then you come with me."

"I'm going, too." Calliope clasped Sport's hand, her face set in sad, but determined lines.

"No, it's not safe," Ed put out his hand to stop her.

She glared at him and growled. "You'll take me or I'll follow you anyway."

"You don't understand. We've been shot at and almost killed out on the bayou today."

"I'll take my chances. I'm going with Sport." She slipped her arm through Sport's and refused to let go.

"Then hurry. We have to get back to town before the kidnapper does something stupid." He didn't even want to think of what might happen to Alex. The men Leon Primeaux hired to do his dirty work weren't known for the mercy they showed their victims. The only bargaining chip he held was Primeaux's ex-girlfriend. The one person whose testimony would put Primeaux away for life, thus saving countless other lives from his ruthless machinations.

The three of them ran back to the marina and climbed into the waiting airboat. Joe cranked the engine and spun the craft around, heading across the water. Clouds had gathered over the bayou, sinking low and heavy, threatening a deluge that would wash away all traces of Alex's scent from the ground. Ed shouted, "Faster!"

"Goin' as fast as this crate will move," Joe shouted back.

They held on as the boat skimmed over man-made mounds delineating different areas of the swamp, through stands of marsh grass, and skidded around an alligator lazing in the middle of a tributary. He and Sport hung off the sides, peering around the giant fan to the rear, searching the bayou for any signs they were being followed.

When he thought the swamp might go on forever, Joe entered the sinister gloom of a cypress forest, where the Spanish moss hung low enough they had to duck to avoid being slapped in the face.

A small dilapidated house appeared, nestled in the watery forest, its eaves sagging, bright green moss growing on its porch rails. Madame LeBieu's home. It never changed.

In the shadows at the side of the house, movement caught Ed's attention. He strained to see what or who lurked in obscurity as they sped closer.

About the time he could make out Marcus's form, the man stepped into the open, carrying an automatic rifle at the ready. Oscar Mills emerged from the opposite end of the house, sporting a rifle and a handgun.

Joe slowed as they neared the rickety dock, and then shut down the engine. They skimmed in, to bump against the wood planking. Ed jumped onto the pier, Sport close behind him, Calliope bringing up the rear.

Ben Boyette pushed through the front door, frowning. "What's happened?"

He stopped and stared up at his friend. "They have Alex."

The man's face paled, his lips tightening. "Damn." He shoved a hand through his hair. "They want to trade for the witness, don't they?"

"I have a name, dumbass." Phyllis Ragsdale shoved Ben aside and stepped out onto the porch. "You told them hell no, didn't you?"

"It's not safe for you to stand in the open," Ben said. "Go back inside."

"I'm tired of being bossed around. I want out of this stinkin' swamp and back to the city where I belong." She stood with her hand on her hip. "And I'm not gonna stand by and let you swap me for some swamp bimbo. I got my rights."

Ed clenched his fists about to launch himself at the bitch, when a large, mocha-skinned woman dressed in a bright red, pink, and orange muumuu with a scarf tied around her head emerged behind Ben and Phyllis and raised her hand. "Silence!"

All eyes turned to the commanding presence of the legendary Voodoo queen he had only heard tales of about from Ben. She was every bit as intimidating as Ben had promised and then some.

"I'm not taking any more orders from some fat lady in a Hawaiian tent," Phyllis stated.

Madame LeBieu held up a hand and clamped her fingers together.

Phyllis was in mid-rant, "Get me out—" her lips moved, but no sound came out. Her eyes widened and she clapped a hand to her throat, her mouth continuing to flap, but blessed silence reigned.

Had he seen right? Ed stared at the witness who'd been non-stop talk since they'd picked her up four days ago. This was the first time the woman was quiet. What had Madame LeBieu done to get her to stop? Magic?

He shook his head. He didn't believe in magic. But he sure wished he could conjure a crystal ball to help him find Alex.

"Dog, come to me." The Voodoo queen waved her hand toward Sport.

He frowned. Why had she called Sport *dog*?

Sport climbed the steps and handed her the pouch he'd been carrying since they'd left Alex's house.

She took the pouch in one hand and reached out with the other to brush her hand across his forehead, pushing the shaggy hair out of his eyes. "What brings you to Madame LeBieu?"

Ed shifted impatiently, ready for this visit to be over so he could head back to town and begin his search for Alex. "Sport said he knew of a dog who could track Alex."

"I say silence!" Madame LeBieu held up her hand. "Let de dog speak."

"What dog?" he asked. "We came to get one."

The old Voodoo queen glared at him until he closed his mouth and waited.

She gave her attention to Sport again, her expression softening. "You want for me to break de spell?"

Sport glanced toward Calliope, his brown eyes sad. When he turned back to the mistress of Voodoo, he nodded. "Sport find Alex, but not like this." He held his arms out.

Calliope flew up the porch and grabbed Sport's hand. "I love you."

Sport squeezed her hand. "We always knew this could not last."

The old woman shook her head. "De dog be right. De *cunja* not meant to be forever."

"Will he remember?" Calliope whispered, pressing her face to Sport's palm.

"No." Madame LeBieu shook her head and reached out for Calliope's hand. "But you will. Do you want to forget?"

Calliope stared up into Sport's eyes. "No." She leaned up on her toes and kissed Sport.

Ed shook his head, the conversation going on in front of him getting more bizarre by the minute.

"Come." Madame LeBieu beckoned Sport to enter her house, holding the door open for him.

Calliope hesitated, but the old woman nodded, allowing her to pass as well.

When Ed started forward, the Voodoo queen blocked him. "De rest o' you wait here."

"But—"

Ben gripped his arm. "Do as she said, and trust her. She's Lucie's grandmother and one of the most respected Voodoo artists in all of Louisiana. Her magic is very strong."

"Magic?" He couldn't believe it. "Alex is missing and we're playing in the swamp with a Voodoo queen instead of searching for her."

The door closed behind Madame LeBieu, shutting him out and Sport and Calliope inside.

His patience at an end, Ed spun and marched back to the dock. "Joe, take me back to Bayou Miste. We don't have time for this nonsense."

Joe stood still, shaking his head. "We go when Madame LeBieu says we go."

"Are you kidding me?"

The marina owner crossed his arms and stood solid.

He searched for the jon boat Ben and Oscar had used to transport the Ragsdale woman to Madame LeBieu's. He spotted it concealed in the brush near the shore, twenty yards away from the house. As he dropped over the side of the dock onto the marshy island, he could swear he heard the beat of drums.

His footsteps faltered and he glanced back at the house.

All gazes focused on the front door as a low melodious sound resonated through the wood siding, growing in strength as it continued, combining with the drumbeat.

Shivers slid across his body, raising gooseflesh on his arms. A buzzing whine filled his head as the sound increased from inside the building. Ed pressed his hands to his ears, his vision blurring and his thoughts growing hazy.

A brilliant flash of light and sound erupted from the house and the front door blew open, the screen door slamming against the exterior.

From the dark interior, a golden retriever leaped out into the open and barked.

Calliope emerged, followed by Madame LeBieu.

"Go," Madame LeBieu said. "Save my Alex from de evil mans."

The dog bounded toward the airboat and jump aboard.

Ben hooked Phyllis's arm. "Come on, we're all heading back and we might need you for collateral."

The woman dug in her heels and shook her head, her mouth working but no sound escaping.

Marcus stalked up the steps, flung Phyllis over his shoulder, and carried her to the airboat, dumping her onto a seat. Ben and Oscar climbed aboard.

Ed heaved himself up on the dock and ran to get into the airboat as Joe started the engine. The huge fan blade spun, the sound echoing off the canopy.

"What about Sport? Isn't he coming?" he called out as Joe spun the craft around and headed toward Bayou Miste.

Calliope bent over, crying, and no one else spoke as the airboat zigzagged through the cypress forest maze and out into the open fields and canals.

Ed, Marcus, Ben and Oscar each held tight to the boat with one hand while pointing weapons outward, ready to take on any assault.

All the way back to Bayou Miste, he prayed they weren't too late.

CHAPTER 16

Alex awoke to the smell of oil and gasoline, her cheek lying against greasy concrete. Pain ripped through her head and her mouth felt like the Sahara Desert. Her wrists were bound behind her back by what felt like a zip-tie and her ankles were bound the same way. She listened for voices or movement, her sight adjusting to the dim light coming from dirty windows. Where was she? Better question—where was the man who'd abducted her?

She lifted her head, wincing at the sharp stabbing pain, and looked around at what appeared to be the interior of an auto shop. Long derelict, the building had old tires piled against the walls, what was left of a hydraulic lift anchored to the floor, and gnawed-on pegboard attached to the wall with hooks. Across every surface was a nasty layer of grime. And she'd worn her favorite baby blue tank top. A car that looked like the one that had hit Sport stood in one bay with a dent in the front fender.

Laughter bubbled up inside her and would have escaped but for the wadded sock stuck in her mouth. Her gaze returned to the metal plate that had at one time anchored the hydraulic lift. One corner of the plate had been pried upward, leaving a jagged edge. Just what she needed to break through the plastic handcuffs.

Rocking back and forth, she built up her momentum and rolled, scooted, and inched across the disgusting, slimy floor to the metal plate. For a moment, she lay still, breathing and listening for the return of her captor. When nothing stirred, she rolled on top of the plate, the jagged edge scraping her arm several times before she wiggled her body into position where her wrists lay over the metal edge.

With awkward persistence she sawed at the tie, gouging hunks of flesh from her arm in the process. Blood mixed with grease, making it even more difficult to hook the plastic. Her arms and belly aching from holding the uncomfortable position, she finally broke through and rolled to the side, rubbing the feeling back into her hands.

Metal scraped against metal as a door opened in the back of the building.

She swung her feet around, jammed the zip-tie over the sharp edge of metal, ripping her jeans in the process. After three attempts, the tie broke and she lurched to her feet, ducking low behind a counter.

A man entered the car bays. Enough light shone through the dingy windows to silhouette his form. He carried a handgun with a very long barrel on it, like it had a silencer attached to the end. "Ms. Boyette, it's time to go."

When he arrived at the location where he'd dumped her body, he grew still and turned in a three-hundred-sixty-degree circle.

Hidden behind the only counter in the shop, she realized it was only a matter of time before he found her. If she wanted to live, she had to get out, now. She felt around on the floor for something to throw, her fingers curling around what felt like a lug nut. With all her strength, she threw the nut to the opposite end of the shop from the door her abductor had entered. It landed near the pile of tires.

The man spun and ran toward the sound. "You can't get away from me."

Oh yes, I can. She balled up her muscles and launched her body from behind the counter and ran, zigzagging toward the back door.

As she reached the exit, something pinged on the metal wall beside her. She ducked and swung the door wide, rushing through and to the right. The back of the shop opened out on the canal. Alex's mad rush gave her so much momentum she plunged over the bank and slid into the water.

Knowing the man with the gun would have an easy target if she came up for air, she stayed below the surface, swimming as fast and as far away as she could. When she thought her lungs might burst, she ran into a bed of lily pads. She tipped her head up, pressing her lips to the bottom of a pad and lifted it ever so slightly, breathing in enough air to go under again.

A bullet pierced the water beside her, so near she could almost feel the current it produced. She pushed away from the lily pads, afraid their movement on the surface would give her position away. As she swam through the dark canal water, she prayed she didn't get hit by a bullet or a boat, or that she'd be eaten by an alligator. When she came to an opening off the canal that led out into the bayou she swam toward it, hoping her attacker would stay on dry ground and give up his chase. As she slipped deeper into the bayou, she heard the sound of a boat engine start. Oh, hell, the man had found a boat. If she didn't find a place to hide, soon, she didn't stand a chance. As she surfaced for another breath, she prayed, *Please, Ed, find me!*

* * *

THE SHERIFF HAD an airboat sitting at the marina when Joe pulled in and practically ran over the pier. "Sorry!" he shouted as he shut off the engine.

Ed didn't wait to explain anything to the local law. As soon as they stopped, he hopped out of the boat onto the dock. The dog leaped out beside him and ran.

"Follow him!" Calliope yelled.

Ben ordered Marcus, "Stay with the witness."

Ed chased the dog across the street, dodging sheriff's vehicles and bystanders. Mrs. Boyette was standing on the porch at Alex's house talking to a deputy holding a notepad.

The dog raced between their legs and into the house.

Ed squeezed Mrs. Boyette's shoulder and said, "We'll find her," then set her to the side, rushing into the building after the dog.

"Hey!" the deputy yelled. "You can't go in there. This is a crime scene."

With Alex's life hanging in the balance, he didn't have time to waste talking to the man. When the dog ran out the back door, he followed, running on blind faith that the animal knew what he was doing.

In the backyard, the dog put his nose to the ground, sniffing. He followed a scent to the edge of the property and beyond, crossing streets and ducking through yards moving farther and farther away from Alex's home.

He kept the animal in sight. He looked back once to see Ben racing to catch up. They spread out, running parallel to each other behind the dog.

At the edge of town, the dog stopped and sniffed the road and a curb. He whined and looked up at him as if he wanted Ed to look there as well.

Ben staggered to a stop, breathing hard. "What is it? What did he find?"

Ed bent to study the dark stain on the curb. "Blood. And by the way the dog is whining, I bet it's Alex's." His gut clenched.

The dog spun in a circle, picked up a scent, and headed for an abandoned building that might once have been an auto mechanic's shop. The metal sides of the building had rusted, what paint was left had long since faded.

The dog scratched at a door. Ed reached for the knob, but the door was locked.

"What is it Sport?" Ben asked. "Is she in there?"

Ben went one direction and Ed the other. When they reached a back door, it was wide open.

"Alex!" He ran inside, picking his way past old tires and discarded, broken equipment to a fairly new car standing at the other end with a big dent on the front panel. As if it had hit something.

Sport circled the car, growling, then he sniffed at the floor, whining. He picked something up with his teeth and trotted over to Ed.

He bent to take what the dog had in his mouth and walked to where

Ben and Marcus stood near the door and held it up to the sunlight. A zip-tie like ones they used in the department. And it had blood on it.

Sport slipped through their legs, pressed his nose to the ground outside, and took off running, barking as he went. He threaded through tall grass that ran along the bank of a canal, pulling ahead of Ed and Ben. The tall grass hid him from view. If not for the incessant barking, Ed would have had to guess where he was.

Ahead in the canal, a boat pulled away from the shore, a man with shocking white hair at its helm.

There was something familiar about the man. The shock of white hair, his height, and the way he carried himself. He turned back at the sound of the dog barking.

"Holy shit, that's Gordon Dean," Ed said.

Ben ran up beside Ed. "Are you sure?"

"I saw his face. It's Dean."

"That bastard's the leak in the department," Ben said, breathing hard to keep up with the dog.

"I'll kill him if he hurts Alex," Ed ground out, sprinting to catch up, knowing that if Dean got too far ahead, he could disappear into the bayou. If he had Alex in the boat, he could dump her anywhere and they'd never find her.

A fork in the canal loomed ahead of the man in the boat. If he made it there, they'd never catch him.

The dog burst through the brush and, with a magnificent leap off the bank, landed on Dean's back. The boat swerved, bouncing against the bank. Dean struggled to straighten the boat as the dog sank his teeth into the man's hand.

"Goddamn dog!" Dean raised the hand holding the gun.

"Don't you hurt my dog!" Alex Boyette climbed up a hassock of dirt and swamp grass, screaming like a raging Valkyrie, her hand loaded with a clump of something dark and dripping, looking suspiciously like a wad of swamp grass, roots and all.

As Dean leveled the gun on the dog, Alex swung her grass and launched it into the air, clipping the man in the shoulder. The gun went off with a soft pop.

The dog screeched and fell into the water.

Ed and Ben ran along the bank of the canal until they were parallel with the drifting boat.

Dean aimed the gun at Alex. "Stop or I'll shoot her."

Ed knelt on the grass, whipped his rifle to his shoulder and aimed at Dean's shoulder. "Put down your gun."

"You really want me to kill her, don't you?"

"You shot my dog!" Alex either didn't hear Dean or didn't care. She dived at the boat.

Ed squeezed the trigger.

Dean's hand jerked, the gun flying into the water as Alex hit him with the full force of her body. She knocked him out of the boat and tumbled into the canal with him.

Ed and the others slid down the bank and into the water.

Gordon Dean grabbed Alex by her ponytail and yanked her neck into the crook of his arm. "Come any closer and I'll kill her."

"Shoot him, Ed!" Alex said. "He killed Sport."

He aimed his gun at Gordon's head, afraid to pull the trigger for fear of hitting Alex.

"Throw your weapons in the water or the girl dies," Dean yelled.

"Don't do it," Alex pleaded.

"I have to. I can't let him kill you," he said.

"Let her go, Gordon," Ben said. "The game is over. You won't get away. You kill her and the court won't settle for anything less than the chair."

Alex wiggled in the man's clutches, her face turning red then purple.

About to toss his weapon to the bank, Ed hesitated, spying movement in the water behind Dean and Alex. "Alex, be ready to swim. There's an alligator behind you two."

Gordon Dean's eyes rounded and he swung his head around, trying to look over his shoulder without releasing his captive. Then his body jerked and he screamed, his hold loosening.

Alex pushed away from him and swam to the other side of the canal.

Gordon splashed and thrashed, his head going under, then coming up spitting water. "Help! Please, help me!"

Behind him, instead of a deadly alligator, Sport snapped at him again, sinking his teeth into the man's shoulder.

Ed ran to where Alex slipped and slid on the bank, trying to climb the side of the canal. He reached out and grabbed her hand, pulling her up into his arms.

"No." She struggled to be free, "I have to help Sport."

Ben chuckled. "Relax, Alex, he seems to be helping himself."

The dog snarled and took another bite out of the crooked cop then abandoned the man and paddled toward the bank where Alex had come ashore.

Ed set Alex away from him and dragged the tired, injured dog up the muddy bank.

Alex dropped to her haunches and hugged the dog. "Oh, Sport, why did you do it?"

"He saved your life." Ed squatted beside her. "That dog is a hero."

"Oh, Sport, you sacrificed so much." She buried her face in is wet fur and wept.

Not wanting to part her from her dog, Ed Sport he needed medical attention. "Alex, honey, he's bleeding. Let's get him to a vet." He helped Alex to her feet and lifted the dog.

Ben dragged Gordon Dean out of the canal and up the bank where he collapsed on the ground, muttering, "Damned dog. I should have killed him."

Ben ran ahead to get a vehicle to transport Sport to the vet and Gordon to jail in Baton Rouge.

After Ed settled the dog into the back of Ben's SUV, he slid into the back seat beside Alex.

She leaned into him, her hand resting on his leg. "There's something I've been waiting all day to tell you." A soft chuckle shook her frame. "I even wore my favorite blue shirt for the occasion."

Covered in mud, grease streaked across her face, and the blue shirt more brown than any other color, she'd never been more beautiful. "Before you say anything..." He kissed her, holding her close, soggy clothes and all. "Alex Boyette, I think I'm falling in love with you."

She glanced up, her eyes shining. "That's what I was going to say."

"Yeah, well I beat you to it." He brushed his thumb gently across her bruised cheek.

"You're not afraid of my huge family?"

"I love your huge family."

"I have a business."

"My job is in Baton Rouge, but I don't mind the commute." He rested his cheek against her hair. "We can play it by ear and find a way to make it work."

Alex sighed. "I'm not afraid to leave Bayou Miste. There's a whole world out there I haven't seen."

"Yeah, but it will be a lot more fun to explore it with you."

THE VETERINARIAN BANDAGED Sport's leg and gave him a mild sedative and a shot of antibiotics to ward off infection. He prescribed rest and a low-stress environment for twenty-four hours. He checked Alex's eyes for concussion, cleaned and applied bandages to her head and wrists, and told her to see a doctor in Morgan City as soon as possible.

She left the vet's clinic in Ben's SUV with Sport draped across her lap and Ed in the seat beside her, his arm over her shoulder. Every time she stared into Sport's soft brown eyes, her heart ached for him and Calliope. Deep down, she'd suspected that the magic wouldn't last, but Sport had sacrificed his time with Calliope to save her.

When they arrived at Alex's house, the adults were waiting. Ben had called ahead to let them know Alex was okay and they all wanted to see for themselves.

As soon as Ben got out of the car, Lucie ran to him, wrapping her arms around his middle, smiling and crying at the same time. "Oh, *bebe*, I'm so glad you're okay."

Her mother engulfed her in a hug so tight, she croaked, "I'm okay, Mom."

She loosened her hold slightly, tears trickling down her face. "I was so afraid of losing you."

Alex hugged her back. "It's over."

Setting her at arm's length, her mother pushed the limp hair out of her face. "*Mais,* then get yourself cleaned up and meet us back at the house. I'm making dinner for everyone." She brushed the tears from her own face and sniffed. "Don't be long this time."

"But I want to know what happened."

"We'll talk about it over dinner," her mother insisted.

She smiled. "I'll be right there."

"We'll stay and make sure she's there on time," Lucie said.

Calliope stood to the side, her bright green eyes dark as the deepest forest and filled to the brim with emotion. "Where's Sport?"

Alex swallowed hard, ready tears springing to her eyes.

Ed lifted the dog's limp body out of the back seat.

Calliope reached out a hand, tears slipping down her face. "Is he..."

"Asleep," Alex reassured her. "He's going to be okay. The vet gave him a sedative. It should wear off soon."

Calliope followed Ed as he carried the dog into the house and laid him on blanket on the couch.

"Ben promised me some clean clothes," Ed grasped her cheeks between his hands and bent to press his lips to hers. "I'll see you at your mother's."

Alex would have preferred he stayed, but she wanted to talk to Lucie and Calliope alone. "I won't be long." She kissed him back.

After Ben left, she turned to Calliope. "What happened?"

Through choking sobs, Calliope told of Sport's demand to undo the Voodoo that had made him into a man, insisting he could find her.

"Madame LeBieu said the magic was never meant to last." Calliope knelt on the floor beside Sport and ran her hand along his fur. "He's more of a hero than any man I've ever met."

"Oh, *ma chère,* I'm so sorry." Lucie dropped to the floor on one side of Calliope, Alex on the other, and they hugged her until her sobs stopped.

"We'd better get going before my mother comes looking for us." She hurried into the shower, her body achy, her wrists raw, her heart sore for Calliope, but full of hope for her own future. Soon, she'd see Ed. She scrubbed her hair, careful not to disturb the bandage on her forehead, and washed the swamp out of her skin with scented soap. When she felt human again, she stepped out of the shower, dried off, applied antibiotic ointment to her wrists, cuts, and scrapes, and found her prettiest sun dress and sandals.

Sport was awake and actually perky when she emerged from her bedroom.

"Can we bring Sport?" Calliope asked.

"The vet said he needed rest, but he appears to be recovered somewhat." She smiled. "Yes, we can bring him. He's as much a part of my family as my brothers and sisters and you."

Lucie pushed out of the lounge chair and rubbed a hand over her swollen belly. "I see I'll have to get to work on something for Calliope next."

Calliope and Alex both turned to Lucie at once.

"No!"

Lucie held up her hands in surrender. "Okay, okay."

"I hope that once you have your baby, you won't have time to dabble in Voodoo," Alex said.

"I can't let it disappear when Gran LeBieu passes on. It's tradition!"

Alex slipped an arm around her friends' shoulders and hugged them. "That kind of tradition we could do without. Come on, the family's waiting."

When she opened her front door, she stared into the dark brown eyes of the man she was falling madly in love with.

He wore Ben's old fishing clothes that were tight across his broad shoulders and a little short on the pant legs. On his feet he wore a pair of bright orange flip-flops.

Lucie and Calliope slipped around her, Sport trotting after them with only a slight limp.

"We'll see you at your mother's," Lucie called out, leaving her and Ed alone on the porch.

"I couldn't wait to see you," he said, gathering her in his arms.

"Are you going to tell me the whole truth now?"

"Since I'm no longer undercover," he held her a little away from him and gazed down into his eyes, a smile playing at the corners of his lips, "ask me anything."

She tipped her chin up and tried to look serious. "What happened to the witness?"

"Marcus and Oscar are escorting her to Baton Rouge where they will keep her in a holding cell until the trial begins tomorrow morning."

"Who was the man who kidnapped me?"

Ed shook his head. "Sad to say, that was our supervisor, Gordon Dean. Crooked as they come and on Leon Primeaux's payroll. Might mean a promotion for me or Ben."

"And you're not a mediator?"

"No. I'm a special agent for the Special Criminal Investigations Unit of the Louisiana State Police."

"All that stuff about growing up in the foster system?"

"True."

"And you've never been fishing before coming to the bayou?"

"True." Ed raised his hand like a Boy Scout. "Scouts honor."

"Were you ever a scout?" she asked.

"No, but I wouldn't lie to you...well, not if I didn't have to."

"Final question." She paused, inhaling a deep breath before continuing. "Were you telling me the truth when you said you were falling in love with me?"

He gathered her closer, his head dipping until his mouth hovered over hers. "You bet your beautiful Boyette buns, sweetheart."

Alex sighed. "One more question."

He brushed her lips across hers. "Really?"

"Do you believe in magic?" she asked.

He laughed. "I have to. It brought me you."

EPILOGUE

Raccoon Saloon, Bayou Miste, Louisiana
Four months later

Alex stared around the big table, filled with her friends and some of her family, realizing she'd never been happier. Jean Dupree had even allowed Sport to join them at Calliope's insistence. The burly, old bar owner had a soft spot for Calliope and let her have her way more often than not.

Leon Primeaux was sentenced to life in prison. Phyllis Ragsdale had entered into the witness protection program and hopefully moved clear out of Louisiana by now. Ben and Lucie had delivered a beautiful baby girl and life had returned to normal in Bayou Miste.

She had been seeing Ed practically every weekend, since he'd gone back to work in Baton Rouge, and falling more in love with him each day. With a grand flourish, she raised her beer mug. "I'd like to propose a toast to the new parents."

A round of clinking bottles and mugs was cheered along with, "Here! Here!"

Lucie and Ben grinned, both looking tired, but elated at the new addition to their household.

Ben lifted his mug. "I'd like to propose a toast to Dolley and Madison for agreeing to babysit tonight so that we could have our first night out since Lilly was born, and so that Mom could come out with us."

More clinking, more cheers and hugs all around.

"Can we join the party?" Joe Thibodeaux and Miz Mozelle stepped up to the table.

"Please," her mother scooted her chair back.

"We'll need room for four," Joe grinned and waved toward a man and woman entering the saloon.

"My nephew Craig and his wife, Elaine, are in town for a visit. Some of you know them," Joe said. "They're expecting their first baby." Joe's chest puffed out as he draped an arm over his nephew's shoulders. "I'm going to be a great uncle."

Her mom made the introductions all around and they made room at the table for the Thibodeauxs.

Ed stood and cleared his throat. "I have an announcement to make."

All eyes turned toward him. "After careful consideration, much haggling and assistance from Alex, I've purchased a house, in White Castle, halfway between Morgan City and Baton Rouge." He pulled a box out of his jeans pocket and dropped to one knee.

Her pulse pounding so hard against her eardrums, she strained to hear his next words.

"I'm hoping Alex will like the house enough to agree to move in with me...as my wife." He opened the box, displaying a beautiful sapphire and diamond ring that took her breath away. "Alexandra Belle Boyette, after one failed marriage, I never thought I'd want to take the plunge again, but you gave me hope. You showed me how to really love someone and that it was worth risking my heart. Will you marry me?"

"Yes!" She threw herself at Ed, wrapping her arms around his neck as he staggered to his feet, then twirled her around, planting a kiss on her lips.

Everyone gathered around, congratulating, hugging, and shaking hands, as Ed slid the ring on her finger. When they finally resumed their seats, Alex glanced across at Calliope, her joy fading. For the past three months, her friend had put on a happy face. But Alex knew her heart would not be mended so easily. Losing Sport as a man had taken the spark out of the normally bubbly and vivacious woman.

Lucie leaned close to Alex. "I've been working with Gran LeBieu on a *cunja* to help bring Calliope out of her funk."

"I don't know, Lucie," she said. "I don't know how much more excitement this town can handle. Neither one of us will be around to bail her out if things get crazy. You know how gullible she can be."

"It'll be okay. I promise." Lucie patted her hand. "There are enough Boyettes in Bayou Miste to help her out of a bind. Besides, look what Voodoo has done for you, me, Craig, and Elaine. Do you think we'd have found our true loves without it?"

Her heart swelled every time she glanced at Ed. "I don't think I'd have changed a thing. I can't imagine my life without Ed in it."

"See?" Lucie winked. "Don't worry. Gran LeBieu and I won't let her down. We'll come up with something."

Alex's mother leaned into the conversation. "I've been giving it some thought, too. I believe we need to find Calliope a man."

"Mommmm." She gave her mother a warning look. "Not everyone appreciates your meddling."

"*Matchmaking, ma chère.*" Her mother lifted her hand. "That's a beautiful ring on your finger, Alexandra Belle." She gazed into her daughter's eyes. "I believe between me, Lucie, and Madame LeBieu, we can help our Calliope find the love of her life."

Alex rolled her eyes and raised her beer. Who was she to doubt the power of love and Voodoo. *"Laissez les bon temps rouler!"* Let the good times roll!

THE END

TARZAN & JANINE

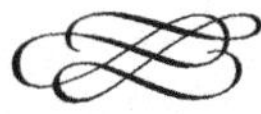

TEXAS BILLIONAIRES CLUB BOOK #1

NEW YORK TIMES BESTSELLING AUTHORS

ELLE JAMES

DELILAH DEVLIN

TARZAN & JANINE

TEXAS BILLIONAIRES CLUB BOOK #1

New York Times and USA Today
Bestselling Authors

ELLE JAMES
&
DELILAH DEVLIN

CHAPTER 1

"Holy Hell." Tanner Peschke groaned.

"My friend, you worry far too much." Rip O'Rourke grinned from across the table but stared through the barroom door.

Tanner rolled his eyes. Rip didn't look as though he had a care in the world—the eye-straining Hawaiian shirt paired with his beat-up cowboy hat pretty much reflected his whole outlook on life.

"Wow, T-man. You couldn't have picked a better place for us to meet."

"I should have known this was a set up." Tanner ran a hand through his hair and stared out into the Austin, Texas hotel lobby hosting the National Beauty Products Convention. "My old man is testing me."

Rip sighed. "This place is heaven."

"It's hell for me." Tanner waved a hand at the plethora of women—slim, curvy, tall, petite, fresh-faced, mature—and in every mouth-watering color scheme available on the planet. "Look at them. All of them. I'll never make the deal he expects."

"Tanner, why don't you just tell your father you quit?" Jesse Jordan sipped his steaming coffee.

The twinkle in his eye said he understood Tanner's predicament all too well. Although women fawned over the young Robert Redford lookalike, he didn't melt like hot wax.

"You don't need Peschke Motors," Jesse said. "You make more on your investments in a month than that place sees in a year."

"I made a promise to my mother—"

"On her deathbed ten years ago." Gage Jenkins, a no-nonsense man with a military haircut and direct stare, leaned over the table. "Dude, a lot has changed since then."

"You could buy ten Peschke Motors with your pocket change." Rip shook his head. "Hell, you could probably buy your own new car manufacturing company with the money you're making in day trading."

"That's not the point." Tanner leaned back in his seat. "Why do you work at the radio station, Rip?" Irritation tightened his throat. He turned to Jesse and waved a hand. "Why do you run a ranch supply store, Jess? And why are you still a member of the Army National Guard, Gage?" Tanner glanced around at the group. "None of us do what we do because we *need* the money."

"That's right." Rip let out a belch, followed by a grin. "Sorry."

Tanner shook his head. "We started the Texas Billionaires Club so we would all succeed."

Rip nodded. "And once we made our collective billion, we are supposed to remind each other what's important."

"Family, friends and, most important, not getting a big head." Jesse counted off, one finger at a time.

"Back to the point." Gage set his coffee mug on the table with a thump. "Tanner made a promise...to his dying mother, who is family, to stand by his father...who is family."

"That's why I called this meeting, my friends." Tanner straightened his collar. "I needed moral support and a reminder of what's important. My dad's counting on me to do this right."

"Well, soldier." Gage threw back his broad shoulders and gave Tanner his best military glare. "Get out there and make that deal."

"I don't get it." Rip's brows furrowed. "What's so hard about buying a load of used cars from an old lady?"

"He's a sucker for a sob story." Jesse shook his head, a grin spreading across his mouth. "This place is filled with women, a veritable field of land mines for our man Tanner."

"You got that right." Tanner stood, staring out at the lobby, dread filling him with each passing second.

Jesse, Gage and Rip stood, Rip leaning in like a quarterback in a huddle. "Keep your eye on the ball. Ignore the other team, and the fact you'll be surrounded and outnumbered by the fairer sex."

"Thanks," Tanner snorted. "I'm ignoring them already." His tone dripped sarcasm.

"You can do it, buddy." Rip pounded him on his back. "Just pretend they're all men in drag and breeze right through."

"We've got your back." Jesse took his turn pounding Tanner's back. "Call us when you're done. We'll give you a cyber high-five."

"I'm on it." Tanner strode out of the bar and entered the lobby. Knowing the TBC had his back gave him fuel to get going.

On his way to the reception desk, several lovelies nodded, smiling as they passed. Others fluttered their fingers in little feminine waves—the kind that made a man's insides curl. All the while, the combined scents of their perfumes increased the dread in his sensory-overloaded brain.

Tanner cleared his throat and straightened his red tie. Time to get serious. This meeting was important to his father's business and crucial to Tanner's future at Peschke Motors. The appointment could be the beginning of bigger and better things...or the beginning of the end.

Passing a large gilt-framed mirror, he checked his appearance. He'd been shooting for honest and down-to-earth to appeal to the matriarch and CEO of Barbara Stockton's Beauty Secrets. Thus the blue chambray shirt, crisply ironed blue jeans, and highly polished cowboy boots. Next to all the beautifully groomed and fashionably dressed women in attendance at the conference, he probably looked like a hick. He got great pleasure in knowing he wasn't just a hick. He had money. Lots of money, but he chose not to advertise that fact. No one in Texas but his banker knew exactly how much money he had. And he liked the situation that way.

Tanner usually didn't give much thought to what he wore or how others viewed him, but his normally take-me-as-I-am attitude had gone for a hike after his father's latest challenge, which he'd delivered just that morning...

"SON, if you're gonna run this company when I retire, you've gotta show me you want it."

That was the hard part. Tanner really didn't want the business. He didn't have Jesse's steadiness, Gage's laser-focus, or even Rip's laissez-faire attitude. He was a man approaching thirty and feeling strangled in place because he hadn't found his life's calling.

Sitting across the desk from his father, Tanner silently groaned and tipped his cowboy hat forward so his dad couldn't detect his impatience. He knew he was in for his father's latest lecture on "Used Car Sales Business: Lecture Number 4123."

Try as he might, he couldn't force the passion his father had for the sales game. But Tanner promised his mother on her deathbed that he'd help his father with the family business. He wished he'd inherited his father's natural used-car-salesman gene. The fact was, he hadn't.

Just once, he'd like hearing his father's praise and admiration of his business prowess. But his father wouldn't sugarcoat what wasn't there for him to see at Peschke Motors.

Too often, Tanner bit hard on his tongue to keep from telling his father he didn't need him or the job or anything to do with Peschke Motors. But his sweet mother's last words always came back. "Take care of your father. Help him. He needs you."

"Tanner!" Joe Peschke's booming voice pricked the bubble of Tanner's memory. "Son, are you payin' attention to anything I'm sayin'?"

"Yes, sir," Tanner lied and decided he'd better give the man his undivided attention, or this could turn into an even longer ordeal than usual. By the look of his father's ruddy cheeks and bristling black moustache, Tanner guessed he'd missed a cue.

His dad rose to his feet, his bulky frame towering over Tanner. "I plan on buyin' a fishin' boat and a house on the beach. In exactly three months, I'm movin' there. Do you understand what I'm sayin'?"

Tanner must have drifted *way* off. This was the first he'd heard about his father moving. "You're moving?"

"Yes, I'm moving."

"But how will you run the business from the coast?"

"I'm won't. I'm retirin'."

"Retiring?" This was new, too.

"Yes, and I wanted to leave the family business in the hands of family. I had high hopes that family would be you, seein' as you're the only family I have left."

Tanner pushed his hat back on his head, every fiber of his being tuned in to his dad's words. He could feel a "but" coming...

"But, I need a quarterback who can lead the team to victory. Problem is, son, I'm just not seein' you as that quarterback."

Wait a minute. Tanner couldn't have heard that right. "You mean, you'd fire me?" he asked disbelieving. A little devil in his conscience leapt for joy, while an angel with a face like his mother's shook her head sadly.

"Not necessarily fire you, but I need to select a general manager. If you're not the man for the job, I can't put you in it."

A cold, hard lump lodged in Tanner's throat. Perhaps now was the time to break it to his father that he was a multi-millionaire and didn't need the job of general manager. But that time had come and gone. Telling his father he didn't need him might break the old man's heart and would definitely go against what Tanner had promised his mother. Caught between a rock and a soft spot, Tanner argued, "I've sold fifteen cars in the last month, Dad. How many other salesmen have sold as many?"

Joe Peschke shook his head, his mouth turned down in a sad frown. "Not a one. Volume's not your problem, son."

"Then what is?"

His father lifted a piece of paper from the stack on his desk and shook it. "Statistics show every car you sold to a woman, you sold *at,* or a fraction above, cost. Which barely pays the bills around here, much less your commission."

Tanner knew he couldn't refute his father's words. "But Dad, you don't understand."

His father shook the paper. "Then help me understand, son." Scanning down the list, he poked a finger at a line. "The green conversion van."

"That would be Mrs. Jenkins." Tanner straightened his shoulders. "Her husband's disabled and they live on a fixed income."

His father frowned and looked farther down the list. "How about that blue, four-door Saturn?"

"Rebecca Pitkin." Tanner remembered the frazzled redhead with the toddler. "Student. Single mom. Needed reliable transportation to get her daughter to daycare. She's trying to make a better life for herself and her child."

With a roll of his eyes, the older Peschke went to the next line. Crossing his arms over his chest, his father slowly shook his head. "Tell me about the F-150 Pickup."

Tanner groaned inwardly. Was this how a frog pinned to a dissecting board felt? "F-150 pickup?" Damned if he could remember the face that went with that vehicle. "Refresh my memory, Dad."

"Micky Freeland ring a bell?"

"Micky... wasn't that a man?"

"I don't know too many men who dot their 'i's with hearts."

"I could have sworn she was a man," Tanner muttered. A sick feeling filled his stomach. His father was right.

Tossing the paper back in the pile on his desk, his father leaned forward. "Truth is, son, you're a marshmallow with the women."

"And that's a crime?" Tanner knew the answer before the words left his lips.

"In the used car business, it is. We're not a charity organization." His father leaned back in his chair, pinching the bridge of his nose. "The word is out. You sold three cars to three generations of Smithson women. And they'll all be tellin' their friends."

"That could be a good thing." *C'mon, Tanner, spin this in your favor.* "Return customers and word-of-mouth advertising is bound to be good for business."

"Won't do the dealership a darn bit of good, if they're all comin' to you, son." His father shook his head, his lips tightening. "Face facts—as soon as a female feeds you a sob story, you're silly putty in her hands."

Tanner hung his head, knowing every word his father spoke was true. He was a soft touch where women were concerned. That wily Smithson grandmother had him pegged the moment they'd met.

For just a moment, he'd held her hand, feeling the parchment-thin skin and smelling the lilac fragrance she'd doused herself in. He hadn't been able to bear the thought of the elderly pensioner making high payments for the vehicle she had her heart set on. Hell, Tanner didn't need the commission. He could subsidize every one of their customers if the action didn't leave a paper trail back to his investment portfolio.

"I have no complaints about your sales volume. You need to work on your profit margin if you want to prove you have the fire in your belly for this business."

Right now, the only fire Tanner felt in his belly was the ulcer he'd earned. Despite the promise he'd made to his mother, he still resisted committing the rest of his life to Peschke Motors.

"You've got three months. Make those months count. And, son, decide what you're gonna do with your life." His father had leaned his forearms on the desk to deliver the final warning. "Don't straddle that fence—all you'll get is bruised balls."

AT TWO O'CLOCK that same afternoon, Tanner was feeling pretty bruised all right. Standing in line at the concierge's desk in the hotel lobby, his stomach still roiled at his father's words. Even knowing he had the support of his best buddies wasn't helping.

Barbara Stockton of Barbara Stockton's Beauty Secrets, or BS-Squared as he thought of her, had requested him specifically for this deal, and that he come to her. Tanner hoped like hell she wasn't Aggie Smithson's friend. This was his chance to make the deal of a lifetime. A chance to redeem himself for all the missed opportunities—if he could keep a hard-core business mind and not be swayed by a woman's woes.

"I'm here to meet with Barbara Stockton. Could you tell me what room she's in?" he asked the busy concierge.

"I'll have to call her room first to verify the appointment. Could you wait just a moment, sir?"

"Sure, I'll wait over there." Tanner pointed toward a potted plant set next to an entryway.

Women moved in surges, ebbing and flowing from the ballroom. Feeling out of place and outnumbered, he swam with the current until he reached the plant. He almost grabbed hold to keep from being swept into the sea of estrogen. More than once, he could swear he felt the soft pat of a hand on his ass.

Tanner stared into the ballroom from his anchoring tree, feeling incongruous as the only male for as far as his eyes could see. The large expanse was partitioned into dozens of booths where women demonstrated various beauty products. Hands in his pockets, Tanner forced himself to relax. He leaned against the doorframe and heaved a sigh.

Why were women his greatest weakness? What about them made him such a pushover? Every last one of them—be they homely or gorgeous, elderly or eligible—left him feeling like he had to protect them, take care of them, and ease their worries. Why did they have that affect on him, and how could he armor himself against it to pull off this deal?

He had a knack for bringing in the customers. Perhaps he should stick to publicity and marketing and let someone else handle the sales. He certainly wasn't helping the dealership if he gave away cars. And Peschke Motors had been a part of the Peschke family for three generations. The place meant a lot to his father, therefore, the business meant a lot to Tanner.

How could he make his father proud and keep the business going? Ideas raced through his head, none seemed substantial enough to impress his father.

"Please notice when Rafael applies the Miracle Hairspray, it goes on evenly, without spitting or clogging."

Tanner heard her before he saw her. Though soft and breathy, the voice carried over the steady hum of hundreds of feminine conversations. And that voice made every hair on his body stand up and cry *halleluiah*.

Because he stood a good foot above the tallest, he didn't have to crane his neck to see over the heads of the women gathered.

A beauty perched on a stool with a mini-microphone attached to the low-cut lapel of her suit jacket.

"Holy hell," Tanner breathed.

When the spraying stopped, the woman climbed gracefully from the high stool and shook her hair back from her shoulders. "See? Every hair remains in place with a springy, natural hold."

Tanner's gaze remained riveted—but not only to her hair. Her entire package captivated him from the top of her golden blonde coif to the tips of her bright pink, Barbie-style stilettos. Every curve and feature in perfect proportion, her beauty was reminiscent of Marilyn Monroe. And that musical, breathy voice made his pulse flutter and his mouth dry. Tanner's blood raced from his heart to his extremities—one in particular.

The cotton-candy pink suit that would have looked feminine but professional on any other woman, clung lovingly to her generous curves. The skirt ended just above her knees—round, pink kissable knees. The three-inch stilettos emphasized delicate ankles and well-defined calves. But just her physical perfection wasn't what drew him, she dripped sweetness.

Tanner gulped and forced himself to look beyond the woman to the enraptured crowd gathering around her. With her voice, beauty and natural talent, she could sell beachfront property in Arizona. *Or...*

A Cadillac of an idea slipped into Tanner's mind and gunned all eight cylinders.

This gifted, eloquent and drop-dead-gorgeous woman could be the answer to all his prayers. But who was she?

Tanner stepped forward, but pressure on his arm stopped him, and he looked to the source.

"Excuse me, sir." The concierge stood at his elbow, drawing his attention from his salvation. "Ms. Stockton will see you now in the

Double Diamond suite. It's on the forty-sixth floor—the first door on your right when you exit the elevator."

"Thank you very much." Tanner turned to treat himself to one last glimpse of the curvaceous blond in the pink suit. "I'll talk with you later," he whispered before heading for the elevator and the dreaded meeting with BS-Squared.

THE TRIP to the forty-sixth floor took only three minutes. Not much time to compose his scattered thoughts. Thankfully, the fifty-something-year-old Ms. Stockton couldn't possibly hold as much appeal as the breathy blonde who waited below. And she wasn't old enough to play to his soft side, like the infamous Aggie Smithson.

Tanner rapped lightly against the door bearing the shiny brass nameplate with "Double Diamond Suite" engraved in bold letters.

When the door opened, he turned up his smile full force. "Hello, I'm Tanner Peschke, you must be..." Tanner's voice faded and his smile slipped.

"Barbara Stockton," she finished for him. "Won't you come in?" Turning, she stepped aside and waved a hand with a flourish, indicating the way.

He gulped, and his heart sank to his knees. "I'm doomed."

"Pardon me, did you say something, Tanner? You don't mind my calling you Tanner, do you?" Barbara Stockton's throaty voice purred. She eyed him with a raised eyebrow and a knowing smile.

"I said, nice room." Edging past her, he entered the lioness's den.

For a woman in her fifties, Barbara Stockton was very well preserved. Her shoulder-length, dark brown hair curled artistically around her face and glinted with beautifully engineered red and gold highlights. She wore a full-length wrap made of a filmy leopard print. Beneath it, she sported a black sports-bra and figure-hugging leopard-print leggings. And if that wasn't enough, the black thong worn over the leggings was the clincher.

Tanner frowned. This was no Aggie Smithson. Barbara Stockton was a very astute businesswoman, a lion in the jungle of gone-by-the-wayside beauty products distributors. What did he have to fear? She didn't inspire him to one iota of protectiveness. If anything, he felt like raw meat being dangled to entice her ravenous appetite.

Pushing back his shoulders, he stood tall, schooling his face into that of a professional businessman. Tanner was sure even a seasoned negotiator like his dad would have difficulty with this feline. With a raised eyebrow, he said in his smoothest voice, "I'll wait by the window while you get dressed."

He could handle this. Barbara's beauty didn't appeal to him. But the blonde downstairs did, and he couldn't wait to return to the ballroom to propose his idea for the dealership.

"Daahhling, you seem awfully tense." Barbara's voice tickled the back of Tanner's ear as her fingers dug into the taut muscles at the base of his neck. "*Relaaaxxxx*."

Tanner inhaled deeply, but it didn't work. How could a man relax when a cat had her claws in him?

"It's awfully warm in here, don't you think? I just finished working out." She slipped the filmy wrap from her sleek, well-toned shoulders and the garment cascaded to the floor in a careless heap. With a practiced turn, she walked toward a cabinet on the far wall. "Can I pour you a drink?"

Think blonde, think blonde. His new mantra had the immediate effect of bringing to mind the pretty spokeswoman in the ballroom downstairs. Thinking of the two women, Tanner realized no comparison existed.

Granted, Barbara Stockton was incredibly hot, but she didn't have the same impact. Her moves were too predatory, too calculated. A feral cougar, he could resist.

"Yes, I'd like a drink." Tanner eased his mouth into a genuine smile, feeling more confident by the moment.

"What's your poison?" she asked with a little flirty glance from beneath her brown eyelashes.

"Whiskey." He smiled wider, confidence restored, a feeling of invulnerability spiking his blood.

With his 'Marilyn' firmly fixed in his mind, he spent the next two hours playing musical chairs among the sofas and loveseats in the suite, while negotiating the purchase of a fleet of cotton-candy pink company cars from the equally determined CEO.

By the end of the meeting, Tanner had won. He'd gotten BS-Squared's handshake—and unsolicited kiss—on a contract that promised the dealership a tidy return once they'd repainted and sold the vehicles. The contract was a coup de grace, and he hadn't had to compromise the company, or himself, to get it.

Exiting BS-Squared's suite with a promise from her to visit the lot, Tanner allowed a little strut in his stride as he returned to the ballroom. He was determined to find "Marilyn". During his time with BS-Squared, he'd begun to think of the blonde as his good luck charm. Somehow, he had to convince her to come to work for Peschke Motors.

Once inside the ballroom, he was disappointed when he didn't see her at the Miracle Spray booth. After five minutes of scanning the multitude in the area, he finally spotted her on a raised dais, astride a mechanical bull.

She'd changed her clothing. Body-hugging denim and gray snake-skin boots were topped with a scoop-necked pale pink T-shirt that ended just above her silver belt buckle.

"As you can see, even a full two hours after applying Miracle Hair-spray, my hairstyle is still in place."

Tanner was fascinated. He hadn't imagined the sexy, breathy voice. Nor had he exaggerated the impact of her voluptuous figure. She spoke with the confidence of an experienced actress and, even more intriguing and definitely arousing, she rode the mechanical bull like a pro.

With a hand gripping the rope tied around the torso of the beast, she held her other arm high in the air in true rodeo-rider fashion. Each rise and fall caused the woman's breasts to lift and dip. That little space of skin between her tiny T-shirt and her belt played peek-a-boo with her audience.

God Bless America—and the inventor of the mechanical bull. Every red-white-and-blue blood cell in Tanner's body rode south. Without thinking, he crossed the ballroom floor and climbed onto the dais. He had to talk to her now.

"EVEN A BUCKING BULL can't destroy the beauty and natural spring." Janine Davis recited her scripted lines without fail. Maybe this wasn't an Academy Award-winning performance, but she gave it her all anyway. Every acting job added a credit to her resume, putting her one step closer to realizing her dream.

"Ma'am, I don't think the hairspray has anything to do with your beauty."

The voice from behind startled her into forgetting her lines and temporarily losing her balance. The bull dipped, and she started to slip. She dropped her arm and grabbed the rough hemp rope encircling the bucking bull.

When she'd righted herself, she glared at the tall man at her side. "Please don't talk to me, sir."

"What if I have a question about the product?" he countered, a smile curving his mouth.

Taking another dip, she loosened her grip and pressed her free hand to the microphone on her lapel. "I have a script to follow, and you're not in it. Please don't distract me," she whispered fiercely, loud enough for him to hear, but not for other conventioneers passing by. She forced a bright smile, directing it toward the audience.

"Pardon me, ma'am. I wouldn't dream of keeping you from your job."

Her gaze narrowed, but he didn't appear to be mocking her. "Good. Now please move along before you get me fired." Janine scanned the room full of people, looking for her boss, before returning her gaze to the man beside her.

He was kind of cute. Tall and dark with a grin that could melt a girl's bones into a gooey puddle. He spread his large hands wide, an innocent look on his smiling face. "Now, how could I get you fired? You're positively brilliant."

Exasperated by his persistence, and at herself for getting all tingly when he was near, she replied, "All I know is I need this job to make my rent money, so don't blow it for me."

"All right, but first tell me your name." He leaned back against the bull's control panel and crossed one ankle over the other.

The man's brown-black eyes held a wicked gleam she found hard to resist. "Janine Davis. Why do you ask?" she said, fighting hard not to notice how sexy he was because the bull's rhythmic motions jounced her breasts and drove her lower parts hard against the saddle. Sensations she had no business noticing began to build along with the thrumming heat flooding her veins.

"I wanted to know the name of the woman I need to thank."

Curiosity won out. Her annoyance at his interruption forgotten for the moment, her head tilted to the side as she continued rocking back and forth on the bull. "Thank me? Why?"

"Because of you, I made the best deal imaginable with old BS-Squared herself."

"Who's BS-Squared?" she asked.

"Barbara Stockton of Barbara Stockton's Beauty Secrets. You know —B. S. B. S..."

Janine frowned.

"Two BS's is BS-Squared." He shook his head. "Never mind. You're my new good luck charm. I just made the best deal of my career."

A movement behind the gorgeous cowboy caught Janine's attention, and her heart nearly stopped. Her boss was headed her way. With her hand squashing the microphone to her breast, Janine whispered, "Uh, sir, don't look now, but..." She jerked her head in his direction.

He ignored her attempt to interrupt and continued, "So you see, I have you to thank for keeping my mind on business with old BS-Squared."

Janine cringed. Why hadn't he taken her hint and shut the hell up? She let go of the rope around the bull's middle and waved, pasting a smile on her stiff lips. "I wouldn't thank me now," she sang.

"Why?" The tall man's eyes widened and his jaw slackened. His gaze locked with Janine's. "She's right behind me, isn't she?"

"Uh huh." Janine nodded. "Uh...hi there, Ms. Stockton." She bit the corner of her lip and fluttered her fingers in a strained attempt at a light-hearted greeting.

The cowboy swung around, his elbow knocking against a lever on the control panel.

The bull leapt into high speed.

Janine squealed and grasped for the rope—for something to hold on to—but her hands flailed uselessly in the air.

After three raucous bucks, the bull spun, knocking the man from the stage to land flat on his butt on the floor in front of Barbara Stockton. At least he'd earned his just desserts.

Janine smirked and would have clapped her hands if she weren't in trouble herself. The bull jerked one direction, then lurched and spun another, flinging Janine through the air.

She screamed and twisted, attempting to land on her feet. Instead, she fell face-first on top of the man who'd caused all this.

"Ooomph!" Their chests met with enough force to knock the wind out of them both. Stunned, and fighting for her breath, Janine resisted the urge to hide her face against the cowboy's broad chest. She wished a gigantic black hole would open up and suck in her humiliated self.

Unfortunately, Janine felt the intensity of her boss's glare before she pushed up on her hands and turned to smile sheepishly. "See? The hair-spray holds even through the worst of conditions."

Ms. Stockton's expression was not amused. "My, my, isn't this touching. The hired help flirting with the used car salesman."

Janine had a gut feeling the tightness on the older woman's face did not bode well. Turning her anger to the cause of this debacle, she glared down at the man lying beneath her.

WHEN JANINE LOOKED down at Tanner, all he could think about was her thighs straddling the only un-stunned part of his body. Her full, rounded breasts pressed intimately against his chest.

Barbara Stockton's outraged expression didn't even faze him when Janine struggled to sit up. He could feel himself harden in response to her denim-covered bottom rubbing against his groin. How much torture could a man take and survive?

A clicking noise next to his ear finally got his attention. The sound was a shoe tapping against the floor—Ms. Stockton's shoe. When his gaze made the trip up the long sleek legs of his client to rest on her angry face, his stomach plunged.

"This whole scene reeks of low class. And I make it a habit to deal only with high-class operations..." BS-Squared's eyebrows rose as she stared pointedly at him, then turned to Janine, "...and individuals. I'm afraid your services are no longer required, Miss Davis. Collect your wages and get out of my sight."

"But Ms. Stockton—" Janine pushed to a sitting position astride Tanner.

A pretty little frown making her even more adorable in Tanner's books.

The CEO held her hand up. "Just leave."

A wad of guilt twisted in Tanner's gut.

"And, Mr. Peschke?" BS-Squared's lips moved with careful, cutting precision. "The deal is off." Executing a perfect about-face, she left the room and the disaster Tanner had created in her wake.

Tanner groaned and let his head flop back against the floor, welcoming the slight pain. His dad was going to kill him.

"Thanks for nothing, mister." Janine finally got her feet beneath her and rose.

Tanner stood and flashed a scowl at the crowd gathered around them, and they quickly dispersed. He turned to Janine. "I'm sorry about that. Hitting that switch was an accident."

"As far as I'm concerned, you're a walking accident looking for a place to happen." Her words were clipped and angry. "Now, what am I going to do? This was the best-paying acting job I've had in a while."

That was his cue. If he wanted to keep his good luck charm, boost profits and do it his way, he had to convince Janine to go along with his plan.

Brushing off his hand against the side of his leg, he held it out. He gave her the smile his grandmother had told him could *tempt the birds from the trees*. "Janine Davis, have I got a deal for you."

Texas Billionaire Club

Tarzan & Janine (#1)
Something To Talk About (#2)
Who's Your Daddy (#3)
Love & War (#4)

ABOUT THE AUTHOR

ELLE JAMES also writing as MYLA JACKSON is a *New York Times* and *USA Today* Bestselling author of books including cowboys, intrigues and paranormal adventures that keep her readers on the edges of their seats. With over eighty works in a variety of sub-genres and lengths she has published with Harlequin, Samhain, Ellora's Cave, Kensington, Cleis Press, and Avon. When she's not at her computer, she's traveling, snow skiing, boating, or riding her ATV, dreaming up new stories. Learn more about Elle James at www.ellejames.com

Website | Facebook | Twitter | GoodReads | Newsletter | BookBub | Amazon

Or visit her alter ego Myla Jackson at mylajackson.com
Website | Facebook | Twitter | Newsletter

Follow Me!

www.ellejames.com
ellejames@ellejames.com

ALSO BY ELLE JAMES

Hearts & Heroes Series

Wyatt's War (#1)

Mack's Witness (#2)

Ronin's Return (#3)

Sam's Surrender (#4)

Brotherhood Protector Series

Montana SEAL (#1)

Bride Protector SEAL (#2)

Montana D-Force (#3)

Cowboy D-Force (#4)

Montana Ranger (#5)

Montana Dog Soldier (#6)

Montana SEAL Daddy (#7)

Montana Rescue

Take No Prisoners Series

SEAL's Honor (#1)

SEAL's Ultimate Challenge (#1.5)

SEAL'S Desire (#2)

SEAL's Embrace (#3)

SEAL's Obsession (#4)

SEAL's Proposal (#5)

SEAL's Seduction (#6)

SEAL'S Defiance (#7)

SEAL's Deception (#8)

SEAL's Deliverance (#9)

Ballistic Cowboy

Hot Combat (#1)

Hot Target (#2)

Hot Zone (#3)

Hot Velocity (#4)

Texas Billionaire Club

Tarzan & Janine (#1)

Something To Talk About (#2)

Who's Your Daddy (#3)

Love & War (#4)

Hellfire Series

Hellfire, Texas (#1)

Justice Burning (#2)

Smoldering Desire (#3) TBD

Up in Flames (#4) TBD

Plays with Fire (#5) TBD

Hellfire in High Heels (#6) TBD

Cajun Magic Mystery Series

Voodoo on the Bayou (#1)

Voodoo for Two (#2)

Deja Voodoo (#3)

Billionaire Online Dating Series

The Billionaire Husband Test (#1)

The Billionaire Cinderella Test (#2)

The Billionaire Bride Test (#3) TBD

The Billionaire Matchmaker Test (#4) TBD

SEAL Of My Own

Navy SEAL Survival

Navy SEAL Captive

Navy SEAL To Die For

Navy SEAL Six Pack

Devil's Shroud Series

Deadly Reckoning (#1)

Deadly Engagement (#2)

Deadly Liaisons (#3)

Deadly Allure (#4)

Deadly Obsession (#5)

Deadly Fall (#6)

Covert Cowboys Inc Series

Triggered (#1)

Taking Aim (#2)

Bodyguard Under Fire (#3)

Cowboy Resurrected (#4)

Navy SEAL Justice (#5)

Navy SEAL Newlywed (#6)

High Country Hideout (#7)

Clandestine Christmas (#8)

Thunder Horse Series

Hostage to Thunder Horse (#1)

Thunder Horse Heritage (#2)

Thunder Horse Redemption (#3)

Christmas at Thunder Horse Ranch (#4)

Demon Series

Hot Demon Nights (#1)

Demon's Embrace (#2)

Tempting the Demon (#3)

Lords of the Underworld

Witch's Initiation (#1)

Witch's Seduction (#2)

The Witch's Desire (#3)

Possessing the Witch (#4)

Stealth Operations Specialists (SOS)

Nick of Time

Alaskan Fantasy

Blown Away

Warrior's Conquest

Rogues

Enslaved by the Viking Short Story

Conquests

Smokin' Hot Firemen

Love on the Rocks

Protecting the Colton Bride

Heir to Murder

Secret Service Rescue

High Octane Heroes

Haunted

Engaged with the Boss

Cowboy Brigade

Time Raiders: The Whisper

Bundle of Trouble

Killer Body

Operation XOXO

An Unexpected Clue

Baby Bling

Under Suspicion, With Child

Texas-Size Secrets